Steven Griffiths serv[...]
Police graduating fr[...]
Squad and on to Sp[...]
VIP protection speci[...]

He now lives in Surrey with his wife and daughter, where he says life is more sedate.

IN GWAN-DAI'S NAME is Steven Griffiths' second book. His first, NIMROD RISING, was published by Futura in 1989 to wide acclaim.

Also by Steven Griffiths in Futura:

NIMROD RISING

In Gwan-Dai's Name

Steven Griffiths

Futura

A Futura Book

First published in Great Britain in 1992 by
Futura Publications, a Division of
Macdonald & Co (Publishers) Ltd
London & Sydney

Copyright © Steven Griffiths 1992

The right of Steven Griffiths to be identified as
author of this work has been asserted by him in accordance with
the Copyright, Designs and Patents Act 1988.

*All characters in this publication are fictitious
and any resemblance to real persons, living or dead,
is purely coincidental.*

All rights reserved.
No part of this publication may be reproduced,
stored in a retrieval system, or transmitted, in any
form or by any means, without the prior
permission in writing of the publisher, nor be
otherwise circulated in any form of binding or
cover other than that in which it is published and
without a similar condition including this
condition being imposed on the subsequent purchaser.

ISBN 0 7088 5346 3

Typeset by Leaper & Gard Ltd, Bristol, England
Printed in Great Britain by
BPCC Hazell Books
Aylesbury, Bucks, England
Member of BPCC Ltd

Futura Publications
A Division of
Macdonald & Co (Publishers) Ltd
165 Great Dover Street
London SE1 4YA
A member of Maxwell Macmillan Publishing Corporation

*To the men and women
of the Royal Hong Kong Police Force.*

ACKNOWLEDGEMENTS

Thanks are due to the following:

To the many friends and former colleagues in the RHKP who made comments or suggestions on the story-line of *In Gwan-Dai's Name*. In particular to those officers operating in specialised units who, for obvious reasons, cannot be named here. You know who you are, anyway.

To the Mass Transit Railway Corporation for their generous cooperation in allowing me free access to what must be the finest underground railway system anywhere in the world. A special thankyou to Fred Y. F. Lam, Area Manager of the MTR City Line for walking me through the control rooms and tunnels featured in the latter part of this book.

Jill Mackenzie and Declan Costello, for their comments and criticisms on various parts of the manuscript. Also to Rob Mack for his specialised knowledge and insights on the Japanese aspects of the story and Yue Shau-shown for his help with triad culture and expressions.

Peter Lavery, for believing I could actually do it.

Last, but not least, thanks to my wife Sue for providing coffee and enthusiasm at the exact moment when both were most needed, and for her patience in repeatedly proof-reading and correcting the manuscript.

*'To Hear the Unspoken and Observe
That Which Has No Substance'*

A passage from the 'Instructions to Police Officers'
by Dai Keishi KAWAJI Toshiyoshi, founder of
the Japanese Police System in 1874.

CONTENTS

GLOSSARY

It would be impossible to write anything that recreates the unique experience of police work in Hong Kong without reference to some of the many Chinese words and idioms which the European officer comes to learn.

Here are explanations of some of those used most frequently in this novel.

Ah Chan	Person from the Mainland; country hick (derog.).
Ah Char	Indian or Pakistani (derog.).
Ah Goh	Elder brother (also used as honorific to a senior).
Ah Gung	Grandfather (also used as honorific to a very senior person).
Ah Je	Elder sister.
Ah Yor	Person who lives on boats; low-born (derog.).
aiyah!	Mild exclamation.
amah	Maid or servant (usually living in the home of the employer).
Baak Chi Sin	White Paper Fan (Triad Master of Administration).
baak pei jue	European (white-skinned pig).
bai Gwan-Dai	Ceremony at which the god Gwan-Dai is honoured.
bai san	Ceremony of worship – general.
blue lantern	Triad follower not yet fully initiated.
bo biu	Bodyguard.

bong baan	Police Inspector.
chai lo	Cop.
chai yan	Policeman.
Chan Fat	Anybody (same meaning as 'John Doe' in USA).
char siu bau	Spicy pork buns (also woman's breasts – slang).
chat	Penis (slang).
cheng sik faan	To host a dinner party.
cheung	Gun.
Chi Gung	Martial art which utilises breath control and internal energy.
chi sau	Pushing hands, also sticking hands. An exercise to develop sensitivity and balance.
Chiu Chau	Ethnic Chinese group originating in the Swatow region of Mainland China.
Cho Haai	Grass Sandal. (Triad logistical support.)
Choh Gwoon	One who sits in charge (triad term). (See also *Shan Chiu* and First Route Marshal.)
da fei gei	Shooting at airplanes (masturbation – male).
da gip	Robbery.
dai dong	Illegal casino.
dai fong	CID duty room.
Dai Huen Jai	Big Circle Gang. Criminal groups originating from the Canton area of mainland China – usually ex-soldiers of the People's Liberation Army (PLA).
dai lo	Elder brother; mentor. Generally used to refer to one's immediate superior. In triad slang *dai lo* means a man's protector.

xi

Dai Luk	The big chunk (mainland China).
dai pai dong	An open-air cooked food stall.
dai sik wooi	Dinner party or celebration (literally, big eating party).
dai siu	Big-Small. Chinese gambling game using three dice.
dang yat jan	Wait a moment.
dim gaai	Why? Also used as noun to mean an official inquiry.
dim sum	Breakfast snacks served in Chinese restaurants.
diu lei lo mo	Fuck your old mother (Cantonese curse).
dui m'jiu	Excuse me. (An apology.)
fai ji	Chopsticks.
Fei Foo Dui	Special Duties Unit (the leaping tigers).
foh gei	Constable (slang).
fong sam	Don't worry (relax your heart).
fung shui	Chinese art of divination (wind and water).
gau cheung	Dog track.
gau dim	Right enough. An expression of satisfaction.
gau meng!	Help! Literally, save life.
ging chaat	Police (formal).
gung on	Inner council.
gwai lo	A European. Originally *faan gwai lo*, meaning foreign devil.
gwai tau jai	An informer or spy.
Gwan-Dai	Chinese martial god. In life a great general and hero at the time of the Han dynasty.
Haak sei wooi	Triad society.
hai m'hai a?	Completes a question: 'Is or is not?'
heung jiu	Joss-sticks.
hing dai	Brothers. Members of the same

	group. Particularly strong in police, triad or martial arts context.
ho	Positive expression: good, right, fine, very.
ho lui mo gin	Long time no see.
hoi cheung	Open fire.
hung gaai	Red Chicken. Name for incompletely refined heroin No. 3, a reddish granular substance. The fully finished product, heroin No. 4, is known as *baak fan* or 'white powder'.
Hung Kwan	Red Cudgel (triad enforcer).
jaap chai	Detective.
jau gau	Yellow running dog. Chinese lackey.
jing ji bo	Special Branch (political police).
jo san	Good morning.
kai do	One-man ferry boat.
kuen wong	King boxer. Common nickname for one who quickly resorts to violence.
lap sap	Garbage. Rubbish.
lor yau	Anus (slang).
lui ging	Woman police officer.
luk ye	Penis (slang).
m'goi (sai)	Thanks (very much).
ma jai	Little horse. A follower.
mat ye si?	What's the problem?
mau saat	Murder.
mo choh	That's right.
mo man tai	No questions. No problem.
mo yuk!	Don't move!
nei ho ma?	How are you?
pai kau	Gambling game using Chinese dominoes.
pu le a moh	Fuck your old mother (Chiu Chau).
puk gaai!	Fall dead in the street! (Cantonese curse).

sai lo	Little brother (also used to refer to the penis).
sair	Snake (also used to describe illegal immigrants).
San Yee On	Chiu Chau triad society.
sap ji	Chinese character denoting the number ten.
Sap Sei Kei	14K. Pro-Taiwanese triad society.
sei gau jai	49 member. Lowest level initiated triad member.
sei yee luk	426 member. Enforcer (See *Hung Kwan*).
Shan Chiu	Master of the Lodge (Chief Triad Official).
si fat	Anus (slang).
si gon	Responsibility.
Sifu	Master or teacher. One who is learned in a particular art or skill.
sik faan	Have a meal (literally, eat rice).
sin saang	Mister. Sir.
siu ye	An evening snack. Usually taken in a group.
sor jai	Crazy guy.
sor mooi	Crazy girl or crazy little sister.
sui	Water. Usually used in slang form to mean money.
Tai Chi	Complete system of health and self-defence (also Tai Chi Chuan – Tai Chi fist).
Tin Hau	Goddess of the sea. Much favoured by fishermen and boat-dwellers.
tin kei	Pray to heaven! (Usage is similar to 'for God's sake!')
tit kuen yam	Chiu chau tea. Iron Goddess of Mercy.
walla-walla	A one-man ferry paddled from the

	rear by a single oar drawn from side to side.
wei?	Chinese response when answering the phone.
Wong Tai Sin	District of Kowloon named after the Chinese god whose temple may be found there.
Wu Chi	The void from which the universe was created.
yam booi!	Drink up! Cheers!
yam jui jau	Drunk.
yam sing!	Bottoms up! Drink to the last!
yau mo gau choh!	Are you kidding? Expression of disbelief.
Yen-lo	The keeper of the gates of hell.
yit hei	The warming characteristic in food which when taken to excess produces stomach and blood disorders and leads to skin eruptions.

BOOK ONE
HUNGRY GHOSTS

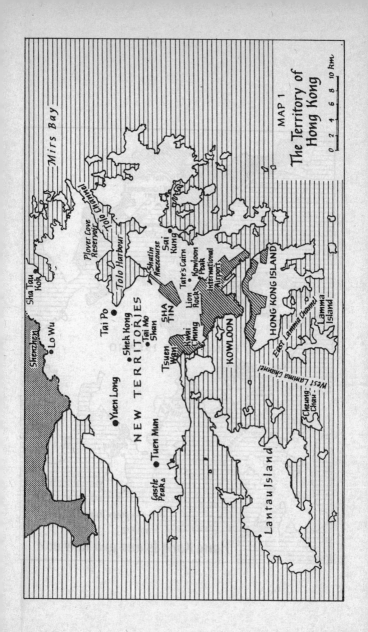

MAP 1

The Territory of
Hong Kong

0 2 4 6 8 10 km

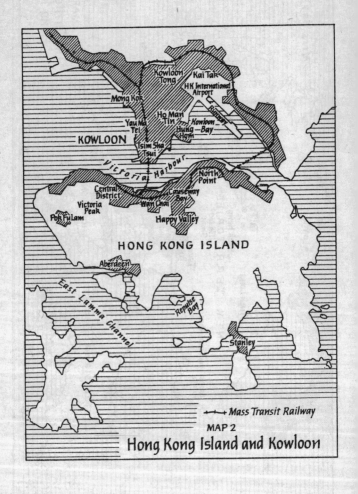

Mass Transit Railway

MAP 2

Hong Kong Island and Kowloon

ONE

It was the first small tremor in the night sky that warned him of their coming. The Hungry Ghosts were now returning.

Then, through the rain-spattered windscreen, he watched their magic begin. Far beyond the harsh glitter of the street, high above the ragged black curtain of the Kowloon foothills, the first muted glows appeared as their dead fingers pressed against the membrane of the sky. Soft explosions breaking in amber clusters and echoing back and forth between burnt black banks of cloud.

Gwan-Dai was hunched in the secure darkness of the vehicle, watching the few last revellers still out on the Kowloon strip tumble homeward through the rain. And as he watched – the lime-green wash from the dashboard LEDs painting his face into a mask of hatred – one hand massaged the hilt of a large hunting knife somewhere near his thigh. Abruptly his thumb strayed across the razor-edge of the blade, drawing blood – and his mind was made up. Thrilled by the spectral presence all around him, he knew now that he must kill again.

For this was not just any night. This was a special night: the Festival of the Hungry Ghosts, when Yen-Lo, the keeper of the underworld, unlocks the gates of hell and sets free a legion of lost souls to torment man. Even now he could sense their distant shrieks as they clawed their way back from the celestial matrix.

Again he listened to the sound of the thunder, like the sharp crack of dry bamboo snapping. And he thought he *heard a deeper groan of ancient locks turning, and stone gates moving against their hinges. Then the dragon's deep-throated roar as it chased the lightning across the South China sky. Receding and ultimately lost within the infinite.*

Time to act, he decided – for the approaching spirits demanded a sacrifice.

As he swung the taxi off the Golden Mile and into Sai Yee Street, fat droplets of rain were bouncing knee-high from the pavement. Kowloon was wet and bright with neon: a whore clothed in tawdry lurex and cheap jewellery, her streets reflecting the multicoloured sleaze palaces ranged along her roads. Through the rolled-down window he saw the small charred piles of joss papers swirl in the brimming gutters ... many-hued paper scraps and the phoney million-dollar banknotes labelled BANK OF HELL which local shopkeepers burned to appease the Hungry Ghosts.

Cruising along the narrow street, where ranks of shabby tenements rose up into the darkness on either side, he dropped the gear-stick into second and studied the lighted bars at street level. Outside them stood Chinese pimps and toughs, gang members mostly, hustling their pitches or dealing a little red chicken – while, inside, their bosses lounged on velvet banquettes gulping five-star brandy. A succession of garish reflections and suspicious glances crossed his windscreen, until at last he reached the strobing purple sign of the Barking Peacock Club, and he pulled into a tight space at the kerb.

It was a part of Kowloon he knew well: Mongkok – a name meaning 'busy corner'. It was that, all right: the most densely populated quarter square-mile in the world. A place where the action was available around the clock, and the police thought twice before answering a local emergency call. The glitzy façades of the nightclubs gave

6

a false appearance of glamour, but behind this fear and intimidation haunted the crowded tenements. This was a place where triads ruled; the police knew that. A place where the gangs preyed remorselessly on local businesses; where rivals fought blade wars for protection concessions, spilling each other's blood to protect their fiefdoms. A place where countless people could come to satisfy any physical need. It was all here: the tiny fifty-dollar packet of China White – ninety-eight per cent pure; the willing young woman with a *cheung saam* dress open to her thigh. Anything you could name – but for a price. The blazing ideograms told their own story: *New Lucky Ballroom ... Special Body Massage ... Hostess Service Provided. All major credit cards welcome.*

Setting the handbrake, Gwan-Dai tuned the radio to an all-night FM station that played mostly Cantonese love songs, and he leaned back in the seat. The female singer's voice was like the whispering of silk as it slid gently in and out of his consciousness. This position was good, he decided; here he could observe the frontage of the Barking Peacock and watch adulterous couples come tumbling out through the motorised glass doors in search of a motel room. And soon even the whores would leave to make their lonely way home.

As he settled down to wait, he let the silky voice from the radio wash over him; he imagined the girl's mouth pressed close to the microphone – full and red, and opening like a flower. Like the girl he now waited for, she would be soft and pretty – and alone. When last he had seen the girl it had been through a pavement throng, but tonight's rain had all but dissolved the crowds. Aside from a few strutting bouncers and the touts poking their weaselly heads expectantly out of doorways, there was almost no one now. Tropical storm Nadia had come up from the Philippines like a wildcat; though narrowly missing Hong Kong, and instead hurling itself against the Vietnamese coastline, it still left twenty-four hours of rain in its wake. Now the streets of Kowloon were deluged, and the rising water-level lapped around the entrances to the Mass Transit underground railway. On the hillsides wooden squatter shacks clung precariously, as if expecting to be swept away at any minute.

Gwan-Dai's left hand strayed from the steering-wheel to stroke the enamelled surface of the mask lying on the seat beside him. It was hard and cool to the touch: an opera mask of red and black, ornately decorated with thin gold lines. The terrible face of the martial god Gwan-Dai. With exaggerated reverence the driver lifted it in both hands, letting the black silk beard spill into his lap. For an electric moment he gazed in awe upon the power of the face, the wildly curving eyebrows, the fiercely down-turned mouth. Placing it over his face, he adjusted the rearview mirror – and saw the god mask come to life.

On the fourth floor of the Barking Peacock, well up from the clamour of the disco floor, four men filed into a darkened room and took their seats before a large video screen.

Even had the light been good, it would have required an educated eye to distinguish between the two Chinese and their guests, for though all four men possessed the same black hair and almond-shaped eyes, one of them was a stocky Korean and the other a slender Japanese.

While the two visitors waited, sucking on their thin cigars, one of the Chinese found the video controller and activated the viewing equipment. The other one, who gave the orders, was taller than the average Chinese, handsome and heavily tanned, and his chest and shoulders stretched the white dinner-jacket. He showed a certain charm when he spoke to his guests, but there was something unsettling, menacing even, about those good looks, which made the others listen carefully when he spoke. The name on his Hong Kong ID card was Kwan

Kui-cheung, a name he had since westernised to Tony Kwan for the purpose of expanding his business into overseas markets. But the other men in the room knew him better as 'Red Cudgel', his official designation within the Society. Something in his manner let one know there was power and money behind him, and violence within.

'Take a long hard look,' growled Kwan, indicating the screen. 'Then tell me what you think?'

He had trouble sounding his consonants: the TH in THINK softened into an F; the TS on the ends of words were swallowed whole. Not that the others were now concerned with matters of diction. All eyes in the room were fixed on the video screen, watching two naked bodies writhe together in the most private of human interactions. The bed was huge and round, with sheets of pale silk. Above their heads a wooden ceiling-fan twirled slowly. From the girl's face, her pale smooth flesh and shining blue-black hair, it was obvious she was Chinese; from the dark curly hair on the big man's back and shoulders as he pumped between her thighs, it was equally clear that he was Caucasian.

'Where are they?' asked Rhee the Korean, throwing back his head to release a plume of cigar smoke towards the ceiling.

'Right above our heads,' answered Tony Kwan. 'That's where they usually go. First they have sex, then they do a little business. The information he gives her is always excellent. I don't want to meet him myself, so we use Ruby as our cut-out.'

'Does she *know* she's on camera?' asked Rhee, wondering how far they had taken her into their confidence.

Red Cudgel smiled thinly.

'Ruby? Of course she does. Forget any worries you may have. She's our property, and safe enough. Just concentrate on the American she's humping with. Phase one of our operation begins tomorrow. We must make up our minds about him tonight '

'I understand, Red Cudgel,' said Rhee. He waved his cigar towards the protagonists on the screen. 'But how can we see who he is, when his face is stuck between her tits?'

'Patience, brother,' said Red Cudgel. 'My Ruby has her orders. She knows what to do.'

Less than a minute later the girl in the bed moaned aloud, struggling to free herself from under the American's weight.

'No good for me like this!' she panted into his ear, rolling the big man over on his back. 'Can't feel nothing. Want you right inside of me.'

As realisation dawned, the American grinned up at her. His face eager, he reached for her breasts.

As Ruby slid down upon him the Westerner's head slammed back into the pillow. A groan accompanied the sudden arching of his buttocks. At that moment, in the room below, Red Cudgel pulled the video camera into a tight close-up of his face, and he operated a digitalised graphics interface which froze the picture. It took another five seconds for the software to rebuild the enhanced close-up and feed it back to the screen, simulating normal lighting conditions.

'Well?' he asked, impatient for an answer.

'That's him,' said Rhee with conviction. Beside him the slim Japanese blinked once, but said nothing.

'You're sure?' pressed the Chinese, adjusting the wing collar at his throat.

'No question about it. That's the American I saw in the club in Metro Manila. He's a Company man, I'm sure of it. There's a chance he might have wandered from the fold, but I'd say that if he's the source for your information, then you've got problems.'

'Meaning?' Red Cudgel continued to press him.

Rhee held his gaze.

'Ask yourself who is using whom.'

Red Cudgel snapped off the video, his irritation

undisguised, and strode to an altar shelf in one corner of the room, where a white statuette gazed benignly down. Tin Hau was goddess of the sea, most beloved deity of the sea-going Tanka fishermen from whom Red Cudgel was descended. The act of lighting three joss-sticks and placing them upright within the brass urn gave him the time he needed to think. By the time he turned around again, he had already decided what must be done.

But first he wanted to hear what these foreign devils had to say – these consultants who had come so highly recommended and for whom he had paid so dearly.

'Tell me, Rhee, what would you do in my place?' he asked.

Rhee studied the glowing tip of his own cigar. 'A double agent is a liability forever. They can never be trusted. Bearing in mind the nature of what you have planned for the next few weeks, you cannot afford to keep him around. Providing he has already handed over the sought-after document, I would wash him away now, before he causes you further trouble.'

The Chinese nodded thoughtfully, and continued to pace the room.

'A sound enough strategy,' he said stopping by the desk to stub out his cigar in a deep crystal ashtray. 'But a wise man judges by actions, not words.'

'Meaning ...?' asked Rhee, stiffening in his seat, ready to seize upon any slight to his reputation.

'Meaning, perhaps, it is time we see how good this man of yours really is.' Red Cudgel's gaze fixed on the Japanese sitting to Rhee's right. Thus far Okamoto had remained silent; his face had registered only mild disgust at the enlarged images of sweating flesh which had appeared on the video screen. Now Red Cudgel thought it was time to see exactly what he had bought.

'What about a demonstration of this absolute commitment you mentioned.'

Rhee kept his composure. For the money Red Cudgel

11

was paying, the man was entitled to air his doubts. And when Rhee studied the young man sitting silently beside him, he sometimes felt doubts himself. The Japanese showed no external capacity for violence; indeed there was a certain meekness in his appearance. His skin was ghostly pale, his lashes were long and fine; his face resembled the delicate features of a girl.

Rhee addressed his acolyte with several rapid sentences of fluent Japanese. The pale young man gave a quick, curt nod of his close-cropped head. He lifted a long leather case from the floor by his feet, and began to pick open the straps at one end of it.

Red Cudgel exchanged glances with the other Chinese – an officer known by his position within the Society as 'Vanguard' – and both men watched closely as Okamoto continued to loosen the knots with his long fingers. Both had been silently wondering what this leather bag might contain. Now their eyes widened as the Japanese peeled back the flap and carefully drew out an ornate sword sheathed in a scabbard of lacquered red wood.

The young foreigner's face registered intense concentration as he drew the hilt a mere four inches from the wood, revealing a gleaming and perfect steel blade with a clover-leaf pattern at its edge. Glancing around him, the Japanese saw their grudging looks of appreciation, though he knew in his heart that these two Chinese gangsters were incapable of understanding the true nature of the *katana* he now held in his hands ... or the enlightened spirit it represented.

It was a sword of the Genroku period: from a time when swords were worn as symbols of social status. This was an example of the art of the master swordmaker Ikkanshi Tadatsuna, and it carried his signature on the blade, along with the date: December 1699 in Western terms. There was a deep sheen to the surface of the steel; relief carvings depicted carp swimming up a waterfall, with branches of plum blossom as embellishment. The sword mountings were also exquisite: lacquered vermilion on magnolia wood, overlaid with lacquered gold. The bindings were of black waxed silk braid plaited over a leaping golden carp device on either side of the hilt, and the pommel was a perfectly polished red stone the size of a quail's egg. To complete the artistic balance, the sword guard had been conceived as a simple blackened surface relieved only by the raised pattern of a single peony blossom in gold.

These Chinese triads were ignorant, reflected Okamoto; they could not begin to know what a masterpiece of the swordmaker's art this piece represented. Or what price he had paid in order to possess it.

The young man inclined his head, then spoke softly so that only Rhee could hear.

Nodding in understanding, Rhee turned back to the two Chinese.

'Red Cudgel,' he said, 'Okamoto presents his compliments and says he awaits your pleasure.'

Moments later, in the upstairs apartment, Ruby Tang's shuddering climax was interrupted by the urgent warble of the telephone. It rang a dozen times more before her breathless voice came on the line.

'*Wei!*'

'Ruby, this is Tony. Finish up and bring our friend back downstairs. I've some friends here who'd like to meet him.'

'*Ho!*' she said, acknowledging the order. 'Give me fifteen minutes.'

'Make it ten,' ordered Red Cudgel. A new note of concern entered his voice. 'Did he bring the document?'

'Of course,' she said, lowering her voice as she fished in her handbag. 'I have it here in my hand.'

'Good.' His relief was audible. 'After you bring Reicher to me, go down on to the dance floor. That crazy little bitch you just hired is playing up again. She's making us look bad in front of our guests from the mainland. Send her home before I have her mouth stitched.'

'*Ho!*' said Ruby obediently. 'I'll attend to that at once.'

Brown eyes burning behind the slits of the mask, Gwan-Dai watched the girl come downstairs into the pink and purple glow of the club entrance. Just as before, she wore stiletto heels and a rose-tinted chiffon dress with spangles across the bodice, but this time she was not alone. There was another woman, equally attractive but too well-dressed to be just another of the club hostesses. As they walked out across the pavement, heads lowered against the drenching rain, he realised the second, older woman was supporting the other, who was clearly the worse for drink. Gwan-Dai set down the mask and watched with interest.

There seemed to be some trouble between them.

Ruby Tang gripped the younger girl by the upper arm, her fingernails biting deep. She scolded loudly as she pushed her towards the red Mercedes sports coupé parked at the kerb. What this girl had done was unforgivable: neglecting her duties and indulging herself in unseemly behaviour with a bunch of young triad 'Blue Lanterns' of no particular standing. She had drunk far too much brandy, becoming loud and unruly, and knocking over glasses, which could bring the club a bad name. Small wonder that Red Cudgel wanted her out now. It did not matter that the kid was depressed – a one-month abortion still fresh in her mind. What mattered was that she, Ruby Tang, was the hostess captain of the Barking Peacock, and this girl was her responsibility. It was Ruby's own face which was now at stake.

'*Sor mooi!* Stand still while I open this door,' she ordered irritably, fumbling in her bag for the keys to the Mercedes.

14

The drunken girl was not listening. Staggering against the front wing, she toppled sideways on to her back, and lay across the bonnet, staring upwards, oblivious to the rain splashing on her face. As Ruby Tang reached for her arm once more, the girl opened her eyes and began to curse loudly.

'Leave me alone, poison woman! I'm going back inside!'

'No you won't,' snapped Ruby Tang. 'I'm taking you home before you cause more trouble. You'll sleep it off alone tonight!'

'Trouble? What trouble I cause? You're crazy!' argued the younger woman.

Ruby shook her head in disgust.

'You're the crazy one. Look at you behaving like a piece of trash. All you had to do was smile and flash your little tits for your boss's guests.'

'Those men were like kids in a candy store – hands here, hands everywhere!'

'Nevertheless, they were special guests.'

The girl's head rolled to one side and the bright red bud of her mouth twisted in a bitter sneer.

'Special! – *Diu lei lo mo!* Wise up, won't you? Those bastards were nothing special. Just *Ah Chan* from across the border.' She raised her head just enough to spit into the gutter. 'Probably illegals! With dirt from the communes still beneath their fingernails!'

Ruby Tang stiffened at the mention of the words *Ah Chan* – a derogatory term for recent arrivals from China. Invariably such men were looked down on by Hong Kong Chinese as ignorant and uncouth, but from their ranks had come some of the most vicious gangsters in the colony. Already the girl had said too much.

'Listen to me, little sister.' Any remaining sympathy was gone now. 'Tonight you were entertaining important businessmen. That's all you'll say if anyone asks – *ming baak?*'

15

But the girl remained abusively defiant, emboldened by the brandy in her stomach.

'What businessmen? You think I'm stupid, think I don't know *Dai Huen Jai* when I see them? *Diu lei lo mo!* Think I can't guess why they're here?'

'Hold that tongue before it chokes you!' cautioned Ruby nervously, reaching for the girl and finding a pair of flailing arms fending her off.

'It has to be something really big. Chan Ming showed me the pistol shoved inside his waistband – big as a fucking cannon!'

In a flash of anger Ruby slapped the arms aside and seized the girl by the hair, lifting her up off the bonnet with a squeal of pain. Ruby's hand then struck like the lash of a whip, catching the hostess across the jaw, spinning her round and sending her sprawling into the gutter with a splash. Standing over her, Ruby Tang issued a final warning through clenched teeth.

'Don't you know what happens to little drunks with big mouths!'

All at once the girl's bravado crumbled. Her head fell forward and she began to cry.

At such an abject sight Ruby felt her heart melt. She had once been a hostess herself, a long time ago. She knew well enough the misery they suffered. Theirs was a life of continual debt, frequent beatings, and the constant threat of greater violence. Finally Ruby stretched out her hand to help the girl back to her feet. She hugged her close, clucking like a parent with a wayward child.

'Sssshhh, it's all right now,' she cooed, smoothing her damp hair. 'Whatever are we to do with you?'

'I'm sorry ... *Ah je*,' the other managed between her sobs, addressing Ruby respectfully now as Elder Sister. '*Yam jui jau* – getting drunk – causing you so much trouble. I really am *sor mooi*.'

Ruby smiled goodnaturedly. *Sor mooi* – crazy little girl. This had been her nickname from the day she arrived at the Barking Peacock, but underneath the bravado and big talk here was just another frightened kid. And one who would catch her death of cold if she did not get home soon.

The taxi appeared from nowhere, pulling into the kerb behind the red Mercedes. The purple light from the club sign washed over its silver roof and red side panels. There was a clunk as the driver operated the autolock, and the rear door swung welcomingly open. It took just a second for Ruby to imagine the girl's wet gown on the new chamois leather of Tony Kwan's car, and to decide that this taxi was the better option.

She bundled the girl into the back of the cab, and stepped around to the driver's window. At first the man behind the wheel avoided her gaze, staring intently at the windscreen.

'Take her to Wong Tai Sin,' Ruby began, detailing the address as she fished inside her handbag and produced a bundle of notes. At first the driver seemed not to hear her, gazing instead at the windscreen in front of him.

'Did you hear me?' she pressed, offering the money. There was something strange about this man: something cold and unresponsive. Then her eye fell on something shiny on the seat beside him. The sight of the mask made her catch her breath, then the man's gaze was full upon her. She sensed danger at once – almost before his hand was through the window, grabbing her arm and pulling her towards him. Her shoulder slammed painfully against the door frame, causing her to cry out as her handbag tumbled inside on to the floor of the taxi. It was then that she saw the hunting knife in the man's other hand, and knew what he intended to do. His eyes were wide and blazing, but she saw her chance and took it – clawing at those staring eyes with her long fingernails. The attacker cried out in pain, and loosed his grip long enough for Ruby Tang to recover her footing and draw back from the open window. Turning, she ran screaming for the safety of the club entrance, with the sound of the taxi's gunning engine in her ears.

'*Gau meng! Gau meng!*'

Breathless with shock, Ruby Tang turned from the sanctuary of the doorway in time to see the taxi disappear into the night with a squeal of protesting rubber. As the glass doors purred aside to admit her, and her brain struggled to comprehend what had happened, suddenly the full shock hit her.

Her handbag! The document!

Invoking the names of all the gods, Ruby ran back into the street, less afraid of the man with the knife than of the swift and certain retribution of Red Cudgel when he heard she had lost the document he so eagerly awaited.

The street was empty, the taxi nowhere to be seen. She had not even registered its full licence number.

As she stared vainly into the neon-clustered night a cold fear began to grip her. Her chances of recovering the document were hopeless. Perhaps Red Cudgel would understand. Surely he had to believe her. The taxi-driver with the madly staring eyes had been intent on murder. May the gods protect *sor mooi*, she whispered aloud, for no one else could help her now.

But all Ruby's experience told her that even if Tony Kwan did believe her, he would still have to make an example of her for the sake of appearances. Gulping back her tears, she made up her mind in the next few seconds.

The rain was still falling steadily on the streets of Kowloon as Ruby Tang turned her back on the Barking Peacock and slipped away into the night.

TWO

There was the unmistakably sweet odour of Pepto Bismol in the room as the Director of Central Intelligence poured a measure of the bright pink liquid into a shot glass and knocked it back in a single loud gulp. The hand which stifled a wet cough was flecked with brown age spots.

'This goddamn ulcer – it keeps me bent double almost half the day.'

'At your age, Phil, and in these times, what the hell do you expect?' Kazinski, the National Security Adviser, expressed scant sympathy for the head of the US intelligence community.

Both men sat in an air-conditioned, electronically-swept office in the Old Executive Building, within sight of the White House, though the DCI would have been the first to admit that he did not let the view intimidate him in any way. Kazinski continued playfully, 'Perhaps it's time that you called it a day. Spend a few years counting the money you've made from that private practice of yours. Enjoy, why don't you?'

Director Kagan looked across the desk and smiled in genuine amusement, his eyes almost disappearing in the folds of his face. He had been an impressive figure as a young man, and a snappy dresser too. Now he was old and, though he still liked to dress well, his measurements had ballooned to a degree that his heart was fighting a losing battle with his weight. Though he was a favourite target for Washington political cartoonists, none doubted the quality of his mind. Even at sixty-three, Kagan was bright as a laser, and a dangerous enemy for any man.

'Retirement is the last thing on my mind. The Agency badly needs a success after our losses of recent years. Something big. The real work is just beginning.'

'And just where do you hope to find such success.'

'New horizons.' Eyes widening in sudden animation, Kagan squared his shoulders against the leather back of his executive swivel-chair. 'Pacific Rim.'

'You mean Asia?'

'That's right. No more of that Central American shit. I'm tired of kicking ass in Spickville. For every kick I give them, I get two in return from the Oversight Committee and another from those bastards in the House.'

Kazinski nodded his agreement, adjusting the onyx-and-gold cufflinks he had received from the President on his last birthday.

'There's plenty of scope. What had you in mind?'

'You know, things are really starting to break up over there. Our policy of containment of the Soviets in the eastern Pacific is looking particularly shaky since those Filipino bastards kicked us out of Subic Bay and Clarke Field.'

Kazinski nodded once more, remembering how the Philippine government had unilaterally ordered a pull-out from the two major bases as part of their settlement with communist insurgents who had been tearing the Philippines apart for years. A high price to pay for national unity, he thought, in view of the billions of dollars the US had previously paid them in rent each year.

'I guess I have to agree: the situation is an unhealthy one. The Soviets will obviously try to strengthen their position. They're gut-sick of having their Pacific Fleet bottled up. That could lead to all kinds of relocations now that we can't field the same forces over there. It could go either way. The Japanese are sharing the early-warning and radar responsibilities but they're not applying any real pressure. They're waiting. We have to be seen to take the leading role in that theatre or, so help me, we're going to see the emergence of new alliances: ones which leave us out in the cold. Japan, China and Korea are a natural power-bloc. They grow closer every year, culturally, economically, militarily. With Jap technology and a fully-developed Chinese economy, they would present a very credible alternative to the Western defence bloc.' Kazinski stopped himself. He had succumbed easily to discussing the Pacific Rim, for it was an area never far from his thoughts these days. The past few years had seen it emerge as the single most strategically-important section of the globe. He checked his watch. 'Forgive me. You didn't invite me over just so we could bad-mouth the Flips.'

'That's right, I didn't.'

'Then why? You know I'm due at the Oval Office in forty minutes.'

Kagan looked his man full in the eye and said: 'Karl, I need your support.'

'Support?' echoed Kazinski curiously.

'Something they're not going to like up on Capitol Hill.'

Kazinski folded his arms defensively. The other man was a political predator if ever there was one. Now was the time to go carefully.

'Phil, I've supported you on many occasions in the past. And come pretty close to getting shit-canned for it.'

'Just bad luck.' Kagan waved a huge paw dismissively.

'Bad luck, my ass! You should have known that witness would turn bad on us in Congressional hearings. I've told you before, I won't do time in the pen for anyone. Not even for him!' Kazinski's finger jabbed towards the window, in the direction of the White House. He watched the old man's face change, enormous grey eyebrows knitting beneath a shiny expanse of forehead.

'Got you out of that mess, didn't I?'

Kazinski sat in silence for a moment, controlling his resentment. Finally: 'Yeah, we all came out virgin-pure. That's another story, though.' A sign of resignation. 'OK, what's on your mind?'

Kagan placed his chin in his left hand and massaged it slowly.

'It's time to look at that Thousand Island mess again.'

'You mean the Spratlys? I thought that was safely dead-locked: Vietnam, China, the Filipinos, all bickering over who owns what. The way I read it, most of those islands are nothing more than reefs and sandbanks, anyway.'

'Let's not be quite so naive, Karl. We both know the importance of these islands in terms of power projection. We're talking six hundred kilometres east of Cam Ranh Bay, a major Vietnamese naval base where Soviet ballistic submarines are berthed at this very moment. China is just nine hundred klicks to the north, and Philippine and Malaysian territory no more than a spit to the south-east. Put a Trident-bearing sub in amongst those atolls and you could wield untold power.' Kagan opened his left hand flat and jabbed it with his right index finger. 'The next time you look at a map, take a pen and draw a circle around the Spratlys, say five thousand klicks or so: the range of one of our Trident missiles.' He traced a circle on his palm and looked up to make sure Kazinski was paying attention. 'Inside that circle you got one third of the world's population. Imagine that.' He closed the hand into a tight, hairy fist. 'A third of mankind under the gun. Don't tell me those little reefs aren't worth fighting over.'

'OK, you've made your point: the area's a powder keg. I know that. But so long as the Chinese don't push the Vietnamese too hard over sovereignty, there'll be no conflict. The Viets just don't want to get locked out of the open sea by a strategic presence of Beijing's subs – or anyone else's either.'

22

'What if I told you the Viets have a survey party on one of the Western groups right now? The strong suggestion is they're doing a feasibility study on constructing a base there.'

'Hypothetical, right?'

'Just answer the question.'

Kazinski opened his palms and made a face.

'I don't know. I guess I'd say national pride had clouded their judgement. Or else Moscow had decided to give them a push.'

'Smart boy! You ought to be National Security Adviser some day,' cracked Kagan. 'Look at it this way. Our Seventh Fleet is currently patrolling that region, with only Hong Kong offering the right strategic and logistical support base. Our profile there is diminishing since our withdrawal from the Philippines. Another four years and the Chinese government will yank Hong Kong back from the British. What then?'

'Looks like Ivan gets a free hand in the Pacific and the leverage to properly threaten important oil supply routes.'

'Both of which would strengthen his hand in the event of an all-out global war.'

'Wait a minute. Who said anything about war?'

'Karl, please don't give me any of that Harvard bull-shit about the age of reason. Our policy has always been to work for peace but to prepare for the inevitable. That's why I've got this thing for those goddamn little islands.' His hand moved to the open attaché case on the side table; he withdrew a grey folder and placed it on the desk. Even reading upside-down, Karl Kazinski could make out the words DIRECTORATE OF INTELLIGENCE, and, beneath, IMAGERY ANALYSIS SERVICE. There were also KH-12 codeword classifications stamped in bright red on the cover. Satellite reconnaissance. Kazinski produced a pair of reading glasses and picked up the folder.

23

Kagan talked on while the other man read the contents.

'Two days ago we moved one of our KEYHOLE assets into position over the South China Sea. Just routine monitoring of military shipping, looking for pictures of the opposition nuclear boats putting in and out of Cam Ranh. During the transmission there was a malfunction, the motors controlling the satellite sent it spinning further south, photographing at random. Results were mostly garbage, but the bird did pass over the Spratly group, and it took these pictures of a survey vessel doing some serious examination of access channels around the western atolls.'

Kazinski examined the folder. A stack of eight-by-tens confirmed what the DCI was saying. The outline of the ship bobbing in the dangerous swell reminded him of Soviet spy-trawlers he had seen years ago when he had been a commander of Naval Intelligence in carriers.

'It could just be routine: keeping an eye on the other players. Or a boat mapping fish shoal migration. Anything.'

Kagan shook his head emphatically.

'Look at picture number twelve. It's a close-up of that survey ship. See the name's blanked out. They've tried to disguise it but I had it matched and, believe me, it's a Soviet ship. They're up to no good, Karl.'

Kazinski just smiled and shook his head.

'You won't convince me unless there's more.'

'Oh, there is. Much more. This morning I received this.' He tossed a typed sheaf of papers bearing the codeword UMBRA on to the desk. 'I had the NSA monitor all radio communications coming out of that ship for the past twenty-four hours. They do a lot of jabbering in Vietnamese, claim they're sizing it up for oil exploration, but their real communications are coded. This is the unscrambled version of yesterday's product.'

He peeled back a couple of sheets and turned the

stack for the other to read. Kazinski felt a twinge of excitement in his chest. He still found it nothing short of miraculous to be able to do this sort of thing: to pluck words out of the air on the other side of the world by Rhyolite satellite, bounce them between the Pine Gap facility in Australia and Rendondo Beach in California, and thence to NSA headquarters at Fort Meade, Maryland. And all in a matter of seconds. His eyes devoured the translation, secretly enjoying the sense of intrigue.

'Visitors request this, visitors request that. Specific mention of foreign consultants in three places. Fraternal colleagues. And what does this word mean?'

Kagan could not restrain a smile.

'Oh, yeah. That's a rather charming Vietnamese word meaning something like "white barbarians". A slip that tells us they have Caucasians aboard: probably Soviet naval engineers with GRU clearance. That's a guess born out by the NSA's analysis, which says they were using an old GRU coded cipher which our Cray computers broke eighteen months ago. The major military installations have got wise and stopped using it, but I guess the word hasn't filtered through to these clowns yet.'

Kazinski quickly read the report by the senior survey engineer aboard the vessel. It spoke of the difficulties of navigation of large vessels between the thirty-some islands. Depths varied, but there were a number of access routes for both surface and submerged vessels. There were references to the routes used by the Japanese navy during The Great Patriotic War: the Russian term for what the rest of the world called World War II. The report closed by saying that navigation beacons had been laid to assist safe passage to the proposed construction site.

'Honest to God,' said Kazinski when he had finished, 'they really are going for it. A forward military base.'

'I wonder if you appreciate the magnitude of this.'

The DCI threw his arms wide to give him a clue. 'If the Vietnamese, and through them the Soviets, can establish a submarine base here, they can control all surface movement in that theatre. They could cut off the Japanese from their Gulf oil routes, could lock off maritime shipping lanes between the Indian and Pacific Oceans, cut all supply lines. Hell, the seabed is like a rucked up bedsheet down there. We'd never be able to detect and neutralise their boomers. They'd hold all Asia hostage!'

'Phil, you have to bring this to the President.'

'Don't worry, Corrigan has things under control on the White House staff. I've asked him to squeeze me in right after your appointment. I'd be grateful if you'd hang around afterwards, because what I'm about to propose could get a little sticky. With your assistance he'll appreciate the problem. I need him to appreciate its importance so he can understand that its worth the risks.'

A dark frown passed over Kazinski's face.

'You're not suggesting military intervention are you?'

Once again the DCI smiled. 'Karl, Karl. That's much too crude. I'm an intelligence officer. My job is to do by stealth what may not be done openly. Nobody's talking about a shooting war when we can achieve the same result by manipulating perceptions.'

'And what does that mean in words even the President can understand?'

'I'm going to work a sting on those bastards so cute that they'll never even know they've been stung.'

Kazinski felt himself infected by the DCI's boyish enthusiasm, as he once more flicked through the satellite pictures. Already his sharp political brain was plotting how to grab a good share of the credit.

'You know,' he said, 'I can't wait to see their faces in the National Security Council. Naturally, you'll be presenting all this at the next meeting.'

Kazinski became aware that the DCI did not answer promptly, and he caught that vague, secretive look on his

26

face: the one the old man usually reserved for his testimony before the Oversight Committee.

'The NSC ... yes,' he said eventually. 'Karl, I'm afraid I can't do that, and I'll have to ask you not to discuss it with anyone but myself and the President. You'll understand why after we speak with him today.'

Somewhere in the street below a car horn sounded as it passed. To Kazinski it sounded like a human scream – or perhaps an alarm bell warning him to take care. Did he know what he was getting into here? Keeping information from the Oversight Committee was a fact of life for Directors of the CIA. If they don't ask you about it, then you don't have to tell them anything. But the NSC was different. The Holy of Holies.

'Karl?' The DCI broke into his reverie. Kazinski's eyes refocused inside the room. The old man was eyeing him questioningly. He thought of the weighty evidence he had already seen that morning, and dismissed his reservations. After all, Soviet nuclear submarines!

'You know you can rely on my discretion, Phil.'

'Thank you.' Kagan smiled infectiously, and they shook hands like two schoolboys sharing a pledge. 'I promise you won't be sorry.'

The National Security Adviser checked his watch.

'I hope not. Now, if you'll excuse me, I'm due across the way. Be seeing you shortly.'

As the door closed, Phil Kagan's old face betrayed none of the satisfaction he really felt. He took a Havana cigar from the carved sandalwood box on his desk, inhaled the tobacco's rich aroma and struck a match.

The cigar was, of course, strictly against his doctor's orders. But, then, Phil Kagan had never been much good at following orders he did not concur with, trusting instead to his own better judgement.

He maintained the exact same attitude towards the many constraints placed on his organisation by the US Congress. Kagan remained true to the one good piece of advice his lawyer father had bequeathed him.

'Son,' the senior Kagan had told him. 'Rules are made for the blind obedience of fools, and for the guidance of wise men.'

Like any loyal son he had done his best to live by this sentiment.

THREE

When he reached the top of Beacon Hill, Becker slowed his pace to a walk and stepped through the trees on to the narrow path, sucking in deep breaths of air to cool his burning lungs. Behind him, the imposing golfball of the radar beacon stood out against the spine of the Kowloon foothills, blinding white in the pure light of the early morning. Before and below him sprawled the mystery of Kowloon, wearing its permanent haze of monoxide fumes like a mantle. He felt the intense burning in his thigh muscles, now that he had stopped, and the involuntary spasm that always followed the uphill battle. The run up to the radar beacon didn't get any easier, he reflected, hawking loudly and spitting the phlegm from his throat. It was no more than a couple of kilometres on a deserted concrete road used only by the occasional government vehicle, but the gradient was consistently brutal and made it a cruelly efficient workout. As usual, the dominant males in the baboon troop inhabiting the trees just off the path had challenged his progress, but Becker had stared them down and continued his pace unbroken through their territory, sending them chattering back into the trees. To his left narrow footpaths snaked away, chalk yellow, across the spine of the green foothills which ended in the squatting bulk of the Lion Rock.

As his breathing returned to normal, Becker began to feel just how tired he really was. He had slept only fitfully the night before, tossing and turning under a single cotton sheet, while he cursed the damn humidity and his broken air-conditioner, until it all became too much. Twice he had doused himself under a cold shower and lain beneath the twirling ceiling fan – his government flat had ceiling fans in every room – but this had done nothing to relieve his discomfort. In the end he had got up and had driven down into the bar area of Tsim Sha Tsui. There he occupied a barstool at the Ship Inn, drinking coffee and speaking Cantonese with the barman. Jimmy was an expert on Sixties pop music, and he and Becker liked to trade trivia of the 'Who sang this one?' variety. When dawn arrived he had driven back home, showered once more, changed into running kit and crossed over the Lung Cheung Road behind Elizabethan Court to work out his frustrations on this routine climb up Beacon Hill.

As Becker walked along the baked path, memories came rushing back like a hot wind through the tall grass. It was eight long years since he had first discovered the secret of 'the Pavilion Without Walls', and those first memories were still as strong as ever. He'd been a second-tour police inspector or *bong baan* then – an aspiring steely-eyed oriental crime fighter, as they jokingly referred to themselves – still striving after the essential spirit of the place and curious to know what made the Chinese so different from themselves. Perhaps wiser, more in tune with their surroundings, more at peace with themselves? Then one day he had decided to take an early run up the Beacon Hill, and had been lured off the path by a sound like wind rushing through a deep cave. Following the melancholic sound, he had come upon a break in the trees where the path opened into a small clearing. Here the urban sprawl below was completely blotted out by intervening vegetation, but the dense cover of trees and young bamboo gave way to one of the most inspiring sights Hong Kong has to offer: Lion Rock thrusting its head upwards against the great blue bowl of the sky, with its rugged Lion's face brought dramatically to life by the unexpected sparkle of the sun upon a hidden eye.

Then he'd realised he was not alone.

In the middle of the clearing stood an old Chinese man dressed in baggy black pants and white vest. The back of his head was flat, the white hair cropped close enough to reveal a spattering of brown freckles beneath. A retired agricultural worker, or maybe a construction worker – anyway, low income group, thought Becker. The man was standing with his back straight and his knees bent at ninety degrees, alternately inhaling and exhaling as his open hands slowly described wide circles in front of his face. At first Becker had the impression of watching a man drowning in molasses but as he continued to observe, he saw the old man turn and centre himself against the outline of the Rock, and then his whole body began to move, feet shifting instinctively with perfect poise and balance. A single joyful and harmonious entity: soft, yet possessed of an immense intrinsic strength, ritualised and yet spontaneous beyond imagination. The slender nut-brown arms drew dynamic strokes in the morning air, like ancient and magnificent calligraphy, and yet it seemed both effortless and formless.

Becker knew enough of Hong Kong to recognise a martial arts exercise when he saw one. He himself had grunted and twisted through self-defence class in Police Training School, but he had never seen anything quite like this before. Fascinated, he crept forward quietly and took a seat on one of the smooth rocks placed to mark the path. But at once the old man sensed the intrusion and came to an immediate halt. For a moment he stood there listening, perhaps trying to sense the intention of the intruder. Becker held his breath and made no sound. Long seconds later the movements began again. This time the old man sped through his ritual dance without pausing, treating Becker to a rare display of perhaps one hundred and twenty separate martial movements. When he was finished he came to rest facing the Lion Rock, letting the sweet warmth of the morning sun wash over his serene, weathered face.

There was a brief moment of silent meditation, and then he spoke.

'Why do you watch me?' he asked in level Cantonese, without turning around. Caught off-balance, Becker didn't answer. 'Why do you watch me?' the old man asked again, his voice a little louder this time. Then he turned, and Becker saw clearly for the first time his blindness; the eyelashes fluttered like summer insects, but the old man's eyes were gone from the sockets.

'*Dui m'jiu, Ah Gung,*' he apologised.

'As I thought: *gwai lo!*' muttered the old man. 'Kindly do not call me grandfather, for we are no blood kin.' His old face filled with anger at the mere thought of such kinship with a foreign devil.

'Excuse me, *sin saang,*' Becker corrected himself, also in Cantonese. 'I meant no disrespect.'

'Your presence is disrespect enough. I did not invite you to watch me practise my art.'

The old man had a lot of fire in his pot belly for such a little fellow, thought Becker.

'Sir, I could not help myself. Your Kung Fu is of the first quality, and yet you are blind.'

The old man cocked his head oddly, following the sound, and then nodded sagely.

'Yes, I am blind. In that respect at least you are right, but in the matter of my art you are wrong. It is Tai Chi and Chi Gung I practise, and how would you, a barbarian, know *first* from any other quality?'

'You heard my footsteps on the path, didn't you?' said Becker changing the subject. 'But how could a blind man guess I was a foreigner?'

At this the old man's face creased like ancient leather.

'*Aiyah!* Yes, by the Gwan-Dai, I heard your elephant feet. But not before I smelled your barbarian odour and felt your outer skin touch mine.' He spread out the fingers of one hand and the tapered fingertips bent sharply at the last joint, giving the impression of a bird's claw.

'You smelled me? That's impossible at that distance ...'

'You must have run up the hill.' He wafted a hand before his nose in distaste. 'The smell of a meat eater is powerful, and it offends the nostrils of one who adheres to a civilised diet.'

'Sir, I meant only to praise your skills. If you will not give me even a little face in return, then I will leave you to your meditation.'

He was about to leave the clearing when suddenly the old man began to laugh.

'*Aiyah!* So young and so proud! Wait, don't go yet. It is unwise to be so sensitive and I, too, meant no offence.'

Becker stopped to listen, though he had to concentrate hard to decipher the Chiu Chau inflection.

The old man continued, 'Your Cantonese is good. I have never conversed with a *gwai lo* before, and I should like to do so. I have taught many fine young men to blow down mountains and wrestle the wind, but never a *gwai lo*. If you are interested, and are also a good listener, maybe one day I will make you my student.'

'Sorry, I'm not interested. Besides, you don't look as if you have that much time to play with.'

The old man laughed again. 'We'll see,' he said, bending down to sit upon another rock with the practised ease of one who knows his ground well.

In spite of himself, Becker stepped forward and sat down next to him, feeling like an awkward kid. The old boy was a powerful talker, and Becker soon found himself mesmerised. Like one of the professional story-tellers who work the crowds on the streets of Canton, he laid out his biography with no trace of modesty. He was sixty-two years old, and his name was Chen Man-kin of the famous Chen clan which originated in the Chen village in Ho Nan Province. As he said this he paused, but when the foreigner showed no recognition of the name, the old man gave a grunt and continued. His particular branch of the family had been farmers for generations, but they had also trained hard to preserve the skills of his ancestor Chang San-feng who was recognised as the founder of Tai Chi Chuan. Again no recognition – but this time the old man continued without a pause.

In youth Chen Man-kin had been trained as a bean curd maker, and for this he had been well known. But by the time he was eighteen he was already one of the finest boxers in the province. Every day some new boxer would come to the village to match skills with him at Chi Sau – 'pushing hands'. This, the old man explained, was an exercise regularly used in training, but it was also the highest test of Tai Chi ability. Two boxers would face each other, lock hands, and attempt to hurl each other to the ground by alternately pushing and retreating and by the expert use of balance: softness to overcome strength. The old man laughed when he recalled how he had once been challenged by the son of a local mandarin who was an intense and fierce student of martial arts, and had travelled many *li* to reach the Chen village. At the venerable one's insistence the contest was held on a wooden plank over a deep and muddy ditch, and the whole village had lined the bank to watch. After long minutes of inconclusive action the son of the mandarin became overexcited and tried to stab at Chen's eyes with his fingers. The sudden violence transmitted through his hand had been sensed by Chen, who deftly withdrew and circled, and then bowled the proud youngster head over heels into the ditch.

The cheers of the villagers had been tumultuous; so

too the loss of face for the loser, who slunk away with his entourage never to return. But that was not the end of the matter. One week later the wooden shed where Chen made bean curd was mysteriously burned down. A week after that, local officials visited the village elders and made threats about increasing their taxes. It was just the beginning, they realised, and they could expect continuing harassment so long as Chen Man-kin remained in the village.

Reluctantly he agreed to leave. He moved to the coastal port of Swatow and began teaching his skills to others under a different name. His gymnasium quickly became famous, attracting many of the young men associated with the secret societies pledged to support the Kuomintang party of Chiang Kai Shek. When Mao's communist forces approached Swatow, Chen knew his name was listed with those of the subversives, and that death by public hanging would be his punishment. There was no choice but to join the refugees fleeing south to Hong Kong. He had no particular love for the Generalissimo, nor any interest in restoring the throne of the Ming dynasty, but still he went. And as he came ashore on a deserted beach, jostled by the crowd of refugees, all he then knew of Hong Kong was that the foreign devils had stolen it a hundred years ago and made it rich through opium. And that now the Chinese called it, with longing in their voices, 'the land where men eat fat pork'.

In Hong Kong he found a wife, and returned to making bean curd. Trading on family connections, and the name of Chen, he bought a strip of land on the hillside beneath the Lion Rock and sold his blocks of white bean curd to the restaurants of Wong Tai Sin below. As the wooden shanties of the squatter villagers grew around him, he moved further up the hillside, seeking isolation. His wife bore four children and it was happiness of a kind, the old man murmured: peace and tranquility and a deserted hillside on which to practise his art.

'You taught these skills to your children?' Becker asked quietly. The old man sighed, then shook his head.

'I started to. My first son was a disappointment, loud and ungainly like his mother, and unwilling to practise. But the second son was gifted: bright, clear-eyed and diligent. And his hands could feel the breath of an attack long before it came.'

'What happened, *sifu*?' Becker realised he had automatically used the traditional title for a master.

'In the summer of 1960 there was a terrible fire.' He stretched out his hand towards the green slopes below the Lion Rock. 'It raged for two days through the squatter villages. It killed many people, including my wife and little ones. I remember clearly, it was very early when the fire began – before dawn. I had risen early to deliver boxes of bean curd to the restaurants, leaving my family asleep. There was no way the authorities could bring engines up the hillside, and water was in short supply that summer. I had to guard the ashes of my wooden hut for days to keep the looters away, but I never found the few taels of gold we had hidden. Truly, I lost everything.'

Becker looked at his feet, absorbing the silence of the old man's grief. He had always considered himself poorly off compared with the overt wealth of many Hong Kong citizens, their shiny cars and their affluence. Suddenly he felt ashamed.

'How did you manage after that?'

'Like the willow that bends with the wind, and thus endures.'

How many times had he returned here after that to converse with the old master, or to visit his wooden hut on the hillside below? Scores, perhaps hundreds. And gradually he had begun to learn what lay beyond the curtain, in that shaded backroom he had dreamed of, where the mysteries of the Orient were kept hidden in small lacquered boxes.

36

Chen Man-kin became first his friend and then his teacher, asking him many questions about the ways of the foreigner, and offering the alternative wisdom of the Chinese. But it was a long time before the *sifu* offered to teach Becker the skill of pushing hands. And by that time Becker had already learned that the art of boxing has very little to do with physical considerations.

Becker now stepped through the ferns and into the open space his *sifu* had once called the Pavilion Without Walls. Fond memory almost led him to hope he might see the old man once more squatting there with his arms flashing about him and the breath thundering from his chest like the wind rushing through a deep cave.

But the old master had died two years ago. A long bout of emphysema had finally finished him off in the dampness of winter. A string of distant relatives, on his wife's side, had seen him properly buried. Later, when his flesh had fallen from his bones, they would take them to be polished, then placed in an earthenware jar on the hillside here, as was the custom.

Now in the Pavilion Without Walls the grass had grown back. Gone were the two bald patches where the *sifu*'s feet had stood at the start and finish of his forms. All his marvellous skills were lost, gone into that void of the universe that the Chinese call Wu Chi. It saddened Becker to think of such experience being lost. The old man's legacy had been one of inspiration and strength, and Becker knew he would never forget him.

Five hours later, Chief Inspector David Becker descended the steps of Caine House, at Police Head-quarters, wearing the kind of well-cut suit expected of an officer of the Special Branch VIP Protection Unit. Beside him walked two burly Americans of the US State Department Security Branch, easily recognisable as bodyguards, who had flown in from Manila just that morning to prepare the ground for the impending visit of William Fredericks, the American Secretary of State. As they reached the bottom step, a dark saloon moved smoothly into position to collect them.

Seated in the back of the vehicle, the two jet-lagged advance men were still enthusing wildly about rosewood furniture when the car pulled into the Wanchai basin and approached the helipad.

Becker smiled indulgently as he directed the two across the blinding stretch of concrete to where a waiting helicopter was already snapping its rotors at the sky. The whoosh from its down-draught was refreshing after the oppressive heat of the street. Humidity was trembling at the ninety per cent mark, according to the weatherman's graphics.

As the aircraft rose above the mirror-faceted glass towers of Central's business district, Becker felt his stomach lurch; the reek of aviation fuel inside the cabin augmented his general sense of nausea. Why on earth had he agreed to take this flight, when his head still ached from lack of sleep? But when he looked down and saw the waterfront road gridlocked by four lanes of Hong Kong traffic all nudging towards the Cross Harbour Tunnel, immediately he knew why. For a brief moment he enjoyed the sight of so many of the city's rich and powerful stranded in their own limousines – then the pilot swung north across the flat blue expanse of the harbour, where the Star Ferries plied back and forth, and his stomach lurched once again. Beyond the harbour the solar-panelled roofs of the five-star hotels in Tsim Sha Tsui East loomed large.

'Christ, it looks like the aliens are coming!' cracked John Divine, a man with a dark blue cast to his jaw but otherwise scrupulous grooming, as they picked up the Kowloon exit of the tunnel and followed the endless traffic crawling north down Waterloo Road for the Lion Rock Tunnel.

'Race Day at Shatin,' Becker explained. 'Gambling is a way of life here. Everyone who can beg, steal or borrow a ticket will be there. Everyone else pays the penalty of the traffic jams. Today will be worse than most: it's the Stewards' Cup. Very prestigious. Lots of face for the winning owner. But don't worry, it shouldn't be this bad when your Secretary of State attends.'

'Even so, I'm glad the Secretary won't have to wade through that lot,' observed Tom Lassiter, the taller, more senior of the two Americans. 'He'll be using the Chairman of the Jockey Club's private helicopter. I'd hate for the Secretary's motorcade to get caught up in that chaos. Traffic here is worse than downtown Manila.'

Becker sensed a nervous apprehension in the advance man's voice. Ever since their arrival, both men had seemingly done their best to raise the temperature of this operation. But that was their job: to hustle the local security team into laying on their best service. And whenever the Americans were in town everything had to be just so. As field commander for the operation being put together by Hong Kong Special Branch's VIP Protection Unit, it was Becker's job to keep them reassured.

'Relax, Tom. Our intelligence people agree there's no major threat here. In the Philippines I could understand your concern: a certain degree of hostility toward the US. But, honestly, Fredericks has nothing to fear in Hong Kong; everybody's far too busy making money. Maybe some hawker will try to sell him a fake Rolex – nothing worse. Unless there's something you haven't told me?'

'No, we don't anticipate any problems. We'd just rather keep our boss out of trouble. What do you have planned in the way of coverage?'

'You needn't worry on that score. Residence security, vehicle escort, EOD team: the full nine yards. We treat them all seriously. Just ask Jack Cinch; he's seen our work.'

Cinch was the Regional Security officer at the US Consulate-General on Garden Road, and was State's senior security specialist in the territory. He had worked closely with Hong Kong Special Branch's VIP Protection Unit, and knew of their close links with the British Special Air Service Regiment who had trained their teams. Pedigrees did not come much higher than that.

'Yeah, we had the Cinch lecturette already. Doesn't make us any happier about surrendering our weapons to another bodyguard unit. If Fredericks collects so much as a scratch we can kiss it all goodbye.'

'As I said before, that's the policy here.' Becker felt his irritation growing, and suddenly there was an edge to his voice. 'No one's asking you to like it. Just get used to it.'

Lassiter checked an urge to retaliate, glanced at his partner, then fell silent.

Beneath the skids, the Kowloon peninsula broadened out into a patchwork of factories and grey tenement blocks. As the Dauphin flew north, climbing away above the islands of exhaust fumes, Becker gazed down at the patches of green on the Kowloon foothills where squatter villages hung precariously from the hillside: raddled old shacks on matchstick legs, somehow defying gravity and seemingly just waiting for the next typhoon to blow them all away. And beyond these rose the undulating peaks of the Kowloon hills, then the crouching majesty of the Lion Rock. This conspicuous yellow outcrop, hewn throughout time by wind and rain into the effigy of a recumbent lion, signalled the end of Kowloon and the beginning of the once rural New Territories – now universally known as the NT.

Beyond this range lay the new, white, skyblock cities where the Hong Kong government had rehoused millions from the urban area. Old NT had all but gone; many of the rice paddies and farms on which Shatin had thrived had been redeveloped for light industry and housing. Even so, Becker could still remember the old Shatin, the rural town famous for its old-style Chinese market. It was a place where, as a probationary inspector, he had conducted midnight patrols with his sergeants, chasing the glow of opium lamps which mysteriously extinguished as they approached. Now Shatin was a city in its own right and, where the market had previously stood, giant new housing estates loomed. The snake charmers and fortune tellers had all moved on, and triad heroin had seen off the last of the old men who nightly sucked on opium pipes. Now younger men burned heroin on squares of tinfoil and sucked in the smoke through drinking straws. This they called 'chasing the dragon' – or, when only a matchbox cover was available to capture the fumes, 'playing the harmonica'.

Once Shatin had been famous too for its rice crop and the restaurants which sold roast pigeon; now it was famous for something altogether different: horse racing. For Shatin was home to the Jockey Club's world-famous all electronic track. Computerised betting. Real-time visual monitoring of each and every race on Asia's first giant video matrix board.

Shatin lay like a jewel at the end of the Tolo Channel looking out towards the sea, to Mirs Bay, and ultimately *Dai Luk* – mainland China – its location in perfect harmony with the spirits of the surrounding hills and of the water. The *fung shui* was so perfect that old men often paid their last dollar to be buried on the adjacent green hillsides. There, in the shadow of Ma On Shan, 'the Horseback Mountain', the Royal Hong Kong Jockey Club had leased a section of water adjacent to the land and built the most modern racetrack in the world. It had literally moved mountains of earth to reclaim that area from the sea.

'Not as big as I'd expected,' Lassiter observed, though still admiring the immaculate green baize turf.

'Nevertheless,' said Becker, feeling a little foolish to

be reacting so defensively, 'on a good day they can take in more cash here than in half a season at any track back home.'

Divine, the shorter of the Americans, who sported a Burt Reynolds moustache, continued to stare down at the concentric loops of sand and grass, and the dazzling white concrete of the grandstand.

'That's hardly surprising if, like you say, this Jockey Club is the only bookie in town. There can't be many places in the world still operating a gambling monopoly. That must be a licence to print money. They must have some real heavy pull with your Governor.'

'Yes, you could say that. But they're an old established institution: part of Hong Kong's power élite. Does the Secretary like to gamble?' asked Becker, changing the subject. It seemed to him that every foreigner who visited Hong Kong took a swipe at the Jockey Club, without realising that ninety per cent of the take from its gambling was ploughed back into the city in the shape of free medical treatment for its citizens and through other community projects.

'He likes the track all right,' said Lassiter grinning. 'Got a couple of good runners of his own back in New England.'

'Yeah, whoever works the right shoulder next week will need to keep a radio line free to the bookie's runner.'

The Dauphin circled twice before moving in to land. Below them they could see a dense mass of humanity surging the last few hundred metres across the footbridges from Shatin railway station into the track. Beneath the footbridges on the Shatin bypass, five lines of limousines, taxis and buses were fighting for three lanes of road. The Dauphin put down on the Jockey Club Chairman's private helipad in Penfold Gardens, a richly landscaped area in the centre of the track. A courtesy limousine then took them to the Stewards' enclosure. At the elevator Rebecca Lee, a tall and striking Shanghainese graduate of UCLA, and the Chairman's Personal Assistant, greeted them with a demure handshake and a soft Californian accent.

'Good afternoon Chief Becker.' She smiled. 'So very nice to see you again.'

'Sorry, Miss Lee,' corrected Becker. 'Only Chief Inspector.' The girl was a China doll: cute and manipulative with it.

'Oh, well, maybe one day.' The practised smile did not falter. 'These two gentlemen must be ...'

John Divine moved in close to take the girl's hand, turning on charm like a geyser.

'Special agents Lassiter and Divine, ma'am. State Department security branch. Glad to meet you.'

The girl appeared impressed. She lowered her eyes for a moment, simpering beneath the intense gaze of Divine's clear blue eyes.

Finally the girl said: 'I understand the Secretary of State will be honouring us with his presence here two weeks from now, as the special guest of our Chairman. You are here to inspect the private box and restaurant for security purposes, yes?'

Though educated in the States, her inflection was entirely Chinese: the statement which ends in a sharp interrogative, so becomes a question.

'That's right, Miss Lee,' said Becker moving between the two in irritation, so that Divine had to drop the girl's hand to let him pass. 'We'd also like to take a walk about up on the Steward's corridor. To get to know the stairways and fire exits, that sort of thing.'

Lassiter gave his partner a frown of reproach.

The girl nodded her understanding, then cocked her head to one side and regarded Becker suspiciously. 'Tell me, Mr Becker, are you expecting trouble during this visit?'

'No, Miss Lee. This is just routine: standard advance security procedure. But I'll have to ask you to treat all this as confidential. Restrict it to those with an absolute need to know, and don't speak to the newspapers.'

'Of course.' Rebecca Lee bridled at any implication of laxity. 'If you'll follow me, I'll show you up.'

In the elevator Becker was amused by the perfume in the air-conditioning, the general aura of affluence and privilege. The Chairman's box was somewhere few people got to see the inside of; it was more difficult to get into than the Governor's mansion. The only reason they'd been allowed to snoop around today was because the Chairman was out of the colony on business.

The lift operator was an old Chinese – probably a retired policeman, judging from the severe haircut. Covertly he examined the three men, racked with curiosity because he knew every one of the stewards and staff with clearance to the Stewards' corridor and these were not either.

'*Bin goh ah?*' he asked Rebecca Lee in a whisper.

'Relax, Uncle,' she answered in playful Cantonese. 'Just some nosy foreign devils who want to see how the men with huge testicles live.'

Becker understood every word and he couldn't resist it.

'*Nei do sik m'do ngoh leung goh!*' he retorted fluently. Hardly very gallant of him, he knew, but the look of mortification on Rebecca Lee's face was well worth it. Seeing her pretty face flush, the old man broke into a loud wheezing laugh.

He was still laughing when the elevator doors opened on to a pink carpeted corridor full of people speaking in loud, monied voices. Becker followed the girl past small cliques of both Chinese and European men who wore sharp suits and gold members' badges hanging from their buttonholes. Their wives, wearing designer labels and imaginative hats, stood to one side nursing long-stemmed glasses full of Moët et Chandon. The double doors leading into the Chairman's box were solid maple and opened on to a split-level air-conditioned dining-room done up in pastel shades. Beyond this a small lounge gave directly on to a tiered balcony overlooking the finishing line. The wall decorations and soft furnishings were all one might expect.

Once inside, Rebecca Lee made it clear she would not be staying. Not after the remark in the elevator. Losing face in front of the old man.

'Please help yourselves to the cold buffet, and enjoy the meeting. When you are ready to leave just pick up the pink telephone and I will arrange for the pilot to take you back to Hong Kong Island.'

'*M'goi sai, siu je,*' Becker thanked her to make the point.

Ignoring him, Rebecca Lee smiled with difficulty to the Americans, closed the door and was gone.

'Boy, is this something.' Divine was already across the dining-room and uncovering the foil-wrapped buffet. Lassiter slid aside the double-glazed door leading to the balcony, picked up a pair of binoculars from a table and looked out across the track. A moment later Becker followed him out, leaving Divine to plunder the food.

'What was that all about in the elevator?' asked Lassiter, watching the riders parade their eager mounts past the grandstand before breaking for the long canter down to the starting gate.

'Nothing, really.'

'You didn't care for her tone did you, Becker?'

'Not really, she's a snotty bitch.'

'You speak their lingo pretty good. What on earth did you say to her?'

Becker put a foot against the parapet and leaned upon the balcony rail. Below him the crowd surged like a bright culture of microbes covering every square foot of concrete, their rolled newspapers fanning the breeze.

'She was telling the old guy we were here to feed from the rich man's table,' he said after a while. 'They have this delightful expression here for someone with money and influence: *dai chuen dui*. It means "one with huge testicles".'

Lassiter put down the binoculars.

'She said that? What did you say?'

'I told her she could never get both of mine in her mouth at the same time. That's when the old guy cracked up.'

Lassiter broke into a wide grin and brought the glasses back to his eyes.

'And there was I thinking you had no sense of humour.'

Becker shrugged. 'It was a pretty rough night, last night. Stick around, I get better.' Then he turned his back to the rail and gazed at the line of glass stewards' boxes spread out like giant fish tanks. 'You know, there really wasn't any need to "advance" this location. We're too high up and too well protected here for anyone to take a swipe at Fredericks. This whole corridor is off-limits to anyone without a gold badge. They have their own uniforms to police that. They're so screwed up about status and privilege here that security inside this area is no problem for us at all. Believe me.'

'Oh yeah?' Lassiter was watching intently through the field-glasses. At strategic locations, within the Members' Enclosure and also in the Outer Enclosure, he could see men in green police uniforms – only these were different. These were wearing blue berets, boots and anklets, and moving stiffly through the crowds in twos and threes. 'So why do I see storm troopers down here?'

'That's just PTU insurance,' said Becker.

'Huh?'

'Police Tactical Unit. Two platoons from Echo Company. They're part of the colony's counter-insurgency force. When there are no riots, we use them for saturation policing. When we get complaints that triads are menacing housing estates, we cordon that area and send them in to kick arses and take names. It's like flushing the toilet.'

'So what are they doing here?'

'The Jockey Club pays government a hefty fee to have them keep order and guard the take. It's official.'

'I see,' murmured Lassiter. 'You expecting a riot, or something?'

'That depends how many favourites win today,' said Becker stepping back to the glass door. 'Come on, let's take a walk around.'

It is afternoon, only a few hours before his next shift begins, and the apartment is broodingly silent. He has not slept well: the anticipation has been almost too much to bear. Beneath the covers his flesh burns like fire. Still he must wait while his mother fusses quietly about the kitchen. Each furtive second ticks painfully away.

When finally he hears the outer door close and the lift descending, his heart leaps as the excitement begins. Outside, the sun is at its fiercest, and his mother now bears a black parasol and a plastic hold-all along Hennessy Road to buy vegetables from the street market. As always, she will prod and feel the produce, and not return until she has gleaned every scrap of gossip to be learned.

Abruptly he rises from the bed, drags a reinforced garbage sack from the space beneath it, then wrestles the whore's inert body out on to a rubberised sheet spread across the floor. A sigh escapes the dead girl's chest as she settles back into an attitude almost of compliance. The only evidence of violence upon her is a slender, purple necklace of bruising around her throat: the mark of the ligature which killed her. The hunting knife had only been a show; a means of forcing obedience.

Inside the apartment the warm air is still and damp, and tinged now with the sickly redolence of body fluids, but he does not object to that. Indeed, he is used to it. He

47

takes a sharpened scalpel and proceeds to cut away the spangled crimson gown, revealing for the first time a perfect pair of lifeless breasts. The girl's body rolls beneath his touch.

He looks down at the floor, at the corrupt flesh lying there, and his only thought is where to begin the cutting.

It was just after the fifth race. On the lower ground floor of the grandstand, in a loading bay protected by a motorised steel shutter, the two armoured security trucks had finished loading the thirty or so reinforced steel combination chests which contained the take. On a signal from the security manager four guards, wearing crash helmets with padded leather neck-guards and carrying loaded shotguns, climbed inside the vehicles and heaved closed the doors, which were over half a foot thick. Immediately locks turned, deadbolts slid into place, and when all was ready the security manager spoke into his radio.

Slowly the steel shutter rose, and the trucks nudged forward out of the artificial light of the loading bay and into the brilliant sunlight at the foot of the ramp. The first driver gave a thumbs-up to the platoon sergeant commanding the police escort at the top of the ramp, and the vehicles began to climb upwards towards the iron gates leading out into the Members' car park. Lining the ramp on both sides were PTU constables specially trained in weapons handling. Each officer carried either a Winchester Wingmaster shotgun or a US-made AR-15 rifle in addition to his police service revolver. The officer in charge, Inspector Jason Leung, stood by the gate supervising, occasionally speaking into his hand-held radio packset, to announce in coded language the departure of the truck.

Inside the police command post, which was deep within the grandstand, the report room sergeant requested reconfirmation of the message. Leung, carrying a crumpled white handkerchief in his left hand, was suffering from the kind of streaming head cold which distorts even the clearest of radio procedure. Behind him the roar of the crowd signalled the beginning of the final race. Their last chance to make a fortune – today at least.

'*Tin kei,*' he muttered to himself as he blew his reddened nose for the hundredth time that day. 'Heaven hope they get this money out before the crowds start moving away.' Security procedure dictated that the trucks leave whilst the punters were still concentrating on the racing, and before the roads out of the racecourse became choked, as they inevitably did for the three- or four-hour period following the last race. Leung knew that a cash truck stuck in Hong Kong traffic was an easy mark for any serious team who cared to take a potshot at it.

Slowly the truck ascended the ramp, its engine protesting under the weight of its load, springs rocking backward on the rear axle. Jason knew that the major job his section had been detailed to perform – that of ensuring the safe loading of the vehicles – was over, and soon he could go home and prepare for Ah Fung's wedding party. It had been months since he had been to a good wedding. Now the thought of mah jong and stewed abalone was uppermost in his mind.

As the two trucks nosed out of the security compound and into the exit road shared by the Members' car park, first one and then the other, Leung heaved a sigh of relief and ordered his section sergeant to close the gates.

'*Gau lan dim!*' called the sergeant with a smile. 'All done!'

Outside on the pavement, still within the sprawling confines of the racecourse access roads, a young scruffily-dressed Chinese man leaned on his mobile hawker cart that offered boiled chicken legs for sale – and watched the truck's approach with interest. It was a hot day, and hot work. Sweat glistened upon his cheeks and neck, and the hawker reached down into the cart for a cloth with which to wipe himself. As the trucks swung out, moving up through their gears, he calculated the gathering speed of the lead vehicle and flipped a switch concealed in the handle of the loaded cart. Then, as the lead truck drew level with him, he braced his rear leg and pushed with all his strength, sending his cart slamming into the truck's radiator grille. Immediately he dived for cover behind the first line of parked cars, hearing the high-pitched squeal of protest as the driver's foot slammed hard against the brake.

The explosion was powerful but controlled. Powerful enough to throw bystanders to the ground, and controlled enough to lift and flip the first truck over on to its side. Yet the noise of the blast was barely audible above the frantic roar of the grandstand, as the India Club's horse came steaming towards the finishing line at odds of fifty to one, cheered on by an exultant crowd.

Disbelief. Confusion. Then, from the private bays nearby in the Members' car park, three white mid-engine vans squealed forward, and stopped close to the smoking wreck.

Behind the compound fence, Inspector Leung spun round in a low crouch. At once his eyes caught the rising column of pale grey smoke.

'*Diu lei lo mo!*' He cursed aloud. 'They're taking the trucks!' Urging his men forward, Leung scrambled for the radio, which had fallen from his grasp. Less than a second later the doors of the three white minivans slid open, and men in blue coveralls came swarming out. At almost the same moment there was another explosion, and the second truck pitched over on to its side. Leung found the radio, and with mounting disbelief barked quickly into the microphone.

'This is Echo Two. We have an Alpha Romeo in progress outside the secure compound!' It was the radio code for armed robbery.

Behind him he heard his men running up the ramp towards the gates, chambering shotgun cartridges as they ran. Then something came skittering towards them from the direction of the truck. Leung saw three green cartridges the size of soft drinks cans, and knew it was tear smoke. Immediately a thick grey smoke began pouring out, obscuring his sight of the gates. Without their own respirators, the firearms section collapsed, coughing and retching. As if in a nightmare, a series of smaller explosions errupted around the trucks, their brilliant flashes lighting up the smoke cloud like a cinema screen, followed by the grinding of fracturing metal. Fighting back his wave of panic, Leung clamped the sodden handkerchief over his face and nose and kicked open the gate, with his revolver drawn. The platoon sergeant and two other constables stumbled after him, almost blinded, holding their breath and crouching low. They could hear the muffled shouts of the robbers and the sound of feet running back and forth.

After what seemed an eternity the radio crackled to life. 'Echo Two, Echo Two, please repeat last message, over.'

'Take cover!' shouted Leung, turning to indicate positions to those behind him. Then, just as the men began to move, there came the ugly report of machine-gun fire – four points of spitting flame – from out of the midst of the swirling smoke cloud. A strangled scream of pain was followed by the thud of boots on concrete. Someone was down.

'Echo Two, Echo Two, please repeat last message, over.'

The platoon sergeant was now beyond the gate, crouching behind one of the police transports. It took only a moment for him to make up his mind; there might be innocent bystanders still in the way but he doubted it. Not with all that smoke. He swung the shotgun up, took careful aim and pumped out four thundering rounds in

51

quick succession. Without the ear protection of the firing range his ears screamed under the assault, but the sheer volume of noise served to bolster his confidence. From out of the churning ball of smoke he could hear the scrape of metal being dragged over tarmac. The attackers were stripping the truck.

The sergeant rubbed his eyes to clear them, then looked back towards the gates, calling out to his men to re-establish their positions. The constables were lying prone beyond the gates, faces streaming, and firing off their weapons with no real targets in view. In the panic which had seized them, no one was sure whether to press forward or to wait for reinforcements to arrive. All the sergeant could think of was where was Leung? Where was the officer? Hell, there was nothing laid down in standing orders about this. No one seriously believed this could happen.

But it was happening. And, even as the sergeant raised his weapon to fire once more, he was ready to admit he was scared to death.

Abruptly the stutter of machine-gun fire ceased, and the sergeant's finger paused upon the trigger. Then, holding his breath, he felt the menace of the silence and saw a small dark object sail over the fence. The first constable to see the grenade reacted wildly, screaming to the others to get away. But as they scrambled clear, the full force of the detonation slammed into the loose knot of young Chinese policemen, scattering them upon the ground and silencing their weapons.

Behind the police transport the platoon sergeant felt the shockwave both inside and out. 'My boys,' he mumbled in disbelief. 'They've killed my boys.'

Above the ringing in his ears the sergeant heard the sound of engines gunning to take flight. Now the tear smoke was dissipating, he could make out the figures: nine, perhaps ten black-masked demons, heavily built like tanka fishermen – the last of them running expertly backwards, sweeping wide arcs of cover with their weapons. Running back towards the minivans which were stopped across the path of the lead truck. That first sight of their silhouettes burned deep into his brain. That impression of expert training and absolute commitment scared him more than anything he had ever seen. Another few seconds and the minivans were accelerating hard for the exit road. The sergeant realised he was sweating hard; a sick feeling in his stomach rooting him to the spot. Then he was not just sweating; he was weeping too. Feeling his anger surge, he jumped up and ran out from behind the transport. He fired the last of his cartridges into the air, knowing it was useless at such a distance. Then, helplessly, he watched the vans roar into the traffic interchange, heading northward towards Tai Po town. He stopped running, his chest heaving, pulse pounding. All at once he became aware of the trembling in his fingers. Shame made him clutch the empty shotgun tighter.

Somewhere behind him someone was shouting. A clatter of boots. Number One platoon, which had deployed nearly half a mile away in the cattle pens of the public transport bays, was running as one man towards the upended security trucks. The platoon sergeant turned, wiped his eyes and mouth, and ran back towards the smoking wreckage. By this time the first few hundred spectators were already spilling out of the main stand, and seeing the scene of devastation, they were drawn straight to it. The sergeant ordered several of the dumb-struck constables to keep everyone back while he looked inside the first security truck.

The driver he found dead at the wheel. They had not even bothered to remove the blue crash helmet from his head; just shot him in the face several times, leaving a red mush inside the helmet. Likewise the other guards. One lay face-down in the back; the other two had been dragged clear, and their bodies thrown to the ground.

53

The guards in the second van had fared little better. Then the sergeant spotted the green uniforms lying scattered on the concrete of the secure compound. Green uniforms with dark patches of blood seeping through. There were men from One Platoon crouching near the bodies, their young faces twisted in horror. A sharp stink of carbonised matter irritated his nostrils. Only one of his men was still alive. One constable rolling over and over, clutching at his back in agony.

'Echo Two, please respond your situation, over.'

The radio lay on the ground next to Inspector Leung's body. The sergeant picked it up, anger winning over shock and despair.

'Echo Two reports. Emergency. Security vehicles ambushed just outside secure compound. Approximately one dozen suspects. Explosives involved – multiple casualties. Call ambulances immediately. Roger so far?'

'So far.'

'Suspects escaped along Tai Po Road or Tolo Highway towards New Territories in three Japanese-make mid-engine vans. All three coloured white. No registration marks. Urge caution, they are armed with automatic weapons. Over.'

'Roger all that, Echo Two. Any further details, over?'

'Just that I'm still alive! *Diu lei lo mo!*' the sergeant exploded. 'Just get those fucking ambulances here!'

The sergeant looked down at the ground where Inspector Leung's beret lay upturned and crumpled beside his head. It was impossible to tell how many bullets had entered his body. His mouth was open, and blood and mucus had run from his nose. The sergeant knelt beside him to check for a pulse, but found none.

Suddenly he was aware of a new presence. When he turned around, he saw a tall European standing by the gate, a police warrant card clipped to his breast pocket.

'Chief Inspector Becker, Special Branch,' the man identified himself. 'What the hell happened here?'

The sergeant's account of the robbery was not a professional policeman's account. It was lurid and distorted, and Becker guessed that shock was already taking its toll on the man. Realising he himself was the senior police officer on the scene, Becker immediately began issuing orders for the treatment of the injured and the preservation of evidence. When he asked after Jason Leung, the sergeant gave him a bleak look and led him over to the inspector's still-bleeding body.

Becker fought back his sense of horror, but lost the fight. Dropping to one knee he checked the body again for vital signs.

'Ah sir,' said the sergeant softly, his voice colourless, bereft of emotion. 'I've done that twice already. It's no good. Inspector Leung is dead.'

Becker took one last look at his friend and, without knowing exactly why, stroked a hand over Jason's still-warm face. Then he climbed to his feet and walked back through the gate. Outside where the other uniforms were forcing back the crowd of onlookers, the two Americans were still watching with cold fascination as the smoke rose from the armoured vehicles.

'Jesus Christ!' said Tom Lassiter meeting him head on. 'I thought you told us there was no threat here in Hong Kong? Difficulty in obtaining weapons, you said? They must have had high explosives to do this.'

At that moment Becker was in no mood to talk, let alone discuss policy on a VIP operation.

'It's just a robbery,' he said coldly, walking on past them. Suddenly he felt sick in the stomach and he wanted very much to be somewhere else. Anywhere but here, and preferably alone. 'Nothing here for you to worry about,' he mouthed blandly. 'No political impact. Like I said: just a robbery.'

The two Americans stared at one another, then at the twisted hulks of the security vans. They did not care for such bland assurances of safety when everything they saw told them otherwise. In the silence John Divine gave a low whistle. Both men were thinking the same desperate thought, but it was Divine who finally voiced it.

'If that was just a robbery, I'd hate to see what a terrorist operation looks like around here!'

FOUR

In the quiet of a Sunday morning, before Hong Kong Island could be said to have truly awakened from the worst excesses of Saturday night, a gleaming black Toyota Princess limousine, bearing a white licence plate with the registration number '1', came off Waterfront Road and slipped smoothly into the sparse traffic making the steep climb up Cotton Tree Drive. In the rear seat of the vehicle James Weldon, Commissioner of the Royal Hong Kong Police, sat scrutinising the Sunday newspaper reports of the Shatin robbery, wincing at each damaging headline, and quietly dreading the ordeal which now lay ahead of him.

Weldon was a powerful man in every respect, a strapping Scot with a commanding, weathered face and a bulky frame which had once played rugby for the Colony fifteen. His was a high-pressure job, by turns policeman and politician, walking a tightrope between Whitehall and Beijing, with Government House looking nervously on. As Commissioner of the Hong Kong force he enjoyed wide civil powers and almost unrestricted access to the Governor himself. If, indeed, enjoy was the correct word. But with that privilege there came a heavy burden: absolute responsibility for law and order and the internal security of the crown colony. Now, as the limousine climbed towards Mid-Levels, he had reason to somewhat regret his elevation to that lonely position.

Usually his Sunday mornings were inviolate, reserved

for his weekly jaunt into rural NT, where he kept a bay gelding stabled at the Fanling Jockey Club. Working the horse over some of the last green areas left in the colony was the part of the week he looked forward to most, but on this particular morning it was not to be. Not after the biggest single robbery in the colony's history. Not after the brutal bloody murder of seven of his officers. Weldon had cancelled a dinner with the Commander of British Forces at the Hong Kong Club to sit at home and personally direct operations. The night had passed quickly as he sat cursing into the telephone, and listening to the empty reports of his subordinates. At eight that morning he had taken a hurried breakfast, and then returned to his office on the fifth floor of Police Head-quarters to hear a briefing from Chan Ham-gar, the Director of Criminal Investigation, in anticipation of the Governor's questions.

Leads had been pitifully few.

As the vehicle passed the Peak Tram tower and the police driver swung off on to Kennedy Road, turning sharp right under the flyover, Weldon's mind was jerked back from the undulating green hills of Fanling to the immediate business in hand. Skirting the tree-lined entrance to the Botanical Gardens the vehicle slid down onto Upper Albert Road, and coasted to a halt outside the white-walled entrance to Government House. Immediately one of the police constables on guard duty at the gatehouse stepped into the road to halt traffic and wave Weldon's limousine through the broad gateway. The house itself was very grand, a dazzling white colonial mansion of immense proportions, with an impressive porticoed entrance and a history almost as colourful as that of Hong Kong itself. The first thing any visitor noticed, coming around the circular drive, was the watchtower growing incongruously out of the roof: a feature grafted on to the building during the Second World War by the commander of the Imperial Japanese

Forces who had made his headquarters there during the years of occupation.

James Weldon, OBE, QPM, had attended GH many times before, often admiring its tropical shrubs and the many species of oriental flowers which flanked the mansion. But as he stepped from the cool of the air-conditioned limousine and felt the clinging damp heat of the morning begin to engulf him, the garden was the last thing on his mind. Shielding his eyes and turning to look back towards Victoria Peak, he saw the myriad stacked towers of luxury apartment blocks gazing down towards the sea. High above these a pair of sea eagles sailed gracefully around the rocky peak in an unbroken canopy of clear blue sky. The morning heat haze told him that this would be another sweltering day but that there would probably be rain in the afternoon to cool the air. Intuition told him he could expect no such cool relief in the Governor's study.

Waiting to greet him at the top of the shallow flight of stone steps, stood Superintendent John Leach, the Governor's ADC. Leach had been chosen for this most coveted and prestigious of police posts because his record of service was beyond reproach; and because he was tall and straight and looked good in the mauve dress uniform required to be worn when accompanying His Excellency the Governor to official functions. At thirty-eight Leach was one of the few European officers of gazetted rank who was still single, and therefore qualified to live at the Governor's beck and call in a small self-contained flat within the mansion. As always John Leach looked as neat and crisp as his uniform, and he came to attention with a slight shuffle and click of heels.

'Good morning, sir.'

'Good morning, John,' Weldon acknowledged, taking his briefcase from the driver. He was wearing a blazer and slacks, so did not return the salute. 'I see I'm not the first to arrive.' He gave a nod in the direction of a metallic-green Mercedes saloon parked in one of the visitor's spaces, its chauffeur languidly misting the windscreen with his breath and then polishing it clean. 'Devereau's?' he asked.

The ADC made a slight face and nodded.

'He's having morning coffee with HE right now.' Then Leach hesitated, wondering whether or not to speak out. Finally he said, 'Sir, I feel I ought to warn you he's in a perfectly bloody mood.'

Weldon squared his shoulders in a gesture of acceptance.

'That's his prerogative, John. Devereau has just lost two hundred and seventy million Hong Kong dollars. How would you feel?'

'Indeed, sir. But I just thought it fair to let you know he got the jump on you. Devereau's been filling His Excellency's ears for the past forty minutes. Scaremongering, loss of confidence – that sort of thing.'

'Just as I expected.' The Commissioner's voice was almost a sigh. Gordon Devereau was Chairman of the Royal Hong Kong Jockey Club, in itself a position of great influence and prestige, but when that same man was also the Chief Executive of the most powerful bank in the territory, and a member of the territory's ruling Executive Council in Central Government, that influence was raised to an even higher level. The CP smiled to himself. 'Thanks anyway for the warning, John. Time to see the headmaster.'

The ADC escorted Weldon in through high, panelled doors to a split-level entrance hall with a marble chessboard floor and a broad and impressive mahogany staircase leading to the kind of upper gallery Weldon always associated with Errol Flynn movies. As usual the Chinese rosewood benches in the hall were adorned with intricate oriental flower arrangements, a particular passion with Lady Mackie. As he waited for the ADC to announce him, Weldon stalked over to a square upholstered easy chair, deliberated a while, and decided to remain standing.

Weldon had been here often enough to lose count of the times he had stood in this same hall. Sometimes his visits were to attend official functions for which the GH ballroom had been filled to overflowing with ambassadorial majesty. But the times he remembered most, those which retained a special clarity, were the private meetings in the wood-polished intimacy of the Governor's study, whenever some threat to public order or internal security reared its ugly head. And many were the times they had averted an economic crisis or a public scandal by a timely arrest, a deportation, or a few well chosen words in a taipan's ear. He had seen it all. You could say what you wanted about the importance or political influence of the hongs – the colony's mighty trading houses which thronged the choice real estate of Central district – GH was still the nerve centre and the base of all real political power in Hong Kong. And stepping through its high doors still gave him a special thrill.

Behind him Weldon heard the ADC's heels click back towards him across the marble floor.

'You're to go right in, sir.'

Weldon patted the silk scarf at his throat, straightened the line of his blue blazer and stepped inside. Immediately he sensed the atmosphere: like a child who enters a room and knows instinctively, from his parents' silence, that he is the subject of their bickering.

The Governor, Sir Andrew Mackie, sat at his desk in one corner of the study, with his back to the red-curtained french windows, as he pored over the headlines of the *Sunday Post*.

'Ah, James,' he muttered distractedly, concern writ large on his thin face. 'Join us, won't you. There's coffee on the sideboard. Have some.'

It had always struck Weldon that the Governor was a rather small man for a position so important. He had a deceptively affable face and soft feminine hands. What was left of his hair was silver and silky fine. But Weldon knew better than to underestimate the man: a hard-nosed career diplomat with a thirty-seven-year stint at the Foreign and Commonwealth Office that had taught him how to keep his people on their toes. Those who worked for him soon knew he did not suffer fools gladly, or allow the same mistake twice. Weldon helped himself from the silver coffee-pot and nodded across the room to where Devereau sat in a leather button-back armchair beside the Adam fireplace, his face set in a frown of contempt.

'Gordon.'

'James,' said Devereau levelly. 'Good of you to come. I believe Sir Andrew would like you to answer a few questions.'

The needling had already begun.

'Thank you, Gordon,' said the Governor, taking off his spectacles and silencing him with a glance. 'Thank you for popping up, James. Shame to cut into our Sunday, but there we are. You've seen the papers, of course?' Weldon eased himself into the leather armchair opposite Devereau's; he set his briefcase carefully on the floor beside him and took a sip from his cup.

'I read them on the way up here, sir.'

'Yes ...' muttered Sir Andrew softly, finishing off the sentence he was reading and suddenly looking up with a fierce scowl, a tactic he used to unsettle his people's equilibrium. 'Shocking, shocking! They're saying that the robbery at the Shatin Jockey Club was like the rape of a favourite maiden aunt. Damn poor taste, I say. But you know the way this place works, and it's bound to affect sentiments. It won't look good in the weekly morale report, but then if the Foreign Secretary will keep us on such a tight rein.'

'Yes, sir,' was all Weldon offered. This was not the time to explain, and he knew better than to interrupt when Sir Andrew was having his say.

'I'm not happy, James. We're only a small place. We can't afford to have this sort of thing going on, you understand.'

Again: 'Yes, sir.'

Sir Andrew peeled off his thin gold reading spectacles and tossed them petulantly upon the folded newspaper.

'It isn't just a matter of one robbery – God I wish it was. There's the wider picture. You know the phrase: prosperity and stability. Hong Kong is such a tiny powder keg of a place that without stability there can be no prosperity. God help us, rightly or wrongly, the British Government has sworn to hand over this place to the Chinese as a going concern. There are six million worried people here, most of them without any form of internationally recognised passport, all crammed into three hundred square miles, and desperately wondering what the future holds for them. That's a dangerous situation. Now this is beginning to look like a rearguard action for anarchy in the run-up to 1997. These incidents are becoming far too common. All it takes is something like this to start the ball rolling and there'll be riots, looting and mob rule – just like we had in '56 and '68.'

Sir Andrew must have felt his face begin to flush, because he paused for breath. Weldon did not need to look: he could feel Devereau watching him closely, enjoying every syllable of the headmaster's pep-talk.

In another moment the Governor was into his second stanza, and Weldon thought to himself: almost through.

'Hong Kong exists to do business,' Sir Andrew was saying emphatically. 'As the third largest financial centre in the world, we stand or fall by that most ephemeral of commodities: confidence. That means confidence in our business community. Confidence in our ability to maintain law and order. Dammit, we've seen too many companies pull up sticks and run – some of our best names. Beijing can make all the promises in the world

63

about basic freedoms and preserving Hong Kong's way of life for a further fifty years, but if sentiment says this place is going to the dogs, then to the dogs it shall go. Then what happens, eh? Tell me that? No, I'll tell you. When big business packs up, our service industries go bust; the pretty swift result being mass unemployment and no damned way to feed these people. Then you'll see a real breakdown in law and order!'

Weldon maintained his silence during this long tirade, reflecting that there was no other man in the colony who could speak to him this way without receiving the rough edge of his tongue in return. But he knew what the Governor said was right. Just as he understood, as well as any man, the knock-on effect security had on economics. Still, the headmaster would insist on having his say.

Without warning Sir Andrew reined in his oration and directed his gaze towards the Commissioner, leaning over the desk in anticipation.

'All right, now we'll hear everything you have so far. I thought it best that Gordon sit in and listen to this. After all, it was his money – or, rather, money for which he was ultimately responsible.'

'Quite,' smiled Devereau sourly. 'Two hundred and seventy million dollars to be precise. I hate to seem bitter, James, but that money was taken right from under your men's noses. We expect better than this from those Blue Berets of yours. They take a hefty slice of the law-and-order budget don't they? Makes a mockery of the whole business if they can't handle the threat when it materialises.'

'With all due respect, Gordon,' Weldon lied, glowering back at the banking taipan, 'are you speaking now as Jockey Club chairman or Exco member?'

Devereau's finger was already up and a vitriolic riposte poised on his lips when the Governor intervened.

'Gentlemen!' The commanding voice was both a

warning and a reminder of where they were, and that he was still determined to keep firm control in spite of Devereau's influence. 'I think we'll skip the name-calling and go straight to the report. James?'

The Commissioner of Police reined in his resentment and took a folder from his briefcase. With an effort of self will, he recovered some composure and began his presentation.

'These are the facts as far as we know them. Yesterday afternoon at 16.17 hours, two security vehicles were attacked while leaving Shatin Racecourse and were robbed of two hundred and seventy million Hong Kong dollars – the property of the Royal Hong Kong Jockey Club. There were at least ten assailants, well trained and exceptionally well armed, probably all Chinese males but certainly very highly motivated. They appear to have used some sort of exploding mine, concealed inside a hawker's cart, to overturn the first security truck, then a different explosive charge to disable the second. It's likely the mine was a piece of military hardware originating from the China mainland. In twenty-two years of police work I've never seen that done before.

'The three mid-engine vans used by the suspects appear to have been parked in the Members' parking bays and driven out at speed as the first explosion went off. The video tapes we took from the security cameras at the gate of the secure compound show just how professional these people were. Cash escort is performed by a single column of eight PTU officers armed with long-barrelled weapons. By all normal standards this is a stern enough deterrent. These suspects used sophisticated shock tactics and tear smoke to neutralise that cash escort. Again, in all my police experience I've never seen this done before in a criminal case.

'They used shaped cutting charges to blast their way inside the trucks, then pumped CS smoke inside, forcing the security staff to come out or suffocate. All the security men were shot dead. At this time there was a total of fourteen armed police officers in the vicinity, nine of whom were deployed inside the compound on cash escort duties.'

'But there were two platoons on duty,' interrupted the Governor. 'That's a lot of men. What were the others all doing?'

Weldon drew a breath, silently counted to three, then patiently set about re-explaining the situation.

'Sir, race day is a big operation, and the biggest threat is that of crowd violence and injuries. It doesn't take much to get the locals going; you know that. Most of Echo company were on crowd control duty in the grandstand, or in the outer enclosure and in the public transport areas. For this duty they do not draw weapons; it's just too dangerous. They keep them locked in column boxes and safely stored inside the police command post in case of riot. This decision was taken after consultation with the Jockey Club Executive. Whoever planned this raid knew that. They seem to have known quite a bit besides. I must say I resent Gordon's point about my men failing to pass muster. It's true some of my officers were armed with long-barrelled weapons, and that they do have special training; even so they came under attack from automatic weapons which kept them pinned down throughout the whole of the incident. As if this wasn't enough, the suspects hurled a fragmentation grenade into the compound, killing four officers instantly. They stood little chance in those circumstances, and had very little opportunity to return fire. Furthermore, examination of the security video shows that the suspects were all wearing some sort of ballistic waistcoat. The inspector in charge of the column had eleven gunshot wounds in his body. Only the column sergeant survived the attack – oh, and one police constable who is now on a life-support machine in Queen Elizabeth Hospital.'

Weldon stopped speaking abruptly, and took a sip from his cup to quell the rage he felt. He strung out the sombre silence, using it as a weapon against Devereau. Damn the man, and damn all the bloody money, too! The Governor was strangely silent, elbows on the desktop, both hands shading his eyes as he looked down.

'This was no ordinary robbery,' continued Weldon eventually, brandishing the report as if it was an indictment. 'The organisation and planning were much too good. The job seems to have had the advantage of a fair degree of inside knowledge, but what I find most disturbing about it all is the sheer bloody audacity: the coldblooded execution of police officers with wives and families, for no other reason than that they could threaten the success of the operation. This tells me that we're dealing with a particular kind of enemy. These were trained military men, specialists – possibly even commandos. They were far too good to be some half-baked local team of toughs.'

Sensing the end of Weldon's speech, Sir Andrew lowered his hands and looked up, his high forehead furrowed with questions.

'What about the follow-up, James? I believe you said it was a rather clean getaway.'

'Clean as a whistle. We set up roadblocks on all major roads, virtually brought the New Territories to a standstill, but we were too late. Nothing. Two hours later Tai Po district traffic patrols found the three getaway vans abandoned on a single track access road just past the Chinese University – only two kilometres from the scene of the robbery. It's a quiet spot amongst the banana groves, with only one house nearby: nobody saw anything. From the tracks we found there, it's fairly clear that's where they transferred the cash and switched to backup vehicles.'

'What about criminal intelligence? Your people are usually pretty good at spotting this sort of thing at the planning stages. Was there nothing to indicate this was on the cards?'

'Nothing. Sir, you know we have an excellent intelligence system. Our surveillance and targeting sections have a very high success rate, but this time there was nothing. They must have maintained exceptional security. Not a single leak – that's rare indeed. Oh, I've asked the Director of Criminal Investigations to trawl for informers, but it doesn't look hopeful.'

Devereau's chair squeaked as he fidgeted in frustration.

'Dammit, James, can't you even hazard a guess at who's responsible for this?'

Weldon appeared to think for a moment, then his tanned face took on a look of seriousness and he glanced between the two: first at the Jockey Club chairman, then back to the Governor.

'There's only one source I know for this kind of mayhem.'

'Well?' demanded Devereau, seeing the Commissioner hesitate to name it.

'The Big Circle Gangs out of mainland China. I can't think of anyone else who'd take on a job like this.'

It was only a matter of time before someone mentioned the Big Circle Gangs – or *Dai Huen Jai*, to give them their Chinese name. They were the toughest thing to hit the territory in twenty years. Hardened young Chinese released from service in the People's Liberation Army, they had formed themselves into efficient strike units for the purpose of infiltrating Hong Kong and hitting the fat banks and goldsmiths there. Heavy firepower was their trademark, and they hit hard and split fast – north, over the border back into China, disappearing into the urban area around Canton. Rich and safe, they lived well, knowing they were untouchable because, in spite of the years of Sino–British talks, there was still no extradition treaty between Hong Kong and the People's Republic of China.

Devereau waded in heavily, his reddening neck bulging against his shirt collar.

'If it is the *dai huen jai*, then it's time something was done about them. They've been hitting us far too long and getting away with it. We can't simply sit back and have them walk in and take what they please!'

'Thank you once again, Gordon,' said the Governor, patiently checking him. 'Let's not go off half-cocked, shall we?' This was a political can of worms which Sir Andrew had no wish to open. Not with the Sino–British talks on 1997 once more deadlocked over the matter of UK passports for key Hong Kong people.

'First things first,' continued Sir Andrew. 'I'm sure you join with me in expressing our sympathies both to the police force and to the bereaved families. I trust there'll be the usual official police funeral?'

Weldon was glad that the Governor, at least, still retained a proper sense of priorities.

'Yes, sir, Wednesday morning. Guard of honour and all brass in attendance, or I'll want to know why.'

'Good. If the one in QE Hospital pulls through, I'll be happy to award a Governor's commendation.'

Weldon felt a warmth within him. Such awards were seldom made, being reserved for acts of bravery by police officers in the line of duty. Those handful who received them were instantly recognisable by the red whistle lanyard they were privileged to wear, hung between left shoulder and breast pocket.

'Thank you,' he said, genuinely pleased by the gesture. It could in no way replace the lives of the dead officers, but such recognition could be a useful antidote to worsening police-force morale.

Sir Andrew stood up from the desk, helped himself to more coffee, and replenished Weldon's cup as he spoke.

'Now, to return to the investigation. I know I can rely on you to do the job. You have your own specialist units

69

capable of dealing with these kind of men. But have you decided how to play it yet? Obviously you'll give this your best men.'

'We'll begin with the formation of a task force. And we'll question everyone involved, and anyone with inside information. Gordon will have to agree to a lot of impertinent questions. Also the Jockey Club stewards. Naturally we'll share anything we find with the insurance investigators.'

Suddenly Devereau shifted in his seat, trying to attract Sir Andrew's attention. When the Governor pretended not to notice, he spoke directly to the Commissioner.

'Look here, James,' he hesitated. 'There's something you ought to know. There isn't going to be any insurance claim. The money wasn't insured.'

Weldon's face wrinkled in sudden disbelief as the bombshell exploded.

'Not insured? You can't be serious.'

But the reddening of Devereau's cheeks showed that he was. Looking away, the words came from his thin lips in a tumble of embarrassment.

'I've authorised a figure of three hundred thousand Hong Kong for information, or one million for the outright return of the cash – pro-rata for a partial recovery. There'll be notices in the English and Chinese press tomorrow morning. That ought to turn up something for you to go on.'

'Not insured! But that's ridiculous!' blurted Weldon, though enjoying the sudden reversal of roles.

'Listen, I'll thank you not to make comments on Jockey Club procedure. The cash was insured whilst in transit between Shatin Racecourse and the bank's main vault here in Central. There was no coverage in the grounds of the racecourse. It wasn't deemed necessary – not with the illustrious Police Tactical Unit on hand to protect it.'

Weldon couldn't quite believe what he was hearing,

but at least now he understood the full reason for Devereau's hostility.

'Then you're a bigger bloody fool than I took you for, Gordon.'

'Fool or not, Commissioner,' the Jockey Club boss snarled back, his sharp finger pointed like a weapon, 'after the showing your boys made I don't think you've much to crow about. So, if you want to keep that job of yours I suggest you find the money, and quick!'

The Commissioner's eyes probed the Governor's comfortable, diplomatic face, wondering to what degree he supported such overt pressure. He did not need to wait long to find out. Sir Andrew's next utterance was a reaffirmation of Devereau's clout.

'I'm sure there's nothing to worry about, Gordon. James is a man of considerable skill and determination, with a force of over thirty thousand officers at his disposal. If I thought for one moment he couldn't properly police this territory, I should replace him immediately.' There was a lengthy pause there to let the implication sink in well and truly before the Governor covered his face with the most benign of smiles. 'Let's just wait and see, shall we? Who do you have down to lead this task force, James?'

'I'm still considering names at the moment, sir,' Weldon answered bitterly, still brooding on the implied threat in Sir Andrew's words. Had it been a bone, he wondered, to appease the man in the opposite chair, or was it a genuine ultimatum?

The dog in the opposite chair took the bone and barked.

'We want someone on it who'll get results fast.' The Governor made no attempt to silence him. 'Since I'm the injured party here, I think I have a right to air my views. I want you to put John Tasker in charge of the investigation.'

The CP bristled. Tasker – not him! Not 'two-gun'

Tasker, the biggest cowboy in the whole of CID head-quarters. Damn it all! His mind searched blindly for the words to express his indignation at such meddling in police operation matters, but the Governor caught him offguard.

'What about it, James?' said Sir Andrew expectantly, returning to his chair. 'I can't say I'm surprised at Gordon's request. I don't wish to sound melodramatic, but Tasker has made something of a name for himself as a – what do the newspapers call them – a gang-buster.' The Commissioner turned his attention away from Devereau to the man behind the desk. The brightness of the sky beyond the French windows caused him to squint, and the Governor became a dark buddha-like silhouette.

'Superintendent Tasker is not necessarily the best man for the job,' he began carefully. 'Yes, he's had his successes. He's flamboyant and he attracts publicity, but the headlines haven't always been good. His rule-bending has landed him in trouble more than once. Two years ago he was very nearly retired in the public interest.'

'But he's a bloody good detective,' Devereau insisted. 'The results prove it.'

'I'll need to check availabilities and ongoing workloads. I've a feeling he may be due on long leave in the near future.' Weldon was smokescreening and the Governor knew it. He was not a man easily fooled.

'James ... James.' The old man's eyes closed briefly, almost wearily. 'Just do as Gordon asks. Sometimes we have to go against conventional wisdom in order to send the right signals. I want this thing stamped out now before it gets any worse.'

'And what if the trail does lead back to the Mainland? You know we can expect no cooperation from the other side. Does the political will exist to do anything about that?'

The Governor smiled that benign smile of his again.

'Let's cross that bridge when we come to it, shall we?'

After that there was no more to be said. Devereau had won. The Commissioner of Police had received his instructions from the highest authority in the territory; had once more been reminded of the political realities of Hong Kong.

Offering only the curtest of goodbyes, Weldon repacked his briefcase and walked gratefully out of Government House into the bright sunlight and the fresher air. Alone on the steps he cursed angrily under his breath as his limousine swung into position. This time, as he looked upwards, the windows of the high-rise apartment blocks seemed to look down mockingly.

Behind him the ADC, caught unawares by his sudden departure, came scurrying down the steps, but he was too late to make any formal farewell. Weldon stepped quickly into the cool of his limousine and was borne away.

FIVE

On Monday morning Detective Superintendent John Tasker reached his desk at Kowloon Regional police headquarters to find an urgent message waiting for him. Slumping into his chair and taking a long slurp of black coffee from a styrofoam cup, he stared blearily across the chaos of his desktop, groaned, then snatched the bright yellow note from his pad. It was 9.45, with distant memories of an empty tequila bottle still jangling inside his brain, and already the day looked like shit.

Without reading it, he knew the note spelled trouble – detective's intuition, call it what you like. A note important enough for the duty officer to both sign it and time it, thereby covering his own behind. Two lines telling Tasker that his presence was required immediately at Police Headquarters over on the Island. By order of the Director of Criminal Investigations: the lord high detective himself. The worry lines on Tasker's forehead deepened. It was not often he got to speak to the DCI, no more than two or three times a year, so why this, and why now? Tasker fingered the paper with growing puzzlement, trying to recall any recent indiscretion which might have precipitated the summons, but he was fairly sure there was none. No battered prisoners or broken bar-rooms that he could remember offhand. Still, it was with a certain uneasiness that he signed out, climbed into his car – after bumming a cigarette from the transport sergeant – and started off for the sweaty monoxide drive through the cross-harbour tunnel to Hong Kong Island.

The headquarters of the Royal Hong Kong Police lies close to the north shore of Hong Kong Island, facing Kowloon across the busy waterway of the biggest deepwater harbour in the world. The high-walled compound, with its quaint colonial turrets (a reminder of years of civil unrest), dominates the whole of Arsenal Street, which itself lies tantalisingly close to the vibrant Wanchai bar district. Within the compound were two distinct blocks: Caine House, the original PHQ, or Police Headquarters; and the more modern May House. Both had been named after Police Commissioners from the Victorian era, and for many years the twenty-floor rise of New May House had made it something of a landmark in the area, standing out like a beacon of law and order. But in recent times the pace of building development along the Wanchai waterfront had served to swallow up New May House in a growing jungle of concrete and mirrored glass. Tasker could not now remember a time when the air in Wanchai was not filled with sand blown from nearby construction sites; but that was true all over the colony. Even with only a few years left till the colony's handover, the developers were still looking to turn a quick profit.

Wanchai was becoming upwardly mobile and cosmopolitan. A new crop of hotels and shopping centres was sprouting up. Now it was beset by Japanese developers. Even the remaining Wanchai whores were after yen. The whole district was struggling to shake off the legacy of Suzy Wong and become an extension of the Central business district.

As Tasker turned off Gloucester Road and on to Hennessy, he felt the buzz of the place: traffic horns screaming in the steaming heat; antique trams shuddering along on their antique rails, plastered with advertising messages for Yeo's seafood sauce and Sanyo airconditioners. Even in daylight the mosaic of movement and colour on these streets threatened Tasker's brain with sensory overload. The streets were hung with vertical hoardings of Chinese characters; so everywhere you looked were these large blocks of painted red script.

And the people who thronged these streets remained a constant source of mystery, from the bent old women in black pyjamas scurrying between home and market, to the fierce, posturing machismo of the street toughs who dominated the tiny chickenwire-fenced playgrounds. How nearly six million people could live in such close proximity and such stifling heat without going crazy had always astounded Tasker. But that was Hong Kong's way, for the Chinese at least: a Confucian imperative towards order and conformity which was sucked in at the mother's breast, and later reinforced in the classrooms of Chinese schools. How else could Hong Kong's countless poor live cheek-by-jowl with the mega-rich unless through an innate, passive acceptance that this was the intended order of things.

Tasker thought of the many thousands of office workers now riding the dragon of the Mass Transit Railway into work, and he truly worried for their futures. He saw in his mind the trusting smiles on the faces of young people commuting in from the satellite towns of the New Territories or the housing estates of the East Island Corridor, to service the colony's financial engines day after day. Their parents and ancestors had devoted their lives and energies to create this unique place and time that was Hong Kong – but which would soon be lost forever. When the time came to leave, he could go to Australia, or perhaps home to the UK, but what of them?

To consider the disrupted lives of nearly six million people was beyond his comprehension, so he turned his thoughts to the future of his own team. Almost to a man they expressed fears for their own safety at the hands of the Chinese People's Liberation Army; yet they carried on with typical Chinese fortitude, always making the best of any situation.

Seeing the gates of PHQ loom large before him, Tasker turned his mind back to the meaning of this morning's summons, and once more he began to wonder. As he slowed the car to flash his ID to the uniformed gate guard, he had no idea he was being observed from a window on the fifth floor of Caine House.

In the first few hours of Monday morning, all the talk around police headquarters was of the Shatin robbery and the rumours that 'Two-Gun Tasker' would be pulled in to clear up the mess. Naturally, as in all forces with specialised units, feathers were ruffled by this suggestion. A job of this size should normally have gone to one of the existing teams of the Organised and Serious Crimes Bureau (OSCB). But there was nothing normal about this case.

At thirty-nine, Tasker was already a legend in the force. Streamed for CID in his first tour of duty, he had shot to the heights of the gazetted officer rank whilst his peers were still struggling to make Chief Inspector. Though his methods were irregular, some thought brutal, his successes against triad and other hard-core criminal targets spoke for themselves. A string of armed robbery cases, handled with guts and a heavy measure of good fortune, had won him promotions and made him a firm favourite with the media. It was the tabloid press that had given him his nickname. That was after an ambush and shoot-out outside a jewellers on Kowloon's Golden Mile. As shoppers and tourists fled for their lives, his team had shot dead three of the robbers. Tasker had been snapped by a photographer while standing over the bodies with an automatic pistol taken from the villains in one hand and his own police revolver in the other. 'Two-Gun Tasker' – the name had stuck.

Headquarters had not liked that image. Headquarters did not like a lot of things about John Tasker. But most of all they did not like his cavalier attitude to discipline and his hard-drinking lifestyle. His hatred of bureaucracy and predilection for rule-bending were famous in CAPO: the Complaints Against Police Office. There it was said that Tasker's only use for the heavy Police General Orders manual was to beat prisoners over the head with it when he could not lay hands on a telephone directory.

But the *foh geis*, the Chinese detectives working under him, worshipped the very ground he trod. Often accused of megalomania, Tasker thrived on this personality cult, neglecting his home life to lead his men on nightly forays through a string of the seedy Mongkok ballrooms where his name was already legend. When they were not rousting informers or needling the local gangs, they were chugging brandy in tall glasses and playing raucous rounds of *chai mooi*, Chinese drinking games, with anyone who would take them on. To his men Tasker was both boss and big brother, their *dai lo*, and through the power of his personality he commanded their absolute loyalty. No other European officer understood half so well the codes and puns of gutter Cantonese, or the arcane system of ethics, motivations and superstitions which ruled their lives. There was a steady stream of transfer requests from *foh geis* wanting to work under him.

When Tasker reached the fifth floor of Caine House he found the Chinese Director of Criminal Investigations waiting to read him his personal fortune.

'This time your colourful reputation seems to have worked against you,' said Chan Ham-gar, the territory's senior detective, with just a hint of smugness. He was a Chiu Chau from the Swatow region of the Mainland; he was bellicose and spare in his manners, and the skin of his face was stretched so tight that whenever he spoke, in

78

precisely correct English, his eyebrows moved in time with his lips. 'Whatever you're doing at the moment, get rid of it. We're giving you the Shatin robbery case. As of now you're back in OSCB. That'll give you access to the Criminal Intelligence Branch computer files.'

'But I still have major investigations into loan-sharking to finish.'

'That's taken care of. Crabtree will take your place this afternoon. You can arrange a handover during the rest of this week.'

'How long will this posting be for?'

'Until it's wrapped up – one way or the other.'

Hardly bothering to hide his irritation at the selection of Tasker for this role, the senior Chinese detective outlined the brief he had been issued that morning by the Commissioner. The primary concern of the Jockey Club was to discover the present location of the money, and to effect its immediate recovery; but Tasker was also being ordered to investigate in detail exactly how the job was done, and by whom. Of particular concern to the CP was the exact source of the weaponry used, and the rather puzzling fact that Criminal Intelligence had not registered so much as a whisper prior to the robbery itself.

'Pick whatever officers you need,' said Chan dismissively as he returned to a draft he was preparing.

Tasker smiled to himself.

'What, no warning about unlawful use of firearms in crowded areas?'

Both men were aware that Tasker was subtly mocking previous reprimands in this very office.

Chan did not bother to smile.

'The CP wants a quick result. So does the Governor. Both of them know your reputation. Read between the lines.'

Tasker pursed his lips and nodded, aware of the implication. Jesus, he thought, this must really have scared them.

'You said I could pick my own team. There'll be resistance from regional CID.'

'If you get any flannelling from anyone, regardless of rank, inform me immediately and I'll have him chasing illegal immigrants back over the snake fence. One more thing, Tasker. You have a reputation for going your own way, but remember who's in charge. I want to know what's going on, every step of the way. If you start any moves on major crime targets, I want to know before you go in and screw up ongoing operations. Is that clear?'

'Whatever you say.'

'You will already have heard speculations that elements of the Big Circle gangs are involved. Anything that looks vaguely political, or otherwise embarrassing, I want to know about it. Is that also clear?'

It was. Perfectly.

That afternoon Tasker was allocated two rooms in Organised and Serious Crime Group (OSCG) on the twelfth floor of New May House: a large one to serve as the *daai fong* or CID duty room, where his team would conduct their interviews and sift evidence; and a smaller one for his own office. Desks, chairs and telephones were allocated faster than he would ever have thought possible. But, then, Chan and the fifth floor were pulling all the strings.

The first thing he decided was to get hold of everything currently known. For this he needed only to take a short walk along the corridor to speak to K. K. Wong, the superintendent in OSCG whose team had caught the case on Saturday evening. Known facts fitted into a disappointingly thin folder. Only two statements had so far been taken: those of the surviving sergeant and of the Shatin Jockey Club's security operations manager. K. K. promised to keep on to it until Tasker had assembled his team and was ready to take over. He picked up a video cassette and tossed it across the desk.

'You'd better take a look at this,' he said stone-faced. 'It's the tape from the on-course video cameras. Better keep an eye on it, because everybody in PHQ wants to view it – ghoulish bastards! Watch it doesn't walk off!'

Tasker called for a machine from Criminal Intelligence Bureau (CIB) and viewed the video alone in his office. It was not a long film, but it was the hardest thing he had ever had to watch. Police officers being cut down like corn, so quick and so ruthless – it made even a hardened officer want to weep. Worst of all was the sight of Jason Leung's bullet-torn body. The other officers he did not know, but Jason Leung had been a probationary inspector under him when Tasker had done his short stint as instructor in the police training school at Wong Chuk Hang. When you have been responsible for someone to that degree, it is hard to watch their death on film.

When it finished, he took out a pen and wrote a list. This did not take long. From the moment they had said he could choose his team, he had known exactly who would be in it.

Five minutes later he was on the phone fixing it.

Tasker wanted Chinese officers first and foremost: men he had handled before, and whom he trusted. He wanted men whose nerve had been tested under fire, for they would be going against a tough team who favoured use of firearms and there would be no free rides.

The first man he chose was Joe Lai.

At the moment John Tasker picked up the phone, Detective Senior Inspector Joe Lai was just across the water, making observations on a Chinese fast-food outlet in the Wong Tai Sin district of Kowloon. Wong Tai Sin was one of those areas not featured on the tourist brochures: a place crammed with aging and grimy deck-access high-rise housing estates, and controlled by constantly feuding triad street gangs.

'That's Dai Pau, all right,' croaked the sergeant in Joe's ear. 'But where's he keeping the white powder?'

The shop Joe was watching was called Bang Bang Fast Food and lay squeezed between a photo-finishing shop and a small general store on a busy side-road just outside the lower estate; territory belonging to the 14K. These places were usually one- or two-man businesses which remained open all day and most of the night, cooking up lunch boxes of rice or noodles with various meats and sauces ladled on top. Because of the steady flow of customers using these places, heroin dealers often staked a pitch outside, and intimidated the owners into keeping quiet. The dealer Joe Lai was watching now was a skinny Chinese, probably in his late twenties, with tight bleached jeans, permed hair, and a sparse moustache on his upper lip. From his sunken appearance and nervous shuffle, as he paced the pavement chainsmoking American cigarettes, Joe guessed the man was probably using some of his own stuff, too.

Joe's information had been pretty good, gleaned from an anonymous informant – probably a rival dealer hoping to move in on the territory. Apparently this man, known as Dai Pau, meaning Big Gun or Big Mouth, had been selling Red Chicken here for the past three months. That meant a reddish granular type of heroin used exclusively for smoking, and nowhere near as pure as 'number four' heroin, or China White. Joe realised the dealer was pretty far down the chain, but that did not matter. What mattered was making an arrest and winning back face for the police. Local residents had begun to have doubts about police commitment to keeping drugs off the street, and one local district board member had even made a formal complaint. An object lesson was needed, and Dai Pau fitted the bill very nicely. Usually he hung around outside the open frontage of the fast food shop, waiting for calls on the public phone hanging on the wall just inside. Apart from one lookout, and an obligatory single fighter well versed in Chinese boxing to protect him and his stash, Dai Pau worked alone.

Directly across the street, peeking through slits in a steel shutter pulled across a metal workshop, Joe Lai had been studying the man's technique for two solid hours. He had to admit it was all fairly baffling, until the target coughed once too often, thereby revealing his secret.

'It's in his mouth,' Joe declared with absolute certainty.

The sergeant shook his head in disbelief.

'*Yau mo gau choh!* Must be kidding! Nobody's that stupid.'

'This one is,' said Joe. 'Just watch.'

It was true. Every time a customer appeared and slipped money into Dai Pau's left hand, he would give a cough, then take out his wallet and hand back change in several small bills. At no time was heroin seen changing hands. Eventually Joe had realised that the hand put up to stifle the cough each time received a tiny heroin packet spat out from inside the mouth. Dai Pau was storing the forty-dollar packets of Red Chicken, probably up to a dozen at any one time, in his cheek cavities.

On Joe's order the team moved in while Dai Pau's back was turned. Before the man could react, Joe had grabbed him by the hair with one hand, and clamped the palm of his other across the trafficker's throat to prevent him swallowing the evidence. Simultaneously two of Joe's men moved in on the fighter, and a third on the lookout. It took two more of them to force Dai Pau to open his mouth, but Joe eventually recovered what he was looking for: eight tiny packets of heroin in candy-striped plastic casing. It was a method of packaging he had only once seen used before: first an ordinary McDonald's drinking straw was filled with heroin; then a heated knife was used to cut the straw into a dozen sections, heat-sealing each. The reason for using plastic was the false belief that if a dealer was arrested he could safely swallow the evidence. Far from it: sometimes the seal was incomplete, and besides stomach acid is strong stuff. Several traffickers had died that way, but there were plenty more to take their place.

Dai Pau may have been luckier than he realised, but that did not stop him sounding off as they led him away.

'You police don't scare anybody now – not after the Shatin robbery. You've no face any more. My protector will settle you bastards, then you'll go the same way as those other police bastards.'

It was the wrong time to speak and the wrong thing to say, though the trafficker could hardly have known the loss Joe Lai had suffered with the death of his friend Jason Leung. The two men had been *hing dai*: brothers. The sergeant saw Joe's eyes flash in anger, and he tried to come to between them, but Joe just brushed him aside. Before anyone else could move, Joe had hauled the dealer inside the shop and thrown him bodily across the counter. Eyes blazing and erupting curses, Joe raised the trafficker's arm and heaved a punch deep into his armpit, causing him to scream in pain.

The man struggled on the counter top, shrieking out at the top of his lungs. '*Gau meng! Gau meng!* Save life! Save life!'

In the next moment Joe Lai had emptied a lunchbox into Dai Pau's face, the tangle of hot sauce and noodles almost choking him, blinding his eyes.

'Take him away' – Joe released the man's hair and turned away in disgust – 'before I make a Hungry Ghost of him!'

As they rode back to Wong Tai Sin police station, with Dai Pau wedged between two detectives, the strong aroma of oyster sauce lingered in the vehicle. Quietly Joe fumed and brooded on the man's remark about the police's loss of face. Back inside the station compound, it was a relief for him to step down and get away from the prisoner.

The first thing he did was check his radio-pager for stored messages. During the stakeout he had turned the sound off, but in the course of the arrest, and his stupid blow-up, he had felt the vibrations of the pager unit's silent call mode. Now he responded to the bleep, and heard John Tasker's tobacco-rich voice calling him to a meeting on the Island. Joe Lai felt a sudden shiver pass through him:

'There's a small job on. I'd like your help,' was all Tasker would say. But when Tasker called anything 'a small job', you knew it had to be far more.

Joe Lai was one of those goodlooking, athletic Chinese men whose true age always comes as a shock to Europeans. His manner of dress, his way of walking and behaving were uniquely Hong Kong Chinese: a showy mixture of exuberance and a confidence which only submerged itself when he found himself around those he truly respected. Which in Joe's case was not often.

A force-entry police officer, Joe had made it to Senior Inspector the hard way: beginning at the bottom at a time when a recruit constable still wore short pants. In fourteen years he had worked in most police formations, and attracted a string of commendations almost as long as the string of complaints. Tasker liked that, he did not trust any man who did not attract some complaints; they were the natural consequence of doing the job properly, and anybody who did not receive them just was not trying hard enough. Joe Lai's family had both money and connections: they owned one of the many goldsmith's shops in Mongkok, and a string of video-game arcades. These connections gave Joe access to the petty underworld as well as a wealth of inside knowledge on what the Chinese high-rollers were currently up to.

* * *

Next Tasker had to choose an NCO to keep the *foh geis* in line. Some one with a reputation. He wanted a young man energetic enough to get a grip on the detectives in the team. Older men had the experience, but too much to protect; they were unwilling to take the kind of risks Tasker knew would be necessary. Experience had taught him that you don't go up against *Dai Huen Jai*, the Big Circle Gang, with a force of backsliders.

The man he chose was Detective Station Sergeant Cheng Tatwah, known as 'Lo Foo Cheng': Cheng the Tiger. He was thirty-five years old, though his well-muscled body looked easily ten years younger. They called him Tiger because he had a way of looking at suspects which froze the blood: wide, alert eyes staring out of a tanned face that seemed carved out of granite. Otherwise a short hooked nose and broad flat cheeks gave him the appearance of an American Indian. Twenty years ago Cheng had been a formidable fighter in a street gang in Western district. Later, when he had joined the force, he had volunteered as a physical training instructor in the training school, where he specialised in self-defence and close-quarter combat. Cheng had the street-fighter's strength and phenomenal speed, but also a tremendous fund of self-discipline. Like Joe Lai, he was one of the true exponents of *wing chun kung fu*, the street-fighter's art.

And yet Cheng was equally proficient with firearms. Few detectives ever reach the rank of station sergeant, a rank known as D-Major. Most spend their careers just grubbing after sergeant's pay and better police married quarters. But Tiger Cheng had made D-Major, working under John Tasker, just three years after gaining sergeant's stripes, because he knew his way around the underworld as if he had a schematic of Kowloon tattooed in his brain. At street level he was known as a gifted tactician, and best of all, the criminal gangs both feared and respected him.

Tasker knew Cheng had a history, some involvement with triad enforcers. But that could only be good, given the parameters of the present case.

At 5.30 that afternoon Tasker threw the folders across his desk. Enough of reading. He took his detective special out of the desk drawer and threaded the holster on to his belt. The leather shone at the edges; it was the same one he had used as a *bong baan jai*, or young inspector, on his first vice squad attachment out of police training school. Like himself the holster had not been much good in those days, a little rough around the edges, and it seemed it had taken a number of years of detective work to wear them *both* in. Tasker checked the load, snapped the cylinder shut, and walked out to meet his team.

The Luk Kwok Chinese restaurant lay in the bustling heart of Wanchai. Joe Lai and Lo Foo Cheng were already playing a hand of *sap saam jeung* at a reserved table on the first floor – the regular alcove for police meetings – when he arrived. Tasker came to the table smiling broadly, and the two men rose and greeted him with nods of the head which to the initiated eye showed the same respect as the full traditional bow. '*Dai lo*,' they greeted him: meaning 'elder brother', 'boss', 'leader', or sometimes just 'senior', depending upon the context. It was a demonstration of respect conveying more than just the officially-required 'Ah sir'.

'*Ho lui, mo gin, dai lo!*' grinned Joe Lai in that boyish manner that made his eyes fade to joyous slits. He lifted the porcelain teapot and filled Tasker's cup to the brim. Like all Chinese, Joe firmly believed in giving face to a senior. 'Long time no see, boss! What's the score?'

Tasker outlined what he knew of the case – and the extent of his suspicions. He proceeded to warn them of the danger, just once, and then would never mention it again. That was the code of honour. That done, he probed another source of concern.

'Jason Leung was in your squad at training school, Joe. Is that a problem for you?'

Joe sucked on the cigarette which always seemed to hang from the left side of his mouth. At first Tasker thought he saw something there, a reluctance to discuss the subject. Then it was gone, and Joe gave a long sigh.

'You know, today I busted a drug trafficker who said the force has no more face out on the street. I can't accept that. I can't accept that kind of contempt for the life of a police officer. And I won't. We owe it to Ah Leung to do this thing right. We owe it to each and every one of the *foh gei* who died.'

Tasker nodded in understanding, and his gaze passed across to Tiger Cheng.

'What about you, Tiger?'

The station sergeant stared fixedly at the green leaves in the bottom of his cup.

'This is still the festival of the Hungry Ghosts,' he said without looking up. 'The ghosts of our men won't get any kind of peace until we catch this team of robbers – or kill them.'

Before breaking up their meeting Tasker gave the remainder of his list to Joe Lai and told him to arrange for detachment of the named detectives. He asked both men to start putting out feelers for information; and not in a passive way, either.

'Gentlemen,' he continued, raising his cup and draining it in salute. Both watched closely as Tasker closed his fist and squeezed the porcelain until it broke with a cough of powder and glaze. 'We're not dealing with the usual street punks waving choppers now. These are a very special, highly-trained crew – soldiers for all I know. And we all realise that anybody who'll take on the Jockey Club must be very well connected in order to get their money laundered. Jockey Club connections will be watching those little blips on the screens in Exchange Square from now on, so our targets will need someone big to help them move it. The Jockey Club wants that money back very badly. Me, I don't give a fuck for all that. These men are cop-killers; it's as simple as that. Wherever they are, whoever they are, I just want their carcases.'

big to help them solve it. The Jockey Club wasn't that
money back very badly, Mr. I don't give a fuck for all
that. These men are cop-killers, it's as simple as that.
Wherever they are, whoever they are, I just want their
carcasses.

SIX

That same evening another of Joe Lai's old squad-mates
from the police training school caught a particularly bad
homicide in Kowloon West, though it was not until much
later that he would appreciate the full significance of the
crime.

Yaumatei lies across the Golden Mile, in an area
bounded by Nathan Road on one side and the floating
hovels of the Yaumatei typhoon shelter on the other.
Between these two points there lies a baffling maze of
narrow streets and alleys whose high buildings have
grown together over the years, conspiring to keep out
much of the daylight. In daytime all you see are the
shops and the street hawkers and thousands of people
milling in and out of restaurants, but at night the place
really comes alive. High above the bustle of the night
markets, within dark tenements bristling with aerials and
bamboo laundry poles, are secreted a staggering number
of commercial enterprises – licensed and unlicensed.
Sometimes crammed into just one apartment space, or
even half a floor, there are nightclubs, restaurants,
massage parlours by the score. Tucked between stairways
there is a profusion of tiny run-down boarding houses,
where the fugitive as well as the merely homeless rest
their heads. And dotted amongst these, well watched and
guarded by the triad armies, are enough one-girl
brothels, illegal casinos, and drug distribution points to
keep the Yaumatei vice squad busy until 1997.

The incoming report had said 'Bad smell found', but when the mobile unit had threaded its way through the crowded backstreets of the Yaumatei dockside, they forced their way on foot into a dump space between two tenements. It was their noses which took them straight to a zinc garbage tank that contained the body of a tall, well-dressed European male.

Yaumatei being one of the more densely populated districts in an already groaning territory, an instant crowd of onlookers quickly reacted to the presence of the blue police transit van. In seconds flat a throng had formed around the end of the alley, and overhead hundreds of faces stared down from the tangled ranks of balconies.

Even as the sergeant in charge of the mobile patrol climbed down from his vehicle, he had recognised the familiar overpowering odour of death. For nothing else in this world smells the same as a human corpse, and, once smelled, it remains locked inside one's brain, never to be forgotten.

Now, leaning over the big man's body, he had to make a special effort not to breathe through his nose as he checked the body for identification. Eventually he stood up straight, tugging at his green safari uniform and readjusting the black leather Sam Browne belt. As he strode back to the police transit a soft curse escaped his lips, and it was with a certain amount of annoyance that he unclipped the microphone from the dashboard and radioed in to Kowloon RCCC – the Regional Command and Control Centre. From long experience he had found that dead bodies usually came with a lot of paperwork attached; now he realised that he and his men would be working until the early hours, instead of catching a few beers and a late massage before heading home to their families.

'Further report to that complaint of bad smell,' he informed the police communications officer in the command centre. 'Change to: *Dead body found. Suspected homicide*. Please inform headquarter units accordingly.'

Roman Fung was not actually watching the TV when the phone rang, though the set was on and a historical Chinese costume drama was playing loudly on TVB Jade. Instead his attention was fixed on the photograph album lying open before him; and his mind occupied by the memories it preserved. It was the graduation picture which held his attention: three ranks of probationary inspectors drawn up outside the main admin block of the Police Training School. Europeans and Chinese all side by side, their new green safari-style uniforms as yet unfaded by the heat and sweat of Hong Kong; leather Sam Brownes gleaming; black peaked caps pulled low over their eyes to shade the sun's glare, but also to disguise their youth and inexperience. The photo caption read *Passing-out squads 197 to 199* in bold letters; and in the heat of that parade square, Roman remembered that many of them almost had. With a fond smile his eyes tracked the faces of those seated in the front rank, recalling the irreverent nicknames they had given each of the three squad instructors, Tasker, Sewell and Dalton. These were seated on either side of the school commandant, nursing official black canes across their knees. That was the last time he could ever remember seeing John Tasker in uniform. He had been a confirmed CID cowboy ever since then... Then there were the baton of honour winners: Dave Becker, Ruth Tavistock, and Roman himself. And in the back row, between Mel Kale the big Australian, and Roman's own personal hero Joe Lai, stood baby-faced Jason Leung, who could never march in time with the police band and who was now a hungry ghost.

As Roman ran his finger over the laughing faces, he was trying to understand that he would never see Ah

Leung again. A part of his group, and therefore of himself, was gone forever.

It took two rings of the phone to break through his thoughts. When he picked it up, the police communications officer at Kowloon RCC identified himself.

'Fung, sir, you're reserve homicide team, tonight.'

'I know that.' Irritation was obvious in Roman's reply.

'Sorry, sir. They've got you a body and it looks like a *gwai lo!*'

The local CID was already out in force when he arrived at the scene. You could not miss them: permed hair and Hawaiian shirts, wearing laminated warrant cards clipped to their breast pockets. They scurried back and forth taking the names of people living in nearby blocks who might have seen someone dump the body. One *foh gei* was making a detailed sketch of the alley on a clipboard, while a second flitted around with an extendable tape measure on a revolving reel. The blue light of the mobile patrol transit rotated silently, sweeping the alley with a weird glow.

Fung gazed around at the dense profusion of dilapidated housing blocks, the debris and filth piled high in the spaces between – and the first question he asked himself was: What the hell was a *gwai lo* doing down here?

'Ah sir. Sergeant Ma, RCU Kowloon.' An old Chiu Chau sergeant from the Yaumatei Regional Crime Unit stepped up beside him, his square bulk covered by a bright green bowling shirt. His head was closely shaven in the regulation cut of twenty-five years ago, so that the silver grey stubble glistened in the glow of the lights. Ma came momentarily to attention as he spoke, giving face to his senior. Fung did not return the courtesy. As far as he was concerned, the older Chiu Chau detectives were all tainted with the drug business and the large-scale corruption of the Fifties and Sixties. Indeed, he looked forward to a day when all Chiu Chau detective sergeants were finally gone from the force, for their presence was a constant reminder of the old days when they had controlled CID and only they were promoted.

'Relax, sergeant,' he replied dismissively. 'DSI Fung, OSCG reserve homicide team. My men will be here soon. Better show me the body.'

The sergeant turned and pushed his way, between two uniformed officers, into the alley where stanchions and tape had been erected to cordon off the area. A woman detective wearing jeans was now keeping the necessary log, and overseeing the security and integrity of the crime scene. Fung gave her his name and formation, and was allowed through immediately.

'He's a big *gwai lo*, Fung sir. Nice clothes but not a scrap of identification on him. Someone took great care to remove the clues. It has all the signs of a contract killing if you ask me.'

'I didn't,' answered Roman abruptly, and the sergeant followed him in silence.

They picked their way through a squelching heap of debris until they reached the metal dump tank. It was waist-high from the ground and twelve feet long, with garbage spilling out on to the ground where the uniform officers had left it. The sergeant flipped on a powerful six-cell torch – the kind Emergency Unit officers carried as an extra baton – and shone the beam into the tank. Flies rose in clouds from the mess of rotting food and sodden kitchen refuse. The evening was warm but the tank generated a heat all its own, which was entirely due to putrefaction.

The smell was appalling.

Gathering his resolve, Fung took an extendible steel pointer from his jacket pocket and began to probe inside. The corpse was undoubtedly European, easily over six foot, and heavy with it. The body lay on its right side, still fully clothed, the back arched and the lower limbs distorted like a discarded shop mannequin. The hands had been carefully bound behind the back with thin-gauge industrial wire twisted many times. As Ma had said, the clothes were well tailored – not the jeans and T-shirt he found on his usual murder victims. Here was class: blue double-breasted suit, expensive leather loafers, white shirt and painted silk tie. The collar of the shirt was caked with a blackened crust of dried blood. Then Fung registered the jutting white projection of the neck vertebra, and around this the oozing raw stump where the head had been cleanly removed.

'Who found him?'

Ma took out his notebook.

'The complaint came from a woman on the first floor. She claimed the stink was keeping her kids awake.'

'I'm surprised they could smell anything with so much crap and garbage around.' The old CID sarcasm: a talisman against horror.

'Fung sir, they're used to that. But this is different.'

Fung was concentrating again on the body; the maggots in the flesh were already well developed. 'Been here a few days, by the look of it, and nobody saw anything – as usual?'

'You know how it is with people down here, Fung sir. The last thing they want is to get involved in anything like this.'

'*Hai ah*, they might wind up missing a whole day's business!'

Fung made his own thorough search of the body but found nothing in any of the pockets: no wallet, no watch, no business card, no credit card and no cash. An enigma, this, he was forced to conclude, or else a well camouflaged hit. Why else would the head be missing? As a grisly souvenir? Or to prevent identification? The one thing he was sure of was that the corpse was indeed a *gwai lo*. The thick black hair on the victim's chest, fore-arms and fingers confirmed it. No self-respecting Chinese would have body hair like this monkey!

Fung stepped back against a wall and pushed the fashionably long hair away from his eyes, brooding on what he had seen. The broad padded shoulders of his cotton seersucker jacket rested against the concrete. A moment later Sergeant Ma lit up a cigarette and joined him by the wall, folding his fat arms across his chest.

'Got to be a *gwai lo* tai-pan: rich businessman. They're bound to miss him tomorrow in Central. Why not leave it until start of business tomorrow morning, and wait for a missing person complaint. Match the two – *gau dim!* Cracked it!' The back of the smoking hand smacked into the open palm of the other in emphasis. Like the uniform sergeant, Ma clearly wanted to get away as soon as possible. Fung watched the red shower of sparks and ash fall to the ground and reacted with quiet anger.

'Put that cigarette out – now. You know the rules about scenes of crime.'

In fact the chance of getting any forensic evidence from the scene of this crime was desperately slim, but he still wanted to make a point. Sergeant Ma responded in embarrassment, his eyes registering a sullen resentment even as he apologised and waddled back down the alley to wait by the police transport.

Then Fung had an idea. Reaching back inside the rubbish tank he forced himself to touch the body, this time flipping open the big man's jacket. What he saw there made him curse his previous stupidity, for it ought to have been the first thing he checked. After all, this was Hong Kong, and the *gwai lo* businessmen all had their suits made to order, with their names stitched under the left inside breast pocket.

The label inside was stitched in gold lettering: HANDMADE BY SAM'S TAILORS, BURLINGTON ARCADE, NATHAN ROAD, FOR MR JAMES B. REICHER.

The corpse had just announced himself.

Fung now knew the man's name. A man who had

been trussed like a turkey, brutally decapitated, and then dumped in the steaming armpit of Kowloon. That did not make it any easier to look at what was left of him now – and it still left a million questions unanswered.

But at least it was a start.

Just after midnight, Joe Lai's red Celica was parked in a look-out off Stubbs Road high on Victoria Peak, with a good view of the harbour. He was thinking about that evening's business and idly watching a walla-walla taking late-returning sailors back to one of the warships that rode at anchor off HMS *Tamar*, when his radio-pager sounded for the second time that day. When he answered the call on his car-phone, the girl on the line gave him a message left by a European, a Mr Becker. The message said simply: 'The Double Dragon – *bai Gwan-Dai.*'

At once Joe's mood brightened. *Bai Gwan-Dai* was just what he needed.

Having left Tasker and Cheng only thirty minutes earlier, he had decided to drive his car up Victoria Peak to smoke and to think, and enjoy the panoramic view of the harbour, before making for the Hilton Hotel's Dragonboat bar to drink and chat with the waitresses he knew there. He had no real wish to drink alone, any more than he wanted to go home to bed yet – not when Jason Leung's murder was still preying heavily on his mind.

The *bai Gwan-Dai* was a ceremony with a long tradition at which policemen offered worship to their patron god.

All hail to Gwan-Dai,
Noblest of heroes,
Defender of the House of Han

But among members of Probationary Inspectors

97

Squad 197 it had always had a further significance. To them it had always represented a squad reunion accompanied by heavy police talk, general bitching about the job, and a lot of serious drinking. It was understood between them that any of the members might call a *bai Gwan-Dai* at any time: to resolve some personal problem of their own or just to get blasted and let off steam. With anxieties over 1997 growing, and so many officers leaving the force, these reunions were becoming more frequent. But after Jason Leung's death it was only a matter of time before another one occurred.

This time Becker had called it and for the rendezvous had named an old favourite: the Double Dragon, a disco bar just off Lockhart Road on the Wanchai strip. The animated neon sign outside showed twin leaping dragons – one green, one red – and beneath this sign tattooed young men in jeans would meet and hustle, and step into nearby alleys to transact their business. Inside the place was a mirror-lined bar that extended along most of one wall. Small tables were ranged around a dance floor where a dark Filipino DJ kept the music so loud one almost had to shout to be heard. Each table was lit by a candle flickering inside a small brandy glass, and inset in the purple walls were booths with padded banquettes for those desiring greater privacy.

Joe Lai left his car by the kerb and walked up the steps, to be instantly swallowed by the relentless thump of the music. Even above the din he could hear the voices of Kale and Doherty arguing the rules of some drinking game neither of them could properly remember. At the bar two Chinese hostesses in topless chiffon gowns were hustling the row of near-drunks slumped on padded barstools. When they saw Joe, both girls smiled.

'Buy me one drink, Joe?'

Their young bodies with tiny, perfect bare breasts competed for his attention. Joe turned around and saw the 'worshippers' collected in the first booth, with a platoon of empty beer bottles on the table and full glasses before them.

'Another round for my friends over there,' gestured Joe, 'and drinks for both of you.'

Becker noticed him first, and waved him over enthusiastically.

'Took your bloody time, you yellow-running dog!' roared Mel Kale, waving a beer bottle in salute. The others responded with cheers.

'I wouldn't have missed it, you pink-skinned pig!' Joe retorted in kind. 'Someone's got to teach you *gwai lo* bastards how to drink!'

When the waiter arrived Joe took the large gin from the tray and half filled it with tonic water before setting it down before Ruth Tavistock.

'Thanks, Joe,' said Ruth. 'Always the gentleman.'

'*Hai la!*'

Chief Inspector Ruth Tavistock was the only woman ever invited to a *bai Gwan-Dai*. The rule was no outsiders, and no wives or girlfriends either, but Ruth had always been counted one of the boys; herself a baton-winning ex-member of Squad 197. And because she was the last European girl ever to be recruited into the RHKP, she was known to the Chinese as the last of the *gwai mooi* – a term meaning 'little ghost sister'. With her neatly bobbed blonde hair, striking good looks and caustic line in wit, it was hardly surprising they could not ignore her. No one could for long.

'Where's Roman?' asked Joe. 'We Chinese are a bit thin on the ground tonight.' He spoke without realising the full significance of his remark, but Becker answered before anyone had time to brood further on Jason Leung's absence.

'He's been called out, mate. I paged him earlier, and he says he won't be able to make it. He's got a heavy date over in Yaumatei with a headless corpse. Still, *we're* all here. How about some sort of a toast to the remaining members of Squad 197? Nearly twelve years now and still going strong!'

Glasses were charged and raised.

'And may we all be out before 1997! *Yam sing* – bottoms up!'

'*Yam sing!*' they all chorused, and drank.

'Stuff the future,' roared Sherpa Davey, waving his glass tipsily. 'I'm staying for the last bloody helicopter out. It will be like the fall of Saigon around here.'

'Yeah, only you won't be able to get to the bloody airport, 'cause you'll be trampled in the rush.' Becker remained sceptical. 'And we won't all get on those three little minesweepers they keep at HMS *Tamar* neither.'

'Well I'm here for the full ride,' grinned Blackdog, taking another drink. Blackdog was always taking another drink. 'I don't care if it's helicopters on the roof of Government House. At least it'll be interesting. What else are we going to do back home? Lazy bastards like us, spoiled by the colonial lifestyle of amahs and room boys. Maybe open a pub or a guesthouse? I'm not cut out to sell filofaxes to bloody yuppies, and we're not trained for anything else.'

Mel Kale made an expansive gesture with his enormous bare arm, beer swilling over the rim of his glass. The white areas on his Hawaiian patterned shirt glowed purple beneath the ultraviolet lamps.

'I've got it all worked out. Last time I was home in Oz, I met this guy who owned a houseboat down on the Great Barrier Reef. Beautiful little place in the Whitsunday Islands with a dozen windsurfers beached out back. Renting them out in tourist season, he makes enough in six months to keep him in grog and sheilas for the rest of the year.' Here Kale sighed and closed his eyes as if picturing it all. 'Think of the address on your mail: Blackstump Houseboat, Magnetic Island, Whitsunday Group, Great Barrier Reef. That's for me, mate.'

Then the rugby songs were struck up again, and

suddenly everyone else was laughing and talking at the same time. Just like the old times – the nights out they had stolen together instead of mugging for police professional examinations.

Almost inevitably, conversation returned to the time they had shared as recruit Probationary Inspectors, or PIs, in the police training school at Wong Chuk Hang, on the south of Hong Kong Island. It was to this place they had all come in the spring of 1980, not quite sure what they had let themselves in for.

The *gwai los* amongst them had all been recruited overseas: the Brits at the Hong Kong Government Office in London's Piccadilly; Mel Kale, the only Aussie, at the same office in Canberra, Australia; and Sherpa Davey in Auckland, New Zealand. They had signed on for an initial tour of three years with the rank of Inspector of Police, the lowest level for a European.

Becker recalled how the Brits had all arrived in the territory jet-lagged and the worse for alcohol, after a twenty-hour flight from Heathrow via Frankfurt, Bahrain and Calcutta. All sweetness and innocence, they had been set up for initiation in time-honoured fashion by a bunch of more senior trainees posing as squad instructors.

Then Frenchie Cook took up the narrative.

'Remember – we'd barely fallen off the plane and they had us going at it. They put us through circuit training, psychological evaluation, barrack inspection and that bloody run up Brick Hill, all in the space of the first hour. I'd just finished an English degree; I couldn't march to save my bloody life. I was ready to throw the towel in right then.'

'That's why they took your passport away,' said Becker, twirling a wooden chopstick between his fingers: an exercise to strengthen them. 'They say some of our predecessors went over the wire on their first night.'

It was true that on occasions new PIs were so scared

101

by the rigours of the initiation ceremony that they had grabbed their gear and hopped a taxi straight back to the airport the same evening. However, those who stuck around soon learned that real training was much more reasonable, and after the lunacy of those first few hours they took what was to come in their stride. Of course, coming halfway around the globe with a group of near strangers, to live in a place never even seen before, is a fairly harrowing prospect. But the RHKP had a way of dealing with this sense of isolation. When the new recruits were finally marched into a darkened chapel singing 'Onward Christian Soldiers', only to find, when the lights went on, that they were actually in the officers' mess, surrounded by hordes of howling trainees, this provided an instant ice-breaker.

Like all recruit inspectors, PI Squad 197 spent over eight months in PTS having the wrinkles of civilian life ironed out of them. For a *gwai lo* the first two months involved intensive Cantonese language training. For the Chinese, who were generally judged to be less independent after having lived their whole lives in the protective shelter of the family home and subject to Chinese education methods by rote-learning, there was a series of expeditions and leadership exercises. When those two months were up, they were brought back together for the long slog of absorbing the Laws of Hong Kong and the mysteries of the policeman's bible: the Police General Orders manual. Discipline was strict: anyone who failed just three of the fortnightly exams was automatically dismissed.

During that long hot summer, when the humidity inside the classrooms nudged into the high nineties, the ceiling fans whirring at full power making little difference, they went about bare-chested and wore a uniform of baggy green shorts, white belt, polished boots and black peaked cap. In lectures they strove not to fall asleep in the soporific heat, while watching an overhead projector, or sometimes the hawks circling hypnotically outside the window, high over the dense green slopes of Mount Nicholson and Wong Nai Chung Gap. There they learned about the historic role and development of the RHKP and of the wide powers of arrest, search and seizure they had been granted for the express purpose of maintaining the rule of law and order.

They discovered that the RHKP has always, of necessity, been a paramilitary force, due in large part to the vulnerability of its booming economy to outside influences and criminal exploitation. The Royal Hong Kong Police was formed in 1841, shortly after Hong Kong Island was ceded to Britain, and right from the very first it was commanded by a soldier, Captain William Caine, who was appointed as Chief Magistrate. Even in the early years, the colony was beset by organised bands of criminals. On land, triad groups terrorised the local Chinese fishing communities; whilst at sea, pirate junks preyed on the tall ships which carried rich pickings from the South China trade routes. As refugees and entrepreneurs alike flocked to the island and business increased, so too did the opportunities for criminal activity. Throughout the Victorian era Hong Kong was deluged with the dregs of the Mainland's criminal classes. Chinese justice often being summary execution by beheading, it was hardly surprising they chose to continue their criminal activities under the more lenient British legal system. In those early years successive police commissioners fought a rearguard action against poor-quality recruitment, and the corruption which was endemic in Chinese society. Often it was a losing battle, but still there was sufficient benefit of law and order to persuade the traders, the colony's lifeblood, to stay.

The PIs were told how, in the Fifties during the aftermath of the Chinese revolution, the colony survived only through the organisation and discipline of its police force. At this time Chinese communists, incensed by the proximity of this freewheeling capitalist enclave, had attempted to destabilise the colony with a frightening series of riots and bombing incidents that raged through the heart of Central district and the Kowloon peninsula.

It was much the same in the Sixties during the worst excesses of the Cultural Revolution. Roads and streets were blocked by burning cars, buses smashed and over-turned, buildings gutted. The seriousness of the situation had forced the Governor to order the police into full Internal Security (IS) mobilisation as a series of divi-sional riot companies, which met the rioters and looters head-on with batons, tear gas and shotguns. Eventually order was restored, but not without blood on both sides. After the horrors of the mob violence, the police force was careful to guard against any reoccurrence.

To this day, police officers are constantly briefed on the dangers inherent in high-density, high-rise living, the collective irresponsibility of the mob, and the low flash-point of Chinese tempers. John Tasker had warned each of them of the perils of getting themselves cornered in the public housing estates they would police. Crowds of a thousand or more could quickly form and any confron-tation between police and public be a potential incident, needing only the merest spark to make it explode.

PI Squad 197 learned all that was expected of them in the classroom, but it was afterwards, in the officers' mess over endless golden glasses of San Miguel beer, that they learned from the old hands what it was really like to be out there. Physical training was rigorous, too. They grew fitter, more confident, more determined to succeed. As they grew in confidence, they were schooled in leader-ship: how to control a body of men, maintaining both morale and discipline – Chinese men at that, with all their alien superstitions and sensibilities.

And they learned to handle a police revolver, as well as the IS weapons. For some who had never held a weapon before, it was a strange and disturbing experience. And with that came a creeping change in personality. By degrees the confirmed liberals amongst them became more pragmatic, more rigid in outlook.

On the day of their passing-out parade they each marched past the dais at the head of a graduating squad of recruit constables, the drums of the police band beating as fast as their proud hearts. Their uniform was now the green safari suit and black-lacquered leatherwork of a full Police Inspector. It made a stirring sight, hundreds of men and women in synchronised motion, the sun glinting off the bayonets of the constable's parade rifles. Yet on that day the *gwai lo* were reminded, by the absence of family or friends, that they were each essentially alone in this colony; that their only family was each other. With a final official graduation photograph, they were committed to the force and to each other. At last they were *bong baan*: Inspectors of Police.

Now they had been almost twelve years in this rank, and it was gratifying to see the hard core still turn up to *bai Gwan-Dai*. All had seen and done much in the intervening years. All had been posted to different units and formations: some to the New Territories on the China border, others to Hong Kong Island, and still others to the teeming hellhole of Kowloon.

David Becker and Ruth Tavistock had moved into Special Branch, where both had been promoted to the rank of Chief Inspector. Roman Fung and Joe Lai were now Senior Inspectors and CID 'cowboys' through and through. Jason Leung and Sherpa Davey had remained Inspectors in uniformed branch, but for different reasons: Jason had relatives in Canada and plans to emigrate to Vancouver, so he was not interested in going any further; Davey was currently a shift commander in EU/Kowloon West (Emergency Unit). Mel Kale had been posted to Operations Wing as training officer of the Special Duties Unit: the force's élite counterterrorist intervention specialists. The fact that Kale had inherited this role only after David Becker left it to reorganise Special Branch's bodyguard teams was a source of friendly rivalry between the two.

A sudden hollow ringing rose above the noise of the dance floor in the Double Dragon as an empty bottle flew off the table and bounced twice without breaking. Mel Kale, now definitely the worse for drink, was attempting to perform Slippery Sam with hand movements. The forfeit was a brandy for each mispronounced word. The others counted off his mistakes.

'Six nubile nuns, naughtily nibbling nuts. Seven slit sheets slit by Slippery Sam, the professional sleet-shitter!'

'Sleet-shitter!' chorused the jeering onlookers. 'Sleet-shitter?'

'Oh, Christ!' he thundered, knocking over another empty bottle. 'Screw it! Give me another drink anyway.'

While all eyes were still on Kale, Ruth turned and touched Joe Lai on the elbow.

'I hear you're on Tasker's team for this Shatin robbery investigation.'

'Around PHQ news travels faster than a speeding bullet,' said Joe coyly, lighting his cigarette and enjoying nevertheless the face this news brought.

'So, do *you* think they're back inside China?'

The question everyone in Hong Kong was asking. Even the DJ on *Talk-Back*, the radio phone-in programme on RTHK Radio 3, listened to by practically every expatriate in the colony.

'That's anybody's guess.' He was lighting a Winston filter as he spoke; the flare of the lighter flame washed over his cheek. He drew deeply before continuing. 'All I know is it's Tasker's case at the Governor's instruction, and this time they've taken the gloves off him.'

For some reason everyone stopped talking and looked in Joe's direction. Perhaps it was caused by the look of intense concentration on Ruth's face as she listened. They listened, too, while Joe explained how Tasker had already set the wheels in motion, but Becker's irritation forced him to interrupt.

'Look, Tasker may have been our instructor in PTS, but I still think the man is a dangerous liability. When you start behaving like a hoodlum you have to examine your motives pretty long and hard.' Becker's professional distaste for Tasker's freewheeling, TV cop-show methods was well known amongst the Gwan-Dai worshippers.

As a Chinese, Joe Lai found such disloyalty to a senior of Tasker's stature rather distasteful.

'Maybe you're right, Becker. But there's a ton of earth to shift on this case, and the *foh gei* won't do it for anyone but him. PHQ's behind him, and they don't seem to care how he brings it off. That will make a lot of people very nervous. Speaking personally, I think he's the only one who could do it.'

Becker gave a heavy shrug, fighting off the sudden memory of the dead police officers in Shatin.

'Well, I hope you're right, Joe,' he said raising his glass in mock salute. 'I hope you're bloody well right.'

SEVEN

Roman Fung came out of the lift at the twelfth floor of New May House, still looking bleary-eyed from lack of sleep. At the front desk, where a detective controlled access, he signed on for duty in the Occurrences Book, greeted any passing colleagues with a halfhearted '*Jo san*', and made his way around the quadrangle of corridors towards his office. The sign on the door said: DSIP FUNG Lo-man OSCG/1/TEAM 3. and beside it someone had written in Chinese characters: *The Abbatoir*.

Since the Police Force reorganisation of 1984, when Homicide Bureau had been absorbed by the Organised and Serious Crimes Group (OSCG), section Number One had handled any dead bodies where violence was involved. Roman Fung was the Detective Inspector in charge of one of the five reserve teams which took homicide cases by turn as they were reported. It was a good unit to work in: no common suicides or street sleepers, and no accidentals either. Just the real thing.

Only these days there was far too much of it – and just recently the killings had taken on a chillingly personal aspect.

On Sunday afternoon a group of picnickers in the Shing Mun country park had spotted a number of plastic sacks floating in the reservoir. When they fished one out, it was found to contain the mutilated torso of a young woman. Eventually the local uniformed branch had recovered the other sacks, and with them the remaining

108

pieces of the grim jigsaw puzzle. Like three other victims before her, the woman had been first strangled with a ligature, then her body carefully dismembered. As with the previous victims, there were obvious signs of sexual assault, the tell-tale bruising and laceration; but, this time, the pathologist was sure the assault had taken place after death. And this time there had been a note.

It was written in precise characters, and addressed to Detective Roman Fung, and signed: '*In Gwan-Dai's name*'.

Almost certainly they were dealing with a homicidal maniac of some sort, and obviously the killer had seen Fung make his televised appeal for information on the RTHK programme *Police Report*. Still it was more than a little disturbing to see his name on the killer's note: as if the man was now deliberately playing with him.

Entering the small office, Fung threw his briefcase on to the desk and tried to shake himself free of his gloom. There was no sense in brooding; he would plant three sticks of incense before the Gwan-Dai shrine in the duty room, and pray for a change in his team's fortune.

Within two minutes of his backside hitting the chair, Sergeant Amy Chan pushed her way through the open door with two glasses of hot sweet coffee made with condensed milk, the way Roman Fung liked it.

'*Jo san*, Roman,' she greeted him with a beaming smile. '*Yam ga fe* – Drink some coffee!'

She wore a light cotton shirt and loose-fit Levi 501s gathered at her slender waist by a broad leather belt with a large buckle. Roman was forced to admit Amy had an exceptionally neat figure for a homicide detective.

'*M'goi nei*, Amy,' he thanked her and gulped the muddy brown liquid gratefully. '*Wah, ho ye!* That's good! Just what I needed.' Then at last a smile came to his face as he put down the glass. He put out his hand to grab the girl's wrist, and pulled her gently round the desk and into his arms, standing up as he did so. The woman

109

sergeant did not resist and he held her closely. Looking into her sweet smiling face he kissed her hard on the mouth. Her soft tongue responded immediately.

'Is this strictly good procedure, Inspector Fung?' the woman sergeant grinned, when his searching mouth at last released hers.

'I suppose not, Woman Sergeant Chan,' he chuckled. 'But, like the coffee, it was just what I needed.'

Amy Chan had been sergeant of Roman Fung's team for the past sixteen months, and she had quickly won the respect of the detectives under her. She was bright and capable, and probably the best-looking woman in CID Headquarters – much fancied and interviewed by senior officers on the flimsiest of pretexts.

Roman and Amy had fallen in love with none of the suspicion and reserve so necessary in their professional lives. They had consulted each other's parents, and had decided they would marry as soon as Roman could save enough money to pay for a thirty-table wedding banquet; for such was the requirement of Amy's family. In the meantime they knew they must keep their plans a guarded secret. Police regulations forbade husband and wife from working together, and frowned on office love affairs. If the bosses ever found out, Amy would have to be transferred.

Suddenly mindful of this fact, she wriggled free of his arms and pushed him back into his chair. After checking the corridor, she slid the second chair in front of his desk, leaving the door ajar to allay suspicions.

'One day you'll go too far,' she warned him, suddenly serious. 'One day you'll try that stuff just as some *foh gei* walks in the door. Then what will I do? *Lok saai min!* Lose my face!'

Changing the subject she reached into the back pocket of her jeans and pulled out her police notebook.

'We think we have a match with Missing Persons Unit on our latest Gwan-Dai victim. The physical characteristics match up with those of a ballroom hostess who went missing last Saturday night.'

'Did you find anyone willing to identify the body?'

'You know how it is. We can't trace the girl's family; she's probably a runaway. So we'll have to get one of the nightclub staff over. So far, we haven't been able to locate the girl's immediate boss; nobody seems to know where *she* is.'

'What's her name?'

'Ruby Tang. Alias Lee Ping-li. Ethnic Chinese raised in Vietnam. She came here in '78 aboard the *Huey Fong* – one of the original boat people. She's done pretty well for herself since then. She's the hostess captain at the Barking Peacock over on Kowloon side.'

'Anything on her in CIB?' A routine file check with Criminal Intelligence Bureau was always the first step.

'Not really. Some early vice offences a few years ago, but nothing serious. But the Barking Peacock is a triad business, San Yee On group, so she must be linked to them in some way.'

'Hmm, I can't see a triad execution here. Not after that particular death note.'

Amy had to agree. 'Maybe Ruby Tang has some *personal* involvement in the murder,' she said speculatively. 'Or maybe she knows who the killer is.'

'Yes, and just maybe she's lying at the bottom of the harbour with all her interesting bits cut out, just like the others. You'll have to keep hammering away until we find her. In the meantime try to get one of the victim's flatmates to ID her.'

Amy pursed her lips and stared at her fingers. 'All right, but she won't be an easy thing for them to look at.'

A shiver ran through her as she remembered the dismembered remains she had viewed at the autopsies. Two of the victims had been kids in their mid-teens – probably runaways trapped by triads into a life of drugs and loneliness. And then to die like that.

111

Roman sensed her uneasiness over these particular crimes. Most of the murders they dealt with were either neat contract killings by professionals – clinical affairs with little chance of being solved – or deaths resulting from domestic disputes or heat-of-the-moment passions. A serial killer with a sex motive was something entirely different. It meant that the streets of Kowloon were no longer safe for any woman – not even a police sergeant.

'Amy, I know you'd really like to catch this pervert, but I want you to watch yourself on late enquiries. No more lone forays into those Mongkok dives you've been prowling, OK? Take Ah Keung and B-jai with you in future. Ah Keung did three years in the Special Duties Unit; even with his eyes closed he can still shoot the balls off a flying fish.'

She managed to force a smile. 'Anything you say ... Ah sir.' Though warmed by his concern, there was still an edge to her voice; she resented any implication of helplessness. Being a modern Hong Kong girl, she found it hard to accept the Chinese idea that she would always need a man to look after her. But she did not feel like arguing the case at that moment, so she changed the subject once more. 'What about your *gwai lo*? Any luck with Sam's Tailors?'

'Solid gold.' Fung's face illuminated with satisfaction.

He had visited the Burlington Arcade that morning on his way into work, and Mr Sam, the Indian proprietor, had graciously agreed to consult his records. His was the most famous tailoring business in the colony – probably in the entire Far East – and among his records were the measurements of countless wealthy and notable men around the world who would have their suits made by no one other than the redoubtable Mr Sam. The record Roman was chasing was fairly recent, and Sam took only a moment to find it.

James B. Reicher had been his client for less than six months, and in that time he had ordered two safari suits, a dozen monogrammed shirts and three lounge suits. Sam remembered him as a forty-six-inch chest who wanted a couple of inches extra 'for comfort'; tailors' parlance for 'space to accommodate a shoulder holster'.

Fung opened his desk drawer, rummaged for a second, and extracted a thin white booklet issued by the Hong Kong Government Printer.

Amy recognised it immediately as the Consular List. 'Reicher was a diplomat?' she asked.

'*Hai la!* I've got a photograph too. It was on Sam's wall next to one of him with the Duke of Kent.' The picture Roman took from his briefcase was one of Mr Sam smiling and shaking hands with a burly, well-dressed American whose own smile was forced and uncomfortable.

'He looks a lot happier here than he was last night. Did you get a job title or a business card?'

'No. It seems Reicher was reluctant to leave one, claimed they were still being printed. Obviously sensitive about his job. But he did leave an address for delivery of his suits: the US Consulate-General, Garden Road.' His fingers found the entry he had been looking for. 'Here we are: *James B. Reicher, Deputy Regional Security Officer.*'

'Deputy what?' Amy Chan was none the wiser.

Roman's face registered sudden insight.

'It means the guy we found last night is actually an officer of the US State Department.'

A few minutes later Roman Fung knocked on the door of the Senior Superintendent and entered. Ordinarily he might have taken the storm warning to Jerry Cunningham, his immediate and dangerously overweight superior, but everyone in the officers' mess knew that Cunningham was suffering from a stress-related heart condition, and had been given mostly admin. duties to perform. Knowing the panic engendered in senior officers whenever crime spills over into the diplomatic field, and not wishing to unduly excite his boss and endanger his health, Roman Fung had gone straight to see Peter Wimbush.

'Holy mother of God!' breathed the Senior Superintendent. 'Why wasn't this in the morning crime report? I've already seen the top man this morning, and told him there was nothing abnormal to report.'

'Last night we had no idea he had diplomatic status. Just another *Chan Fat*.' Fung used the term for an unknown Chinese male.

'How can anyone mistake a bloody great hairy Yank for a *Chan Fat*?'

Fung was familiar with this insulting discrimination between the scores of Chinese homicides, which raised hardly an eyebrow, and the death of a single European, which was always a major source of concern. Sensibly he said nothing.

Wimbush threw his weight back in his chair, tossing his pen on to the blotter.

'Just what the hell was this Yank doing anyway, poking around in darkest Yaumatei?'

'We won't know that until I meet with their Regional Security Officer.'

'Not the kind of hellhole a *gwai lo* normally frequents, is it? See what you can dig up on a possible joint investigation with other Hong Kong police units. It could tie in with the passport and visa racket the Americans have been digging into. Have you informed anyone else yet?'

'I'm drafting a First Information now.'

'Good. Copy it to the CP's office, the DCI's office, Protocol Section of Government – and don't forget the Director of Special Branch. With the Secretary of State's visit to Hong Kong coming up soon, no doubt Special Branch will want to examine this for any political motivation.' Wimbush allowed himself a brief, ironic smile as he mentioned the Branch. Like many hardcore CID men, he gave the 'secret squirrels' no face at all. 'This should make a change for them from the crossword puzzle of the *South China Morning Post.* That's all for now – but keep me appraised.'

The primary contact between the United States Consulate-General and the RHKP was the former's Regional Security Officer. As RSOs go, Jack Cinch was better than most: smart and cooperative. He was a grade-eight State Department security branch officer with experience in the Manila and Bangkok embassies, and four years of roving VIP protection with the Secretary's personal detail. His current duties comprised a mixed bag of passport and visa frauds, extradition problems, and general commercial crime, and in these matters he worked closely with the Hong Kong police and the local branch of Interpol.

At ten o'clock Roman Fung called Cinch's third-floor office at the Consulate-General to give him the bad news about his deputy. The quiet statement came as no great surprise to Cinch, who had noted Reicher's absence these past three days but had failed to report it; however, as he agreed to identify the body and then put down the phone, he knew he would need to think fast. Cover the trail.

Instructing his secretary to cancel all his morning appointments, Cinch headed up to the fourth floor, where all office windows were fitted with externally mirrored glass. He strode along the carpeted corridor hung with portraits of past presidents, and stopped outside a door with a coded lock. When he pressed the buzzer, a secretary inside checked the security monitor on her desk, then released the automatic door lock.

'What is it, Jack? You look like you've just been called upon to testify.' The silky voice belonged to John Prioletti, who emerged from the inner office to meet him. Prioletti was heavily tanned, short and square, and he

115

wore his silver hair a shade too long, so that it curled on to his collar. As usual, he wore red suspenders and a blue-striped shirt; the bow-tie at his throat was red with white polka dots. Because of his patriotic colour-scheme, he was known down on the third floor as 'Uncle Sam'.

Silently Cinch steered him back into the inner office and closed the door.

'I just had the police on the phone. Homicide. They've found Reicher.'

The older man's face fell about ten floors. His thumbs crept behind his suspenders, and he began to tug nervously against them.

'Jesus Christ,' he whispered. 'Where?'

Cinch told him.

'Jesus Christ,' he repeated louder this time. 'What else did they say? What did they find on him?'

'How should I know?' said Cinch curtly, beginning to pace the floor in irritation. 'They're taking me to the morgue for an ID. Maybe I should tell them to see you instead?'

'That wouldn't be very sensible, Jack.'

Cinch could see that Prioletti was worried. His eyes flicked from side to side as he considered the situation.

'Maybe I don't feel like being sensible anymore.' Cinch turned the screw. 'What are you going to do?'

'I don't know yet. I'll have to refer back to Washington. You'd better go along with them. But keep cool and stick to the cover story. Try to discover what they already know before we start offering anything voluntarily.'

Cinch turned to leave, then paused to point an angry finger.

'I'll do what I can, but it's *your* problem, John. You'd better get your freakin' act together.'

Roman Fung was sitting in a white OSCG Ford Cortina in the car park when Cinch came down. They exchanged brief greetings, and a moment later the car turned and swept out through the motorised steel gate, and into the dense downhill traffic of Garden Road.

Cinch hardly spoke a word, keeping his eyes fixed on the silvered walls of the Bank of China building. The towering structure, with its oddly angled panels and futuristic pylon, seemed ill at ease with its environment, but even Cinch knew it had been deliberately constructed to cast a spell of ill-fortune on the rival banks on Queens Road; the geomancers had guaranteed it. Outside Police Headquarters the white saloon took the flyover and swooped down on to Gloucester Road, joining slow-moving lines of traffic heading east for the cross-harbour tunnel to Kowloon.

The journey to Kowloon public mortuary in the Hung Hom district was a distance of only a few miles, but took over forty minutes. The only sound inside the slowly-moving vehicle was the roar of the airconditioner.

'Is that him?' asked Fung, when the attendant had swung open the door of the huge walk-in refrigerator and rolled back a clear plastic sheet covering the body. The fridge smelled of disinfectant and wet metal; its walls were lined with wide shelves made up of thin wooden slats, so that fluids would drip on to the tiled floor, then follow a pair of drainage channels to a grille in the far corner. That particular morning there were only three bodies on the shelves: two Chinese street-sleepers and the huge headless body of James Reicher.

Cinch scanned it up and down. Parts of the corpse had already taken on a waxy appearance where the body fats had begun to marble, but what grabbed his attention was the stump of the neck. For a second he gagged.

'You neglected to mention that his goddamned head was missing.'

His shock was clearly genuine, but Fung noticed there was no trace of sadness or regret in the American's reaction.

117

'Yes, I'm sorry,' he said unconvincingly. 'I didn't like to mention it over the phone. You know, switchboard operators ...'

Cinch nodded, his eyes continuing to roam over the familiar hairy knuckles, the heavy stomach, the deep chest. He coughed once.

'So,' prompted Roman quietly, 'is it Reicher?'

'Jesus Christ, who can tell for sure? It looks like him – and those were his clothes. Let me have a set of fingerprints and I'll get them confirmed by our central personnel.'

Fung pushed his hands deep into his pockets.

'So, Mr Cinch, when was the last time you saw James Reicher?'

'Saturday morning. We both worked a half-day. Where's the head?'

Fung looked up from his notebook and saw the American's eyes fixed again on the bloody stump. He perceived no grief, only professional curiosity.

'It wasn't found at the scene. But we're still searching. Forensics are doing the best they can down there.' Fung returned to his notes. 'Mr Cinch, when did you first notice his absence from work? I mean, he does work for you? I can't find any record of a missing persons report.'

The American turned away, obviously having seen enough, and stepped back out into the white-tiled room. Roman Fung followed.

'Yes, he did work for me, but Reicher had a heavy case-load this month. He sometimes went a couple of days without coming into the office. That was no big thing. If I hit the panic button every time he failed to make breakfast in the commissary...' Cinch made a gesture of futility to underline his point.

'Yes, I see. You mean you gave him a free hand?'

'Not really. But he more or less took it. He was a maverick: he liked to work alone. I'd give him shit for

118

not reporting in, but that didn't seen to work.'

Just then, two skinny attendants in blue overalls and leather aprons wheeled a trolley into the room, and began to man-handle the corpse of an old woman on to a vacant table. Cinch used the moment to break eye-contact, and he walked a few paces towards the door. The stratagem was not lost on the detective.

'Perhaps,' said Fung, 'it would save us both a lot of time if you just told me what Reicher was working on.'

'I'm sorry', responded the American. 'I can't discuss my work. You don't have the clearance.'

'Mr Cinch,' said Fung stiffening, 'this is a murder enquiry. It would take only a short time to secure that clearance.'

'Don't bet on that,' threatened Cinch.

Roman Fung tried a different tack.

'Tell me about Reicher. Did he have any personal problems?'

'No more than the next man.'

'But he *was* working on something very important?'

Cinch gave a sigh, appearing to concede the import-ance of the detective's questions.

'Jim Reicher was assigned to our office just over six months ago as part of an investigation into passport forgeries. We'd had a big jump in the numbers seized at US airport immigration points. Hong Kong Chinese and Filipinos mostly. Some forged US visas in false Indonesian passports, too. They were good, but not quite good enough to stand up to ultraviolet scanning. Reicher was sent out to help me get on top of it, and try to locate the source.'

'Did that involve undercover work?' asked Fung significantly.

'Sometimes,' admitted Cinch reluctantly. 'We know there's a group of very wealthy Chinese involved, but we don't know who they are. Anybody in their way seems to

119

get chopped. Reicher was running his own operation, trying to get a connection – offering official stamps and blanks for sale.' He checked himself, as if he had already said too much. 'Obviously this is highly confidential. I'll have to pass on what's happened, and check just what's been compromised, before we can progress the investigation. It would help my report if you could share with us what you have so far.'

This sudden switch in approach and lowering of barriers seemed to soften the Chinese detective's attitude. Cinch noticed the hard lines in his face relax.

'We don't have much yet. Certainly no witnesses. The autopsy is due some time this morning, though, with his head cut off, there seems little doubt as to the cause of death. As I said, Forensics are examining the scene, but amongst all that garbage ...'

Fung sensed something in Cinch's manner as he stroked his nose.

'There is one other thing,' the American put in.

'Yes, what is it?'

'We think Reicher may have had classified documents with him when he disappeared. Did you find anything of that nature – a briefcase or anything?'

The urgency of the question was only thinly disguised. Fung's immediate assumption was that this man was now scared stiff of a breach-of-security enquiry.

'Nothing so far. I've got detectives wading through the piles of *lap sap* right now. I'll have to let you know on that. But I'm afraid I'm going to have to ask you for details of that undercover operation. It might tell us who got to Reicher.'

'Fine,' said Cinch, clasping a friendly hand on Fung's shoulder – no doubt feeling he had succeeded in handling the situation. 'Just as soon as I get clearance from my boss in Washington.'

Roman shot him a sideways glance, and for the first time cracked a brief grin.

'*Diu lei lo mo*, do you Americans have to ask your President everything?'

EIGHT

There was no shortage of leads on the Shatin robbery –
not after the Jockey Club's million-dollar reward notice
was splashed all over the front pages. It was an unheard
of amount of money – and inevitably it attracted much of
the wrong kind of information.

From out of the hothouse of the Kowloon slums came
a deluge of gossip and speculation: a symphony of
whispered malice. Within the first three days the special
hot-line set up for the case was inundated with calls from
Chinese citizens suspicious about a neighbour's new car
or expensive holiday, or the increased indulgence of his
gambling habit. Tasker leafed through the information
sheets, cursing softly, then flung the whole sheaf into the
slop bucket where they emptied the teapots.

He had a feeling about this one, detective's intuition,
and it told him he could expect no casual informer's help
this time. This time he would have to go for it himself,
play rough and tumble with the underworld, if there was
to be any progress at all.

Those in a position to know any real information kept
remarkably quiet in the first few days. The street hawkers
from Yaumatei to Wong Tai Sin, who hear more gossip
than they should; restaurant waiters who while away
their slack time in illegal gambling dens in run-down
apartments; and the 'fishball' girls in their old-fashioned,
dimly-lit ballrooms. These women were so-called
because their young breasts were still small enough to
resemble the fishballs sold with noodles at cooked food
stalls.

It was the sudden and complete clamming up of this section of the community – normally a fertile source of criminal intelligence – that convinced Tasker he was dealing with a very powerful enemy indeed.

And with power being exercised to such a degree, he knew the triads had to be involved somewhere along the line.

When Tasker entered the *dai fong* – the CID duty room where the detectives mustered and conducted most of their routine interviews – he knew at once his men were ready to begin their task. There was an air of breathless expectation there, like they knew they were all here for a special reason and were eager now to settle a score. As Tasker began checking the faces one by one, he found himself recalling past cases they had worked on together, but it was not until his eye fell upon the last and most important member of the team that he finally pronounced his approval.

The last team member was not to be found staring back at him from the assembled chairs – but instead from a ceremonial altar recessed within a tall redwood cabinet which dominated the far end of the room. Within the cabinet, beneath a single red bulb, was a figure no more than eighteen inches high which represented the most psychologically charged image in the police psyche: the martial god Gwan-Dai. It gazed out from the altar with eyes that burned like hot coals, missing nothing. Gwan-Dai the great. Gwan-Dai the just and powerful, clothed in warrior robes of green and gold. The visage was twisted in a fierce frown, the long black beard and moustache trailing down to reach to his deep manly chest.

In China's classical past, Gwan-Dai had been a mortal, a famous general renowned for his loyalty, judgement and bravery in battle. In death these outstanding qualities had led to his deification, and his rapid adoption as patron god of many diverse professions. But, above all, Gwan-Dai was inextricably tied to the police force, specifically the god of all detectives. He was seen as their lord and protector, and the embodiment of all they aspired to. In other *dai fong* his image was often no more than a framed painting on mirrored glass, but for his team Tiger Cheng had insisted on a proper glazed porcelain statuette. It was a matter of face.

Tasker had not needed to mention it. It was just expected there would be a Gwan-Dai shrine, and Cheng had arranged it. For without Gwan-Dai, it was generally held, no CID team could function properly and all manner of ill-fortune might befall them.

Every officer had contributed to the cost according to his rank and salary, and when it was finally placed within its altar and the bowing and supplication completed, everyone agreed the *dai fong* had now been properly dedicated. The statuette itself was magnificent: brooding and terrible as it should be, threatening untold retribution to wrongdoers. The traditional pose was of a noble general, back straight, head high and proud, with the first two fingers of the left hand extended; and in his right hand the long bladed halberd with which to ward off evil.

As was the custom, the altar in the task force *dai fong* was now strewn with small ritual offerings. A dish of small oranges, a porcelain cup filled with *woo lung* tea and a shallow bowl of sand out of which grew many stands of smoky yellow *heung jiu*, joss-sticks arranged in multiples of three: the mystic number. The detectives had already made their petition to Gwan-Dai for a swift end to the case and retribution for the murderers of their dead colleagues.

Now it was time to go to work.

'Two hundred and seventy million dollars,' breathed Tasker with utmost respect. '*Ho lan doh sui!* That's a lot of water!'

As usual Tasker found himself speaking to his men in

Canto-babble, an expressive mixture of Chinese slang and English used by detectives of both races. *Sui,* or water, was what they called money out on the street – though the Cantonese have as many different words for money as the Eskimos do for snow. And in Hong Kong *sui* is the water without which life cannot continue.

He was now standing before a briefing board which covered most of one wall of the *dai fong,* twirling a felt-tipped marker pen thoughtfully between his fingers. Abruptly he uncapped the pen and began to write on the white board.

'For those of you who've been in a coma for the past few days, last Saturday it was the Jockey Club's turn to lose its shirt at the race-track. No tears of sadness, I see.'

The laughter that followed the joke seemed to ease some of the tension, and when it had died away Tasker turned and drew two square boxes on the board to represent the security vans. 'I have to say from the outset that it was a very thorough and professional job. The film from the on-course security cameras was enough to make your blood run cold. But it did give us a very clear picture of what we're up against. There were ten of them, all dressed in some kind of black military jump suit, and one accomplice in plainclothes posing as a hawker. Unfortunately none of the faces were visible because they were all wearing full-face respirators.'

Tasker turned back to the board and drew eleven small circles, one for each suspect, spaced around the security vans he had already drawn.

'There were four getaway vehicles, all white Isuzu mid-engine goods vans, but only three of them were used.' Three small rectangles were placed in line beside the first security van. 'The fourth was obviously a backup, and that shows the degree of preparation and planning here. They knew exactly what they were about. They grabbed the cash and made the switch early. Where was it they found the three getaway vehicles, Joe?'

Joe Lai, seated just to Tasker's right, consulted a slim folder containing the reports from the scenes-of-crimes officer and the duty forensic investigator.

'Less than a mile from the scene, on a single track road leading down to a small pier. It's close to the Chinese University, a place where those rowed ferry boats cross over the water to Ma Liu Shui. As we expected there were no prints inside any of the vehicles, just traces of plastic cement on the steering-wheels.'

No one showed any surprise. Every one of the detectives had worked on armed robbery cases and they were all familiar with the practice of criminals smearing airplane glue on their fingertips. When it hardened, it covered the ridges perfectly and left no prints.

'The vans themselves,' continued Joe, 'were all reported stolen within the forty-eight-hour period preceding the robbery, so the dirt and dust found inside can't help us. The government chemist is currently analysing the fibres found on the seats and on the door frames.'

'And the tyre tracks?' prompted Tasker pacing back and forth before the board.

'They confirm that a much heavier vehicle, probably a goods truck from the traces of diesel oil found at the scene, was waiting there to receive the steel chests. Beyond, there were footprints in the mud leading down to the pier. Heavy tread soles, with a pattern similar to US-style jungle combat boots.'

'That's not going to help us,' added Tiger Cheng, leaning backwards to balance his chair on two legs. 'Ever since the Vietnam war those boots have been available all over Asia. You can get them in at least half a dozen surplus outlets down in Sham Shui Po alone.'

'So basically they got clean away with enough *sui* to set themselves up for life.' Tasker could not resist a snort of appreciation. It was the kind of stunt the perverse side of his nature found gratifying. Were it not for the murdered police officers, he might have even felt a twinge of admiration.

'Not a clean getaway, *dai lo*,' remarked Joe. 'They left behind something very important.'

'Oh yes,' said Tasker realising he had overlooked one very significant piece of evidence. 'Where is it?'

Their one stroke of good fortune so far – an event attributed by Tiger Cheng to the direct intervention of Gwan Dai – had been the discovery of a single weapon in one of the getaway vehicles. In the robbers' haste to escape it had been left behind, stuffed beneath the driver's seat and apparently forgotten.

'We got it back from Forensic this morning,' said Joe. 'Nothing special: the odd hair and not much else. When a weapon is that clean, you know the man who used it has been well trained. No prints there either. This morning we're down for a ballistics report.'

'Good.' Tasker jabbed the marker pen in Joe's direction. 'It's an ugly piece of work, that rifle. Looks like a Soviet assault weapon but I'll bet a thousand bucks it's another one of those Chinese copies we keep picking up. Either way, Len Rice can soon tell you what's what.'

At the mention of firearms a buzz of conversation began between the detectives, leaving Tasker in no doubt about their feelings toward those armed robbers who had shot dead police officers for no other reason than that they stood between them and the money. Tasker could feel their outrage growing by the minute. That was good, he thought; that was the emotive force he needed to drive them. The superintendent decided to needle them a little further.

'Pretty damn good, though, these guys. First they outgunned us, and then they outran us.' Aware that he had their undivided attention once more, he continued. 'So while this goods van – or whatever it was – doubled back and joined the traffic on Tai Po Road or the Tolo Highway, these robbers hopped into a boat and quietly

127

disappeared out to sea. *Ho lan ye!'*

Another hubbub of discontent erupted. Some of the detectives gave him querulous sideways glances. Suddenly Tasker bellowed at the group.

'You'll have to do more than just talk about it!' he thundered. 'I happen to believe that talking rarely solves anything! You all know how little face you have on the street right now that every bloody triad in the colony – however young or dope-ridden – is laughing about this. Laughing at you.' He could see they did not like that, but then he was not in it for the popularity ratings. 'Seven police officers dead. Seven families devastated. It's up to you now to do something about it.'

In the awkward silence that followed Tasker turned back to the board, wrote down the word WEAPON in scruffy capitals with a question mark alongside it, and replaced the pen on the desk.

'So what happened after the money switched vehicles?' asked Joe, gently leading his boss back to the subject.

'Thank you, Joseph. I was coming to that. Where's the map?'

'Ah-sir, *hai ni do!'* Tiger Cheng indicated a typhoon warning map which had been Blu-Tacked to the wall above the tea table. Beneath it the thermos jugs and drinking glasses were lined up like soldiers.

At that moment a radio-pager went off, bleating loudly, and disturbing the quiet of the room.

'Shut that bloody thing off!' thundered Tasker as the detective hurriedly reached for his belt.

The map covered the whole territory, extending from Po Toi Island, far to the south of Hong Kong Island, up through Kowloon and NT, and over the border into the Shum Chun Special Economic Zone of China.

'They must have had power boats waiting here, close to Ma Liu Sui. A short hop up the Tolo Channel and out into the open sea.' He knew the boats would have had to be fast enough to outrun the Marine Police launches in a pinch. But that would not have been difficult. All the best stuff, the Zodiacs and rigid raiders, were deployed in North Sector on snake duty. 'Snakes' was how they referred to illegal immigrants who slipped beneath the border fence and slithered into the colony.

'They probably laid up on one of those islands for a day or so, just to make sure they weren't being followed. There are bloody hundreds of little beaches to put into there.' Tasker was looking at the north-east corner of the map, his eyes tracing the easy route they would have taken up the Tolo Channel towards Mirs Bay. 'Either way it's a certainty they'd have made it into mainland China by now. For the time being that puts them beyond our reach, so we shall have to unravel this thing from the Hong Kong end.'

This was by no means a revelation. Ever since the British first pried Hong Kong from the grip of the Chinese Emperor, all manner of Chinese pirates and bandits had been drifting into the colony to commit crimes, then fleeing back into China to evade capture. Even now, a hundred and fifty years later, there was still no proper extradition treaty between the two governments.

'Right then,' said Tasker, breaking the reflective mood which had suddenly formed. 'Let's not waste any more time sitting here scratching our balls. Get out there and shake the tree!'

The ballistics section covered one whole floor in New May House. It housed not only the laboratory, where microscopic comparisons were made, but also a fully equipped indoor shooting range and the force firearms museum. It was this latter facility which usually caught the interest of visitors, for the many weird and arcane exhibits on show there. Locked into wooden racks mounted around the walls was a fine display of rifles, shotguns and machine-guns dating back to the Second World War and beyond. Beneath these, the locked cabinets contained drawer after drawer of every type of handgun ever made, ranging from the single-shot pearl-handled derringers to the Magnum revolvers and self-loading military pistols which had either been seized in raids or else given up during general firearms amnesties.

Joe Lai made a point of delivering the seized assault rifle personally to the force ballistics officer for examination. He knew that if they ever made a case of the Shatin robbery and took it to trial for the murders committed in the process, this weapon would be a crucial piece of evidence. For this reason he was going to make damned sure it did not get lost or somehow 'mislaid' during the investigation. Firearms have always commanded a high price on the Kowloon City black market due to the difficulty in obtaining them, and at the back of Joe's mind was the fear that such a price might, perhaps, be high enough to turn the head of a detective with bad gambling debts or financial worries about his future.

Like all potential exhibits its progress through the system had been meticulously logged, and statements taken from anyone having charge of it for however short a time. This was all part of the procedure governing what was called 'The Chain of Evidence': a procedure intended to guarantee that the weapon produced in court was the exact same weapon picked up at the scene, and that it had not been tampered with in the period intervening before the trial. But beyond this Joe had an added interest in the weapon. Somewhere in the back of his mind he suspected it had killed his friend Jason Leung.

Entering the laboratory, cradling the large sealed polythene packet in both hands, he approached a long bench laid with thin metal files and cleaning rods where Kiwi Rice, one of the senior Force ballistics officers was assiduously working at restoring the mechanism of an antique pistol.

'Isn't that an old Mauser?' asked Joe, admiringly as he put down the bag. '*Ho leng.* It's beautiful.'

Rice looked up, flashing a quick smile.

'Yes, she's a beauty all right. A couple of amateur divers found her on an old freighter wreck off Cheung Chau island.'

Rice was a big, rawboned man with a head of shiny silver hair, an overgrown bushy moustache still flecked with brown – and a well-known disregard for any form of departmental bullshit. Though an equivalent-rank to Senior Superintendent, he cherished his civilian status and called everybody – apart from the Commissioner himself – simply 'mate'. Kiwi's expertise with firearms was widely known and respected, not only in Hong Kong but also in many other police forces throughout Asia.

He was one of the dwindling band of experts the force had recruited from overseas back in the late Seventies. Originally a captain with the New Zealand Army, Kiwi had come to the colony on very attractive expatriate terms and with the promise of a large say in the organisation of the ballistics section.

'Should have been rusted to buggery by rights,' he said wiping his hands on a piece of cotton waste. 'Lucky for me she was tucked away in an air pocket. Probably belonged to a China Sea pirate, I shouldn't wonder. Used to be a lot of those freighters pirated off Cheung Chau. Buggers used to hide amongst the crew and take over the ship in open sea. That's where the junks would be waiting to rob everyone and offload the cargo. They had a thing for these Mausers, all right. Bet this one could tell a few good tales. Probably got left behind when they scuttled that old rust bucket ...' Realising he was rambling now, he stopped himself and looked over at Joe. 'So, what can I do for you, mate?'

'I've got the Shatin weapon here for examination and report.'

'Is it properly signed off by Forensics? I don't want to get my dabs all over it if it isn't.'

'It's OK. They've finished. Nothing much on it anyway except a hair of Asian origin stuck to the stock. Even that could have belonged to the traffic PC who found it.'

Len Rice consulted his watch and noted the time on a desk pad before breaking open the seal of the packet. Drawing the weapon out, he immediately removed the magazine and proved it before laying it down on a clean sheet of cartridge paper which would show up clearly any parts or screws which either fell off or were subsequently removed. After casting an appreciative eye over its length, he picked the weapon up and felt its weight with both hands.

'Soviet design assault rifle with collapsible metal stock,' observed Rice mechanically. 'Introduced in the mid-Fifties mainly for airborne troops and motorcyclists.'

'AK-47, *hai m'hai a*?'

'Not this little beauty. This is the newer AKM design. But there's something wrong here. The weight's not right. The Soviet model is supposed to incorporate plastic parts and newer metal stampings, but this one doesn't. See, the grip is wood – not plastic. That makes it heavier. And, another thing, it doesn't carry the Soviet serial numbers. That means it's almost certainly a foreign model.'

'Tasker thought it might be one of those Chinese copies,' said Joe uncertainly. 'What do you reckon?'

'Sorry to disappoint you, mate,' said Rice lifting the weapon to inspect the metal body. 'No Chinese serial numbers here, and no communist star. Besides, the Chinese model would be smaller than this.'

'*Hai me*?'

'For sure. No file scratches, either, to suggest the markings have been removed. So what we have here is a little bloody enigma. Let's strip her down and take a closer look.'

132

Quickly and confidently the ballistics man braced the grip against his thigh, located the body locking pin, and broke the weapon down. It came apart easily, allowing him to draw out the bolt carrier assembly and lay it on the white paper.

'Jesus Christ,' he grunted at the greasy brown smears upon his fingers. 'She's clean enough, but somebody ought to tell these jokers to be more sparing with the gun oil.'

Next he fished inside his drawer and pulled out a small hand lens which he used to look inside the hollow body. At first he saw nothing and a frown descended over his face. Then, almost as an afterthought, he flipped the weapon over and looked inside the magazine housing. What he saw there brought the Kiwi smile back to his face.

'Take a look at this, Joe.'

The small indentation punched into the metal had a distinctive crescent shape to it. Beneath it was a seven-digit serial number, also punched into the metal, and below that a series of seemingly random squiggles scratched into the metal with a scriber.

'Does that mean something to you?' asked Joe, totally defeated by what he saw.

'Too bloody right it does. This might look like a Chinese copy, but those marks mean it's almost certainly a Pakistani model.'

'But isn't Pakistan Western-aligned? Their army uses American weapons.'

'True, but this had nothing to do with the government or the army,' beamed Kiwi Rice. 'This is strictly black-market stuff. Ever hear of a tiny little place on the North-West Frontier called Derra?'

What Joe knew about Pakistan was not worth remembering.

'No.'

'Not many people have. It's just south-west of

133

Peshawar, in a closed area that's still under tribal law. Afghanistan to the north – and just a stone's throw to the north-east is the Khyber Pass. The town of Derra has only two industries: cannabis and weapons. I went through there on long leave three years ago. Professional curiosity. Mate, it's like Dodge City: dirt roads and broken-down shacks, and every so often there's the sound of gunfire somewhere up the street as somebody haggles over a purchase. Been that way for a hundred and fifty years or more. Everybody carries weapons in the tribal areas – the warrior caste and all that. There must be a couple of hundred small factories and work-shops, some of them no more than garden sheds, all making their own weapons and ammunition. When I was there the most popular items were the AKM and the Tokharev Soviet officers' pistol. Back then a lot of their stuff was going to the Mujaheddin fighting the Soviets just over the border. They must still be churning them out by the crateload.'

'You think this one came from there?'

'Almost certainly. This crescent marking is an Islamic symbol and those scribed lines look to me like Urdu script.'

'*Mat ye wa?* Say what?'

'Pakistani,' explained Kiwi Rice. 'It's a safe bet those squiggles are the signature of the gunsmith.'

With those few words it seemed a door had just swung invitingly open; though where it led, Joe Lai could not even begin to guess. Two questions immediately sprang to mind. Why would a hit in Hong Kong need guns from Pakistan? And which of Hong Kong's many illustrious operators had imported them into the territory?

'Is there any way of tracing the manufacturer for certain.'

Rice pursed his lips, then nodded slowly.

'Could be. Could well be. I know a guy with the police ballistics department in Islamabad. But even if they could

134

trace the manufacturer I don't know whether that joker would be too keen to give us the names of his client. God only knows how many handling agents and middlemen might be involved in the operation.'

'Listen, we have everyone on our backs from the Governor down to the DD Crime, and we still don't have a single lead yet. Anything you can find out would be useful.'

Rice gave another quick nod.

'OK, mate. We'll see what we can do. A lot will depend on how fast Interpol is able to set things up, but I'll get it organised today. Leave this with me. I'll have the comparison results by tomorrow morning.'

'*M'goi sai, dai lo,*' Joe thanked him. 'Remind me I owe you a beer sometime.'

It would be difficult to explain just how John Tasker knew there was triad involvement in the Shatin robbery. But he knew all right, just as sure as he knew his own name; just as sure as he knew he would need to put the bite on them from the outset.

That a crime of that scale could be committed in Hong Kong without triad knowledge was for any detective of Tasker's experience inconceivable; indeed his only problem lay in deciding which of the many triad groups to actually put the bite on. But in order to understand why Tasker was so certain in his belief you had to go back a hundred and fifty years or more and look at the development of the triad power-base in Hong Kong.

No one knows for sure just how the Chinese triads first came into being. Their ultimate path of corruption into becoming a powerful and durable criminal empire is now a matter of public record, but their exact origins still remain shrouded in legend. And that is one of their strengths.

There are as many versions of the story as there are triad offshoots hustling the streets of Kowloon. Some scholars maintain that triad lore began in the late seventeenth century with the destruction of the fabled Shao Lin Buddhist temple, judged by the then-ruling Manchu emperor to be a focus for treason and insurrection. It is said that five martial monks – known as the first Five Ancestors – escaped from the burning building by a series of miraculous revelations, to later found the five lodges of the Triad Society and rally support against the Manchu invaders throughout China. But ask any two Chinese where the Shao Lin temple is supposed to have stood and you will receive three different answers.

Equally, there are those who maintain that the secret societies are really much older, dating back as far as 300 BC to the Han dynasty, and beginning with the Green Pang brotherhood of Northern China, or else with the mythical hero-bandits of the Water Margin. The only thing people seem to agree upon is that the original aims of such societies were entirely worthy and patriotic: that is, the liberation of China from oppressive foreign rule.

The triads were already well established in Hong Kong in 1841 when Britain first wrested control of the island from the Chinese Empire. These were the subgroups of the Second Triad lodge known as Hung Obedience Hall of the Golden Orchid – district of Kwangtung and Kwangsi provinces. Throughout the remainder of the nineteenth century the increasing commercial exploitation of the island saw a vast influx of Cantonese-speaking Chinese from the Mainland. These people found work servicing the China trade as coolies, both aboard ship and in the many storage houses, or 'godowns', which flanked the docks. But they found the language and customs of the barbarian British difficult to understand, and their general distrust of officialdom caused them to look to their own elected headmen and elders for leadership. This led naturally to the formation of a series of associations and guilds to protect self-interest and resolve disputes. The Triad Society, with its strict organisation, patriotic image and emphasis on Chinese fighting skills, was ideally placed to seize control of these organisations for its own purposes.

Using the guise of an anti-British resistance group, the Triad Society organised uprisings and planned attacks on barbarian homes and property. But beneath this guise they moved quickly to consolidate their control of the labour market, selling employment, extracting protection fees, and levying fines on workers. Where extortion money could not be squeezed from employers, strikes were organised and property damaged. The small local police force was powerless against them. That was hardly surprising. Consisting of only a handful of British officers and Chinese constables of dubious loyalty, the Hong Kong police were ill-equipped to make any significant impact on the growing triad problem. When they did gain a lead in some crime, the true perpetrators often remained shielded from discovery by the coded language of their secret rituals and by the general fear and reluctance of their victims to speak to the authorities.

Small wonder, then, that the influence of the triads grew virtually unchecked throughout the early part of the twentieth century. So great was their influence in the British Crown Colony that, prior to the Japanese invasion in 1941, Japanese intelligence officers secretly met with senior triads and secured their cooperation in return for a free hand in their control of the vice industry under the subsequent Japanese administration.

Of course, by this stage any pretence at a patriotic motive had long since been shed. Their rallying call had always been *fan Ching – fuk Ming* – 'Overthrow the Manchu and restore the house of Ming' – a sentiment worthy of an underground resistance movement set up to repel invaders. But, with the establishment of the Chinese Republic in 1912, Dr Sun Yat Sen, himself a senior triad official, had finally visited the tombs of the Ming ancestors and declared China free of Manchu rule.

Its original aims achieved, the Triad Society ought to have quietly dissolved. Instead it split into factions divided along ethnic lines – Cantonese, Hakka, Shanghainese, Chiu Chau – and began a series of bloody battles for spheres of influence in criminal activities. The ultimate irony seems to be that even as leaders of the Wo Group were concluding their secret agreements with Japanese intelligence, Japanese Imperial forces on the China mainland were engaged in a series of massacres and some of the worst atrocities of war ever witnessed. But that no longer seemed to matter to the triads: business was now far more important.

Yet still these newer criminal organisations clung on to the ritual of the original Triad Society, retaining its many secret hand-signals, codes and poetry, and trading on its mysticism and its obsession with numerology. Those societies affiliated to the Second Lodge continued to use the same official titles and numerical designations associated with the legends of the Five Ancestors. Best information available confirms that each triad society is still organised into five sections: General Affairs, Recruiting, Organisation, Liaison, and Education, with a senior official commanding each. The four basic ranks within the Triad are still the Red Cudgel (426), the White Paper Fan (415), the Grass Sandal (432) – all of whom are equivalent in status – and the Ordinary Member (49) often known simply as a 'forty-niner'.

But access into the Hung Family, as it is also known, is no easy matter. Each recruit must first find a senior official to sponsor his application and thereafter act as his 'protector'. This relationship will involve the payment of a fee (some multiple of the mystic number three) and henceforth the recruit remains the follower or retainer of this particular officer. The protector is bound to give aid and assistance to his follower in times of threat or trouble.

The triad initiation ceremony was once a long and

complex affair, but is now less so. It still involves the swearing of a blood oath of loyalty to the society, though the length and number of historical references have reputedly been severely curtailed. Recruits must still swear the thirty-six oaths and symbolically cross the mountain of knives, the two-planked bridge and the fiery pit negotiated by the Five Ancestors when fleeing the Emperor's soldiers, but they will usually complete these tests in a single night instead of the three days they used to take.

Prior to initiation the young recruits may or may not be told the full story of the Five Ancestors – nowadays it seems less important – but there are certain aspects of the lore which are always imparted: the significance of the Yellow Gauze Sheet which appeared from heaven during the fire at the Shao Lin monastery and covered the Five Ancestors, saving them from the conflagration; the Grass Sandal which later turned into a boat when the Ancestors fled the ruins of the monastery, allowing them to cross a broad river and escape the Manchu soldiers; and the Red Cudgel once used by the abbot of the monastery to chastise errant monks, and which is still retained by any triad society as a symbol of discipline and punishment. Above all, the new members are warned of the certain fate of anyone who betrays his brothers – death in every case. This threat is echoed in the symbolic beheading of the three legendary traitors: the Manchu emperor; the government official who led the attack on the Shao Lin monastery; and the renegade monk who divulged to the attacking force a secret way into the monastery. All this is to ensure that the responsibilities of membership are not taken lightly – for, once initiated into the Hung Family, the only way out is by death.

Tasker had often mused on the difficulties faced by previous generations of Hong Kong police officers in combating the triads. They must have felt they were trying to bail out a sinking ship with a thimble, he concluded; but they had had it easy compared to what was still just around the corner. The real crunch came in the Fifties when the scourge of opium was usurped by the more virulent white powder from the Golden Triangle. How much greater was the triad problem now. For the triads, heroin had seemed a gift from heaven; a hundred times more powerful and more addictive than opium, the white powder had revolutionised the illegal narcotics industry. Heroin was lighter and therefore easier to store and transport than the sticky, sweet-smelling opium gum. Possessing virtually no odour once refined, heroin was therefore impossible to detect without sophisticated chemical analysis. It was heroin that had put Hong Kong on the world map in the Sixties. With its busy air and sea transportation routes and its unparalleled world-wide communications, the port had quickly become the main distribution point for Asian heroin to a worldwide market tightly controlled by the Hong Kong triads. And bloody violence was the means by which each group secured its own share of the trade. Indeed it was only the in-fighting between opposing triad groups which now prevented them from uniting under one banner to wield absolute power in the colony.

A lesser detective might have shied away from engaging such an enemy; a man with more discretion and a due regard for a healthy retirement at the end of his career. But Tasker was not noted for his discretion, and since they had chosen him specially for the Shatin job he felt bound to hand them a result. In order to do that, he decided he would need to put all the societies on notice.

It was Joe Lai who suggested the Barking Peacock. It was one of the best clubs in Kowloon: a place which had become fashionable in the last six months amongst top triad bosses who used the place to conduct business, to demonstrate their current alliances and generally to be seen. For all these reasons it seemed the perfect place to begin.

Tasker ordered the whole team across in three CID vehicles, and sent four detectives inside the club first to cover the exits. When these men were in position he led the remainder of the team through the glass doors and up the stairs into the main room, brushing aside five burly doormen as they went. Once inside, there was a long moment of confusion while the detectives fanned out and Joe Lai attempted to locate the manager. Immediately heads turned at the tables surrounding the dancefloor, and some of the men in lounge suits rose to their feet as if trying to decide whether to run. Quickly Tiger Cheng approached the DJ and ordered him to cut the disco music blaring from the throbbing speaker cabinets.

A moment later the house lights came up and Tasker could discern each of the tight triad groups thronging the booths along the walls. They were men dressed in well-cut suits, like real businessmen but not; each with the obligatory handful of soldiers at his beck and call, and a selection of well-dressed tits and thighs also present for his amusement. The air was thick with menace and cigarette smoke.

'Licence check,' announced Joe Lai, raising his police warrant card for all to see. 'Thank you for your cooperation.'

'*Mai lan ye!*' shouted someone, outraged by the intrusion. The triad soldiers fidgeted uneasily. Beneath the exit signs the detectives turned back a stream of escapees as their colleagues began checking ID cards at the tables.

'Any underage girls or illegal immigrants working here?' demanded Joe Lai when the manager appeared. But no one believed for one moment that Tasker's men were there for such a trivial reason.

'Ah sir,' fawned the manager, a balding Chinese with

an obvious family look about him, who had been nominated to act as front-man for such occasions. 'Trust me, the place is clean. What do I want with that kind of trouble? If I lose my licence I have to answer to my boss.'

'Who needs a licence,' sneered the detective, 'to run a toilet like this?'

Joe brushed the man aside, stepping between tables to where Tasker stood glaring at the occupants of one of the wall booths while those in the adjoining booths looked on. Joe knew his boss had been looking for a stooge, someone to make a public example of, and now he had found him in Whistling Ming.

Ming was a lower- to middle-ranking official of the Wo Shing Wo. Though once a very powerful force in both the Yaumatei dock area and the watering holes of Mongkok, Ming's particular branch of the Wo Shing Wo had over the past five years been forced to cede control of both areas to the emergent Chiu Chau groups. Now they were only peripheral players, allied to the Chiu Chaus but operating as a kind of wholly-owned subsidiary force with a much smaller area of control. And though he still liked to pretend otherwise, Ming and his brothers were now quite definitely second league.

As John Tasker's eyes burned across the table, Whistling Ming lounged behind two ranks of cocktail glasses. He was sitting at the centre of a group of young men all dressed in sportsjackets and open-necked shirts, staring silently back at the detective – and grinning.

'Good evening, gentlemen,' Tasker began with feigned bonhomie. 'I'm presently conducting enquiries into a major robbery. Perhaps you could be of some assistance?'

A collective grunt of disdain rose from the table. One of the forty-niners muttered something sounding like an obscenity and turned away.

'Are you kidding me, Superintendent?' mocked Ming, the words whistling through the crack between his front teeth. 'You know better than to come here hassling honest citizens when there are armed gangs running around out there.'

'I just wanted to give you the chance to make it easy on yourselves, and save everyone a lot of trouble. Take your time. Think about it.'

The response came immediately, as Tasker had expected.

'I've already thought about it. Here's my answer. Go fuck your mother, Superintendent!'

Tasker heard the sniggers from Ming's followers, and even smiled himself at first. Then he picked up the nearest cocktail glass, removed its little umbrella, and hurled the drink straight into Whistling Ming's face. In a booth to the left a woman squealed in surprise. Then, before the triad's eyes had a chance to clear, Tasker slapped him hard twice on the face. At once Joe Lai moved closer, seeing one of the sportscoats make as if to rise. But Tasker's raised index finger was enough to stop the young forty-niner in his place.

'You so much as make a fist, boy!' threatened the superintendent, and I'll bounce your arse off all these four walls!'

Immediately the forty-niner relaxed in his seat. Tasker took a long look round at the tableau of stunned faces. Now he had the undivided attention of every triad in the place. When he turned again, Whistling Ming was dabbing at his bloodied nose with the serviette that accompanied his drink, and was wearing a look that suggested he was now in a more receptive state of mind.

'What is it you want, Tasker?' Ming asked in a low voice. 'What's this shit all about?'

'You know what I want. A name for the Shatin job.'

'You're fucking crazy, Tasker. You want information? This isn't how the game's played, *dai lo*. This is our place – you know that. You try pushing us around here you know what will happen.'

143

'Attempting to intimidate a police officer, dear me. Better forget what's gone before, Ming. We play by my rules now. And this is just the beginning. That goes for all of you here!' he announced to the hushed room. 'I'm going to shake down every major triad haunt on the Golden Mile until I get what I'm after.'

'You're wasting your spit, Tasker. I don't know shit about that robbery – and if I did ...'

Tasker smiled darkly.

'Better ask around then, hadn't you? Speak to your brothers, your affiliated societies and all that crap. See what you can find out.' His final remark was directed to all the other booths ranged along the wall: 'Because I swear by Gwan-Dai there'll be no peace for any of you until I have a name.'

Satisfied that he had made his point, Tasker signalled his men to break off and leave.

As he walked towards the exit Whistling Ming's voice rose again in a final warning.

'You better be as tough as you talk, Superintendent. When this gets out they're going to burn you!'

Tasker neither broke his stride nor turned his head, but he replied automatically, 'Let's just see who burns who, *sai lo*,' and he was gone.

Over the following two nights Tiger Cheng took a selected group of detectives out into the lowest dives Kowloon had to offer. Their intention was to stir up the cesspit and press home the message of Tasker's determination to uncover the gang responsible for Shatin. His men knew well enough where the low-lifes hung out: the small cabaret restaurants that boasted a microphone and 'live' girl singers and little else, or the amusement centres, pool-rooms and video arcades. And that was where they began asking questions – none too gently. Forty-niners were summarily yanked out of the mah-jong schools they frequented and interviewed in side alleys with an arm around their throats. Dragon-chasing addicts were grabbed even while the last coils of heroin smoke still rose from their tin-foils. In the one-girl brothels triad informants were ambushed and lifted bodily from between the hookers' thighs. Everywhere the word went round that Tiger Cheng was stalking.

For his part, Joe Lai let the word percolate down to the lowest levels before making his own move. Then one evening, while the *foh gei* were still out systematically hassling street gangs, he made a call to the one man he knew was guaranteed to know something – if anyone did.

Joe's best information had always come from Tsui Chi-keung: a man he had met twenty years ago when both were just kids studying *wing chun kung-fu* under the same *sifu*. Sharing the same teacher in any martial art creates between fellow students a particularly close bond – a relationship best described in terms of *hing dai*, or brothers. Down the years, *hing dai* retain certain loyalties to one another however widely their paths might diverge, and this still bound the two men together in later life, despite their ending up on opposite sides of the law. Tsui had joined Shaw Brothers studios in his teens and built a sound reputation as a stuntman and later actor in the kung-fu movie business, where he was known by the nickname Siu Din Din, 'Little Thunder'. Like all kung-fu actors in Hong Kong, Siu Din Din was naturally allied to a triad group, where his traditional Chinese fighting skills would be fully appreciated.

In Tsui's case he had eventually sworn the thirty-six triad oaths with the Honourable Brotherhood of the 14K in return for immediate promotion to the rank of Red Cudgel, 426 triad enforcer, within the Wong Tai Sin district. As such he was one of three top officials in that area, with specific responsibility for extortion, discipline and the defence of the society's turf against all other triad incursions. In his six-year tenure he had never been known to lose a single battle. One on one, no other *Hung Kwan* in Kowloon could live with him. Now his fame was such that even other enforcers referred to him as *Ah Goh*, or elder brother, as a sign of respect to one judged their senior. More recently, Siu Din Din's position within the 14K had been bolstered still further by his promotion to *Seung Fa*, or Double Flower: the highest rank a fighter may achieve.

When Joe Lai met with his brother, Little Thunder, it was in a high-rent nightclub occupying the sixth and seventh floors of a commercial building just off Nathan Road. Both men arrived alone, without the usual retinue of followers known as *ma jai* – little horses – and they were accorded all the proper respect by the manager of the club. The latter clearly understood it was his responsibility to prepare a suitable place and provide tea and cups on the table for the ritual giving of face. He had cleared an alcove lined with red and gold silk bunting so their conversation would be neither disturbed nor overheard.

The nightclub's decor was a vibrant mixture of hi-tech and traditional themes, dragons and phoenixes rendered in luminous perspex. The main room was bustling with stylishly dressed couples in flamboyant evening wear and groups of businessmen entertaining clients with endless bottles of French brandy. Joe knew the place was on file with Criminal Intelligence Bureau as one of the 14K's more legitimate operations.

Joe poured some tea first, and immediately both men emptied the small, delicate cups in a single gulp. Siu Din Din then reciprocated the gesture, and once again both men drank.

Face given, and face received.

'What's this I hear, brother?' began the triad enforcer, holding himself stiffly and formally. 'A lot of people seem very upset with you. These people are wondering if you and that boss of yours plan to take on the whole of Kowloon?'

'Maybe,' shrugged Joe. 'If that's what it takes.'

Both men kept their faces expressionless: unreadable.

Siu Din Din wore an expensive silk tie with his suit and gold cufflinks with his shirt. His haircut was fashionably short, the way Hollywood tough-guys were wearing it now, and looking at that strong handsome face you could understand how he had once been a minor star himself. And also, from the livid red scar running down one cheek and across his throat, why he no longer was.

Joe filled the cups a second time, only this time neither man drank. Face had already been satisfied. Instead Siu Din Din called a waiter and ordered a bottle of Remy Martin.

'So, Tasker's been set to find the Jockey Club's money,' murmured the enforcer as he poured two stiff measures into ten ounce glasses. 'Doesn't surprise me, that *gwai lo* is crazy enough for anything. What does surprise me is that you'd let yourself get mixed up with him again. He's bad news. Doesn't know when to stop pushing. If he chases this one it can end only one way, and their money's not worth dying for. Take it from me.'

'It isn't the money,' corrected Joe. 'That means nothing to us against the lives of seven dead police officers. Tasker's committed to making a fight of it unless we get some help from the societies.'

There was a brief flare in the enforcer's eyes.

'Harsh words, brother. But understand one thing: if I decide to help you it is because we are *hing dai*, and not because of any ludicrous *gwai lo* threats.'

While Siu Din Din sat measuring Joe's reaction, on the dance floor a Filipina girl singer stepped up to the glittering podium and began to sing a Karen Carpenter number.

Finally Siu Din Din said: 'All right, but I require a favour in return.'

Joe's hands opened in an expansive gesture. 'Name it.'

'My uncle's fourth son has a problem. Last month he

was arrested with eight small packets of white powder. The kid has no society involvement, I swear it. He's just finished high school and wants to study in Canada. A criminal record would kill his chance of a student visa – and with it any chance of relocating his family to Canada before the communists get here. The kid was stupid; he carried a package for a friend, and got stopped in the street. The friend has already been dealt with.' The enforcer made a single chopping movement of the side of his neck with the edge of a calloused hand. 'My uncle is seeking a way to prevent his son's conviction.'

Joe made a face and shook his head.

'If they have the heroin, there's nothing I can do. That's what they call "simple possession". The prosecution doesn't need to prove anything more than that the kid was carrying.'

'Yes, I know.' The enforcer leaned forward in his chair. 'But wait, what if the white powder went missing from the police station before the trial. The magistrate would then have to kick the case out of court.'

For a moment the detective considered this. He had every sympathy for anyone trying to escape the colony before the takeover, but he had too much respect for the office he held to consider misappropriating evidence. On the other hand, he pondered, might this not be worth it just to find the killers of Jason Leung?

'What you say is true,' he answered after the long silence, in which he lit a cigarette. 'However, what you ask is impossible. I don't mind bending with the breeze, but I'm still a police officer.'

'Then you refuse to help a brother.'

'I didn't say that,' countered Joe, sensing he might be about to lose what he hoped to gain from this man. 'I'll take a look at the evidence and see how strong a case they have. District drug squads are just uniform officers on temporary assignment, and some of the inspectors in charge of these units come under so much pressure to get figures that they screw things up. They occasionally get carried away and forget the proper procedures. A good lawyer can tie them in knots, get the case dismissed. So your uncle may have nothing to fear. Rest assured I shall advise you how to proceed. That's the best I can offer.'

Siu Din Din nodded. He knew Joe Lai pretty well, and he had not really expected him to agree to outright subversion of the legal process – but it was always worth a try.

'That will be acceptable,' he said in a lowered voice, his battlescarred face suddenly serious. 'Now, as to the information you require, let me warn you well. You are yapping at the heels of the high dragons. There are influential people involved in this robbery, people with clean faces and dirty hands. They have much to protect, and they'd just as soon kill you and Tasker as take a piss. So don't go into places with only one exit. Understand?'

Face dictated that Joe show not the least anxiety at this warning.

'Thanks for the advice. Now tell me about the robbery.'

'One thing I know for sure is they used hired muscle from over the border to lessen the risk of anything being traced back to themselves.'

'A contract?'

'Yes. The Big Circle Gang. Everyone in Kowloon knows those fucking *Dai Huen Jai* will do anything for a straight fee of five thousand dollars American. They say this is the hardest team ever to come out of Canton.'

'Ex-PLA soldiers?'

'Not just any old soldiers. The best. Ever heard of Division 17?'

'Should I?'

'They were a commando unit put together to work out of uniform behind the Vietnamese lines when the border disputes were raging. Their job was to ambush military convoys, gather intelligence, perform assassinations.

When they got out of the army, about fifteen of them moved back to Canton and decided to make it their rice bowl. They've pulled three big jobs down here already, but back home they keep their underwear clean.'

'Where do I find them? How about some names?'

'Sorry, that's as far as it goes. You'll have to do the rest yourself.'

Lai nodded his understanding.

'You said something about high dragons. Exactly who?'

'That's why I'm warning you to be careful. I'm no *gwai tau jai*' – there was a sneer on his lips as he uttered the triad term for an informer – 'but I'd hate to see a brother like you taken by such filth as the San Yee On. Take a lesson, brother: it's hard to dance with only one leg!'

All at once, with the mere mention of the San Yee On, he had split the case open. That was the name of the fastest growing and most violent of the Hong Kong triad societies. A Chiu Chau group up to their necks in the white powder trade.

'Let me get this right,' blustered Joe. 'The San Yee On commissioned the Shatin dinner party, is that what you're telling me?'

The enforcer looked over his shoulder and gave a nervous shrug of assent.

'Ah Joe,' he whispered, 'Don't waste your time trying to chase it back. You'll never pin anything on the San Yee On. The way is barred for you. Their leaders are very respectable now. The First Route Marshal is a businessman of standing, with a massive financial empire. His identity is known to only three or four top officers, but I hear constant rumours of his political connections. Some have it he's a district board member – others say he goes as high as the Legislative Council.'

'Wouldn't be the first time I'd heard that rumour.' Joe shrugged.

150

'Distrust speculation if you must, but this much I *know* is true. The lodge of the San Yee On is protected by the fifth floor of Police Headquarters. Don't ask me who. I don't know.'

Joe made a hurried check of the dancefloor and the nearby tables.

'Are you saying that one of the San Yee On dragons is a senior police officer?' He wanted to add: 'Bullshit!' but he knew this *Hung Kwan* would not waste his breath on idle talk.

'For heaven's sake, don't put my name on any reports you write. I can handle myself, all right – you know that – but I don't need any more of these.' He indicated the scar on his face.

'You didn't need to say that,' said Joe, somewhat irritated by the suggestion. 'You know anything you tell me is unattributable.'

'See that it remains so, *dai lo*.'

Joe left the meeting in a state of some confusion. It was the first time he had known Siu Din Din to behave that way. Clearly then even the enforcer was intimidated by what he had heard. And with good reason, thought Joe, if the San Yee On was involved.

NINE

The Headquarters of the RHKP Special Branch is in Caine House, a seven-storey, T-shaped, white and grey building which it shares with the Police Force Directorate, whose offices are on the fifth floor. To the rear, Caine House looks out over the harbour, but to the front it directly faces the taller New May House across the headquarters compound, and every morning a sea of smartly-dressed men and women flows through its doors to fill the hundreds of desks and offices there. It is a scene repeated in the office blocks all over Hong Kong; however a careful observer will notice that the workforce entering Caine House is far from normal. To begin with there is a high proportion of young European women, a ratio almost unique in Hong Kong where about ninety-eight per cent of the population is Chinese. These women are the trusted secretaries, executive assistants and registry girls who have been cleared to handle intelligence material graded up to TOP SECRET, and they are often the wives or daughters of British servicemen working on military bases. The men, also predominantly European, are the many intelligence officers who man the desks of the colony's political police force.

Initially formed to monitor the subversive aims of the Chinese Intelligence Service (CHIS) in Hong Kong, the Special Branch is quite different from its namesake in the United Kingdom. Unlike that body it has taken on board full responsibility for all intelligence matters, counter-subversion and counter-espionage, which in the United

Kingdom are the province of the Security Service. In this respect SB more correctly resembles MI5 than any branch of a normal police force, but also with full police powers of arrest which MI5 does not enjoy. This combination of power renders it one of the most effective forces anywhere in the world.

David Becker was sitting at his desk on the fourth floor of Caine House, contemplating the thickness of the William Fredericks file lying in his in-tray, when a registry messenger delivered the buff-coloured envelope. He turned it over and eyed it indifferently. In the RHKP all official documents have a 'Pol' reference number. First information sheets are called Pol 159s, and in times of major crisis they are sent to absolutely everybody from the CP right down to the barrack-room coolie. Often these documents contain nothing more significant than the news that the Commissioner has ordered the seasonal change to blue winter uniform. So it was with scant concern that he tore open the envelope to read its contents.

What he saw made him immediately reconsider his opinion of Pol 159s. This one was to advise the Director of Special Branch of the suspected homicide by decapitation of a US diplomat.

'Oh, shit,' he muttered to himself, a sense of foreboding beginning somewhere in the pit of his stomach. 'That's all we need.'

Becker's section, bearing the official designation G4, was one of the largest in Special Branch, and was responsible for the physical protective security of Government and Consular premises and their attendant staff. This had always been the first priority on their section charter, but by far the greater part of their time was taken up in mounting protective security for a succession of visiting heads of state, politicians or other dignitaries. Bodyguards, in fact. G4 was that group of smart-suited and discreetly armed young men, all wearing the same lapel badge and radio earpiece, who on the TV news were usually seen surrounding whatever foreign leader was currently in town, and gently fending off the overzealous cameraman.

At that moment Becker's desk was piled high with correspondence relating to the visit of William Fredericks, the US Secretary of State, for which G4 section would routinely be providing coverage. Grimly he reflected that there was still a mountain of work to get through before the visit could take place. There were still buildings to be checked, accommodation and transport to be cleared, routes to plan (both primary and back-up); and everyone likely to come within arm's reach of William Fredericks during his visit would need to be record-checked against SB's index of known terrorists and political activists. All this to do – and with only two weeks before Fredericks' plane arrived from the Philippines.

Now, suddenly, this small sheet of paper seemed to threaten all the preparation that had gone before. Rereading the Pol 159, Becker found questions stacking up in his head. Why had this James Reicher, a US Federal Agent, been found dead in a part of the city where *gwai los* just did not go? Who would want to kill him? And why? It was a Homicide case, certainly, but the diplomatic passport Reicher carried had now brought it squarely into G4 domain. Two words had leapt off the page and seized his attention: *State Department*. Jesus Christ! This was one of William Fredericks' own men.

Grabbing his jacket, Becker headed straight for the office at the end of the corridor where the section head lived. On the way he tried to determine exactly what it was about this operation that bothered him so. Regrettably Fredericks' visit had already been announced in the local press, but that was only to be expected. Becker was always unhappy about giving such clear advance notice to any potential attackers – it gave them all the time needed to plan their move – but, on the other hand even he recognised the politician's need for publicity. But this was a particularly sensitive visit; if the press were to somehow find out about Fredericks' secret appointment in the New Territories, then local passions would doubtless be aroused – and then anything might happen. It would have been far better to hold back the press releases until the very last moment. But, then, politicians are there to be seen.

It was not the size or the importance of this VIP party which bothered him. The visit of the Prince and Princess of Wales had ballooned into a nightmare of planning and bureaucracy, but the visiting couple had been popular and, in spite of some ill-feeling over the 1997 issue, they were universally well received. The Americans were another story. Of late US foreign policy in the Far East had come in for heavy criticism in the Asian media as being divisive and even provocative. So provocative and so widely criticised, in fact, that it was now felt the Secretary of State merited particularly tight personal security coverage during this stay. State Department fielded its own bodyguard detail to protect the Secretary during his world travels, but the moment Fredericks landed in Hong Kong that responsibility would pass to the men of G4.

The SY advance men, Lassiter and Divine, were now ensconced on the seventh floor of the Hilton – the hotel selected as the VIP residence for the duration of the visit. Right now they would have their hands full just allocating accommodation and fixing up a fleet of hire cars for all the American units involved in the operation. Now because of the Pol 159, Becker knew he would have to speak with the two Americans later that day, and find out what, if anything, they knew about the circumstances of Reicher's death. But before that he needed to bring this whole matter to the attention of his immediate boss.

Stephen Lee Kwok-wing read the Pol 159 with a shrug, then handed it back to his subordinate before returning to the report he was drafting.

'Very interesting. Make sure CID keeps us informed of any developments.'

Becker was not so easily satisfied.

'I was thinking of doing a little more than that,' he pressed, settling himself into the easy chair his Chinese superintendent reserved for guests. Stephen Lee continued writing, one elbow on the desk top, a hand shading his eyes. He wore a crisp white long-sleeved shirt and a fashionable necktie of hand-painted silk.

'Like what, for instance?'

'Digging around some. I'm not happy. First the Jockey Club, and now this. Two incidents touching my operation, however tangentially, seems too much of a coincidence for me. It makes me nervous.'

Lee put down his pen and sat back, reining back a smile.

'What's this, a case of *gwai lo* paranoia. You know there's really nothing to link either incident with your operation.'

'I want to know what Reicher was doing down there in Yaumatei – way off the beaten track.'

Stephen Lee pursed his lips, his small black eyes flicking from side to side as he stared at the wall, considering the question.

'It could be any number of things. Economic intelligence units get up to some pretty weird antics. But even if he was, say, meeting an agent, what business is it of ours? We've never tried to restrict them in that field. They have their targets and we have ours. We've always pooled our intelligence product – up to a point.'

'I don't have any problem with that. The thing that bothers me is: what the hell have they been doing down there to get one of their own men carved up so badly? If the Americans are running something covert, something

156

sweet and sour, then it's bound to impact on my operation.'

There was a stridency in Becker's voice that he had not intended, and he checked himself, shrugging slightly. Steve Lee let the silence gather a moment before answering. Handling Becker's outbursts was becoming increasingly more difficult these days.

'Look, Dave, I understand how you feel, and I know this is your operation, but just lately you've been very heavyhanded where the Americans are concerned. That last meeting we had, you almost tore Cinch's head off.'

Becker examined his wristwatch, then looked away. Lee continued: 'Sometimes there's a temptation to read too much into these things. I want you to leave this alone for now and concentrate fully on preparing for the Yank's visit. We'll get our liaison desk to raise the subject with the RSO at the Consulate-General. That's the proper channel.'

Steve Lee was always one for the proper channels. He was what they called a 'banana policeman': yellow on the outside, white on the inside. Very definitely Westernised in his habits, with a preference for Italian clothes and French cuisine; his exaggerated diction and speech patterns suggested that somewhere along the line he had taken elocution lessons. He had been section head for just over one year: a smart young seven-year superintendent with all the right social connections. Promoted to *ging si* while still in his mid-thirties, he had always been considered something of a 'flier'. Some time ago the powers that be had decreed that by 1997 all senior police posts would be occupied by Chinese officers, a policy known as localisation, and it was known that Lee was exactly the kind of officer the force wanted to promote to fulfil this aim. But, instead of shooting for the top, Lee had confounded the directorate by opting to take over the VIP Unit: a post which, though it builds a certain reputation, does little to advance an officer's career.

Becker knew he had no possible grounds for complaint – that was the annoying thing about Stephen Lee: procedurally he was always dead right. But Becker had always been his own man. He had his own set of rules, which fitted neatly over SB ones like a photographic transparency, and he realised that this was going to be one of those rare occasions when he would simply have to say 'Yes, sir' and go do it anyway.

'Don't worry,' his Chinese superintendent assured him. 'Ruth Tavistock is like this with their RSO. She'll get the unofficial word for us, if anyone can.'

Becker was aware of the heat of the room. The air seemed stale and the sweat beneath his rubber watch-strap irritated. Now that he'd made up his own mind what to do he wouldn't push any further.

'OK, if that's how you want it played, we'll leave it to Ruth Tavistock.'

Stephen Lee cocked his head to one side and his eyes narrowed in suspicion. The sudden capitulation made him feel uncomfortable, but he knew he had no grounds to issue a more explicit warning. For a Chinese, to imply that his own subordinate might actually disobey him was in itself a loss of face. Toying with the heavy gold-nibbed fountain-pen the superintendent leaned back in his chair.

'So, tell me, what is the current status on the American party?'

'The latest information says Airforce Two arrives just before midnight on 1 October with a party of forty-six. They'll use the long-term parking apron at Kai Tak. It's to be a full-blown SY detail with EOD and secure communications teams. Some additional personnel will be drawn from the Manila and Bangkok stations to fill in. As usual, the Hilton will be swarming with military technicians. They're setting up a secure microwave link from the hotel to the aircraft-carrier *Carl Vinsen*, and from there back to Washington.'

158

'Handling their own baggage?'

'Yes, thank God! We'll put an armed officer with the baggage convoy, but they'll get their own people to marshal it.'

'Has Cinch made it clear to the advance party that we'll have to collect all their weapons at the airport?'

'Yes, we agreed that their detail leader could collect them before debarkation and surrender them at the hotel rather than waste time out there on the apron – to avoid distractions. Lassiter and Divine weren't happy about any of that, which is understandable. They'll be tagging on to our operation completely unarmed, like so many human shields.'

'It's no different for any other team we play host to.'

'They've never seen our section work before – we don't have the high profile of some of the other units – and after the Shatin robbery they're very jumpy. I get the feeling they think they're coming back to Saigon or something. Lassiter would like us to let them keep a couple of Magnums per shift, as token reassurance.'

'Absolutely not!' Steve Lee sat forward in his seat. 'The laws of Hong Kong forbid it, and I can't risk one of our boys shooting one of theirs if he catches sight of a weapon.' As usual this was exactly by the book. But there was more to it than just that: once again there was face. 'Maybe you should do something to restore their confidence.'

David Becker nodded in agreement.

'There's a range course booked at Castle Peak this afternoon. I thought I'd take Lassiter and Divine along to see the boys shoot. Take them through a few of our drills.'

'Perfect. See that you put on a good show.'

Judging that the interview had concluded, Becker made as if to leave, but Lee waved him back into his seat and pulled a thin orange folder from the pending tray on his desk.

'Here, might as well take this with you for inclusion in your file.'

'What's this?' asked Becker, opening it.

'Just what you requested: authorisation for the Mass Transit Railway phase. The Corporation has agreed to lay on a special train. No press, no public – just the VIP and his immediate party.'

'That's good. I wonder when we'll find out just what the Secretary of State intends to do on this little trip out to the New Territories? It's not the regular thing for a visiting politician.'

'Oh, we already know that,' said Lee evenly.

'We do?'

'Of course. Last week I received a call from the NCNA.'

Becker's puzzled expression deepened into a frown of concern.

'The NCNA? What do they want?'

Just the mention of the New China News Agency was enough to set cogs turning inside Becker's head. For many years that organisation, which occupied an aging grey building in Hong Kong Island's Happy Valley district, had been the mainland China government's only official representation inside the British Crown Colony. Since China had never officially recognised the original treaties which had ceded Hong Kong to Britain, a full consulate was obviously out of the question. For this reason the NCNA had become the focus for all official and unofficial contacts between the two administrations. The Chinese had always kept up the pretence of high journalistic endeavour there, but every last hawker in Hong Kong knew that the building housed the resident section of the Chinese intelligence service, that this was the base from which they had launched their many attempts at subverting British rule, and that most of the old men in Mao suits who posed as senior information officers were in fact senior CHIS officers.

With the ascent of Deng Xiao Ping, however, relations between Beijing and the Hong Kong administration had warmed a few degrees, to the point where there were sometimes polite, if severely restrained, contacts between Special Branch and the 'officials' at the NCNA on matters affecting their mutual security. On several occasions over the past few years, SB had provided protection for Chinese cabinet ministers visiting or transiting the colony. Becker had to confess he could not see the connection between the NCNA and William Fredericks.

Stephen Lee steepled his fingers and concentrated on Becker's face, secretly enjoying the reaction he had produced.

'They wanted to arrange a meeting to discuss arrangements for confidential talks between the Secretary of State and one of their own senior cabinet men.'

'They have got to be kidding?'

'No joke. It's their Foreign Minister.'

'That wasn't on the programme Lassiter gave me.'

'That's because Lassiter doesn't know about it. Few people do. Only a handful on either side. They wouldn't have told *us* if they could have somehow got around it. Apparently it was scheduled months ago, and deliberately screened out of all communications. It's about as sensitive as anything we've ever handled: discussions about increased military cooperation in the mid-Nineties. The exact location hasn't been disclosed yet, but it's to be somewhere in the NT, fairly close to the border. They'd like to meet us to tie up the timings and so on.'

'I suppose we shouldn't be too surprised, considering the military cooperation between the Soviets and the Vietnamese in the Pacific.'

'Yes, the East-West thaw doesn't count for chop suey out here in the Far East theatre.'

In fact, the breaking-up of old alliances in the Pacific and the formation of new power blocs based upon economic muscle meant that *nothing* now came as much of a surprise. These days the Pacific was a mad scramble for power and influence, with partners changing almost every other day.

Stephen Lee sounded a note of caution: 'You realise how damaging this could prove if this meeting became public knowledge. Damaging for both sides.'

'I think I can imagine,' said Becker.

'China is still suffering this bloody left-wing backlash after the student uprising of '89. On top of that, the crumbling of the Communist empire in Europe scared the old men in Beijing pretty bad, by all accounts. They're at pains to stress their continuing commitment to Communism.'

'So they don't wish to be seen cosying up to the Americans – yes, I see that.'

'Not after Washington's punitive economic sanctions against Beijing and some pretty bad mudslinging over human rights violations.'

'So why has the State Department arranged this visit? And why now?' quizzed Becker. 'Obviously, we're not getting the full story.'

Stephen Lee sensed *gwai lo* paranoia returning.

'Ours is not to reason why ...' Lee smiled. 'The first I knew of it was their phone-call. I routinely passed the request up through the Director of Special Branch, but nobody at Central Government Offices knew anything about it. There were a lot of red faces there, I can tell you. Discreet representations are being made at this very moment. Anyway, you better keep tomorrow free: I want you with me on my trip over to the NCNA.'

'I won't be much use to you. I can get by in Cantonese, but I don't speak any Mandarin at all.'

'You let me worry about that. You know what they're like. I can't go without a *ma jai* – I'd have no face at all. When dealing with the NCNA, face is always the most important thing.'

Becker knew he was right. The men from the People's Republic of China would field an impressive group of officials for this ritualised meeting, and on his own Stephen Lee would be overwhelmed – he might have to agree to almost anything. Therefore he would need his own sidekick to back up his authority and help balance the negotiations.

Becker nodded. 'And when they see you have a *gwai lo* for your *ma jai . . .*'

'You get the picture: big face.'

'So wear your oldest, drabbest, worst-fitting suit, and fill the pockets with mothballs; that way you'll blend right in.' Becker couldn't resist this one small dig. Nowhere was the gulf between the two cultures more apparent than in the shabby dress-sense of the PRC men.

Steve Lee decided to share the joke. 'I'll do my level best. In five years' time one of those buggers could be running this place.'

For Becker the joke stopped there.

'God help Hong Kong when that day comes. I'm only glad I won't be here to see it.'

When David Becker's car pulled up outside the plate-glass doors of the Hilton Hotel, Tom Lassiter, changed into T-shirt and jeans, was already waiting for him in the upstairs lobby.

The hotel, one of the most luxurious in the colony, was situated in the heart of the business district, sandwiched between the competing giants of the Hong Kong Bank building and the Bank of China tower, at the bottom of Garden Road. Just a few hundred yards lower down the hill from the US Consulate-General, the Hilton had always been popular with American visitors – tourists and government officials alike – and so it was the obvious choice to accommodate the Secretary of State's party.

Taking the escalator up to the main lobby, Becker

enjoyed the expensive feel of the place: polished marble, thick Chinese carpets, light beams spilling in soft, golden pools over velvet upholstery and varnished redwood.

Lassiter was seated in an armchair, reading the cartoon strips in the *International Herald Tribune*.

'Divine won't be coming,' he said, rising to greet Becker with the same affable smile he always seemed to wear. 'He has an appointment with some guy in Tsim Sha Tsui who deals fake Rolex and Cartier watches. We promised the boys back in the Washington field office.'

Becker shook his hand, then led him down to the waiting SB vehicle.

It had been four days since their last meeting, on the day of the Shatin robbery, and Lassiter started in with questions as soon as the car moved off, heading for the New Territories.

'So what's all this Big Circle stuff?' he began. 'The papers are full of it?'

'Just speculation. There's nothing so far to link it to them – apart from the particularly violent m.o.'

'I appreciate what you're saying, but my office has been asked to comment on the situation. Anything you can give me would be appreciated.'

'It involves teams from mainland China. Most of the heavyweight stuff does these days. It began back in 1984 with small groups of demobilised Chinese Army soldiers. For some time the people over the border had been picking up our TV programmes: shows that depict rich lifestyles; game shows where you can win piles of money. Gradually the word got around that the streets down here are paved with gold. It's one of the reasons we've always had so many illegal immigrants. So when these demobbed soldiers saw pictures of fat jewellers' and goldsmiths' shops with the bare minimum of protection, they started to make their way down from Canton, to jump the snake-fence on the border by night and lie up in some flat or guesthouse arranged by an advance man or a local collaborator. As a rule they bring automatic weapons, which are more easily available in China than here – sometimes grenades, too. A quick hit and they're gone; back into the People's Republic within a matter of hours, with a fortune in gold to spend. Think of the buying power of gold in an economy like China's!'

'And those are the kind of people who hit the Jockey Club?'

'That's what everyone's saying. These are not just ordinary robbers: they're military-trained and they're hungry. If you're going to pull a job, this is the place to do it. The average sentence for armed robbery here is twelve, maybe fifteen years.'

'And in the PRC?'

'Thirty-eight – just behind the ear. No appeal.'

'I see.'

Lassiter fell silent for a time, gazing out at the high-rises of Sham Shui Po and Cheung Sha Wan districts on both sides: slab after slab of sky-high resettlement blocks, all strung with bamboo washing poles and TV aerials. Every street was choked with people moving purposefully about their daily business with an energy he himself could barely emulate in this debilitating heat. He listened with interest as Becker, pointing to the giant walls of windows, explained that each one was a government flat housing an extended family of grandparents, aunties and children all crammed into a few hundred square feet of space. Lassiter wondered what kind of life they could enjoy under such extreme conditions.

Gradually the tenements fell away, and the car overtook a line of green and yellow PLBs, or public light-buses, climbing out of Kowloon and heading north for the New Territories. There was nothing 'new' about the New Territories. The lease on this mainly rural and hilly area had been granted ninety-four years previously, and for most of that time it had remained a backwater – set apart from the main urban sprawl by the mountains separating it from Kowloon. In recent times, however, a staggering number of people had been rehoused here in a rapid and enforced urbanisation programme needed to accommodate the burgeoning population. Thousands of families who had previously lived in dangerous hillside squatter villages had been relocated in New Towns which had exploded on to the map in just a few short years.

Although the area of the New Territories was many times bigger than Kowloon and Hong Kong Island put together, the vast majority of it was too rugged and unsuitable for building, so these New Towns had sprung up along the east and west coasts only, on the sites of old rural villages. Much of the central area remained agricultural, but there were numerous examples of villagers who had grown rich by selling off parcels of their ancestral land for building development.

Their car took the Castle Peak Road along the western coast, continuing north through industrial Kwai Chung with its modern container terminal, and on through the sky-block forest of Tsuen Wan crouching beneath Dai Mo Shan, the highest mountain in the territory. On the Tuen Mun highway, Becker was not surprised to see that drivers still drove like highschool kids on a chicken-run: at top speed and seemingly taking as many risks as possible. Now they were out of the grey concrete jungle, and away from the bewildering array of Chinese hoardings which assaulted the eyes from every angle, Lassiter found himself relaxing and enjoying the sight of the green folds and gentle undulation of the hillsides.

The combat range was a British Army facility set well away from population areas, in five acres of cleared ground surrounded by thick groves of young bamboo. In the heat of the afternoon one could actually feel the waves of hot damp air rising out of the sweating expanse of lush vegetation. At the gatehouse Becker showed his warrant card to the Gurkha on duty, and they were allowed through into the restricted area.

When they emerged from the changing room, wearing camouflage-pattern fatigues, they found the G4 section men already assembled and going through some kind of group martial exercise. Lassiter stood and watched quietly, as an eight-by-six matrix of young Chinese men swam slowly through an extended series of movements in perfectly synchronised motion. Each man was stripped to the waist, well tanned and possessing the slender muscular definition normal in Chinese, yet with no trace of tension in their muscles. There was something hugely impressive about it all: serene and yet profoundly dynamic. Each push and circular sweep of the hand was cleanly articulate, each step and turn perfectly balanced.

'What's that all about?' asked Lassiter finally, when they finished, wondering privately whether Becker was actually relying upon Chinese boxing skills to keep the Secretary of State alive.

'Tai Chi. In G4 we use it to aid relaxation and concentration. We find it also enhances body coordination skills, and these group exercises foster a valuable sense of teamwork. You can take it a lot deeper than that, if you care to, but we just find it helps the men shoot better.'

'Why is that?'

'Tai Chi teaches breath control; it also reduces anxiety and excessive tension in the upper body, and that means fewer hand tremors. Result: increased accuracy.'

Becker excused himself and broke away to issue orders for the range practice to start. The men arranged themselves in groups of six, collected weapons and ammunition from the range officer, and put on polarized sunglasses to reduce glare from the concrete facing and white paper targets. Some of them wore black baseball caps with their nicknames stitched on to the peaks in gold thread: *Rocky – Julius – Ah Jack – Saliva Man*. They were all young men with serious faces. As the first group stepped up to the firing-line the rest looked on,

167

with ear-defenders casually clamped around one leg or perched on top of their heads.

They fired courses in rotation from a variety of starting positions: standing, kneeling, prone. The first two magazines were aimed warm-up shots at a black silhouette target on a white background set twelve metres away. After that, each exercise began with a fast draw of the holstered weapon. For a bodyguard, who is unlikely to get any warning before engaging the enemy, practising any other way would be a waste of time. The men practised turning from left and from right to engage the target, and then turning fully about. As Lassiter watched their fluid movements, he realised now the importance of the Tai Chi training. Each time they pivoted, on the ball of one foot, their arms came up already locked in a Cooper-Weaver grip, and two shots in rapid succession pierced holes in the target paper within two or three inches of each other.

Groupings of hits on the targets were consistently tight and accurate, at four inches or better. Each time, Becker checked the results and nodded his approval. When the next detail donned ear-defenders and moved up to the line, their movements proved just as smooth: drawing and firing off double taps in a single continuous motion. After many thousands of practice rounds, most of Becker's men were rock solid from every angle – the movements trained into their muscles like a golfer's practised swing.

Lassiter had to admit he was impressed by the standard of shooting, though he deliberately chose not to comment, out of bodyguard's etiquette. Instead, sitting on top of an ammunition box, he launched once more into questions.

'I'm curious. How do these gangs from the mainland fit in with local organised crime outfits. I understood the triads had the lock on things around here.'

Becker came and squatted beside him, scratching the

ground at his feet with a discarded twig as he continued watching his men shoot.

'Not exactly. Two years ago there was big trouble. Some *Dai Huen Jai* – it means Big Circle Gang – decided to stay on after a raid, and carve out an area of influence for themselves.'

'How did that sit?'

'None too well. There's only a limited amount of turf to be had, and triads always defend theirs with blood. For a time there was a spate of attacks, choppings mostly: severed hamstrings and shoulder joints – aiming to disable rather than kill. But then the elders stepped in and prevailed upon the younger men to organise settlement talks with Big Circle. After that there had to be a formal council of war. It seems funny to us that these groups would sit down in a restaurant in neutral territory to talk it out, but that's actually the way they did it.'

'What happened?'

'Neither side would concede an inch. When talks finally broke down, the triads pulled out twelve-inch beef knives, intending to finish it there. Only the *dai huens* were one jump ahead. They pulled .45 calibre autos and shot dead four of the 14K's best-known fighters!'

Lassiter studied the line of constables now pasting squares of paper over the holes in the targets. The more he heard the less he liked it.

'What happened then?'

'After that things quietened down a bit. The Big Circle gangs split and splintered. Now there are lots of other offshoots. Our intelligence indicates there is a degree of cooperation between them and the triads. It's not exactly orthodox but Lodge Masters have used *Dai Huen Jai* as hired help on a straight fee-paying basis.'

'For robberies?'

'Sometimes. Some contract killings, too.'

Lassiter turned to look at Becker, his eyes widening.

'Assassination! Lordy Miss Claudie, my detail leader's

going to love that!' He shook his head and spat into the dust. 'I had hoped you could offer us some reassurance, but everything I've heard so far seems bad!'

'I'm sorry. That's the way it is.'

Becker realised that now the other man was really worried, and that was good. He needed to convey the respect that attached itself to the *Dai Huen Jai*. They weren't just a bunch of pig farmers on a day out. Nor were they as naive as the many illegal immigrants who flooded across the border with the mud from the rice paddies still between their toes. Without a tip-off, the police had little chance of apprehending them. Even when they did, it usually ended in a gun battle with the threat of innocent bystanders being wasted by stray bullets.

'Big Circle is always a wild card,' continued Becker, snapping the twig with which he had been toying, 'but what concerns me most now is the Reicher killing. I was hoping you could help me with that one.'

From the reaction he got, Becker guessed that the American had been expecting this question. He also sensed a degree of bitterness in the answer.

'You're not the only one who'd like answers. I've known Jack Cinch a long time, but getting anything out of him on this has been next to impossible. There should be no problem about secrecy; I'm cleared to the same level as him and its obvious I have a genuine need to know about anything sensitive they might be running. Still I'm convinced he knows more than he's telling me. He keeps saying how there's nothing to worry about; how it's not the Department's problem.'

'Whose bloody problem is it, then?' Becker stood up, massaging one knee. Looking up into the cloud-strewn sky above the green hillside, he could see passenger jets circling – stacking up over Lantau Island for the final descent into Kai Tak airport.

'Did Cinch tell you what Reicher was working on?'

'Something about a visa fraud operation, but I don't buy that.'

'Oh?' said Becker turning his gaze back on to the American. 'Why not?'

'It just doesn't feel right. Undercover is not our style. Our work is high-profile; there's too great a risk of being recognised. It's more like something the FBI would go for.'

'What about Reicher? What was he like? Did you know him?'

'No. Never ran across him before. Never even heard his name. I called the detail leader in Manila this morning and he didn't know him either. That's pretty strange.'

'Why's that?'

'Well, because we're an exclusive club at SY, everyone knows everyone else, but no one seems to have heard of Jim Reicher. He must have been a new guy. The funny thing is, new guys usually first do at least a year at home before getting an overseas posting.'

Becker pondered these words inside his head, his suspicions beginning now to crystallise. If Tom Lassiter did not know him, and Reicher was not a new guy after all, then who the hell was he? And why was Jack Cinch, an officer of good standing, covering for him?

Suddenly Becker became aware that someone was calling out to him from up on the firing-line. The previous detail had finished firing, and the range officer was calling him and Lassiter forward to shoot. Raising a hand in acknowledgement he led Lassiter over.

'I don't know.' He shrugged. 'Maybe my boss is right; maybe I am just acting paranoid.'

'I thought that's what the job was all about,' said Lassiter drily as they reached the range officer's table and saw the lines of GLOCK 17 automatic pistols laid out in neat lines beside the extended ammunition magazines.

171

TEN

Ruth Tavistock came out of the bedroom, wearing just the white cotton sheet they had spent the last hour creasing between their bodies. She found him leaning bare-chested against the window, watching the ferry-boats butting through the blue water in the harbour below. Her first impression was of the changes in the room itself. There was now the smoky fragrance of jasmine which had not been there before; incense burning in a glass bowl on the antique Korean chest, its snaking trails of white smoke weaving patterns through the rays of sunlight spilling through the window. Some-where in the background Pink Floyd was playing softly, like the accompaniment to a continuing dream.

Quietly she padded across the parquet floor until she was standing directly behind him, close enough to hear his breathing. Like a spy she stood there watching, noticing the restless way his angular frame moved against the window: one muscular arm resting high up on the glass, his forehead laid against the arm. Something was troubling him; she knew that from the series of short exasperated sighs which escaped him, and the longer one punctuated with a muttered 'shit!' It was the same distraction she had noticed in his eyes just before their lovemaking.

Under present circumstances she was hardly surprised.

She was a honey blonde, made blonder by the tropic

172

sun, with eyes as arrestingly blue as the South China Sea. Her tan, a perfect caramel hue, was the result of regular tennis and a hundred or more beach parties – with just a dusting of freckles on her muscular shoulders. She was not a natural athlete, but having decided on the body she wanted for herself, she had singlemindedly jogged, swum and lifted weights to achieve her goal. Swathed now in the creamy whiteness of the sheet, her tan appeared even darker, the toned legs even longer than usual. But Jack Cinch was lost in a world of his own, and too troubled by his problems to notice.

It was a faint rustle of the sheet that made him turn his head. The easy, confident smile was there on his long face in an instant. His smooth, hairless chest was still slightly flushed with the evidence of their lovemaking.

'Hi, there. I thought you were asleep.'

'Not at 2.30 in the afternoon.' Her arms went around his waist from behind, her chin burrowing into the bunched muscles around his shoulder-blades. She loved the smell and texture of his skin.

'What is it, Jack?' she asked with concern in her voice.

'Huh?' he answered, half distracted by something in the water below: a passenger ferry from the US aircraft-carrier berthed out in the Western anchorage.

'You seemed far away. Is it something you're not telling me?'

'Not especially.' He turned and kissed her half-heartedly, then looked her full in the face.

She noticed how the sun lit up the close-cut hair around his temples: short fair stubble like sparks of gold.

'It's just the job – you know how these things go.'

Ruth sensed that the Reicher homicide had affected him badly. Just a short while ago she had lain in his arms and listened to him describe his visit to Hung Hom public mortuary, the muscles in his neck bunching tighter as he spoke. Obviously the sight of his subordinate lying on the slab was a memory that would not easily go away.

She hugged him closer, hoping she might help him forget what he had seen.

'I think you should put it out of your mind, Jack. Reicher was obviously out of control. He was playing both ends against the middle and he came unstuck. That's the price you can pay here in Hong Kong. He must have known the risks.'

'Yes, but unfortunately it doesn't end there.'

The look of resignation on his face made her wonder.

'Oh, come on, Jack, they can hardly hold you responsible.'

'Don't you believe it.' He turned back to the window. 'I was in charge. Back in Washington they're bound to say that I blew it.'

'Relax. It's just another investigation.'

'Uh-huh. With the Secretary of State on his way in, how's it going to look? State Department officer mixed up with local crime bosses. I can see the press coverage now. I just hope you can cut us some slack at your end. Help stage-manage things a little?'

'You're worried about the newspapers?'

'Amongst other things. It's me who answers for any bad publicity which mars this visit. There might be a lot of awkward questions I couldn't easily handle. It would certainly help a lot if we could somehow redefine the circumstances of Reicher's demise. Suggest a robbery motive. Maybe even link it to this Gwan-Dai killer who's going around.'

At once her grip slackened and she stepped away from him, turning towards the window. A shiver ran through her. He was asking her for something that did not quite feel right. During her time with Special Branch she had occasionally been required to withhold information in the public interest, but this was the first time she had been asked to help in propagating a lie.

'The Gwan-Dai thing wouldn't work. That's a straight sex thing. Strictly female victims.'

Cinch sensed her unease in the tightness of her voice. He moved immediately to dispel it, lowering the sheet and laying one hand against her shoulder.

'Ruth, in the past we've always been there for each other. You know I wouldn't ask if it wasn't really important.'

As he turned her back again to face him, the cotton sheet slid down far enough to reveal the strong swell of her breasts. One delicious hard nipple now pressed against his chest. Unsure what else to do, she kissed him hard.

'All right,' she said at last, her eyes searching his face for something to believe in. 'If it means that much, I'll do it this once, for you. But don't ever ask me to do it again.'

He raised one hand in a scout's promise. 'Swear to God and hope to die.'

This time the boyish grin didn't quite work, and when Ruth did not laugh Cinch moved awkwardly away from the window.

'Care for some coffee? It should be ready now.'

She pulled the sheet back up beneath her arms and shook her head. Now it was she who had the faraway look in her eyes.

'Sorry, I'm due back at Caine House in twenty minutes, for a meeting.'

'Just one cup of coffee,' he said, appealing to her. 'That's a small price to pay for good bilateral relations with your American cousins.'

'I suspect that if my bosses knew the exact nature of those bilateral relations, they'd have something more telling to say about these extended lunches of ours. I'd better just shower and go.'

She forced a smile, but it was obvious they were both uncomfortable with the situation. Suddenly she wanted to be away from the music and the smell of the incense.

Heading back to the bedroom, Ruth took a shower

175

and put on her clothes. She found herself reflecting upon the information her visit to the Consulate earlier had produced. She had gone that morning at David Becker's urgent and unexpected request, aware that both he and Roman Fung were dissatisfied with what the Americans had so far told them. In Cinch's third-floor office the meeting had been extremely businesslike, but afterwards the excellent lunch at the Mandarin Hotel Coffee shop and this subsequent extracurricular visit to his apartment in Mid-Levels were anything but a duty commitment.

Ruth Tavistock was section head in charge of Intelligence Liaison: the funnel and filter for anything going to and coming from the allied intelligence services stationed within the Crown Colony. That was how she and Jack Cinch had first met, swapping terrorist alerts and threat assessments, until one night they had fallen into the same bed. That had been the night of the annual US Marine Corps Birthday Ball, the previous year, and they had been lovers ever since.

That was over six months ago. She and Jack had continued to meet, keeping their affair even more secret than the documents they exchanged professionally. For both of them it was a dangerous and foolish involvement; perhaps that was what had made it so exciting in the first place. Involved in the intelligence world where such liaisons are strictly forbidden, both of them could easily lose their top-grade security clearance because of it. Worse still, Cinch might even be recalled to Washington.

She fastened the Rolex Cellini on to her wrist and, noticing the time, began to hurry. Her meeting with David Becker and Stephen Lee was scheduled for three o'clock and an undefined sense of guilt made her anxious to be on time.

'I'll call you when I know what's happening,' she said, grabbing up her briefcase.

Cinch left the sofa and followed her to the door, a coffee cup still in his hand.

'You cut me some slack on this and I'll make it up to you,' he said, gently seizing her elbow. A smile flashed over his face. 'How about dinner tonight? We could take the junk across to Cheung Chau island for some of that glorious seafood. No one would know us there.' Cinch's thirty-foot motorised Chinese junk was his pride and joy. He kept it moored at the yacht club in Causeway Bay.

'Sounds great, but I'm busy tonight.' She wondered if the lie showed in her face.

'Then tomorrow night. I'll pick you up eight o'clock, Queen's Pier,' he insisted. 'It's the least I can do.'

At that moment it occurred to Ruth that their affair had always been based on a series of similar minor debts, and perhaps little else.

'All right,' she conceded finally, without enthusiasm. 'But now I really have to go.'

As she hurried out he was still saying something about steamed crabs and tipsy prawns, but all she wanted was to get away – to be on her own long enough to catch her breath. She had kissed him before leaving, not because she wanted to but because not to do so would have revealed too much about her current true feelings.

On Robinson Road the mid-afternoon sun was fierce, reflecting harshly from acres of glass and concrete all around. Slipping on dark glasses, Ruth flagged down a prowling cab and slid gratefully into the airconditioned comfort of the back seat. As the vehicle negotiated a tight series of bends and dropped down on to Garden Road, she was already replaying in her mind what Jack had told her and what he had asked of her. Her feeling of unease was increased when, glancing up from the window, she caught the cab-driver's eyes studying her furtively through his rear-view mirror.

During her years in Hong Kong Ruth had grown used to being stared at; it was the yellow hair that did it. Chinese girls were pretty enough but uniformly dark in colouring. Understandably the Chinese men were curious about Western women. And the way blondes were always portrayed in Asian movies did not exactly help either.

She ignored his gaze, concentrating instead on the glass towers that lined their route; but as they passed the Botanical Gardens the driver began to speak to her in halting English.

'Sorry, madam. Is it you are friend of Roman Fung?' The question caught her off balance, and when she did not answer at first the driver turned his head slightly and asked again. He was a thin young man with spots around his mouth, and a moustache so sparse it could have adorned the upper lip of an old woman.

'Hong Kong has many Fungs and many Romans,' said Ruth in guarded Cantonese, her eyes wandering back to the window.

'Wah! Your Chinese very good,' the driver responded solicitously. There was something about his nervous and ingratiating manner Ruth did not care for. The young man seemed to undulate eel-like in his seat, occasionally flashing tiny yellow teeth. 'My meaning is Roman Fung Lo-man: Detective Inspector,' he managed with difficulty.

'Yes, I know him,' she conceded. 'He's a colleague of mine. Why?'

The driver nodded furiously in satisfaction. He switched to Cantonese, though his voice was no less solicitous for that.

'I thought I recognised you. I'm Roman's younger brother. We met once before at a celebration dinner in Luk Kwok Restaurant. You were one of Roman's classmates in the police school, weren't you?'

Ruth threw up a hand. She had been to so many Chinese banquets in her time that there was no way she could remember every one. Often the great round tables were packed with relatives of her Chinese friends, and in most cases being introduced to them merely meant raising your brandy glass in a toast, followed by much hand-clapping and moving on to the next table. This driver was no more memorable than any of the others.

'*Dui m'jiu,*' she apologised politely. 'I'm afraid I don't remember.'

The driver looked a little hurt. 'But you asked me what I planned to do for a rice bowl. I said I would be a detective, like Roman. Remember that?'

'*M'gei dak.* I do not remember.'

At the bottom of Garden Road the cab climbed the flyover to rise above the Hilton Hotel, high above the steel tracks and the trams which rattled their way towards Kennedy Town. She would have happily ended the conversation there, but outside the New Supreme Court Building the traffic had slowed to a crawl.

'As you can see,' said Roman's brother, again flashing his yellow teeth, 'now I'm a taxi-driver.' At this he swung the steering-wheel from side to side, the way a child mimes driving a car.

'So what happened to the police career?' she asked in spite of herself.

'*Diu nei lo mo,*' he muttered, cursing routinely. 'Sorry, madam, for my foul languages, only it makes me angry enough to die. Somebody injected poison against me with the authorities. This was my bad fortune.' Ruth was too savvy to be fooled by that old line. More likely he had failed the entrance exam or else the preliminary interviews in which they weeded out such oddities as this. The lie about his referees bad-mouthing him was just a convenient defence for his ego.

She sensed that the rejection had been a heavy blow to the young man's expectations. The loss of face would have been considerable, particularly when his elder brother had been so readily accepted, and had become so successful in his police career.

Ruth made the appropriate sympathetic noises, and when the taxi finally pulled into Arsenal Yard to stop outside Caine House she got out and began fishing in her wallet.

Seeing this strategic opportunity eluding him, Roman's brother rolled down the window to continue the conversation. 'I was thinking perhaps you could help me.'

'What kind of help?' asked Ruth distractedly, looking for another ten-dollar note.

'Maybe an important lady like yourself could introduce my virtues to the police selection board, is it possible? I'm sure I could make an excellent and virtuous officer.'

'I don't think so.' She smiled apologetically. 'I have nothing to do with applications.'

All at once the young man's face grew serious – full of cunning. Almost that of a different person.

'If it's a question of *heung yau* ...' he said scratching his nose and looking around to check he was not overheard.

Ruth's eyes blazed. It was the first time anyone had ever offered her a bribe, and she had not at all expected it. The fact that this offer was wrapped up in a Chinese phrase meaning 'fragrant grease' did nothing to hide its stink.

A moment later she recovered her poise. Pulling the exact fare from her wallet, she dropped the notes through the car window. The thought of touching this young man's hand made her flesh crawl.

The driver's reaction was one of confusion.

'Please, please, there's no need to pay,' he said, more than a little hurt by the obvious rebuff. 'I know how to give face to authority. I know how the game is played. You can have this one on me.'

At that point something snapped, and Ruth gave vent to every Cantonese obscenity she had learned in her twelve years on the force. Immediately the driver pulled his head back inside the cab, his mouth open in

180

confusion as he thought to himself: *Aiyah*, what can a civilised person do with these *gwai lo*?'

By the time Ruth reached the first floor, her mood was no better. As she clipped on her SB security pass and stepped in to the main office corridor, David Becker fell in beside her.

'You're late,' he said without inflection.

'I know that,' she answered coldly, and kept walking.

When they reached her office he followed her over to the desk, sitting down without waiting to be asked.

'So where's Stephen Lee?' she asked impatiently. 'If I've held things up, then he ought to be here already.'

Becker folded one leg across the other and smiled.

'He's been called up to Protocol Section at Central Government Offices. There's a flap on with the NCNA.'

Glancing across the desk he saw that Ruth's mouth was set rigid, her hands balled into fists with the knuckles showing white. He considered asking her what was wrong, but sensed the question would be ill received. Instead he simply asked: 'So, what did you get?'

She took her time in answering. Removing her jacket, she placed it on a hanger, then adjusted the files on the desk top, and finally pushed her handbag into the bottom drawer. When she felt more composed, she smoothed back her hair and sat down.

She leaned back in her chair, obviously choosing her words with care. Becker had never known her so circumspect – or so angry.

'They have something of a major problem up at the Consulate-General. It could be extremely embarrassing for them.'

'Gee, that's a shame.'

'David, you have to appreciate the impact this could have. James Reicher was not working undercover on visa fraud, or anything else for that matter. He was actually selling visa blanks himself to a Chinese syndicate. The story they gave to Roman Fung was cooked up the morning after we found him, in order to save face. Naturally CID were not privy to any of this, but they always intended to level with the Branch.'

In spite of what Cinch had asked of her, Ruth had decided she could not keep the story from other sections in the Branch who had a pertinent interest. But she could still fight Cinch's corner and try to reduce any outraged reactions.

Becker showed a disconcerting lack of visible reaction.

'I see. Any ideas who the buyers are?' he asked.

'No, but I've been promised a list of the people Reicher ran around with. They've known about this for a couple of months. Apparently the man went off the rails shortly after arriving here in the colony. The spirit of capitalism perhaps. It was all being handled internally; their own people put a tail on him, hoping to get a lead. It seems he was too clever for them. Being a trained agent and all.'

Becker folded his hands behind his head and studied the ceiling, his broad chest straining the buttons of his shirt. Ruth found herself watching his movements, trying to gauge his reaction, and she realised then just how alike he and Cinch were in their mannerisms as well as in their looks. The only real difference between them was that one was fair and the other dark.

She sensed he had yet to be convinced.

'So, how did they get on to him?'

'I don't know that. Cinch just said he received a coded telex from Washington: intelligence gained from a reliable source. I understand one or two of a missing batch turned up in Hawaii. Chinese couriers attempting to enter the US with heroin packed inside tins of talcum powder. Most likely it came from the Drug Enforcement Administration; they get a lot of good information from their work up in the Golden Triangle.'

'What else do they have on Reicher's extra-curricular activities?'

Now that she was in full flow she felt herself beginning to unwind a little, her professional cool returning.

'Reicher wasn't just your regular Wanchai bar-fly. He used to hang out at some pretty strange places for a *gwai lo*, and he always had the same girl with him. Floating poker games, cricket fights, full-contact tournaments – you name it.'

'He went to the fights?'

'Anything that involved gambling. Reicher loved to bet, and he usually lost. Jack Cinch gave me pictures of him at an unlicensed boxing tournament up in the Kwai Chung container terminal.' She saw Becker was nodding his head now, as if in recognition. 'I see you know about that.'

'I've heard. It's a triad operation, naturally – all about money and about face. Completely illegal, so the location keeps changing. Basically groups of men with money to burn sit around and lay bets while two kids go at it inside one of those empty shipping containers. Thai boxing, kung-fu, hap ki do – anything goes, but the conditions tend to favour the society's fighters, who all fight *wing chun*: close in.' His hands came up close to his chest as he spoke, their shape changing in a stylish sequence of economical movements. 'It's pretty brutal, of course. No rules, no referee; they just keep going at it until one of them is too cut up to continue. As you'd expect, the money changing hands is counted off in thousands.'

The truth was that Becker had done far more than just hear about the fights. He had actually been inside the cage himself. It was Joe Lai who had first introduced him to the fights, for Joe reckoned it to be the ultimate test of unarmed combat skill. It was that all right. He had had several bouts in his time, but the one that always stuck in his mind was the time he had been up against a dark-skinned Indonesian who fought *muay thai* kick-boxing. It was an experience he would never forget.

Suddenly he noticed Ruth was gazing at him and realised he had allowed his thoughts to wander.

'You mentioned a girl. Who is she?'

'Hard to say; there was never an identification. Take a look for yourself.' She opened the desk drawer and found the photographs Cinch had given her, laying them on the desk in a bundle. 'Mid-twenties, possibly more, very attractive and Vietnamese or possibly ethnic Chinese out of Vietnam. Cinch said his people reported her as having a bit of a body, whatever that means. You'd assume from the clothes she's wearing that she's out of one of the nightclubs. I'm all set to recommend this stays with the CID; their chances of tracing her are better than ours.'

Becker continued flicking through the sheaf of pictures, saying nothing.

'Since this appears to have no direct impact upon your forthcoming operation,' continued Ruth cautiously, 'I intend to also recommend to the Director of Special Branch that we help Cinch out wherever we can, by maintaining the cover story they began.'

Suddenly Becker looked up from the pictures and threw them back upon the table.

'Oh, no, it's not going to be that easy for them. Not by a long way.'

Ruth's eyes flared with blue fire.

'What on earth are you talking about?'

'You're not doing anything until you've heard what I have to say about your pretty boy up at the Consulate.'

'And exactly what is that supposed to mean?' she blustered, feeling her cheeks flush. 'You're not making any sense.'

Becker got to his feet and began pacing the floor.

'Ruth, I have to say I've known you a long time, and I've usually found your judgement to be sound. But where the Americans are concerned, I'm beginning to have my doubts.'

'Perhaps you ought to examine your own motives before questioning mine.'

'For God's sake don't try pretending there's nothing going on between you and Jack Cinch, because I know there is.'

'Really, David,' she said feebly. 'You have a very fertile imagination.'

'Drop the façade, will you. You were seen together on the deck of his junk out at Gin Drinker's Bay about a month ago. One of my friends saw you. Oh, don't worry, I made him promise to keep it quiet. I've no intention of screwing your career.'

This time she knew she was trapped and her eyes fell to the desk, anger overcoming the tears which threatened.

'That was very noble of you, I'm sure,' she answered bitterly, suddenly hating everything about him.

But Becker was not finished yet.

'Leaving aside any personal involvement for the moment, doesn't it sound suspicious that Reicher was missing for three whole days and they never thought to report it! Roman tells me that Cinch just pretended he was still reporting in every day.'

At that moment Ruth did not quite know what to think. All she felt now was anger at his presumption in lecturing her. Instinctively she attempted to bolster Cinch's story.

'I've already told you, Reicher was out of control.'

'That's what they told you.' His voice was almost a sneer. 'What if the gentlemen up at the Consulate had him killed?'

'That's bloody ridiculous for a start.'

'Maybe,' countered Becker. 'But who's to know? If we were to take everything Jack Cinch tells you as gospel, we'd never find out.' There was a hardness about his face now, the planes of his cheeks like a granite surface. 'First they were lying, but now they're not, is

185

that it? They'd give Roman a fairy story, but not dearest darling Ruth – no, not Miss Tavistock. Well, I don't believe a word of it. I'm telling you, they've been running something very naughty in our own backyard. Something that got screwed up badly. Now they want our help to hide their blushes. If they won't share it, then it has to be something bad.'

'A trifle paranoiac, David.' She was attempting to dismiss his suspicions even before she fully understood them.'

He threw up his hands. 'God, I wish people wouldn't keep saying that stuff about paranoia.'

Ruth adjusted her cuffs, intent on appearing the one still in control.

'Look, if you have grounds for doubting the validity of the story given by the Regional Security Officer, you'd better let me hear them.'

'All right, try this. Yesterday afternoon I was discussing the situation with Lassiter. He's been with the State Department for five and a half years, knows just about everybody there is to know, but he's never heard of Reicher. Nor have any of his colleagues on the Secretary of State's detail. That made me suspicious, so I checked with the USIS library in Admiralty Centre. They have a register there of State Department employees worldwide. Surprise, surprise, Reicher wasn't on it.'

'That proves nothing. Those registers are usually out of date by the time they leave the printers.'

'All right, have it your own way for the moment. When I checked the diplomatic list I found that our man's had a diplomatic passport for the past ten years, and has been through most of the Asian missions at one time or another: economic adviser in Tokyo, information officer in Seoul, visa section in Ho Chi Minh City. If he was FBI, DEA or Customs and Immigration, it would have been there. Even Naval Intelligence officers have their positions announced as attaché roles. He's definitely not a State Department officer, so tell me who the hell else he could be working for?'

There was a momentum building in his argument, a rapid sifting of possibilities and the exercise of an intelligence officer's nose for a false legend. Ruth followed it, too, gradually awakening to his suspicions. She pushed back her chair and walked to the window, hugging herself against a sudden chill that made her shiver involuntarily. As she looked out across the grey yard and the pale blue stretch of harbour beyond, she was trying to work out what to believe – and who. She could still feel the pull of Jack's arms around her, but not so strongly now. She wondered vaguely whether that meant anything.

Becker waited for her thoughts to return to the room. At length she turned around, keeping her arms folded defensively.

'You think Reicher was a Company man.'

There was a certain quiet confidence about Becker's manner that made it all the more infuriating to her: an understated arrogance.

'That's what I think,' he said quietly. 'And so do you, if you're honest with yourself.'

'Not at all,' she continued, but her denial was unconvincing. 'It would be altogether too flimsy a cover for a CIA officer if anyone could spot him by casually leafing through a few US government publications.'

A frown cut deep into Becker's forehead.

'That's already occurred to me. But we're not talking about a general policy here. This is one man planted carelessly or in haste; one man who came unstuck, so now they want to cover up the mess. Spare me the bullshit about CIA being too clever for that. Look how many of their cock-ups have hit the newspapers in the past ten years. It's a mistake to assume any man is intelligent just because he works in intelligence.'

She wanted to say that none of this was true, could

187

not possibly be, because Jack had told her otherwise. Standing up straight and staring Becker in the face, pride made her cling to the belief that Jack had not lied to her. Reason told her that, if he had, she would surely have sensed it. With a perversity of imagination she began to consider whether she was the kind of person to be blinded to truth by her own feelings. If trust had been breached between them in this matter, then in what other ways might Jack Cinch have deceived her?

She would need time to herself to think that one through.

'It's ridiculously circumstantial, of course, but what if he was a Company man? What's to be gained by publicising a failure? Aren't you forgetting that we're allies? Aren't our aims ultimately the same?'

There was a bitterness about the way Becker laughed at that.

'Look, if the CIA is undertaking covert action in Hong Kong without informing us, then it's our duty to find out what the hell's going on. There are two things you can do to settle this. First, call the SIS station chief – what's his name?'

'Anthony Lethbridge.'

'Yes, call Lethbridge. Get him to run Reicher's details through their files in London. They should have a record of all CIA men in Asia.'

Becker would have done this himself but he knew Ruth had the only proper liaison channel below Assistant Directorate level.

'And the second thing?'

'Check with Operations and find out what joint ventures are currently under way between us and the Americans. If he was put in under State Department cover, then I'll guarantee they didn't declare Reicher to us at all.'

For the first time he felt Ruth was beginning to have her own doubts about Reicher. But, more than this, he sensed a certain fear about her – fear, perhaps, of what her investigations might turn up.

She spoke softly, as if with a great effort of self-will.

'All right, I'll speak to Lethbridge first thing tomorrow. We'll take it from there, one step at a time.'

'Fine,' he said, suddenly hating himself. She seemed so confused at that moment, just a shadow of her former fiery self: a ship with a broken rudder. Christ, he thought, she must have it bad for Jack Cinch. What made it worse was that he knew he had not even attempted to spare her feelings. He wished to God now that he had.

'Look, I'd better go,' he muttered and strode for the door. 'Perhaps you could give me a call if you hear anything further.'

'Of course,' she answered with something of a forced smile. 'That's my job, isn't it?'

For a moment he considered an olive branch. Why not have a drink together, maybe dinner? – something like that. But in the end he just stood awkwardly for the briefest moment, then walked quickly from the room.

Before he had reached the next office, he heard her feet crossing the floor and then the key turning in the lock.

ELEVEN

In the red glow bathing the *dai fong*, Joe Lai stood alone, head bowed respectfully before the Gwan-Dai. It was early morning and outside the sun was already burning away the mist that hung above Victoria Peak; yet inside the room remained dark. The blinds were still drawn from the night before, and at that particular moment Joe was in no mood to open them. The only light he needed now was the single red bulb burning in the alcove above the Gwan-Dai's head.

One by one, he pressed three smoking joss sticks into the soft sand of the urn, the smoke undulating like dragons' tails as it drifted up against the crimson visage of the warrior god. As the god stared back, the porcelain eyes seemed even more hooded than usual, the dark brow more deeply furrowed, and the flaring nostrils those of a charging steed.

Almost without realising, Joe began to recite the poem he had spoken as a child in thrilling games of heroes and demons:

'Gwan-Dai stands alone in robes of green and gold. Noblest of all heroes, he protects the House of Han. Protect and favour us now, Lord Gwan-Dai. Be thou implacable in judgement and swift to strike the enemy. And should the heroes fall in battle, guide their souls unhindered to eternal heaven.'

When the kettle was boiling, he lifted the lid of a terracotta teapot beside him and filled it to the brim, watching the dark leaves twist like fish within the water. Quietly he watched the plumes of steam rise, and after a minute more he took the pot and filled three porcelain cups with the thick red-brown liquid. The aroma was harsh to his nostrils, but he knew that was just as it should be. He placed one cup on either side of the incense burner and one in the middle: a balanced offering. Finally he took a dozen orange kumquats and laid them on a dish between the cups, arranged in a sort of pyramid.

The smell of the fruit was sharp and sweet, but it did nothing to uplift Joe's spirits. Solemnly he pressed his palms together and spoke a silent petition to the god of detectives.

He almost did not hear the door opening behind him.

'Is that you in there, Joe?' Tasker's eyes had not yet grown accustomed to the dark. The light spilled across the floor of the duty room in a broad wedge, but it did not reach the corner where the altar stood.

'It's me, *dai lo.*'

For a moment Joe stood rigid before the altar. Tasker, realising the importance of the ritual, remained quietly observing but saying nothing.

'I heard about the PTU constable,' said Tasker, when Joe finally turned around. 'Is this for him?'

'For him – and for the others. There are eight of them now: eight hungry ghosts. They'll need something to sustain them on their journey.'

Tasker pursed his lips in silence, examining the offerings on the altar table.

'What's in those cups?' he inquired at last.

Joe sounded very tired when he spoke, as if he had not slept in days.

'*Tit kuen yam*: Iron Goddess of Mercy – the bitterest of teas to take away the taste of death.'

Tasker did not know what to say to that. Sighing heavily, he crossed the floor and lit three joss sticks of his own, pressing them into the sand beside Joe's. 'A bad business all round,' he said eventually. 'The doctors say this one eventually succumbed to heart failure. That doesn't seem fair; not when he'd already survived a grenade blast.'

Joe fixed his gaze on Gwan-Dai's face, and said nothing.

'You look like you've been up all night,' commented Tasker.

'Just about. It was a useful meeting. I came in early to type up my source report.'

'I look forward to reading that,' replied Tasker enthusiastically. 'We're not but a few days into the investigation and already the Governor is looking for signs of progress. Comes of my having a reputation as a thief-taker. Not always helpful, that. I hope you got more from your informant than I got from those tight-arsed stewards at the Jockey Club. I'm assured everyone there is beyond reproach.'

'Don't worry, *dai lo*. I think you'll find what I have written very enlightening.'

The source report was everything Joe had promised. Seated at his desk, Tasker read the typewritten sheets with interest. To protect the informant's identity, his name had been replaced with a code number, which was cross-referenced to an entry in Lai's police notebook. Still, Tasker knew immediately by the quality of the information that it must have come from a top triad office-bearer.

By the time he had finished reading, he was wearing a very worried look.

'*Haam gar chan!*' he cursed softly. 'Do you realise what this means?'

'I think so,' said Joe, straightfaced. 'You'd have to be a fool not to realise that.'

For some reason Joe could not understand, Tasker needed to spell it out clearly.

'The Shatin robbery was an operation both sanctioned and procured by the San Yee On.'

'And if that wasn't enough,' added Joe with irony, 'one of their High Dragons is flying a fucking desk right here at Police Headquarters. I don't know what this is going to do to the constables' morale.'

Tasker shot him a glance.

'Never mind that, what worries me more is the possible compromise of long-term CID intelligence operations. The whole lot might be shot to pieces. Every single undercover man we have could be in danger.'

Picking up the phone, Tasker summoned S/Sgt Cheng to his office. Experience told the superintendent that he would need to act quickly to shore up their operational security. Cheng would be the one to coordinate that.

'Tell the *foh geis* to restrict their notebook entries to the bare minimum,' Tasker warned his station sergeant, 'going on duty, off duty, that sort of thing – and any queries from senior officers are to be referred directly to me.'

'*Ho ah!*' agreed Cheng.

'Joe, I want this thing sewn up so tight it squeaks.'

The detective lit a cigarette and sucked on it thoughtfully, a look of black amusement on his face.

'What's on your mind?' Tasker inquired.

'I was just wondering which of them it is – the spy I mean? Kwan, Lee – maybe its Yue Kwok-sum.'

'For the moment it's only speculation.'

'Yes, I know, but it makes you think: which of our illustrious leaders?' Joe mouthed the words with scorn. 'Certainly it will have to be reported. Police General Orders are very clear on allegations of corruption and on membership of a proscribed society.'

Suddenly Tasker's face grew very red, and a vein in his neck began to pulse.

'Stuff that! And risk losing this whole investigation to the bloody ICAC? I'll show my arse in China Products before I'd do that!'

In Hong Kong the Independent Commission Against Corruption was the Governor's much-vaunted public watchdog, which existed for the sole purpose of investigating corruption within the public service. Time and again, over the years, the police had found themselves targeted by this body – to the extent that any malicious complaint by a member of the public could easily lead to suspension and a full-scale enquiry. Understandably a degree of mistrust and suspicion had grown up between ICAC and the police, and often police attitudes reflected that. '*We're* going to do this ourselves,' continued Tasker, his determination now evident. 'There are ways of winkling this bugger out, but it's going to take time. It could be any of those buggers up there in Caine House – anybody above senior superintendent rank. That means twenty or more officers to choose from.'

'Not at all,' corrected Joe Lai. 'A High Dragon would have to be Chinese. The societies are becoming more progressive, but they still wouldn't trust a *gwai lo* to hold high office.'

'Yes, almost certainly a Chiu Chau,' added Cheng, following Joe's argument. 'That's if it *is* a San Yee On dragon.'

'All right, but that still involves at least a handful of suspects,' said Tasker doubtfully. 'Before we go screaming our heads off, let's just wait until we know who we're gunning for. Until then this information stays just between the three of us.'

'If that's the way you want it, *dai lo*.' This time it was Joe's turn to look doubtful. 'But I hope you know what you're doing. If things go wrong we could all end up in the shit.'

But Tasker wasn't at all ruffled. Far from it, he was actually enjoying this. And the knowledge that he was operating outside the rules made it that much sweeter.

'They gave me a free hand, don't you remember?' he said with a sly grin. 'And, as you Chinese say, the mountain is high and the Emperor is far away.'

'So how do you want to play things from here?'

The superintendent did not even need to think about that one: the answer was obvious.

'We focus on the society itself, making exclusive use of all undercover assets, and we zero in on the Shatin and Tai Po districts. See what Criminal Intelligence Bureau has on their current status, then set up an immediate debrief of anyone they have who is close enough to hear the whispers of the San Yee On office-bearers. Don't bugger around with small fry; they only end up wasting our time.'

'Right,' said Joe stubbing out his cigarette. 'I'll go see Sandy Buchanan and get that set up.'

CIB, the Criminal Intelligence Bureau, belonged to the Organised and Serious Crimes Group, and was its most jealously guarded jewel. It consisted of some sixty officers, headed by a senior superintendent, and was charged with the acquisition of intelligence on organised crime. In practice that generally meant triads, though there was always interest in the many foreign fraternities attempting to infiltrate the colony. A highly secretive unit, it was divided into two sections: the first responsible for obtaining information such as current strength, order of battle, planned operations and long-term aims; the second responsible for the often complex task of sifting and analysing raw and apparently unrelated items of intelligence.

But this was not simply another criminal records bureau – far from it. Their information would never be used in a court of law, being constructed out of hearsay and rumour – or else obtained by methods a court might wish to question. Drawing upon a network of informants and agents, and relying upon sophisticated methods of data collection, over the years they had amassed millions of computerised records on areas such as triad society membership, patterns of operation, areas of influence, and current feuds and alliances. They had literally thousands of individual dossiers on criminal targets ranging from street-level bookmakers to wholesale drug-exporters. But inevitably their best stuff was related to triad office-bearers, for that was their bread and butter – or, perhaps more appropriately, their rice bowl. In one of these computerised records you could find details of initiation and promotion dates, favourite restaurants, known associates, even down to who they were sleeping with these days.

The San Yee On was well known in CIB as potentially the most violent and dangerous of the societies operating inside the Colony. The 14K might be the most notorious, and the Wo Sing Wo one of the longest-established, but for sheer ambition and the speed of its expansion, the San Yee On took some beating. Ruthless and clannish, like all the ethnic Chiu Chau criminal groups, it had originated in the coastal fishing port of Swatow on the border between Kwangtung and Fukien province. In 1949, under cover of the great Chiu Chau refuge migration, its members had come swarming across the border, pushed by the onward sweep of Mao's victorious forces. At first, like all triads, they had worn the guise of a nationalist organisation, pledged to assist Chiang Kai Shek regain China for the Kuomintang. They called themselves the Yee On, a name of significance in Chiu Chau culture, and used the rituals of the old secret societies, the patriotism and mystique of the Shao Lin temple, to sow fear in their enemies and bind themselves together. Even now they still claimed to represent Old China in an outcrop of land which had been stolen by the *gwai lo*.

But they had not been tolerated for long. In the Fifties, Special Branch soon grew tired of the bitter infighting of these political, and increasingly criminal, groups on what was now British sovereign territory. They were known to be subversive – even terrorist – groups who funded themselves through extortion practised on the local population. SB cracked down hard, declaring them proscribed organisations, and deporting many of their leading lights to Taiwan. After that the Yee On Commercial and Industrial Guild went underground, emerging as a full-blown triad society with the name San Yee On, meaning the new Yee On. It was no longer a nationalist organisation, but a leaner, more sinister animal. Its avowed intention being the forging of a powerful criminal fraternity that would capture, through extreme violence, the most lucrative slices of Hong Kong crime: extortion, gambling, vice, racketeering and, of course, drug-trafficking.

The computer files at the Criminal Intelligence Bureau told the whole story of their sudden growth: their meteoric rise to prominence throughout the Seventies and early Eighties. After being one of the also-rans of the Fifties, there had been an explosion in recruitment. CIB reckoned there were now over six hundred office-bearers and in excess of thirty thousand soldiers: a force equal to the size of the Royal Hong Kong Police! With that burgeoning membership came power – power that had gained for them a stranglehold on the Yau-Tsim kui, the glitzy, high-rent tourist and commercial districts of Tsim Sha Tsui and Yaumatei. That was an Aladdin's cave where swanky nightclubs, restaurants and international hotels competed for a constant flow of disposable income.

Joe Lai made his request for close surveillance of the top five San Yee On targets direct to Superintendent Sandy Buchanan, the officer in charge of CIB operations. Buchanan was a bellicose Glaswegian whose corned-beef cheeks bore the marks of a life's devotion to Scotch whisky. Though in his youth he had once been a sprinter of some renown, looking at the huge stomach and sunken backside you would certainly never have guessed it. You could even say that the eighteen years he had spent behind a desk had taken their toll upon his body, but that would be to dismiss the man unfairly. As a police officer he had forgotten more about the collection and analysis of data than most other detectives had ever learned. There seemed to be almost nothing that went on in the colony's underworld that he did not know about before it even happened.

'On whose say so?' he demanded in that most belligerent tone he customarily used. Whether speaking in English or Cantonese, he retained the same unfathomable Scottish accent.

When Joe Lai showed him the Deputy Director of Crime's authorisation Buchanan nodded grudgingly, the cigar-stained corners of his moustache turning down.

'Aye, I reckon that'll do. Though, if you ask me, you're wasting time. You should be looking north of the border at those bloody Big Circle Gang people. What did you have in mind: shadows and ears?'

'Sorry, Sandy, it's going to have to be everything.'

'You mean the cars and telephones as well?' At this Buchanan took the cigar out of his mouth. 'Dear God, man! You don't want much, do you?'

'We need to know what the new patterns of communication are between them, so we'll also need a frequency analysis for calls from every telephone number at those target addresses. That might tell us who's been doing the leg work between the inner council and the Big Circle boys. Say, the last six months' phone bills. That should give us a rough idea of who the planners were.'

'That's at least a dozen lines to start with, plus another half dozen portaphone units.'

'Yes, I appreciate the work involved, but we've just got to have it. The whole of the fifth floor is waiting for results on this. I also need an update on San Yee On activity in eastern NT.'

Buchanan cast his eyes over the authorisation once again, and he groaned.

'If you hang on twenty minutes I'll put the whole bloody thing to music.'

'Cheers, mate.' Joe grinned back at him, remembering past times when he had misunderstood the superintendent's deadpan delivery. *Gwai lo* humour was a strange animal, he told himself, particularly in the mouth of a Scot.

Twenty minutes later there was still no music, but there was a detailed breakdown of San Yee On officials known to have visited the town of Tai Po in the two weeks immediately prior to the Jockey Club robbery. It amounted to quite a gathering of top men, most of whom normally stayed south of the Lion Rock Tunnel, well within the confines of Kowloon's Golden Mile.

'We can give you a full analysis of your targets' movements and contacts, if you give us a couple more days.'

'Why the delay?' Joe Lai wanted to know.

'The computer terminals are pretty tied up with data captured from the raid we did at Forsythe and Lowe.' Sandy Buchanan could not resist a small gloat. The second-string law firm of Forsythe and Lowe had offices in the Exchange Square complex in Central district, and had long been suspected of links to the San Yee On. Their preference for defending cases prosecuted against Chiu Chau villains was suspicious in itself, but nobody had suspected the full extent of their involvement with the triad. Getting a judge to agree to a raid on the premises had been nearly impossible, but when the warrant was finally obtained the wealth of documentation found there fully justified police suspicions. In addition to records of dubious financial transactions, Forsythe and Lowe's computer had also contained a partial database of San Yee On membership records. Not a full one, of course, but enough to be of inestimable use. It seemed even an organisation as traditionally minded as the San Yee On had gone for the silicon chip in a big way. In the officers' mess they were saying that the technical operator who found it had let out such a whoop that the detectives present had flipped and drawn their pistols in terror.

'That must be worth a commendation, isn't it?' said Joe, stroking the other man's ego.

'Yes, but not for myself. All credit to the operator who checked their computers for deleted data. You see, the stuff was on a PC, and one of the clerks must have deleted all the files while we were still kicking the door down. Stupid bastard did not know enough about the operating system to realise that the disk directories could be recreated and the files recovered, using any one of half a dozen data-recovery utilities.'

'Strange him not knowing that,' said Joe, equally baffled. Then he grinned, his eyes turning to dark slits. 'What's a bloody PC, anyway?'

'Aye, you're learning,' observed Sandy as he caught the irony. 'We'll mak a guid Scot o' ye yet!'

While still on the man's good side, Joe turned to the most important part of his request.

'Look, Sandy, I have to tell you I've also been authorised for emergency access to our Cancer Cell in Tai Po.'

Sandy Buchanan looked suddenly grave. Taking the cigar from his mouth again, he spat a flake of tobacco on to the floor.

'Is that another little idea backed up by the DD Crime?'

'It is.'

'Dear God, I hope you know what you're doing, Joe.' Buchanan pointed the cigar at him for emphasis. 'You disturb his cover once too often and it'll kill him just as sure as any bullet.'

It was a thought which had already occurred to Joe Lai. The warning merely underlined his own fears.

The Cancer Cells were a CIB facility: agents infiltrated inside the triad societies over many years, for the purpose of destroying them from within. They were all volunteers, young men carefully selected from recruit constables at Police Training School to undertake this dangerous role. CIB were looking for very special young men: they had to be intelligent, independent and emotionally stable enough to carry out the job without being lured into the triad fold. Those who agreed knew they would be outcasts, shunned by all but a handful of police officers who knew their true purpose. Some were quietly kicked out of PTS on a pretext, others were interviewed but never hired. All of them endured great loss of face amongst families and friends. And within the societies they faced certain death if they were ever discovered.

'I don't like it, Joe,' protested Buchanan. 'Those cells are under my direct control. I'm responsible for their debriefs and for their protection. I know every one of those lads, and they trust me. I'd be betraying that trust if I didn't ...'

'I'm sorry,' interrupted Joe, pointing again to the authorisation, 'but Tasker has the full backing of Government House for anything he wants to try. We need access to this asset – that's all there is to it.'

Buchanan fidgeted in frustration.

'Government House, eh?' he sneered, balling up his fist. 'Well, just you tell Tasker from me, if he screws this up, the pair of you better find a nice quiet safe-house, because I'll surely have your guts for violin strings.'

Back at his desk, Joe Lai studied the CIB report. It was better than he had expected. There had been frequent visits to Tai Po by high-level targets, but they had all been centred around a tiny squatter village on the Tin Kok Road, called Kwong Tau Shan. That intrigued him. Kwong Tau Shan was really nothing more than a collection of fishermen's wooden shanty shacks located about a mile and a half along the bay from the town of Tai Po. It had no special significance except for the thriving *dai dong*, or illegal casino, there which Shatin district anti-gambling squad had never managed to crack. Why, he wondered, should *it* attract such attention from the lodge grandfathers? That was a question only Philip himself would be able to answer.

As he came to the end of the report and turned the page, Joe's eyes widened in triumph. The last insert was a small strip of teleprinter paper which had been torn off and inserted into the file as an appendix. He had to read the message twice to be sure he had read it right.

Reported by Immigration Department (Kai Tak): Targets 12883, 8744 and 11072 departed Hong Kong at 1220 hrs on Sunday 15th September by CAAC 005 for Guangzhou. All returned by CAAC 011 at 10.50 hrs the following day.

Coming the very next day after the Shatin hit, Joe Lai was sure it was linked to the robbery.

And it had to be more than just mere coincidence that target 8744 was also the resident operator of the Kwong Tau Shan *dai dong*.

While the television in his bedroom plays a favourite video of Japanese cartoons, Gwan-Dai locks the door and turns up the volume to drown out the snoring of his aged mother in the room beyond. Glancing back at the screen, he sees robots waging war far out in space; sparks fly from their metal fingers – the way they sometimes do from his own, when it rains.

It is early evening on his one day off and, thankfully, there is no need to go to work. Silently, he removes his clothes and kneels beside the rubber sheet – aware of his nakedness, and of hers. He has spent an anxious after-

noon walking the streets, with the incessant bleat of traffic horns in his ears. He was buying film, carefully choosing a new filter for his camera, but the one thing on his mind has been the dead girl hidden like buried treasure beneath his bed. Nothing else seeming to exist. Finally he is home again and the bedroom door is locked. His treasure lies before him now, as naked as himself, but her flesh is pale and cold where his is hot. He reminds himself that this is the same costume-painted whore he found selling her sex last night from a darkened doorway down on Temple Street. He recalls his excitement as he watched her pick up a client and hail his cab for the short trip to a nearby motel. Then how he had waited outside to take her home.

She had seemed very tired – though not too tired to fight for her life. They were never too tired for that. This one had fought like a tiger. Such strength for one so slight. Strength inspired by terror. The hot sting of her pleading tears remained with him even now, as did the struggling of her body as she fought desperately against the wire.

Remembering those tears, his hand describes the flattened contours of those lifeless breasts. Flesh once capable of inspiring evil in men's hearts. Filled with loathing, he raises her legs to part them and the knees sound like a pop-gun. He enters her roughly, and her jaw jumps to one side with the force of it. The cold kiss of her sex makes him shudder at first, but it is a feeling he has come so much to enjoy. A moment later he is working to a frenzy, his pelvis thrusting back and forth as he tries to reconjure the pitch of her dying screams – the twist of her mouth and the flare of her nostrils. The flames burn only briefly, but there is satisfaction in knowing he has claimed her – in Gwan-Dai's name.

Suddenly he is aware of the dark eyes staring up at him, and his loathing is now turned inwards. He wants to cry, but no tears will come. Now he feels her plundered limbs mocking him, from the broken fingernails to the neat appendix scar on her belly. The shadows on her face mould the black-lipped mouth into a bitter sneer. She is exultant, haughty, vindicated. She wears the look of one who knows this moment was inevitable. As if it was she who had planned it, and not he. This is the measure of her evil intent.

Now he decides to cut her.

Angrily he selects a sterilised scalpel – cuts out her eyes. Freed from her terrible gaze, there is no stopping him. With Gwan-Dai to guide him there is nothing he cannot do.

The honed edge is an artist's brush between his fingers. He is mesmerised by the granular feel of grey fat deposits beneath her skin. What the books he has studied call 'subcutaneous'. Fascinated, he delves further into the mysteries, just as he once dismantled his father's broken pocket watch, lured on by the glint of gilded cogs and springs.

In the intervening years he has sharpened his skills. He has learned to catch stray cats and strangle them before they can make a sound. He has worked with a wire. Making the switch proved easier than expected – stray cats and stray women having much in common. But there had been help from an unexpected quarter and even now he can still remember the first time he heard the rain-voices talking to him.

'Her blood is for Gwan-Dai,' he explains, glaring into the TV screen. 'This woman's body was a temple inhabited by evil. I have silenced the devils and claimed it back in Gwan-Dai's name.'

As soon as the moon disappeared behind a cloud, Chan Chi-fai stepped around the side of the wooden hut, unzipped his greasy denim cut-offs and urinated into the bushes, sighing with obvious pleasure while his brother kept watch upon the road. He had been standing guard over the *dai dong* for the past four hours, smoking continuously and taking occasional pulls from a bottle of San Miguel beer. Now it was just after two in the morning, and as usual he was bored. As he zipped up his shorts, he stared around at the sheer rockface which reared up behind the village, black and imposing against a vast star-filled sky. Suddenly a noise made him start. It was a sound like the scurrying of a small animal somewhere on a ledge high up in the rock. He listened hard for a moment, but then it was gone.

Cursing softly in the harsh Chiu Chau dialect, he returned to his post and settled down upon a stool in front of the hut.

Within the village they called him *Juk Sair* – the Bamboo Snake – a name awarded him by the brotherhood of the San Yee On, and tonight, as always, he and his younger brother sat outside their wooden hut at the top of the main stone staircase leading into the village of Kwong Tau Shan. The night was unusually oppressive, the smell from the sewer pipes leading down to the beach particularly pungent, as they sat there in sweat-stained vest and shorts, swapping stories of sexual conquest and enjoying the breeze off the water. The glowing red tips of two cigarettes were the only visible light.

The job they had been assigned was simple: to remain at this post and make sure the Vice Squad did not get close enough to raid the casino now in full swing at the rear of the village. What made the job easier was the fact that there was only one road leading to Kwong Tau Shan. The Tin Kok Road snaked around the bay out of Tai Po towards Plover Cove, and at this time of night it was always dark and deserted, so that the lights of any Vice Squad vehicles would be seen lighting up the sky well over a mile away as they swung around the bay. Because of this, the police had never managed a surprise raid, and the casino flourished – one of the safest illegal gambling establishments in the territory. Besides this, the Bamboo Snake knew every one of the Vice Squad cars by sight, and the instant he saw one he would push the plunger of the pneumatic rape alarm he kept by his feet. One burst from that horn and any evidence of gambling would immediately vanish away into the surrounding wooden huts in a well-rehearsed routine.

'How many big-money men in tonight?' muttered the Bamboo Snake, sauntering over to the top of the stone stairway to count the Mercedes and BMW vehicles squeezed into the tiny bus bay at the foot of the steps.

'Maybe two dozen or more. I reckon they'll drop half a million between them tonight.'

In the darkness the Bamboo Snake tossed his hair.

'By the look of those fucking wheels down there, I'd say they could all easily afford it.'

At times like this it seemed clear why they had given him his nickname, for the Bamboo Snake possessed glittering black eyes that never seemed to blink; a broad mouth and poke-hole nostrils completed the air of reptilian menace. But in fact this was not the real reason. The multicoloured snake tattoo which wound its body around his left leg was the true reason; the creature's head was poised to strike up on his thigh; its tail coiled provocatively out from his groin, suggesting the power of his manhood.

Like his younger brother, the Bamboo Snake was a *sei gau jai*, a forty-niner: one of the lowest-grade foot soldiers of the San Yee On triad society, who were usually given only menial tasks to perform. Secretly, however, he harboured a burning ambition to one day amass a following of his own soldiers, and to extract protection money from each of them. But first he would need to win promotion, and the blessing and permission of his own protector.

Within the organisation every rank had its own two- or three-digit number which commemorated some mystical aspect of triad culture. Foot soldiers and new initiates were called '49 members' because of thirty-six solemn oaths they had to swear as part of the initiation ceremony: $4 \times 9 = 36$. The higher officials, allowed to maintain a personal following of *ma jai*, were those with the designations of Grass Sandal (415), Red Cudgel (426), and White Paper Fan (432). Each had a well-defined role in the hierarchy: Grass Sandal handled logistics and hospitality; White Paper Fan was the financial director; and Red Cudgel, as the most formidable fighter and tactician, was responsible for marshalling the forces in battle.

At eighteen years of age, already the Bamboo Snake was known for his Snake Bite: the deadly kick he had developed in close-quarter fighting. It was an explosion of power that came from nowhere and slipped effortlessly beneath the leading elbow of his opponent's guard, to crush his ribs. Many fighters had heard of it, and not a few had come to fear him. That was vital, he knew, if he ever hoped to reach 426 rank; for fame and reputation brought followers, and the more followers a man collected, the more his power within the organisation would grow.

As he sucked hard upon his cigarette, the red tip illuminating his sunken cheeks, the Bamboo Snake tried to put aside such ambitious thoughts and instead concentrate upon the broad sweep of the Tin Kok Road. Beyond the road lay the blackness of the Tolo Channel, and he watched the orange lights of the Tanka fishing boats move listlessly across the water. In the grass at the water's edge the cicadas chirped soothingly, reminding him how tired he was after four hours of watching. Beneath the rockface the wooden huts lay in darkness, the villagers all asleep. But the village was far from silent.

Outside hut sixteen, under a canvas awning, the regular knot of Chinese gamblers all wore gold chains and designer silk shirts. And each time the black tiles clattered upon the polished table top, a cheer of delight rose up into the night. There, in the stark, brilliant glow of two hurricane lamps – for the village was without electrical supply – the big-money-men, 'the men with huge testicles', were playing *pai kau* with no holds barred: Chinese dominoes at ten thousand bucks a hand. With each new round, the dealer expertly shuffled and stacked the tiles in a single black cake, slicing off a slab of four to each of the four major players. Those with less skill, money or nerve laid bets in support of one or other of the players, while the banker sat back and cut a steady percentage of each pot.

It was all very safe and very civilised, and each of the businessmen present knew he was under the Society's most excellent protection. They were all of them *yau chin lo*, rich men: entrepreneurs with one foot in the underworld and a personal introduction to White Paper Fan, the keeper of the *dai dong*. While the wads of yellow notes fluttered back and forth across the table, there was much hawking and spitting and the air was thick with cigarette smoke and squealed obscenities.

Behind the dealer, flanked by several 'forty-niners', the White Paper Fan himself sat quietly watching the proceedings. He was a man in his late thirties, studious and well groomed, with a tie of patterned silk and a shiny suit of silver and black sharkskin which gave him the look of a successful company lawyer. Each time the black tiles turned, his eyes quickly assessed the spots, observing looks of elation and despair, letting the curses wash over him with indifference. Immune to such casual emotions, he smoked constantly, only breaking his calm silence to permit credit or settle a dispute with either a nod or a flick of the hand. To his right sat a man much younger, early twenties with punch-permed hair and a neatly trimmed moustache, which he stroked repeatedly as he calculated the odds; the rolled-back sleeves of his white sports jacket were vaguely reminiscent of a Japanese pop singer he had once admired and now copied.

'Let's make this next round for twenty thousand,'

roared the winner of the last game, flushed with his success. He was a dumpy individual with sagging cheeks, who wore a huge ring of dark green jade on his middle finger. Before each game he would wipe the sweat from his palms on a towel he kept upon his knee. Then he would begin to stroke the tiles, his ring clicking irritatingly against them, perhaps hoping to thus out-psyche the other players. 'I feel the god Wong Tai Sin himself sitting right here on my shoulder! Any of you losers want to challenge me?'

The White Paper Fan glanced at the young man lounging in the chair by his side, and he smiled thinly.

'Look here, Ah Sin,' he said for all to hear. 'Fat Boy Fok has fortune on his side tonight, *ha m' hai ah*?'

'*Hai a!*' agreed Ah Sin with a flicker of menace in his eyes, enjoying the sudden look of discomfort now on Fat Boy Fok's chubby face. 'Perhaps we should increase the payment due from him next month; his club must be doing better than we thought.'

Fat Boy Fok grinned nervously, unsure whether to join in the joke or not. Instead, for a moment he silently fidgeted with the jade ring on his finger; then, feeling the eyes of the other gamblers upon him, he determined to try to save his face.

'Before you talk about more tea money, first keep the police away from our doors. Twice this week the detectives of *Kuen Wong* have disturbed my guests: putting pressure on my people to find those Shatin robbers. That's very bad for business.'

Ordinarily the White Paper Fan would have been disposed to punish such disrespect but, seeing nods of agreement pass between the other gamblers, he decided to answer this challenge more diplomatically.

'You have all suffered police harassment; the Society understands that, but I assure you it is nothing serious: *sap sap sui*. It is all a mere show for the Governor's benefit. Believe me, when their detectives realise they have no chance of catching those robbers, they will cease snatching after ghosts and all will return to normal.'

Emboldened by the success of Fat Boy Fok, a second gambler joined the fray: an older man with a lucky mole on his cheek from which erupted a wisp of dark hair.

'All well to say that, White Paper Fan, but we *were* promised protection. You assured us that your control over the police was absolute; now we see it is not. Must we in future look to the patronage of the 14K?'

The triad's response was measured but immediate. Laying both hands carefully upon the table he speared the old man with his gaze.

'I would not do so if I were you. At your age major changes tend to upset the body's equilibrium. The result could be harmful to your health.'

The old man had heard such veiled threats many times before, and he realised the danger in crossing these men. But he had always gained a perverse kind of pleasure in baiting the triads, so he could not help but push just a little further.

'It's true, an old man may die of many things,' he murmured. 'Yet it is also said that the 14K provides excellent health insurance.'

'If you think that,' demanded the White Paper Fan, 'then why not take your money to a 14K casino?'

'That's easy,' interrupted Fat Boy Fok, again growing in confidence. 'Their casinos are unsafe. And this one has never been raided.'

'How long will that be true, I wonder,' grunted the old man in disgust. 'With all this robbery business, and Crime Squad detectives turning everyone over, I tell you nowhere is safe. Nowhere.'

By now White Paper Fan had heard enough, and he silenced the discussion by ordering the dealer to cut the black cake and begin a new game. As the gamblers laid down their money and picked up the tiles, the triad reflected again on the rumours of the past three days. He had heard much whispered speculation about John Tasker's team, and the threat now posed to San Yee On authority by this one crazy *gwai lo*. Even the most decrepit old man in his casino felt free to speak his mind without fear of retribution. If things had come to this, then it was a situation to be corrected immediately – with an object lesson to restore confidence in the Society.

Red Cudgel would know what should be done.

Masking his concern with a false enthusiasm, he began to urge on each gambler in turn.

'Come along, Fat Boy Fok, put up some cash or forfeit your seat. You know the rules: no money, no talk.'

On the periphery of the game, the young fighters continued to move in and out like barracuda, watching the hand signals of White Paper Fan. Ready, as always, to step in.

Out in the bay, Tasker counted them off through the lenses of a powerful pair of binoculars. He was a hundred metres off shore, standing in the bow of a commandeered fishing boat which showed no lights. Soon he spoke into his packset radio.

'I make it twenty-five, what about you?'

'Confirmed. Only about a dozen fighters. The rest will make a run for it as soon as we move in.'

Joe Lai and four detectives were lying in the grass on the hillside behind the village, harnesses buckled and ropes fed through the karabiner, looking down from the sheer sixty-foot rockface that protected the rear approach to the casino. A birds-eye view of hut sixteen which lay close beside the rock face.

'Standby, then.' Tasker turned and gave the signal to Tiger Cheng, who was crouching in the stern with three other men. They paddled in rapidly, striking barely a ripple from the water's surface.

'Maintain positions, Joe. Don't make a move until you see us up on the road. *Ming baak mei?*'

'*Ming baak!*'

As soon as the boat grated on to sand, the detectives sprang forward and started running hell-for-leather across the road for the stone staircase. As if in a dream, the Bamboo Snake caught their silhouetted movements flitting across the paleness of the road surface and he fumbled unsuccessfully for the alarm canister. The next moment he screamed out a warning: '*Jau! Jau! Chai lo!* Run, run – Police!'

Bolstering his nerve with a strangled obscenity, he rose from the stool to meet the first detective rushing up the stone steps. Checking his step, he gave a queer sideways skip and his leg shot out, skewering the detective in his mid-section. Crumpling sideways off the staircase, the cop hit the banking and rolled back down into the drainage ditch beside the road. Glancing quickly to one side, the Bamboo Snake saw his brother come forward, swinging a rice flail in a figure of eight. The second man up the staircase was bigger than the first, and, when the Bamboo Snake tried a second kick, this time Tiger Cheng caught the leg between the armoured vice of his two wrists and pivoted in a tight arc, launching the triad out into the darkness like an Olympic hammer.

When the first shriek came, Joe Lai had already given his own men the signal. Five ropes spewed over the edge of the rockface and five men sailed after them. They fell rapidly, clearing the distance in three easy kicks against the rock-face. As he came down, Joe saw the silhouetted gamblers start up in terror and begin to grab back their table money. Unclipping the karabiners Joe's men ran towards the harsh glare of the hurricane lamps, aware of the giant leaping shadows moving across the walls of the wooden huts. Joe reached hut sixteen just seconds before Cheng, both men shouted in the same breathless instant: '*Mo yuk, chai yan!* Don't move, it's the police!'

The disintegration was instantaneous. The table was upended, sending hurricane lamps, tiles, and glasses of brandy in every direction. As the police moved in, a patch of burning spirit erupted across the concrete path. The gamblers were the first to scatter through the warren of narrow passages that ran between the lines of huts. But the police had no real interest in them; instead they moved to encircle the group of gang fighters who had formed a defensive wall around the senior triad officials. Nobody moved at first, but when Cheng seized the first fighter his hand could reach and slammed him against the side of a hut, the triad force leapt into the attack.

A mêlée errupted in the space between two wooden huts, their walls literally shaking as bodies crashed into them. In the darkness it was hard to tell who was who. Each time Joe Lai caught a glimpse of an unknown face, he struck out hard against its throat and watched the body fall. Then, within the chaos and violence, someone reached beneath a shirt to produce a blade. It slipped easily into the gang fighter's hand, and before Joe could anticipate the attack, the triad had fetched him a slashing cut across the face. Detecting the assault too late to evade it, Joe twisted away in anticipation and raised his left arm in a defensive reflex. The blade connected with his bare forearm, peeling back the skin like the flesh of a ripe mango.

Then he saw it: ten inches of surgical steel with a serrated edge that glistened with his blood. There was no immediate pain, only the sudden intense nausea he always experienced whenever he saw his own blood. Then there was rage. All control lost, Joe feinted a finger jab to the fighter's eye, and when the man moved to protect his sight Joe lashed out with a crutch kick that lifted him clean off his feet, following up with a back-hand swipe that slammed the fighter's head into a wooden upright.

The blade hit the ground with a dull ringing sound. The triad scrambled in his agony to reach for the weapon but the next sound he heard was the cocking of Joe Lai's detective special. Glancing up, he saw his own death mirrored in the policeman's eyes.

'Leave it,' snarled Joe, pushing the barrel into the man's cheek, 'or follow your ancestors.'

In an instant the milling crowd was still.

'Everybody over against the wall. Move!'

As the fighters reluctantly complied, Joe breathed a covert sigh of relief. It was over before it had really begun, and he was glad of that.

A voice from the shadows broke the tension. 'OK, Cheng, let's kick arses and take some names.'

John Tasker appeared, walking casually along the cement path as if he was out for an evening stroll. He glanced at the line of triad soldiers now spreadeagled against the side of one hut, and he nodded his approval.

'Nice work, lads. You all right, Joe?'

'*Mo man tai.* No problem,' he answered automatically. Reholstering his weapon, he grabbed the back of his attacker's T-shirt, ripping it off to wrap up his injured forearm.

As the search commenced, a selection of choppers and beef-knives clattered on to the cement floor.

'Really, boys,' Tasker mocked, 'don't you know it's dangerous to play with knives?'

The man in the sharkskin suit and the one who looked like a Japanese pop-star at his side had not moved an inch during the mêlée, knowing resistance at this point was useless, but unable to restrain the more impetuous of their *ma jai* in time.

'Superintendent Tasker,' he began in Hong Kong accented English; he had immediately recognised the officer. 'There appears to be some misunderstanding. I hope you didn't expect to find an unlawful casino here. That would be an unfortunate mistake. I trust you have the necessary authorisation.'

His delivery all seemed terribly well rehearsed; like

the pre-arranged drill which had already vanished the tiles, markers and table money.

The superintendent approached the table and hauled up the grinning triad boss by his shiny lapels. He spoke in rapid fluent Cantonese for all the triad soldiers to hear.

'Don't smart-mouth me, you worthless piece of shit.'

Forced to react now by this blatant loss of face, the White Paper Fan's eyes filled with fire.

'Our Society has given face to you in the past, policeman, just for the sake of appearances, but you don't know how to give face in return. You push too far, *gwai lo*. You upset the natural order, and it can only mean trouble for you.'

At this Tasker slapped the triad's face sharply twice, drawing a thin trickle of blood from the man's lip. There was an immediate intake of breath from the other triad prisoners. Then the superintendent pressed an index finger hard against the man's nose, squashing it almost flat against his face, and completing the ritual insult. Even Joe Lai winced at this. He knew what Tasker was doing, deliberately challenging the reputation of the Society, but to him the finger on the nose seemed way over the top.

'Don't start that fucking triad mumbo-jumbo with me! I don't care if you're the lead soprano with the Vienna Boys' Choir, you're coming with us. And if you try anything funny – anything at all – I'll drop you like an empty cigarette packet. Clear?'

Silent, burning rage was the initial response.

'*Ming baak mei?*' Tasker demanded. 'You understand?'

'*Ming baak.*' It was spoken quietly, grudgingly.

The White Paper Fan said no more. This *gwai lo*, he concluded, was dangerous. His behaviour was so totally, ridiculously unsophisticated that something would have to be done about him – and soon.

After Tasker's men arrested the White Paper Fan and his *ma jai* with the rolled sleeves, they were led away to

215

the stone steps where a police transit from Tai Po police station was now in position. Inside the vehicle the Bamboo Snake was already sitting handcuffed between two constables, cuts and bruises on his face and down the side of one bare leg.

White Paper Fan glanced back at Tasker and this time spoke with calculated respect.

'I trust we shall be allowed to summon a solicitor?'

'Eventually,' muttered Tasker darkly. 'But first let's talk about dead policemen. After that we can talk about day-trips into China. I hear you're the man who knows about that.'

The nightshift uniforms were just back for their *siu ye* break when Tasker's team arrived in Tai Po divisional station and took over all three of the interview rooms. The shift commander, a very young one-pip *bong baan* who clutched a clipboard self-importantly, recognised Tasker at once, so gave him the run of the station.

Inside interview room number one, the White Paper Fan sat quietly watching through the window as uniforms buzzed back and forth in the report room. He was unconcerned by what was going on around him, knowing it was only a matter of time before a lawyer would appear to demand his release. Lodge headquarters were pretty hot on that point: top-class legal representation in all court cases.

John Tasker and Joe Lai were holding an impromptu conference at a vacant interpreter's desk in the back of the report room, well out of hearing range of the uniform men. Joe Lai sucked on a soft drink carton which had been pressed on him by the duty officer.

'Jesus, how can you drink that stuff?' Soya-bean milk was one thing Tasker had never developed a taste for.

'Full of protein,' said Joe Lai, inspecting the sterile dressing on his arm. 'Stops my face from turning pink.'

The arm hurt like hell.

216

He looked across at the Chinese face behind the window of the first interview room. 'What do you suppose he's thinking now?'

'Just what I want him to think: that he's been rousted by a crazy *gwai lo* who doesn't have a shred of evidence but has high hopes. Where's Philip?'

'Third interview room down. I told Tiger to rough him up a bit. Do you want me to sweat the big man?'

'I'd better do it myself. We wouldn't like him to think he wasn't the main target, would we? Might as well start now.'

The instant they were through the door, the triad started in with his own questions: the kind of questions intended to rattle a less experienced officer.

'I think you ought to tell me exactly what this is about. My lawyer will be pushing for wrongful arrest as soon as he gets here.' Joe Lai sensed uncertainty in the triad's voice. He was tired and out of his element; the voice was thin and cracked, lacking conviction.

Tasker gave him the once over and shook his head, unimpressed.

'Save it, son. I could think of a dozen or more things to charge you on – that's before I even start planting stuff. Suspicion of keeping an unlawful gambling establishment; suspicion of MOTS; suspicion of conspiracy to commit armed robbery; and suspicion of getting right up my nose. Take your pick.'

The White Paper Fan sneered, 'We both know you have no evidence. Our lawyers would walk all over you in court.'

'Maybe so, but once charged I could tie you up in knots; get you remanded in custody for weeks pending trial. I'd enjoy that.'

This seemed to have more of an effect.

'*Yau mo gau choh!* That's ridiculous! This bust is bull-shit. That Shatin robbery must have made you crazy or something. Now you're just shaking the tree to see what falls out!'

But the triad official knew that what Tasker threatened was perfectly possible. The way the court calendars were running these days, he might be off the street for months. The White Paper Fan considered his position carefully. If Tasker was willing to risk being kicked off the force, or even going to prison for fixing up evidence, then obviously he meant business.

'All right, if it's just a talk you want, let's talk.'

'Good. Start by telling me everything you know about the robbery at Shatin Racecourse on 14 September.'

'What do I look like: a fortune-teller?' The man looked away as if he had decided not to speak – then changed his mind. 'I know as much as the papers tell me.' He shrugged, and attempted to smooth creases from the rumpled sharkskin jacket. 'Looks like another Big Circle job. They're a vicious bunch those *Dai Huen Jai.* Shame about the policemen.'

'Save the sentiment!' snapped Tasker, taking the chair directly opposite the prisoner. 'What about your trip to Canton on 15 September?'

There was a second or so of hesitation during which Tasker guessed he was making up his mind whether to bother denying it. But ultimately he must have realised they could verify his movements with immigration, because he decided to play along.

'Let me see, now. Ah, yes, I remember.'

'Was it business or pleasure?'

'Both. I visited a member of my family. My uncle has a metalwork shop; he makes kitchen implements – that sort of thing. We're hoping to export to Australia. It's potentially a very big market, you know.'

'Save it,' said Joe Lai sarcastically. 'We know exactly what the San Yee On wants to export to Australia: about a ton and a half of white powder every quarter.'

Without waiting for a reply, Tasker fired his next question.

218

'I understand the other gentlemen we arrested went along with you. Why was that?'

'They work for me. I had something very valuable to deliver, and I needed protection. One can't be too careful up there with all those *Dai Huen Jai* around.'

'What was it you had to deliver?' persisted Tasker.

'Moon cakes,' answered the White Paper Fan, stifling a smirk. 'It'll soon be the mid-autumn Festival. That wouldn't be the same without them.'

Behind him Tasker heard Joe swear softly under his breath. He tried a different tack.

'It's my belief you actually met with officers of a unit called Division 17. You know them?'

'A rock band, perhaps? I'm a businessman, Mr Tasker. I don't get much time to listen to music. Being a traditionalist, Chinese opera's more my thing.'

Both policemen sensed the triad was beginning to warm to this verbal pingpong.

'You know who they are: soldiers of the People's Liberation Army. Commandos. I'd say you could tell me quite a lot about those gentlemen if you had the mind to.'

'Then you'd be wrong.'

Without warning Tasker banged his fist hard on the table. The triad flinched in surprise, wondering what the *gwai lo* would do next. Tasker's eyes bulged with exasperation.

'You know we never give up on cop killers – or those involved with them.' Slowly he extended one finger in warning. 'I'm going to have you, you piece of scum. You and all your kind. The next time you lot meet to dress up in those red hankies of yours, tell your bosses this: until I get the Shatin robbers I'm going to be on the San Yee On's case night and day.'

From the look on the *gwai lo*'s face White Paper Fan had no reason to doubt his word.

* * *

It was another hour before they turned their attention to the two remaining prisoners. It could have been sooner, but the crack about the moon cakes had really got under Tasker's skin. When finally he beckoned Joe and strode from the room, he let the door bang shut with a great show of frustration.

In interview room three, however, it was a different story.

As they entered the room, the man with the rolled-back sleeves sat wringing his hands. His soft brown eyes had the look of an injured animal caught in a trap.

'What's going on?' he hissed angrily. 'Are you trying to get me killed? I'm not due for another twelve days.'

Philip was their most precious asset in San Yee On northern district, a young agent of immense nerve but still very conscious of the many dangers he faced: of being a man on the edge. Suddenly raising his voice, he barked off a string of defiant insults which could be heard all over the report room.

'Relax,' said Joe, turning his back to the glass wall. 'We went to a great deal of trouble to get you in here.'

'You're not kidding. That place has never been raided before. It sounded like the bloody army crashing in.'

'We needed to get you out quick, and with a minimum of suspicion. I had to promise Buchanan we'd do it right. Now your White Paper Fan is convinced it's him we're after.'

'Let's hope you're right, or this is the last time you'll ever see me.'

Tasker folded his arms and looked the agent square in the eye. What he saw there made him uneasy: it was fear, pure and undiluted.

'No bullshit, Philip. We have to ask you about the Jockey Club hit.'

'*Diu lei lo mo*,' he cursed running his fingers nervously through his punch-perm. 'I thought so. Somebody got a cigarette?' Joe threw a pack of Marlboro on to the table between them, and offered his gold lighter.

Immediately the agent picked up the packet and threw the entire contents in the superintendent's face.

'Shove 'em up your *si faat.*'

Tasker's face remained unmoved. It had been a nice little touch by someone who did not want to appear too cooperative in front of a report room full of witnesses. Glancing around, he noted the staring faces of the report room staff, any one of whom he realised might be a triad informer – from the civilian interpreters right down to the canteen staff and the station cleaners.

Already Philip was beginning to wish he had accepted the cigarette; his nerves were shot to pieces.

'You obviously know it was a San Yee On operation or you wouldn't have come to me.'

'Go on,' said Joe guardedly.

'The detail is pretty hazy. The Big Circle is like a gun, see. You only have to aim them at a target, give them the word, and they'll do the rest. Still, you have to hand it to those bastards; they pulled the job all sweet and clean. I heard they were back on Mainland soil within four hours. Not bad going, *hai m' hai ah*?'

'Who are they, Philip?' There was an almost imploring note in Tasker's voice.

Philip gave a dry laugh that smacked of resignation.

'They're the hardest team in Canton, or anywhere else, as far as I can make out. Soldiers, as you'd expect. Most of them were decorated in the Sino-Vietnamese border conflicts in recent years. Division 17 was an incursor unit which performed sabotage and selective assassination of Vietnamese political cadres. When they got out of the forces, things were harder back in civilian life than they'd anticipated. For them crime was the answer. There's about fifteen left of the original twenty-four members. The others are either dead or else serving time at hard labour. The leader is their old NCO, a real hard case called Chan Ming. You can't miss that one: about six-one with a stubbly beard and a soldier's shaven head. He must be on file somewhere with military intelligence. Most veterans of PLA special forces are.'

Tasker's gaze flicked sideways catching Joe's stern reaction.

'All right, so where is Chan Ming now?'

'About half an hour outside Canton there's a town called Foshan. It's famous for a statue of the Buddha which once stood on the hilltop, but it's also famous for metal casting and handicrafts. To the north of the town there's a casting workshop that doubles as their base of operations. Each time they pull a job, that's where they return to. The local Public Security Bureau chief is into Chan Ming for a big percentage, so forget about interagency cooperation.' Philip shook his head in resignation. 'Believe me they can't be touched.'

'And the cash, what about that?'

'The money stayed here; swallowed up by lodge headquarters, they say, for a very special project. After laundering they realised about twenty-five million US dollars. They used a small Chinese commercial bank which has offices in every offshore haven in the world. Don't ask me why they did it, I don't know, but something big is being planned.'

'Long-range project?' suggested Tasker speculatively.

'I don't know. But I've heard bad things just recently. All kinds of things that make no sense; stuff about American spies. On top of this, somebody inside the lodge has been picking up hotel bills for a group of Japanese tourists. I tell you it doesn't make any sense.'

'Japanese? Listen, we're going to bring you in to the Shatin safe-house next week, but in the meantime you'd better know we believe your friends have someone very senior inside PHQ.'

Philip looked from one man to the other.

'How high?'

Tasker felt he owed it to the man to level with him completely.

'High enough. Fifth floor – CID.'

Philip's mouth gaped fish-like, as if he were drowning in the air he gulped.

'Then if you don't get me out, I'm as good as dead. I ought to have known. I've heard the rumours, but I thought it was just so much cyanide spread to keep the forty-niners in line. To stop them giving evidence against the lodge.'

'So you don't know who it is?' persisted Tasker. 'No ideas?'

'Oh, I have ideas all right. How about a long holiday in Canada for a start, and maybe a new face to go with it.'

It was beginning to sound quite bad to Tasker. Philip seemed ready to plunge into a trough of self-pity, and that was dangerous for all concerned. He reflected for a moment, then said: 'The relocation comes later. Unless, of course, you think you can't handle it.'

At that moment Tasker picked up one of his own cigarettes and lit it. He could tell without looking that he had angered the agent. It was the intended result. Joe Lai looked down at his feet, where the plastic tiles were stained with cigarette burns.

'I can handle it,' replied Philip hotly.

'Good,' said Tasker evenly. 'Because, without you to find the name of this infiltrator, we'll be stuffed at every turn. Whoever it is, he's going to be monitoring our movements. Don't worry, we won't keep any records of your involvement in the operation. Just let us know the instant you have a name. After that you can walk into the safe-house and we'll have you out in a matter of hours.'

At length Philip sighed deeply and shook his head. Then he looked into Joe's eyes, wondering who, if anyone, he could trust now. Perhaps only the Gwan-Dai, he told himself bitterly.

'All right, I'll find out what I can. But we have to make it look good.'

For a second Tasker was confused by this. Slowly, Philip stretched himself and stood up, taking a step towards the door.

'You see,' he said matter-of-factly, 'my cover and my reputation demand this.'

Without a word he went for the side of Tasker's head with his elbow, smacking the *gwai lo* backwards into the window. The glass pane broke, exploding over a passing uniform and showering on to the report room floor. Tasker took two more punches, one in the chest and one on the side of the jaw, before Joe Lai grabbed Philip's shoulders and pulled him backwards. Then, regaining his balance, Tasker swung a short hook into the side of the prisoner's face and, grabbing the permed hair, he knee-dropped his chest and hurled him bodily through the broken window.

'You little fucking shit!' he snarled dabbing the blood from a cut below his ear.

Suddenly the whole report room was frozen in shock.

A second later the duty inspector came running over, followed by the desk sergeant and two uniform constables. Immediately they grabbed the prisoner and hauled him out of the debris – for his own safety.

The inspector stared back incredulously at Tasker, all previous admiration now lost. At length he turned to the prisoner and, in the full hearing of the whole report room, asked him: 'Do you wish to make an official complaint against any police officer here present?'

The inspector's gaze fixed upon the superintendent.

When Philip came up off the floor his nose and mouth were covered with blood, his moustache clogging with red. Seeing the White Paper Fan standing now at the window of interview room one, he proceeded to complete the show. He forced a cold laugh, showing pink teeth edged with scarlet and spat a gob of blood and mucus on to Tasker's shirt.

'*Ngoh diu lei lo mo! Ngoh diu lei lo mo!*'

'Fine by me,' said Tasker between breaths. 'My mother's seventy-nine years old. I'm sure that would be quite a treat for her.'

White Paper Fan watched in open admiration, his eyes taking in the glass on the blood-stained floor. His *ma jai* had put up an impressive fight against the crazy *gwai lo*, and now he was fucking the man's mother for all to hear. Great face indeed.

'Any complaint?' repeated the inspector, his pen poised above his clipboard. 'I assure you there is nothing to fear.'

'No complaint,' said Philip with difficulty, his lips now beginning to swell. 'Would you expect a tiger to scream if a mosquito bites his arse?'

The inspector made no attempt to hide his disappointment.

'Have you finished with these prisoners now, *sir*?' he asked, putting ironic emphasis upon the last word. 'I don't suppose you'll be laying an assault charge of your own, will you?'

'Yes, I'm finished with them, son. Check for any outstanding warrants, then kick all three.'

The inspector's eyes traced the spillage of shattered glass from the window frame, right across to the duty officer's desk.

'Very good, sir.'

Tasker snorted, and strode towards the door, with Joe Lai following. He hoped to God that the White Paper Fan had found the painful charade as convincing as the young inspector obviously had. Still, he could not resist one parting shot. Halfway through the door, he stopped and called back to the duty inspector.

'You know, you really ought to clear this place up a bit. It's like a bloody pigsty.'

TWELVE

Aléxander Au-Yeung Wing-fat, Chairman of Bright Star
Holdings, rose at 5 a.m., swam twenty easy laps of his
private pool on a breakfast of dim-sum and black dragon
tea, and was at his desk in the Au-Yeung building on the
Wanchai waterfront by 7.30 sharp. At that time of day
the traffic was light, and his chauffeur, Ah Ming, piloting
the Rolls-Royce Silver Spirit smoothly over Wong Nei
Chong Gap and down the switchback mountain road
towards Central, was only dimly aware of his boss's
movements. All he saw was the glint of gold cufflinks in
the mirror, as the rich man turned the pages of the *Asian
Wall Street Journal.*

It seemed a day like any other, a day of peace and
calm, another working day for the Au-Yeung business
empire. Only Au-Yeung himself knew the full gravity of
the situation his organisation was currently facing.

During the short drive from his Spanish-style villa
tucked in the folds of a green hillside along the Repulse
Bay Road, Au-Yeung had been scanning the business
pages with concern. His big blue-tinted spectacles
reflected the print in huge caricatures as he attempted to
gauge the temperature of the Hong Kong stockmarket.
There was brisk trade in both directions for Bright Star
shares, indicating a disturbing degree of uncertainty
amongst investors. But the Hang Seng Index continued
to nose still higher, in spite of all the pundits' talk of an
imminent 'correction'. So far so good, he had told
himself, relieved to see that Bright Star Holdings was still

receiving a favourable press. 'Bright Star still the darling' quipped one financial journalist. 'Au-Yeung in bank acquisition rumour' insinuated another.

Silently, he thanked the god of good fortune. For he knew that as long as he was the focus of so much positive speculation, there was little to fear.

Reaching his tai-pan's desk in the Au-Yeung building on the Wanchai waterfront, he removed his jacket and turned the swivel chair to face a mirrored glass window that ran the whole length of the wall. The view opened like a picture book on to a clear expanse of blue water almost a mile wide, flanked on one side by the golden turrets of Exchange Square and on the other by the vast, tinselly shopping plazas and first-class hotels of Tsim Sha Tsui. It was a sight often called the most expensive view in the world; and with office space currently ten per cent higher than in either Tokyo or New York there was some justification for such a boast.

But as he sat pensively stroking one flaring eyebrow, Au-Yeung was not looking outward, he was looking in. Never before had he known a time so fraught with dangers. Never before had he felt quite so vulnerable.

Beneath the window sat a hundred-gallon tropical fishtank with twin scorpion fish sailing endlessly back and forth between smaller, purple flashing damsel fish. Absently he patted ants' eggs on to the water's surface, and watched the fish rise to take them. As he watched he noticed, as usual, how the larger, more aggressive, scorpion fish rose quickly to capture the greater share. There was something reassuring in that, he thought: reconfirmation of the natural order of things.

Bright Star Holdings now stood on the threshold of a success Au-Yeung had long dreamed of, and he knew the next few weeks would prove both crucial and dangerous. The property market – basis of the Au-Yeung empire – was again teetering on the peak of a phenomenal upswing; and it would need the most careful manipulation, perhaps even some disinformation, in order to maintain the good will of his investors. Without that, Au-Yeung knew Bright Star was dead. For it was thanks largely to Hong Kong's bullish investors that the shares had been parleyed up three hundred per cent in two short years. What they did not realise – what nobody realised – was that there was actually precious little to back it all up.

Starting as an unknown, with a little cash and a lot of anonymous credit, he had pulled off two hostile take-overs and a string of speculative real-estate deals which had made the financial pundits' heads spin. At a time when everyone was still recovering from the crash of '89, his nerve and audacity had turned the depressed market around, and set prices climbing again into the bargain. Since that time he had been the golden boy, much wined and dined by credit bankers. His companies now rep-resented the 'new' Chinese money which would see the territory right through the turbulent years ahead – as against such old colonial trading houses as Jardine Matheson, Swires and Hutchinson Whampoa who might well be tempted to up-sticks and move out in the run-up to Chinese rule.

The thought brought a smile of satisfaction to his lips. To think that *gwai lo* tai-pans now came cap-in-hand to see him, and that credit bankers were beating down his door for a piece of his action. His deals were so exciting to the market that in the past year he had been offered unlimited credit by every major finance house in the colony. And all of this secured on nothing more substan-tial than his own good name – and that of Bright Star Holdings. It was fortunate indeed that Hong Kong law required none of the normal disclosures about share ownership which other countries demanded. How many of those merchant bankers would choke on their execu-tive lunches if they knew the true source, and the limited extent, of the money actually behind him.

How different it all was from the hungry years, he mused.

To the business fraternity, Au-Yeung was one of the colony's greatest success stories; to the common man a bright promise of what might be achieved through hard work and self-denial, without the benefit of family fortune or wealthy connections. His parents had fled Swatow back in 'fifty-nine, and arrived in Hong Kong as refugees with nothing but a small bag of millet and a faded photograph of his paternal grandparents. Penniless, the family had borrowed money from a Chiu Chau mutual aid group and set up a cooked food stall in the Wanchai district, bringing breakfast, lunches, dinners and even late snacks for the stevedores in the cargo basin. The work had been backbreaking, the hours long, and his father had been content to work them for little more than the price of inflated loan repayments.

But his mother was a different story. She had come from loud, boisterous merchant stock who had dealt textiles in the markets of Canton before the communists came. For her, success and happiness were things that jingled, and from her the boy had learned how to fight for that success. He never forgot the important lessons of self-reliance and the ambition drilled into him by his aggressive mother, and as he grew he learned to work with the mutual aid groups, which he saw as providing the crutch the Chiu Chau people needed to pull themselves up out of the gutter. As he struggled to help his parents' business grow, he saw the true extent of the loan sharking being run by the Aid Groups which fed off the poor Chiu Chau community – actually no more than a front for organised crime – and he determined it was better to be part of them than continue to be their victim.

He joined the triads as a matter of course, the way other businessmen join the Lions Club or the Jaycees, for the many benefits that membership provided. With San Yee On help, he expanded the cooked food business into a restaurant – then two. When premises became

229

available on the Wanchai strip, he paid a hefty price in 'fragrant grease' for a liquor licence, and opened up his first bar just when the American GIs were beginning to use Hong Kong for a spot of R and R from the hellhole of Vietnam. Importing young girls from the Philippines to staff this bar, it didn't take long for him to recover his initial outlay. After the serious money came rolling in, Society membership provided an opportunity to branch into a small construction firm whose workforce was kept firmly in line by San Yee On intimidation.

At forty-six years old Alexander Au-Yeung ran a company which now owned a sizeable portfolio of some of the colony's best commercial real estate, including, to his pride and satisfaction, the twenty-six-floor office block that towered over the very spot in the Wanchai cargo basin where his father's Chiu Chau noodle stall had once stood. That was the Au-Yeung building.

Through the success of his business he now had access to legitimate funding for speculative property purchase. In Hong Kong's few hundred square miles there is only a small and finite amount of commercial real estate available. Twice he had bought in at massive prices on prime buildings in Central district. That was just after the company went public. He had carved the properties up, selling them off floor by floor for a handsome overall profit as property prices soared. That had sent the new shares through the roof. Everybody wanted them. Every exciting portfolio had to have them. Au-Yeung himself, however, knew the fragility of the property market. Supply and demand. The problem he now faced was this: if the bubble should burst, if the market suddenly began rejecting the billion-dollar building contracts, the outrageous office rents which his company had created almost single-handedly, then how would he meet the crushing loan repayments entailed?

The ensuing crisis in confidence did not bear thinking about. Everything would go!

But, never one to be caught out by a sea-change, Au-Yeung had taken precautions to protect his personal fortune. The past few months had seen him carefully unloading the assets of the companies he had captured, and secretly absorbing them through the books of the holding company. If the change came, then any companies that went under would be those owned by the speculative investors who had hyped the shares. Let them choke upon their own greed, he told himself. His own profits and assets must be safeguarded at all costs. And so they would be, through nominee companies, for under Hong Kong law the owners of such companies need not be declared, and in the event of liquidation of the holding company any assets hidden within the nominee company would be untouchable. Thank all the gods! For the money was not strictly his own, no not his own at all, but that of the Society: funds for which he had been granted charge and responsibility. To lose any substantial portion of the Society's assets through speculation would bring a swift and sure end, and Au-Yeung realised that his own fate was now inextricably linked to that of his business.

A warble on the intercom yanked his thoughts back to the present.

'Yes, what is it?'

'Excuse me, Au-Yeung sir, a Mr Hung wishing to speak with you urgently.'

'Put him on at once.'

Au-Yeung listened to the agitated voice on the other end of the line for almost a full minute, his grip gradually tightening upon the receiver as he digested the full impact of the news.

Suddenly he turned to scowl through the window, and barked an instruction into the phone: 'Meet me at the Star Ferry, Hong Kong side, in thirty minutes.'

* * *

They exchanged signals outside the bookshop on the ferry concourse and went separately through the turnstiles, followed by their respective *ma jai*, who occupied themselves in studying the faces of fellow passengers, most of whom were Japanese or European tourists. When the gates opened and the crowd surged aboard, both men found seats on the upper deck, but as soon as the ferry was underway they sauntered casually to the rail and stood side-by-side looking west along the harbour front, where the jetfoils came and went from the Macau ferry terminal.

The second Chinese was a pit-bull of a man, a shade shorter than the tai-pan, with the same moonfaced look, flat features and broad mouth, as Au-Yeung himself. But where the tai-pan wore a well-cut business suit, the other affected a more relaxed mode of dress: light-weight bomber jacket of white leather with designer jeans, patent-leather cowboy boots, and a heavy gold dog-chain around his neck. Both men wore sunglasses against the faint possibility of either being recognised.

'Was it so very urgent,' breathed Au-Yeung in irritation, 'that it could not wait until the meeting tomorrow evening?'

'*Ah Goh*,' said the second man in deference to his elder brother, placing both hands upon the rail. 'We cannot bear this any longer. *Kuen Wong* has intensified his campaign of insult and harassment against the Society. I feel we must act now, otherwise we have no face left at all.'

The tai-pan looked down at the other man's hands with distaste. They were a fighter's hands, of course, broad at the base with strong fingers that tapered almost to points at the fingertips. Each finger joint was a swollen, discoloured knot of calloused tissue, and between the knots the skin shone like tanned leather. But it was the knuckles of the fists which made him uneasy, the obscene swellings of bone and gristle which were the product of many years of conditioning – punching an iron plate. When a man spends all his time preparing for violence, mused Au-Yeung, it is all too often the first and only option he considers.

Tony Kwan was eight years younger than Alex Au-Yeung, and actually his half-brother. He was both heavier and more athletic; an essentially brutal man with an intimidating manner – and with none of his half-brother's talent for business, inherited from a different mother. He was the product of their father's union with a second wife, a nightclub singer, a practice common in Hong Kong at the time of their childhood. In accordance with Chinese tradition their father's second wife was accepted by, though remained subservient to, Au-Yeung's mother, who remained the *tai tai* or supreme mistress of the household.

When Kwan's mother died in childbirth, however, he had been packed off to live with distant relatives in the Yaumatei typhoon shelter who had no sons of their own. His childhood spent aboard a fishing junk had been very different from that of Alex Au-Yeung. For years he had run with the street gangs, taking the family name of his dead mother but always aware of his connection with the rising businessman Alex Au-Yeung.

By the time he was sixteen Tony Kwan was dealing Red Chicken from a pool hall in Yaumatei, with a small gang of fighters of his own to protect his patch. At seventeen he was the 'closed-door' student of a leading exponent of Choy Lei Fat, one of the better known branches of Shaolin boxing; and his fighting skills quickly won him notoriety amongst the other youth gangs.

One evening around the time of his eighteenth birthday, he had received a secret summons to go to his brother's nightclub in Wanchai. They had not spoken a word in eleven years, but on that same night he learned he was to be sponsored for San Yee On membership. Seated between two of his own fighters, Alex Au-Yeung

233

had stressed the importance of kinship and self-reliance amongst the ethnic Chiu Chau, and the strategic importance of their alliances against the expansion of the 14K triad. He explained that he had heard of Tony Kwan's fighting skills and of his particular reputation for violence – one rival gang member thrown off a rooftop after a kung-fu duel, and a second carved to the bone with a pair of butterfly knives – and now he wanted him within the society.

But there was one small problem. Au-Yeung was already a name respected in the business community, and for that reason no one could ever know the two of them were brothers. Kwan had readily agreed to this provision, for although he was not a businessman he was a gifted tactician and he instinctively understood the politics of that decision. He knew that the power of the San Yee On was growing year by year, and that his brother was now on a fast track to both the top of the society and a major place in the business community.

'Let it be so,' he had agreed. 'Treat me well, *Ah Goh*, and I will do all the things you may not do. I will be your darker side.'

And it had been so, ever since.

Now Alex Au-Yeung held the supreme office of the San Yee On triad society, a position bearing the code number 489 and the title of *Shan Chiu*: First Route Marshal. His first action as chairman of the *Gung On*, the San Yee On inner council, had been to install his younger brother as senior Red Cudgel enforcer, a 426 officer with the elevated status of *Seung Fa*: Double Flowers. Now his own position within the Society was unassailable, controlling both the decision-making process in central council and, through his brother, the many thousands of foot soldiers who were the real power behind San Yee On.

As the ferry neared the centre of the harbour a second ferry rocked past, heading back towards Hong Kong

Island with tourists at every window and rail, all busily photographing the view. Au-Yeung followed their gaze back towards the waterfront skyline, and sighed deeply. Beside the Macau Ferry Terminal Building the sun reflected off the second-phase redevelopment of Au-Yeung Plaza. If the anticipated downturn in the property market materialised, this development would never reach completion.

'What is John Tasker to us?' asked the tai-pan with irritation. 'A minor inconvenience – nothing more.'

'No, it's gone beyond that now. We thought we could control him through CID Headquarters, but this time they were overridden by the Police Commissioner. He's getting too close to us.'

Au-Yeung took off his sunglasses and began to polish them thoughtfully.

'Tell me, what is it that bothers you so?'

Tony Kwan described the previous night's events in great detail: the raid on the village, the arrest of his people, and then the long, apparently pointless interrogation of the White Paper Fan.

'They know about the visits to Canton,' he continued grimly. 'It's obvious they've made some connection between us and the Shatin robbery, but I'm not sure what they know about Chan Ming and his brothers.'

'Where did their information come from?' asked the *Shan Chiu*, replacing his sunglasses on the bridge of his nose and neatly folding the silk handkerchief back into his top pocket. 'I thought we had tight security on this one.'

'We did. Only a dozen or so people knew anything, so somebody must have talked. Don't worry, *dai lo*, we'll find out who. My main concern is the effect of Tasker's outrageous behaviour on our standing within the community. He made us look very bad.'

'Not as bad as I was made to look when that little whore of yours went missing. My special Vietnamese

235

guests were most put out not to receive the papers I had promised them. They had the greatest difficulty in believing Reicher's story without the promised documentary evidence. Now Reicher is dead we have only Ruby Tang's word that the story is true.'

'It's true enough. I saw the document myself, just briefly, before she disappeared. Things were pretty mixed up that night. We were preoccupied with getting the Japanese to identify Reicher.'

Imperceptibly Au-Yeung's voice took on a more menacing tone.

'Yes, a great pity you let her out of your sight. See you get that document back soon. I wonder if you appreciate how delicate the situation is? When the market turns we're looking at an estimated shortfall of eighty million dollars. That's American dollars! We're going to need the white-powder earnings to preserve our cash-flow, every last cent of it – but without the Vietnamese our heroin supply routes cannot be guaranteed. Now do you see why we must keep them sweet?'

'The Vietnamese would withdraw their favour, after all these years?' Kwan sounded incredulous.

'Yes, they would,' said Au-Yeung, 'if things go badly. But their generosity will know no bounds if they get what they want.'

'And what is it they want, exactly?' asked Kwan displaying once again some frustration at hearing only half the story.

'You will know soon enough.'

'It's got something to do with that Japanese. That's why you brought him here, isn't it?'

Au-Yeung shot him a look of reproach, then looked away to the purple industrial haze rising above the power station on Tsing Yi island in the distance.

'For the moment just keep the Japanese safely locked away where he can do no more harm.'

Kwan ground his fist against the rail, making the joints

crack. 'And what are we to do about Tasker? The White Paper Fan is my personal follower; I recruited him and took his thirty-three dollars more than ten years ago. As his protector, my personal reputation hangs in the balance. I ask leave to do what is right.'

'Will public complaint not suffice?' asked the *Shan Chiu* wearily. 'We can have Tasker removed from the case just like that.' The tai-pan snapped his fingers.

'No, Elder Brother, not now. Tasker has information implicating us with the unwashed ones from over the border. Besides, Tai Po district demands action – before the delicate harmony is put out of balance.'

After long years of triad politics the older man understood the implications of a failure to act. The seeming loss of potency, the apparent slackening of grip that might be interpreted by enemies as a lack of resolve to defend their turf. The return of the blade wars; nobody wanted that.

'Very well, little brother,' he said. 'We treasure harmony above all else, especially now. Wash the barbarian. But see it is done well!'

Tony Kwan smiled for the first time that morning. Already he had decided how he would handle it. It would be a very public demonstration of power by the Master of the Dragon's Fangs.

Seated in the waiting-room of the Tang Siu Kin Government Clinic in Happy Valley, Roman Fung's mind seethed with the possibilities of the Reicher murder. It haunted and intrigued him, teasing him to solve this darkest of riddles. Beside him the old lady, his mother, chuntered on, occasionally tugging at his arm. Absently he fixed his eyes upon an AIDS poster on the wall in front of him. The thick black characters, like fat insects, stressed the importance of condoms and warned the unwary against sexual contact outside marriage. Yet his eyes saw nothing, and only his mother's gentle nagging pulled him back from the deepest of thoughts.

'What for you look at that, Roman?' The old lady rebuked the poster's decadence. 'Disgusting *gwai lo* diseases! Listen to your mother, it has nothing to do with us Chinese. We are civilised.'

'Ssshhhh, Ah Ma,' he complained, sensing heads turn in the packed waiting-room.

He had taken a half-day off, which he could ill-afford, to bring his mother here to harangue the doctors in the Government Families Clinic about her recurrent chest complaint. In her left hand she carefully nursed a small jar wrapped in plastic, containing dubious samples the nature of which Roman could only guess at. She was healthy for a woman in her mid-sixties, rudely so, and she wore a flower-patterned pyjama suit of pale lilac with a grey cardigan which made her seem somewhat younger than her age. That is, until you noticed the stooped back and bent neck, symptoms of calcium deficiency in earlier years and a general protein deficiency throughout her life. Yet she was still full of fire on all subjects relating to her family, and the old lady had not finished telling him what a good thing it was he had come with her.

'Ai-yah! But for you, Roman, they'd have had me sitting here all day like a sparrow on a fence. Even so, they ought to give the mother of a police inspector more face.' She tapped the rubber end of her walking-stick on the floor. 'I've a good mind to report that young nurse!'

'*Suen ah.*' Roman stroked her shoulder placatingly. 'Just a little while longer, Ah Ma.'

Like all Chinese, Roman respected his mother almost to the point of reverence, as indeed he had respected his father up until his death. His mother had always taken good care of herself; even now she went every morning to the small public garden outside their block to perform callisthenics with the other biddies. But his father had burned himself out before his time. All his life the old man had dragged his wiry frame around one construction

238

site after another, rigging bamboo scaffolding as the concrete giants rose out of the earth: hotels and apartment blocks. But the old man had continued labouring long after he ought to have been looking for a watchman's job or nursing a bird cage on his knee in the park. Too proud to slow down, his heart had given out ten years ago, leaving three kids for his mother to manage. Fortunately, by that time Roman had already joined the police force, earning more money than his father had ever done, so was able to support the family.

A soft fog lingered before his eyes as he sighed for the past. Grit and rice times they had been, but happy times for all that. Saving for anything at all was difficult back then; most of his money had gone straight to his mother. But now it was different: his sister was married to a senior chef at the Mandarin Hotel – not bad face that, a master chef – and his younger brother was working all shifts as a taxi driver. Now his mother received money from all of them, and it eased the burden. At last he could save enough table money for his and Amy's wedding banquet.

'Roman, you're not listening to me!'

'Sorry, Ah Ma.' He jerked back to the present.

'Why don't you do something for your little brother? You know how much he wants to be a police officer. Sitting in a taxi all day and all night will bend his spine and dull his spirit. Do you want him to look like me?'

Roman felt uneasy. The same old question begging the same old answer.

'Ah Ma, there's really nothing I can do. He failed the interviews and that's that.' His mother had conveniently forgotten that her youngest son had also been convicted of indecently assaulting a waitress inside a public lavatory, but he had not the heart to remind her. It had been a stupid fumbling act by a stupid mixed-up kid, but it was enough to get him a criminal conviction and three months of psychological counselling by the government probationary service. That's what had really kept him out of Police Training School.

'Such a good boy. He watches all the cop shows on the magic-shadow machine. It broke his heart when they turned him down. He'd give anything to be a detective like you.' His mother took his hand and squeezed it with pride.

Mercifully, the nurse called out her name, 'Madam Fung', and she scuttled off through the consulting room door, still clutching her plastic bag and sample jar.

After twenty minutes the old woman re-emerged, bowing and fawning to the doctor. As usual, she grasped her prescription paper proudly, though after four years of such visits she still had no idea what ailed her. Whenever Roman badgered her on the subject, she reminded him that doctors were important officials and it was impolite for a patient to be nosy about things that did not concern them. 'Just take the medicine and don't ask questions!' she chided him. That was the Chinese way.

When Roman Fung arrived at Police Headquarters, Amy Chan was sorting the pile of folders on his desk, filing witness statements and scanning a sheaf of reports just back from the Government Chemist.

'How's your mother?' she asked with some concern. 'Still strong?'

'Very. Especially the tongue. The doctor gave her four types of pills. It made her very happy.' Amy covered her mouth politely as she laughed, then reached for a typed report and placed it before him.

'These are the results of the forensic examination on the American. The pathologist confirmed that the cause of death was traumatic decapitation, but he also found a high concentration of alcohol and traces of cocaine in the victim's blood.'

The forensic report itself fleshed out these bald circumstances of Reicher's death. Forensics had found

240

smudges of makeup on the jacket, Vietnamese food in his stomach, and traces of semen on his underwear. It had obviously been quite an evening for the deceased: wined, dined, and entertained sexually by a lady of some energy. Among the visible signs on his body was a series of long fingernail scratches on the man's buttocks and thighs, teeth marks upon the head of his penis, and a further bite in the flesh just over the hip-bone, which had bruised into a perfect dental record of the donor. Contact analysis had also found that the skin surface had been massaged with a perfumed oil produced by a Korean manufacturer.

'The dental image shows a small mouth, with one upper incisor that's crooked.'

'Which one?' asked Roman, responding with interest.

'The right, why?'

Quickly Roman searched for a manila envelope in his intray, then pulled out the photograph which Jack Cinch had provided. It was a head and shoulders close-up of Reicher's girl, smiling broadly.

'There we are: right upper incisor. It matches.'

Amy Chan jumped down from the edge of the desk on which she was perched.

'Let me see.'

While the woman sergeant studied the photograph, Roman filled a teapot with hot water from a thermos jug always on hand. He poured tea into two cups almost immediately, while the brew was still light and refreshing.

'So it looks like he probably spent his last hours in her company,' said Amy Chan.

'Yes. I'm more than ever convinced she's going to be the key to this case. We *have* to find her.'

'If Reicher was working undercover, she could be the link to the passport fraud syndicate. It could be she even set him up, and then these other people murdered him.' Though she did not realise it, Amy was still working to the false assumptions handed to Roman by Jack Cinch.

241

'Let's not jump to too many conclusions,' he warned. 'If she'd had murder on her mind, she'd need to be a pretty cold-blooded bitch to sleep with him first. But then again it takes all kinds...'

His eyes strayed across the desk top and fell upon a white envelope. Lying amongst the stack of buff-coloured government envelopes it stood out easily.

'What's that?' he asked suspiciously.

'It came with the morning mail – addressed to you personally in Chinese characters, and marked private and confidential.'

Roman examined the envelope carefully, sniffing it and even holding it up to the light.

'Let's treat this girl as just another witness for the time being,' he said. 'Take the photograph and have IB make two hundred copies. Give one each to the *foh gei*, and send some to the Public Relations Bureau for inclusion in the TV bulletins. Have the team check out all the Vietnamese restaurants, to find out if anybody saw the two together on the night Reicher died. Let me see, that would be Saturday night to Sunday morning. Start on Kowloon side, then do the Island if necessary. After that, start checking the nightclubs and massage parlours. It looks like she gave the American a very fancy rub-down, so chances are she was a professional at some stage. It's just possible one of the other massage girls might recognise her picture.'

At that moment Roman Fung's face screwed up in a grimace of horror.

'What is it?' Amy demanded.

As he'd been talking, Roman had opened the envelope and emptied its contents on to the desk. There was a folded sheet of white paper inside, but the first thing to catch his eye had been the square polaroid colour picture which accompanied it.

'It looks like a woman,' he answered, recovering from the initial shock. 'But there's so much blood it's hard to tell.'

242

Amy took the picture and studied it carefully. She gave a small gasp and clamped one hand firmly to her mouth. It was a woman all right – or at least what was left of one. The naked body lay upon a white sheet which was spattered with blood. Behind the small heap of body organs which spilled from the woman's belly, Amy could see that the lower torso had been split by a single incision extending upward from the pubic bone for eight or ten inches. She gazed in horror at the wet mass of exposed red tissue by the left pectoral muscle, where one of the woman's breasts had been cut away.

'Merciful *Gwan Yin*...' breathed the woman sergeant.

Then, staring aghast, she heard Roman read aloud the contents of the letter.

'Attention Inspector Fung Lo-man, homicide detective. Please accept this modest offering of my latest work. The light was not good, but then the girl was not especially pretty. Still, there are many hundreds more to choose from, so I will endeavour to do better next time. Unless, of course, you find me first. We shall have to see which of us is really the cleverer. Please do not feel too badly about the girl; she was ready to sell herself, and quite obviously deserved to die. The rain voices told me, but in the end I made the decision for myself – in Gwan-Dai's name.'

* * *

The drive out of Washington, along Inter State Sixty-Six and out into the rolling Virginia countryside, made a pleasant change to the National Security Advisor's usual afternoon schedule, but as his driver swung left off the road, taking the Oldsmobile limousine into the Manassas Park entrance, he felt more than a twinge of discomfort.

It was a bright, sunny day and the rough grasslands of the old Bull Run battlefield were studded with wild summer flowers as far as the eye could see. In the visitors' car park, Kazinski dabbed his streaming lids and wondered which he disliked most: the hayfever from which he now suffered, or the fact of having to meet and deal with Kagan. There wasn't much in it, he decided – except that with hayfever at least you knew what you were letting yourself in for. Dry-swallowing two antihistamine tablets he ordered his official escort to remain in the car, clunked the door shut, and set off walking along the marked route through the knee-high grass to the far viewing point where Kagan stood alone staring at the greens and browns of the adjacent hillside.

When he heard the grass rustle behind him the old man half-turned in acknowledgement, then continued to stare ahead at the line of trees just below the brow of the hill. In spite of the heat of the afternoon, he was wearing a voluminous grey wool suit which possessed only marginally more shape than he did himself.

Coming alongside, Kazinski glanced down at the metal plate on which was inscribed a map and a narrative explaining the significance of this patch of ground. They were standing on the site of an engagement which the world had come to know as the Battle of Bull Run. At the start of the American Civil War the Union army had advanced here to Manassas to engage the Confederate forces then marching on Washington. Not wishing to miss the great spectacle, Washington's gentry, and even their ladies, had attended in their open carriages to see what they mistakenly believed would be an easy victory over the rebels. At first the day went well for the Federal forces, and the enemy was turned and put to flight. But then the rebels had rallied behind General 'Stonewall' Jackson, and turned the day into victory, chasing soldiers and gentry alike all the way back to Washington. To this day the battlefield remained a grim reminder for those who would too easily underestimate their opposition.

It was a lesson which Kagan himself was fond of reviewing.

Pressing the button on the display pylon before him,

Kazinski listened to an audio-tape loop which described the historic combat.

'Must have been quite a sight,' said Kagan when the tape finished, his great balding head nodding towards the far distance. 'Those Union skirmish lines making their way down through the trees, and the rebs just sitting here watching 'em, waiting to open up with their cannon.'

Kazinski assented politely and blew his nose on a linen handkerchief, dabbing at the corners of reddening eyes.

'The strategic ambush,' he mused disarmingly, 'is that what's waiting for Bill Fredericks on his Far East tour?'

Kagan appeared to find that amusing; his chest wheezed like an old bellows when he laughed.

'Oh, I doubt that. Fredericks is very well respected over there. He'll get the usual glad hand wherever he goes. Only this time he'll be doing us some good for a change.'

'Us?' queried the National Security Advisor sceptically. Then he turned to look back towards the parking lot. There was only a handful of cars there and two of those belonged to Kagan's entourage; his three minders were dispersed around the battlefield, trying to look inconspicuous in lightweight suits. The few real tourists were either poring over the exhibit cases in the visitors' centre or scattered around the acres of rough ground.

'You and me!' retorted Kagan shortly. 'We're in this thing together – don't you forget that. It might have been my idea, but it was you who sold it to the President. If anything goes wrong now, it's both our asses!'

It was barely a second of confrontation, and as usual Kazinski was the first to look away, cowed by the venom in the older man's gaze. He cleared his throat.

'I've read your latest on the Spratlys situation. It seems that you were right about Vietnamese intentions: those concrete structures have a certain air of permanence about them.'

'Don't expect Ivan to wait until the base is finished, either, before he starts moving in his boomers.' The old man chuckled, regaining his humour. He might as well have been discussing the tactics of his favourite football team as the deployment of Soviet nuclear submarines.

'That thought had crossed my mind,' countered Kazinski, needled now by Kagan's obvious delight in calling the shots. 'We now have a detachment of the Seventh Fleet on station less than two hundred miles south of the archipelago. Nothing too heavy for the moment: a missile destroyer and two frigates. Just enough to show we're there.'

'No, no, *no*!' protested Kagan, his features in a wrinkled scowl. 'For Christ's sake, we have to send the right signals to these slants. Get the big guys in there, the whole damned carrier group if possible. Really put the fear of God into them. The success of the operation I'm running depends on a high naval profile.'

'That's all very well,' argued the younger man with his normal caution, 'but what about those four Chinese frigates you picked up. They appear to be shadowing us; they must know something is going on. You know the Chinese always get jumpy where sovereign territory is concerned.'

Kagan waved his hand dismissively. A moment later he hawked and spat into the long grass.

'They won't do jack shit – not when our own Secretary of State has virtually promised Beijing as much advanced computer technology as they can handle. With Fredericks in there assuring them of our best intentions...' He left the sentence hanging in mid-air, punctuating it with a self-satisfied grimace.

Kazinski was not convinced.

'We're placing Fredericks in a difficult situation,' he insisted, 'by not warning him of our intentions. He's a politician of considerable ability, but even he will find it dangerous if things blow up while he's out there.'

Kazinski was beginning to feel misgivings about the deep animosity Kagan harboured for Fredericks.

Kagan removed his glasses, breathed hard on each lens, and began to polish them with a small treated cloth. His fat face seemed somehow naked without the heavy black frames. His eyes were small and glassy, the whites shot through with blood vessels, and they reminded Kazinski of the marbles he used to play with as a boy.

Suddenly a sneer formed on the old man's lips, and Kazinski was touched by a sense of dread.

'He'll have to take his chances like the rest of us. We all have to make occasional sacrifices – for the sake of safeguarding our beloved democracy.'

Perhaps the old man actually meant what he said, Kazinski could not tell anymore. After a moment's silence, in which he watched the grass ripple on the far hillside, Kazinski sighed aloud. An empty sound of resignation.

'You know, Phil, sometimes you scare the hell out of me.'

'Like I told you before: don't worry. Everything is under control. The operation is well under way.'

'Maybe. But I wish you'd flesh out the detail for me a little. This undercover guy of yours, how's he doing so far – the one out in Hong Kong I mean? From what I understand, we're relying on him very heavily for the success of this whole operation.'

The question was enough to bring the CIA Director back to earth. Briefly he remembered how he had reacted on reading John Prioletti's report on the murder of their agent: how he had hurled a water jug at the wall. Something would have to be done to correct this, he had decided. Masking his true feelings, Kagan just smiled.

'If it makes you feel any better, two days ago Reicher contacted his controller and reported a successful first phase. That means they've taken the bait. The way I hear it, he's got them eating out of his hand. In fact, the Hong

Kong Station chief should be receiving my instructions for the second phase at this very moment. Don't worry, the operation is still a runner.'

Kazinski allowed the CIA Director to link his arm and they set off, heading back along the path towards the visitors' centre. As they walked along, with the warm sun on their faces, Kazinski was already planning what he would say to the President that evening. The news would be good, and he realised suddenly that his hayfever attack had all but passed. Already he was breathing easier.

Inside the secure communications cage on the fourth floor of the United States Consulate-General on Hong Kong Island, John Prioletti watched Langley's coded reply finish printing out from the teletype. Impatiently he tore off the paper before even the cipher clerk could read it.

Waiting for the reply to break over the satellite had been like waiting for an impending typhoon to hit. His nerves were jangled and on edge. He had coded his own report to Director Kagan, advising him of the murder of Jim Reicher, over twenty-eight hours ago. Exactly whom Kagan had consulted in the interim, Prioletti had no way of knowing; just as he had no real knowledge of who else in the White House cabinet was privy to the details of the operation itself – but he had a shrewd idea it went to the very highest level. From that he could also imagine the alarm engendered by his report in the offices out at Langley; and the kind of vengeful act Kagan would now demand. Kagan was like that: a real bastard when he chose to be.

Prioletti produced steel-framed reading glasses and read the single flimsy sheet. It was headed FLASH TO CHIEF OF STATION HONG KONG. The reply was short and to the point:

*Details of your communication duly noted. Proceed
exactly as planned. Commiserations on your loss.
Arrange measured and equivalent response in kind.*

*Imperative the ball get back in play soonest. Trace
progress of 'compromised text' and take all steps
necessary to preserve local credibility. Kagan.*

Prioletti thanked the clerk and went back to his office.
There he secured the sheet of paper inside his safe. As he
spun the combination wheel, he was deciding what to do
next – mentally checking out weak links in the operation,
more aware than ever that Jack Cinch was still an
unknown quantity. He was still Fredericks' man and with
the Secretary due in soon, the SY men would be sensitive
to anything that upset the balance of their security:
paranoia would soon set in. He mouthed a vague
obscenity. Prioletti did not like using men outside the
company domain, men whose first loyalty was not
towards Langley – for they were always a liability. But
Cinch was involved and, like it or not, the show had to
go on. The cable was quite clear: *Proceed exactly as
planned.*

Only now there was an extra dimension. Kagan
wanted some measured and equivalent response in
payment for Reicher. In Company terms that meant
blood for blood.

Still wrestling with the problem, Prioletti grabbed his
jacket from the chair back and made for the outer office,
where his confidential assistant sat behind a computer
screen, wearing audio headphones. She was a honey
blonde in her late thirties: one of the army of neat,
precise and totally discreet ladies the Company sends all
over the world to handle its paperwork. At the sound of
his voice she slipped the audio phones down around her
neck and looked up.

'Anyone been looking for me this morning?' he asked.

'Two people,' she answered immediately. 'First there

was Miss Tavistock from Special Branch. She called early this morning; said she needed to see you fairly urgently.'

Prioletti made a grimace. He could guess what she wanted to discuss. He waved that aside.

'And the other one?'

'Mr Walters – or rather his secretary. She called to remind us you're lunching with the Consul-General today. It seems he's also very keen to see you.'

'I'll bet he is,' said Prioletti ruefully. Yesterday Cinch had been ordered in to brief the C-G on the Reicher homicide. He had flannelled the old man just like he had the local police; only the old man had been around the block a couple of times and he had insisted on knowing more. That was when Cinch had covered himself by saying that, since it involved the CIA, detailed disclosures on the matter could only be authorised by Prioletti himself. So now the C-G wanted it straight from the horse's mouth. There'd be all kinds of awkward questions, he told himself, but, after all, Walters was just another of those tweedy Ivy League duffers State Department liked to promote. And the day he couldn't run rings around those bastards would be the day to hang up his spying hat.

'Don't worry,' he told her. 'I'll be there. Now call the apartment and tell Bowman I'm on my way over.'

'You'll be on your bleeper?'

'Right here,' he said, patting the small device clipped to his belt.

Prioletti signed out a pool vehicle and drove down the hill, then east through Wanchai towards Happy Valley, carefully considering his response. This was one of his favourite parts of the Island, home to his favourite handful of restaurants, and the best place on earth for Peking Duck. Amongst the din of car and bus engines, clanking trams gonged their way through the bustling street markets which spilled out amongst the dense traffic. Then, of course, there was the Jockey Club. In the early years of British rule the Europeans had chosen this place, one of the few areas of flat land on the island, to lay out the Colony's first racecourse. Back then there had been only a handful of wood and stone huts nearby, inhabited by the indigenous Hakka population, and each race-day had been a thrilling social occasion. Even now there was still the same sense of intrigue and excitement about the place, only the valley had been completely absorbed into the greater urban area, and the once secluded racetrack, now totally modernised, was overlooked by a multitude of high-rent, high-rise developments.

The apartment which Prioletti was looking for was on the twenty-third floor of Baguio Court, a plush and prestigious block perched on the steeply rising hillside to the south of the racetrack. It was a much sought-after location, commanding a five-figure monthly rent, and from the apartment's broad picture window in the main living-room a breathtaking view of Happy Valley unfolded below.

The apartment's interior was furnished to Prioletti's own specification with deep Taiping silk carpets and rare Chinese antique furniture, and with air-conditioning throughout. It was just the kind of apartment provided by multinational companies for their expatriate senior executives: a cushion against the mad hustle and clamour of the Crown Colony.

Only this apartment was not intended as living accommodation – except for such operational teams as found themselves deployed there. Nor was their interest in the view restricted to the jade-green turf of the Jockey Club track, but rather to a prestigious new building which faced the stadium across Wong Nai Chung Road. For the apartment had been rented, and equipped at great expense, as a CIA surveillance facility for the sole

251

purpose of monitoring clandestine activity run from the suite of offices that housed the Cuban Consulate.

When Prioletti buzzed the apartment, Wes Bowman, agent in charge of the operational detail, triggered open the outer door lock, and came to meet him by the lift. Bowman was early forties, a little overweight, with sandy hair grown long and combed across to hide a thinning patch. With his heavy jowls and sad watery eyes, Bowman resembled a harmless and faithful family pet, but behind this mild appearance was a seasoned field agent with half-a-dozen Asian languages and a kill tally measured in dozens. In fact Bowman was one of the Company's unannounced operatives – one of those whose name did not appear on any consular list, thereby allowing the CIA the luxury of denying his activities if necessary.

The two men exchanged routine pleasantries, and Prioletti stepped inside, acknowledging with a brief nod the two young agents monitoring the surveillance equipment. The air inside the apartment was rank with the smell of stale beer and cigarette butts, and on the dining table, amongst the debris of a takeaway pizza meal, lay the coloured plastic pieces of a Trivial Pursuit set. The young agents responded by standing up, but Prioletti waved them back to their seats. Both were WASPs only a few years out of college, and they sat at a table pushed well back from the window of the spacious living-room. On the black lacquered surface before them a large Japanese video screen echoed the street scene at the entrance to the Cuban Consulate, and beside it the most expensive audio deck Prioletti had ever seen.

Bowman indicated a jug of coffee and a box of fresh doughnuts. Prioletti helped himself to both, and walked over to the broad floor-to-ceiling window.

'Get any good pictures last night?' asked the station chief routinely, parting the lace curtains and casually looking out.

'With a set-up like this, they're all good. I could get a job with 20th-Century-Fox tomorrow.'

Prioletti forced a smile.

The video camera was mounted on a black tripod, poking through the curtains and aimed directly down on to Wong Nai Chung Road. Its telescopic lens, like a black arm, captured a razor-sharp image of the target building, which was then projected on to the screen being carefully watched by one of the young agents. Beside the video camera stood a second tripod with a still camera, and another long lens, which could at any time be fired remotely from the agent's keyboard to produce good-quality hard copy.

'Well?' said Bowman to the back of his boss's head. 'What did they say?' He had long since given up addressing him as sir. Vietnam had taught him that the title was meaningless.

Prioletti saw the other two agents look up. Slowly, he sipped his coffee to wash down the last of the doughnut.

'Oh, I think you can guess the answer to that one, Wes,' he said eventually. 'We're to carry on with the operation.'

Bowman feigned surprise.

'After what happened to Jim Reicher?'

'That's right.'

'Just like nothing happened?'

'"Proceed exactly as planned" was the precise wording.' Prioletti's manner invited neither opposition nor comment. 'Now, tell me what you have on the Korean.'

Bowman tried hard not to show his disgust, but it was there in the heavy lines on his face. The initial phases of the operation had gone well, but when Reicher's headless corpse turned up that had really scared him. He had been convinced it would change things. It had not. Obviously, then, this operation was of greater importance than he had realised. Though he had only known Reicher slightly, the agent's horrific death had caused him to lose sleep; had thrown a ripple across the calm surface of his operational thinking.

Still, what the fuck, he now told himself bitterly, everybody dies sometime, and I'm still here dunking doughnuts! He shook himself free of the moment. It was unproductive. And as a volunteer Reicher had known the score.

Bowman reached for the operational log and snapped his fingers, pointing at the video kit to indicate to the young operator to cue the tape.

'After three nights scratching our asses here, the Korean finally showed up. Ortega worked late last night. His clerical staff worked their usual day, and they had all left by 6.30. About 11.30 Ortega took a phone-call from a cellular phone. Ten minutes after that an unscheduled visitor turned up.'

At this point the screen flared into life, and the magnetic image of the Cuban Consulate filled the screen. A tracking line appeared briefly as the tape was rapidly advanced – ordinary pedestrians flashing past the Consulate entrance at a frenetic pace. There were short comic clips of the staff arriving to work in the morning ... followed by their lunch breaks ... messengers' visits ... and finally the evening departures. Then, as darkness fell, the visitor described by Bowman entered the frame, and the operator froze the image. By now they were working with image intensification, and the picture glowed with a luminous pale green wash.

The station chief came to the table, put on a pair of half-lens spectacles and carefully studied the frozen image. He checked the subject's build and features, hardly able to believe his eyes. Male, clean-shaven, five feet seven, and a very solid 170 pounds. The man wore a brown tropical safari suit and carried a gent's wrist-bag of leather and gold – the kind the agents called a 'fag bag'.

'My God,' breathed Prioletti. 'It *is* him.'

'Just like in the photograph,' put in Bowman. 'But who the hell is he exactly?'

John Prioletti spoke in a hushed, even reverent tone which Bowman had seldom heard him use before.

'That's Rhee Joon-kil. Not a man to fuck with. North Korean military intelligence gave him every dirty job going when they were trying to sabotage the South Korea-China trade rapprochement back in the eighties. He nearly succeeded, too. Specialist in low-intensity operations: sabotage, assassination and psy-war. Got one hell of a fuckin' brain on him.'

'Sounds like someone we ought to be taking serious interest in.'

'Oh we are, Wes,' said Prioletti quietly. 'And for a very good reason.'

'I'm listening to every word.'

'That's good, Wes. Very good. Because I believe he's the man who took Reicher out.'

The words had the required effect. Wes Bowman turned to fix his gaze a second time on the image. He whistled tunelessly. For a North Korean this was a stone slab of a man.

Satisfied with the effect of his words, Prioletti continued. 'This must be the specialist Reicher warned us was coming; the organising influence they talked about. The Chinese he dealt with were pretty nervous themselves.'

'Obviously Rhee's reputation precedes him,' mumbled Bowman. 'But I'm wondering why he now suddenly turns up to see Ortega?'

'Yes. We didn't know he was coming, did we?'

'Absolutely not,' confirmed Bowman, his face still fixed on the screen. 'We record every word uttered in that office. Take it from me, Ortega spoke to no one about this guy.'

Prioletti considered this carefully.

'Then it must mean one of two things: either he knows

about the room bug, or he's been using another channel of communication.'

'Amounts to the same thing, doesn't it?' said Bowman disparagingly. 'It's possible he knows about the bug – but I doubt it. It's too well hidden. I placed the fucking thing myself, and he's never shown the slightest interest in it. Not that it's *too* well hidden: it's just a real cute placement.'

Bowman spoke with a degree of professional pride. He was an agent who had learned his surveillance techniques the hard way, by tagging after KGB and CHIS officers all over the Pacific. Here in Hong Kong a *gwai lo* stuck out like a sore thumb, but he had still maintained an impressive record, and the Cuban Consulate was his most satisfying job to date. Due largely to the reticence of Beijing, there was no official representation in the colony for any of the governments that had once constituted the Warsaw Pact; a situation carefully designed to limit the possibility of espionage by the KGB and other so-called hostiles.

Cuba was the only Soviet ally which maintained a presence, and although the Cuban Consulate was staffed by Cubans and Chinese locals, it was actually controlled by the KGB from the Soviet Embassy in Hanoi. Bugging the Cuban Consul's office had actually been child's play. Hector Ortega was primarily a diplomat, with no training in active measures, and as far as Wes Bowman could tell there was no security officer on station to assist him. Ortega functioned as a passive conduit and a shared asset, taking his orders from whichever senior intelligence officer contacted him.

The Cuban was a handsome and dapper Latin, middle-aged and much given to fits of temper. He liked two things fresh and readily available: women and Cuban coffee. That was the first thing Bowman had noticed about him. It was a weakness, and for Bowman it was his way in. Indulging in his weakness, Ortega always kept a coffee-maker on the sideboard beside his desk. Just eight days after the diplomat moved in, Bowman burgled the office and replaced the voltage adaptor which connected the coffee-maker to the mains with an identical one containing a powerful radio transmitter. The beauty of the arrangement lay in the fact that, whereas previous bugs had been battery-powered transmitters which had a lifespan measured in hours, necessitating a regular series of break-ins to replace them, this bug drew power direct from the mains supply and could transmit indefinitely – even when the coffee-maker was turned off. The result was an ear inside every meeting held inside the room, and a steady flow of valuable information on Soviet, Vietnamese and North Korean activity in the Far East theatre. The photographic set-up at the apartment therefore put faces to the names that were discussed openly inside the office.

'If you're sure the bug's safe, Wes,' said Prioletti, leaning heavily on his agent, 'we'll have to take Ortega's silence up to now to mean a heightened security rating for whatever they're working on. What did they talk about?'

'Same thing: the bag and the documents. Ever since that Tang woman went missing with them, Ortega talks about little else. He'd hardly be doing that if he thought we had ears on him, now would he?'

'OK, OK. Go on.'

'They're both pretty pissed about losing contact with the girl Ruby Tang. Because she works for him, Alexander Au-Yeung lost a lot of face over that. It's just speculation, but it's beginning to look like that horny little bitch took one look at the papers Reicher was carrying, decided she'd stumbled on a gold mine, and went to ground – probably looking to sell them back for a fortune. If those guys ever catch up with her, it won't be pretty. I once heard of a triad executioner who used a melon knife to slice the skin off his victim one layer at a time. It took the guy a day and a half to die; his hair turned completely white.'

'Do you think she knows what those papers are worth to the Viets?'

'I said she was horny – not dumb. Of course she knows.'

'Damn!' Prioletti rubbed the back of his neck. This was the worst thing that could have happened. 'Those papers are the key to this whole operation. If they don't get to Au-Yeung, the whole thing could collapse. Any leads as to where she might be?'

'Strong possibility she's somewhere in Macau. That's where her sister lives – but they have no address, of course.'

'Of course not, otherwise they'd be over there right now tearing her fucking eyes out.'

Prioletti began to pace the floor, thinking. Reaching the far side of the room, he took a seat on a sofa beneath a colour print of tea-clippers in Hong Kong harbour, then indicated that Bowman should join him. A stern look in the direction of the two young CIA men made them return to their duties.

Bowman studied Prioletti's thin face; it was heavy with anger and frustration.

'Wes, I'm afraid we're losing it.'

'How's that?'

'The operation, dammit!'

'Maybe a little.'

'No, a lot. The Viets are preparing for large-scale construction on the Spratly Islands because they believe we won't try to oppose them. That's an impression we must disabuse them of at once. Kagan aims to fool the Viets into believing the US and China are planning to invade the Spratlys to kick them out. Make them withdraw, leaving the way clear without firing a shot.'

'So that's it?'

'We looked around for a mark, and selected Au-

Yeung because of his links to Vietnamese intelligence. Then we put Reicher in close to the Tang woman, and made him vulnerable to blackmail by having him sell blank passports through her to the Au-Yeung syndicate. For that we had to arrange State Department cover, and involve the RSO. Cinch didn't believe the story we gave him, but we could hardly tell him the truth.'

'Why not? He's cleared for classified material?'

'Loyalties, Wes. Cinch is so straight it's downright nauseating. He was bound to have referred back up the line, and you know Fredericks' position on black operations. If he'd ever found out, he'd have had all our asses in a sling. Congressional hearings, crusading senators: there would have been no end to it.'

'OK, so Cinch is cleaner than Kleenex. What then?'

'Au-Yeung's syndicate bought the passports all right, and it didn't take long to get around to discussions about secret documents. We sold them some pretty imaginative stuff, and spiced it up with some genuine low-grade material. Everything pointed to a growing relationship between Washington and Beijing. Then came the crunch.'

'The briefcase?'

'Right. Reicher was carrying a sheaf of papers which purported to be copies of agreements signed between us and the Chinese. Economic stuff mainly, but in there somewhere was an agreement that the US Navy could continue to use Hong Kong as a docking facility after 1997, and share in the spoils if we assisted them in clearing out the Spratly Islands and establishing a joint facility there to lock up the Vietnamese coastline. That would severely hamper Soviet submarine deployment from Cam-Ranh Bay, and keep those bastards honest.'

'Who'd ever believe that?' asked Bowman incredulously. 'The Soviet threat has diminished to the point where global war is now almost unthinkable. Why should China drop its pants and bend over for us?'

Prioletti gave a long-suffering look and continued patiently: 'You ever hear of Nan Yang?'

'Of course,' the agent answered, still none the wiser. What CIA operative in Asia had not heard of it? 'Nan Yang is a Chinese military ideal. The Middle Kingdom as principal military power in Asia and centre of the civilised world. They believe it's their responsibility to police and protect the Pacific and the South China Sea.'

'Yes, and in order to do that they intend over the next twenty-five years to build for themselves the largest navy anywhere in the world. They're committed to it.'

'So how does that square with them agreeing to support the presence of US naval units?'

'A simple marriage of convenience. They receive our help in unseating the Vietnamese, and also economic and technical aid in developing the Spratlys. Their own oceanographic mapping capability dates back to the Mongol invasion.' Prioletti allowed himself a derisive sneer. 'Plus we support their claim to sovereignty over the islands the next time it's raised in the United Nations. We're playing Fredericks' visit as the occasion for cementing the relationship and signing all the agreements.'

Bowman let out a low whistle. It was the kind of bluff which would have appealed to only the most seasoned of poker players – or the bloodiest of fools. Phil Kagan's own fingerprint. But there was something that didn't quite match up with his image of the Secretary of State. After all, wasn't he the very whitest of the doves in the current administration?

'How come Fredericks bought in? Surely not *his* style.'

The station chief allowed himself a tiny smirk.

'Fredericks doesn't know anything about it. You know how he hates Phil Kagan. He'd throw him to the Oversight Committee as soon as look at him. Then we'd all be facing charges.'

Bowman took a moment to assimilate everything.

'Jesus Christ, John! This really *is* high stakes poker.'

'You want out now?'

'I didn't say that. I just wish I'd known all this sooner. At least now I see why you brought Reicher in.'

'The obvious choice, since he'd never worked out of Hong Kong before. His disinformation work back in Manila bordered on genius. He knew instinctively how to give a genuine feel to a document. He just ... knew. Pencil notes in the margins, sweaty thumb prints, the works. Yes, he was our most experienced agent.'

'Until they killed him.' Bowman felt a small jolt in his chest – unsure whether it was fear or excitement that gripped him.

'That's the most puzzling part of it. Why would they kill a high-grade source like that, and blow it wide open.'

'Maybe they weren't as sure of him as you think.'

'That's possible, but they'd have had to be *pretty* sure he was a triple to take him out. They could have milked him or sent back their own disinformation ... anything. No, I think there was something else. This Tang woman making a run for it convinced me of that. It all blew up on the night Reicher took the girl to the fights, and now, if we're not careful, we're going to lose it altogether. I don't like it when we're not in control.'

'I don't think they planned the last move. The Tang woman just blew up and went for it. Nothing else makes any sense.'

'Nevertheless, it's bad. The girl just stole the initiative from us. Fredericks is already on his way, and there isn't time to set up another Reicher, so we have to get that briefcase back in play. You're my head of operations...'

The station chief looked at Bowman with hard eyes. Bowman stroked the hair across his forehead as he considered. His answer was swift.

'OK, we still have another twelve days before Fredericks gets in. Time enough to tear Macau apart. I'll get over there today. We can use our police contacts there to locate the sister. After we house Ruby Tang, we pass the address anonymously to San Yee On and let them do the rest.'

'Good. That sounds very good,' enthused Prioletti. 'Get on it right away. Do whatever you think necessary to preserve the operation.' Prioletti stood up and walked slowly back across the room, drawing Bowman with him. 'But before you leave for Macau, there is one other thing I'd like you to take care of.'

Bowman listened intently as the station chief described the tone of the signal from Langley and the kind of retaliatory action which Kagan had demanded. Prioletti had already made up his mind what the target should be, and as he described the details of his intended plan Bowman's face glowed with a kind of exultant fire.

'It would be a pleasure,' breathed the agent. 'I'll do it tonight – personally. Hell, I'd do that just for laughs!'

'Thanks, Wes. I knew I could rely upon you. We have to teach these bastards a lesson. Show them nobody fucks with the Company. Least of all a bunch of...' He let the words trail away to nothing and checked his watch. 'By the way, was there anything on last night's tape about why the Korean is here?'

'Uh-huh.' Bowman shook his head. 'Ortega keeps pumping him about the mission but he won't give word one. Whatever it is, he's not sharing it. Rhee has a tight schedule; he's asking for meetings to be set up within the next four days.'

'That's not much to go on. What do you think it is? It can't be routine agent recruitment. If he was planting stay-behinds for the future, he'd hardly be in such a lather about it.'

'True. Au-Yeung's name keeps coming up but they both seem wary of meeting him face-to-face. Ortega is picking up the tab for Rhee's room at the Hyatt Regency Hotel in Tsim Sha Tsui.'

'That's strange. You'd have thought he'd go for the Peninsula or the Regent if someone else was paying.'

Bowman pulled a grimace.

'Maybe he prefers a view of Nathan Road. Who knows? Anyway, whatever the operation, it just got a hefty injection of funds.'

'What about Ortega, has he contacted his Soviet control?'

'If he has, he didn't do it from the Consulate. Maybe he used a dead-letter drop. We know he also uses a PO box at the central post office at Star Ferry, but we don't have the number yet. Probably has someone else fill and empty it for him. More coffee?'

'Thanks.'

Bowman grabbed the jug, poured two cups, and set it back on the heated plate. He took a sip from his own cup.

'And another thing, how come the Special Branch didn't inform us of Rhee's arrival? I thought they're supposed to keep us current on all intelligence officers landing here.'

'You're goddamn right,' agreed Prioletti. 'I'm going to double-check my intray when I get back, but I'm fairly sure we didn't get anything. I'd say that was a serious omission. Perhaps I'd better lunch Ruth Tavistock this week.'

'If you're thinking of trapping the Blonde Rat, you'd better take a groin guard with you. That lady doesn't fight fair. We had a run-in six months back. I was going to tear a strip off her, but by the time she'd finished, it was me who was apologising. Smart move putting that sweet face in the front line.'

'I can handle Miss Tavistock, Wes.'

'Course you can, John. Ask her nice and she'll walk all over your naked body in spike-heel shoes.'

They were not the first men to speculate over the girl from Special Branch. Nor even the first to notice with amusement that Ruth Tavistock's initials on official communications spelled RAT.

'Looks like I'm already on the lady's hit list,' grinned the chief. 'She's been leaving messages with my secretary. It appears Special Branch is getting suspicious about Reicher's cover.'

'That's to be expected,' said Bowman, 'but better be very careful with that one; she doesn't let go.'

Prioletti didn't quite like the implication that he might not be able to handle the local flatfoots – especially when the flatfoot in question was a woman.

'I think you underestimate my influence over Miss Tavistock,' he replied with a smug expression that suggested he knew more than he was prepared to disclose.

Less than half a mile from the same CIA apartment, on a busy corner facing the racetrack across Morrison Hill Road, a long white saloon car broke out of the thrumming log-jam of taxis and public light buses and drew up outside the New China News Agency Building. When the door opened Stephen Lee and David Becker stepped from the rear of the vehicle, buttoning their jackets and looking carefully around.

While Lee stooped to give the driver his further instructions, Becker gave the shabby, nondescript building a glance up and down, steeling himself for what was to come. The first thing he noticed were the ugly blotches of scrubbed stone where daubed slogans had been removed. Whenever he saw these Becker was reminded of the tragic student demonstrations of June 1989, the senseless and bloody conclusion to a democratic dream. Here in Hong Kong the demonstrators had turned out in their tens of thousands to lend their support and their voices to the pro-democracy movement, encouraged by the initial restraint and tolerance of the Chinese politburo. Then, when the killing began, they had taken to the streets in angry despair, daubing slogans of accusation against Beijing upon the walls of the NCNA building. A sandblaster had removed the words, but the shame lingered on; and Becker knew that Beijing could never now remove the images of Tiananmen Square from the people's minds. For the Hong Kong people those blood-stained bodies would remain the threat of things to come.

'Come on, then,' said Stephen Lee, brushing past him. 'Let's get it over with.'

Becker shook himself, and walked briskly through the doorway and into the Holy of Holies.

Visits to the NCNA by Special Branch officers were very few and far between – and with good reason. Practically the first thing an SB man learns is that somewhere behind the grimy curtained windows, hidden amongst an army of drab-suited officials and journalists, lives the full-blown apparatus of CHIS: the Chinese Intelligence Service, a very capable and professional body indeed. Historically, relations had always remained civil, with the Hong Kong Government pretending to believe that NCNA men actually dabbling in trade-union affairs were in fact just reporting the news. A kind of mutual face-giving had always prevailed, but it was a matter of common knowledge that most of the political and economic subversion practised by China over the years against the tiny offshore colony had been planned here.

In more recent times, however, there had been a cautious thaw in relations, to the point where there was now official contact on matters of security. The most frequent kind of cooperation related to the movements of mainland Chinese politicians. The NCNA now routinely passed advance details to Special Branch of visits to the Colony by senior Party members, and accepted for them, albeit grudgingly, SB protective security. After Tiananemen Square the secrecy surrounding the visits of even low-level Chinese VIPs bordered on paranoia, and Lee and Becker judged that their summons here today was in order to be briefed on just such a low-grade operation.

But they were wrong about the level concerned.

When at last they were greeted – not by a flunky but by one of the senior intelligence officers, a diminutive grey figure wearing the standard Mao suit and a demure expression – Becker knew at once this was no regular operation.

The man introduced himself as Lin Qi-feng, a name that did not tally with his SB dossier. He ushered them into a windowless conference room and served them tea. He spoke Cantonese instead of the official Mandarin for the *gwai lo*'s benefit.

'Gentlemen, thank you for coming.' He eased himself into a large, square-backed easy chair that made him look like a ventriloquist's doll, for his feet did not reach the floor. 'I thought it would be to our mutual benefit to discuss security arrangements for this private lunch between the American Secretary of State and the Foreign Minister of our People's Republic.'

There was a moment of stunned silence while the two Special Branch men glanced meaningfully at one another and the Chinese official registered their surprise.

'Excuse me, Mr Lin,' said Stephen Lee cautiously. 'Are you saying that the US Secretary of State and your Foreign Minister are to hold an official meeting here in Hong Kong?'

Lin's face wrinkled in amusement.

'Nothing official – a private lunch, that is all. Something in the way of a personal visit between old comrades. I gather you have not been informed?'

'The US Consulate neglected to mention it,' said Lee, attempting to hide his embarrassment. 'Perhaps you could share with us what you know?'

'Of course. I'll be happy to oblige.'

266

Becker flipped open the filofax balanced on his knee and began to take notes. Something told him this visit was going to prove a security nightmare.

'As I said, this is an unofficial visit. The news media are not being invited to cover it. Just a few close aides on both sides. The meeting itself is set for 2.30 on Thursday 2 October. The location will be a house in the New Territories.'

Lin peeled an information sheet from the folder on his knee and handed it to Stephen Lee.

'The exact address?' asked Becker.

'Fung Chik Sin Villa,' said Lee, studying the sheet. 'It's just outside Tsuen Wan at 14$\frac{1}{2}$ milestone on Castle Peak Road.'

'I know the place,' said Becker confidently. 'It used to be a police mess for single expatriate officers once.'

'Indeed,' said Lin, 'and now it is owned by our Government, as a hostel for junior staff of the Xinhua News Agency.'

The SB men nodded as if they had just learned something, but both had known about Fung Chik Sin Villa and its many functions for quite some time. It was their job to know.

Lin adjusted his spectacles and referred to a sheet of Chinese characters.

'The Foreign Minister will arrive by train with a party of four, and an unspecified number of security officers, shortly before noon. He will disembark without formality at the border town of Lo Wu. I trust you will smooth things with your immigration department?'

'Of course,' said Lee.

'He will then proceed by armoured limousine to Tsuen Wan. The meeting is scheduled for two hours' duration, but may run to four depending on various factors. The Foreign Minister will remain there after the meeting and depart at 1800 hours exactly, returning to Lo Wu by the same limousine. His train will depart immediately. I'm sure you'll agree this is a simple operation. Provided absolute secrecy is observed, there should be no reason for either of us to lose any sleep, yes?'

Stephen Lee looked thoughtful.

'If the information remains restricted, then I foresee no problems. Anything you'd like to say, Dave? By the way, Mr Becker will be field commander for this operation.'

Becker looked up from his notes and saw Lin nod approvingly, then he spoke.

'Yes, a couple of things. First the proposed route: Lo Wu, Tsuen Wan. There are a number of significant blind spots and at least one transmission blackspot where we might lose radio contact with SB control. We'd like to see the route plan, and have the opportunity to comment or suggest changes where necessary. Also, I'd like one of our officers inside your limousine, and a follow car to escort you there.'

Stephen Lee's face remained straight, but inside he was grinning. You had to hand it to Becker, he thought; the man's a trier

The Chinese Intelligence officer smiled uncomfortably.

'My answers are "yes" to the follow car but "no" to the man inside the Foreign Minister's vehicle. I know the thinking behind such a request, nevertheless I must refuse it. His presence would be too, shall we say, inhibiting. We will be solely responsible for the Foreign Minister's vehicle, and for the inside of the hostel itself.'

'With respect,' said Becker, feeling none, 'your Foreign Minister may be satisfied, but before the US Secretary of State sets foot inside that hostel, we have to search it for explosives, incendiaries and surveillance devices. Please understand, it's not just me; the American security team will insist upon that, too.'

The old man flushed as the good humour suddenly drained from his face. Becker was pushing his luck now, and he knew it. The villa was probably wired for sound in every bloody room. There was no way they would be allowed to sweep it electronically first. Lin shifted awkwardly in his chair, his feet still dangling like a doll's.

'In this matter I think you will find you are outvoted. I have already spoken to the US Consulate – their regional security officer – and we are in full agreement. The hostel is *our* responsibility.'

Cinch, again, thought Becker. Damn the bastard.

'That's settled, then,' said Stephen Lee, shooting a disapproving look in Becker's direction. He had gone far enough now. 'However, I'm sure we'd appreciate all that in writing, Mr Lin.'

'Of course, Mr Lee.'

'Just to clarify the extent of our own coverage and to prevent subsequent misunderstandings. A contract, if you like.'

Becker reined in his anger. 'Just in case some of the local students decide to make your party go with a bang,' he muttered in rapid English.

If the remark was caught at all, it was most definitely ignored.

On the way back to Arsenal Street, Becker apologised to Stephen Lee for provoking the old man.

'I know it was wrong of me, but the little bastard was winding me up. Sometimes it seems these people don't want our protection at all, just someone to clear away the traffic and save them a bloody parking spot.'

'All part of the service,' said Lee. 'Try to remember that. Anyway, we now have a much bigger operation on our hands.'

'With the added complication of secret talks between China and the USA,' said Becker darkly. 'That raises all kinds of questions. Do you think he expected us to buy that bullshit about a private lunch with an old friend?'

'I don't know. Maybe. One thing's for sure, he

wouldn't release this information to us if it hadn't first been sanctioned from above in Beijing.'

'Jack Cinch should have informed us of this earlier. Once again he's been holding out on us.'

'Again? What else?'

'The State Department officer who was murdered last week...'

'What about him?'

'It turns out he's a CIA man in extended cover.'

'What!'

'Yeah. Cinch denies any knowledge of the operation the man was running, but he's obviously lying – and I'd like to know why. I can't help feeling there's a tie-in somewhere with this Chinese affair. Perhaps if we knew who killed Reicher then we'd have the key to all of this.'

The white saloon slid inside the gates of Police Headquarters, Stephen Lee acknowledging the gate guard's salute.

'Key or not,' said the Chinese superintendent, 'in twelve days' time William Fredericks arrives here from Manila, and we'd just better be ready.'

THIRTEEN

Outside the Sacred Heart Catholic Primary School – set amongst the drab grey-green structures of Kowloon City, and directly beneath the roar of the airport glide path – a glut of small white microbuses thronged the narrow street waiting to pick up the first groups of school-children and take them home. Directly opposite the school entrance two young Chinese women, wearing blue jeans and blouses, sat watching the gates from the cab of a yellow minivan.

The vehicle had been double-parked on the corner outside a herbalist shop for only a matter of five minutes, hardly long enough to attract the attention of the beat patrols; and although it bore none of the red characters stencilled on to the sides of the official buses, the occupants knew that, being women, they would attract no special attention.

The little girl they were waiting for was eight years old. She lived just three blocks from the school, and whoever her parents were, they clearly felt she was big enough to find her own way home on foot. The two women in the van knew all this because they had made it their business to find out. Silently they watched a stream of little girls begin to push their way out through the doors, and examined each bright young face. Each wore a spotless white uniform dress: blue school badge on the chest and blue piping around the collar. Because of the fierce competition for high school places, every kid was loaded down with homework carried in colourful satchels with cartoon motifs. Neat ankle-socks and frills completed the picture.

'Don't they look sweet? Couldn't you just eat them?' said the driver with a small sigh.

'*Hai ah!*' confirmed the second. 'Dear little ducklings.'

A moment later they saw the little one with the HELLO KITTY satchel, and both sat upright in their seats.

She wore her short hair in bunches, tied with elastic bands ending in red plastic balls. She walked through the school gates alone, threading between the knots of chattering friends and out along the pavement. At once the driver slipped the column shift into first, watched the little girl disappear behind the first of the school minibuses, then pulled out into the flow of traffic.

They turned the corner into Lion Rock Road and saw the girl, standing outside the Golden Pavilion toyshop, staring at the Japanese robots hanging in the window.

At the precise moment the van pulled in to the kerb, a Cathay Pacific 747 jet made its final turn from Chequerboard Hill, and came in just a hundred feet over the streets of Kowloon City. For local residents it was a regular occurrence, the screaming of jet engines that blocked out every other sound, including traffic, and they had learned not to even hear it any more. The woman passenger was out on to the street in a moment – and around the van before the child even noticed her. Any scream she offered as she was grabbed and bundled inside the van was lost in the roar of jet engines.

Fifteen minutes later, a stocky dark-suited businessman, eating lunch alone at a table in the Silla Korean restaurant in Tsim Sha Tsui, received a call on his portaphone. Calmly he lifted the last piece of *kim chee* between his chopsticks, mixed it with the rice in his bowl, then scooped the moistened ball into his mouth. He listened to the urgent warble of the instrument on the table, then he swallowed, burped, patted his lips with the cotton napkin and picked it up.

'*Wai?*' His Cantonese had a slight northern inflection. Even so, it was obvious from his stature that he was not Chinese but Korean.

'*Rhee saang*, this is the shipping agent. The container is loaded and under immediate dispatch.'

'Thank you,' said the Korean. 'All in good condition, I hope.'

'Of course. Such delicate cargo is always well packaged - to protect it in transit. You may proceed without worry.'

The Korean put down the phone-set, pleased by what he had heard. Now came the delicate part. He poured fresh tea into his cup and rinsed out his mouth, then he took a wooden toothpick to probe his upper molars.

He had been in the colony only six days: observing, liaising and planning. From Bangkok they had plucked him without warning, sending him here to oversee the pre-operative phase. The scale of it all had made his head spin. They explained that he would be working alone, but he did not mind that. The hotel was comfortable, the local units cooperative, and there was no language problem: he had fluent Cantonese as well as Mandarin and Thai. So far it had all gone smoothly. He had taken due receipt of the funds, made the deposit with the North Korean People's Bank, and arranged for the same amount to be made available at two separate Chinese commercial credit banks. The transactions would be secure and untraceable. Still, he was not altogether complacent about his job: he knew that working with criminal groups was never as 'solid' as having military intelligence units to back him up.

Deliberately he picked up the portaphone and tapped out a number.

On the upper concourse of Tsim Sha Tsui underground station passenger flow was predictably swollen during the lunchtime rush. Behind the glass window of the control room, at the northern end of the concourse, the station master checked his two video monitors showing the hundreds moving through the ticket activated turnstiles. All around him was shining stainless steel, ceramic tile and armoured plastic. Suddenly he felt a surge of pride. It meant a lot to be part of the Mass Transit Railway Corporation: one of the safest and most secure underground rail networks in the world.

Just then his thoughts were interrupted by the ringing of a telephone, but as usual he let his subordinate answer, keeping his own eyes on the lighted indicator board mounted to the left of the monitors. This board was his most valuable piece of equipment; it showed the movement of trains through the IT – the Immersed Tube – running along the sea-bed of the harbour. A concrete structure that connected the Island with Kowloon peninsula. Lighted studs indicated each train's progress through the mile-long tunnel.

'Ah-sir, for you. Man says he wants to speak only to Station-Master Cheung. A personal matter.'

Casually Cheung took the call, expecting to hear from one of his friends looking for a fourth player for mah jong. Money being so tight this month, he knew he would have to bow out.

'Cheung speaking.'

'Listen carefully. We have your daughter. But don't get excited or you'll never see her again.'

'What? Who is this?' A choking sensation seized his throat.

'Stay cool, little man. Raise the alarm and the little one dies within the hour. Understand?'

Station-Master Cheung took two deep breaths.

'I understand.'

'Ah Ping is safe for the time being – and unhurt. Cooperate and she'll stay that way.'

'What is it you want?' The Station Supervisor gave a

suspicious sideways look then returned to checking his clipboard. 'Who are you?'

'No more questions! Here's what you must do. After I hang up, phone your wife. She'll confirm that the little one is missing, so tell her what has happened. Warn her not to contact the police. If anyone asks where the girl is, say she's sick – staying with a relative or something. Use your imagination – understand?'

'I understand.' Cheung was responding without thinking, prepared to agree to almost anything to protect his child.

'You finish work at 5.30, I know. Normally you ride the dragon back to Kowloon Bay and walk home from there. Only, tonight you don't do that. Tonight you meet me at the Ocean Terminal. Take the steps up to the roof; I'll be waiting at the far end of the car park at six o'clock exactly. We can speak privately then. No police. If you're late, or I think you're being followed, that's it for the little one.'

'I'll be there. But how will I know...?'

Before he could finish, the line was disconnected. He replaced the handset, the harsh tone still buzzing in his ear like the purr of electric tigers.

At that very same moment, at a busy intersection between Wanchai and Causeway Bay, Bamboo Snake sat lounging in the bucket-seat of a flamingo-pink Porsche 911, squeezing a squash ball in his right fist and watching the crowded tables of an open-air cooked food stall.

Unlike on the night of the Gwong Tau Shan raid, Bamboo Snake was now fashionably dressed in designer jeans and a brightly-patterned silk shirt. Gold rings on eight of his fingers and around his neck a flat disc of white jade with a gold double-happiness symbol in the middle. He had to wait fifteen minutes, watching the rear-view mirror through a pair of dark Raybans, before he was rewarded. His contact was a tall Chinese in his late twenties, with slightly rounded shoulders and the smart, pressed look of an office worker: white shirt and dark tie. Cautiously he looked around him, as if afraid of the milling crowds, then he bought a copy of the *Oriental Daily News* from a news-stand and sat down at a table near the roadside. Bamboo Snake raised his dark glasses with a languid movement of the wrist, just long enough to confirm that Yip Suen had arrived, then he got out of the car.

At midday the Wanchai street restaurants were always heaving, and extra tables and chairs seemed to appear from nowhere, spreading like some virus along the pavement and into the road. In the busy churning atmosphere of savoury steam and clacking chopsticks, office workers mixed easily with construction workers and school-kids. Skinny young men in greasy vests scurried between tables carrying plates of food and trays piled high with bowls of rice, while fat cooks stood sweating over great iron woks. Seeing that Yip Suen had already found a table, Bamboo Snake skipped between the line of traffic crawling along Lockhart Road, and joined the man at his table.

Yip Suen began with an apology. '*Dui m'jiu, Ah Goh.* There were problems.'

'*M'sai.* Forget it. I have just arrived myself,' lied Bamboo Snake, determined to preserve face and at the same time demonstrate his generosity. His eyes remained concealed by the sunglasses.

When the waiter appeared, he ordered a mixture of light lunch dishes without consulting Yip Suen. Then he called for a large bottle of San Miguel and two glasses. The pleasantries continued as Yip Suen took bowls, spoons and chopsticks and rinsed them with hot tea to strip away deposits of grease. Serious conversation did not begin until all five dishes of food were on the table.

Yip Suen aligned his chopsticks and launched in with gusto. His first thrust was for the flash-fried prawns, one of which he deftly caught up, dabbed into a tiny dish of red chilli sauce, then pushed into his mouth. For a moment his mouth churned, then he spat the empty shell on to the brown Formica.

'*Gam dim a?*' asked the young triad, ostentatiously lighting a Dunhill cigarette with a Dunhill lighter, and staring at Yip Suen through the blue smoke. Black Rayban eyes unblinking.

Yip Suen had already filled his mouth with rice before he realised the other was not eating. He swallowed without enjoyment, suddenly reminded of the serious nature of the meeting.

'The matter is beyond my control, elder brother. The duty lists are not my *si gon.* Those *gwai lo bong baan* assign duties; I'm just a reserve for the close protection party.'

The other man suddenly took off his dark glasses to clean them.

'Very well then. If you cannot worm your way on to the Secretary of State's security party, then get me the list and I will arrange for a vacancy.'

Yip's chopsticks paused in mid-air; a segment of spring roll slipped between them, clattering into a dish of soy sauce and splashing the table with pungent brown liquid.

'*Dui m'jiu,*' he excused himself once more, taking a packet of paper handkerchiefs from his top pocket and mopping the spill.

'Clumsy of you,' said the Bamboo Snake.

'A small slip. Nothing serious.'

'And yet small slips lead to greater mistakes – or so they say. Take care, little brother.'

'I will,' mumbled Yip, well used to the other man's word games. It was as clear as any warning he was likely to receive. After a moment his chopsticks continued. 'What do you mean: arrange a vacancy?'

'I think you know what I mean.' The other man smiled

thinly. 'Clearly, if *you* are only a reserve for this operation, then we must arrange a small accident. One man becomes unavailable for duty and another steps into the gap. What could be more natural?'

For a brief second Yip's eyes registered stark horror.

'*Diu lei lo mo!* You want me to finger one of my own brothers?' He looked quickly around, but diners at the nearby tables were chatting noisily, concentrating upon the serious business of eating. 'Look, I don't mind helping you – I admit my gambling debts were substantial – but I'm not that cold-blooded.'

The other man stroked his bicep, faintly bored by the untoward display of loyalty.

'Take it easy, little brother. There is no question of washing faces. It will be a small accident. Just enough to require a week or so of sick leave and recuperation. I promise it will be something trivial. Come, tell me who you like least.'

Just then a scrawny waiter appeared and collected some empty dishes and bottles from the table. Yip Suen considered carefully. When the waiter had gone, he took out a notebook and pen and tore off a sheet of paper in slow gestures of betrayal. The pen was a local copy of a Dunhill, on which the fake gold barrel was beginning to flake. The other man looked away, busying himself with his cigarette while checking the street, his Porsche and the other tables. Satisfied with the random motion of the crowds on Lockhart Road he then contemplated his Italian leather shoes while Yip placed two lines of characters and a police Unique Identity number on the paper.

'This *hing daai...*' He paused, self-consciously, clearing his throat and spitting into the gutter, cursing the devils which made him speak the words. 'This man is about the most arrogant in the unit. He likes to joke and lose my face before my brothers.'

He folded the sheet in two and pushed it quickly

across the damp surface of the table. The other man's expression did not change as he opened the sheet, looked at it disinterestedly, and placed it in the top pocket of his shirt.

'Bad manners cannot be tolerated, *hai m'hai a*?'

Yip did not answer at first, there was a pain in his stomach now and his appetite had suddenly disappeared. When he did finally answer, it was without enthusiasm.

'He is also about the third best shot in the unit. A dangerous man in a firefight.'

'Then it is better he is not around on the day,' said the Bamboo Snake coldly, 'or we might be forced to kill him. You're actually doing him a big favour.'

The triad noticed the newspaper on the tabletop lay open at a feature on the Shatin robbery. Casually he picked it up and began to read. Yip Suen marshalled his chopsticks once more, nervously, and made another attempt at the remaining dishes.

'What's the latest news on this Shatin robbery?' Bamboo Snake asked when he had finished reading the article. 'The whole Territory is buzzing with it. You work at Headquarters, you must have heard something.'

There was a pause while Yip stripped the flesh from a piece of chicken and spat the bone into a small pile of prawn shells beside his bowl. On this subject he felt much safer.

'One or two good tips, they say. The rest is total bullshit. Two-gun Tasker's men are getting rough with their informants. Blood on the floor of the *dai fong*, I heard. Some of the usual informers have had to skip town for Macau or Taiwan. In the past Tasker always liked to play it rough, but this time...' Yip shook his head. 'This time he's not holding back. Complaints are already starting to flood in. For heaven's sake, don't get yourself picked up.'

Bamboo Snake smiled at the irony.

'I don't think we have anything to fear from the *gwai lo*.'

'Perhaps, but this guy is *chi sin*.' Yip tapped his forehead in a universal gesture of insanity. '*Nobody* is safe in his office.'

'So I hear. They say his fingers itch: a big man when carrying a gun and surrounded by his little horses. But they also say he drinks far too much. That's a weakness.'

'Show me a cop who doesn't,' countered Yip defensively. 'Nevertheless, he'll find those robbers.'

'You're sure?'

'Positive. Everyone in PHQ thinks so too. Providing the complaints office doesn't get to him first. His file is already thicker than the Kowloon telephone directory.'

'Then perhaps his arse is made of stone.'

Yip Suen grinned. It was a graphic Chinese expression meaning one immune to disciplinary procedures – for whatever reason.

'They don't worry too much about the niceties when it involves the deaths of police officers.'

The Bamboo Snake snorted in derision.

'Though his arse be made of stone, still a strong wind enters every orifice.'

'So they say. But how big a wind is your boss: the *shan chiu*?'

He sensed right away that he had gone too far. The Bamboo Snake reached across the table and grabbed him by the knot of his tie, twisting hard enough to constrict the man's breathing.

'Never mention him again in public, little brother. *Ming m'ming baak?* Do you understand?'

'I understand!' gasped the policeman. 'Please ... you're choking me.'

The other released his grip, aware of the power of his right hand, and enjoying the intense pain it had inflicted.

'Good. I don't like having to repeat myself. Your association with us is under review – as is the status of

280

your loans. The person to whom you refer is no mere wind. I'd say he is the biggest fucking typhoon ever to reach this territory.'

Keeping the constable under the glare of his shaded eyes, he pushed him back on to his stool.

'Unlike you, I chose my allegiance with care. You now have a second chance. Stay with us inside the City of Willow, and prosper.'

The triad was pleased by the terror he observed in Yip Suen's face. The frightened mouse beneath the paw of the cat. *Diu!* This was indeed a fortunate catch: a constable of Special Branch, but better than this, a *bo biu* – a member of the VIP Protection Unit. In other circumstances the constable might have jumped at him for what he had just done, but he was in far too deep to try anything foolish. If anyone at PHQ found out about his visits to the loan sharks, or his association with the San Yee On, his career would be over. And with it would go his government flat, his police pension and his right of abode in the United Kingdom after 1997, already guaranteed by the British Parliament. Now, thought the triad, reviewing his strategy; now we possess the means to make the *shan chiu*'s plan a reality.

The triad saw a scowl appear on the policeman's face, indicating the depth of resentment swirling beneath the superficial deference demanded of him. Regretting now that he had twisted the other's collar quite so hard, he attempted to lighten the atmosphere.

'Come on, Ah Yip. Let's have a drink!' The policeman raised his glass, reluctantly at first, and took a mouthful, then the triad offered him a cigarette, from the red and gold packet. The colours were perfect: an omen of prosperity for all concerned.

Silently, the policeman took the cigarette accepting the triad's authority, knowing he could do no other. He had already made his choice.

The ping of the lighter as it flipped open reunited the

two of them. Yes, thought the Bamboo Snake exultantly, how sweetly it was all falling into place.

'So, what do you want from me next?' asked the policeman, studying the burning tip of his cigarette.

'Remain as quiet as a shadow and keep your head down. No hard drinking, and no more gambling ... at least for the time being. Don't give your bosses any reason to suspend you from duty. We need you on that detail when the moment comes.'

'Don't worry, I know how to behave.'

'I'm sure you do,' said Bamboo Snake, ignoring past indiscretions. Dammit, he had to give the man a little face! 'No changes to the schedule?'

'No changes to the part you're interested in.'

'Good. So how long before we have the timings on it?'

'Another day or two – three at most. I saw a reply from the Mass Transit Railway this morning, but so far I haven't had any legitimate reason for requesting sight of the file. The inspectors get very suspicious if you start reading sensitive documents at random. And don't call me again – it's too risky. For all I know CIB could be watching you.'

The triad nodded his agreement. After the Shatin robbery, they would be trawling deep for information, and who knows what else they might inadvertently stumble across.

'Very well, little brother. When you have the details, put them in an envelope and use the usual box at the main post office beside Star Ferry. It will be another few days then before we contact you again.'

'How?'

'On your radio-pager.'

'But all messages are logged.'

'Don't worry. We will only place a wake-up call with the bureau. When they call you, then you call my car phone number. I'll be waiting.'

Bamboo Snake stayed and watched his man melt

away into the street before calling the waiter and paying the bill with one of the thousand-dollar notes he always kept in the breast pocket of his shirt. Then he gathered up the change and, leaving a handful of coins on the steel tray, walked back to his Porsche.

When he reached the vehicle, there was a parking ticket attached to the wiper. Without a second thought he tore it up, scattering the pieces into the road.

Ruth Tavistock stepped out of the taxi at the Star Ferry Terminal on Hong Kong side and into the crowd thronging the concourse. Automatically she gave a furtive glance over her shoulder. There were the usual crowds tumbling off the ferries, the shambling knot of rickshaw men courting the tourists, and the same squatting groups of Filipino guest workers, twittering amongst themselves like birds. Business people in smart designer-label clothes lined the taxi rank, but she saw no one recognisable. Even if anyone had been watching her, she thought as she walked quickly through the open area of Edinburgh Place, she would be hardly likely to know about it: not in a Hong Kong crowd. She tried to banish her neurotic fears and concentrate on what she would say to him.

When she came to the covered shelter by the water-front directly opposite City Hall, where the Queen's Pier faced Kowloon across the open harbour, mechanically she checked her watch. Realising she was over twenty minutes late, she uttered a curse beneath her breath. She was a very precise person, who hated bad time-keeping in others as much as in herself, but this time the delay had been unavoidable. Those extra twenty minutes had provided her with the information she needed to confront Jack Cinch. It was Lethbridge, her contact inside *HMS Tamar*, the Royal Navy Base less than fifty metres from where she now stood, who had provided the full details.

The keenly-awaited response to her trace on James Reicher had come into *Tamar* in the late afternoon, and it had been relayed to her just twelve minutes ago. The coded signal from MI6 Central Registry, just south of the River Thames in London, had confirmed Becker's suspicions about this whole US Consulate business. It had also confirmed her own worst fears about the man she had believed she was in love with.

Yet even now, despite firm evidence, she was unsure how to approach the problem. Had this been strictly business, her course of action would have been crystal clear. She would have kept quiet and allowed his lies to pile up until she was in a better position to kick the legs from under his story. But her feelings were too tightly involved, and deep inside she hoped he might be able to explain it all away harmlessly.

That would preserve everything – including her own self-respect.

She saw him waving from the wheel-house, and she managed to wave back as if there were nothing wrong between them. The junk, a 30-footer, with russet-brown varnished timbers and that characteristic square Chinese hull, was standing off from the stone boarding steps, riding the swell with a handful of other pleasure craft awaiting passengers.

Cinch engaged the engine and eased the vessel up to the pier. Trotting down the steps, Ruth tossed him her tote bag and leapt nimbly aboard. When he tried to catch hold of her hand and kiss her, she gently brushed him aside.

'Not here. Too many eyes. I'll go below until we're past Green Island.'

Green Island lay off the western end of Hong Kong Island, quite a long way out towards Cheung Chau, and Cinch was somewhat surprised by this sudden new precaution. Nevertheless he could not fault her logic.

'OK, there's beer in the fridge and chips on the table. I'll call you up when we're clear.'

She went below and closed the cabin door, shrugging off her skirt and blouse and replacing them with a swimsuit which she covered, for the time being, with a loose T-shirt and shorts. The room was cheerful and neatly scrubbed, reminding her of other, happier times spent aboard. It still smelled of varnish and creosote, and she remembered the ache in her arm the time she had helped him paint it.

By the time he called her up on deck, she had finished her first San Miguel beer. She came topside holding two more cold cans, and pressed one into his hand.

'Thanks,' said Cinch with a broad smile. 'We're clear of land now, and there's not a police launch in sight. Do you think your honour's safe?'

He received only the most perfunctory of smiles. This was not like her, he thought. Ruth went forward and sat on the upper deck, folding her long legs under her. Cinch continued to watch her just sitting there, proud against the blue of the water and the red sun now dipping fast over Lantau Island. He enjoyed the way the light painted the edges of her silhouette: a coral pink glow around face and arms; and blonde hair shining like spun gold. Still, even in that romantic light he could see the hard set to her chin, and he knew she was angry about something. Best to let her come around in her own time.

So they crossed the West Lamma Channel without speaking, and forty minutes later dropped anchor just off one of the long, flat beaches of Cheung Chau Island. Before the anchor had even touched bottom, Ruth dived into the water and swam aggressively for land. Staying aboard, Cinch opened another beer and watched her wade ashore and walk further along the beach. She was wearing a blue *Speedo* swimsuit which both covered and flattened her breasts – not the stunning high-cut red bikini she usually wore, and that seemed to suggest something, though what he was not sure. Just as it had become too dark to follow her progress along the beach, there was a splash of foam and she came swimming back to the junk. As she climbed aboard once more, her smile seemed a little easier.

He tied up the boat at the restaurant's private moorings. Cheung Chau is a small dumb-bell-shaped island with hills at either end, and beaches and habitation ranged along a thin strip in the middle. Ruth and Jack had been coming to the island for intimate dinners ever since the start of their relationship, and they had always made straight for the same place: Inky's Kitchen. Though little more than an open-air cooked food stall, it enjoyed a prime spot on the waterfront, with its own moorings and an unsurpassed reputation for seafood. The owner's name was actually Ng Kei but everyone called him Inky which was far easier to pronounce. As usual, the tables were packed with local islanders and their families. Inky himself, a squat dumpling of a man with a fierce crew-cut and a mole on his left cheek from which trailed a tail of black hair, came out of the kitchen and greeted them both warmly, a huge cleaver still clutched in his left hand. Two gold teeth flashed his delight at seeing them both.

'Good evening, Goddess of the Golden Moon, happy to see you.' As always he fawned unashamedly. 'Same old table?'

'*Yau hai gam hau fa fa!*' said Ruth, gently poking his stomach. 'Still the same old flatterer.'

Inky laughed still louder.

'*Wah!* It's absolutely uncanny,' he chortled. 'If I closed my eyes I'd swear she was Chinese.' In truth her command of Cantonese was only reasonable, but Inky was one of that older generation of Chinese who found it flattering and amusing that a *gwai lo* should learn to speak a civilised language.

Their table stood on a raised concrete dais by the water's edge, where the gentle lapping of the tide and the chirping of cicadas made a soothing music. Above them the canvas awning was drawn back to reveal stars over-head, and the wooden frame was hung with Chinese lanterns and hundreds of coloured fairy lights. Candles also flickered on the tables, echoing the flaring of Inky's wok as he tossed tipsy prawns and caught them expertly. The smell from the kitchen was heavenly. They watched Inky's fat aproned body dance around before the stove. A splash of rice wine was ignited inside the red-hot pan, and the sizzling prawns were churned with a large metal spatula before being doused in a secret sauce, then flicked out on to an oval plate and presented at their table. Inky served only beer or tea with his food, and never tired of explaining why.

'Too much fried food very bad for health. Chinese say *yit hei*: that means hot air trapped within the body giving rise to all kinds of bad effects. Chinese drink tea or beer to cool the blood. Take away the *yit hei*. Feel better. Healthy, *ah*!'

As they ate, Ruth began to unwind, and she realised it was Inky's banter and cooking which had once again worked their magic.

'I'm sure going to miss this place when my tour's up,' Cinch said airily, leaning back in his chair. 'How about yourself? Think you'll still be here come July 1997 when the boys from Beijing are in command?'

Ruth toyed with her glass.

'Isn't it a little naive to think they aren't in charge already? They control all the key industries in one way or another. Even the tai-pans line up to kiss their hands.'

'All right then, I'm not looking for an argument. The question was about you.'

She flicked her hair away from her face. Though it was still wet when they sat down, the warm breeze off the South China Sea had now dried it completely, and it shone a rich gold in the candlelight.

'Hard to say,' she began. 'Everyone says there's no future for us *gwai lo* here, and England keeps calling me back. Not the real England, of course – the place as it is now – but the place I left twelve years ago. Fields and meadows; crisp autumn days; the crunch of snow in the lane. You know what they say: there's no patriot like an *ex*patriate. Who knows whether the communist cadres will allow us to keep our jobs. Besides, I'm not sure I could work under their kind of government.'

'You don't trust the assurances of the People's Republic?'

'Like I trust my horoscope in this month's *Cosmo*.'

'The way I see it, you Brits have had a good run here to say you practically pirated the place out of Chinese hands.'

The old criticism. She had heard it many times before, especially from Americans.

'The Opium Wars? Yes, we stole this place. But just look what we created from a barren rock. Come 1 July 1997 we'll be handing them back the most exciting and vibrant financial centre in the world: fair compensation I would have thought. I can see this place as the biggest financial market in the world come the second millennium, when those one billion Chinese consumers begin exerting their full economic muscle. I mean mega-rich.'

'And you don't want to stay around and be a part of that? I'd say you have a pretty strong hand. A Cantonese speaker with a straight line to the inside track. You know practically everyone worth knowing here, and as an intelligence officer you have a genuine head-start.'

'Are you suggesting I ought to abuse my position, breach confidentiality for personal gain? A betrayal of trust.' Suddenly she realised what she had said, and stopped abruptly. Cinch looked quickly away across the water before she could judge whether her missile had found its mark. Then, just as abruptly, he turned and fixed her with his eyes.

'Come on, Ruth, let's not be so coy. You're smart enough, for God's sake, and in Hong Kong all the rest is contacts. You have plenty of those.'

For a moment her heart leapt and she wondered guiltily whether he knew she had been checking on his own name as well as that of Reicher. But, of course, there was no way he could know.

She fell silent. A bicycle passed by, ridden by an old man in a clean white vest, and she watched its quiet progress along the waterfront road; the toddler balanced on the crossbar might have been his granddaughter.

Without warning, Cinch asked her directly: 'Ruth, is there something wrong?'

'No, nothing,' she lied, hating herself the instant she said it. 'I'd like to go back now, if you don't mind.'

On their way to the junk, Ruth's mind churned with a hundred different ways of confronting him. Once they were aboard, Cinch threw the engine into reverse and puttered away from the jetty, occasionally glancing at her and wondering.

They were well into the swell of the Lamma Channel when he decided to find out. Coming close up behind her, he slid both arms around her waist and bent his head to kiss the soft skin behind her right ear. Ruth was taken by surprise, and for a moment was near to pulling away. But then she let herself be turned, and even responded warmly when he kissed her on the lips. Immediately he slipped an exploratory hand between the buttons of her blouse and began to trace the smoothness of her stomach. At once she let out a soft moan of encouragement as his fingers tugged at the elastic of her panties. Then, as he pressed forward she clasped her own hand tightly over the back of his and dropped onto one knee, bringing the full weight of her body to bear against his cocked wrist. The sudden intense pain made him cry out.

'Jesus Christ! You're breaking my hand!' he gasped as she swept him to the floor, his fingers numb as his hand slipped out of her clothing – pain shrieking along the whole length of his arm.

'Not nice, is it, Jack? Being set up, I mean.'

She stood over him, her blue eyes glittering coldly in the light of the boat lamps.

'What's gotten into you?' he demanded angrily, rising to his feet. 'What's this all about? You've been somewhere else all evening.'

'Today I discovered something that was very hard to accept, Jack. It was hard to accept because it proved my judgement had been unsound, and that's something I'm not known for.'

He stopped massaging his wrist. 'Go on.'

'Jim Reicher, your State Department colleague. It was a lie, wasn't it? I had him checked out, Jack. Reicher wasn't working for you at all. You were working for him – both working for the CIA.'

Cinch inhaled deeply, then let the breath out slowly. Choosing his words carefully.

'Look, Ruth, I don't know what this is all about but I don't think this is the time to start playing heavy psych-games.'

His evasion only fuelled her resolve.

'Why not? It's as good a time as any. Since I don't anticipate being alone with you much in the future.' She let that sink in, and watched his reaction before continuing. 'You told me Reicher was sent here to help you clean up a counterfeiting ring, but that was a lie. Why did you lie to me, Jack? I found out that Reicher had a long history of black operations in Vietnam. Not actual combat, but clever little propaganda and disinformation exercises. He was in Manila propping up the Marcos government until the last minute; after that he helped circulate rumours about the advanced state of Star Wars technology to try to stampede the Russians to the negotiating table. He even sold virus-infected military software to non-aligned governments, which would cause missiles to explode on launch. It's hardly surprising somebody eventually killed him.'

'Ruth, please, you don't understand...' Cinch reached for her hand but Ruth smacked it away.

'You don't think so? Perhaps you'd care to explain why the CIA had to place Reicher in State Department cover. Was it to make him seem as squeaky clean as you are? Or should I say used to be?' Damn! Why had she begun personalising this. That was stupid. 'You know the rules; all black operations in our backyard must be cleared through Special Branch first. If the CIA is running one undeclared, there'll be more trouble than the Consul-General's seen in years.'

Cinch knew then that further denials were a waste of time. There was a smell of putrefaction on the night breeze as the junk passed the crowded tenements of Kennedy Town.

'Ruth, this is my job, for Christ's sake! Sometimes it gets a little messy.' His whole body was tense; his face lined with guilt. Suddenly he was no longer the Ivy League student. Now he was the intelligence agent.

'I don't accept that, Jack. I've contravened Branch orders for you; supplied you information classified NUSN – No US Nationals – when I thought it necessary. I put my trust in *you* before my own career, because I thought we had an understanding. But you used that trust to further your own career. I was willing to help, but instead you told me a direct lie, asked me to smooth things over – just cover up the mistake. That wasn't you talking, Jack; that was John Prioletti. You always said you'd never work for the Company, that you couldn't trust them. When did you become their pawn, Jack?'

'You can believe what you want, but it wasn't like that. I was ordered to provide cover for Reicher. That's all. I have no idea what he was working on or why he was killed.'

'I'm afraid I don't believe you anymore.'

'That's your privilege,' he said coldly. 'When they found him butchered that way, I did what I had to do to protect the reputation of the State Department.'

Without waiting for him to finish, she returned to the attack.

'And what about me?' she blurted. 'Wasn't I worth protecting? Why did you have to make me a part of it?'

'You're making this into something that just wasn't there.'

'Am I? All I know is I'll never be able to trust you again. There'll always be a doubt in my mind, and that's not the kind of relationship I'm looking for.'

'Hey, now, wait a minute. This has nothing to do with us.'

'Doesn't it, Jack?' she almost shouted. 'I don't agree. You lied to me even while we shared the same bed. That hurts, Jack.'

Cinch's hand tightened upon the wheel. Beyond all expectation, that last remark had hurt him, too. Suddenly he despised himself, but more than this he despised John Prioletti and his sordid little world of lies and dirty tricks. Prioletti had made him dirty, too.

'OK,' he said, his face assuming a martyred look. 'If that's the way it is.'

'That's the way,' she snapped. 'From now on it's strictly business between us. First thing tomorrow you'll receive a memo requesting official clarification of the work Reicher was committed to, and if I'm not happy with your answers I'll take it straight to the Consul-General.'

'You'd really do that?'

'You bet I would, Jack. Here endeth the special relationship.'

It took Wes Bowman's team just half an hour to locate Tony Kwan's red Mercedes sports coupé in the underground lot. There were only a few places it could possibly be, and one of those was the VIP car park beside the swank Chiu Chau restaurant in Tsim Sha Tsui

East, where they eventually found it. Bowman listened with satisfaction to the radio confirmation from his junior runners, but as the team moved in to take preliminary observations they found another team already running a covert action against the same vehicle.

'What the hell are those guys doing?' asked Bowman of no one in particular. He was observing two Chinese men wiring some kind of electronic device into the battery circuit, while a third stood guard.

'Could be a new heating coil,' offered the young blond agent sardonically. 'But I doubt that somehow. Looks like somebody else has an interest in Tony Kwan.'

They kept well out of sight until the three-man team had slipped quietly out through the service stairs then, cautiously, they moved in and carefully lifted the bonnet to see for themselves.

They searched for fifteen minutes and still they found nothing.

'Whoever they were,' breathed Bowman respectfully, 'those guys were good. Not a sign of a charge anywhere, nor even an initiating circuit. That can mean only one thing.'

'Technical surveillance?' asked the blond agent.

Bowman grinned broadly in assent.

'They must have bugged this baby. Wired a transmitter to the battery circuit for long-range tracking.'

'What do you think – local cops?'

'Almost certainly. Should have anticipated this. Kwan's so far into the white powder that the Narcs probably follow him everywhere.'

'So what now? Still want to lay the charge?'

'You bet your ass.'

Twenty minutes later Bowman's team was relaxing in a big Holden saloon vehicle parked just across from the Shangri-La Hotel, and still in sight of the VIP car park.

'Just a little something on account,' said Bowman,

taking the radio detonator from his jacket pocket.

'Hey, Wes,' interrupted the young blond agent. 'Mind if I do this? I've never done one before.'

Bowman smiled indulgently and handed over the detonator.

'Sure, man, be my guest.'

The agent threw the switch and a boom reverberated through the concrete vault of the underground car park. Bowman caught the first small flash of light spilling up from the entrance ramp, and smiled again, watching the uniformed attendants race down the ramp to where Tony Kwan's beautiful red Mercedes now stood engulfed in flame and black smoke.

'This time it's only your car,' Bowman grinned acidly. 'But before this thing's over, Mr Red Cudgel, it's going to be your ass.'

The stolen four-door Mazda sports swung out of the evening rush of Hennessy Road into a side street of glitz-fronted buildings, and stopped – double parking beside a line of ramshackle goods lorries and micro-vans encroaching on the pavement.

Wanchai. Where everything was for sale. Even the space at the kerbside. The throng of Japanese hatchbacks on this side street were waiting to sell the space they occupied to the prowling limousines, because in Wanchai parking was a nightmare.

Still, none of this mattered to the driver of the Mazda, for he would not be staying long.

The vehicle had been boosted from the public car park up at Middle Gap on the Peak of Hong Kong Island and kept out of sight in a lock-up garage in Kennedy Town until darkness fell. Now the driver was in position, and he kept the engine running, only once lowering his window to flick a lighted butt into the gutter.

Looking out across the street, Bamboo Snake jerked his head in the direction of the huge Chinese restaurant which dominated the street front opposite.

'*Goh gaan ye. Yee lau*,' he said to the rearview mirror. 'That's the place. First floor.'

The two Chinese men in the back had a brief exchange of words before one got out and walked quickly across the street into the restaurant.

Inside the foyer a girl in a green and gold *cheung saam* greeted him, indicating the red-carpeted stairway to the upper floors. In the back of the car the remaining passenger sat quietly, looking straight ahead, fixing cold fish eyes on the neon striplights in front. It was time to make ready. With ritual slowness he raised both hands in front of his chest, as if holding a heavy stone jar, closed his eyes, and began to breathe deeply. Concentrating. With each successive breath there came a sound which seemed to come from the pit of his stomach. A sound like wind rushing through the pit of a deep cave. After four such breaths the process began: the warm glow emanating from the centre of his palms, moving outwards until he felt both hands vibrating with the surge of energy passing between them. In his mind he saw ice-blue sparks leaping the gap between his hands, completing the circle of energy – releasing the reservoir of his inner power.

The Bamboo Snake watched and listened in fascination, saying nothing, hardly even daring to breathe himself, for he too had studied the secret arts and knew better than to upset the vital flow of *chi*. He firmly believed that one of this man's fingers pointed in his direction would be sufficient to end his life. Nervously Bamboo Snake licked his lips.

One minute later the first Chinese returned and slid quietly into the vehicle, keeping a respectful silence until the breathing process was complete and the other man's eyes had again flicked open. Then he spoke softly. Addressing the other by the title Master.

'*Sifu*, the way is prepared.'

295

'Is he there now?'

'Yes, he is there.'

'How is the place marked? There must be no mistake.'

'Do not worry, *sifu*. The place is marked by the *sap ji*.' The second triad used the index finger of each hand to form a simple cross: the Chinese symbol for the number ten. 'The chopsticks will be crossed upon the table before him. This will be the sign.'

'Good,' said Red Cudgel, with energy shining through the portals of his eyes. 'Then I am ready.'

It was 9.45 in the evening, and Wanchai was an inferno of neon and crystal. Inside the Luk Kwok Restaurant business was booming.

Like all the bigger Chinese restaurants, or *jau ga*, the Luk Kwok's exterior was a riot of exotic colour and symbolism, the doors and windows decorated with the colours and emblems of good fortune and prosperity. There were three large floors, and most of the fifteen hundred chairs were filled by groups of office workers or family groups enjoying dinner parties. At the main entrance, the smoked-glass doors were motorised, whisper-quiet and surrounded by a carved wooden border of entwined chrysanthemums carefully overlaid with goldleaf. The three plate windows on the ground floor were embellished with the neon outlines of a fish, a prawn and a crab, and between these windows lacquered murals depicting plum blossom and singing sparrows climbed gracefully to meet the gold lettering above the doors which proudly announced the restaurant's good name. To ensure continued good fortune, red silk bunting hung in the windows and from the tables in the foyer, each strip of it carefully lettered with gold calligraphy.

In keeping with tradition, there was a bamboo *pai lau* at first-floor level: a neon-lit board which extended over the street on bamboo scaffolding and was decorated with green and gold tinsel and inscribed with giant red characters. Beneath the *pai lau* a thick crimson carpet covered the floor of the main foyer and spilled out on to the pavement in extravagant welcome.

Units from police headquarters had a long-established relationship with the Luk Kwok. It was a place that always gave face to cops, allowing them discount and a privately sectioned area in which to unwind, out of the public gaze. The food was always excellent (the poor man's chicken exceptionally so); and, being just a few minutes' walk from New May House, the Luk Kwok was a convenient place for PHQ cops to celebrate a promotion, a wedding, or even just a job well done.

On such occasions it was traditional amongst Chinese for the host of the celebration to *cheng sik faan*, that is to invite the others to eat at his expense. At office parties it was always the boss who paid; with family groups, the wealthiest and usually senior member. Only amongst groups of equal status was the bill divided equally. It was a matter of face. The host always gained immense face as he peeled off hundred-dollar bills, the recipients of his largesse politely extolling his virtues the while. The larger the bill, the greater the face. Occasionally good-natured fights would even break out as rivals competed for the privilege of paying – some of the constables cheerfully blowing half a month's pay at a throw, and counting it a wise investment to confirm his standing within the group.

After its raid on Gwong Tau Shan the special OSCG task force was more than ready for a celebration, and Tasker had given strict orders, when they booked a screened-off section of the first floor, that nobody was to *cheng sik faan* but he himself. The *foh gei* complied with a grinning 'Yessir!'

Protocol was strict, even within the informality of a section bash – or *dai sik wooi*, literally a 'big eating party'. Face demanded that Joe Lai and Tiger Cheng each supply two bottles of brandy for the obligatory *yam sing* toasts. In addition it was the station sergeant's job to arrange the menu and the seating plan, observing proper protocols, and that all the five basic tastes were catered for in the menu. Choosing complementary dishes was a tricky business, and every mother's son in Hong Kong is an expert in the business of food. The meal might begin with sliced roast pork, followed by a selection of pork, chicken, beef and seafood dishes, with fresh steamed or stir-fried vegetables. The boys would all take care to eat something from every course for fear of offending the host. Likewise they would not dream of embarrassing themselves by taking more than their share, or by fighting for the tastiest pieces on the plate.

Amid the raucous banter, the lively conversation and the drinking they would pick sparingly at the dishes. After a dozen or more courses, the waiters would divide up dishes of fried rice and noodles between the revellers, and the banquet would usually end with sweet red bean soup and sweet pastries. As a final gesture, dishes of oranges would be offered, to indicate that the meal was ended and it was time to leave. Tasker always referred to these as the 'piss off' oranges.

The party began at 5.30, with the team splitting into fours for the usual two hours of what they loved most – mah jong. The game was one of the few kinds of so-called 'social gambling' which the law allowed, and they lost no opportunity to play. The tables were square, like card tables, with a Formica top and drawers set into the edges in which the players could keep their stake money. When the players were seated, a steel box of tiles was emptied noisily out on to the table, and everyone pitched in, shuffling and turning them face-down. Then the players each stacked their own share of the tiles, with much clattering, into a long wall, and these walls were pushed together in the centre to form a box from which each player's hand of tiles was selected. Nimble fingers caressed and expertly manipulated the tiles as they were drawn and discarded in turn. Every move invited much table talk and frequent grunts of disgust, until finally someone made a winning hand and slammed it down in triumph.

The banter and advice flowed freely, as did the stream of obscenities when fate cheated a player. After each successive win, the folded green tens and twenties were tossed across the table and gathered exultantly into the winner's drawer; then the exaggerated shuffling began anew. The *foh gei* loved every hand – win or lose. They loved the noise and show and the pantomime of it all. They went on like this for hours, only stopping, reluctantly, when the food was ready, and the waiters brought in pre-laid table tops and manoeuvred them into position over the game tables.

As soon as the first course arrived, the brandy bottle was opened and the toasts began. When each glass was charged with an inch or more of Remy Martin each man took his glass between two hands and raised it in salute. *Yam booi!* Then the expensive liquor was knocked back like orange juice, and all glasses were slammed down upon the table with cries of '*Ho ye! Ho ye!*' Great stuff! That done, the chopsticks were seized up and the food itself came under attack.

Tasker was sitting in the place of honour, next to Joe Lai on the main table near the top of the stairs, enjoying the free-for-all in the centre of the table. Between courses, individual constables approached him and demanded that he drink a toast with them. Flattered, he complied, taking great care to finish off his glass first each time, thereby gaining in face. Not until the fifth glass did he acknowledge that the *foh gei* were up to their usual tricks, trying to drink their boss under the table.

'OK, enough, you bloody munchkins,' he roared. 'Feed your faces!' His team responded with whistles and jeers.

Between the fifth and sixth courses a rest was

declared, and Tasker turned to talk to Joe Lai in a low voice.

'It's a bastard of a situation, Joe. We've got an excellent lead, and the promise of more when Philip reports in again. But I'm buggered if I know who to trust with it all. We could easily get that kid killed if the information gets back to their High Dragon at our headquarters.'

'You have to brief the DD Crime, right?'

'Yeah, but what if Lee's the one – or if it's Chan Hamgar himself?'

'The Director? Both of them are Chiu Chau. But which one to trust? It could be either. Let it slip to the wrong one about Philip, and the boy is dead.'

'Yes, you're right. I guess we've no choice but to go straight to Weldon himself. I'll tell him everything, and get him to order me to report direct to him in future. It's the only way to safeguard Philip and restrict access to his intelligence.'

'Talking of intelligence...'

Abruptly Tasker jabbed Joe's elbow, warning him of the approach of a waiter. Wearing a short red uniform jacket and black bow-tie, the man came through the screens and moved rapidly around the table, replenishing drinks and removing empty beer bottles. Nobody paid him much attention as he loaded up his silver tray, or even noticed as he broke open a spare packet of chopsticks and laid them crosswise in front of Tasker's place setting. A moment later he was gone, and Joe continued speaking.

At the top of the stairs the waiter paused, put down his loaded tray, and removed his red jacket. He rolled it up and pushed it between two potted palms, then, looking around anxiously, he walked quickly down the stairs. At the first landing a shabbily-dressed man in a dark green sports jacket leaned against the handrail with his arms folded. As he passed him, the waiter stopped just long enough to give the sign of the phoenix claw with his right hand. He continued on down the stairs and out into the street.

Red Cudgel glided up the stairs, almost as silent as a ghost. A second man fell in beside him, ready to clear away any obstruction – or man – in his way. As they reached the first floor, they glanced around, then moved towards the first dining section, pausing outside the red and gold screens just long enough for Red Cudgel to slip a red opera mask from beneath his jacket and extract a pair of steel chopsticks from his inner pocket. The mask he slipped over his face; the chopsticks he laid upon his right palm with their shafts crossed. When he closed his hand into a tight fist the two points jutted out between his fingers, extending some twelve centimetres beyond his fist.

Dragon fangs.

Tasker was just emptying his brandy glass when the two scruffy Chinese emerged between the screens. Two, three, four steps – the first man reached the table and swiped the glass away from Tasker's mouth.

'What the fuck . . .' he yelled in protest.

There was a microsecond of stunned inactivity before the bigger Chinese grabbed Tasker by the hair and yanked his head sharply backwards, cracking several vertebrae with the force of the movement. The superintendent's face became a frightened mask, and a strangled cry rattled in his throat as the brandy discharged into his air passages.

His cry was echoed by some of the *foh gei* at the table, but their dulled senses worked far too slowly to prevent what followed. Only Tiger Cheng and Joe Lai reacted at all. Caught off balance, Joe turned on his chair.

Cheng was almost on his feet when the second Chinese pulled a pair of PLA officer's pistols and jabbed one into each of their faces, screaming, '*Mo lan yuk!* Don't fucking move!'

Red Cudgel moved against Tasker with awesome

301

speed; so fast that not one of the drunken *foh gei* had a chance to help him. There was a sudden blur as the killer's ugly calloused right hand rose and fell above the superintendent's upturned face – driving the two steel rods down through his eyes and deep into his brain.

With the first agonised scream, blood spurted on to Red Cudgel's sleeve. Tasker's limbs went into immediate spasm as Red Cudgel toppled the chair and let it fall backwards. The bloody steel rods still protruded from the policeman's eyes like obscene antennae. His limbs bent awkwardly as he writhed in his death throes. A few seconds more and he lay still, legs splayed wide apart like a puppet whose strings had been cut.

Without pausing to retrieve his weapons, the killer turned and rushed for the exit. His accomplice backed out after him cursing aloud and still sweeping an arc with his automatic pistols.

Moving as if in an opium dream, his brain shrieking outrage, Joe Lai rose from his seat and grabbed for the pistol that was not there. *Diu lei lo mo!* All weapons had been returned to armoury on Tasker's orders, for they knew they would all be drinking far too much! Helplessly he hurled a brandy bottle at the disappearing form of the accomplice. It smashed against a screen, toppling it, and revealing the assassination scene to the view of the whole restaurant.

Heads turned, and for a second there was horrified silence. Then the real screaming started. Suddenly waiters were running everywhere.

Someone was screaming over and over: '*Mau saat! Mau saat!* Murder! Murder!'

At the table no one moved.

In the next second, Joe Lai let out a roar of anguish. John Tasker lay in a crumpled heap at his feet, and he could not yet believe it.

'Ah Keung, call it in,' he shouted. 'Ah Cheng, follow me!' He took off hurtling down the stairs, with Cheng

302

and two others following him. Murder in his head now, Joe ran out into the street, barging guests and waiters aside in his headlong flight. Out on the road a public light bus braked hard, swerving to avoid him, and careered sideways into a parked Mercedes, buckling its door panel. But the two Chinese were already in the yellow Mazda sports and halfway down the road when Joe saw them. Their getaway driver had moved up to the entrance right on cue. The yellow Mazda was now skidding down the street, tyres smoking as it weaved madly between the traffic.

All at once the rage exploded within him. He screamed from the pit of his stomach. '*Dai lo!*'

In frustration he turned and swung his fists, raining blows against the side of the light bus, kicking at the driver's door. By the time S/Sgt Cheng had grabbed and restrained him, both fists were already skinned and bleeding.

'*Dai lo!*'

'It won't do any good. Not now.'

'They killed him, Ah Cheng. San Yee On. I know it, you know it.'

'*Hai,*' said the sergeant quietly. 'He pushed them to the edge, and they had to do something. But he knew the risk of what he was doing. He knew it might come to this.'

'I swear by Gwan-Dai I'm going to find whoever did this! No matter who, no matter where.'

'Joe-sir, better look after yourself. This is still the season of the Hungry Ghosts.'

In the pained and confused silence that followed, Cheng slowly released his grip and Joe's hands came up to cover his face. Heaven help them all now, he thought. Now that their Elder Brother was gone.

In the gloom, and with hot tears filling his eyes, Joe realised he had not even glimpsed the car's licence plate.

* * *

James Weldon was dining with his wife and niece at the prestigious Hong Kong Club on Jackson Road when the news came. The coffee was just being poured when the captain glided to the table and discreetly invited the Commissioner to take a phone-call in the restaurant manager's office. Without further ado, he rose from his chair and excused himself.

He listened intently to the voice of the duty officer speaking from the first-floor control centre at PHQ. Headquarters PolMil was the coordinating centre for all major incidents, and the duty officer always kept an availability register to speed up notification of senior officers in times of crisis. He had already phoned the Director of Criminal Investigation and other senior detectives, in accordance with set-down procedure. Each had confirmed that the CP would need to be notified, particularly since Government House was monitoring the case which Tasker was working on. Weldon put his hand to his forehead, stunned by what he was hearing, then his training reasserted itself and he responded with a series of terse orders before replacing the handset. As he walked back to his table he asked the captain to summon his police driver.

'I'm sorry, darling,' he apologised to his wife. 'Something's just come up and it can't wait. Why don't you two stay and finish. I'll send the driver back for you.'

After twenty-eight years' marriage to a top police officer, Claire Weldon was philosophical about such interruptions. Like her husband she was a Scot by birth, redheaded, but unlike the fiery stereotype she possessed a great fund of patience; her soft green eyes had always looked with sympathy upon the demands of her husband's long career. One look at the set of his features told her all she needed to know. Something had set his eyes ablaze, but it was no use asking him until he was ready to confide in her.

Quickly, he kissed her, and left.

There were already half a dozen police vehicles and a large crowd outside the Luk Kwok restaurant when the CP's limousine arrived. The restaurant was still fully lit up, but had been evacuated and cordoned off by uniformed officers from Wanchai station; the District Commander was directing operations. Weldon acknowledged various salutes, and was escorted up to the first floor where Chan Ham-gar, the Director of Criminal Investigations, and Lee Ming-kwai, his deputy, were in conference with the senior superintendent commanding Organised and Serious Crimes.

'Good God above!' he breathed when he saw the body. It was like nothing he had ever seen before. He clenched his hand into a tight fist, recalling how he had warned Devereau and the Governor against assigning Tasker to this case. But not even he could have predicted this.

A description of the assailants and of the getaway vehicle had already been circulated to all stations. RCU Hong Kong Island were handling initial enquiries, but this had the look of a ritual slaying by a professional triad assassin.

The steel chopsticks used in the killing were the real giveaway, those and the red opera mask discarded in the main foyer when the killer fled. Weldon knew that triad hitmen were very hot on tradition. They preferred traditional Chinese weaponry to guns: usually a blade but any piece of arcane equipment would suffice. It would need a huge stroke of luck or some specific tip-off to catch them now.

Weldon listened to the DCI's version of events, then asked to see the witnesses. They had taken one of the large round dining tables, and those who were not still writing out their own statements were sitting quietly staring into space or else slumped wearily across the table. There were glasses of green tea and a fresh pot. The Commissioner noticed Joe Lai, leaning upon one elbow, staring into his glass, a cigarette burning between his fingers, its ash almost an inch long. As he approached, Joe looked up and tried to stand but Weldon pressed him back in his seat and refilled his glass from the teapot. Joe tapped the table politely, grateful for the small gesture of understanding.

Weldon took the seat beside him.

'I don't quite know what to say, Inspector,' he began sympathetically. 'Perhaps there are no words at a time like this.'

'I know he liked to play with the rules, sir, but he was the best police officer I ever knew. He had a big heart. And he understood his men.'

'I believe you have some ideas about why this happened. A connection with the case you were investigating?'

'Yes, sir.'

'But you refused to speak to any of your senior officers about it.'

'That's right.'

'Care to tell me why, lad?'

'Because I don't trust those bastards!' Joe felt his anger rise.

Be calm, he warned himself; any show of hysteria would only weaken his argument. 'Tasker was unhappy about the channels of reporting on this case, and the amount of interference he was getting from CID headquarters. He was about to request a meeting with yourself.'

Weldon was puzzled. 'What about?'

'He wanted to cut them all out of the chain – to report direct into your office. He felt that would be safer.'

'Why safer?'

'Because ...' Joe Lai stole a glance around him, then rose. When Weldon rose too, he steered him to an empty table at the far end of the room. There was mild interest from the knot of senior officers, though no one tried to

306

follow them. Joe's face was suddenly tinged with cold hatred. 'Because we found out that the San Yee On were the ones behind the Shatin robbery and we now know one of their senior office bearers is also a senior police officer – someone on the fifth floor in PHQ. Tasker didn't feed that through channels, for obvious reasons.'

'I presume we're talking about a Chinese officer, otherwise you wouldn't even be talking to me. Do you have a name?'

Joe shook his head.

'Not yet, but we have an undercover asset working on that.' Joe moved his chair, bunching his fists. 'Sir, he's very well placed and he's given us top-grade intelligence. He confirmed the link between the triad and the Shatin robbers. We now have the location of the gang's base outside Canton.'

'That's why Tasker had to die,' said the Commissioner, nodding with bitter understanding. 'To cover their trail and that of their bloody triad sponsors.'

'No, sir.'

'Then why?'

'For the future. At first I thought like you, but just now it came to me, sitting over at that table. It was like John Tasker's ghost was talking to me, here in my ear, reminding me of the facts, adding them up. Now I'm sure of it. He wasn't killed to protect the past, but to safe-guard the future.'

'You'd better fill in the blanks, laddie. I'm not with this at all.' For a moment Weldon wondered whether shock had unhinged the inspector's mind.

'Our source warned us something very big was being planned here in Hong Kong, but he didn't know what. He still doesn't. But he said the Shatin robbery was just the fund raiser for what was to follow. The triads were afraid any attempt to trace these connections would uncover the existence of this major operation. *That's* why they pushed his eyes through the back of his head!'

Joe's fist banged hard upon the table. Then his hands shot up to cover his face. James Weldon patted Joe's shoulder, attempting to steady him, realising the bond that must have existed between the two men. He sensed how hard it must have been to have witnessed Tasker's appalling murder.

For long minutes Weldon sat with the detective, listening to the man's most private thoughts. By the time Lai's cigarette was finished Weldon had made up his mind.

'All right, laddie, I think I'll take over from here.'

Joe looked up, staring into the Commissioner's hard grey eyes.

'What do you mean?'

'From now on you report exclusively to me. Is that clear?'

Joe nodded gratefully.

'*Ho ching choh*, sir.'

'See me in my office at 8.30 tomorrow morning. I want every scrap and detail you have on the case. We're going to crack this thing by hook or by crook. Aye, and we'll have this bloody so-called High Dragon of theirs to boot.'

Joe appreciated the rhetoric, but there was one very important point Weldon seemed to have forgotten.

'Sir, the San Yee On have closed every door we've knocked on. The only way left now is through the *Dai Huen Jai* and they're still holed up outside Canton. I hate to say it, but unless the Chinese change their mind about extraditing them we can't move at all.'

As he stood to leave, Weldon's manner seemed that of a man whose course of action was already decided.

'In that case, Mr Lai,' he said quietly, 'when you see me tomorrow you'd better have that address with you. Chinese territory or not, I still mean to have a result.'

BOOK TWO
CLAWHAMMER

FOURTEEN

The following morning the Tasker assassination was lead story in every one of the colony's forty-odd newspapers. TOP DETECTIVE MURDERED IN RITUAL GANGLAND SLAYING trumpeted one banner headline. That was enough to shake the Civil Service community to its foundations. All over Hong Kong, police officers woke to the RTHK news bulletins, hardly able to believe their ears.

John Tasker, the living legend – no more.

For some old hands it was like the known world had been turned upon its head. Attacks on police were rare enough, but attacks on expatriate officers were practically unheard of. In police messes from Stanley Fort to Lok Ma Chau there was speculation that the rule of law might finally be slipping. So much so that Europeans contemplated anxiously their future in the colony. Many had already noticed a subtle deterioration in attitude towards the *gwai lo*, prompted, some thought, by the British Government's bad handling of the sovereignty issue and its divisive policy on the granting of British passports to only certain key Hong Kong Chinese. Inevitably some of those who had vowed to stick it out until 1997 brooded darkly on whether *now* was the time to make the break.

Joe Lai was in and out of the Commissioner's fifth-floor office before most of the directorate staff had even arrived for work. He came well prepared with every last detail Weldon had demanded, and was ordered to continue low-key investigations alone without involving any of his team. It was important, warned Weldon, that whoever had been trying to sabotage the Shatin investigation should believe they had succeeded.

In the meantime the Commissioner intended to progress the investigation by a much more radical method, known as 'Clawhammer'.

Soon after Lai had slipped quietly out of Caine House, Weldon was on the phone to two of his most senior officers: the Director of Special Branch and the Director of Operations.

Henry St John-Black, the DSB, was the first to arrive, a spare, ascetic-looking man with a pinched grey face and few remaining wisps of hair on the shining dome of his head. He greeted Weldon politely and took a seat at the conference table in front of the Commissioner's desk, his long fingers drumming expectantly upon the table top. At directorate level unscheduled meetings of this kind were rare, but St John-Black had seen the newspapers that morning and he knew how difficult was the Commissioner's position. What he could not quite fathom was the reason for involving his own department, which was, after all, the political arm of the Force.

A moment later the square bulk of Ray Doogan, the uniformed Director of Operations, appeared in the doorway. Weldon came round from behind his desk, waving the new arrival across to the conference table. Doogan nodded a surprised greeting to the DSB, clearly as intrigued as St John-Black about the latter's presence.

Weldon lost no time with pleasantries.

'Gentlemen, cards on the table. We have a situation.' His favourite euphemism. 'One which I feel demands the deployment of our Clawhammer capability.'

Straight away both men looked thunderstruck. Clawhammer was a very emotive word.

In fact it was the codename for a joint tasking group dedicated to covert action of a highly sensitive nature.

Normal criminal cases entailed predefined responses executed in line with standard Force organisation; but Clawhammer was an *ad hoc* unit few people knew about, made up of skilled specialists drawn from Special Branch and the Operations Directorate, with the added assistance of CIB and TSB technicians. They were activated only on the Commissioner's express orders, to conduct operations too potentially embarrassing or just too damn dangerous to trust to other units.

St John-Black moved uncomfortably in his chair and glanced across at Doogan, who artfully occupied his attention in packing and lighting his briar pipe.

'Would this be in response to the death of Tasker?' asked the DSB.

Weldon gave a curt nod.

'Partly. But there's a great deal more to it than just that. And what I have to say goes no further than this office. "Round eyes" only, is that clear?'

It was. No Chinese involvement whatsoever.

His briefing was concise, covering first the details of Tasker's murder, without apparent emotion; and then explaining the extent of Joe Lai's information about the possibility of a triad source within the PHQ directorate.

'I'm authorising you, Henry, to treat this as subversive penetration. I want you to root out this rotten apple, and I want him found quickly.'

'A senior Chinese officer,' mused Ray Doogan, blowing a cloud of smoke above his head. 'I was about to ask why the Deputy Commissioner isn't with us. Now I see.'

'Indeed.' Weldon shifted his gaze to the D. Ops, who was now listening intently, with arms folded in his lap. 'As for you, Ray, I have a very special task for your men.' He paused as if choosing his words with care. 'We've lost too many officers already to this particular gang of thugs. Last night was a total outrage. I can't have it, do you hear? This office I hold carries too many responsibilities for that; not just to the Governor and the people of Hong Kong, but also to the men and women under my command.'

'Understood, sir,' agreed St John-Black.

'So it's not just the robbery anymore?' Ray Doogan took the pipe from between his teeth.

'Yes, it goes much deeper than that. I learn now from the death of one of my officers that something very big is being planned on our patch.' Weldon stared past them at a point on the far wall. 'This bloody territory has just five years to go before we hand it back to Big Brother. I'm damned if I'll see it degenerate before then. Not under my regime. That's why we have to act. That's why your men are going to infiltrate the Chinese mainland and hit that address in Foshan.'

'What?' Doogan's surprise was evident. Then a faint smile shone through, as his pipe now jiggled from one side of his mouth to the other. 'You mean go into the People's Republic of China?'

'I think you heard me, Ray. We can't expect help from Interpol in Canton, so we'll have to help ourselves. Go up there and bring those *Dai Huen Jai* back – alive if possible. They're the key to this whole bloody mess.'

Doogan continued nodding as he considered the potential outcome of handling such political dynamite.

'Excuse me, sir, but what does CGO make of it? I mean are they with us?' This was a reasonable enough question, since all covert actions were supposed to be cleared first through the Secretary for Security in Central Government Offices.

But not this time.

Weldon scowled back at his Director of Operations.

'I have not consulted them. Nor shall I be doing so. I'm taking this on my own back.' He spoke with the finality of a judge passing sentence. 'I'm *ordering* you to deploy the Special Duties Unit.'

It was like a small electric jolt. Each man in the cool,

air-conditioned room sensed it: the sudden heat of adrenalin. The Director of Special Branch swallowed hard.

'Let me get this straight. You're sending our counter-terrorist weapon into the PRC? Are you sure you know what you're doing, sir?'

Weldon did not waver.

'I always know what I'm doing, Henry. This operation will be restricted to only those officers with Clawhammer clearance. There'll be no senior uniformed or CID officers involved, other than we three at this table. I want it properly coordinated through Special Branch, using the Clawhammer format. SB will handle all security aspects: code-words, reconnaissance, communications and intelligence gathering. Henry, do you have suitable agents in place in Canton?'

'Close enough. Yes, I don't see any problem. It's just that ... well, look here, James, I'm speaking as a friend now. If our men get caught inside territorial PRC kidnapping Chinese citizens, there'll be hell to pay. They'd have to construe it as an act of blatant terrorism. Who knows what repercussions that could have upon Sino-British relations. Apart from screwing up your own career, the 1997 agreements on Hong Kong could go right down the Swanee, too.'

Weldon was no fool and he had spent half the night considering these very things. But his mind was now made up. He eased himself back in his chair, propping a beefy sunburned forearm on its handle and resting his jaw in one huge hand.

'Thank you for sharing those thoughts, Henry,' he said. 'Then you'd just better make bloody well sure that nobody gets caught, won't you?'

Seen from the dozens of passenger aircraft that swooped hourly over Kowloon peninsula towards Kai Tak airport, the South China Sea looked the same deep, luminous

315

blue that was captured in the tourists' picture postcards. But off the west coast of Kowloon, in the busy channel between Yaumatei and Stonecutter's Island, the water was always thickly clouded with silt; a greenish, brownish soup constantly churned by the giant screws of container ships steaming their way out from Hong Kong's vast harbour, heading for the open sea and the consumer markets of the world.

At a depth of twelve metres visibility was poor, the light dim like some science-fiction movie shot through a green filter. It was diffused, confusing and, to the unskilled diver, extremely dangerous. Aside from sudden storms of jellyfish and the occasional shark, there were enough scuttled or abandoned wrecks to terrify even experienced swimmers – everything from small wooden junks blasted by typhoons to monstrous steel-hulled freighters, the casualties of insurance fraud.

At the first dark shadow Mel Kale stopped and turned upright in the water to check the luminous compass clamped over the left wrist of his dry-suit. Instinctively he also checked the velcro fastening that held his H and K machine pistol in position above his weight belt, and then readjusted his bearing towards the stern of the ship. Having located the leviathan above him, he yanked on the two-metre buddy cord attached to his right elbow and received a double tug in response, telling him that Haak Jai, his diving buddy on the other end, was OK. He sucked hard on the demand valve in his mouthpiece, realising that the oxygen bottle was running low, and then moved on through the dark water with long fluid beats of his speed fins. They swam in tandem, communicating only by touch, and leaving no trail of bubbles behind them. A spring-loaded reel in Kale's left hand rotated, paying out a command line for the other pairs of divers to follow.

There were eight men in the assault team. Each wore a black, one-piece, hooded dry-suit without markings, and each was equipped with a special rebreather rig consisting of a rubber lung fed by a small oxygen cylinder mounted on the chest. Unlike normal sub-aqua breathing gear, with a rebreather no gas was expelled into the water to give away one's position to an enemy. Expelled air went back into the bag to be recycled, and the oxygen was topped up from a small metal cylinder. Stealth and camouflage were of vital importance. All their metal equipment and fittings had been painted a matt black to evade discovery, and instead of the coloured buoyancy jackets normally demanded of divers, they wore black flak jackets fitted with ceramic-tiled body armour. It was a cumbersome rig and, with all the other kit they carried, a float was just too expensive a luxury. It was a danger-ous situation to be in – but then it was a dangerous job. That's why the SDU recruited only the best and fittest swimmers for its Water Team – or created them out of the few exceptional individuals who each year managed to pass the SDU selection exercise. Like élite units the world over, the Special Duties Unit looked for men without phobias who could work underwater in total darkness, often in confined spaces, without the risk of being seized by panic. For in their particular line of work one man's panic could kill a whole team.

Every year eager young police officers of all ranks would sign on for the exercise, hoping they possessed the character and stamina to make it into Hong Kong's premiere special forces unit. Only a handful of inspectors applied at any one time, and those who did knew what to expect: the roughest, most miserable time of their lives. If they failed, there would be no loss of face; they would still be treated with respect by their peers, for there was no shame in being turned down or in failing to complete this exercise. The simple act of applying said a lot about a man. But if successful, the inspectors knew they would command and lead assault teams in one of the world's top counter-revolutionary warfare units. A unit which regularly exchanged officers with the British SAS Regiment, and who cross-trained with the USA's Delta and Seals.

As he pulled himself through the cold darkness of the water, fingers blanched and numb and his jaw aching from the pressure of the rubber mouthpiece, Mel Kale still asked himself what the hell he was doing here. Why was he swimming through half the excrement of west Kowloon, while friends and colleagues in the Police rugby team were at that very moment enjoying the fleshy delights of their Bangkok-Manila tour?

Mel Kale and David Becker had both volunteered for SDU in their mid-twenties – a decision taken one fateful dawn following a monumental *bai Gwan-Dai* neither man would forget. It was a pact they had sealed with *mao tai*, an evil Chinese rice liquor that tasted like airplane glue. Neither could now remember which of them had suggested it first, but whichever one it was the other would have been bound to follow. That was the way it had always been between them, friendly but determined rivalry.

The first time they had locked horns was back in training school. All recruit inspectors had been subject to regular fitness tests, and in the school gymnasium neither man would concede a point to the other. Kale was obviously the stronger; an Aussie ex-lifeguard with a classic V-shaped musculature, he excelled in all upper body exercises. Becker, leaner and a shade taller, always had the edge in endurance, especially at distance running and on the assault course. Together they played excellent rugby for the Police first fifteen, but put them on opposite sides in training and the sparks would fly. In training school every range course became almost a grudge match, each fitness test another battle in their ongoing war. That was how both had begun to test each other in running marathons. After that came triathlons, swimming, cycling and road running. Both became tougher, leaner and still meaner. Their many personal contests became a talking point in police messes across the colony. In the end SDU selection had seemed the toughest challenge either of them could think of next.

Twelve candidates had begun the selection exercise. Checking into the vacant barracks at PTU HQ in the heart of rural New Territories, they were given the oldest, most faded green bush kit the SDU barrack sergeant could find. Only those who made it would be allowed to wear the tailored black jumpsuit reserved for those on the inside. The first few days were hair-raising. There were in-depth stress interviews followed by a series of phobia tests to weed out the psychologically vulnerable: the dark and smoke-filled tunnel; the gut-wrenching leap from the fire services training tower; a swim through the narrow water-submerged pipe; and a dozen other tortures. All of that cut their numbers in half straight away. Those who remained then suffered a further eighteen days and nights of gruelling physical torture.

With little or no sleep they endured endless rounds of speed marching, sprint running and circuit training, interspersed with bizarre pointless tasks designed only to irritate and harass. On night marches in the rural areas, they were given bivouacs and told to sleep if necessary. The smart ones built themselves hides out of available vegetation, but those who took no such precautions were ambushed, beaten, and left tied to a tree, to be picked up ignominiously the following morning and returned to unit. Those who kept marching were also ambushed by hidden assailants. There was never any relaxation.

When they were sore enough, and well softened up, each candidate was allotted an operation to plan and a team of SDU men to brief, to test how well his brain functioned under pressure, and how well he could field a volley of well-informed questions from the rank and file – questions aimed to challenge his leadership. For within the SDU a team leader needed to *earn* the respect of his men, not simply rely upon the pips on his shoulder to get his orders carried out. If a man could not build up a rapport with the *foh gei*, then rather than upset the harmony of the team this potential officer was returned to his unit.

After eight days of this treatment most of them knew the sweeping green hills of the New Territories all too well: the Pak Sin mountain range and the heights of Tai Mo Shan. Distances covered with pack, rifle and compass gradually increased, as did the loads carried. As exhaustion set in, rest breaks became more frequent, but with the examiners always watching. The onus was on the candidates to outdo each other: work harder, take shorter breaks, be the last to sit down and the first to stand up. Everything to be noted down on clipboards.

Periodically the instructors would single a man out to have a quiet, insidious word in his ear. 'Doesn't look like you're going to make it, mate. Just say the word when you've had enough.' Becker just grinned at this ploy; Kale's reply was more colourful. Another tack was tried: the examiners taunted them individually, singling out some sensitive area to probe. They told Kale he was a flake with a short fuse, that he carried far too much weight, that his body-type was wrong for the climate. Becker, with his political science degree, was subtly accused of being on some intellectual masochistic trip, informed that his sneering élitism was not wanted here. In both cases there was a grain of truth which gave them pause for thought in their private moments. But both carried on all the same.

It was at this time that some of the seemingly toughest guys packed it in for no apparent reason and disappeared without a word. Somehow Becker and Kale became even stronger. Neither would countenance defeat while the other still remained. And, through the near delirium of fatigue and heat stress, each was watching the other carefully, hiding the true extent of his own exhaustion.

They knew well enough they were competing for just one or two available places; that between them they had out-psyched all the other candidates. What they did not know was just how much longer they would need to hold out – two more days or twenty? They were never told. So still they just hung on, blistered by the heat of the sun, drenched by their own sweat, and driven by something ever closer to hatred. Hatred of the instructors, of the towering hills they plodded, hatred of each other and, above all, of defeat. Always waiting for the other to be the first to break.

At that point fitness was no longer the factor. Their arms and legs were crying out for rest, and refusing to move; their brains were reeling in a dreamlike state of fatigue. The sun and sky had become a dizzy blue blur above the sweltering humidity of the grassland that sang in the late spring heat. Only their individual force of character could see them through now.

The end came as an overwhelming surprise and relief to the three who lasted it out. They had been walking most of the night, using cover to avoid roaming search parties. When they stumbled back into tactical unit HQ at first light they were given forty minutes for breakfast, then taken off to the foot of a steep hill just outside camp, which they knew as the 'A' Course.

'Here we are, gentlemen,' said the training officer levelly. 'A couple of laps up and down this bugger with rifles held above your heads will warm you up.'

Both Becker and Kale knew that the third man, Higgins, was about all in, so it was no surprise when he slumped down into the grass and said: 'Fuck it, that's me done.' He had had enough.

The training officer gave him two chances to change his mind, then drew a neat line through his name on the clipboard. He turned to the two remaining men.

'Looks like it's between you two lads, now.'

They eyed each other suspiciously, like boxers between rounds, wondering how much each still had left.

The training officer looked up from his clipboard. 'Right, there's the hill. If you look up to the top, you can just about see Sergeant Lee. Would you like to show me, gentlemen, which of you can get to him first?'

They did not wait for him to say 'Go'. Both took off hell-for-leather, attacking the grassy slope in a mad, weaving, exhausted gait. The grass was long and each stumbled frequently in sudden dips and over hidden rocks.

Becker could hear Kale's laboured breath beside him – then slightly behind him as he pulled ahead. The next moment a hand grabbed his ankle and yanked him back. He slid down fifteen feet before he managed to grab hold of a tussock and force his legs to propel him back up the hill. Cursing, he charged after Kale and snatched at his leg. Kale kicked backwards, his boot thudding into Becker's chest. Becker clamped his arms around the other's calf, lifting it clear off the grass and hurling him sideways, then dived after him. The next moment they were grabbing for each other's throats, rolling back down the hill with feet and fists flying.

At the first sign of blood, the training officer stepped in, satisfied that he had seen enough.

'Hey, leave it out, you two. I should have known it would come to this,' he shouted. 'It's over now!'

But in their frenzy they could hear nothing but the blood pounding in their own ears.

'Come on, Ah Lee, before they kill each other!'

They were wrenched apart by two regular SDU men, applying vicious grips on nerve points, and thrown into the grass. The training officer had looked them both over: gashed lips and bloody noses but otherwise intact.

'OK, that's the last of your tests, lads.'

'Some joke,' heaved Kale, determined not to fall for another sickener tactic. 'What's next? Another fifteen-mile jog with a pack full of rocks?'

'Believe me, it's really over.'

Slowly realisation dawned. Becker's eyes narrowed as he looked up, waiting for a decision. A decision that would elate one of them, and tear the other apart.

'So what's the score? Who's in, him or me?'

The training officer stifled a faint grin.

'You'll have to wait to hear officially from the OC...'

'Screw that!' Kale snatched up a small rock and hurled it into the long grass.

'However, unofficially I'd say you both made it.'

'What do you mean?'

'After what I've seen, I'd say we can't afford to turn either of you away. Most of those who make it this far are too tired to even button their own fly. You two would have killed each other there if I'd let you!'

He cracked a small grin, enjoying their success the way he had once enjoyed his own. 'Go get cleaned up, and be back in the briefing room in thirty minutes. You're with the hooligans now!'

That had all been seven years ago, but still that sharp sense of achievement remained with them both. They had since proved to be the backbone of the unit's officer cadre. Dubbed 'the dynamic duo' by those on the inside, they graduated from assault leaders to team leaders, until the post of training officer fell vacant. It was Becker who was given this, the most experienced officer's post and functional second-in-command of the unit; and it was perhaps a sign of their new understanding that Kale was the first to shake his hand and congratulate him. When Becker moved out and joined Special Branch there was never any real doubt about who would succeed him. Now Kale had all he had ever wanted, for it was he who set the standards of the unit. The officer commanding might well be the titular head of the SDU, but the training officer was its heart and its soul.

* * *

As Kale's fingers brushed the first of the giant links of the ship's anchor chain he came upright again, and secured the command line to it. Soon the other divers loomed out of the murk, grouping close, and responded to his hand signals. The ebb and flow of air from the demand valve roared loudly in Kale's ears, amplified by the watery silence all around. They had been submerged for thirty minutes and their body temperatures were dipping.

One by one they surfaced in the shadow of the bow. They removed speed fins and breathing gear, secured them to the anchor chain, and carefully began the back-breaking three-storey climb up to the ship's main deck. In full kit the climb was exhausting; each chain-link was almost as high as the man hauling himself up it.

At the top they stopped to fit respirators and after a final weapons check Kale gave silent directions. All at once the order was GO GO GO. He launched himself over the side, leading the lithe black figures across the freighter's deserted deck – making for the main hatchways in two groups. It had been prearranged that the sniper group would take down the three deck watchmen with head shots at the GO command, so the way to the captain's bridge was clear.

Once they made the hatchways, it was over in a matter of seconds. Stun grenades ruptured the silence below decks, followed by surgically precise bursts of SMG fire and the panicky yelling of hostages as they were rushed on deck, to be pushed face down and handcuffed. The gunfire continued for a further thirty seconds, before the assault team withdrew back into the sunlight.

When the whistle blew, the video camera teams stopped filming. It had been a pretty good operation: once again, bold strokes. The training report would read: *Twelve 'doves' freed; seven 'crows' neutralised.* The real analysis would come later, during the debrief, when the video would be put under the microscope and all mistakes revealed and made known.

Kale pulled the respirator off his head and smoothed back his fair hair, aware suddenly that one of his men was shouting to him and pointing over the side. He shaded his eyes against the sun and the golden glare off the South China Sea. He could see a launch approaching off the starboard bow, its black hull topped by a cabin of duck-egg blue, stencilled with black characters. *Sui ging*. A police launch.

Once the launch was alongside, three men climbed the stairway. The first two, in black fatigues, were easily recognisable as the officer commanding SDU and his Operations Officer. The third, however, wore plain clothes, and Kale wondered who it was they could be bringing into the exercise area. The moment they were on deck he saw that the man in the well-cut light grey suit was David Becker.

'That looked about right from where I was, Mel,' said the OC.

'Thanks, boss.' Kale brushed aside the compliment. 'Better check through the video before handing out any commendations.'

The OC nodded agreement. These were Kale's men, after all, and the relationship between them was about the tightest anywhere in the Force. Any plaudits or bollockings would need to come from him alone. He inclined his head in Becker's direction.

'As you see, we have a visitor from the ivory towers of Special Branch.'

Kale forced a lopsided grin.

'What's this then, mate? You joined the Force Inspection Wing – checking up on us?'

'Yeah, just checking you weren't out waterskiing again off the back of the *Zodiac*.'

Kale laughed out loud; his thick moustache moved up to reveal an impressive line of teeth of which Becker knew the two front pegs were removable. Rugby.

'You heard about John Tasker?' asked Becker, suddenly businesslike.

Kale's grin quickly disappeared.

'I heard it on the radio this morning. Couldn't believe it at first. I always reckoned him for a bit of an arsehole, you know, with all that cowboy stuff, but no way he deserved that.'

'Yeah, that's about the way I feel. Joe's pretty cut up. He was sitting right there when it happened.'

'Good God. Someone better organise a *bai Gwan-Dai*. He's going to need it.'

'I've already tried, and he's not answering his pager. But there's something else to think about now.'

'So what is it?' asked Kale, intrigued. He reached back to tug at the heavy-duty waterproof zipper that extended across his shoulder blades. There was sweat visible on his upper lip. 'Jesus, let's get inside before I start to melt.'

While the remainder of the unit collected and stowed the equipment for their departure, the three men went inside the wheelhouse. The vessel had been mothballed for the past three years; left anchored there on the understanding that it could be used periodically for SDU's maritime counter-terrorist exercises. It was an ideal location: two miles out from shore and not subject to observation by prying eyes.

'They've activated Clawhammer,' said the OC without ceremony.

Kale's pulse quickened at the mere mention of the word. He folded his arms, affecting a calmness he did not feel.

The OC continued: 'Dave is here on DSB's orders to set up a "head shed" with us for the operation. The planning from our end will be down to you.'

'Fine by me,' said Kale feeling his interest grow. 'What's the job? Are they finally going to let us take out those *Dai Huens*?'

Becker gave a thin smile.

'Funny you should say that ...'

In the basement car park in Tsim Sha Tsui East, Tony Kwan stared quietly into the burned-out wreck of his red Mercedes and felt a murderous urge welling up inside him. A moment later he leapt forward, punching wildly at the twisted door. The car park echoed to a stream of Chiu Chau obscenity.

The handful of *ma jai* with him stepped neatly aside, out of arm's reach.

When he was finished, Red Cudgel looked menacingly around him, holding up the huge misshapen ball which was his right fist. 'Tell me who it was. Was it the dogs of the 14K?'

'*M'ji, Ah Goh,*' his first lieutenant answered quietly. 'Nobody knows. Nobody saw anything. They came and left like shadows.'

'Like shadows, eh?' Kwan muttered, eyes still fixed upon the blackened remains of his beautiful car. Once its colour had been a source of joy, but now the steel chassis was burned into hues seen only on the surface of oily puddles. The handstitched leather hung shrivelled and black, like strips of charred flesh.

It was not so much the car itself that bothered him; that could easily be replaced. But *face* could not. Still worse was knowing that the bomb which destroyed it might easily have been placed to explode while he was at the wheel. But it had not – and that had been deliberate. A very sophisticated mind was at work here. Someone was playing games, trying to throw a scare into him.

But who?

With an effort of will he recovered his outward composure.

Inside his rage still smouldered away like a burning incense stick.

'So, a very bad night then, last night,' he attempted philosophically, appearing to brighten.

The lieutenant looked sheepish.

'There's more, *Kwan-goh*.'

'What more?'

'*Hai a*.' The words came painfully slow. 'Last night someone torched one of our video arcades down in Mongkok. Three guys in masks, pouring kerosene everywhere. Then they grabbed our street enforcer and made a candle out of him, too.'

Kwan's anger deepened once more, like a rumbling volcano about to burst upon the heads of those around him. In inarticulate rage his broad jaw quivered as he fought to regain control. Finally, clasping both hands firmly behind his head, he paced back and forth.

'What is this? Somebody trying to rattle me?' he snarled. 'Some kind of a challenge, eh?'

The lieutenant hung his head.

'*M'ji do, Kwan-goh*. I don't know.'

When he managed to look up, he saw Kwan's eyes were blazing.

'All right then, never mind that for the moment. What about the one in charge here? The one set to watch over this car of mine. Where is *he*?'

The lieutenant called out in the direction of the lift lobby, and immediately two forty-niners stepped from the shadows, clutching between them a Chinese man wearing the blue and white uniform of a car park attendant. As they hustled him forward into the light, the man's body was shaking; his shoes dragged reluctantly on the concrete.

Up close, Red Cudgel saw just how pathetically skinny and frightened he was: a Hakka some way past forty, with the small wrinkled features of a spider monkey. Probably he would have kids – maybe even grandchildren. He saw the submissive bow of the man's head, the fearful droop of his lower lip as he mumbled apologies. But most of all he smelled the heady perfume of the man's fear.

As the infinite seconds of torture ticked by, Red Cudgel pushed his face close against that of the prisoner.

'You know who did this?'

'No, *Kwan-goh*,' whimpered the prisoner. 'I saw nothing. I swear it.'

The enforcer looked the man up and down, considering his next move.

'Tell me, *sai lo*, do you understand exactly what it means to be *Hung Kwan* and to have tasted blood and crossed the Fiery Pit?'

Suddenly the prisoner's eyes widened in fright; he was now almost too scared even to answer. A savage wrench of his shoulder forced his reply.

'*Aiyah!* It means ...' he stammered, wincing with each painful twist of his arm. 'It means you are supreme enforcer of San Yee On, and sworn to protect the reputation of the Society.'

'Exactly so,' smiled the triad.

Checking his watch, Red Cudgel pointed a tapered finger at the big BMW in which they had arrived, instructing one of his followers to start her up. A second later a deafening roar erupted from under the bonnet.

'I'm glad you understand these things, *sai lo*,' he told the prisoner. 'It's better that way.'

In the next instant all the ambiguous warmth drained from his face as he strode towards the waiting BMW.

'What about *him*?' The lieutenant indicated the cringing figure in the attendant's uniform.

'Break both his legs,' came the immediate, slightly irritable reply. 'Then go get me a newspaper. I want to read some more about the unfortunate death of that *gwai lo* policeman.'

Later that evening Red Cudgel took a team of trusted *ma jai* across on to Hong Kong side for a very important meeting. They had dinner at a large restaurant in Happy Valley, then when darkness had fallen they climbed into two vehicles for the steep drive over Wong Nei Chong Gap, to reach Alex Au-Yeung's Spanish villa on the south side of the island.

Once inside the house, Red Cudgel was offered tea and congratulations on a job well done. 'A very clean kill' were Au-Yeung's exact words. He seemed particularly well pleased by the headlines the event had produced. Red Cudgel then made his report, predicting an imminent collapse of the police investigation against them – while attempting to minimise the importance of Ruby Tang, who was still missing. The torching of the video games arcade he attributed to some renegade faction within the brotherhood of the 14K, who would in due course be hunted down and made to pay. Wisely he decided to say nothing of the car bomb. At this point he badly needed to give an impression of total control.

That was what the Vietnamese would need to hear tonight.

Red Cudgel saw the car headlights fill the blackness of the Repulse Bay Road long before the limousine turned to sweep on to the gravel drive. He took a moment to confirm the vehicle's number plate on the CCTV monitor, then ordered the gilded iron gate to be opened. He stepped out on to the porch, flanked by four of his followers. As they stood, casting giant black shadows across the lawn, the car pulled slowly forward towards the steps. At the end of the drive, the gate closed once more with a soft whine of its motors.

As the car doors opened, Red Cudgel stepped forward to greet the two thin and bespectacled Vietnamese. Both were dressed in white tropical dinner-jackets and carried slim leather briefcases with gold clasps. A moment later a third Vietnamese stepped out of the car, glancing quickly about him; an altogether rougher individual, with the characteristic bearing of a military man. Red Cudgel looked him up and down, guessing this man to be some kind of security escort for the two high-ranking intelligence officers.

'Nice to see you, gentlemen.' With an effort he smiled at his brother's honoured guests. 'Please come inside. Mr Au-Yeung is waiting.'

Drenched in floodlighting, the Au-Yeung house was an impressive sight with its red pantiled roof and white adobe façade, both of which in daylight stood out dramatically against the lush green foliage of the surrounding hills. It was perfectly located, on a roadside half way up the valley facing out towards the sea, where both the view and the *fung shui* were excellent. For although Au-Yeung was first and last a businessman, he was still Chinese, and he knew the value of being in harmony with the surrounding elements. Though loving the house at first sight, before agreeing to buy it he had first engaged his personal geomancer to check that its location did not disturb the dragon. By Chinese belief, dragons slumbered in hills such as this, and to build a house on the dragon's head would bring all manner of misfortune – and possibly ruin. Luckily this villa was considered to be sheltered from the dragon's wrath by the many folds and undulations of the hillside.

As soon as Au-Yeung had moved in, he had arranged for the grounds to be relandscaped. The house itself was now sheltered from the Repulse Bay Road by a high white stone wall, with a security camera mounted at the gate and a screen of tall rhododendrons to damp down the noise of passing cars. Inside the wall a bank of floodlights carefully traced the edges of the lawns, eliminating shadows and leaving no place for concealment. It was the first thing the Vietnamese security man had looked for, and he was impressed.

After a slamming of car doors, the three men followed Red Cudgel up the marble steps and into the house. They passed through a hallway furnished with mahogany, and dominated by the stuffed and mounted head of a

Royal Bengal tiger. But if the Viets were impressed, they certainly did not show it. Finally they reached Au-Yeung's study. In contrast to the rest of the house, a cornucopia of foreign styles with its many European antiques and Islamic treasures, the study was decorated as a scrupulous reproduction of a Chinese Pavilion of the Ming period.

When the door opened, they saw Au-Yeung sitting cross-legged and imperious on a bench of black-laquered wood. He was reading a collection of the philosophical poems of Lao Tzu. Unlike the urbane Western dress of his guests, he wore a traditional Chinese jacket of blue silk with broad sleeves and toggle buttons. The false white collar and cuffs edging the garment lent an air of formality to his appearance. On his feet were white socks and the soft black pumps known as *gung fu haai*. He glanced up at them, affecting a look of concentration disturbed, then smiled broadly and closed his book.

'Gentlemen, welcome to my humble home.' Standing, he came forward to greet them. 'So happy to receive you.'

Red Cudgel followed the other men into the study and closed the door.

'Honoured to be received,' said Van Nguyen, the delegation leader, with a polite inclination of his head. He was a thin man with a pallid complexion and a slight shoulder stoop that gave him the false impression of frailty. Au-Yeung knew different.

'Please forgive the ostentation of my study. I like to remind myself of all that is best in Chinese art.'

'A most sublime arrangement,' said Van Nguyen noticing the expert use of filled and empty space. 'Calculated to uplift the observer's spirits. And unmistakably Ming.'

'An educated eye is very rare. There are few people who know how to *look*.'

'Party membership does not dull one's appreciation of true beauty.'

'Just so,' murmured Au-Yeung. 'I trust you have remained well since our last meeting in Bangkok.'

He shook the hands of the two who carried briefcases, and waited to be introduced to the third, whom he had not met before. Van Nguyen inclined his head.

'This is Tranh. He is responsible for our security.'

At that precise moment a wrinkled Chinese amah entered the room, carrying a blue porcelain teapot and Chinese cups on a tray. The old woman wore the traditional long single plait and white jacket of a domestic servant. She bowed first to Au-Yeung, then poured the tea with care. A moment later she bowed again and faded from the room like a ghost.

'No problems since your arrival, I hope.'

'None at all so far.'

All three had flown in from Bangkok the previous evening, on Thai passports, posing as investment bankers in search of projects to fund – which in one sense was what they were. They had checked into pre-booked adjoining rooms at the Mandarin Hotel in Central district, and during the following day made preliminary contact with the Cuban Consulate through one of Ortega's runners. This brush contact had taken place on Cloth Alley, a narrow pedestrian thoroughfare off Des Voeux Road lined with a myriad of tiny tailors' shops that in a matter of hours churned out finished garments from the bolts of cloth on display. Even by Hong Kong standards Cloth Alley was congested – always choked with people moving in every direction at once. Physical contact there was unavoidable, so a newspaper exchanged in a brush contact went completely undetected.

Back in his hotel room Van Nguyen, the senior officer, had decoded the message, using a one-time pad which operations branch had secreted for him inside a bar of soap. The message told him that his team had not been detected by the authorities, and to proceed therefore to meet with Au-Yeung that evening.

'Before we go any further,' said Van Nguyen, looking suddenly serious, 'there is one small precaution I would like to take – if you have no objections.'

'Just as in Bangkok,' smiled Au-Yeung. 'Very well, please proceed.'

Aware of the embarrassment created by a security sweep, Tranh got quickly to work. Snapping open his briefcase he removed a small radio-signal detection device no larger than a pack of cigarettes. After a few passes around the room, and no significant deflection of the needle, he replaced the device in his case. Next he unscrewed the mouthpiece of Au-Yeung's desk telephone and checked for extraneous wiring. Nothing. Lastly he took up the connection cord between his fingers and traced it back to the wall connection.

Au-Yeung drummed his fingers, his face betraying none of the impatience he really felt. Tranh knew it was a simple matter to turn a phone into a permanent live microphone, using an off-the-hook switch. There was no reason to believe the phone was tapped, but Tranh yanked the cord out of the wall socket anyway, and the phone went dead.

Au-Yeung watched and smiled thinly at the professionalism of the Vietnamese, then he turned his attention to Van Nguyen.

'I have awaited this visit most eagerly. As you know I have a great deal invested in our project. If you read the newspapers you will also know that my side of things has run smoothly so far.'

'Indeed. We have monitored your progress. The Shatin robbery went very well. However, some of my superiors still doubt the wisdom of attacking so controversial a target. The extra attention from the authorities could prove counter-productive. I understand this Jockey Club is something of a sacred institution in Hong Kong, *hai m'hai a*?'

'As are all financial institutions here.' Au-Yeung

334

made a gentling motion with one hand. 'You may assure your senior officers that the authorities here know nothing of our purpose. As I told you before in Bangkok, the Society's man in Police Headquarters is closely monitoring the investigation. He says they are blundering around in the dark, cursing themselves that they cannot reach into the mainland.'

'Very well. What of Chan Ming and his group? We would do well to clear up that matter. I find it difficult to trust them up there in Canton, beyond our reach. Particularly after their refusal to be involved in the second phase of the operation. It was a mistake to involve Chan Ming so deeply. If we do not control them, then we have to remove them.'

'Of course. I had planned it so. But that is a complicated matter. One must wash them all out at the same moment, or risk later reprisals. I should not like to think those killers were stalking my shadow.'

Au-Yeung used his eyes to signal to Red Cudgel that the guests' cups were empty. Dutifully, Tony Kwan went between them, carefully refilling each cup to within a centimetre of the brim, so giving the triad chief an opportunity to change the subject.

'Forgive my presumption, but may I ask whether your superiors have now authorised the financial arrangement we spoke of last time?'

'Yes, they have,' said Van Nguyen, adjusting his black bow-tie, 'subject to certain other criteria being met.' Obviously he was not going to be pushed.

The Chinese masked his suspicions with an inoffensive look.

'Criteria? What criteria?'

Van Nguyen shifted in his seat. The lacquered wood was hard and uncomfortable beneath him, not like the padded seats of his office at the Economic Intelligence Bureau back in Hanoi. Having changed position he continued.

335

'Firstly we need the papers you promised. The intelligence gathered from the Americans by your agent was first-rate, but we need to see the draft agreements. Without those we cannot hope to convince our government that the Chinese are prepared to cooperate with the US against us.'

'What is so improbable about that? The Spratly Island group has long been claimed by China. You must expect any attempt to infringe Chinese sovereignty to be fiercely resisted. As for the Americans, they still suffer the shame of the war. Everyone knows they would go to any lengths to regain their face.'

'Nevertheless, I need the papers. Do you have them?'

'Not with me.'

Au-Yeung saw the flash of concern in Red Cudgel's eyes. Word was already out on Ruby Tang, though so far there had been no clue to her whereabouts. Red Cudgel was aware of acute shame in having failed the *Shan Chiu* in this matter.

'Oh?' said Van Nguyen meaningfully.

'But I can get them. No problem,' said Au-Yeung. 'What else?'

'Full access to your accounts for my colleague, Mr Chien.'

'What!' The leader of the San Yee On glowered from his perch on the lacquered bench, ignoring the quick head bow of the second Vietnamese. Though his own head now swam with rage at the impertinence, he reined in his anger and chose his words with care.

'Mr Van Nguyen, in a relationship of delicacy and trust such a request is ... inappropriate.'

'You think so,' said the Vietnamese. 'Please tell me why?'

'I have already outlined my position. Bright Star is a property-based company. In Hong Kong that's as good as a goldmine. It's just that at the moment we are severely extended. Commercial rents have slumped by

336

sixteen per cent in the past three months, and we can no longer service our debt repayments. As you know, the property market is cyclical. There will be a turnaround and we will again make big profits. What could be simpler or safer?'

'Simple for you, maybe. Mr Au-Yeung, I have been working in economic and commercial intelligence for the past fifteen years. Mr Chien has twelve years with the Vietnamese Bank of Commerce. Before we allow you a revolving credit line equal to the gross national product of a small third-world country, we have to be sure you are a good risk. Without access to your books – both sets – there can be no credit facility.'

'And without my help, what of the second phase of the operation?' There was a trace of a tremor in Au-Yeung's voice that told Van Nguyen he wasn't sure of his ground.

'Please, don't go any further, Mr Au-Yeung.' The Vietnamese looked suddenly serious. 'I should hate to be drawn into responding to a threat you do not really mean. Need I remind you it was you who came to us with this project in the first place?'

Au-Yeung knew he dared push no further.

'Please excuse me. No threat intended. I was merely speculating how unfortunate it might be if all your own work were to be wasted at this advanced stage. And the blow to your prestige within the Party. Of course you may see any and all of my papers. I shall ask our company lawyer to prepare a briefing for Mr Chien first thing tomorrow. There, is that all your criteria met?'

'All except one,' said Van Nguyen. 'If the Hong Kong financial press hears any breath of a connection between your company and our service, or if phase two is compromised by your people, we will feel free to terminate the agreement immediately. Is that understood?'

'Of course, of course,' said Au-Yeung feigning

bonhomie to cover his relief. 'Now let us drink a real toast – with French brandy.'

Red Cudgel brought the glasses forward and poured from a bottle of VSOP. Alexander Au-Yeung held his glass between both hands and raised it in front of his face in the Chinese way.

'To the US Secretary of State,' he said grandly. 'May sun and favourable winds guide his airplane safely into Hong Kong. And may he not drop dead before next week!'

The Vietnamese laughed in spite of themselves, and everyone drank.

Three days was barely enough time to plan and execute a hostile incursion into the mainland, but that was all the time the Commissioner decided Becker and Kale could reasonably afford. That narrowed the possibilities considerably. Kale studied a map of the Pearl River Delta in the operations room at SDU headquarters, and immediately ruled out a water-borne operation. Apart from the main branch of the Pearl River itself, there were a hundred or more tiny tributaries winding their way from the coastline up into the port of Canton.

The team could have gone in at night, in fast inflatable boats, but there was just too much distance to cover unsupported, both ways, at the mercy of Chinese naval patrol craft, to make this a realistic option. Neither was a slow, camouflaged infiltration possible within the time-frame allowed. In the end Becker's finger came to rest on the pink block that was the city of Canton, and traced a short line south-west to the small black dot that was the town of Foshan.

'That's the way to go,' he said. 'Simple and direct.'

Kale considered a moment and then agreed.

'Fine by me. Less chance of a screw-up. Let's do it.'

Success, they decided, would depend on a minimum of equipment and a minimum of fuss. The KISS mentality: Keep It Simple, Stupid. Using scheduled public transport they would infiltrate as tourists, make the hit, and exfiltrate with whatever prisoners they managed to keep alive aboard a ship of the Ho Tung freighter line. The Ho Tung line ran goods from Canton docks to Hong Kong, and was well used to carrying undeclared passengers both ways for Special Branch, without asking too many questions. Provided they made a clean hit, the departure would be smooth as silk.

As they talked over the mission briefing, something seemed to preoccupy Kale. After some silent brooding he finally voiced his apprehensions in a guarded question.

'What are the rules of engagement?' he asked, aware that the DSB had already briefed Becker downtown at PHQ. 'Specifically, I mean what are the kill parameters?'

Becker's face hardened. He did not want to answer that, he knew this would go down like a Bangkok hooker, but there was no other way.

'Self-defence only,' he said, steeling himself against the anticipated response. He was not disappointed.

'You mean wait for the enemy to shoot first? You know we don't work that way.'

'I mean if there's a fire fight, we go for it. But there'll be no bloody executions.'

'What?' Controlled outrage. 'After the bloody mess they made of Jason Leung, and then the chopstick lobotomy this hitman gave John Tasker? That's fucking great!'

'Listen, nobody is convicted of anything yet. Mission briefing says we need them alive for interrogation. Some of them, anyway. This is no vendetta. The whole damn reason for going after them is to find out where the money went and who's behind the planning. Tasker got close enough to put a real scare into them. This isn't just an ordinary robbery anymore. The Commissioner thinks that whoever was behind the Shatin robbery is also funding a major black operation that's going to knock the colony on its arse.'

An awkward silence fell between them. Finally Kale shrugged, hands on hips, and spat out a glib line which belied his real frustration.

'Fine, have it your way. Just as long as the bastards don't have to be capable of independent motion when we bring them in.'

'It's not *my* choice, Mel. These are orders.'

Becker saw the resistance that still remained in Kale's swollen neck. He had seen it before and he knew that while Kale would not directly contravene orders, he would need careful watching.

With an effort, Becker forced his mind back to the most urgent area of concern, the lack of hard intelligence on the target: the men, the buildings, and the immediate area around Foshan. That would need to be remedied immediately. Using the secure computer link from SDU headquarters, he fed through a requirements order to Clawhammer control in Special Branch, with a 'most urgent' flag attached.

Late afternoon the same day, while the two Europeans were choosing and briefing their assault teams, an advance collection unit of four Chinese officers was put together and sent into Canton to locate a suitable holding area, and assemble photographs and information. They sat apart from one another during the two-hour hydrofoil trip, which left from the Canton Road terminal on Kowloon side, and did not come together until they had all cleared immigration at the Zhoutouzi pier and checked into the People's Mansion downtown on Yanjiang Lu. The guesthouse was fairly upmarket, a white tower with views south over the Pearl River estuary and north across the hazy low-rise sprawl of the city. It was a mid-range establishment, comfortable and sufficiently anonymous for their purposes.

They were a mixed unit, composed of a sergeant and a woman constable from operations directorate who were there as agent handlers, a civilian technical expert attached to Special Branch, and an SDU intelligence officer who would brief his unit on tactical aspects of the mission. Sergeant Wong, the senior agent handler, would call the shots during the initial phase.

On the first evening they decided to eat dinner in an open-air pavement restaurant near the Qingping Market. The market faced Shamien Island across the canal, and was a noisy, manic experience; a place famous for the livestock it sold: monkey, owl, civet cat and pangolin, all of which could be ordered from the restaurants nearby. They took their seats among the early evening throng and watched family groups stroll by, laughing and joking. In the near distance they could hear the laden barges hooting their way back from the docks along the river.

When the waiter came to their table, Wong interrogated him about the menu before finally ordering dog. It was a delicacy he rarely tasted back in Hong Kong, where consuming dog-meat was now illegal. Though frankly he could take it or leave it, he knew the guest he was expecting was fond of well braised dog, and he was going to need that man's help.

Just as the food arrived, and the white rice was steaming in their bowls, the man they had been waiting for approached out of the market stalls, accompanied by his 'little horse', and joined them at the table. The sergeant filled their tea cups as they exchanged the mandatory pleasantries.

'*Nei dei ho ma?* How's it going?'

'*Gei ho, mo chuen mo laan. Nei ne?* Not bad, nothing torn, nothing broken. Yourself?'

'*Do ho. Ho foon hei gin do nei.* Same. Good to see you again.'

The sergeant turned to Sung first, the one in the dark, Western suit but no necktie, giving him face because he

341

was the primary contact. Sung was a most valued agent, a Hong Kong businessman whose own assets on the mainland included a soft toys factory located just outside Foshan. He was a street-smart native of Canton who had hopped a freight train to Hong Kong in the early Seventies and quickly built up his business from street hawker to importer. Trading on family and childhood friendships he had got back into the mainland as an export agent for Chinese handicraft goods, and was now well connected with business and trade organisations in Guangdong Province. For the past six years he had been supplying economic and political intelligence to SB on the understanding that a full British passport would be his in 1997.

The man with him wore the white shirt, drab trousers and harsh haircut of a local, and Wong knew him as Lau Bing, the manager of Sung's Foshan factory. Lau was a relative of Sung's wife, and acted as general *ma jai* and gopher whenever Sung was north of the border on business. Lau was a quick, birdlike individual whose ready smile was accompanied by nicotine-browned teeth. He had proved helpful in the past, but his chief use on this operation lay in the fact that he lived in Nanpu, the Foshan suburb where the target premises were located.

Sung looked down at the meat steaming in earthen-ware pots on the table and immediately his broad face brightened.

'*Ah, Saam Luk – ho ye!* Excellent for the balance of internal energy.' His enthusiasm was obvious. He adjusted his gold spectacles and took up his chopsticks with relish, seizing a piece of tender meat, dunking it into the thick brown sauce, and dropping it on to the small hill of rice in his bowl.

Sergeant Wong smiled at the expression he had used: 'Three and Six.' It was one of the many vague and arcane slang expressions used by Hong Kongers to confuse officialdom. Three plus six is nine, and in Chinese this is *gau*; but the word for dog, with a slightly different inflection, is also *gau*. Anyone invited to a private dinner where Three and Six was on the menu knew exactly what to expect: tender young chow puppy.

'Relax, Ah Sung, you may call it dog here.'

The others at the table laughed.

'Yes,' responded Sung quickly, aware that he was being gently baited by the sergeant. 'Here I may call it dog, and *you* may eat it, *hai m hai a?*'

Sung enjoyed the irony of seeing police officers also breaking the law. More laughter.

'*Mo choh*,' nodded the sergeant, wisely conceding this point. 'Absolutely. Now let's eat.'

Good manners dictated that serious talk could not begin until after the food was finished. When the waiter had cleared the table, they sat and picked their teeth with mint-tipped wooden toothpicks; one hand discreetly covering the mouth while the other probed. Then the questions began. Wong and Sung did most of the talking.

'About tomorrow?'

'All in hand. We pick you up in the morning at 7.00 and drive to the factory. Takes less than an hour. After that we go to Nanpu – Lau's place.'

'My colleague over here would like to look over the factory.' Wong jerked his thumb towards the slim, muscular Chinese from the SDU, who had so far said nothing. 'He has his own specific requirements. Is that a problem?'

'No problem. What sort of room would you like?'

'Something big and uncluttered,' said the SDU man. When he spoke every muscle in his face seemed to move. 'One with a good lock, direct access from the outside, and a direct-line telephone.' This he knew would be required as a connection port for high-speed transmission of coded data. The small lap-top computer he had brought was fitted with an internal modem for this purpose.

Sung sniffed and shifted his position in the chair, assessing the man with a single glance. He had close, razor-cut hair and the clear, dark, weathered skin of a construction site coolie. The alert brown eyes shone back at him unblinkingly, and he sensed in the impossibly soft-spoken manner an implicit violence. Realisation struck like a hammer.

'*Fei foo dui*,' he breathed almost reverently, eyes widening slightly. '*Diu lei lo mo!* You are Special Duties Unit!' *Fei foo dui*! The Leaping Tigers! He knew their reputation, as did most people in Hong Kong but he had never met one. The young man's jaw muscle flexed as he shot a look at the SB sergeant.

Wong knew well enough that operational security was his responsibility, and in a second his meaty hand reached out and grabbed Sung's wrist. He leaned close, transfixing the agent with a reprimanding stare.

'Speculation is dangerous, *dai lo*. Just watch your own *wok* and we'll watch ours.'

It was as much of a rebuke as he dared give. Keeping discipline was one thing, but scolding Sung in front of his own *ma jai* was quite another. That would have caused him to lose face – badly. Wong understood his agent well enough to know that if he lost too much face they would not see his fat arse for dust. Come morning he'd be back in Hong Kong, and no one would blame him for it. The sergeant relaxed his grip, having made his point, and Sung straightened the rumpled sleeve of his jacket.

'*Ho!*' he conceded, shaking his arm. 'No need to get excited, *dai lo*.'

Wong lightened his manner, and everyone relaxed once more.

'Right, let's talk about cover. Did you arrange it already?'

'You kidding? Of course. Very simple and straight-forward. You're our guests: potential buyers looking for a manufacturing source. Nothing new there. We bus in dozens of them to see the factory. Some of them stay over at Lau's home. People in Foshan won't bat an eyelid.'

'I like it,' nodded Wong approvingly. 'Ah Lau, what do you know about the target? Which part of town?'

Lau drew himself up in his seat, taking full advantage of his sudden importance. Then, as if remembering himself, he made a quick apologetic jerk of his head which was more of a nervous tic than the bow it was intended to be. Lau was a man who did not easily forget his place.

'Wong-sir, you know Foshan. The town is booming now, no longer just the collection of craft workshops it once was. My village, Nanpu, has been fully absorbed as a suburb of the town. Two years ago these people bought up the largest metal-casting business in Nanpu. The place is a little way out from us. Four or five solid stone huts in a big open yard. A quiet area with fields on three sides, where the kids used to play. It's overlooked to the rear by the greenest, greenest hill, with the sweeping back of a bull elephant.'

'Tell me about the men.'

'They're dangerous. About fifteen, twenty of them, I think. Rough types. Somebody said they were soldiers once, and to see them you can believe it. Nobody bothers them. They do all kinds of businesses, from scrap metal to spare parts for goods lorries, but everybody knows that's just a cover for what they really do: the criminal activity. Some of them did time in the work camps for drunkenness and brawling, but now they're big friends with the Public Security Bureau. They never get caught for anything serious. That's what we're supposed to believe, anyway.'

'How do you know they're in good with the Public Security Bureau?'

Lau laughed out loud with an odd whistling sound, flashing brown-flecked teeth once again.

345

'Everyone sees them. They drink wine with the local *bin yee*.' Wong knew this was the name for the Chinese policemen who worked in plain clothes. 'The Big Circle Gang laugh and joke with them, flaunting their friendship in public.'

'That's pretty bad,' said Wong, sympathising with the man from Nanpu.

'You cannot know how bad. My neighbours hear gunfire from their place at all hours of the day and night. They fear for their safety and their children, but nobody dares to complain. My brother-in-law lives just half a mile from them, and they shot his best pig last month – shot the animal where it stood in the field. When he went over to retrieve the carcase, two of them were standing over it and running their fingers around the bullet holes like a couple of doctors. Discussing the wounds, damn them! They told the Security Bureau the pig tried to savage them … Of course the case was dropped.' Lau paused for breath and shook his head. 'What can we do when the law turns its back on us?'

Wong noticed the hatred that filled Lau's narrative as he talked of the *Dai Huen Jai*. But his narrative was wandering, so he eased the man gently back on course.

'Mr Lau, it would help us greatly if you could give us some proper descriptions and names.'

'I could give you possibly half a dozen of the swine,' said Lau, indicating the number six by extending the thumb and little finger of his right hand. 'But they're not important. The one you want is Chan Ming. He's their leader. He's famous around the new bars in Canton: a big man with a close-shaved head and stubble on his chin. He wears a dark moustache and he likes to dress flash, like a Hong Konger. He used to be a good fighter, probably still is. They say he got a chestful of medals down on the Vietnam border. They also say he never goes anywhere without an officer's pistol stuck in his

346

waistband. The story I heard, it belonged to his platoon officer before Chan Ming killed him.'

Further descriptions were taken down on paper by the woman constable, as Lau held forth with a mixture of fact and hearsay. As he continued, spicing his report with anecdotes, one thing became clear: this team had a big reputation around Canton. In the minds of the locals they were virtually untouchable.

The SDU intelligence officer had been staring into his cup as if deep in Buddhist meditation. Now he spoke softly, without looking up.

'Mr Lau, how far from your home is this metal casting shop?'

'Ah-sir, a walk of five to ten minutes along a dirt road, on the outskirts of Nanpu.'

'Is this road lit at night?'

'Only by moonlight.'

'What do you think?' asked Sergeant Wong, inclining his head towards the other police officer.

The SDU man finally looked up, with a faint smile now forming.

'I think the lads are going to enjoy this one.'

They left the People's Mansions hotel at 6.15 the next morning in one of Sung's small company vans. Lau Bing drove carefully through the early-morning tangle of cyclists that clogged the road. He took a route along Renmin Nan Lu, past the Cultural Park which was thronged with the elongated shadows of Tai Chi boxers, and turned west on to Zhongshan Lu, heading out of the city across the Zhujian Bridge. Beside the road a railway line ran straight into the countryside, and from time to time steam locomotives thundered past, shaking the ground all around them.

Foshan lay twenty-eight kilometres south-west of the city, along a highway much travelled by tour groups eager to see one of China's four principal craft centres.

347

Foshan's porcelain and decorative paper-cuts were legendary.

As a preparatory step Sung's factory was inspected and well photographed, then the group moved on to Lau's home, one of a handful of detached stone dwellings on the edge of Nanpu suburb. If the residents walking around suspected anything, they gave no sign of it. After a hearty meal cooked by Lau's wife, the intelligence group dressed up as farm labourers and set out on foot to climb the Elephant Hill which rose to the rear of their target location. From this vantage point they could confirm with binoculars all that Lau had described. The dirt road leading to the stone buildings of the casting shop was deeply rutted; the open yard to the rear was cluttered with scrap metal and discarded engine parts. Some little way from the main building a single figure wearing military fatigue pants and nothing else appeared to be hoeing a vegetable patch.

Without a word the technical officer unloaded his camera from the wicker food-basket and prepared to shoot.

Back in Sung's factory, the photographs were first developed, then enlarged to A4 size, and finally transmitted back to Special Branch on the businessman's portable fax machine. Becker received the pictures less than one hour later, and was encouraged by what he saw. This was a rural base, quiet and out of the way. That meant less chance of their being detected or challenged by the locals, especially the Public Security mob.

The SDU intelligence officer's assessment came through separately, coded of course, and was picked up by one of the desktop computers up at SDU headquarters. It contained both a very detailed description of the stronghold and a security grading based on comparison with other strongholds SDU had previously encountered. Because the buildings were well isolated and easily accessible under cover of darkness, and because surprise would lie with the assault team, the grading he gave to this operation was C+.

Becker's reply was short: just two bald sentences prefaced by the codeword HILTON. From this terse communication Sergeant Wong understood immediately what he must do next. It was time to move up to the forward command post, and prepare to receive the Clawhammer assault team within the next twelve hours.

FIFTEEN

Foshan, People's Republic of China, 01.17 hours. The night was moonless above the undulating grassland, and beyond the stern stone walls the outline of the great Elephant Hill was just discernible against the hollow blackness of the sky. In silence and in shadow they had come at last to this point, and from the edge of the west field the 'tigers' deployed in their pairs across the last grassy stretch of open ground. Muscles taut, ears straining above the song of insects, fingers gently bending back the soft grass blades so as to leave no trace.

They crossed the low outer wall at a lope and re-formed in three tight groups at the first stone outbuilding. An observation post equipped with an image intensifier had already reported that the perimeter was clean and free from look-outs. There were lights burning in only two of the five stone dwellings, but that meant nothing. Becker knew such obvious signs should never be taken for granted. They would have to clear every building if they wanted to eliminate any possibility of surprise.

And once the first noise erupted, it would all need to be executed very fast – the teams coordinated to the second.

The components of the assault group were well used to one another. Each team consisted of two pairs, trained to operate together on the same target building. Each pair would assault a different entry point: the first man in covering the majority of visible targets, and the second man handling the remainder. Becker's final words, before ordering them forward, had been a reminder that they needed these prisoners alive. But he knew also these were not just ordinary criminals, so he told them to take no chances; they must neutralise any *Dai Huen* who drew a weapon.

Since Becker was the field commander, it was agreed that Kale should lead the assault on the main building. Silently Kale positioned his team to cover both front and back, then he made the necessary radio checks. The station sergeant would lead the assault on the second building, while Becker's team would secure the outside of each building, ready for the extraction of prisoners. Responsibility for clearing the other three, darkened, buildings was split evenly between the two assault teams. They were allowed ten seconds per room, after their primary targets had been secured.

As they pulled on black ski-masks, Becker's only thought was getting his teams safely inside the *Dai Huen* stronghold with the maximum of surprise and momentum. When the final pair of black-clad figures had moved through the shadows of the open yard and melted against the dark stonework, Becker got on the radio. He carried the same lightweight headset consisting of earpiece and stick microphone as that used by tele-phone operators.

'Move up to entry positions. Report when ready.'

Kale felt his pulse-rate move up a gear, realising he had no idea what to expect inside the stronghold. The opposition would be well armed, and probably had been trained to the same degree as himself, but the actual number of 'crows' and the extent of their armoury had not been definitely confirmed. Nor could the presence of Public Security Bureau men in the building be discounted. For a few seconds the acute sense of danger made him lightheaded, his fingers numb and his throat dry. As usual, what bothered him most was the slender prospect of running slap-bang into a wild headshot. Then there was another prospect, if the operation went wrong, of being caught here on Chinese soil and subjected to summary justice at the hands of the PSB.

Attempting to clear his mind of such thoughts, he touched a hand to the earpiece taped inside his ear. There was more distortion than usual, he thought irritably; the batteries must be fading. The wire from the earpiece ran down his neck, and inside his black overall, to a personal radio mounted on the back of his belt. Another wire connected to the transmit key was fed down his left sleeve, and taped to his left wrist where he could easily reach it.

Three more paces across the yard, and he flattened against the wall at the rear of the main building. The back entrance was just an arm's length away. A double-leaf hardwood door with heavy brass hinges and the usual paper scrolls pasted on: two door gods to protect the entrance from evil spirits. The sound of laughing voices spilled out from under them, and he could feel *their* presence now, just feet away from where he stood.

Kale used his fingers to indicate their estimated numbers and location to his partner. He had counted at least four male voices. The doors, he guessed, would be bolted top and bottom. The sounds emerging were those of an informal gathering: single voices mixing in discussion, with the occasional clink of glasses.

Carefully, Kale removed a small gob of plastic explosive from his hip pouch, split it in two, and pressed one piece against each of the two door hinges. Next he pressed electric detonators into the plastic, and fed the wires back to a small handheld initiator which he then carried around the corner of the building. Holding the initiator in his left hand, his thumb poised over the button, he drew his Browning and slipped off the safety. Ready.

Kale felt his partner's hand come up to rest lightly on

352

his right shoulder confirming their relative positions in the dark, and telling him that his partner was also ready.

At this point any vocal response was out of the question. He squeezed the transmit key twice, sending clicks down the line to inform Becker they were locked in.

Immediately there came three more clicks from the second team, followed by four clicks from the third. Becker knew they were on. He took a breath of Republican Chinese air, then spoke clearly into the slim microphone.

'Standby. Standby. *Go!*'

What followed occurred so fast as to defy description. Kale's thumb touched off the initiator, and the doors blew clean off their hinges, landing at a low angle and blocking the doorway. In an instant they leapt over these obstacles and were into the main room beyond, pistols high, staring down at their stunned targets.

There were six stocky Chinese males relaxing at the table: some still in work clothes, others in vests and underwear. There were strangled cries and looks of total surprise when they saw the black figures suddenly before them. A second later came the sound of breaking glass as the second assault pair launched themselves feet-first through the kitchen window and bounded forward. In that moment one of the *Dai Huens* shouted something and hurled himself to the floor. In less than a second the other targets also split and reacted – diving for the cover of the furniture.

Kale knew then that there would be trouble.

'*Mo yuk! Mo yuk!*' he bellowed from behind his black ski-mask, but nobody was listening. His brain screamed hellfire. One of the targets, a solid figure with a shaved head and stubbly jaw, lunged from behind the sofa and made a grab for the pistol lying on a low table nearby. But Kale's foot connected with the man's face first, sending him backwards along with the upturned table, in a shower of lotus seeds. By now the second assault pair were in the main room, grabbing two targets off the floor and pinning them against the wall. Kale's partner caught another man from behind, throwing him to the floor, then kicked the feet from under a second, subduing both prone figures by aiming the Browning into their faces.

But the distraction had given yet another of the targets, crouching behind the table, the time he needed to draw his weapon. Reacting in blind panic he jumped up, swearing at the top of his lungs. Swinging the Chinese automatic up in front of him, he aimed for the chest of the assailant who had kicked Chan Ming's face. Kale was still covering his fallen target, but above the noise of the general struggle and the tumbling furniture, the sound of a cocking pistol went straight to the core of his brain. Jesus, too slow, he thought. The man was already sighted! Then in an instinctive reflex he dropped and twisted. The weapon's roar seemed to hit him full in the face, and he saw the muzzle flash even while the bullets were tearing into the window casing above his head. He would not get a second chance. From a kneeling position Kale squeezed off a double tap that ripped into the *Dai Huen*'s white vest, pitching him backwards across the sofa.

Suddenly all movement ceased.

Within five seconds the remaining targets had been forced to the floor at gunpoint. Kale then checked the remainder of the building, before calling down the line to tell Becker that all was secure. Beneath the ski-mask he was sweating hard. It had been a bloody near thing. Glancing at the window he saw how the bullet intended for him had chewed through the wooden casement. Fear and aggression boiled over inside him and he kicked the nearest target in the ribs, enjoying the sound of his cry.

'Don't move, you bastards!' he warned the captives in loud Chinese as the second assault pair bound their wrists behind their backs with plastic handcuffs. Remembering the second objective, Kale then summoned his partner and they moved out across the yard to check the storage barn. It was empty. As they came out again, still probing for hostiles, Kale heard his radio come to life.

'Talk to me, Delta One.'

'Delta One, primary and secondary targets secured,' he answered breathlessly. 'Five live crows, one dead one.'

Still in position near the outbuildings, Becker heaved a sigh of relief. The sound of gunfire had set him on edge. Worse still was that from there he could only imagine what was happening inside each building. The second assault team had already made its report: they had encountered immediate resistance from the four men they encountered. Two of the *Dai Huens* had pulled pistols and were shot dead where they stood. The other two had then raised their hands in surrender.

'Right, get them all out into the yard,' ordered Becker. 'The reception vehicles are coming in.'

Becker's team worked quickly, searching the live prisoners for other concealed weapons and identification. That done, the prisoners were gagged and hooded and left in the yard while the assault team collected up shell cases and any other evidence of their presence.

On the prearranged radio signal the first white van, driven by Sergeant Wong, drove up and the *Dai Huen Jai* were bundled into the back, with two of Becker's team as guards. Two more vans followed, in which the SDU men and the three corpses would ride back to Sung's factory. There would be no further contact with Lau Bing – for his safety's sake.

As they parked and disgorged their prisoners into the deserted factory building, Mel Kale caught sight of Becker's face for the first time since the assault had gone in. Becker came over, but before he could speak Kale held up a hand.

'Leave it out, Dave. All right?'

Sitting in the lead vehicle on the way back, Becker had already heard what had happened from Kale's partner, how close it had been. All he felt now was an overwhelming sense of relief.

'I only wanted to say it was good work back there. That and how I'm glad you didn't miss.'

Nothing more was said.

They had already lost too much time winding things up, so now they had to drive fast along the road to Canton, to be there before dawn. Most of their equipment had been left at Sung's factory, to be shipped on later. The first mate of the Ho Tung freighter was waiting for them at the main gate, together with a uniformed wharf security guard he had bribed. The three vans were cleared right through to the dockside, where the first mate supervised the secure berthing of the seven prisoners. By this time the assault team had changed into blue jeans and vests, and could mingle easily with the crew.

As the sun appeared on the horizon, the captain received port clearance and the ship steamed out into the grey-brown flow of the Pearl River. She was carrying a routine cargo of cherrywood furniture, metal kitchen hardware and cheap sports shoes, but, as Becker was soon to find out, the true value of their other cargo was beyond measure.

Just two days after they buried John Tasker, morale within Organised and Serious Crime Group began to unravel, and this showed itself in one telling little incident.

It was burning frustration that caused it: frustration stoked by one careless remark. Worst of all it had happened right in the middle of the OSCG duty room in Police Headquarters, where officers were supposed to be subject to the tightest discipline.

Tiger Cheng arrived just as Haak Jai, a dark-skinned stump of a man with a punch perm and a smart mouth, had gone berserk. Cursing loudly, he had just grabbed a steel kettle and used it to lay open the forehead of Ah Jak, another detective. Luckily the sound of the brawl and of overturning furniture had brought Tiger Cheng running before too much blood was spilled. The station sergeant quickly hauled the two apart, threw them into an interview room, and threatened to flay both alive if an explanation was not forthcoming.

Both men's faces were bleeding, and their heads now hung in shame. It had all been a question of face.

It had begun with a poor joke, born of the custom that Chinese couples may not live together until after a wedding banquet has first been provided for the bride's family. Typically, such celebrations could take as long as three years to save up for on a detective's salary. Both the brawlers were newly married, but Ah Jak and his wife, lacking the necessary cash, had yet to provide the wedding banquet, and so were living apart in their respective parents' homes. Unfortunately the banter in the *dai fong* had got around to comparisons between the two brides, and when Ah Jak's new wife received the majority of compliments, Haak Jai had seized upon this moment to crow about the joys of unrestricted conjugal access.

'*Ho chaam, ah nei! Ah Jak. Git joh fan do mo haai diu!* Pity you, Ah Jak. Married and still no cunt to fuck!'

The joke had drawn only a ripple of bored sniggers.

'Never mind,' Ah Jak had responded brightly. 'I still have you!'

At this the other detectives fell about laughing – which was enough to cause severe loss of face. The fight was almost inevitable.

Though Cheng did his best to patch things up there and then, he knew that Tasker's death was bound to affect the men badly. Their aggression, now turned upon each other, was an outward sign of the intense grief felt by all of them.

In this respect Joe Lai was no different from his men.

The official funeral service was held in St John's Cathedral on Garden Road and attended by representatives of all police formations, dressed in full uniform and medals. The Commissioner himself arrived at 10 a.m. sharp, looking predictably sombre, attended by the collected mandarins of Police Headquarters. Media interest was intense but Weldon had no comments to make, and a group of ushers and stewards worked hard to keep reporters at bay and to marshal the madding knot of newspaper photographers thronging the entrance for a final glimpse of this police legend. In the bright sunshine outside the cathedral, the band of the Royal Hong Kong Police in dazzling white tunics played 'Will ye no' come back again'.. Inside, the Commissioner delivered his eulogy praising John Tasker's bravery and tenacity, while Tasker's young Chinese widow and two Eurasian daughters wept softly at the front.

A whisper ran around the Cathedral: 'I didn't even know he was married.'

Many of the congregation departed almost too dispirited to speak.

Later that same day, in the offices of OSCG, Chinese and European officers alike assembled in the duty room to give face to tradition. Tiger Cheng had arranged for a Taoist priest to come and put in a fix that would exorcise the ill fortune which had befallen both the team and the investigation. At the Gwan-Dai altar the mottled old priest in his crimson robe chanted through his dirge-like ritual, swinging an incense-burner and blessing all the endeavours of the detectives. All around him the joss sticks in triplets of remembrance bled their rich fragrance into the room, until the *dai fong* was thick with curling smoke trails.

358

It was, for many of the detectives, an act of re-dedication to the very spirit of the Gwan-Dai and all he stood for.

Two days after they put Tasker in the ground, the inevitable backlash began: a wave of harassment against San Yee On premises and members. The detectives on Joe Lai's teams were sent out every day to brandish the battle pennant and to extract information. They invaded countless restaurants, bars and mah jong schools manhandling and intimidating triad elements wherever they found them, though with no real expectation of any direct leads. Both Joe Lai and Tiger Cheng realised that the killers would be virtually untraceable, but that was not their aim. Morale was dangerously low, and there was now a real danger of the team's disintegration. They had to do *something* positive.

Besides, the detectives now had to regain lost face or risk losing the informants each had cultivated over the years. The San Yee On triad had dealt the whole investigation what they hoped would be a fatal blow, and in Chinese eyes their audacity had shamed the police team and diminished every officer within it. Knowing his men could not work under such a negative burden, Joe turned them loose and looked the other way.

Meanwhile, the heads of C department (Criminal Investigation) were brought together in PHQ to discuss the worsening situation. In a hurriedly-convened meeting in Caine House's fifth-floor conference room, Chan Hamgar, the Director of Criminal Investigation, outlined in detail his fears of an impending all-out war between his department and the triads.

Chan was a humourless figure: a man with the short powerful build of a Chiu Chau, and a fiery temper to match; one whose neatly oiled appearance and deadpan mortician's face were known to strike terror throughout the Force. At fifty-four years old, he was the most senior

Chinese officer, and a committed Anglophobe. It was generally known that he bitterly resented Europeans who had been promoted over him (unfairly he believed), and, unlike the majority of his Chinese colleagues, he steadfastly refused to adopt a European forename.

Chan was anyway something of a controversial figure. For years there had been a rumour circulating in police messes about Chan's connection with one of the five fugitive station sergeants now living in Taiwan. His name had even been mentioned in the now famous Yaumatei fruit market corruption scandal which had led to a full-scale investigation by the ICAC, the Independent Commission Against Corruption. Whatever the truth of such allegations, there had been insufficient evidence to convince the official board of enquiry back in '77; they had found no reason to taint his reputation or restrict his police career. The cynics maintained that Chan had only saved himself by threatening to reveal the contents of his police diary, thereby implicating other officers in past misdemeanours. In short, they reckoned that Chan had the goods on some other very powerful people.

Despite all this, the DCI was acknowledged as a tough, intelligent officer with a passion for criminal investigation and an instinctive understanding of the moods of his men. Following the Tasker funeral he now detected a very dangerous undercurrent of discontent. The contract killing of any police officer produces in brother officers an understandable urge for retribution, but in the case of John Tasker, who had been built up as some kind of hero figure, this was doubly true. Chan Ham-gar realised that the Force would be looking to CID to respond to the challenge.

Even without the information withheld by Joe Lai (on the orders of James Weldon), the territory's top detectives were in no doubt they were dealing here with a triad assassination. The very location was a good indicator: restaurants were among the favourite killing grounds of the societies – being places where members of the public would witness triad power and be terrorised. There were other pointers too, like the crossed chopsticks laid on the table by the finger man, and the fact that a firearm was not employed. Triads always used traditional weapons in their murders.

At this meeting the Deputy Director of Crime, Lee Ming-wai, pressed hard for himself to take personal charge of the case and to have direct control over Joe Lai, without the usual superintendent intervening in the chain of command. Director Chan would have liked nothing more, but after the Commissioner's personal intervention he could not agree to this.

'It's out of my hands,' said Chan bitterly, as he glanced around the table. 'Weldon has taken it upon himself to exclude us here in this room. It's some kind of sensitive operation, I'm told, which cuts across a number of specialist areas.'

There were polite smiles of amusement from those at the table. Chan's little clique evidently enjoyed the mocking tone he used. Every man there was Chinese, and had been elevated through the DCI's personal patronage.

'Even so,' Chan continued, 'I want you to maintain a watching brief, just in case the Commissioner proves a little too enthusiastic for his own good. Sometimes Weldon fails to appreciate the delicate balance at work in this territory. Triads have been with us for a very long time, and their position is well established. Containing them is one thing, but the anarchy we would see if it ever came to an all-out war ... that is quite another. We in this room must distance ourselves from whatever disasters Weldon might provoke.'

'Of course, Chan-sir,' said Lee Ming-wai obediently. 'No surprises. I have my own sources. I'll find out what Weldon's up to.'

It was no secret that DCI Chan was an ambitious man, a consummate politician with designs on being the next

Commissioner of Police after the 1997 takeover, and in truth he seemed well placed to take up that position in the Special Administrative Region that Beijing had planned for Hong Kong – provided he could continue to maintain his successful image. He recalled briefly his last meeting with the commissioner, and his acute embarrassment at having the case removed from his department's responsibility. Nevertheless, the case was turning into a bloody liability, so perhaps there was some advantage in this latest turn of events. Henceforth none of the blame could possibly be his.

'Use all means necessary to find out what is going on,' he instructed his deputy. 'I have the feeling there is more here than just a robbery investigation. It has aroused an exceptional degree of interest and I know for a fact that the Director of Special Branch is being consulted. That bothers me.'

'Why should Special Branch concern itself with a robbery?' asked Lee with concern.

'I can't tell yet, but Special Branch *is* taking a very close interest. Furthermore there are to be no senior Chinese officers involved in the special investigation. That usually means a sensitive political angle; you know how little the *gwai lo* really trust us Chinese.'

Lee Ming-wai nodded his agreement.

'*Mo choh*. Too right! Still, have no fears, Chan-sir.' He smirked. 'All shall be revealed. I know a little "sparrow" inside Special Branch.'

Chan Ham-gar's eyes widened in appreciation.

'And can he sing, your sparrow?' he asked.

'Indeed, Chan-sir. This bird sings a note of exceptional clarity.'

Across Arsenal Yard, on the eleventh floor of New May House, Joe Lai sat smoking his eighteenth Winston of the day, and contemplating the small windowsill aquarium through a dense blue fog.

362

In the silence of what had been Tasker's office, and sitting in his old chair, Joe felt utterly devastated. Like one of the painted eggshells in the China Products Store – empty. On his shirt was pinned the traditional scrap of black silk – a symbol of mourning – but grief and the funeral had wrung him out to such an extent that now he no longer knew quite how he felt. Was it four days now – or five? He could hardly remember. The more he sat and thought, the more the personal recriminations came crowding on him. Why hadn't he moved? If only he had carried his personal issue revolver with him. If only he hadn't drunk quite so much. If only ... he kept on repeating. If only! Blind, impotent rage alternating with self-laceration.

Finally exhausted by such brooding, he sought refuge in his work. The two most pressing matters now were the safety of Philip, their undercover officer, and the outcome of the CIB covert surveillance operation. The first priority was well in hand: Joe himself was set to meet Philip at the Shatin safe-house at 9.30 that evening; he had already decided to pull his man out. Too many police officers had died already and he did not want Philip also on his conscience. Three phone messages stuck to his desk diary told Joe that the second matter now needed his urgent attention. Marshalling his thoughts, he first phoned Sandy Buchanan at CIB, and was told to get down there right away.

Reaching the CIB office, he quickly understood why.

In the interim, intelligence had been building up steadily, to the point where interesting patterns were beginning to emerge. Ever since the fortunate discovery of the San Yee On membership database, CIB detectives had been logging double-digit overtime in just cross-referencing data on known criminal targets. As in all cases involving organised crime, computers had played a major role. There were hundreds of personalities listed on the criminal indices, together with thousands of fragments of information gleaned from informants. Relating them together was a monumental task for any human being, but with smart software programmed by experienced detectives, related information could be quickly extracted and used to fuel hypotheses.

What had emerged was a pattern of meetings just prior to the Shatin robbery, between the leading lights in Tai Po district and their seniors in Tsim Sha Tsui. Some of the names and locations had been given up by informants, including Philip; others had been gleaned through Sandy's unique menagerie of customised bugs and directional microphones.

'Come and look at this, Joe,' said Sandy Buchanan, pouring himself a large measure of scotch into a teacup. He was clearly elated by what he had discovered. 'There's no bloody question in my mind. It's down to those Chiu Chau bastards, all right.' He paused just long enough to knock back the scotch, and then continued. 'But I reckon you're in for a surprise when you see where it all leads.'

Joe slid into a chair in front of the CIB man's desk, and watched as his fat fingers stabbed the keyboard of a neat, futuristic personal computer. When the screen opened up into livid colour Buchanan's face took on a glow, and he seemed to fall through it into another world. His world. The Scotsman gave the monitor a nonchalant shove with his hand, causing it to rotate upon the articulated extension arm to a position where Joe could see it better. This time Buchanan used an electronic mouse to point at and operate the mosaic of icons layered upon the screen.

Joe caught the first line of a program logo which read: LINK ANALYSIS FOR LAW ENFORCEMENT, but before he could read any further Buchanan had already clicked the mouse and selected a file which exploded upon the screen like a coloured wiring diagram.

'*Wah! Choi sik yee da lei fan,*' said Joe with a touch of Cantonese sarcasm when he saw the graphic display. Multicoloured spaghetti.

'Spaghetti that might save your *si fat,*' responded Buchanan testily, keeping his eyes fixed on the screen as he adjusted the zoom factor on the selected chart. 'Do you want to see this, or not?'

'If it'll help provide the cure for a bad case of San Yee On ... What's so special about this, anyway? Another new toy?'

'No, just newer software; a few more bells and whistles, but basically the same principles as before. Are you familiar with link analysis?'

'Of course. Diagrammatic representation of information. It can be any information, but in our case it's criminal organisations and associations. Circles stand for criminal personalities; and a box around a number of personalities indicates joint participation in something: a company, an association, a society, maybe even a robbery.'

'All right, Sherlock.' Buchanan grinned darkly. 'You've passed that test.'

Sandy Buchanan filled the screen with a box that was labelled in dark script: SAN YEE ON – TSIM SHA TSUI DISTRICT. Inside the box were eight named circles. Joe read off the names of the officials, reminding himself of the reputation of each of the hard men who kept Tsimsy screwed down tight. Eddy Kwok, the nightclub and restaurant owner with a four-year stretch in Stanley Jail behind him for wounding, section seventeen. His brother-in-law, Johnny Yau, a so-called businessman actually involved in loan sharking and prostitution: the most they had ever managed to lay against him was attempting to interfere with court witnesses in the trial of one of his own *ma jai.*

But the one who really caught his eye was Tony Kwan. Half-brother of the famous Alexander Au-Yeung, property speculator and head of Bright Star Holdings. Au-Yeung had been the subject of considerable police speculation over the years, but not much else. He had always been an enigmatic figure: a brilliant businessman whose successes had consistently excited the property market, and whose personal influence extended all the way into the Royal Hong Kong Jockey Club.

Tony Kwan was another story, a known 426 officer of the San Yee On, and for that reason alone he had to be responsible, one way or another, for every one of the choppings in the Yau-Tsim district over the past five years. It would be Kwan who controlled the protection rackets and planned the intimidation of businessmen. It was he who had the plate-glass windows smashed as a warning, the limousines vandalised in car parks, and the buckets of human filth thrown in top-class restaurants. Not even the newspaper seller could operate without his say-so – and that would mean a monthly donation of *bo woo faai*, tea money or whatever they chose to call it.

Knowing all this was one thing, but proving any of it was something else. There had never been any evidence against Tony Kwan because, like all Red Cudgels, he had surrounded himself with an impenetrable curtain; a curtain of followers who were willing to take the fall on his behalf. These young men were the *sei gau jai*, or the forty-niners, kids in jeans and sneakers who were the foot soldiers of the organisation. Hotheads mostly, with no proper jobs, they were men who sweated their mornings in kung-fu gymnasiums but staffed the society's amusement arcades, bars and brothels in the evenings. Loyalties were such that the *sei gau jai* would *ying* – that is, plead guilty – to almost anything in order to shield his protector. After all, convictions bought an immediate reputation in the criminal underworld. And, of course, triad time in prison was always easy time.

Joe Lai's fingers itched. One day the curtain would part and he would pluck this Red Cudgel like a flower. In Gwan-Dai's name he swore it.

'These are the names,' continued Buchanan, 'and the "head shed" that planned it – right down to the last detail. Johnny Yau, Eddy Kwok and Tony Kwan.'

'What's your source for all this?'

'Johnny Yau.'

'You kidding me?'

'Not me, boy. Yau's been a saturation target for most of this year, due to his alleged control of drug shipments to Australasia. Last February we got a diving team to bug his yacht for the Narcotics Bureau – and got some excellent intelligence without compromising the transmitter. When your investigation began, we just pooled the product from the NB operation.'

'Your chart shows all three of them linked together. Are they all in the distribution chain?'

'Surprisingly, no. But their close business associations with each other have been a subject of great interest. All three are directors of each other's companies. Dozens of companies – decorating contractors, travel agencies, caterers. All these boxes represent legitimate companies they control between them.'

Buchanan played the pointer upon the yellow circle that was Yau, and all the links extending out from it suddenly began to flash in reverse video.

'In the light of recent events, we started to re-evaluate previous product from that bug. With hindsight it's bloody obvious what they were planning, though at the time we had no idea. They must have thought they were pretty safe, because on the tapes Chan Ming is mentioned twice by name. They talked about powerboat engines, and how fast the marine police boats could go.'

'Why didn't we have this earlier?' snapped Joe Lai, without thinking.

'You know how long it takes to wade through weeks'

worth of product, man. There's a bloody great wodge of transcripts in my bottom drawer, if you care to read for yourself – and that's just the edited highlights.'

'OK, give it to me straight – no frills. I don't have the time right now.'

'Yau was the liaison man: he's got legitimate business interests but he also knows some very bad boys in Canton. It was these contacts who first told Yau about this *Dai Huen* gang, how they'd all been Division Seventeen soldiers in the Chinese army, and all that that meant. They arranged the introduction. As Philip told John Tasker, Chan Ming was always the driving force behind that team. Apparently, Yau fenced some stolen gold for him after that spate of goldsmith robberies two years back. He's got his own smelter hidden somewhere in Kowloon.'

'Is there anything that he isn't in to?'

'Nothing involving children or animals.'

'Very upstanding of him.'

'Kwok was involved to a lesser degree, but it seems to be Tony Kwan who really called the shots. Kwan's men set up the usual restaurant meeting just eight weeks ago – practically summoned Chan Ming down here.'

'How did he take that?'

'Not too well, but he was intrigued enough by the number of zeros being discussed to swallow his pride. They took him for a ride to Macau, where they all gambled and screwed around. Kwan painted a pretty picture, saying there was inside knowledge of the security procedures, volumes and timings. He even outlined the escape route – a path well worn by refugees and illegal immigrants from China, only in reverse. Chan Ming liked the idea.'

'I don't know,' said Joe with a slight grimace. 'Something doesn't quite fit. Why does the great and powerful San Yee On need a bunch of rag-arsed country boys from the Mainland? What's the big operation? What's behind it?'

'Two hundred and seventy million, I heard. That's worth reckoning. Oh, I agree with you, laddie. Last night proved that much.'

'What happened last night?' asked Joe, intrigued by Buchanan's secretive manner.

'Last night one of my teams finally succeeded in placing a tracking device in Tony Kwan's car. An hour later somebody firebombed that same vehicle in an underground car park in Tsim Sha Tsui East.'

'Any idea who it was?'

'No, and neither has Tony Kwan. Some passer-by called the police, and Tsimsy police station called out the Force bomb disposal officer. He reckoned it was a very professional job – highly sophisticated detonator – and not just your average inter-triad dispute.'

'So, somebody else is mad at Tony Kwan. That's good. I only hope they don't finish him off before I get a piece of him.'

Joe stood to leave, readjusting his belt holster for comfort, and Buchanan's gaze fell upon the brown butt of his detective special.

'If I were you, Joe, I'd keep that bloody thing close to hand from now on.'

'Really?' said Joe Lai without much interest. 'Why's that?'

'Because these boys are bad bastards. They don't give a stuff about police officers. You keep on going, and they might think about giving you what they gave John Tasker. Don't be a fool for this job, Joe. You'll get no thanks for it. We can't even be sure our own side isn't bent.'

A sound enough warning, but Joe had heard it all before. In any case, he mused, it was no longer just duty that drove him. Now it was personal.

'Thanks,' he muttered as he got up to leave. 'I'll bear that in mind.'

After two hours of questioning, Chan Ming broke his stone-faced silence. Without warning the *Dai Huen* leader sat bolt upright in the chair and demanded to speak with the Commissioner of Police.

The four Special Branch men in the cramped, whitewashed room – David Becker, a Chinese interrogation specialist, and two armed constables – looked at one another with a mixture of disbelief and suspicion. Each member of the reception team knew the prisoner was special forces trained; that meant he would be schooled in resistance to interrogation, so normal police methods would in all probability be wasted on him. Psychologically, David Becker had already prepared himself for an uphill battle. This newest twist, however, caught him completely off guard.

When no one moved or answered, Chan Ming's face reddened visibly and he began to tug in frustration at the handcuffs that bound his wrists to the chair-back.

'*Diu lei lo mo haai.* You shoeshine boys!' He spat on the floor. 'I've got important information to trade. Bring Weldon. I speak to nobody else.'

Becker pushed away from the wall and came forward.

'What kind of information?' he asked sceptically.

'Good enough to buy me immunity,' the prisoner answered defiantly. 'That's all I'm saying until I see your Commissioner.'

Then the stony silence resumed.

Sensing the glimmer of a breakthrough, Becker walked from the room and called Special Branch operations, asking to speak to the DSB. A woman constable brought him a glass of thick, sweet coffee made with condensed milk while he waited for the return call.

The Clawhammer team had been back in the territory less than six hours, but Becker's knotted neck muscles told him he had been on duty for about the last hundred years. Chan Ming had been identified from amongst the prisoners by the factory manager in Foshan, and therefore singled out for special consideration. The other *Dai Huen Jai* were being held in separate rooms, their movements and conversations all recorded on closed-circuit TV. Their removal to the facility had been accomplished with a minimum of fuss. An undetected transfer of the prisoners from the Ho Tung ship to a police launch the moment they reached Hong Kong territorial waters; after that an unmarked transit brought them under armed guard from Aberdeen marine police base to the Special Branch detention facility known as the Victoria Reception Centre, in the far west of Hong Kong Island.

Chan Ming was all that Becker had expected: tall and solid, with the well-muscled frame of a welterweight and the burned brown features of a farmer. His tough appearance was emphasised by the shaved head and the small ears that stuck close to a bony skull. He was half a head taller than the rest of his soldiers, the kind of natural leader who is used to getting his own way by force. Yet behind the granite exterior there was something more: the quick, narrow ferret eyes that missed nothing; a cool glitter of intelligence often described as low animal cunning. Above Chan Ming's right cheek a discoloured swelling marked the place where Kale's boot had sent him sprawling as he had reached for his weapon. For a moment Becker wondered how well he would have reacted himself in Kale's position – but it was over now. Nor did it make any sense to keep brooding on the Shatin robbery. Still, like Kale, he could not help thinking: 'One of these men shot Jason Leung.'

Was it Chan Ming?

It came as a relief when at last the phone rang, and Henry St John-Black came on the line. There was no mistaking his clipped tone.

'What seems to be the problem, David?'

'It's Chan Ming, sir. He's turned up good as gold.

371

There we were all geared up for sensory deprivation, and then he chucks it in.'

'Hardly what one would expect from his type. What's his game?'

'Immunity. He wants to do a deal. Claims he has important information for the CP's ears only.'

'Immunity for someone accused of manslaughter and armed robbery? Bloody ridiculous. Perhaps your chaps roughed him up a little too hard in transit, David. His mind is obviously gone. What's *your* assessment?'

'He knows we have him bang to rights, but he also knows we can't bring him to court or our foray into PRC would come out. That gives him the leverage to cut himself a deal.'

'You really think he's sophisticated enough to grasp that fact.'

'Oh, I think so, sir. There's a brain in there, all right.'

'Then what's he worried about?'

'I think he suspects he's a candidate for a quiet firing squad. I think we should call the Commissioner and listen to what Chan has to say. He says it's important.'

St John-Black took just fifteen seconds to make up his mind.

'Very well. We'll be with you in about an hour.'

In fact the Director of Special Branch's limousine pulled into VRC just thirty-seven minutes later.

'Looks like the old man's pretty keen,' murmured Becker as he watched James Weldon leap from the rear seat and march inside, the DSB scurrying after him. David Becker had commandeered the office of the section head who ran the facility, for an informal briefing with his superior officers. But Weldon waved away the details, insisting on being escorted immediately into the small cell where Chan Ming was being detained.

As the cell door opened the prisoner was sitting quietly staring at a damp patch on the wall. Weldon gave him a measured look and took a seat on one of the wooden chairs facing him across the table. Becker and St John-Black followed him inside. The only other officer present was the interrogation specialist, a Chinese station sergeant, who sat at one end of the table acting as Weldon's interpreter.

Weldon lost no time in ordering the handcuffs removed. That done, he produced a pack of cigarettes from his blazer pocket and offered the prisoner his lighter. Chan Ming massaged his wrists, assessing the *gwai lo* and finally he accepted the cigarette and with it the face the Commissioner was offering. Becker realised then just how personal an interest Weldon was taking in this case.

'My name is James Weldon, I am the Commissioner of Police,' he said grandly – more for the prisoner's benefit than for his own gratification. 'Let's not waste each other's time, Chan Ming.'

He placed both huge hands upon the table, as if ready to leap forward and devour the man. There was a pause, which all Hong Kong policemen learn to accommodate, while the interpreter echoed back his words to the prisoner.

'You are already in very serious trouble. We know you were responsible for the Shatin robbery and the deaths of eight police officers. Murder carries the death penalty here in Hong Kong, just as in the mainland. That is the reality for you. At this moment I'm intrigued enough to want to hear what you have to say. I'm wondering what you could possibly tell me that could affect your position.'

The interpreter translated rapidly, adding his own personal emphasis. Chan Ming sucked on his cigarette and glanced cautiously around the room at the faces watching him. There was a sink and soap in one corner of the cell but Chan Ming had not so far troubled to use them, and his grimy appearance and darting, suspicious eyes only underlined a sense of the hunted animal at bay.

'Commissioner, don't bullshit me,' he said at last with quiet bravado. 'I know as well as you that in Hong Kong the death penalty is always commuted by the British Queen. Do not think you can scare this chicken with such a threat.'

Weldon fixed the other man's eyes, which were brown and hard as pebbles, but said nothing. After a moment of challenge Chan Ming lowered his lids and looked away, then, adjusting his position on the chair, he sucked again on the cigarette and continued speaking.

'It all depends, doesn't it? I could say I'll give you names – maybe even the name of the tai-pan behind this whole fucking operation. The one who paid my men and me a shitty few thousand bucks and took the rest of the cash for himself. But I doubt that would impress you sufficiently. Not when police officers were washed away.'

'It might,' said Weldon, growing increasingly more irritated, 'depending on what else you had to back it up. But suppose we choose to shake that name out of you instead. As a soldier you must know there are ways. Even a soldier breaks down, eventually.'

Leaning back in the chair, the soldier's body stiffened. All at once his eyes had narrowed to nothing, and the arrogant sneer returned to his lips. For a long, long moment he seemed to consider Weldon's threat, nodding slowly as he contemplated the end of his cigarette. Then, without warning, he casually leaned forward and laid his bare forearm upon the table. He sucked once more upon the cigarette, to bring the tip to a hot red glow, then slowly, deliberately, while his eyes held Weldon's, ground out the lighted end against the soft flesh of his inner forearm until it was completely extinguished.

Dear God! Becker winced as his nostrils caught the reek of burning flesh.

Only the barest flicker of pain showed itself in the soldier's face.

'Yes, no doubt you'd get it eventually,' he said, swallowing hard. A bead of sweat tracked his throat. 'But eventually is not always soon enough, is it?'

The message was clear, it would be a long time before anyone broke Chan Ming. Becker moved forward and grabbed the man's arm to inspect it, wondering whether this was one of those kung-fu stunts involving mind control. It was not. Beneath the grey smudge on the prisoner's chestnut-tanned arm there was a small livid crater of burned flesh, and a blister was already beginning to form. Tilting the arm, Becker saw the light play upon five small circles of shiny scar tissue where the man must have demonstrated the same trick before. Chan Ming regarded the new burn without interest and sniffed.

'We've got a right headbanger here, sir,' said Becker disgustedly as he released the arm.

Chan Ming, who did not understand English, ignored the tall European and turned his gaze on the Commissioner, his self-assurance now growing.

'What if I offer the name of a senior police officer: one who for the past eight years has been an office-bearer of the *Hung Mun* – specifically, the San Yee On. What then?'

Though his brain was clamouring inside his head, Weldon fought to maintain the same faintly bored expression on his face. St John-Black's enquiry was still in its infancy, with no clear leads. Now Chan Ming was offering the whole issue tied up with string.

Weldon silently counted to ten before answering.

'That's an old story. The last time I heard that rumour, it was the 14K who had a spy in the Force. The time before that it was the Wo Shing Wo. It's very good for recruitment, they say – the triad propaganda machine. However, if you have such a name...?' He laid the scepticism on thickly.

'Unfortunately not,' said Chan Ming mockingly.

At that moment Weldon realised he had badly under-estimated the intelligence of his man. That the soldier and one-time farmer was playing with him. Worse still, everyone else in the room knew it, too.

'Perhaps a little softening up, sir,' suggested St John-Black, sensing the Commissioner's discomfort. Weldon considered the question, then discounted that option, silently reappraising the situation.

In another instant Chan Ming's mocking manner became totally serious.

'There is no name, yet,' he told the Commissioner. 'But what I do have is serious information about a terrorist operation. One set to take place here in Hong Kong within the next month. One so grand, so eye-catching, it will scare the stockmarket to death. Would that interest the Lord of Police?'

A sudden jolt like electricity was felt by every police officer in the room.

Weldon turned to the interpreter, angered by the game the prisoner was playing. The man was too clever by half, but he was also too dangerous to ignore. His information gelled uncomfortably with what Joe Lai had already said and with Weldon's own personal fears of what was being planned.

'Tell the man to save this striptease for other eyes. If he's got something to trade, let's hear it now. Otherwise I'm going back to my office and he can bloody well rot here.'

The Chinese watched Weldon stand and turn as if to leave, and he needed no translation to understand that he was being issued with an ultimatum.

'Commissioner, I am not a fool,' he said urgently, now not quite so self-assured as before. 'Before I give away what I intend to trade, I require certain promises. If I tell you what I know, they will risk anything to kill me.'

Weldon stopped at the door and half-turned.

'You'll be well protected here.'

'No! You do not understand. You must personally guarantee my safety. Change the guards – *gwai lo* only. I cannot trust any Chinese police officer. San Yee On brothers are everywhere.'

'Is that all?' Weldon leaned heavily on Scots irony.

'No. The *gwai lo* government must promise me immunity from prosecution. Then I will give evidence against those responsible. In addition, you must arrange my resettlement overseas. I want an Australian passport with a new identity, and cash – lots of cash. After that you will hear no more of me.'

The Commissioner was back at the table and listening hard. He sat down and considered the offer. Two hours ago he would not have believed he could so soon consider bargaining the freedom of a man responsible for killing eight police officers against advance warning of a major terrorist incident. Under the circumstances he felt no qualms about lying to the prisoner.

'Before I can agree to any of that, I'll need something to bargain with. If you have any information concerning acts of terrorism I strongly advise you to tell me now. After that I'll do whatever I can to help your situation.'

Chan Ming was nervous. He asked for another cigarette, and was given one. He did not really trust the *gwai lo*, but he knew he had to offer something or there was no hope. Still, the words of betrayal did not come easy.

'Very well. About two months ago I had a meeting in a restaurant in Sham Shui Po with two men who were looking for firearms – people with special forces training. Apparently I had been recommended by a mutual acquaintance. We talked for some time about the mainland, and mutual friends, before getting down to the real business of the meeting.'

'Which was?' the interpreter prodded in Cantonese.

'They said they were planning a two-phase operation that required a dozen or so good men. They expected it to be very violent, and they said it was important for security that the men came from outside Hong Kong. The first phase was to be a robbery: an armoured cash escort vehicle. The second, the kidnapping of a VIP for political purposes.'

The words caused a sudden flood of adrenalin in Becker's bloodstream.

Chan Ming continued, oblivious. 'There were other meetings after that, some on a yacht with some rich bastards, others in hotel rooms. There were other people there I'd never seen before. Too many people; it made me nervous. Some of them were Japanese, and one I think was a North Korean. That one never said a word while I was around, but you could see the others thought he was somebody important.'

'Why was that?'

'Because of the way they all behaved. They gave him face, gave him the seat of the honoured guest, all that shit.'

'Go on.'

Chan Ming concentrated on his cigarette as if it was a lifeline, taking short, frequent puffs upon it, perhaps to soothe his nerves. He spoke in rapid bursts.

'The details of the first phase were discussed only after I'd made a commitment to the operation, but the second phase was only hinted at, because I said I wasn't interested in involving my team in political matters. On top of that, I said I wasn't prepared to work with those fucking Japanese.'

That last remark surprised no one. Amongst traditional-minded Chinese there was still open mistrust of the Japanese, whose forces had invaded and brutalised China both before and during the Second World War.

'They told you this phase would be political, these men?'

'Yes. The VIP, they said, would be a top official of a foreign government, heavily guarded and well protected; but there was nothing to worry about because they had

378

found a weakness in the man's protective security. It was going to be very easy, they said.'

Becker could contain himself no longer.

'Was the VIP mentioned by name or by nationality?'

'No, never,' came the indignant reply. 'But I know who they were talking about. And so will you the instant I receive my assurances.'

Weldon caught Becker's eye, silencing him with a stern look.

'Go on, I'm still listening.'

'After that we didn't speak about the political phase again. I learned that it was being controlled by a separate group. The ones in charge were the North Korean and a second man, a Japanese, name of Okamoto. I heard from one of the planners that the Jap boy had spent time in Pyongyang – political refugee or something.'

The director of Special Branch moved quietly forward to the table.

'Do you know anything else about these two men – or who they were acting for?'

There was a long irritating delay as Chan Ming appeared to answer the question and the interpreter cross-examined him to check the answer. Weldon drummed his fingers, fuming. Interpreters had a habit of taking over an interrogation if given half a bloody chance.

'I know the man who controls them,' said the interpreter translating Chan's answer. 'He is a man of considerable wealth and power, a Chinese tai-pan. But I know he is working for someone else – possibly another government.'

Weldon was leaning across the table now, the DSB at his elbow.

'So phase two will be conducted some time within the next month, is that right?'

'*Hai a! Mo Choh!*'

'Yes. Correct.' The interpreter echoed needlessly.

'A group led by a Japanese male named Okamoto and another man believed to be a North Korean will attempt to kidnap a visiting politician?'

'*Hai a!*'

'Yes.'

'And the man behind the operation is the same prominent Chinese who engaged your services to rob the Shatin Jockey Club?'

'*Hai a! Mo Choh!*'

Weldon raised his hand, silencing the interpreter before he could speak. Becker smiled to himself. If it had not been so grotesque – that they had pulled this man out of China to face justice, and here he was cutting himself an escape window – he might have laughed out loud.

The old man continued with relentless pressure.

'All right, Chan Ming, you have our full attention. Now if you know the identity of the VIP, the method of attack, or any other details of this operation, I strongly advise you to tell us now. It will strengthen your case considerably.'

But Weldon had come to the limit of his powers, and now he was asking for assistance. Chan Ming recognised at once the strength of his own position and he decided to close up.

'No! Not another word. I have no need to strengthen anything. No more information until I receive a formal undertaking signed by the Governor of Hong Kong.'

James Weldon pushed back his chair and stood as if to leave.

'Then I will consider your offer and speak with the Director of Public Prosecutions, the Secretary of Security and His Excellency the Governor.' The prisoner seemed impressed by the list. 'But I'm warning you. The next time we speak I expect the name of this Chinese tai-pan, the name of the VIP concerned, and a whole lot more besides. If I don't get them, I may just let Mr Becker here

380

have his way.' Chan Ming eyed Becker warily as the interpreter explained. 'Mr Becker thinks it would be wiser all around just to have you taken out and shot.'

Weldon walked quickly from the room, closely followed by the DSB. Behind them Becker paused a moment before leaving too. Just long enough to aim a pistol-like finger at Chan's head and produce a soft click with his mouth.

In one of the Victoria Reception Centre's meeting-rooms James Weldon turned to David Becker with a look of concern such as the Special Branch bodyguard had never seen before.

'It's bloody serious,' he said with typical British understatement.

'Yes, sir, I know,' replied Becker. As the man responsible for VIP security on the ground, he did not need to be told just how serious.

'We thought we were dealing with a firm of armed robbers. We now know there's more to it than that.'

St John-Black thrust one hand into his trouser pocket, the vast expanse of his forehead wrinkling as he pondered.

'Hmmm. Sometime in the next month, he said. David, I'll need your considered assessment as soon as possible, so we can get the warnings out to consulates of likely targets.'

'I can narrow it down here and now, sir,' said Becker.

'Oh?'

'There are only two possibilities. One is the Portugese Deputy Foreign Secretary – he's transitting Hong Kong on his way to Macau.'

'Small fry,' said St John-Black dismissively. 'And the other?'

'William Fredericks, US Secretary of State.'

Weldon reacted at once, as if stung by a wasp.

'Good God! It's got to be him.'

'Yes, sir. It looks that way, doesn't it?'

'Today's Friday. How long exactly before Fredericks arrives?'

'Coming Tuesday 2 October,' answered Becker from memory. 'The day after Chinese National Day. Just four days away.'

'Sweet Jesus!'

The Director of Special Branch touched Becker's elbow.

'David, I want you to take this as your number-one priority now.'

'But, sir, I'm in charge of Fredericks' personal security detail,' Becker reminded the DSB. 'I can hardly do both jobs properly at the same time.'

'Forget the man's personal security for the moment. Stephen Lee can handle that. I want you to mount an investigation based on Chan Ming's allegations. I'll put someone else on to Chan Ming's debrief, but I want you to chase down this Japanese connection. I don't like the sound of that one at all.'

'Yes, sir. But it looks as if Chan Ming – he won't say any more until this immunity thing is processed.'

'Leave that to me,' said the Commissioner. 'It'll take between twenty-four and forty-eight hours to get a decision from Central Government Office. In the meantime we go with what we have. God knows that's little enough.'

'At least we have a starting point,' commented Becker.

'What's that?' asked Weldon. 'You mean the San Yee On?'

'No, not them. This man Okamoto, the Japanese political refugee. If he's spent any time at all in Pyongyang, the chances are he's been through the mill with one of the left-wing Japanese terrorist groups.'

'If that's true,' said Weldon sternly, 'then we'll be going against the first team. Henry, you'd better get the chaps from the US Consulate in ASAP. Special relationship and all that. See if we can't persuade them to cancel Fredericks' visit, or at least postpone it for a while. Just until we have things straightened out with Chan Ming.'

'I'm not sure about that one, sir,' said St John-Black, shaking his big shiny head. 'Comes at a difficult time, don't you know?'

'No, I don't. Obviously you know more than I do about the situation, so I think you'd better let me have your thoughts on paper. What about you, Mr Becker, what's your next move? Just how do you plan to keep our American guest alive, eh?'

'I think my first move is liaison. I have contacts at the Japanese National Police Agency in Tokyo. They spend every waking moment tracking the Japan Red Army across Asia. They'll know the current whereabouts of this Okamoto guy, if anyone does – and his current paymaster.'

'Good, I'll authorise any overseas travel you feel necessary – short of two weeks in Hawaii.' Weldon was winding up like a jet engine. 'We'd better hold off declaring a full terrorist alert for another forty-eight hours and keep the information within the Clawhammer format. Let's not forget we still have an internal security headache.'

'No progress on this High Dragon allegation, sir?' asked Becker.

'Not yet,' said Weldon. 'And I'm not at all sure Chan Ming knows the answer to that one either.'

'Agreed,' said Becker. 'He'd surely have told us, if only to protect himself from the retribution of the San Yee On.'

'Quite so. Still, I believe Joe Lai is close to something very interesting. Our best chance of cracking the High Dragon problem will undoubtedly come from his undercover agent.'

Becker saw the two senior officers out to their

limousine, then walked over to his own vehicle. As he unlocked the car door, the duty sergeant in charge of detainees came out into the yard, wearing a worried look. 'Ah-sir, respectfully suggest we need more staff. Too many prisoners, not enough *foh gei* in my section.'

'All right, Sergeant, leave that to me,' said Becker, rubbing his face in an attempt to stay alert a little longer. 'As soon as I get back to the office I'll arrange for some of the G4 constables to cover.'

'*M'goi sai, Ah-Sir.*'

Climbing behind the wheel, Becker pulled out of Victoria Reception Centre and took the Pokfulam road back towards Police Headquarters. For the moment at least, any thought of sleep would have to wait.

In the rear office of the Barking Peacock nightclub Tony Kwan was in conference with Johnny Yau and Eddy Kwok over a glass of French brandy, when the urgent bleat of the house phone interrupted their discussions.

'Yes, what is it?'

'Excuse me, Kwan-goh, we have a problem.'

'What kind of problem?'

'There's an Inspector Fung here from CID Headquarters. He's asking questions about Ruby Tang. What should I tell him?'

'Nothing. I'll be out in a moment.'

Roman Fung and Amy Chan were standing beside the captain's station just inside the entrance, when Tony Kwan appeared. As he approached across the empty dancefloor, where an old Chinese maid was busy sweeping up, he noticed both officers glancing about them with vague expressions of disapproval.

'Good afternoon, officers,' he began smoothly. 'Kwan Kui-cheung, managing partner. How may we help you?'

Roman Fung indicated the laminated warrant-card clipped to his jacket breast-pocket.

'Inspector Fung Lo-man, CID Headquarters. We'd

just like to ask a few questions about an employee of yours, a Miss Ruby Tang.'

'Yes, very unfortunate. You know, she used to be my most reliable girl before all this happened. I can't understand it. We're obviously very concerned about her, what with this sex-killer on the loose and everything. Of course we'll cooperate in any missing-person enquiry. You'll take a drink?' He made a show of ordering the best champagne and beckoning them both towards a table. Then Roman made an even greater show of declining and opted to remain standing. For a police officer it did not do to be seen accepting hospitality from the likes of Tony Kwan. Kwan knew that, too. It was all part of the face game.

'Mr Kwan, this is not a missing-person enquiry,' Roman corrected him. 'We're investigating the suspected murder of an American diplomat named James Reicher.'

'Murder?' Kwan affected a mild surprise which the police officer found immediately suspicious. After all, the murder had been reported in all the newspapers, so he ought to have known about it.

'I understand,' continued Fung, 'that Miss Tang and Reicher spent a lot of time together. In fact I understand the two of them were lovers. Certain evidence has come to light suggesting they were together on the night he was murdered; she may well have been the last person to see him alive. We're obviously very anxious to interview her, but I gather you've no idea of her present whereabouts.'

'None at all, I'm afraid.'

'That's too bad.' For a moment Fung looked speculative. 'Do you know if Ruby Tang ever brought the American here, to the Barking Peacock?'

Kwan shook his head firmly.

'Most unlikely, I would have thought. Ruby was a very hardworking girl. Frankly I wouldn't have thought she even had time for a boyfriend.'

'Indeed.' Roman sighed deeply, now more than a little

irritated by the game Kwan was playing. 'Well, if you do hear anything we'd appreciate a call at Headquarters. Ask for either myself or Woman-Sergeant Chan.'

'Of course, Inspector.'

Kwan saw them both to the door. As he watched them walk down to the street he was feeling distinctly pleased by his performance. What fools these police officers were.

When he returned to his office there was a call holding from the White Paper Fan in Tai Po region.

'What is it now?' he demanded.

'It's Ah Sin,' came the uncertain reply.

'What about him?'

'I think he might be a cop.'

'*What?*' At once there was deep concern in his voice. 'Are you sure?'

'No – not sure. We've been trying to plug the leak out here. There was something I didn't quite like about our arrest at Kwong Tau Shan. That business between him and Tasker.'

'Did you set somebody to watch him?'

'Yes, a group of forty-niners – *sei gau jai* he's never seen before.'

'And ...'

'He's been trying to shake them for the past two days. Could be he's trying to get away to meet his contact.'

Kwan chewed on his lower lip.

'All right, then, go ahead. Bait a trap and see what you snare. If he is *gwai tau jai*, an informer, don't waste any time. I can't have any loose ends at this stage of the game.'

'Does that mean you want him washed, Kwan-goh?'

'Do you really need to ask?'

It was early evening as Joe Lai reached Shatin, and his Celica finally found a kerb-space in the busy Lek Yuen housing estate. Thankfully, he had missed the worst of the rush hour, but there was still a steady stream of commuters spilling out from the bus and railway stations, heading home. The more ambitious of the local population was already fighting its way back out to evening classes.

As he locked the car and joined the flow moving along through the estate, threading between the circus of hawker carts and cooked food stalls, he was trying hard not to brood, but one thought kept returning; the threat of danger. Not for himself but for Philip, his agent. The potential guilt of it was the worst thing, but still he held fast to the belief that Philip's information was crucial to his case. And to finding Tasker's killer.

He climbed the stairway to the elevated shopping precinct, and leaned against a parapet to light a cigarette and take in the view. As he put away his lighter and pulled on the cigarette, he glanced around him, checking for coincidences – a familiar face or maybe just the same face too many times. No one. There was the usual sample of street furniture: construction workers with soiled jeans, neat office girls in chiffon blouses, old ladies wearing their flowered pyjamas and carrying string bags full of fresh vegetables. But no one with an obvious association – *mo liu do*, as they said in the CID.

Joe let his gaze travel upward, drawn by the clatter of mah jong tiles, to the ranks of high-rise apartments surrounding the precinct. Through the bamboo-pole tangle of laundry, children were chasing noisily along the balconies. One grey old woman gazed out into space; there was isolation in her forlorn manner. Sad, thought Joe, perhaps her kids had abandoned her; maybe gone overseas to make a future – to escape the Communists. He wondered briefly, from bitter experience, whether this old woman would be Shatin station's next rooftop jumper. They had always called them 'acrobats' back when Joe was a patrol inspector – the ones who went over the side, or more frequently off the roof. Suicides.

Many of them had been moved in from the rural villages and just could not take it in these boxes. Sad to be crammed in so close together, he reflected, but, after all, this was Hong Kong.

No more space left. Too little land. Too many refugees from the mainland. *Diu lei lo mo!* The Government had resolved to create these New Towns, and stack them high like vegetable crates in the market.

But Lek Yuen was modern. Lek Yuen was one of the first of the low-cost sky-block housing estates to be built in central Shatin. All amenities provided: community centres and playgrounds. The estate was linked to two shopping centres, and the neighbouring Wo Che estate, by a series of aerial walkways. Above the roadways, at pedestrian level, there were landscaped gardens and activity playgrounds for the kids, but, as in all such housing estates, these had become the natural congregation points for street gangs and drug traffickers.

Joe detoured through two restaurants and out through the yard of a kindergarten, before crossing over into Wo Che estate, satisfied for the time being that he was unobserved. The sun had already dipped behind the mountain of Tai Mo Shan; and beneath the square tower blocks, where all the real street action was, the cooked food stalls were bathed in harsh electric glare from unshaded bulbs. At this time the tables were mostly empty. Business would pick up later when the night creatures came out to quarrel and sell their souls.

He checked his watch once again, took a deep breath, and made his move towards Block Three.

He was just inside the hollow quadrangle, near to the district housing office, when an old familiar voice called out to him.

'What's this I see?' It was a queer croaking utterance. 'A tiger stalking in a jungle of stone?'

Joe looked up abruptly. There, hunched over a folding table, surrounded by his regiment of split bamboo brushes, brass ink-boxes and swatches of red paper, sat Wong Yiu-shan, the old calligrapher and letter-writer of Shatin Market. Everybody in Shatin knew him affectionately as Wong-suk – Uncle Wong.

'Ah Joe-sir, *dim yeung*?' the old man enquired, his watery eyes twinkling massively behind thick spectacle lenses.

'*Mo chuen mo laan, Wong-suk.* Nothing torn, nothing broken.' The stock answer.

'*Jan hai! Ho lui mo gin!* Really. Long time no see!'

'Not so long. Perhaps your bloody mind is going,' Joe beamed back, infected by the old man's happy face.

'*Waak je.* Perhaps.' The other grinned ironically. 'But these old eyes still miss nothing.'

It was a good face, an antique face, dappled with age spots and on his cheek one great hairy mole which the old man cultivated as a herald of good fortune. But the most splendid thing about this face was the agreeable way it collapsed in upon itself around the jawline whenever Wong-suk laughed, because he refused to wear his false teeth.

Uncle Wong was an important landmark in the community. 'Turn left by Uncle Wong's table,' the locals would say. That's how Joe had first come to know him; because *he* knew everyone on the estate, or at least knew about them. Back in '81 when Joe had been a freshly graduated police inspector posted to this new town, such knowledge had proved invaluable.

Wong-suk had occupied this same spot, tucked against the wall of the housing office, facing the water gardens, for the past nine years – observing a world framed by apartment blocks, and receiving a steady stream of customers. For some people he was an oracle, dispensing his homespun wisdom; for others he was their surrogate voice on official documents. He was the closest Shatin could claim to a modern soothsayer. Before that he and his father had occupied a hereditary pitch in the old run-down Shatin Market, in the days before electricity and when there was only a handful of poorly-educated farmers living here. Equipped with horse-hair brushes and his family's secret formula ink, he claimed to have bamboozled officialdom for over fifty years; and, with his own exquisite ideograms, to have melted the hardest lady's heart. Love letters had always been a speciality; his Dragon and Phoenix style was instantly recognised by all the best matchmakers. At once serene and dignified, his scholarly figure bent before the flimsy table was a pleasant link with the old days and the old ways.

Wong-suk's laugh degenerated into a wet, hacking cough.

'*Aiyah!* Nothing torn, nothing broken, you say. Except for the small door.' His face collapsed again in a lecherous grin, and this time Joe laughed with him. 'Still fornicating with *gwai mooi*, the foreign girls, are you?' he asked hopefully. He had always asked this since he once saw Joe chatting to a European woman inspector on attachment to the division. The old man had drawn his own conclusions from this chance observation.

'How they must love our Chinese bodies,' mused Wong-suk. 'So clean and civilised compared to the male barbarians. No disgusting body hair. Giving those girls no rest and no sleep, I'll bet?'

'They say the wind blows through any hole it can,' answered Joe with a wink, providing the old man with exactly what he wanted to hear.

He shook his head and closed his eyes.

Joe slid on to the stool opposite, and rested his back against the cement wall.

'Got any messages for me, Wong-suk?'

The old man's face was suddenly serious. Looking quickly about him he reached down into a small camphor-wood box at his feet and took out a pink envelope – the kind the banks used to contain fancy gift cheques presented by guests at wedding parties.

'Here is one from a close friend.'

'How close?' asked Joe.

'Very close indeed.' The old man raised a pair of wispy grey eyebrows in the direction of Block Three, overhead.

'*Gam yeung*. Did you see anyone else?'

'Yes. He was followed.'

'What?' Joe tried to cover his concern, though it must have registered in his face. 'How many?'

'Four of them. Not very sophisticated. They waited until he was inside the elevator, then they slipped into the lobby. I saw them checking the floor on the lighted panel.'

'What did they do then?'

'Went up the staircase like panthers. Big fellows, *ho dai jek*.' Wong-suk simulated the bulk of a gorilla as best he could.

Joe felt a sudden cold flush of fear. Not again, he prayed. In Gwan-Dai's name not again! He grabbed the old man's arm, the full extent of his anxiety now obvious.

'What did they look like – *Dai Huen Jai* or the local gangs?'

'Locals, I think. Flashy shirts and cowboy pants. Young street trash. But not from Shatin.'

'What do you mean?'

'They looked like *Ah Yor*.'

'*Ham gar chan*,' whispered Joe at the connections. *Ah Yor* was the old derogatory name for the seagoing tanka fishermen. Many of them had settled in villages such as Gwong Tau Shan, and their offspring were now the mainstay of the Tai Po chapter of San Yee On. Evidently it was Philip's own people who were shadowing him. He was already under suspicion.

'How long ago was that?'

'Ten minutes, maybe fifteen.'

'*M'goi sai*, Wong-suk.' He thanked the old man and raised himself from the stool.

Deciding that the elevator and main stairs were too dangerous, Joe Lai took the alternative staircase at the far end of Block Three. At the tenth-floor landing he leaned against the handrail, his heart and lungs heaving painfully in his chest. Too many bloody cigarettes, he told himself, and not enough bloody sleep! When he reached the eighteenth floor, he continued up another two – for safety and to get a better viewing perspective of the apartment. Leaning out a bit from the stair lobby to view the internal quadrangle, he could see the safe-house two floors below. There was a light on somewhere in the apartment; a faint glow in each of the windows. All seemed quiet.

Cautiously Joe leaned further out from the stairwell, using a concrete pillar for cover as his eyes roamed the decks, trying to locate the four watchers. When he found them, he had to smile. More from relief than any amusement. Two of them, in flowered shirts and black acetate jackets, loitering on the eighteenth-floor balcony – one of them close to either staircase, pretending to read kung-fu comics. The third and fourth were up on the nineteenth, one floor below himself, seeking the same overhead view. They were all as tough and ugly as Wong-suk had said.

Silently, Joe gave thanks that he had climbed that one extra floor, but he had to admit it did not look good for Philip. This apartment had so far played no part in the agent's false triad biography, so what was he doing here? They were bound to ask that. Philip already had a place in a building in central Tai Po, and the Society had long since checked out his family and friends. That he had obviously lied to his protector in order to get away for this meeting would also go heavily against him.

Nothing else for it, thought Joe; he had to call Shatin

police station at once and get uniformed help in pulling the agent out.

Just then there was a soft whistle from the deck below. Joe saw the men on the eighteenth floor signal an acknowledgement, then move back into the main stairwell. A minute later all four men were in whispered conference on the floor just below him. As Joe padded along the balcony, darting selfconsciously between pools of light from apartment windows, he pondered what he might need to do if some unsuspecting neighbourhood-watch member were to challenge him.

Now directly above them, Joe looked down at their arms resting on the metal balcony rail. Lying down upon the concrete floor, he was just a few feet above them. They spoke softly but still he could hear every word.

'What do you think, *hing dai*?'

'Looks like they're already inside.'

'I told you that before, you arsehole!'

'All right, so what now?'

'We've housed the traitor. I say we kill him.'

'Fuck it! Kick the door down. Chop him, and anybody else who's in there with him.'

'What do you think, elder brother?'

The third voice was resolute as iron.

'*Gau dim kui.* Give it to him now.'

'Wound or kill?'

'What do you mean? He is *gwai tau jai*; he broke his oath. The penalty for informers is death by ten thousand swords.'

There was a heavy silence. Joe shoved his face still closer to the rail, straining to hear. The stink of dried urine wafted from the concrete floor to fill his nostrils. He could see more now: the permed buds of black hair and the angry movements of their hands. Suddenly, as one man, they reached behind their backs and pulled out what resembled flattened rolls of newspaper, which they had been carrying under their jackets, tucked inside the

393

waistbands of their jeans. Instantly Joe recognised the shape of the weapon, and the danger it signalled. There was the barest whisper as each man snapped his roll downwards towards the floor and the paper slid off, revealing a gleaming fifteen-inch blade of surgical steel.

'Ah Cheung, you tackle the door,' the third voice commanded softly. 'Remember, kill everyone inside.'

With that the group moved back into the stairwell – heading for the safe-house, and for Philip.

Not again! Joe's brain screamed. Not this time!

As if experiencing some terrible recurrent nightmare of death, he felt himself rolling over and over, scrambling to get to his feet. There was no sound from below as the four men crept along the deserted balcony towards their destination. Downstairs in the open quadrangle somebody was kicking a football, and a child squealed. Joe sped back to the staircase, missed his footing and slid down the first flight of steps, crashing painfully against the metal handrail. As he regained his balance he caught sight of running feet coming out on to the eighteenth landing below him. He took the next flight of steps in a kind of blind panic, two and three at a time, his legs almost refusing to cooperate. His chest heaving painfully again, only this time from something more than just exertion. '*Tin kei*. Not again,' he mumbled.

He leapt down the last eight steps and came into the open balcony of the inner quadrangle at full pelt, the slap of his feet echoing loudly in the hollow stairwell. The sound caused one of the triads to stop and turn. When he saw the hurtling figure of Joe Lai coming towards him, he shouted in warning. Joe saw one dark shape hurl itself against the flimsy door. He heard a rendering crash as the joists split and the wooden door catapulted inward. The first two black figures were through the doorway in less than a second.

The third and fourth men turned on Joe in a kind of

leopard stance, raising their blades high enough to make a clean throat strike. Joe saw the first blade sweep towards him and went in low, feet first, grabbing the triad's lower body in a scissor grip with his own legs. As the man hit the deck, Joe flipped over, grabbed for his opponent's face and thrust two fingers into the soft sockets of his eyes. Automatically his left hand seized the wrist of the hand holding the knife, twisting it until the grip was broken and the weapon came free.

He was halfway up again when a kick caught him on the right rib-cage, spinning him about; but by that time he was too scared and angry to feel any pain. He continued moving towards the open doorway, brushing the other man aside like a charging bull, barely stroking the triad's windpipe as he passed. Yet it was enough to fell the man in a groaning, gurgling heap.

As he stepped across the threshold, the shouts and sounds of crashing furniture and breaking glass seemed to come from the main room. He lurched through an inner doorway into the living area. In that second he saw Philip cowering on top of a double bunk bed, his back pressed against the wall. A trail of wrecked furniture traced his retreat from the sofa to the corner of the room where the beds stood. Now he was trapped by the hacking blows of the other two triads, desperately trying to fend off their blades with a blood-soaked pillow. Seeing blood streaming from Philip's forearms, Joe felt his own blood surge out of control.

'*Gau meng!*' screamed Philip. 'Help! They're killing me!'

Just then two quick hands caught a flailing leg and started pulling him down off the bunk.

'*Mo yuk! Mo yuk!*' roared Joe. '*Chai yan!* Don't move! Police!' Why did no one ever listen to that!

'*Diu lei ge chai yan!* Fuck your police!' came the hate-filled reply. 'We are the brothers!'

The blade bit deep into Philip's leg, slicing the upper

395

calf-muscle, and he screamed in bitter agony. The second triad's blow struck at the wrong angle, and bounced off his kneecap.

This was as much as Joe could stand.

He saw the pistol rise into his field of vision, without actually being conscious of drawing the weapon. Suddenly there was nothing to think about; the decision had already been made for him. Arms raised and locked in a tight triangle with his chest he squeezed the trigger once, twice, three times.

The first triad gave an involuntary cough as the bullet hit him. It struck just below the armpit, burrowing into his left lung. He pitched sideways, a look of twisted terror on his face, and fell face-down upon the lower bunk. The second assailant took a bullet somewhere in his abdomen and toppled forward, sprawling over Philip's body.

Both men were still moving. Screaming and panting, but still alive.

Joe holstered his weapon, then, pulling the second triad off him, he helped the agent into a chair. Using a torn piece of bedsheet as a tourniquet, he tied off the arterial wound in the back of Philip's leg at a point just above the knee. Outside on the balcony he heard the slap of running feet as the other pair of assailants made their getaway, but he had no interest in chasing them now. The sight of the other two triads writhing on the floor had already absorbed any hatred he had previously felt. All that was left was a mixture of nausea and utter relief.

His hands were trembling as he picked up the phone, though he could not tell why. He did not feel scared any more. Not now Philip was safe. Perhaps it was the fear of what might have been had he arrived just a few minutes later.

'*Wai!* Shatin Police Station?' he gasped into the mouthpiece. 'This is Detective Senior Inspector Lai,

OSCG.' There was a beat as the constable acknowledged his rank. 'Get me the DO – immediately!'

SIXTEEN

Joe Lai closed the splintered door and waited in the wreckage of the apartment, nervous and unsure about what would happen next. His greatest fear was of a San Yee On back-up team, but in the event no one else came. Within minutes the balconies were lined with gawping residents whose curious heads bobbed in at the open windows.

He greeted the first police siren with a sigh of relief. Next came the reassuring flashes of blue light from the street below. Then the familiar green uniforms of the Emergency Unit. Thankfully, the sergeant in charge knew his business well, and procedure took over before shock could take its toll.

The two men with bullet wounds were transferred under guard straight to Queen Elizabeth for emergency surgery, and admitted to the custodial ward. Philip was taken in a separate vehicle to the casualty department of the same hospital, with firm instructions that those guarding him should not let him out of their sight under any circumstances. By a stroke of good fortune the third and fourth members of the gang had been lifted by a mobile patrol while fleeing the scene, and were brought back in handcuffs to Shatin station to be banged up. It would depend on the advice of Crown Counsel but Joe had every intention of charging all four men with attempted murder. Let the Society's fancy bloody lawyers bargain the charge down to 'wounding seventeen', if they could.

Shatin CID took initial responsibility for the case enquiries, though it was clear that OSCG would pick it up in the morning. Because this involved triad activities, the wounding case would be handled by the experts at CID headquarters. The case of 'police open fire' was another matter: that would be handled separately by the Assistant Divisional Commander Crime (ADVC/Crime) for Shatin.

Immediately the incident was reported, the ADVC/Crime was bleeped at a dinner party and called back to the station to take possession of Joe Lai's personal-issue firearm. Joe did not like that very much. It was, of course, standard procedure in accordance with the Police General Orders manual, but the way the weapon was sealed in an exhibits bag for later examination by one of Kiwi Rice's force ballistics officers gave him an uneasy feeling – like he was also one of the bad guys.

Under normal circumstances Joe knew he could expect to be placed on desk duties pending the outcome of the investigation, but somehow he did not think that would happen.

He found an empty office and tried to phone the Commissioner at home. When all he got was an answer-phone, he called the control room at Headquarters PolMil, knowing that the duty officer there would always know the CP's availability.

He finally tracked Weldon down at Government House and, after a moment's hesitation wherein he deliberated upon the protocol involved, he asked for the Governor's ADC. Weldon came straight on the line without ceremony, and Joe felt a powerful sense of relief at hearing the Commissioner's voice, a lifeline back to his own protector. He realised then what Tasker had really been to him – and what was now missing. Without Tasker's leadership, he now felt himself leaning heavily upon the Commissioner himself for support.

'I see,' said Weldon when the detective had finished

his story. His voice filled with concern, 'And are you all right?'

'Yes, sir. Like they say, *mo chuen, mo laan.*'

'Good. Here's what I want you to do. Stay with Philip, take him somewhere safe and debrief him as carefully as possible. Don't tell anyone where you're taking him – not even me. Are you wearing a radio-pager?'

'Yes, sir.'

'Good, then I'll bleep you if I need to contact you quickly. For your ears only, Joe – not your men's – Chan Ming is now in custody and looking to do a deal.'

'But how?'

'Never mind that. Our little conversation the other day seems to have been borne out. We now believe there is a strong possibility of terrorist action in Hong Kong. If Philip has knowledge of what's coming up, or of this so-called mole at PHQ, then I want it as soon as possible.'

'Don't worry, you've got it.'

'What about a weapon? Are you armed?'

'No, sir. I surrendered my weapon. Procedure.'

'Stuff procedure!' thundered Weldon. 'I'm the bloody Commissioner of the Royal Hong Kong Police. You're to draw another weapon immediately, and if you have to use it to keep Philip alive, then bloody well do so. Now, let me speak to the duty officer there.'

Joe sat in the hospital waiting-room for three hours, turning over in his mind the events of the evening, wondering whether there had been any other way. He knew that, in the court case which would inevitably follow, it would emerge that Joe was an accomplished martial artist. The defence would be bound to question why he had not waited longer before opening fire, and why he had not first attempted to subdue the prisoners physically. Of course it had been a judgement call, and he had decided in the heat of the moment that the risk to

400

Philip had been too great. Nevertheless, in the quiet of the courtroom the defence would find a hundred reasons why he ought not to have fired.

But Joe remained convinced in his own mind that it had been a time for guns, not fists.

It was one in the morning when Philip was finally released from casualty. The doctor who patched up his leg with a total of forty-two stitches told Joe that, despite the amount of blood lost, there was every chance of his regaining full mobility in the leg. They gave Philip crutches to keep his weight off the wounded limb, and told him to rest as much as possible.

Philip lowered himself painfully into the passenger seat of Joe's car, tipping the seat back and placing one bandaged forearm over his face. As Joe got in and buckled up, he knew by the long heartfelt sigh that Philip was now practically wasted. Understandable after what he had been through. A moment later he felt the seat beside him tremble, and when he looked he saw the young man quietly weeping.

'*Diu lei lo mo*,' cried Philip. 'Get me away from here, OK?'

'Where do you want to go?'

'Anywhere. Just get us out of here!'

It might have been some nagging pain in his leg and hip, now that the local anaesthetic was wearing off, but Joe thought it had more to do with heartfelt relief at being back on the inside at long last.

'*Fong sam, dai lo*,' he said softly, placing one hand firmly on Philip's shoulder. 'You can relax now, brother. You're with us, and everything's going to be okay.'

As he eased the Celica out into Wiley Road he knew, as surely as night follows day, that the Society would be watching from now on. Waiting for him to surface; waiting for a chance to kill the undercover man and finish what they had already begun. To *wash* him, as they put it. And already they were not wasting any time.

When Joe had called Shatin station from the hospital, one of their legal eagles had been there trying to get one man bailed out. Casually the brief had also asked after the arresting officer, and, when told he was not there, had offered one of the report room constables five hundred Hong Kong dollars to tell him where the injured person had been taken. Stone-faced, the constable had warned the dapper lawyer about the provisions of the Bribery Ordinance, then thrown the money back in his face, reporting the incident to the DO to cover himself.

All that only strengthened Joe's feeling that it was far too risky to go back to his own apartment. That would be the first place they would look. Right now what he needed was a place to hide his future witness: somewhere anonymous where they did not ask too many questions.

He drove north through Kowloon, along Waterloo Road towards the Lion Rock Tunnel, and turned off left into Kowloon Tong.

Kowloon Tong was one of the more well-to-do areas of the territory, with expensive low-rise housing that boasted small, neat gardens and high white stone walls. Among the buildings were a smattering of the better schools and kindergartens, and even the odd film studio, but the place was really famous for the love motels whose neon signs burned all night long. Here no distinction was made between the innocent young couples with nowhere else to go and adulterous lovers whose spouses would be none the wiser.

The Garden of the Playful Cats was one of the better known establishments. A veritable monument to bad taste, it boasted eighteen rooms attuned to a variety of erotic tastes, each with rotating water bed, shower, jacuzzi, and the ubiquitous giant colour television screen. The television was central to the whole business; evidently Hong Kong Chinese liked their sex in front of the screen, for when a boy asked his girl to 'Go Kowloon Tong watch TV', she knew exactly what he meant.

The Sikh desk attendant barely batted an eyelid when Joe and Philip checked in. It was not his business to ask questions, just to take their money and provide a neat pile of clean towels.

'Excuse me, *sin saang*, may I see your identity cards?' His huge turbaned head bobbed. 'Very sorry. I need it for our records. It is the law.'

'My name is Wooi Fung,' said Joe, drawing two red notes from his wallet and pressing them into the Sikh's hand. 'This is my ID.'

Recognising the Cantonese name for the Hong Kong Bank, the Sikh quietly pocketed the money, his huge head continuing to wobble from side to side.

'As you like, sir. Room number seven. If you'll just follow ...'

'That's OK. We'll find it ourselves.'

As Joe locked the door and inspected the room, Philip hobbled across to the bed, laid aside his crutches, and eased himself carefully on to it, propped against a pillow. Seconds later he had found the remote controller and began flicking through the TV channels. That did not surprise Joe at all. Most Chinese kids grew up with the TV on all day, whether anybody was watching it or not. Philip was now snatching at the familiar. He found an old black-and-white Chinese opera in which the heroine was squawking loudly about her lover who had gone away to war. Almost immediately he was bored, and began thumbing through the stack of soft-porn magazines in the bedside drawers.

Joe turned the volume down and began checking the walls for hidden video cameras. Some of these places, he knew, went in for home movies with a healthy little side-line in blackmail. He found nothing.

'Got any cigarettes?' asked Philip agitatedly.

403

There was a basket on top of the TV and Joe rummaged through the complimentary packs of toiletries, creams and contraceptives until he found what he was looking for: the usual pack of Marlboro. He lit one and threw the pack over to Philip.

'*Nei yi ga dim yeung a?* How do you feel now?'

'*M ji. Ho kei gwai.* I don't know. Feels strange. You know, after three years. There's a lot happened. I don't know where I belong any more: whether I'm on the inside or the outside. Understand?'

'I think so.'

'There's not much difference between the recruits in police training school and the Blue Lanterns running those streets out there for the Society. It's all about brotherhood and membership; our group versus their group.'

Joe relaxed into a low armchair, draping one leg over the arm, and preparing to soak up whatever the agent now threw at him. He had always known that when Philip finally came in, he would be desperate to talk – like a clockwork toy with an overwound spring. Talking would be his way of winding down, and as agent handler it was Joe's job to be there. But after what Joe had been through himself in the past seventy-two hours, he guessed they probably needed each other about the same.

He sucked gratefully on the Marlboro and watched Philip flick the pages of a Japanese copy of *Playboy*.

'Once or twice we thought we'd lost you.'

'When was that?' He didn't look up.

'First time was when they put you in charge of the massage joint in the Tai Po Centre. Buchanan was really worried. Good pay, promotion, and all the girls you wanted. Why shouldn't he worry? That's when you started to speak with affection about your protector. Buchanan said you actually seemed reluctant to give information about your *dai lo*.'

404

Philip put down the magazine and looked up.

'What else should I feel? He saved my life.'

'*Hai me?*'

'It was a dispute with 14K over decorating contracts in a new block in Shatin. The big wheels met in a restaurant for talks, but it broke down after just thirty minutes. We drafted reserves from Tsimsy for a blade war and they brought in reinforcements from Kowloon. Ever hear of a Double Flower called Siu Din Din?'

'I think I've heard of him,' said Joe matter-of-factly. 'Wong Tai Sin chapter?'

'That's him. Almost took my head off with a butterfly knife. Would have done, too, if not for ...' Suddenly he stopped and seemed to withdraw inside himself. 'Anyway, what does it matter now? That's all over.'

'You were a volunteer, one of our best,' said Joe believing that Philip had the right to hear it after all he had done and all he had been through. 'You undertook the most dangerous role we could ask of any police officer. You knew it would be difficult; you were warned it would be impossible to avoid getting involved. All we asked was that you hold fast to the knowledge that you were still one of us. Not their animal but a police officer.'

Philip turned his head away and slid down until he was lying flat, facing the rotating fan on the ceiling.

'Was I a police officer when they pulled me into Tai Po station and kicked me all around the cells? Was I a police officer when they shoved their fingers up my arse to look for packets of heroin? Or when they threatened to cut off my balls?'

'I know it was rough for you.'

'Believe me, you don't know how rough. Do you know how it feels to be thrown out of training school – the loss of face? Or to know that your own parents call you triad scum, and they're actually ashamed to be seen with you?'

405

For a long time Joe said nothing, and both men sat listening to the muted wail of the Cantonese drama on the television.

'We can sort that out,' he said eventually. 'Your family I mean. We could get one of the high-ranking detectives from CID HQ to explain it to them, if that's what you want.'

At first Philip seemed to be considering this, then he seemed to change his mind and spoke softly, almost guiltily.

'I was sorry about John Tasker. A bad way to go. A man ought to die at home in bed, aged ninety-nine, with all his family around him. There was nothing I could do to warn you. It was handled from Tsim Sha Tsui. I never heard a whisper until it was done.'

'That's OK,' said Joe with a heartfelt sigh. 'What's past is past. But it must have been something very big, otherwise they'd never have dared risk all-out war with us. There'll be a reckoning of that score some day. What's important now is the information you're carrying in that head of yours. And I need everything you have tonight.'

'All right,' said Philip, leaning up on one elbow. 'So let's start right away.'

Joe stubbed out his cigarette and forced a crooked smile.

'Not so damn fast,' he said laconically. 'What we both need now is *siu ye* – first we have the eating. Then we can do the talking.'

Warning Philip to lock the door, he drove down into Wong Tai Sin and stopped at a *dai pai dong*, one of the street restaurants which stayed open extra late to catch the shift workers. He ordered roast duck and pan-fried noodles with spring onions, and, while the greasy owner churned his wok over the roaring gas burner, he looked around and wondered how much longer he would have to watch himself this way. It was quiet. Just one or two *fei jai* sitting in front of heaps of gnawed bones, dirty plates and half-finished bottles of San Miguel beer. Joe recognised the night-shift Emergency Unit transit parked a little way up the street, and then the uniforms – a sergeant, two constables and a *lui ging*, woman police officer, at a table under the awning, taking an early meal-break.

As a constable, Joe too had placed great importance on the choice of food stop: the highlight of the shift. On day and evening shifts the public was only too keen to complain of unseemly behaviour, but on the night-shift it was quieter and things were more relaxed. The proprietor would treat them well, and claim to friends and competitors to be well in with the police; for him their presence was a powerful talisman against triad extortion. And the odd free meal was a small price to pay for such reassurance.

For Joe reassurance lay in knowing exactly what was going on at all times. Right now only Philip could fill in the gaps for him.

They ate the noodles out of the brown wrapping paper, with rough wooden chopsticks borrowed from the desk attendant. The duck was succulent and the skin perfectly glazed a rich dark reddish brown. Three tall bottles of San Miguel – well chilled – completed the feast. As they shared the food Philip's mood seemed to lighten, and Joe sensed his man had come through whatever personal crisis he had been suffering. There was once again a sense of shared purpose.

'It was only a matter of time before they latched on to me ...' Philip began, pausing to wash down some duck with a mouthful of cold beer. 'When you ask questions you get yourself noticed.'

'Did you ask questions?'

'*Gang hai la!* You bet. First of all I tried to find out what was behind this connection between San Yee On and the Big Circle. That was difficult. Nobody seemed to

407

know much. Then two nights ago I was in Tsim Sha Tsui accompanying my *dai lo* for a meeting of the districts. There was a lot of drinking – you know what those affairs are like: brandy, brandy and more brandy. But I kept a clear head and latched on to some of Eddy Kwok's men.'

'How did you manage that?'

'The old trick. I made sure I fetched the drinks: brandy in their glasses; cold tea in mine. Same colour. It's stupid but it never fails. Besides, they were already too far gone to notice.'

'And what did they tell you, these drinking men?' asked Joe.

'They kept talking about some people from Manila; people who had been brought in special because Chan Ming's Big Circle men had lost their *chuen dui*. They said these people – one of them said there were six only, but he couldn't be sure – anyway, they were being kept under guard somewhere in the Yau-Tsim district. I asked as discreetly as possible, using coded language, if there was another robbery planned, but they just laughed at that and said it was something much bigger.'

Joe had now lost interest in the food and was listening closely to every word, probing his mouth with a wooden toothpick.

'What's bigger than the Shatin robbery?'

Philip shrugged.

'That's just it, I don't know. And I don't think they did either. They weren't of the first rank – not even district officials. I doubt they were trusted with any more details than what they told me.'

'And these people were Filipinos?'

'No. I said they were from Manila. Kwok's men said they were very dangerous. They said these six brought a dungheap full of plastic explosive with them through airport customs.'

Joe Lai could hardly believe his ears. He spat the toothpick on to the floor.

'Plastic. *Diu lei lo mo!* Did you get any names? Did they mention what day these people arrived?'

'Within the past two weeks, is all they knew. No names, no descriptions. Sorry. The information came third-hand.'

'Where from?'

'One of Tony Kwan's fighters.'

Anger flashed like lightning in Joe Lai's face. Just the name sent a shudder through his body.

'Who was this fighter?'

'His family name is Chau, but everyone knows him as Ah Baai.'

The limping one.

No need to guess where he got the limp, thought Joe: more battle honours of the urban blade wars. The nickname would be enough to go on for the moment; enough to start a trace. If he was Tony Kwan's man, then he was bound to be on record in CIB. He felt something like hope grow in his lower belly. The odds of a reckoning were beginning to improve already.

And the name of the Red Cudgel came like the smell of blood in the water to a prowling shark. Tony Kwan's spoor at every turn.

The blue cigarette smoke gathered in clouds between them as Joe listened to the pain and the anger in Philip's words. Nodding, agreeing, empathising. Occasionally touching his arm or shoulder in reassurance. Understanding the needs of his agent, the way Tasker had understood his needs. Aware, more than ever before, that, for a Chinese, leadership and paternalism are inextricably linked. It took most of the next hour before the jumbled stream of information that tumbled from the agent's lips had lost its intensity. At that point Joe knew he could begin to make progress.

'*Ho la.* Good. Now we're going to begin again. Only this time put the emotion to one side for a while. This time I want detail.'

'*Mo maan tai!* No problem.'

The detective's manner was now totally serious. It seemed as if he had said these things a thousand times before. Witnesses in criminal cases only gave what they thought they remembered. It was up to the skilful interviewer, or interrogator, to probe the dark recesses of recollection and bring forth the truth.

'This could take a few hours, or it may take all night. I know those cuts are bad – do you think you can take it?'

'*Gang hai la!* Of course.'

The night air was unusually oppressive. Joe opened all the windows, lit another cigarette, and threw off his shirt. Beneath it he wore a white vest with red graphics and a police crest, the kind of vest designed and worn by the PTU training companies. Even Philip recognised the diagonal red band of Foxtrot Company: the customised logo which depicted a pair of red foxes amorously mounted, and beneath it the English motto *Why Tango in Paris when you can Foxtrot in Kowloon?*.

'Never mind how long it takes,' said Philip dismissively. 'I told you already, I'm a police officer; this is my job.'

'I hoped you would say that.'

'Just don't make it *too* long. We both need some rest. And there are still other vital matters to speak of.'

Joe had found some headed paper in a bedside drawer and was preparing to take notes. He looked up suddenly.

'What vital matters are those, brother?'

Philip leaned back against the wall, measuring Joe's hunger, then he rolled his eyes upward, examining the ceiling as he scratched his throat.

'There's this Vietnamese *choi*, Ruby Tang. Tony Kwan wants her very badly. When he finds her, she's dead. It will be a very bad death.'

'Who is Ruby Tang?'

Painfully, Philip raised his hips off the bed – just high enough to pull a slim leather wallet from the back pocket of his jeans. He flipped through a sheaf of betting slips until he found a small coloured photograph which he pitched on to the bed in front of Joe.

'She's one of Eddy Kwok's girlfriends. He made her captain of the chickens at the Barking Peacock in Mongkok.'

Joe studied the photograph. The girl had everything in the right amounts and in the right places, too. And if she was tied up with the Society, it was a safe bet she had had a lot of practice using it already.

'*Jeng ye.* Nice bit of stuff,' breathed Joe appreciatively. 'Why do they want her? Something more than just these tits here?'

'She stole something very valuable from the Society.'

'Money?'

'No, something far more valuable than that, apparently. They now seem to think she's in Macau, but they don't know where. Like I said, when they find her ...' The sentence tailed off and Philip drew his fingertips down across his throat to demonstrate the woman's certain fate.'

'So. What's her connection with our business?' asked Joe impatiently.

'Perhaps nothing, but they say she was opening her precious small door for an American at the Consulate. Some of the forty-niners are saying it's the same *gwai lo* who lost his head down in Yaumatei.'

'That was San Yee On?'

Philip shrugged his shoulders. 'All I know is Eddy Kwok and Tony Kwan set her up with an American guy. I heard such stories about her. *Aiyah!* They say she can blow a man's flute until he walks on clouds and the Eight Immortals appear.' Philip's eyes widened with delight at the thought of such ecstasy.

'*Tai jue, sai lo!* Careful, little brother, or you'll burst both our stitches.'

411

A small groan of frustration escaped Philip's lips. '*Mo gong siu*. No kidding, she's one very smart piece of vegetable, that one. They were using her *wok* to distract the American. The deal she was nursing through was sanctioned by the inner lodge. That's why I couldn't find out anything about it. Something seems to have gone very wrong – don't ask me what.'

'How long has she been missing?'

'She disappeared the night before they took the Shatin Jockey Club.'

'Eeeee,' growled Joe in frustration. 'You're as big a teaser of the male stalk as she is. What did she steal exactly?'

'Ask Confucius,' snorted Philip, as if only a sage could know the answer to that one. 'Listen, *dai lo*, I've told you all I know. The rest is up to you. The girl is as good as dead. Find her and offer her protection, then you'll get everything you want on the inner lodge. She has nothing to lose now, has she?'

An instant surge in the detective's pulse. More doors were opening: connections being made which both expanded and deepened his fear. Cautiously he hid his thoughts, looked at the photograph once more, then tucked it into his wallet behind his warrant card.

'You did well, *sai lo*,' he said, striving to keep cool in the face of so many leads. 'I won't have to exaggerate when I tell your father how important you've been to us.'

Philip lowered his head and looked at his hands, embarrassed by how much those words actually meant to him. Seeing him so vulnerable made Joe almost equally embarrassed.

'Now, before your head swells too big, tell me the last piece of information. The one I know you've been saving.'

Philip's grin was broad, his eyes shone with triumph, and behind the carefully clipped moustache his face seemed younger than ever.

412

'Oh, I always save the best until last.'

'Then let's have it, little brother,' demanded Joe, still trying to keep his voice calm and matter-of-fact.'

Philip's eyes narrowed and his voice dropped to a low whisper, indicating the importance of what he was about to say.

'The house is unsafe when a dragon enters. He brings death upon those that dwell within. Prepare to slay your dragon, Joe-sir. I have discovered his name.'

In one of the first-floor offices of Caine House, Senior Superintendent Brian Evans, Stephen Lee's immediate superior, sat pouting speculatively across his desk at the other intelligence officers present.

'From what you say, I think we have to presume that William Fredericks is the intended target.'

'That's if we believe Chan Ming's story,' offered Stephen Lee, unbidden.

'Yes,' said Evans slowly as his mind began to churn. His eyes contained a faraway look, as if he was playing movies in his head, trying to foresee the outcome of any decision he might have to make. 'How long do we have, Mr Becker?'

Becker cleared his throat.

'The Secretary's plane arrives at Kai Tak this Monday evening at 8.30,' he said. 'That gives us less than sixty hours.'

'Sixty hours!' Evans slumped back in his chair and threw his pen across the blotter. 'Good God! What are we supposed to do in sixty hours!'

Becker glanced around him in irritation, first in the direction of Stephen Lee, then briefly at Ruth Tavistock, who sat balancing a personal organiser on her lap, with pen poised. Both avoided his gaze and for a moment he wondered whether he was alone in feeling frustrated by all this bureaucratic rumination when time was so very short. In fact, Becker had already made his calls to the Japanese Consulate and hooked up with Ito, their National Police Agency representative. Ito had made the necessary preparations in Tokyo, and all Becker wanted to do now was to get on with it. But Evans, the Group Head, was suspicious of overseas visits, and even now he insisted on playing judge and jury first.

Evans was a big, ruddy-faced man, his large head topped by a neat cap of slicked and parted hair. Wherever he went in Caine House, his approach was invariably announced by the smell of Brylcreem. The pockmarked look of his large jaw matched the often craggy nature of his character.

'I'm not much for kneejerk reactions,' he said finally. 'And from what you say this Chan Ming character sounds capable of anything. Why not a nice little slice of fiction to save his grimy neck?'

'He may have been lying,' said Becker trying to remain calm in the face of such provocation, 'but I don't think so. In my opinion he was just plain scared to death. Take it from me, Chan Ming is no cream-puff, so whoever or whatever is behind this has got to be fairly impressive. Right now all Chan wants is somewhere safe to hide. After what they did to John Tasker, who could blame him?'

'Allowing for your intuition, Mr Becker, did he give any reason why these people might wish to kidnap the Secretary of State? Or do they just dislike Americans – like the rest of us.'

That was meant to be funny, but nobody laughed.

'Let's not forget our last visit to the New China News Agency,' interrupted Stephen Lee, quiet and businesslike as ever. 'Regardless of the overt reasons for Fredericks' visit, the Americans will be holding talks with the People's Republic. That gives us a very good political motive: disruptive action.'

Evans thought about that for a moment, then looked expectantly towards Ruth.

'What about this meeting? Did you take it up with the RSO as I requested?'

Ruth saw Becker's interest flicker at the mention of Jack Cinch's title. She uncrossed and recrossed her legs nervously.

'Yes, I did. "No comment. State Department business." He maintains they planned to inform us on Monday morning, to give us time to make the necessary arrangements.'

'Much good that would have been. What about Prioletti, what did he say?'

'The same. Only not nearly so polite.'

'Your assessment?'

'At the moment?' He had a habit of putting her on the spot this way and she had developed the ability to think quickly on her feet. 'Difficult to tell. It could be tied in with naval landing rights for US warships after 1997. Since they've been shut out from the Philippines, the Seventh Fleet has doubled the number of its visits to Hong Kong. When Beijing takes over, they have no other base from which to maintain psychological pressure on the Vietnamese military ports. Although economically the US and China are still cooperating, on the diplomatic front relations are still strained. US support for the pro-democracy movement really put their noses out of joint in Beijing. It's possible exploratory talks would have to take place in secret.'

'So the Chinese Foreign Minister slips quietly over the border for a bit of a chat,' broke in Evans with heavy irony, 'and no one's any the wiser. Yes, sounds quite reasonable – except that too many people seem to know about it already.'

'Sir?' said Ruth quizzically.

'You don't whisper a secret through a bloody megaphone, do you now?' said Evans rather smugly.

There was the puzzle: a covert meeting under threat from a terrorist source. But from where had the terrorists gained their information?

'All the same, sir,' offered Stephen Lee, 'it does make for a particularly sensitive operation. If anything should go wrong, and it were shown we had prior warning and did nothing ...'

Evans digested the problem.

'All right, against my better judgement I'll go along with what you say, Stephen. As for you, Mr Becker, if you expect to be released from the operation in order to fly to Tokyo, I hope you have something useful to go on.'

It sounded more like a threat than a hope. Becker shrugged it off.

'Chan Ming gave me a name: Okamoto. I believe he's talking about Kazuo Okamoto, one of the younger members of the Japan Red Army. Our most recent information on him is nearly three years old. It's believed he was one of the team responsible for bomb attacks on US banks in New Delhi and Bangkok back in 1989. He was never arrested. Presumed gone underground somewhere in Asia. With help I think I can trace where he is now. There are also other corroborating circumstances which support Chan Ming's information. However, I'm not at liberty to discuss them at this time.'

The Group Head bridled. He knew Becker was a designated Clawhammer officer, and that such a security set-up cut right across the normal lines of command.

'In my opinion, Mr Becker, we seem to be a little too ready to scream Japan Red Army these days. But that's just my opinion.'

He nodded towards the phone on his desk. 'It seems both the Commissioner and the DSB have decided to give you your head.'

'Yes, sir. I trust there's no problem.' Becker looked back at him levelly, aware of the Group Head's resentment, knowing that if it was up to him, the information would have been graded *Source Unreliable*, recorded at the back of the operational folder, and thereafter forgotten.

At once Stephen Lee sensed what was developing and moved quickly to distract Evans with the latest amendments to the Secretary of State's programme. When he had finished he returned to the subject of Becker's investigation.

'I've released David from the operation so as to chase down the lead with the Japanese. Last night we checked with Ito, the National Police Agency representative here at the Japanese Consulate. His office carries only broad details of Red Army activities – historical mainly. He had to telex Tokyo and set up a meet with their counter-terrorist people. David's booked on a JAL flight for this afternoon.'

Evans's eyes shrivelled to two black points and, as he collected the papers on his desk and tapped their edges straight, he gave a soft snort.

'I trust you'll keep us appraised of any developments, Mr Becker,' he said to the desk. 'Just don't stay there too long. Mr Lee is going to need you here. These liaison trips do have a habit of deteriorating into pleasure jaunts if we're not very careful.'

Evans' resentment was there for all to see.

'Thank you, sir,' said Becker levelly. Anything more would have been stupid, and would have jeopardised his operation.

Sensing his powerlessness to influence events now, Evans brought the meeting to a swift close.

'In the meantime, Miss Tavistock, see Jack Cinch and give him our amended threat assessment. Find out how their Consulate would feel about cancelling Fredericks' visit. Make sure you record the meeting in your source file, and put a copy in the operational folder for the visit. If anything does go wrong we don't want them claiming they weren't warned.'

Afterwards, in the corridor, Ruth put her own questions to Becker.

'Just how sure are you about this kidnap threat?'

'About as sure as I've ever been. The investigation we're on goes deeper and wider than anything I've dealt with before. So wide that James Weldon is handling it personally. That's what bugs Evans so much.'

'Why is Weldon involved?'

Ruth knew that the Commissioner's time was usually taken up by ceremonial and political duties, leaving no time for him to involve himself with the individual problems of policing the Colony.

'Let's just say because of what happened to John Tasker ...'

'But –'

'... and leave it at that.'

Ruth seemed deflated. She was aware she had no proper clearance to enquire further, but for some reason she badly needed to share something important with him.

Becker's face was set deadpan, but his eyes flashed with childish mischief.

'Can't tell you any more, Ruth,' he said in a whisper. 'If I do, then I have to kill you.'

Ruth groaned. It was an old joke between Special Branch Officers.

'Isn't it time for another *bai Gwan-Dai*?' she said as they came to the outer door leading to the stairs and the lift lobby.

'Sure, I'll give you a bell as soon as I get back. We'll get all the old team together.'

She smoothed the hair back from her face, clutching the folder tight against her breasts.

'I'll look forward to it,' she said softly.

But he was already gone.

* * *

In Hong Kong, Saturday afternoons are sacred. When an end is called to the morning's business, the expatriate community disappears like morning mist before the crowds can overtake them. Those with boats escape to the quiet of the outlying islands, where there are still deserted beaches and clear blue water that is cooling to the skin. Others of a more energetic and gregarious persuasion join the very pukka social clubs and vent their frustrations on the sportsfield in games of rugger, field hockey or cricket, then drink the sun down in the clubhouse, all tanned and spent from the day's exertion. There have always been clubs in Hong Kong for those who can afford them. The frantic pace of life in this sweating, jostling, dinning, cheek-by-jowl bedlam of the east was always such that major banks and trading houses feared executive burn-out, so usually included automatic club membership in their benefits package for expatriates.

From the imposing structure of the famous Hong Kong Club, wherein the great and the good mix their cocktails with conspiracy, and seek to influence the lives of others ... to the middle-ranking Kowloon Cricket Club where civil servants don whites and are somehow more British as they wield the willow, and dream of sleepy Surrey village greens – each maintains a sense of sanctuary from the jungle of the streets. Membership is limited, of course. And so the *gwai lo* repairs to his club, or his boat, in the sincere belief that without these he would either leap from a building or go stark raving mad within the month.

Yet on that Saturday afternoon – as David Becker was outward bound from Kai Tak for Narita Airport; and Joe Lai was wondering what his next move should be; and somewhere in the far west of Hong Kong Island an ex-PLA commando with a secret to sell awaited the Governor's answer – there was little thought of social diversion in the minds of certain police officers.

Ruth Tavistock knew with depressing certainty that her date with a sculling partner down at Middle Island rowing club had already been shot to pieces. Right now it was more important that she meet with Jack Cinch and set him straight. The exigencies of the job, as they put it in Police General Orders. There were just sixty hours to go before William Fredericks' arrival, and she could not help wondering, as she slipped the papers into her handbag and closed up her safe, whether the coming Monday would see the ageing statesman walk into an ambush of world-shattering consequences.

For someone more used to merely pushing papers back and forth, it all seemed so unreal.

The phone rang fifteen times before the operator at the US Consulate answered it, Ruth's anxiety growing steadily with each ring. When she finally got hold of someone responsible who had not already left for the weekend, it was the Gunnery Sergeant in charge of the Marine security contingent. Luckily Ruth had met him before at the Marine house, where Friday evening was Happy Hour for consular staff and invited guests. Being directly answerable to the RSO on matters of security, the 'gunny' always knew where Cinch was to be found.

'He went by the Hilton Hotel, ma'am. 'Bout an hour ago. Something to do with the confirmation of details for Monday evening. You know how it is.'

'Yes, I do. Thanks, Carl. Have a nice weekend.'

'Not me, ma'am. I'm on duty now until Secretary Fredericks leaves next Friday.'

She took the escalator up to the main lobby and found him by the main desk with the banqueting manager, poring over the seating plan for a charity dinner in the grand ballroom. William Fredericks was to be the guest of honour, and evidently there was some problem over

420

which of the prominent Chinese businessmen with US trade links should be seated at the Secretary of State's table.

'All right, so we'll get a bigger table. Take care of it!' he said with ill-disguised exasperation.

'Certainly, sir.' The Chinese banqueting manager, perfectly attired in immaculate black jacket and pinstripes, inclined his head and disappeared through a group of people all of whom appeared to be dressed for an afternoon's golf.

When Cinch looked up again from the seating plan, it was to see Ruth standing there looking her usual self: the picture of cool efficiency.

'I think you need a drink,' she said, casting her gaze over his slightly creased and wrinkled suit, which matched exactly his slightly creased and wrinkled face. She noticed how his hair was mussed in front; the boyish good looks appeared decidedly dulled today.

Cinch did not know how to react to her. Their last meeting had been anything but friendly, and since then they had exchanged only a few official words over the phone. Cinch was finding the abrupt change from a hot afternoon of lovemaking to the coldest of cold shoulders personally very unsettling. He thought perhaps a drink was not such a good idea.

''Fraid there's no time for that. I'm up to my eyes.'

'Oh, what's wrong now?' she said, choosing to save her own news until she knew the extent of his present troubles.

He blew out his cheeks, tugging uncomfortably on his shirt collar despite the hotel's excellent air-conditioning. This was not the usual Jack Cinch.

'Where should I begin?' He counted off the problems on his fingers. 'First there was the screw-up on the room bookings: we ordered twenty-four and, thanks to this morning's cable, now we need twenty-seven. Then we find our transportation agent can't supply us. Can you believe it? This town has the finest collection of swank automobiles in Asia, and I'm busting my ass to scare up another two stretched Benzs for hangers-on. Add to that the two Marines who went sick last night after a night down in Wanchi – sergeants, I might add, who ought to know better. Then there are these two Chinese *tai tais* who refuse to be seated within scratch-and-spit distance of each other at the charity dinner. To top that all off, there's a tropical storm scheduled to follow the Fredericks plane all the way in from the Philippines, with a possibility that he may get diverted or postponed. Now I have to organise a complete wet-weather programme – just in case. By the time his plane lands, we could all have drowned out there on the apron. Who knows, with a little luck ...?'

Ruth grinned at the black humour.

'Come on, you really do need a drink.' And if you don't *now*, she thought, you soon will.

Cinch allowed himself to be steered the few steps into the Dragonboat Bar, off the main lobby, where they both found vacant stools by the counter.

There was a good mixture in the place: the usual gaggle of middle-aged American tourists in loud leisure wear, the younger ones with designer jeans and gold rings, and the usual large number of Hong Kong businessmen who had stumbled from their offices in Central straight into the bar, and showed every intention of staying there the whole evening. There was a pleasant hum of spirited conversation.

Part of the attraction of the place, apart from the stunning waitresses in their tight silk cheong-saams, was the bar-counter itself. It was moulded in the shape of a dragonboat and ran the length of the room, ending by the glass doors with a magnificent rearing, roaring dragon's head. As they hoisted themselves into raised stools halfway along the great serpent's back, Cinch's eyes began to wander after a waitress sheathed in

422

turquoise silk. A conditioned reflex, mused Ruth as she caught the barman's eye and ordered two of their coldest bottles of Tsing Tao beer. It was Ruth's preferred drink, apart from champagne – a light beer made from Lao Shan mineral water in a brewery originally located in the German concession of the mainland. That was an excellent pedigree for any beer.

Their glasses came straight from the freezer and there was a chilled film of condensation on the bottles in which you could almost write your name. The barman was one of those precise Chinese who sought perfection in the most apparently insignificant of tasks. He poured the drinks with tantalising slowness, watching the head rise like a surfing wave.

'*Yam booi!*' said Ruth, raising her glass. 'Cheers!'

Then came that glorious burning-cold ecstasy that almost numbs the throat.

'Jeez! That's better!' said Cinch with a long grateful sigh. His eyes concentrated upon the glass as he set it back on the bar. 'I guess I was getting pretty wound-up back there.'

'That's understandable. It'll be your work that makes the Secretary's visit a success or a failure.'

'How true. Care to write my next evaluation?' He grinned and took another long pull from his glass. That tasted even better than the first.

'By the way, where are the leg-men? I don't see them anywhere. Shouldn't they be doing all this.'

'If you mean Lassiter and Divine, the bastards ran out on me. They're over in the China Fleet Club ordering enough rosewood furniture to fill the next aircraft carrier bound for San Diego.'

'Not a very responsible attitude, under the circumstances.'

Cinch bristled at this first sign of criticism. Ruth could be fairly withering, given the opportunity, and he felt a natural urge to protect his own people.

'Wait a minute. It's their advance, OK? What you British would call a perk. Those guys on the Fredericks detail spend months away from their wives and families every year in some of the shittiest garbage-heaps in the world. When they're on post it's backbreaking work. Long days, and precious little sleep sometimes. A few days on advance to the next location gives them a chance to rest up and recharge. I know, I did it myself for five years.' He might have added 'That's why my marriage went down the toilet' but he chose not to.

'Point taken, Jack. What say we call a truce here?' There was no giveaway inflection in her voice.

He took another drink and said: 'Fine by me. What did you mean by "under the circumstances"?'

Turning her glance to meet his, she leaned closer, dropping her voice to a soft whisper that even the barman could not hear.

'Let me tell you a little story ...'

Five minutes later, when Cinch had listened to the revelations of Chan Ming and had had a chance to order a second round of drinks – this time with a bourbon chaser – he had turned deadly serious.

'Come on, give it to me straight,' he whispered hoarsely. 'No Special Branch bullshit now. Is this reliable? I have to know.'

Ruth had never seen him look quite so worried before, and that immediately made her worried too.

'As far as I can tell,' she said, jerking her arm free of his grasp. 'For God's sake, stay calm. We've no intention of holding out on you.' There was a subtext to that remark, and Cinch received it loud and clear: *We're not the ones who withhold information – you are!*

Ruth snapped open her handbag and took out a sanitised copy of Becker's source report, placing it on the bar beside his elbow.

'This contains everything I've told you. Perhaps you'd let us know if you or Prioletti have anything more on file.

In the meantime I've been asked to strongly recommend you do what you can to get this visit cancelled. Speak to the Consul-General, or something.'

Cinch turned back to the bar-counter and concentrated on rotating the glass between his two palms.

'That's out of the question.'

'But why?' asked Ruth, as if that had been the obvious solution. 'It may not be safe for him here.'

'Because the C-G would never try to dissuade him from coming. Any visit by a cabinet member is a special occasion, but when it's the Secretary of State you've got something akin to Christmas, birthday and Fourth of July all rolled into one! There's too much face at stake for him.'

'Isn't there another reason also, Jack?'

He shot her an acid-filled glance, realising now that her sharp brain kept on ticking even as she sat there supposedly relaxing and shooting the breeze.

'So you know about that, huh?'

'The Tsuen Wan meeting? Yes, I know.'

'Is there anything you don't know?' Cinch was irritated. A droplet of sweat from his upper lip flicked on to the bar with the force of his words. 'Listen, this is a Special Visit – far-reaching consequences. Setting it up with Beijing took a lot of persuasion, and if we pull out now Fredericks might not get another chance during this Administration.'

'I still think you ought to try.'

'Look, I'm due to speak to the detail leader again at five this afternoon, but I don't hold out much hope.'

'Why not, Jack?'

'Because I know just what he'll say: what's the hell good of spending millions of dollars on security each year if the Secretary of State can't go wherever the President sends him? And he'll be right.'

'Why do Americans persist in this belief that the

world is their playground,' asked Ruth, 'and that they're somehow different from the rest of us? What makes them so special?'

'Listen, honey, the sun set on the British Empire a long time ago,' mocked Cinch. Then, affecting a clipped British accent, he added, 'Envy is such an ugly emotion.'

She realised that she had probably deserved that, but she was angry nonetheless.

'All right, have it your own way.' She tapped her sapphire ring against the beer glass. 'Of course, that's a decision for your government, and we'll respect your wishes.'

'Yeah, like you had a choice.'

Ruth ignored the sarcasm. 'But I'd be failing in my duty if I didn't ...'

'Yeah, yeah, I know. He'll be a goddamned sitting duck here in Hong Kong, and you can't guarantee his safety. I know you're right.' His responses were growing steadily more aggressive now. 'Just don't keep telling me my fucking job.'

There was a heavy measure of pride behind the bitterness of his outburst – much of it bound up in the ruins of their affair.

'Let's not make a personal issue out of this, shall we, Jack?' she said between clenched teeth. 'I'm sorry if ...'

'Don't apologise!' he cut in quickly. 'For God's sake don't apologise.'

He reached for the papers and began to study them again.

The threat assessment had been upgraded from '*No known threat*' to '*Likelihood of a specific threat*'. The neatly printed paragraphs tied it up in Special Branch's own eloquent brand of English. In a space between the third and fourth paragraphs the name Kazuo Okamoto had been rendered in both Roman script and Chinese characters, and underlined in red pencil indicating that he had been located in the SB terrorist index. The Chinese characters were also accompanied by their four-figure numeric codes, which were used to distinguish between ideograms with a similar phonetic sound.

'So what are your people doing about this?' he asked when he had finished reading. 'Or should I say, how do they plan to stop his ass being blown clean across the harbour?'

'We're talking hostage-taking, not assassination. At this moment David Becker is on his way to Tokyo. The National Police Agency has a high-powered intelligence unit with the sole task of tracking the Japanese Red Army. Finding Okamoto and his cell will be our first priority.'

'And in view of this new threat you'll be stepping up your security?'

'Of course. Five teams from the VIP Unit, including dedicated CAT team support, together with rooftop-sniper cover from Tactical Firearms Support. We even have PTU on standby for cordon and search duties – house to house – if any leads are turned up. The whole nine yards.'

Cinch nodded his head, apparently satisfied with these arrangements. He finished his drink and folded the papers into his inside pocket. He had heard more than enough for the time being, and there was much to dwell on besides.

'Thanks for the drink, and the information,' he said without looking at her. On an impulse he asked: 'Will you be contactable this weekend?'

'In what sense?'

Cinch shook his head and got up to leave.

'Forget I asked,' he snapped.

She watched him walk away, looking like a man carrying a heavy rock upon his back, and she was glad to find she felt no guilt over what she had said – only relief that she was now free of that particular relationship.

SEVENTEEN

In the foyer of Caine House a middle-aged Chinese stepped out from the senior officers' elevator wearing a very worried expression. He barely acknowledged the bellowed 'Ah-sir' from the duty sergeant as he stood on the front steps lost in thought, tugging distractedly on the cravat at the open neck of his tailored safari suit. From the shadow of the front steps his eyes searched the parked cars in Arsenal Yard, flicking left and right: checking. Then, satisfied, he stepped out of the main gate, walking at a fast pace, and darted smoothly into the maze of side-streets leading into the heart of Wanchai.

As he hurried along a street lined with metal work-shops and tiny cubicle-like garages, he glanced behind, looking for patterns in the churning motion of the bodies. Seeing nothing, he walked on into the tangled passageways of the bar district. He circled one particular block twice, an area patrolled by whores and white powder cowboys, and by the regular groups of American sailors who used both, then he turned abruptly down a covered alley. A patch of sweat now showed dark between the shoulderblades of the safari suit. His heart beat faster as he checked his stride, stepped over an old wretch lying propped against the wall, ignoring the plastic begging cup, and ran the final few yards to the safety of the steep staircase. A smell of warm, damp earth pervaded the inner courtyard as steam rose from the potted plants on the balconies all around.

The apartment building looked about as run-down as

they get in Wanchai. Like most of them it was managed by a private landlord, and the few hundred square feet cost him all he could spare from his monthly salary. Not even the Society knew about this place, he told himself – even they could not find him here. On the sixth-floor landing, an area no bigger than an average office desk and littered with the carcases of a dozen varieties of cockroach, he fumbled for his key – the key his wife knew nothing of – and opened first the metal grille and then the inner wooden door. A sigh of relief!

The first thing he saw as he strode through the door was an unmade bed, and on this the plump, well-rounded bottom of a young girl lying naked but for a pair of bikini pants. The girl looked up from the Cantonese video movie she had been watching and rolled over to face him with a look of resentment.

'*Gam lui mo gin, la!*' she chastised him, twisting her bright, young face into an agreeable pout.

She was just seventeen and the most beautiful thing he had ever owned, but her voice when she scolded him was like the wailing of gulls. To think one so young could sound like the oldest fishwife in the market.

'Be glad I am here now,' he snapped angrily. 'Do not nag me, girl! This fine apartment could very quickly find another occupant! Think on that.'

The girl sensed his rage, but after five days left all on her own she was desperate for his attention. After all, she was his *chip si*, his concubine, and it was her role in life to nag after him – to fill his thoughts as well as his bed, and to distract him from his boring wife. Artfully she softened her approach. This time, gently cupping her breasts in her small hands, she looked up at him, squirming like the kitten he so often required her to play.

'Is Ah Ba angry with Bing Bing? Does he want to play horses, or maybe take shower together?'

'Not now, you little idiot,' he thundered, embarrassed by the memory of his own avid sexuality. 'I have

430

important business to transact. Just lie there, and may all the gods unite to keep you quiet.'

Sliding into a chair beside the telephone, he turned his back on her and punched out a number. Realising she had failed to spark his interest, Bing Bing blew out her cheeks and slapped the mattress in exasperation. In the next moment she was back to watching her video movie and cracking another handful of lotus seeds between her teeth.

The senior police officer with more secrets than was good for a stomach ulcer waited, breathless, for the phone to be answered. He counted the rings, feeling the stomach acid begin to pump.

Finally an old voice answered. The servant.

'*Wai, wan bin goh a?*'

'*Cheng man, Ah Gung hai m'hai do a?* Respectfully request to speak to the Grandfather.'

'*Dang yat jan.* One moment. Who shall I say looks for him?'

'*Ma jeuk si foo.* The Master of Sparrows.'

He lowered his voice to a guarded whisper, fearing the girl might be listening, but the swordplay on the screen had by this time reached fever pitch, and she lay, totally absorbed in the action, spitting discarded shells of lotus seeds into a growing heap on the floor.

A moment later the deep, unmistakable voice of the *shan chiu* came on the line, a trace of irritation behind the commanding baritone.

'Yes, what is it?'

'*Ah Gung*, a serious complication.'

'What complication?'

'Chan Ming. They have him in custody.'

'What! Who has him? The Public Security Bureau?'

'Not the mainland. Here – he's here!'

'There must be some mistake. For sure he is safely across the border in *Dai Luk*.'

'No, Grandfather. He is at this moment being held

431

inside the maximum-security facility of the political department. Most of his best men were captured along with him.'

'How? By whom?' Surprise and disbelief were evident in his tone.

'*Fei Foo Dui.*' The words were an explanation in themselves: the Leaping Tigers – the name the media had given to the police counter-terrorist force. 'Regrettably, Weldon ordered them across the border.'

'Is it confirmed all were taken?'

'You know the reputation of the Special Duties Unit.'

'But have you seen him? Do you have proof?'

'No. Only a few officers have clearance. Even fewer have access.'

'*Po lei ah moh!*' cursed the Grandfather in Chiu Chau dialect. 'Has that unwashed scum talked yet?'

'I do not know. Special Branch have skilled interrogators; they will break him, given time. Yet Weldon spent time last night with the Governor, and this morning I tried to call his office and discovered he was at Central Government Offices with the Attorney-General. Through judicious use of my spies I discovered that the Secretary of Security also attended that meeting. From this we may infer some kind of deal is being cut. If that is the case, I would guess Chan Ming is presently withholding his information and bargaining for his own neck with ours.'

'Let us hope that is so and there is yet still time.' There was a beat while the *shan chiu* thought. His heavy breathing purred down the line like the hum from high-voltage wires. 'Very well. There is too much at stake to gamble on the strength of Chan Ming's bladder. I never did trust "recent arrivals"; they have no sense of honour.' The sentence was short and succinct: '*Sai kui.* Wash him.'

Wash away his life.

When the handset crashed into the cradle, there

followed the loud purr of the disconnection tone. The Chinese policeman sat in his secret apartment in Wanchai, still clutching the phone to his chin. The order was clear, but getting to Chan Ming would not be easy. Not with the degree of Special Branch security presently surrounding him.

And yet there was one way.

He tapped out a second number; this time it was that of one of the major radio-paging companies in the territory. When the telephonist came on the line he said: 'Call two five double seven, *m'goi*.'

'The message, please?'

'Please call the family. Grandfather is ill.' He gave his number at the apartment, and then hung up.

As the police officer walked over to the bed, silencing the video and turning the young girl's face towards him, a pager was already bleeping in the VIP Unit duty room in the basement of Caine House. Immediately Yip Suen turned aside from the hand of cards he was fanning and checked the message flashing in the window of his pager unit.

He recognised the emergency-code phrase at once.

Thirty seconds later he stood up from the table, casually collected up his winnings, and walked out to find a telephone in an empty office – knowing it was time to pay off his gambling debts.

When he returned, Yip Suen resumed his seat and rejoined the game. But not immediately. First he approached his team sergeant with a request to work overtime that weekend. Chief Inspector Becker had already asked for eight men to assist with guard duties over at the Victoria Reception Centre. High-security prisoners undergoing debrief was all he had said.

Yip was happy to volunteer. He said he needed the money.

At 8.15 that Saturday evening David Becker found

himself in the back seat of a very large Mitsubishi saloon cruising through the stark electric video board jungle of Tokyo's Ginza district. The man beside him – the one who had met him at the customs point with such scrupulous courtesy and so much bowing, then steered him to his official car – was a senior officer of the NPA's Terrorist Research Executive. Mishima was Becker's personal contact on all matters involving low-intensity operations, and had been so ever since the Japanese had turned up at Caine House fifteen months ago, looking for a *sekigun* recruitment cell rumoured to be interviewing students in one of Hong Kong's five-star hotels. On that occasion the search had led them up a blind alley, but not before these two officers had formed an understanding about the importance of shared information.

A broad, stocky man in his early forties, Mishima was good looking in a boardroom sense, and something of a power dresser. He was one of those precise and perfectly groomed products of his culture, with a strong, perpendicular nose which set him apart from the majority of his fellow countrymen. Soft-spoken and always under restraint, like the string of a crossbow, yet with eyes full of animation and warmth. Becker's first impression had been of a powerful man held in a straitjacket. Still Becker had liked the man instantly and had made it a personal project to dig deeper than the superficial front the man erected. Only after eight or ten scotches at the Club Volvo in Kowloon East, when the operation was over, did the façade eventually slip.

As their car pulled into an underground lot of an anonymous building close to NPA headquarters, David Becker felt glad to be back working with Mishima, but already he had learned there would be another man waiting to brief him: a specialist.

'Nishimura returned only a few hours ago, after eight weeks away on continuous assignment.'

434

'Where's he been?'

'Following the wind. Bangkok mostly, Kuala Lumpur, Cheng Mai. Ended up in a Metro Manila guesthouse counting the cockroaches. He's just about the toughest guy on our team. Very knowledgeable about *sekigun* matters.'

Like all the Japanese law men Becker had ever met, Mishima never used the name Red Army, even when he was speaking English. It held none of the intrinsic meaning that had attached itself to the Japanese name during his six-year search for the left-wing terrorist group.

'I'm grateful you could spare him for this.'

'Actually, we can't,' said Mishima firmly. 'But it's a waiting game now. The cell he and his men were tracking has been moving continuously for the past ten days. One day in Cebu, the next in Angeles City. When Ito called from the Consulate, the trail had already led back to Manila and our targets had disappeared. Gone underground once again. I pulled Nishimura back because he was waiting for them to resurface, and there was therefore a breathing space.'

Becker nodded slowly. Aware that this man's information must be the most current available anywhere.

'Just the kind of man I need to speak to. I don't have any time to waste.'

'Obviously. It will be an honour to help.' Mishima gave a sharp, dignified incline of his head that was in no way subservient. 'Please make whatever use of him you can.'

They took a glass elevator to the eighteenth floor and came out into a lobby lined with patterned ceramic stonework which suggested more the offices of a top law firm than any government department Becker had seen before. He could not read the gold lettering on the plate-glass doors, but the armed security guard on duty and the doorway arch with its built-in metal detector confirmed that these were in fact the offices from which Mishima's task group operated.

Mishima led the way into a room where the artificial light was twice as bright as any office he was used to. Between the slats of the acrylic blinds Becker saw a cartoon show of animated neon blazing away outside the window – a garish preview of the consumer-led future.

Mishima picked up a phone and spoke a few harsh words of Japanese into it that let Becker know he was speaking to an underling. A moment later the door opened and in walked a man with a five-day growth on his face and a cigarette dangling carelessly from his lip.

'Nishimura, this gentleman is David Becker of the Royal Hong Kong Police, Special Branch.' It sounded long and clumsy in Japanese, but still Nishimura looked impressed. He removed the cigarette with his left hand and hid it behind his back, then he made a quick 45-degree bow and offered his hand.

He was almost as tall as Becker, with long limbs and shoulders much wider than the average Japanese; and one sensed immediately in the assured manner and the deep-etched lines around his eyes that there was not much he had not seen. As he approached the chrome and leather couch where Mishima sat, he gave a perfunctory bow, just low enough to satisfy protocol – no more. Becker guessed immediately that here was a man who had power and influence far beyond his rank, and that Mishima would accept more from him than from his other men. You could easily take him for one of those Tokyo movie stars who like to play gangster roles. He had hair brushing the collar of his red and green Ralph Lauren polo shirt, and a loose pair of well-faded denims that were pulled tight at the waist by what Becker recognised instantly as a black Bianchi holster belt of plaited leather; but for the moment at least he carried no gun.

In fact Nishimura looked more like a gangster than a cop, right down to the slouch and the careless cocking of his head. Perhaps it was natural, but then again maybe it was a pure James Dean rip-off – like the way Japanese kids picked up on anything Western. If he had not known Nishimura was undercover, he would have tagged him for Yakuza right away. Except that there were no tattoos on his brawny arms, and he could not be *boryokudan* without at least a few pictures.

'You have a problem concerning *sekigun*,' said Nishimura, looking the Hong Kong cop full in the face, his voice a low growl that began somewhere in the pit of his stomach. 'And you need our help?'

Becker explained only as much of Chan Ming's allegations as was necessary for the other to appreciate his situation. 'We expect them to move some time within the next week.'

'*So desu ka?*' breathed the Japanese ruminatively. 'There will be much to check and discuss. It would be better to wait until the research department is manned on Monday morning. But obviously you don't have the time for that.'

'No, I need to be back in Hong Kong by Monday afternoon latest.'

Nishimura looked the Hong Kong cop up and down once more and for the first time he cracked a grin.

'Then we'll have to combine business with pleasure, for you cannot leave Japan without first experiencing *O'Chaya*.'

Twenty-five minutes later the three men removed their shoes to step inside a little-known teahouse in the Shimbashi district. Though the place was not nearly as grand as those places where the great corporations fêted their business guests, it was no less select in its clientele. Recognising the possibility of intelligence officers and other senior officials being compromised whilst 'at play', an enlightened government had provided this house of pleasure and made it both discreet and totally secure.

Within these paper walls, government officials could relax out of the public gaze without fear of being observed or overheard.

Mishima was quick to point out that each of the twenty-six geisha who glided between the rooms, their silken kimonos sighing against the tatami floor, had been specially selected and vetted for the job. Discretion had always been a part of the geisha code of conduct, but the women of the Graceful Willow teahouse were also de facto members of the intelligence community.

The room was twelve tatamis in floor area, one of fourteen available for entertaining and for official meetings. They sat on three sides of the low laquered table, with a girl serving them *suki-yaki* from the remaining side. A second girl in the corner, wearing a kimono of soft duck-egg blue and salmon pink, plucked a soothing melody from the stringed *shamisen*. Listening to the sound, and looking upon the purity of her white face and cherry-painted lips, Becker felt a twinge of conscience over time spent so agreeably.

Glancing up from his bowl, Nishimura asked: 'Is this your first visit to Japan, Becker *san*?'

'Actually, I've been here twice before,' said Becker. 'The first time was official liaison. The second time I came here was for a little over three months. I suppose you'd call that one a pleasure trip.'

Nishimura sensed that Becker's reply was partly evasive, and seeing the frown on his subordinate's face Mishima broke in and offered an explanation.

'What Becker *san* is loath to say is that he is a student of Zen. He came here to walk the Eighty-eight Temples of Shikoku.'

At once Nishimura's face registered disbelief, but, when he saw his boss was serious, the look changed to one of unqualified admiration.

'You actually walked the Eighty-eight Temples? That's nearly fifteen hundred miles!'

Becker stared into his cup, knowing that to have said anything at that moment would have been immodest.

The ancient pilgrim's route around the vast rural island of Shikoku was well known to all Japanese, though few had actually completed the pilgrimage. It was a route first trodden by the great Zen priest Kobo Daishi, who had also founded many of the temples along the way. For those seeking spiritual enlightenment, the 1500-mile journey over arduous terrain was the ultimate test of fortitude. Becker had made the trip in an extended leave period between tours of duty. Walking every day with a backpack and tent, spending the evenings in fractured conversation with monks in the temples, it had taken just over three months to complete the circuit.

Nishimura pursued the point, intrigued to know why a foreigner should be moved to follow the path of Zen.

'Quite an achievement for a *gaijin*,' he conceded. 'Did you learn anything from your journey?'

'If you mean did I receive Enlightenment,' shrugged Becker, referring to the Buddhist concept of ultimate truth, 'the answer is no. But I think I found a few answers to questions I'd been asking myself for a long time.'

Sensing Becker's embarrassment, Mishima broke the silence by calling for more sake. When it arrived and the girl had filled their cups, they drank a toast. From that moment on Becker knew he had been accepted.

'Now to business,' said Nishimura, setting down his cup. For a moment he said nothing, considering his words carefully and wiping one powerful hand upon his jeans. When he did finally speak, his manner was grave. Serious.

'There are many in the West who believe the organisation known as *sekigun* is finished. Be in no doubt, Becker *san*, it is not. It functions more strongly today than ever, with a tighter structure and a new generation of experience on which to draw. There were always two

439

factions within the movement: the main line and the equally dangerous offshoot *sekigun-ha*. The main line was formed out of the cadres of disaffected youth which many countries experienced back in 1968. In our case it was the Tokyo student body which provided this fund of revolutionary fervour. Their stated objective was and remains world revolution. A Marxist-Leninist revolution. To further this objective they committed a number of attacks in Japanese cities, but very quickly linked up with other terrorist groups, notably the PLO, and thereafter expanded into Europe and the Middle East.

'One of their earliest successes was the Lod Airport massacre of May 1972. You may remember how three of their number infiltrated the airport arrivals hall in Tel Aviv and sprayed disembarking passengers with machine-gun fire, killing twenty-seven and injuring another seventy-six. It was an event which propelled them to the centre of the revolutionary stage. In September 1974 they seized the French Embassy in The Hague and succeeded in freeing one of their number from a French prison. A commandeered plane flew the terrorists and their freed comrade to Damascus, where they were greeted as heroes and allowed to disappear from view.'

'And the second group – the splinter?'

'*Sekigun-ha*. They moved to North Korea in grand style back in 1970. There they were welcomed home, for it was there most of them were originally trained in guerrilla warfare camps – along with numerous Palestinians and Eritreans. North Korea has always been their ideological homeland. Even today, as we track them through half of Asia, we know North Korean Intelligence provides intelligence officers to support their operations abroad, and to warn them when we are close.'

Nishimura paused and sipped miso soup from a lacquered bowl. For a moment he rotated the bowl between his fingers, staring vacantly at the table as if

440

reminded of some previous, thwarted operation. Then just as quickly he put down the bowl and continued his narrative.

'The nucleus of this splinter organisation, which hijacked a Japan Air-Lines jet and flew to the North Korean capital, consisted of just nine men and women. Two of the original number are now in custody, and it is believed a third may have died of an illness, but the remainder are still at large. Once back in Pyongyang, the student group immediately fell under the influence of the North Korean Intelligence Service. They were given sophisticated covers and further specialist training, and relaunched into other Asian capitals to strike at the soft targets of the industrialised nations. But Pyongyang provided little financial support. It was a matter of honour that the reborn *sekigun* should finance itself by stealing the enemy's own money, and using it to destroy him. They used extortion to swell their bank accounts – widespread kidnappings of industrialists and top executives of multinationals. The hijackings virtually died out, but once they had the funds they needed they began assassinating selected targets to reinforce their image as a secret and deadly organisation capable of striking anywhere.

'In the past six years recruitment amongst the disaffected youth of Japan has been phenomenal. As Japan becomes richer and more powerful, so the conscience of these idealists pushes them into the arms of the revolutionaries. You see, the organisation blames our country and the United States for the world consumerism which is killing poorer countries. Those original core members are now the ruling executive of a considerable network, with cells and agents throughout Asia. They have no interest in joining the political process. Their aim is world revolution, sparked not by the ballot box but by a steadily rising tide of violence.'

While Nishimura spoke, Becker sat silently listening,

aware both of the man's voice and of the exquisiteness of the *shamisen* music flitting at the edge of his consciousness. Becker had heard intelligence men speak of terrorist ideology before – usually they did so in detached, academic terms – but there was a thread of violence in Nishimura's self-restraint: a deep and bitter hatred of the poison the *sekigun* was spreading. The emotion was translated through his words into a barely perceptible quivering of his powerfully-muscled upper body. Mishima's eyes remained fixed upon the stem of the small yellow sake jar as the geisha lifted it and once more filled the tiny yellow cups.

In the brief silence which ensued as everyone drank, the geisha looked into Becker's eyes, perhaps wondering who he was and what they were speaking about. On both points she remained ignorant, for she spoke no word of English. The girl made no attempt to lighten the mood with the witty conversation for which she would have been well regarded. She knew it was inappropriate. Silently, gracefully, her fingers tilted the flask once more, delighting in the soundless excellence of her pouring.

The European muttered his thanks but this time left his cup upon the table. Instead he began to retell his own story, precising it down to the salient points – emphasising the uncertainty and the unreliability of the source, but stressing the importance of the potential target. Nishimura's eyes flashed briefly in response to the name of the American Secretary of State.

'All we really have to go on is a name: Okamoto. That, and a story that this man has been based until recently in the Philippines. I understand you've been there yourself in recent weeks. Do you know the name?'

Nishimura made a face, and drew a quiet breath through clenched teeth.

'Not especially. It's a common enough name.'

'How did you first make contact with *sekigun*?' asked

442

Mishima, characteristically turning the problem on its head.

'Something overheard by our informant,' admitted Becker. 'Okamoto was the organiser, the one in charge. Red Army membership was his pedigree. They said he had been flown in specially from the Philippines to take charge of the operation in Hong Kong. I felt sure you'd know something about him, if he was that good.'

A frown creased Nishimura's forehead as he stared at a tiger-moth which fluttered inside one of the paper lanterns. Suddenly the moth fell into the candle flame and something flared within his memory, like the fragment of a song just outside of consciousness.

'Okamoto,' he whispered to himself speculatively, turning to face Mishima. 'When we first arrived in Metro Manila we spent three nights gambling at a club for Japanese expatriates. One of our men was posing as a writer of revolutionary poetry, looking for admission into the Nagata line of *sekigun*.'

'One of the many cells operating in Manila,' explained Mishima for Becker's benefit. 'A deeply committed group comprising mainly artists and writers whose revolutionary fervour is not limited to brush and ink.'

Nishimura looked impatient to continue.

'What we heard was that the cell had been split by internal dissent on the best way to achieve the goals of the organisation. Recriminations had been bitter, they said. One half of the group decided to abandon passive and largely political discussion in favour of more direct action. I feel sure, now, that Okamoto was the name of the leader of this dissident faction.'

'Do you know what happened to him?'

'He and his group – certainly no more than fifteen hardcore members – dropped out of sight over two months ago. One of the gamblers who claimed sympathy with members of the organisation said Okamoto was now nothing more than a common criminal: that he was extorting money from Japanese businessmen in Manila to support his group. Speculation had it that he was leaning towards organised crime, but it's doubtful the Yakuza would accept him or his men. They pride themselves on an ultra-nationalist orientation and Okamoto's background would rule him out. The Yakuza despise anything that smacks of communism.'

'If Okamoto's group is now for hire, they could be the ones we're looking for. Would there be any ideological barriers towards working for a Chinese paymaster?'

'Not on grounds of race. But Okamoto would need to believe the operation fulfilled at least some of his group's aims. Do you know what the aims of this operation are?'

The question brought Becker up short. He shifted awkwardly: seated on his heels upon the floor cushion, one knee was beginning to seize up. What the hell did he really know? It was all suspicion and speculation so far. And what made him think he could trust Chan Ming anyway?

'No, I'm afraid not. Our information suggests a kidnapping, not an assassination, so we presume the object is to pressure the US into doing something they don't want to do.'

Mishima seemed slightly embarrassed by the question he had decided to ask.

'Excuse me, Becker *san*, if these powerful Chinese businessmen are the ultimate backers, doesn't that suggest a home-grown problem? Perhaps the territory's future?'

The man from Special Branch nodded thoughtfully. It was one of the first things he had considered. Though he did not rule out the possibility, something told him there was far more involved than passports for Chinese.

'It's true there's discontent over the future of Hong Kong, and a general dissatisfaction with the attitude of Britain and her allies towards accepting refugees. But it's not the powerful businessmen who will suffer. With the money they control they could buy their way into any of the industrialised nations on a special-investment visa. I'm prepared to be wrong about this, but I think the answer lies buried deeper than that.'

'And for the moment Okamoto is your only lead?'

'Yes.' Becker felt once again the poverty of his situation. 'May I respectfully request you provide me with everything your intelligence people have on him and the other members of his group: photographs, fingerprints, details of training and expertise. I presume your Manila operation can provide his movements and contacts?'

'*Sa,*' breathed Nishimura noncommittally. '*Dekiru kedo.* We could, but ...'

'Good, how soon can I have all that?' Becker pressed, a trifle too pushy for the Japanese's liking.

Nishimura looked to his superior for guidance. Mishima nodded his head just once, indicating that full cooperation was to be given. The next moment he turned to the geisha and spoke a few words of Japanese. The girl immediately bowed and left the room, returning a minute later with a cordless telephone.

'The profile of Okamoto's group will be available by midday tomorrow. The other details you asked for may take a little longer, depending on the speed of response of our Manila unit.' As he said this, Mishima handed the telephone handset to Nishimura and told him to call Manila. At once.

Nishimura tapped in a number and sat waiting for the international operator to come on the line. In his own mind he believed the Manila unit could be of little use to the SB man on this occasion. They were already in too deep on their own mission to get involved in another manhunt. But Nishimura remained unconcerned, for he had already decided on another approach.

If Okamoto was the quarry, then there was a far better source of information than any police unit: a man who maintained his own intelligence network and already had excellent personal reasons for wanting to find Okamoto.

Nishimura's only worry now was whether his source would consent to speak to the *gaijin*. That was by no means a foregone conclusion. But already he had an idea.

For Chan Ming it began in his lower abdomen as a slightly bloated feeling. A mild irritation which caused him to pass wind, nothing more. Then, all at once, the pain struck like a bayonet twisted in his gut and he slumped backwards on the low wooden cot, bent double and gasping for air.

The bowl was the first thing to go: the first agonised thrash of Chan Ming's arms sent the rice and boiled vegetables it contained halfway across the narrow cell floor. Then he noticed with a sudden sensation of panic that his peripheral vision was a blinding mass of coloured lights, and that now he could barely see the hand in front of his face.

Marshalling his remaining strength the *Dai Huen Jai* tried weakly to call for the guard, but the effort of it almost tore him in two.

Outside the cell, the Chinese constable on duty, checking the monitors at Victoria Reception Centre, had been warned to expect trouble. The section head had briefed all his men that the prisoners were to be carefully watched. They were all of them highly motivated and highly dangerous characters who would employ every trick and method to effect an escape. None more so than Chan Ming himself.

Yet in spite of his briefing the constable was concerned enough by what he saw in the security monitor to put down his pen and step inside the square blockhouse which contained the maximum security cells.

When he opened the viewing slit, the first thing he saw was Chan Ming lying on his cot groaning, with his knees drawn up in a foetal posture. Naturally, he was prepared for a trick.

Only this was no trick.

'Help ... me,' gasped the prisoner. 'It's *burning*!'

The visual signs were alarming enough in themselves. The prisoner's face was pale and drawn; a cold bloom of sweat shone upon his cheeks and forehead, and he looked nothing like the man they had brought in on Friday morning. Now there were dark rings around both eyes, and the eyes themselves seemed to have sunk within his head. Suddenly Chan Ming cried out again and rolled to the edge of the cot, vomiting painfully on to the hard stone floor.

'*Fai di, giu yi saang lai!*' shouted the duty sergeant, before he realised that the resident duty medic had already gone off duty. Any medical emergency would now need to be sent to Queen Mary Hospital for treatment. 'Never mind that. Call out the reserve driver. If anything happens to that prisoner it's my *loh yau*!'

Within minutes the sergeant – who had himself suffered a ruptured appendix and thought he recognised the same symptoms in the prisoner – had the man carefully stretchered into the back of a police transit. Observing the rules and taking no unnecessary chances – not where a *Dai Huen* was concerned – he had the prisoner checked first for concealed weapons, and then ordered the prisoner's right hand cuffed to the escorting constable's left wrist.

'Are you both armed?' the sergeant asked the escort and driver.'

'*Hai ah.*'

'Good. Watch this bastard.'

The tall metal gates swung open, and the transit pulled out into the darkness of Mount Davis Road. It was a stretch overlooked by a great rural hillside with few houses or dwellings in the vicinity, and the driver took the bends at speed, swinging wide on the deserted road to avoid overhanging trees. Each time he heard a moan behind his head, the police driver checked his watch and

447

muttered to himself. It wasn't far – less than a mile away. Even allowing for the traffic on Pokfulam Road they would reach the casualty department of QMH in under ten minutes.

Or so he believed.

They were just half a mile away from the Victoria Reception Centre when a powerful motorcycle roared up from behind and overtook the transit, going much too fast for the sharp bends. The rider wore T-shirt and shorts and flimsy plastic slippers. As he zoomed ahead out of view, the transit driver muttered something reflexive about crazy kids getting themselves killed.

In the next few moments those words were to seem highly prophetic, for as he entered the next bend he was forced to stamp on the brakes when he caught sight of the big machine lying sprawled in the road with the rider lying twisted beside it. Reacting instinctively to the emergency and without thinking, he brought the transit to a skidding halt, cursing as the wheels locked and slid broadside into the motorcycle, missing the fallen rider by a matter of feet.

As the vehicle slewed to a halt, the escort constable pitched forward off the bench; the prisoner shackled to his wrist screamed out in pain.

'*Mat lan ye?*' shouted the constable, reeling forward. 'What the fuck ...' In the sudden tangle of limbs he then landed on top of the prisoner. Chan groaned, clutching his lower belly in agony.

'TAPI,' shouted the driver as a reflex: the standard code for Traffic Accident with Persons Injured. He heaved on the handbrake and stabbed the locking mechanism of his seat belt, scrambling to get out to help the fallen rider.

It was then that the escort in the back sensed something very wrong. At once he shouted to his colleague: 'No! Stay where you are!' But by then it was already too late.

448

At that moment two cars parked in the darkness beside the unlit road turned their lights on to full beam, blinding the occupants of the transit. Immediately the driver covered his eyes.

In another second a figure dressed entirely in black stepped calmly up to the passenger door and levelled a heavy calibre automatic pistol at the window. Against the glare of the headlights the driver's head formed a perfect silhouette. With barely a thought the killer pumped three rapid shots through the glass and the driver's face disintegrated, along with the window beyond. There was a strangled scream from the rear of the transit as the escort constable suddenly understood what was actually happening.

Seized by blind panic he grabbed at his ankle, where his detective special sat in its concealed holster. But now the bike rider was on his feet, and his great helmeted head was leaning through the now shattered glass of the driver's window. In a briefly-glimpsed half-image the escort thought he saw something clutched within the rider's fist, and the terror burned into his stomach. Desperately he fought to release the pistol. At last it came reluctantly into his shaking hand and he began to raise it, half knowing he was finished. As he looked up through a fog of red fear, the last thing he saw was the maw of the semi-automatic.

There were four rapid explosions, four bursts of flame in the dark, and the escort's head split open, spreading fragments of shattered bone and brain tissue everywhere. The force of the full-metal-jacketed rounds slammed the corpse backward against the transit's rear doors, pulling the prisoner after him on to the floor of the vehicle.

Chan Ming heard the policeman's revolver hit the floor directly in front of his face and he realised it was his only hope of survival. Summoning the last of his strength he struggled to get free of the policeman's bleeding weight. In the dark his fingers touched the butt of the revolver, closing around it exultantly.

Responding to the pump of adrenalin, he somehow found the strength to lift his body, and even managed to aim the pistol above the line of seats, in the direction of the driver's window. But all he saw of the bike rider was a single arm. Extended inside the vehicle. Fingers opening. Releasing something. Then, in the madness of expanded time, he saw the ugly black egg falling. Heard the dull note as it hit the floor and began to roll.

Beyond that there was only the sound of running feet.

Chan Ming felt the weight of the dead policeman tugging at his wrist, and knew then beyond all doubt that he too was going to die.

When the grenade did explode, it blew out the remaining windows and a sheet of liquid flame flew after them. The petrol tank went almost in the same instant, completing the inferno and lighting up the banana palms in the plantation beside the road.

At the edge of the plantation, the men sitting inside the two parked cars watched the police vehicle burn with a definite sense of satisfaction. Tongues of reflected flame glinted off their own metallic paintwork. The motorcyclist and the man in black hurried back across the road, climbed inside the first car and waited for the inevitable questions.

In the front passenger seat, Red Cudgel seemed in no particular hurry to leave.

'*Nei ying dak kui?* Did you recognise him?'

'*Yat ding.* Definitely. It was him all right.'

For a moment Red Cudgel looked thoughtful, musing on how the fragmentation grenade had provided a most appropriate end for Chan Ming.

'*I shall die by ten thousand cuts,*' he quoted aloud for all present to hear, '*if I reveal the secrets of the San Yee On.*'

Then, satisfied with the night's work, he barked out an order to the forty-niner who was driving.

'*Jau!* Let's go!'

The two cars pulled away from the inferno with engines gunning hard. Leaving the fallen motorcycle still in the road, they roared off along Mount Davis Road, turned right on to Pokfulam Road, and headed south towards the Aberdeen Road Tunnel.

On the opposite side of the harbour, Red Cudgel was met by another of his *ma jai,* driving the new gold Mercedes 500 SL sportscar which he had purchased that day to replace the one which had been firebombed. Twenty minutes thereafter, he was back at the private mah jong party he had left only an hour ago. The men inside the private room of the New Chiu Chau Restaurant and Nightclub could all swear that he had been there all night.

By the time the first blue flashing lights were on the scene at Mount Davis Road, the two stolen ambush vehicles were already lying crushed at the bottom of a steep drop beneath Tate's Cairn Mountain. Later that evening, relaxing over a glass of French brandy back in the Barking Peacock, Red Cudgel called his *shan chiu* on the telephone and in coded speech reported that Chan Ming had been silenced. Permanently.

'Sleep well tonight, *Ah Goh*,' he said with satisfaction. 'The harvest is in. The cane is cut!'

It was the best news Alexander Au-Yeung had heard all week.

In a small ryokan in the Gotanda district of Tokyo, David Becker awoke from a troubled sleep to the sound of the rice-paper door panel being gently drawn aside. For a moment he was confused by the strangeness of the surroundings, and the unmistakable sweet smell of rice straw from the tatami beneath him only deepened his sense of confusion. Then, as he rolled over on the cotton futon, he looked across the tiny room and saw the owner's wife kneeling at the doorway, dressed in a traditional kimono and apron, and sliding a tray of green tea into the room. Seeing him rise from under the bedroll the old lady's face creased agreeably as she gave a formal bow.

'*O'hyo gozaimasu.*'

'*O'hyo gozaimasu,*' said Becker returning the greeting, and the door slid quietly shut.

Pulling the tray towards himself he checked his wrist-watch: 7.15. Leaning on one elbow to pour the tea he thought about the previous evening, remembering now that Nishimura had agreed to collect him at eight o'clock sharp. It looked set to be a busy day. His plane out of Narita was scheduled for 22.00 that night, which did not leave much time for idle gossip.

He pushed back the light cotton quilt, noticing the exquisite quality of the workmanship within it. It was patterned with green ferns on a background of scarlet and gold, all of which lent a gentle rustic feel to the pine-boarded room. Rice-paper walls and an arrangement of dried flowers completed the whispered elegance of the place, and in ordinary circumstances he would have felt more able to enjoy his stay.

But these were not ordinary circumstances. He had to keep moving.

Noticing the dull grey glow which penetrated the mosquito-screen window, Becker began to feel uneasy. The morning sky seemed too dark and threatening; the atmospheric pressure was low and the air pregnant with moisture. 'Thunderstorm in the offing,' he murmured to himself hopefully. 'Nothing more.' But he knew this was the season when typhoons often raged throughout the South China Sea. He forced himself not to think of that possibility.

He had passed the previous evening at a ryokan in the Gotanda district where traditional Japanese hospitality could still be had at a reasonable price. The meeting had concluded at 1.30 in the morning, after which they had said goodnight to Mishima. Nishimura had then steered him to a late-night *karaoke* bar. Following a succession of toasts from a seemingly bottomless bottle of Suntory whisky, and one highly secretive phone-call, the Japanese had insisted upon driving him here to the ryokan owned by his wife's family. Drunk as he was, Becker had been pleased by the simple elegance of the two-storey wooden building, and even now he could still feel the effects of a hot bath in clear steaming water that came up to his chin. Muscles unknotted, he had slid into bed totally relaxed and ready to sleep. Or so he had thought.

At 4.00 a.m. he had started awake from a very weird dream. Inexplicably it had unnerved him, which was strange because he was not the nightmare type. He could remember walking naked through a narrow tunnel in total darkness, following a shadow that was not really there – whether man or monster he was not sure now. But in the depths of the tunnel he had stopped to listen to the beast's laboured breathing, growing louder and louder now, and realised the thing had turned round. A blast of warm, foetid air that caught him full in the face had told him, all at once, that the thing was now stalking *him*. Seized by a kind of blind panic he had turned to run, legs refusing to find purchase on the rails beneath his feet. Then, behind him, the grinding scream of machinery had risen to a thundering crescendo. One foot struck a rail, the other skidded on something slippery underfoot, and in the next instant the ground smashed into his face. Just as the oncoming evil threatened to engulf him, he had cried out, and sat bolt upright.

In retrospect, as he lay there drinking green tea from a porcelain cup, the madness of the vivid dream made little sense. Just a stupid nightmare – but still it had troubled him enough to disrupt his sleep, and thereafter he had dozed only fitfully.

Nishimura arrived early, as Becker knew he would.

But this time he was clean-shaven and wearing a dark business suit of impeccable cut. Becker's eye was immediately drawn to the small hexagonal gold pin he wore in his lapel.

'Very neat. Why the Sunday threads?'

'I have arranged an important meeting for this morning. Please dress formally as a mark of respect.'

'Respect for who?' asked Becker, suddenly intrigued.

'For a man who is one of the most important political figures in all Japan.'

'Anything you say,' Becker shrugged. He tried to sound casual as he asked, 'Why the lapel badge?'

Nishimura brushed aside the question with a grimace of mild irritation.

'That is not important. You will understand everything soon enough. Do not be cautious about advertising your own status here. As a police officer you are naturally reticent. But in this instance it will prove a positive asset.'

Becker did not fully understand the gist of this, but when he had finished knotting his police tie in place and had slipped into a blazer, Nishimura indicated obvious satisfaction. What appeared to please him most was the richly embroidered crest on the blazer pocket: the gold wreath and crown of the Royal Hong Kong Police Force.

Becker caught the look on Nishimura's face.

'Just a little conspicuous, don't you think? I could wear something else?'

'No, not at all,' said Nishimura at once. '*Chodo ii*. That will be perfect.'

Nishimura's Subaru was parked outside in the shade of an old elm tree. Immediately they climbed inside, the Japanese flicked open the glove compartment and took out a thick brown envelope marked with the official stamp of the National Police Agency's research department.

Thankfully he had arranged for the material to be

translated first. As they drove back into the Ginza district, Becker sat reading from the five close-typed sheets of information, while Nishimura negotiated the heavy traffic. It was all there: a complete breakdown – biographies, training histories, modes of operation, and known affiliations, including a dozen photographs of suspected members of what the NPA now called 'the Okamoto Cell'.

On top of the stack was an enlarged black-and-white photo labelled 'Kazuo Okamoto' – a picture of a young man attending a political rally in one of Tokyo's many parks. Though not quite sure what he had expected to see, Becker was surprised by the youthful, intelligent face which stared back at him. Slim and ascetic, with a long straight nose and a narrow jaw which suggested fragility, it was almost inconceivable that this serene young face could belong to the man he now sought. Somehow it sent a shudder through him.

'So that's him?' asked Becker uselessly.

'Okamoto is not as you expected?'

'Not exactly. How old is the picture?'

'Four years.'

'Four years?' Becker checked the picture again. No wonder he looked so young.

The face was pale and handsome, with a prominent bone structure perfect in all respects; no dark shadow on the upper lip or jawline. A touch feminine, he thought. Were it not for the short cropped hair and the distinctive Adam's apple, Becker could have sworn he was looking at the face of a girl.

The Japanese policeman gave an odd laugh.

'A disarming beauty, *ne*? Okamoto is blessed with the appearance of a monk, but be warned the man is dangerous. And he has charisma too. It is said that he radiates it like the sun, and that all who bask in that glow come under his influence. That is how his group came into being.'

'Funny – he doesn't look capable.'

'Not capable? Listen to me. Three years ago – before he ever went to the Philippines – Okamoto murdered the person he loved most in all the world.' A slight grimace of distaste. 'One of the lesser-ranking kabuki actors from the Kabuki-za here in Tokyo. It was all in the papers. The young man's name was Honda.'

'Hmm, I see.'

'A skilful young man and the son of an important businessman. It was a bad scene. Okamoto wanted him to go off to the Philippines with him, but Honda refused. Next day Okamoto called at his *aparto* ... hmm, apartment,' Nishimura corrected himself. 'After they did what such people do in bed, Okamoto took out the sword and killed the young man. The Metropolitan Police said it was a very neat, single cut: decapitation.'

'Jesus Christ. You mean sweet-face, here?' Becker's imagination could still not quite connect this picture with the horror of the man's reputation.

'You are surprised, Becker *san*? Don't be. Okamoto claims strong Marxist ideals but he is still very Japanese: old-fashioned ideas about death and honour. You should remember that well, and use this knowledge.'

'What else did you find out?'

'Many things: we had more on him than I thought. A student rebel, underground leader, political activist and finally terrorist. A very bright student; exceptionally bright, he attended extensive cramming classes and qualified for Tokyo University; Todai is our most highly respected university. He studied computer and electrical engineering.'

'Bright boy!'

'Exceptionally so. The family was upper middle-class. Father a senior partner in one of the major brokerage firms. The son seemed set to join one of the information technology giants, until in 1982 he joined the Japanese Communist Party. The outrage this created in a family of near samurai rank was enough to cut him off from them completely. In 1983 he attended a kind of extended interview held in Macau – your area. That was during his final year of school. When he returned, he became enmeshed within *sekigun* and went underground. The list of outrages in which he was involved I will let you read for yourself.'

'According to this,' said Becker scanning the pages, 'Okamoto should still be in the Philippines. Can you confirm that?'

'Unfortunately not. But there is one who can.'

At first Becker had thought they were heading back towards the NPA counter-terrorist research centre in the Ginza, but when the car pulled into a multi-storey car park wedged between ranks of glass and steel monoliths, he realised he was actually in west Shinjuku business district. He knew about this area from previous trips: a section famous for its bars and brothels, and its close control by the Japanese crime families. From the four-teenth level he could see a dense glut of glass and concrete pylons richly studded with multicoloured Japanese kanji writing and beyond these the welcome green of the trees lining the water in Shinjuku Park.

Gazing at the familiar towering, crystalline structure of the Sumitomo Sankaku building, Becker decided it was now time for some explanation.

'Look, suppose you tell me what this is all about? Where are we going, and who is this special source of yours?'

Nishimura's explanation was short and succinct.

'On the street below us is the Chobei House: the headquarters of Sakaguchi-gumi. That is where we are going. And we are expected.'

Becker realised at once the reason for all the secrecy. Even a foreigner like himself had heard of the Sakaguchi-gumi: a criminal fraternity of vast member-ship, and the most powerful Yakuza clan in all of Tokyo.

Just three minutes later they were heading down a street densely packed with an assortment of porno cinemas and gay bars, into the heart of Yakuza territory. It was an area even the Tokyo Metropolitan Force did not venture into without back-up. At the end of one row of bars the string of bobbing red paper lanterns gave way to a broad alley ending at a small open gateway. This led into a small ornamental garden dominated by two Japanese elms.

It took only moments for four *chinpira* to appear in the doorway of the house: probably the time needed to respond to a closed-circuit screen. These were the rougher young punks employed by the Yakuza to perform menial tasks, and they dressed in conspicuous gangster fashion: white trousers and jackets, with black shirts with loud neckties – photo negatives of the business community they so despised. Their shoes were loafers of white leather, with decorative gold chains.

There was barely a moment's eye contact between Nishimura and the *chinpira* before they were escorted up through the doorway and into the Chobei House. Silently Becker followed Nishimura's lead in removing his shoes at the *genkan* and stepping through on to the tatami, aware of the intense stares of the *chinpiras* behind him. It all seemed so easy, but he had noticed the metal-detecting equipment installed in the door-frame.

To Becker's eye the house looked not much different from the ryokan back in Gotanda: a traditional wooden construction with a raised porch in front, and a screen and half-curtain covering the entrance. Above the doorway hung a framed piece of cloth whose black-on-white calligraphy announced the name of the Society. It all seemed so open – in contrast to Hong Kong where the triads would never dream of announcing themselves thus. The Yakuza was altogether different: for the past hundred years they had remained a powerful and hidden force behind organised crime and right-wing politics.

An older Japanese now approached and exchanged greetings with Nishimura. Then he turned and led both men down a narrow, creaking corridor where the rice-paper walls were lit by the soft sheen of daylight beyond, and they eventually came into the main assembly-room. Still standing slightly behind Nishimura, Becker took in the empty room: the blond-wood floor, the patterned cushions lining either side of the room, and the panelled paper walls hung with photographs of stern-faced old men in wing-collar shirts. The grand old men of the Sakaguchi-gumi. On the wall at the far end of the room two black banners painted with silver calligraphy were hung vertically above a raised podium covered with the very best unblemished tatami. At the centre of the tatami area was a low, square table with four cushions around it. To the left of this dais an open door gave on to a long porch, and beyond this Becker could see the edge of a tiny green pond in a small neat garden.

Before he could finish inspecting the assembly-hall, a panel in the right-hand wall slid aside and a procession of sombre-suited Japanese filed into the room. They were barefoot to a man, though some wore tinted sunglasses. Without a word each walked quietly to one of the cushions by the side walls and knelt, sitting back on his heels, back ramrod straight; palms laid comfortably upon thighs. Becker looked at Nishimura for clues, but all the police officer did was indicate that they too should kneel and wait.

The next thirty seconds dripped slowly by in raw silence, until the creak of floorboards on the outside porch signalled an end to their waiting.

The *oyabun* approached.

The instant he entered the room, everyone bowed low from the waist – including Becker. As the bow was returned, he straightened up and found himself looking at the venerable godfather of the Sakaguchi-gumi. This was probably the ugliest man he had ever seen. His head, covered by a layer of silver stubble, was flat and smooth as a river stone, and beneath large, languid eyes his heavy jowls jutted outwards around a wide, fat-lipped mouth. This, thought Becker in the silence, was one of the most feared men in Tokyo.

The *oyabun* moved on to the dais with a heavy rolling gait, and sank into a sitting position behind the low table. Becker put him at about sixty years old, and about six inches too short for the two hundred pounds he carried.

He caught little of the exchange that followed between Nishimura and the *oyabun*, except for the word Shikoku, the name of the island where he had completed his pilgrimage of the Eighty-eight Temples. He guessed that, Nishimura was now telling his host of the foreigner's achievement and, judging by the facial reactions, the old godfather seemed impressed. Even the *oyabun*'s top lieutenants, seated respectfully in their two lines along either side of the hall, glanced around at one another in near astonishment that this *gaijin* should undertake so arduous a task. Scanning their ranks, Becker observed that their lapels all carried the same small badge that Nishimura wore: a gold hexagon which echoed one of the shapes on the two black banners gracing the far wall.

Nishimura had to undergo extensive questioning by the *oyabun* before the interview could begin. Then, when all the questions were answered, he bowed in gratitude and turned to speak with Becker in English.

'The *oyabun* has said he will provide whatever information he can.'

'That's good,' said Becker, somewhat relieved to be included once more in the proceedings. 'Why all the questions just now?'

'The *oyabun* wanted to know exactly who you were. The Yakuza oath prevents him from lending aid to or seeking intervention from the police. But since you are an intelligence officer working for the Hong Kong government, and you too hunt the *sekigun* ...'

'That makes a difference?'

'All the difference in the world. It bestows honour on him. The Yakuza has always engaged in espionage and subversion: the Dark Ocean, the Black Dragon. For generations they were the cornerstone of right-wing, ultra-nationalist politics. Our conquests of China and Korea were stimulated by a climate of imperialism largely brought about by their efforts. Do not believe anyone who tells you they are merely gangster extortionists. That is simply not true. At the end of the war even the American intelligence service was heavily reliant upon them to root out the communist fifth-column.'

Becker eyed the old man with interest. A black operations intelligence force? This was a side of the societies he was largely ignorant of.

'What about yourself? Aren't you a policeman?' Becker was being purposely as blunt as he knew how.

'My family has had more than a passing involvement with the banner of the Black Dragon. We still believe in the Emperor and the old order. In the sixties we formed the Corps of Heavenly Sincerity. Our main interest was in protecting Japan from Marxist elements. This caused us to place some of our resources with the NPA's counter-intelligence and counter-terrorist effort.'

Becker could hardly believe his ears. *A union of the country's security services and organised crime, for patriotic purposes!*

'And Mishima knows about this.'

'Undoubtedly. Why do you think he chose not to join us today? He knows my intelligence is excellent, because it comes from inside the Sakaguchi-gumi. If he does not know, then he certainly ought to. He pretends otherwise merely to prevent any possible loss of face.'

'Then you are also Sakaguchi-gumi.'

'You may judge for yourself. I say no more than this.' Silently David Becker nodded his understanding.

'Please, feel free to ask any questions you wish,' said

Nishimura with a small inclination of the head. 'Your presence here confers honour upon the *oyabun*.' Looking up he saw the suspicion clouding Becker's face: the policeman fearful of accepting the helping hand of one so steeped in crime. 'I beg you, if you have reservations, save them for another time. To refuse the *oyabun*'s generosity would be a great insult. Take it as freely as it is given.'

Hesitantly, Becker looked around him at the frail walls, the undulating banners, and the two lines of *kobun* sitting obedient and listening. It was the first time he had sat amongst such revered and infamous company and, along with the sense of unease, he now felt something else he had not anticipated: a heady cocktail of excitement and fear.

'Very well,' he said at last. 'Respectfully, I ask the *oyabun*'s help in discovering the whereabouts of the Okamoto group.'

That was all it took. A sense of relief bloomed like a soft flower, and its perfume pervaded the whole room. Nishimura's shoulders sagged an inch or two as he relaxed. It had been important that Becker use his own tongue to ask for help. Tremendous face for the godfather.

The *oyabun* of the Sakaguchi-gumi set his old and toad-like face in a benevolent smile, the eyes almost disappearing into long sloping furrows of flesh. He then spoke at length, like someone giving a lecture, pausing frequently for Nishimura to interpret his words. Amidst the two lines of *kobun* one man scratched his knee covertly, but otherwise no one moved.

'Perhaps you do not know who we are,' the *oyabun* began, looking Becker full in the face. 'Perhaps you think we are men of evil.' The suggestion appeared to amuse him. The European's long face showed no reaction. 'Allow me to explain. We were born in fire out of the societies of the Dark Ocean and the Black Dragon. This society has a great name and a long, proud tradition; a well-deserved reputation for violence where necessary, but also one of upholding this nation's ideals: *giri* and *ninjo* – duty and compassion. Liberal governments have always feared and shunned us, although, in our own way, we have always provided benefits for ordinary people: the ones who walk in the sunshine while we walk in the shade.

'We stress the ties of brotherhood, the bonds of family, care of the weak and, most important, obedience to the Emperor. Our strength began as the strength of outcasts, gamblers and pedlars, without wealth or nobility. Our doors were opened to all other outcasts shunned by those who walk in the sun. True, we lived by the people's labours, but we gave back to the nation tenfold whatever we took from them. Dreams of power and greatness. All eight corners of heaven under one roof.'

The old Japanese stopped and stared blankly, becalmed for the moment in an ocean of past dreams. He looked down, caught himself, and continued.

'After the great and terrible war, Sakaguchi-gumi joined with other secret societies to safeguard the nation. Nationalism was a word not spoken out loud and, while the Emperor surrendered to humiliation, the communist subversives crept out from under their stones. The Americans were there to see it all, and they feared the reds as much as we. Together we worked to break the back of this new menace. And this we did ... ruthlessly.'

Fire blazed in the *oyabun*'s sloe-black eyes, defiant and unapologetic. Becker was reminded of the words of an old triad: his claims of their patriotic battle to save the nation from Manchu invaders. How attractive such societies were, he reflected, to young men without purpose – the disenfranchised and discriminated against. And how easily and inevitably was their power and fervour corrupted.

463

'Our methods and rituals are the old ways,' argued the old *oyabun*. 'Our values are the old values. We appreciate the beauty of established order over negotiated chaos, respect for age and seniority.' He glanced slowly around at his *kobun*. 'Respect for the family and its rules. *Sekigun* believes in none of these virtues. Theirs is a force for evil; their revolution a threat to order and civilisation. That is why we hunt them. That is why we offer our knowledge to the intelligence agencies.'

Becker noticed the argument progress with quiet vehemence, realising that this was no ordinary lecture, neither was it solely for his benefit. For the *oyabun* it was an opportunity for him to reaffirm the society's beliefs and principles before his followers.

The old man's next words were a question aimed directly at Becker.

'Does that answer some of your questions about us?'

'Yes,' said Becker earnestly. 'Now I understand much better.'

'That's good. I was pleased by Nishimura's telephone call. He tells me you are allied to the British Intelligence. The honour is great.'

So, Nishimura had played upon his master's vanity – a subtle gesture and finely judged, too. Nishimura, then, was guile and mystery in one.

'As for the Okamoto group.' The *oyabun* adjusted his robe, tasting his words like bitter herbs. 'You are not alone in that quest. Though they are difficult to trace, still many seek them out; some to prosecute their downfall, others merely to buy their services.'

'Can they be bought?' asked Becker, rather naively he felt. 'Is such fanaticism for sale?'

'The Okamoto group has for some time been selling its services as a death squad. Their leader was himself trained in assassination and sabotage by North Korean Intelligence, and now he has spread his knowledge amongst his followers. This year alone they have killed five men and two women. Two of them were officials of a Malaysian bank sent into Manila to investigate fraud. Another was a mayoral candidate whose ideas were too bold; another, an army officer whose ideas weren't bold enough for his colleagues. The last was, I understand, an Australian nightclub owner who refused to work with the bosses of the Filipino water business.'

When Becker's eyebrows knitted in confusion, Nishimura hurriedly explained that *water business* was the Yakuza way of describing bars and nightclubs. The SB man smiled. It seemed appropriate.

'And the two women who were killed?' Following the traditional Japanese view of women as decidedly less important, it seemed the *oyabun* had already forgotten them.

'One was the wife of a ranking police officer; the other a Catholic nun. Both deaths were examples to encourage onlookers. In the Philippines politics can be a dirty business. And in all these cases the bodies were found in the lowest of places, hands bound with wire, heads cut clean off.' His bladed hand made a fierce slash behind his neck.

'Decapitated,' added Nishimura. 'A kind of liberation for the victim's spirit.'

As if speaking to a child who understood little of the adult's world, the squat Buddha-like figure patiently elaborated each case. His ideas and reactions were those of a Japanese who treasures the old ways, so there was no trace of revulsion in his descriptions of death – merely profound respect for sound procedural sense.

'In addition to his many other skills, Okamoto is an accomplished swordsman.'

'He is a master of the blade?' Becker ventured.

'No, not a master – merely a superior student. A devotee.'

'Unlike kendo, where blows are exchanged between heavily armoured opponents, *Iai-do* is a solitary form of

465

devotion. Its goal is the single perfect stroke which both confounds and destroys the enemy. Its highest objective is true enlightenment. The release of the mind from all earthly distractions. It relies heavily on Zen techniques of meditation. The perfect blade wielded by the perfect mind.' Nishimura finished his explanation and fell silent once more leaving Becker to absorb the importance of this information.

'Was Okamoto's family of samurai rank?'

Hearing the word 'samurai', the *oyabun* demanded to know what Becker had said. His response was a sneer which Nishimura translated in expanded form.

'Definitely not. But he believes that in a previous life he was *hatamoto*. Many would like to believe they came from greatness, but with Okamoto it is a passion. One which they say affects his belief in the manner of his ultimate death.'

'Meaning what?'

'One day he wants to die a warrior's death. Not like ordinary people, but as a samurai would die – killed in some great battle by another swordsman whose technique is superior.'

Becker felt himself being sidetracked into the realms of fantasy. He knew he had to get the conversation back on an even keel.

'Please ask the *oyabun* to forgive such direct questioning, but I must know Okamoto's present whereabouts and associations. Tell him the information is vital if I am to prevent the kidnap of a senior politician – an American.' He added this last on vague impulse, hoping that the society's relationship with the US would kindle some spark of commitment.

At that moment a breeze ruffled the banners draping the back wall. Silver emblems floated upon a raven-black sea. The *oyabun* waited until the whispering voice of the silk fell silent.

'Through my enquiries I have discovered that

Okamoto and seven of his people left Manila in the last week of August, bound for Hong Kong. My source has it they were engaged to perform one or more assassinations which their sponsor did not wish attributed to Chinese gangs.'

'Then it *is* triads,' said Becker. 'Does your source identify which of them?'

'I have drunk tea with the triad Brotherhoods – and secured fast friendships with some of their number – but if I knew which of them consorted with these red scum, I would readily break all such ties and tell you immediately. All I know is that the sponsors were Chiu Chau speakers. Three of them accompanied the cell into Hong Kong. Check your airport records for the last week of August and you will find them. Look for cheap tourist accommodation; Okamoto likes to be close to the underbelly of the city. Okamoto's controller was not present at their departure, so presumably he made other arrangements.'

'You know his controller?' asked Becker, somewhat astonished by the depth and breadth of the Sakaguchi-gumi's intelligence.

'Of course. Rhee Joon-kil is a North Korean intelligence officer, attached to the group to monitor their activities and provide support where Pyongyang deems appropriate.'

'Excuse me once again, *oyabun*, but are you absolutely sure of this?'

'Of course.' A grin of satisfaction.

'May I ask how?'

'The American Embassy here in Tokyo informed us.'

Becker caught his breath. This time Nishimura broke in and explained the CIA's uneasy relationship with the society, how they routinely passed on information on terrorist targets and expected good value in return. The Americans were priming organised crime to chase the *sekigun*; it was appropriate, then, that the latter's target should be the US's principal foreign policy maker.

'One piece of advice for you,' added the *oyabun*, extending an index finger and using it to brush aside the air. 'Take no chances with Okamoto when you discover his hiding place. The other creatures are fickle, their chief motivation is financial reward, but Okamoto is different. He is a fanatic. That is what prevents him from truly mastering the sword. There will be no arrest for that one – only death.'

The words had an infinitely resonant quality on the *oyabun*'s lips: more the words of a sage than of a gangster.

A timeless silence elapsed before the old Japanese glanced at Nishimura and nodded to indicate that the interview was over.

'*Arigato gozaimasu*,' said Becker, using one of the handful of Japanese stock phrases he had managed to pick up – mostly from Japanese air hostesses he had dated in the past. 'I extend my deepest thanks.'

While the followers looked on, the *oyabun* rose quietly from the floor and, using that same rolling gait, walked slowly back out into the garden.

The drive back into the Ginza seemed no more than a blur of traffic as David Becker meditated upon all he had learned that morning. He was mentally composing a confidential telex to be sent direct to the Special Branch communications centre, when Nishimura broke his reverie.

'Have you yet worked out why he agreed to help you?'

'Because of the Eighty-eight Temples?'

Nishimura smiled.

'No, not because of that, though it made him very happy to hear about it; he now considers you a civilised man with a good heart.'

'Why then?'

'Because the young man Okamoto murdered was actually one of his own grandsons.'

'The *oyabun* wants revenge?'

'Of course, but there is more to it than that. The sword Okamoto used to kill Honda was a present from Honda's grandfather, an antique blade of the Genroku period, very precious. Okamoto still carries .e same sword with him: a sword he has stolen from the Sakaguchi-gumi.'

'I see. I can't bring the kid back, but if the sword were to be returned ...'

'Precisely.'

Suddenly, without warning, the storm broke, and the heavy leaden sky opened up overhead. Nishimura flicked on the radio, cursing loudly as he tuned to a news programme and waited for the weather forecast. When he had listened to the report, he cursed louder still.

'What is it?' asked Becker. 'Is there a problem?'

'Yes, for you there is a very big problem.'

'Is it William Fredericks? Is it about the Secretary of State?'

'No. But you can stop worrying about making your plane this evening. That was a typhoon warning. They've just closed Narita airport and cancelled all international flights until further notice.'

EIGHTEEN

In Hong Kong that Sunday evening, while the typhoon still raged over Tokyo, three Mercedes limousines entered the darkened road beside the Yaumatei typhoon shelter and halted under a pool of street lighting. Beside the road, which was quiet at this hour, a row of metal railings parted to give access to a ramshackle landing-stage leading down to the murky water. As was usual in summer, the breeze wafting in from the sea was sickly sweet with putrefaction and bore with it the foul, cloying reek of effluence from the battalions of ancient boat dwellings ranged within the basin.

After several seconds the driver of the first vehicle flashed his headlights, just once, and out of the darkness sounded the put-put of a small engine.

The water-taxi, a ramshackle canvas-covered wallah-wallah, butted its way through the black, stinking water and approached the short pier at the south-east corner of the typhoon basin. Nimbly the pilot sprang forward to grip the creaking wooden beams at the edge of the pier with his weathered hands, made strong through the hauling of nets. He was a stocky, barefoot tanka, and wore only a white singlet and dark, baggy shorts that came down to his knees. He was in his mid-fifties, and brown as the timbers he now trod, yet he possessed easily enough power in his broad shoulders to steady the dangerous roll of his craft beside the concrete pilings.

There was a series of muffled sounds as car doors

closed, then four Asians slipped quietly aboard – moving quickly under the green canvas awning. Red Cudgel and Eddy Kwok, together with the two Japanese. The pilot threw the engine into a sputtering reverse motion, sliding back into the darkness.

The wallah-wallah showed no lights as it floundered between the densely-packed ranks of boat dwellings in the typhoon shelter. The craft which surrounded them were mostly ancient wooden sampans and square-keeled junks, all lashed together to form long floating streets. But at this time of year – typhoon season – the basin was packed to capacity with a motley collection of other seagoing craft. Some of these still made a living from the sea, fishing or hauling freight or ferrying passengers; but most of the old boats, which had once been the homes of itinerant fisherfolk, were now merely the cheapest accommodation to be had in the territory.

As the wallah-wallah passed through these lanes of junks, Red Cudgel gazed out across the open decks which surrounded him and thought of his own past. The night was hot and damp, and in the harsh glare of swaying hurricane lamps whole families of tanka people squatted in tight circles around linoleum-covered tables, attacking dishes of steaming rice and vegetables. With each successive family group they passed he was reminded of his own early days: the hardships of life in the typhoon shelter. He could still remember the sickness and the blisters, the struggle to defend their place in the basin; but most of all he remembered the terror of the typhoons which claimed so many boats every year. It was no fit place for people to live, he now knew, for, permanently draped with washing and plagued by disease and squadrons of cockroaches and rats, the creaking craft bobbed in a soup of their own human detritus.

This was what he had been escaping from when he had joined the Society – from all the filth and squalor, but most of all from the oppressive poverty. San Yee On

471

had given him money and power beyond his dreams – things he might otherwise never have attained.

Brooding on these memories, he looked up suddenly and the unexpected sight of a toddler staring back from the bow of a raddled fishing junk brought a fond smile to his lips. Chubby and diaper-less, the kid stood gaping at the wallah-wallah, balanced precariously at the edge of the deck, with mucus trails glistening on his upper lip. Red Cudgel laughed a little as he saw the infant penis trail an arc of gold into the water below, one hand clamped around the curling tail of a Chow mongrel dog for balance. In his heart he hoped one day that kid would also escape this terrible mess.

Out beyond the boat dwellers, to the north side of the shelter, they came upon scores of Chinese cargo vessels tightly huddled and riding gently at anchor. Their shapes made them easily identifiable as *tans*: black shallow-draught hulls with green box-like superstructures, and brick-red derricks towering above. The *tans* were unique to Hong Kong, and they plied back and forth between the city and nearby Macau, keeping the Portugese colony supplied with foreign goods.

The wallah-wallah now edged alongside one of the few vessels showing deck-lights. Two scruffy Chinese crewmen shoved their heads over the rail, and then rushed to secure a boarding ladder. On the main deck, two triad guards appeared to usher the party respectfully aboard.

'*Ah Goh!*' said the first forty-niner, acknowledging Red Cudgel the moment he appeared. The forty-niner's eyes then flicked suspiciously over the two strangers, for he disliked foreigners, especially Japanese. But wisely he kept his misgivings to himself and merely reported: 'All quiet here. No problems.'

'*Ho ye,*' said Red Cudgel routinely. 'Very good.'

Glancing around at the surly faces of the crew, who were half-naked in the sweating heat of the evening,

Okamoto and Rhee stepped on board and followed Red Cudgel down a companionway. Somewhere below a generator chuntered mutedly.

Inside the main cabin, lit by naked bulbs, there was the briefest exchange between the triad enforcer and the master of the vessel. Instructions were brusquely given, then the latter turned meekly away to open a storage hatch in a recess bay, beckoning the visitors inside.

The storage area was pitch dark until another dusty bulb lit up. As the light came on, cockroaches scuttled for cover. Okamoto stepped inside, assessing what he saw there with care. The space was damp, windowless, and easily less than fifty cubic metres in volume. But what surprised the Japanese most was the stack of wooden crates which stopped just short of the low bulkhead in a solid tarpaulin-covered block. There was barely space for a man to walk around it.

Okamoto raised one eyebrow quizzically.

'It will be cleared in time, I hope?'

'I think you misunderstand. The cage is already prepared,' came the self-assured answer. Red Cudgel gave another order, '*Hoi mun.*'

The vessel master bobbed his head in acknowledgement, pulled back the tarpaulin, and depressed a combination of wooden pegs along one side of the stack. Immediately a section of the crates, forming a wall eighteen inches thick, swung outwards on hinges to reveal the hollow recess at the centre of the hollow stack. A concealed lightswitch was activated, and the Japanese stepped into the cubicle within. There was just enough space for a double-bunk bed and latrine bucket. While Red Cudgel stood and watched, the North Korean also leaned inside, examining the intricate mechanism of the lock. When they were both satisfied, Okamoto and Rhee looked at one another in tight-lipped and grudging admiration.

'He will remain here safe and secure until the

operation is concluded,' explained Red Cudgel, taking charge once more.

'It is genuinely reliable?' asked Rhee.

'It would take the authorities weeks to search every *tan* in the typhoon shelter – assuming they even knew to look here. In the past, this has proved reliable enough.'

What he did not say was that this hollowed stack had been used many times before, sometimes to smuggle weapons or high-paying clients in and out of the territory, but chiefly to bring in No. 4 heroin from Macau. Fifty kilos at a time. Heroin brought out of Thailand aboard fishing trawlers.

Nodding his approval, Okamoto started to check the wooden walls, looking for loose boards or protruding nails or dangling wires – anything which might provide a means of escape for the prisoner. Or suicide.

'Don't bother,' said the vessel master, rubbing the back of his neck with a grimy sweat-rag. 'The wood conceals sheets of steel alloy. The inside of that stack is both bomb-proof and fire-proof. Rubber seals around the door mean we can make it watertight, too, if necessary. Take the upper hatch off and swing the hook in, and we can drop the box in the water – then collect it later.'

'That will do, Ah Ying,' breathed Red Cudgel, irritated that his follower's explanation may have suggested the box's original purpose. Foreigners were to be trusted only up to a point – particularly the devils from the eastern sea! 'I feel confident that such extreme action will not be necessary in this case.'

Rhee had correctly understood the reason for the enforcer's irritation but made no comment; he concentrated instead upon the concealed prison, testing the soft wooden panels of the door and feeling only unyielding metal within.

'Congratulations on a very professional arrangement. It will be perfect for our purpose. Is the crew reliable?'

'Of course. There are eight altogether; I chose these,

people myself. Every one has served the San Yee On for at least five years. We check our people very thoroughly.'

'Very sensible. Informers and government agents are always waiting for an opportunity. We must be sure to consider even the smallest details if we are to succeed. Have you made the arrangements we discussed?'

'Yes ... I have.' Irritation was building steadily at thus being questioned before his men. 'There will be the normal deck watches when we put out into the West Lamma Channel. In eleven hours we will be safely anchored off Macau, and within the safety of Chinese territorial waters. No *gwai lo* bastard would dare follow us there. Below deck the men will take six-hour shifts in pairs, attending to the prisoner's needs. On land we will keep contact with the *tan* via portable telephone. The society has leased a place on the Rua da Praia Grande.'

Rhee discussed the arrangement with Okamoto, explaining that the Rua da Praia Grande formed part of the southern waterfront, less than a kilometre from the famous Hotel Lisboa. There was an uninterrupted view of the channel between Macau and Taipa island and the long humpback bridge connecting the two points of land. Both agreed the location was good. To the west lay wholly Chinese waters, bounded by the rural mainland and a scattering of green islands. With binoculars they would be able to observe the *tan* make its way under the bridge and take up position midway between the two islands.

'The villa was leased through a cut-out?' enquired the Japanese cautiously. The triad indicated that it was. 'Good. Communications must be intermittent and kept to an absolute minimum, to prevent eavesdropping by the intelligence units. We don't know how well they would cooperate – or whether CHIS would choose to involve itself – but it's better to take no chances. If they intercept the line, they will trace you in a matter of hours. What about the hostage's welfare? Have you made provision for medical attention? It would be a pity to lose the man from a heart attack before extracting the concessions we require.'

Red Cudgel remained self-assured.

'A wise general thinks of everything. The chef aboard this vessel is a doctor of Chinese herbal medicine. We often use him when the hospitals would be bound to ask too many questions. Please relax on that score; he knows his business well enough.'

The Japanese pronounced himself satisfied.

'The weapons?'

'No problem. This boat has a concealed armoury of pistols, shotguns and fighting irons. On deck there is a mounting for a heavy-duty machine-gun. Ah Ying can also build fishing bombs from black powder and tin cans, in case anyone comes too close. They have a very nasty effect on diver's eardrums when they go off underwater.'

'That's good, but what about the weapons for my soldiers?'

Red Cudgel barked another order. He lounged against a bulkhead as two of the crew removed a bilge hatch and leapt nimbly into a recess in the floor. A blast of foul air rose from the hole as the rapid movement of their bodies pushed the stale air around the cabin. A dozen or so plastic sacks were passed up and stacked carefully. The last items were two cardboard boxes of cartridges, which jingled as they hit the floor.

The Japanese looked down at the pile without comment, nodded to himself, then turned to go.

'Aren't you even going to check them?' asked Red Cudgel, raising his voice for the first time. He was irritated more than ever by the cool arrogance of this man.

The Japanese stopped at the hatchway, his eyes narrowing to sharp slivers of ice.

'No. Why should I? If there is something wrong, it is your problem not mine.' He paused just long enough to make his point. 'Now, have someone load up the wallah-wallah. I've seen what I needed to see.'

Thirty minutes later they were back inside the Yaumatei apartment, where Okamoto and his men had remained virtual prisoners for the past three weeks. As the assault rifles were distributed, the seven earnest-looking Japanese cadres listened with rapt attention to Okamoto's instructions, then they set about stripping and cleaning the weapons. Most of them were pretty familiar with the Soviet design, having learned weapon handling from experts at an army base in Pyongyang. Some had even used this weapon to kill before. Still, Okamoto had his doubts about the quality of the Pakistani rip-offs they had been given, and he insisted that everyone practise field stripping and clearing stoppages, in case that would turn up any defects in construction.

Watching them operate, the triad enforcer knew he had chosen his team well. The confident slap and smack of the mechanisms being checked reassured him of that. Clearly these people knew how to handle themselves in a firefight.

When all was checked, Rhee and Okamoto exchanged a few brief sentences of Japanese then moved towards the first bedroom, indicating that only Red Cudgel should join them for this meeting. Inside the bedroom Rhee was the first to speak, but not before he had closed the door and switched on the air-conditioner to drown out their voices.

'Okamoto and his men are satisfied with the weapons. They are not first quality but good enough, and if what you say is true they will be untraceable. The boat is a nice touch. It means we can move the hostage around at will without undue problems of sedation during transportation.'

Red Cudgel pulled on his cigarette, then used it to point in Rhee's direction.

'So what about your end?'

Here the Japanese broke in, answering with quiet assurance.

'That has already been solved.'

Once again Red Cudgel felt the man's gaze burn into him. It was unnerving in a way he could not quite fathom. Though only slight of build, with every syllable he spoke the muscles of his jaw and neck showed up like in some anatomical diagram.

'How shall it be done?' asked Red Cudgel trying to meet Okamoto's eyes with his own.

'Time is a critical factor,' explained the Japanese. 'We must have two expert drivers capable of cutting through the Tsim Sha Tsui traffic at high speed. We need to cover the distance to the typhoon shelter in under four minutes.'

'That's going to take very special skills. You know Tsim Sha Tsui is one of the main tourist areas: very congested. People, cars, trucks and buses. One slip of the wheel and the vehicle goes ploughing through a crowd. Bodies everywhere. Very messy.'

The Japanese batted his eyelids in irritation.

'Can do, or no can do?'

With an effort Red Cudgel controlled his flickering temper.

'Of course can do. I'll give you two of the back-up drivers from the Shatin job. They're the best we have. But you still haven't said what you intend to do. I must have certain details first: where and when, and the type of vehicles you want.'

'Just send the drivers to me tomorrow morning and I will give them their orders. The rest is not your business.'

Real anger flared in the triad's face – anger at this constant evasion: Okamoto's refusal to disclose what had been planned. All at once something snapped inside him, and he flicked the lighted cigarette butt in Okamoto's face, showering sparks upon his shirt.

'Diu lei lo mo chau hai! Ham gar chan, yat boon gwai!'

At that moment Rhee saw the triad begin to advance with hands balled up into two massive, ugly fists. Quickly he stepped between the two men, attempting to forestall the confrontation he had already known was coming.

'Gentlemen,' he implored, 'let us remember our manners and good behaviour. How would such things appear to those who follow us?'

In sharp contrast to the Red Cudgel, Okamoto still stood rigid and unblinking, displaying none of the other man's open emotion. Though outwardly the Japanese looked cool and calm, in Rhee's mind at least there was no doubt he had been equally ready to fight. The Korean knew Okamoto was at his most dangerous when like this, and he had noticed Okamoto's slender hand slide under the back of his Hawaiian shirt, to close over the hilt of a short Japanese dagger with a razor edge. Whatever the outcome, it could have proved extremely bloody, and Rhee had known at once that he must intervene for the sake of the operation.

Luckily it took only a few more sentences of soothing words to calm the situation, and the confrontation evaporated as rapidly as it had arisen. Rhee realised then it had been a matter of face for the triad. Now it seemed face was restored.

'I assure you no disrespect was intended,' continued Rhee placatingly. 'Okamoto is merely unused to sharing information with others. It is one reason he and his group have never been apprehended.'

'Nevertheless,' said Red Cudgel, 'the *shan chiu* must know what will happen.'

A brief look of suspicion passed between Okamoto and Rhee, and in reply the Korean shrugged his assent. Okamoto turned the air-conditioner on to full power, and took a seat on the edge of the bed while he explained.

'The US Secretary of State is a powerful man protected by many layers of security and defensive intelligence. Of necessity the full details of our plan must be restricted to the very fewest people necessary to carry it out. Therefore I must insist you say nothing to anyone else unless it directly concerns him.'

Somewhere wrapped up in this warning was a blunt reminder of the traitor they had harboured in their midst for three years: Joe Lai's undercover man who had escaped in Shatin.

'*M'sai gong la!*' snapped Red Cudgel angrily; all this went without saying.

'In the open he will be closely attended by bodyguards, and they will be well prepared. Were it merely a question of a simple assassination, that could be easily managed with a high-powered rifle. But kidnapping is another matter – more dangerous for all concerned. We have to take him from under the noses of his security men. Therefore we do it when they least expect: when he appears at his safest and their guard is down. Aboard the train.'

'What? Are you crazy?' It seemed too fantastic to be true. 'You're planning to steal the man away while he's riding an underground train?'

'It seems pointless to make premature judgements before you have heard the plan,' said Rhee coldly.

The Japanese then continued slowly, as if speaking to a child of limited understanding.

'Your informant within the Special Branch gave us a full list of timings and locations for the American's Tuesday programme. Fredericks will fly to his appointment in New Territories in an army Wessex helicopter, but the return journey will be via the MTR underground train system. He boards at Tsuen Wan station. The local uniform police will temporarily clear the station and concourse while the Secretary's party boards. The train will be a special service: no members of press or public.

The journey will be non-stop to Central station on the Island. The security party will bring the man out at the Chater Garden exit, where the usual armoured motorcade will be waiting to take him the short distance back to the Hilton Hotel.

'Both Special Branch and the State Department bodyguards will expect whatever trouble there is to occur at either end of this journey. Those are the most dangerous times in a VIP's life: arrivals and departures. They will have people covering every building which has a clear view of Fredericks' head. Everyone who comes within twenty-five metres of him will have first been security-screened and checked with both metal and explosives detectors.' Okamoto suppressed the ghost of a smile. 'But underground, aboard the train, they will be feeling safe from bomb and bullet.'

The Japanese paused and allowed the silence to grow – waiting for Red Cudgel's questions.

'So how will you take him from them? The train will pass through fourteen stations between Tsuen Wan and Central, without stopping once. It will be moving at around sixty miles per hour the whole time.'

'An average of eighty kilometres an hour, actually,' the Japanese corrected him.

'Nevertheless, all doors will be locked and there will be armed uniformed police on all the platforms – Yip Suen has confirmed this. How will your men get aboard – by leaping on to a moving train?'

'No, not by leaping.' Okamoto stood up and walked the few steps to a built-in wall closet, placing his hands upon the door handles. 'Thanks to the cooperation of the Tsim Sha Tsui station master, we now have a thorough working knowledge of the MTR: its structure, operating procedures, and even its computer control systems. Armed with this knowledge we will attack the blind spot in their security... But you are right, first we must get aboard.'

With that the Japanese tugged on the door handles and the hinges squeaked open. His curiosity aroused, Red Cudgel stood up to examine the inside of the closet. There was an ordinary rack of clothes hanging there, but to one side hung a number of sets of orange overalls bearing MTR badges. But what really caught the triad's attention was the life-sized plastic mannequin leaning against the back wall, dressed in a set of the orange overalls and wearing an orange helmet. Leaning closer he saw that the helmet also bore the logo of the Mass Transit Railway, and the patch on the dummy's chest said Track Maintenance Crew.

'You haven't met *gau lo* – plastic man,' Okamoto said drily. 'He will be the ninth member of our team, and I guarantee he will get us aboard the train. With a little technical assistance of course.'

At once Red Cudgel's mood lightened. He shrugged and even laughed forcefully. For the first time he was beginning to think it could actually be done.

At Police Headquarters, James Weldon read the Special Branch situation report for the third time, hoping to find some crumb of comfort hidden there. He was in the foulest temper anyone could ever remember.

'I don't fucking believe it!' he thundered, and his fist came down upon the desk. At the briefing table in front of the desk, the chiefs of Special Branch and of Operations both wisely said nothing. When Weldon was in this mood, it was the best thing to do.

'We knew the directorate had been penetrated, but, dear God, not to this extent.' His gaze turned to the Director of Special Branch. 'Care to tell me, Henry, how SB's maximum security facility was so easily compromised? What do we think we're running over there, a bloody Vietnamese refugee camp?' The dour Scottish voice spat out the questions like slashes from a straight razor.

The DSB paused to look quickly at his briefing notes, remembering how he had asked the same bloody question of his Support Wing not thirty minutes before. The notes in front of him – like his Support Chief – offered no clear answer.

'No excuses, sir.'

Weldon was even grateful for that. He despised senior officers who were unwilling to shoulder blame for a screw-up. Like most things, the Chinese had an expression for that: *juk juk bok,* meaning to drop the shoulder. St John-Black's shoulders remained broad and straight.

Weldon tossed the sheets upon the table. He drew a hand across his mouth, then leaned back in his chair, folding his hands across his stomach. 'Very well, then, I'll settle for what you've discovered so far. Pray enlighten us.'

St John-Black knew his department had sinned, but he also knew the Commissioner had scant regard for those he could too easily push around. Chastened, but unbowed, he chose a firm, measured tone for his words.

'You have the facts, Commissioner, as far as we know them.' This was no time to use first names. 'Somehow persons unknown succeeded in tampering with the prisoner's food. It's unclear when this happened exactly, but it must have been either during the food's preparation, or in transit between the kitchen and the cell. The remains left in Chan Ming's bowl have been analysed and found to contain a vegetable alkaloid poison. Doctor Ong informs me this was almost certainly responsible for the intense abdominal cramps evidenced by the prisoner. Painful but in itself not sufficient to kill the man. My men were concerned for Chan Ming's welfare and decided to send him under escort to the casualty department of QMH.

'Whoever arranged the poisoning also arranged a fake motorcycle accident to halt the SB vehicle on Mount

Davis Road. We shan't know the full details until the intelligence collection unit concludes its investigation, but it seems clear from marks found beside the road that two, possibly three other vehicles were parked there. It has all the hallmarks of a very well planned operation. Just like with Tasker. They had everything on their side, including the element of surprise. All three victims suffered multiple lacerations by fragmentation grenade. The two constables were shot through the head with a .45 calibre weapon. By the time the emergency services arrived there was nothing left but burnt toast.'

'Yes, quite,' said Weldon distastefully, now leaning forward on his elbows. 'All of which gets us precisely nowhere. Any ideas who brought in this poison?'

'The prisoners' meals are prepared on site in the canteen kitchen. There are two senior constables permanently assigned to catering duties – both recommended for light duties on medical grounds. They seem straight enough; both have over fifteen years' service. All meals are ordered by the guard sergeant in charge of the shift, collected by two of his constables, and delivered to the cells on individual trays. Since only Chan Ming was affected we can rule out tampering in the kitchens, because the cooks don't know who each meal will go to.'

'So meals are allocated randomly?'

'It should be randomly. All they count is heads, and everyone gets the same food: boiled vegetables and rice, and a plastic mug of tea.'

'Then it had to be one of the two men who delivered the meals,' suggested the Director of Operations. 'Or both.'

The DSB answered with a long-suffering look that said: don't you think we've already considered that! What he actually said was: 'So it would seem. However, one of them was unfortunately handcuffed to Chan Ming when he died, and the other is currently under sedation after a suicide attempt.'

'What?' exclaimed Weldon.

'Oh, yes,' said the DSB turning to face the Commissioner again. 'He tried to eat his own revolver as soon as he heard he was the main suspect. Apparently the man has wept constantly ever since. Keeps trying to injure himself. Keeps screaming *jing gwoo*.' That was a common expression for police ears; one even used by European officers in preference to the English word 'frame-up'.

'Do you think he was *jing-gwoo*ed, Henry?' asked the Commissioner quietly.

The other shook his head and shrugged noncommittally.

'To be perfectly honest, sir, I don't bloody know. Maybe the dead guard was the accomplice, I really don't know. Maybe he was a stooge paid to help spring the prisoner. Maybe he didn't realise what a liability he'd be thereafter. Anyway, I've ordered an investigation into Breach of Security. Since Chan Ming wasn't officially in the territory, what else can I do? With all those *Dai Huen Jai* in custody, we had to provide cover from other sections. It's possible some of the others had unsupervised access. We'll have to wait and see. I've ordered every officer concerned to be revetted: bank accounts, personal habits, affiliations, everything.'

Weldon knew just how thorough Special Branch could be when the need arose. If there was any character defect or quirk of circumstance which had left one of his men vulnerable to blackmail or coercion then Henry St John-Black would certainly uncover it. He pursed his lips thoughtfully, somewhat mollified by what he had heard.

'I need hardly remind you both how little time we have left. Just twelve hours before the Secretary of State arrives.'

'Excuse me,' interrupted the DSB. 'I'm sorry, but it's less time than that. The arrival's been brought forward to nine o'clock this evening, and if that typhoon shifts in direction the time could change yet again.'

Weldon cast his eyes heavenwards.

'Damn it, we needed this one. Now we'll never know what else Chan Ming had to sell.'

'At least we're now alerted to the threat. That's something,' offered St John-Black hopefully.

'Nice try, Henry. Just pray to God this mistake doesn't turn out to be the one which cost the Secretary of State his life.' Weldon forced a laugh of bitter irony. 'To think, I was due to see His Excellency this morning for a decision on Chan Ming's case. He's been waiting for a response from the Foreign and Commonwealth Office in London, and you know how long those bastards take. Now it will be a very different meeting, and if you think I've been hard on you, Henry, just remember this has been nothing compared to the session I'll get up at Government House.'

Everyone knew that even if Weldon had seemed severe with them, with his own superiors he always shouldered full responsibility for the actions of his men.

Doogan sucked on his pipe thoughtfully.

'They must have wanted him dead pretty badly to take him out inside police custody. Surely that tended to corroborate his claims. Shouldn't we simply prepare ourselves for the worst, and worry about the fine detail later?'

'Oh, I'd say the threat is real enough,' Weldon responded gravely. 'Henry received a signal from Tokyo yesterday. This Okamoto character Becker's been chasing appears to have already entered the Colony. How's that progressing, Henry?'

'I've got my best people working night and day on it, trying to get a lead on where this cell might be holed up.'

'Who's coordinating it?'

'Chief Inspector Tavistock. She has teams checking records at every immigration entry-point. I've also asked her to furnish possible scenarios: anything that could help us understand the reason for their targeting Fredericks.'

'What has the US Consulate had to say?' asked the Commissioner.

'Prioletti seemed at a loss for words. That's a first for him.'

'I must confess, Commissioner,' interrupted the Director of Operations, 'with all the uniformed and plainclothes policemen we'll be fielding, I fail to see how they intend to get at him. Saturation policing around the Hilton Hotel, the US Consulate and in Tsuen Wan. There'll also be CID action squads on hand, mingling with the crowd at public appearances. An assassination is one thing, just bang and run for it, but a kidnapping – especially in Hong Kong – that takes some imagination.'

The Commissioner deliberated the chances of pulling a VIP out of a motorcade without anyone noticing and he had to agree. Now that he actually thought about it, the threat had a slightly improbable ring to it.

'Yes, I tend to agree. Henry, for the moment I want you to treat it as an assassination threat. That should concentrate the minds of your VIP Protection officers, and it will hopefully cover the kidnapping threat at the same time. By the way, how is security for the Chinese meeting? Are there any gaps?'

The DSB was quick to answer.

'None, sir. The Chinese are fielding their own team at Fung Chik Sin Villa. That place should be bound up tight, so I don't anticipate trouble there. We have a Wessex helicopter laid on for the outward journey to Tsuen Wan, and the return journey will take place a hundred metres below ground on the MTR. Special train for immediate party and security only. You couldn't hope for better cover.'

'I pray to God you're right,' said Weldon wearily. 'What time did you say he arrives tonight?'

'It will be 21.30 – and it looks like heavy rain.'

'That's putting it mildly,' commented the Commissioner deadpan.

On a flat rooftop above a kung-fu gymnasium in Kowloon City, Bamboo Snake stood beneath a canvas awning, which sagged under the weight of rainwater, and watched the sky. All around him the incessant beat of raindrops rang in his ears as he stared eastward, screwing up his eyes to visually penetrate the bright, smudged beads of neon lighting up the tall buildings. Occasionally he raised a pair of powerful Zeiss binoculars to check the lights in the sky.

At 21.50 precisely his patience was rewarded. The aircraft came gliding out of the darkness like a ghost, its spot-beams picking out the fall of the rain, growing brighter by the second. Taking the usual approach path, it dropped to two hundred feet and banked steeply over Checkerboard Hill, dropping down, down, down through the grey tenements, almost like a stone. The approach was steep, wheels almost clipping the Prince Edward Road flyover as it roared in. Then, as the silver-grey giant passed directly overhead and the rooftop began to vibrate in sympathy, Bamboo Snake heard the scream of the engines change to a lower, spent frequency, and he caught sight of the aircraft markings he had waited for. The blue background and spread eagle crest of the US State Department.

In a sudden frenzy of excitement he grabbed up the portable telephone lying on the table under the awning, and pressed the first memory dial key. Behind him the plane hopped over the airport perimeter fence, engines screaming in protest at the violent manoeuvre, until the wheels met the gleaming wet runway just two hundred metres beyond Olympic Avenue.

The electronic warble ceased abruptly as Bamboo Snake's call was answered.

'*Wai, wan bin goh a?*'

488

'This is the observatory. I have a typhoon warning,' said Bamboo Snake, standing out in the downpour now and squinting away towards the runway.

'What number is the signal, little brother?'

'Number ten,' he answered excitedly. 'The typhoon is upon us.'

The line went dead without further reply.

The 747 turned at the far end of the runway and taxied back through the torrential rain to the long-term parking apron at the north-east corner of Kai Tak airport. As it approached the parking bay the powerful spotlights picked out the fat droplets of monsoon rain, and in the distance the vehicles lined up for the greeting party. In spite of the weather a full cordon of the Airport Security Unit – counter-terrorist troops armed with SMGs – was deployed upon the apron, in dripping anoraks and berets. As the aircraft coasted to a shuddering halt, they backed into defensive positions around it, and the line of limousines moved up to the boarding steps.

Closest of all was Stephen Lee, standing between the front passenger door of the Secretary of State's vehicle and the foot of the steps, where he could easily observe his own men positioned around the VIP's limousine, facing outwards. There were three SB mobile escort teams on the tarmac, ready to depart the instant the VIP climbed aboard. Satisfied with the cover Stephen Lee turned to look at Jack Cinch, who was huddled beneath a large golf umbrella with Lassiter and Divine. Lee gave a quick nod to signal that all was ready. With this signal Cinch raised a Motorola packset radio and spoke to the leader of the Secretary's detail, at that moment standing on the flight deck of the State Department jet, waiting for permission to disembark their VIP.

'Status green, proceed with disembarkation.'

'Roger that,' came the reply, wrapped in a jacket of electronic crackle and hiss.

The cabin door opened and light spilled out. First to come loping down the stairs were two security men, who immediately took up outward-facing positions at the foot of the steps. Neither had seen Stephen Lee before, but they recognised from the cord of his earpiece and the colour and shape of his lapel pin that he was the field commander of the local protection unit. Both were careful not to obstruct him.

Lee was aware now of the thumping in his chest. Nervously he checked the line of the perimeter fence, for about the hundredth time that evening, then the rooftops of the terminal buildings where ASU sniper-men lay with night-scopes. Then he pressed the transmit key of his personal radio.

'Alpha one, two, and three, *yue bei*. Stand by.'

In the next moment William Fredericks himself appeared in the doorway, dressed in a fawn raincoat. Guiding his wife by the arm he stepped out into the wettest Hong Kong night he had ever seen. On the apron below he saw the two black Mercedes limousines open their doors to disgorge the Consul-General and his deputy, with their two wives. As this greeting party formed up under a platoon of dark umbrellas, Fredericks could spot the CIA and FBI men at a glance: those standing somewhat aloof from the official group, and appraising the Chinese protection officers as they went quietly about their job.

For Stephen Lee, the Secretary of State's arrival on solid ground was a blessed relief. True, the incessant whine of idling engines kept his nerves on edge, but at least now he could stop worrying and get on with the job. He watched the handshaking and the toadying that followed with controlled impatience, anxious to hurry his charges along and out of the open as quickly as possible.

Taking the initiative, he pulled open the rear door of the VIP limousine.

'This way please, Mr Secretary.'

Without another word William Fredericks – who knew the value of good security and cared little for the sycophancy of such occasions – took his wife's arm and steered her into the back seat. A second later Lee was round the other side of the limousine, climbing into the front passenger seat, where he operated the car's central locking mechanism. Taking their lead from Alpha Commander, the three escort teams also boarded their vehicles.

'OK, we have the package we need,' said Lee speaking into his radio in Cantonese to avoid giving offence to the VIP sitting directly behind him. 'Let's move out.'

'Ah-sir,' came the reply from Alpha Two, the rear escort commander. 'The Consul-General's party isn't ready yet; they'll miss the motorcade.'

'That's just too bad,' snapped Lee, irritated. 'We're here to protect the Secretary – not organise a fucking tour group. Every extra second we're out here allows a further opportunity for someone to hit. Now move out.'

'Roger, Alpha Commander.'

The motorcade moved out of the East Gate, heading for the airport tunnel, with the Secretary of State's Mercedes sandwiched between two long, white five-litre-engined Special Branch vehicles. At the perimeter fence they picked up two uniformed motorcycle outriders from Kowloon traffic, and exchanged greetings on the District Radio Net. Lee was glad of this escort. Traffic branch had arranged a green phase on all traffic signals in the district, to prevent any hold-ups. The last thing they needed, with a current high-grade threat hanging over the principal, was to get stuck in a traffic-jam. Hemmed in, boxed out, or cut off they would be vulnerable, lacking any means of escape from ambush. And after the attack at Shatin Racecourse the possibility of a vehicle ambush still remained uppermost in Lee's mind.

The journey went smoothly through the cross-harbour

tunnel, then along Gloucester Road on the island itself, Lee scanning the roadside and the adjoining buildings all the way. Up ahead, the blue beacon of the lead escort vehicle winked intermittently, and beyond that the gleaming helmets of the outriders peeled off to block feeder lanes as they passed. In his earpiece Stephen Lee was reassured to hear coded location reports being fed back to SB control by his men. Each point passed brought them one step nearer to the safety of their destination.

At the covered entrance to the Hilton Hotel the vehicles formed up for an orthodox set-down, and Lee watched the lead escort team leap from their vehicle to form up in a rapid box cordon around the limousine. There was the usual collection of photographers and reporters hanging around the main doors, along with a handful of hotel guests who had happened to see the cars glide up to the entrance and were lured by the flash of blue lights. Some of them even recognised the Secretary of State. It was the job of Lee's men now to make sure none of these onlookers came too close.

'Alpha One. *Gau dim.*'

'Roger.' He noticed a group of local press spill out of the hotel's glass doors. 'Alpha Two, keep an eye on the cameramen. Remember, polite but firm.'

'Roger, Alpha commander.'

Trying to remain relaxed and alert, Lee deactivated the central locking and stepped down, looking casually around him for anything that might set his mental geiger-counter clicking. Already the rear escort team had deployed into an open V formation inside the first box of security men, and the SY team was scanning the gawping crowd for trouble. Lee opened the Secretary's door to an immediate volley of camera flashes. When Fredericks stepped down on to the pavement, instead of moving straight inside he turned to help his wife, who had recently undergone a hip operation, climb slowly and painfully from the vehicle.

The press of the crowd made Lee's stomach churn. Arrival and departures, he kept thinking, over and over, those were the most dangerous times in a VIP's schedule. Seemingly an eternity later the couple stepped arm-in-arm through the double glass doors, to be greeted by the hotel manager. In another ten seconds the procession had swept through the lower arcade, bypassing the main lobby, and boarded two elevators which had been reserved for their exclusive use.

'Almost there,' Stephen Lee heard himself breathe. Lord Gwan-Dai keep him safe – and get David Becker back here soon!

The elevator lights climbed the numbered panel: five, six, seven. Lee pressed the transmit key of his radio once more, and demanded a report from residence security up on the VIP floor. Before stepping out on to the corridor, he needed to be sure there were no surprises awaiting them.

'Alpha Four, *dim yeung ah*?'

No reply. Immediately beads of sweat broke out across his back. Something was wrong. His right hand strayed inside his jacket to the butt of the Glock 17 automatic. Secretary Fredericks was chatting obliviously with the deputy US Consul-General, while Stephen Lee sweated. Without a favourable response he would have to instruct the lift attendant to return to ground level and proceed with emergency evacuation. Embarrassing if it was a mistake!

He tried once more. This time the station sergeant came on the radio immediately.

'Alpha Four, *mo maan tain*. No problem. Residence floor secure.'

A sigh of relief.

When the lift doors opened, two Special Branch bodyguards stepped out on to the corridor to proceed ahead of the Secretary of State, forming a protective screen. Next, Stephen Lee stepped out and invited Fredericks and his party to follow. The procession floated along the corridor towards suite 825. Stephen Lee heaved a sigh of utter relief as he watched the principal and his immediate party disappear inside the room.

Outside the next-door suite, which was the Special Branch command post, Alpha Four approached Stephen Lee with a hurried apology.

'*Ho dui m'jiu*, Lee-sir. Sorry. I was in the bathroom when you called. Couldn't reach my packset.'

'Never mind that now. Has there been word from control about Chief Inspector Becker?'

'Yes, sir. Earlier today they spoke with the Japanese observatory. This typhoon is a very lazy one. They still have wind speeds of a hundred and sixty miles an hour. It won't clear Tokyo until dawn tomorrow. With luck he may get a flight tomorrow afternoon.'

'That means he won't be here for the most important part of tomorrow's programme.' Lee's voice was calm, hiding the dread he actually felt for what might be awaiting them the next day. 'Thank you. Give the teams staggered meal breaks, and continue with your duties.'

'Ah-sir!' responded the station sergeant.

Lee sat upon the bed in suite 823 and decided to call Special Branch control himself, knowing that the Director would be at his desk waiting for word of a safe arrival.

'Good evening, Mr Lee,' intoned Henry St John-Black as he came on the line. 'I trust you didn't find it all too boring ...'

Inside the VIP suite William Fredericks shucked off his jacket wearily and approached the drinks cabinet with more enthusiasm than anything else he had done that evening. It had been a long, hard day and, in line with his doctor's orders, he had avoided all alcohol. Now the day was shot to pieces and he could finally relax. He selected a heavy crystal tumbler, flung a fistful of ice into it, and poured himself a generous measure of bourbon.

'Jesus, that's better,' he said after a good stiff pull.

Sighing heavily, he turned to face the Consul-General, who had finally arrived and was still standing attentively at the other side of the room.

The decor of the room was a mixture of powder pink and Wedgwood blue and the Secretary found the pastel colours soothing after the day's tribulations. Aside from Dan Fluherty, Fredericks' own personal private secretary, there was no one else present. Even Mrs Fredericks had discreetly withdrawn to the bedroom in response to one of those apologetic nods her husband used with her whenever there was business to discuss. The remainder of the greeting party had been dismissed on arrival.

'Fix the C-G a drink, Dan,' said Fredericks waving a hand towards the bottles in the well-stocked bar. Fluherty's moves were slick as ever as he poured bourbon into two more glasses. A moment later the three men were seated in a small sitting-room adjoining the main room looking at each other across a large mahogany coffee-table. The easy chairs were of a semi-regal style, richly upholstered in the same pink and blue as the walls and drapes, with polished wooden insets on the arms and backs. Somewhere in the background an air-conditioner hummed comfortingly.

Not quite sure of what was to follow, the Consul-General allowed his nervousness to show in the most facile of questions.

'And how was your meeting with the Philippine President, Mr Secretary? Not too difficult I trust?'

Fredericks, often described in the American press as everyone's favourite grandfather, was an ex-Marine with a wide, open face and a usually bluff avuncular manner to match. But tonight there was little of the good humour for which he was so well known. Tonight he seemed tired and tense. Seated opposite his guest, one hand cradling the heavy glass, the Secretary snorted lightly. The other hand came up to his face, momentarily shading the eyes which were puffy from lack of sleep. Then with a finger and thumb he probed his temples before he shifted forward in his seat.

'Sorry,' he said, 'what was the question again?'

'The Philippine President, sir ...'

'Ah, yes, not too bad, I guess, considering the circumstances.'

Consul-General Walters did not quite know what to make of this reply. Still he resolved to make an attempt.

'Yes, I understand they're not happy about the speed of our withdrawal from the bases.'

Fredericks sighed once more, not really concentrating upon the question – fingers agitating his glass, watching the golden liquid wash back and forth across the ice-cubes.

'They won't be happy until the last man and the last jeep have gone, and that's only to be expected. But you just can't shift that many men – that amount of hardware – in an instant. It can't be done. Their President appreciates that fact well enough; it's just those gangsters they have masquerading as local politicians. Nationalist knee-jerk, nothing more.' Fredericks gulped at the tilted glass and swallowed hard. 'Nothing to be done. Still it means I have to listen to a lot of bluster and bullshit about how our middle bureaucrats are dragging their heels.'

'And are we dragging our heels, Mr Secretary?'

It was a brave question for a diplomat who had not yet attained ambassador rank, but Fredericks liked honesty and he rewarded it now with a straight answer.

'Frankly, yes,' he grinned. 'A little.'

His tone invited no further probing and the Consul-General merely nodded wisely. He took a sip of his own drink and said airily: 'They're going to hurt when we're gone – without Uncle Sam's subsidies. And without the

496

military's spending power, an awful lot of small local businesses will close.'

'Sure, but who's to say the increase in their national pride won't be worth it?' said Fredericks looking suddenly bored with the whole conversation. The Consul-General waited, confused now as to his chief's line of thought. He glanced at Fluherty, who was silently examining his fingernails, then back to the Secretary of State. Finally he made a conciliatory face.

'I guess you have a point there, sir.'

Fredericks' head jerked up.

'No I don't,' he snapped, suddenly irritated by such flacid agreement. 'It's all bullshit. You know it and I know it.'

'What is, sir?'

The Secretary of State put down his glass and stalked to the window, leaving the other man more confused than before. On impulse he drew back the layers of curtain and peered out across Cotton Tree Drive at the illuminated angles of the Bank of China Building. Far above, atop the column which symbolised Chinese pride and progress, a red safety beacon winked back mockingly.

'This whole Far East tour ...' he muttered to himself barely audibly. 'What the hell am I doing here?'

'Attempting to open negotiations with the Chinese, I believe, sir.'

Jesus Christ, thought Fredericks, this Consul-General was either incredibly naive or annoyingly obtuse. He turned and let fly the volley which had been building steadily since the door had closed.

'What the hell for? Chinese concessions on human rights have been minimal. I swore not to set foot inside the People's Republic until there was some concrete proof their Politburo had mended its ways. Now I'm ordered here to conduct secret talks with their Foreign Minister, as if Tiananmen Square had never happened.'

Caught off guard by this sudden outpouring, the Consul-General wisely held his tongue. Such self-disclosure had embarrassed him to the extent that it had robbed him of any reply. His back still turned to the room, Fredericks continued. 'No specifics, of course; just general niceties – and, by the way, please may we continue to use your harbour after 1997. Damn it all, how does that make us look? Make *me* look?'

In spite of his years, William Fredericks could still muster a head of steam when required. As he turned, the fire in his eyes and the look on his face suggested a bitter cup indeed.

'Like a paper tiger, I'd say,' murmured the Consul-General nervously. 'Soft on human rights violation.'

The Secretary of State shot him a piercing glance, not quite sure whether to feel insulted or vindicated. It was the response he expected senior diplomats all around the world must be whispering about him right now. Fredericks the master of compromise.

'More like a jellyfish,' breathed Fredericks bitterly. Concentrating once more on the building across the street, he swirled the ice in his glass, and took another mouthful.

'But sir,' put in the other insistently, 'that's the whole point of holding *secret* negotiations: no press announcements; everything strictly controlled. That way the Chinese government isn't embarrassed about talking with capitalist imperialists, nor the US Government about having to deal with a bunch of murdering gangsters.'

Both men still remembered the furore in Beijing at the time of the student uprising over so-called British and US interference in Chinese internal affairs. Few people who had seen the news reports could forget the orgy of violence that resulted when the army went in to clear Tiananmen Square – or the sight of a line of tanks being brought to a standstill by one brave young man brandishing only a pair of flimsy white carrier-bags.

Appalled by the extent of Chinese atrocities the Western intelligence agencies had pulled every string to help effect the escape of student leaders now under threat of death for counter-revolutionary crimes. They had slipped out through Hong Kong, to turn up during the succeeding months in a number of cities across the USA, preaching opposition to the Beijing regime. After that, relations between the USA and China had never really moved past the lukewarm stage.

Gangsters, thought Fredericks. It was a fitting enough epithet.

'Thanks for that, Bob, but it doesn't make me feel any easier about talking to them. If the President hadn't asked me to undertake this mission as a personal favour, I'd have offered my resignation over it.'

'I'm sure the President appreciates your loyalty, Mr Secretary.'

Fredericks almost snorted aloud at this, but he checked himself against such self-indulgence before a subordinate. The only people the President seemed to appreciate – or listen to – these days, he thought bitterly, were Don Kazinski and Phil Kagan. Between them they had come to monopolise access to the Oval Office, and with that their control over the President's world perception was absolute.

Fredericks' own requests for equal-time, regular one-to-one meetings with the President, to discuss his own foreign policy initiatives, had met with only partial success. Immediately after these meetings, he had learned, the National Security Adviser was always on hand to help the Chief Executive sift and reformulate his options. In short Fredericks did not have the sole responsibility for foreign policy which he had been promised when he gave up his senior post in Stuyvesant-Lynch to join the cabinet.

'I'm sure you're right, Bob,' said Fredericks, softening a degree or two. 'But I can't help believing I'm only here now because Kazinski thought there was some good to be had from it.'

'I always thought Kagan was the real one to watch,' said Walters, moved to offer his true opinion after the Secretary's own candour.

'True, but that old fox needs Kazinski's support to really make things happen. Always has done. I don't trust either of them. They both view the world at arm's length. They both fear *glasnost* because it diminishes their own importance. That worries me – it encourages all kinds of dangerous initiatives.'

'You're dead against this present initiative then, Mr Secretary?'

'Yes I am,' snapped Fredericks. 'Hong Kong is of marginal importance to the US; it could never cope with the size of naval deployment we had going in the Philippines. We get an agreement to berth fifty ships a year – so what? And in exchange for this we offer a package of agricultural assistance and information technology worth over two hundred million. It's absolutely ludicrous. We should be operating a trade embargo for what they've been doing.'

'With respect, sir, China is set to become a very important member of the economic world over the next seven years. We could hardly cut ourselves off from such a massive market: one point two billion consumers.'

'I've thought about that. Yes, like everyone, we have a price – and that price is economic survival. But I wonder how this military cooperation will be viewed in Hanoi. China and Vietnam still have an awful lot of differences; and the Vietnamese could easily misconstrue what is happening as an alliance against *them*.'

The true depth of Fredericks' concerns was now beginning to show. It was a game of perceptions. One in which he feared the worst possible outcome. A perception of provocation to the Soviet-Vietnamese alliance.

'I'm sure the Soviets will keep them on a tight rein,

500

sir,' suggested Walters encouragingly. 'They stand to lose too much if tensions increase in the Pacific.'

Walters waited for a reply, but the Secretary of State merely finished his drink and placed the glass back on the table. A soft clap of his great hands showed that the subject was closed. His expression brightened.

'So, how are we received *here* these days? I understand the British are getting a hard time over their immigration policies, but what about us?'

'The locals are still very pro-US, I'm happy to say. Stateside is still the preferred destination for those with 1997 jitters. Come and see the line around the block outside the Consulate's immigration section.'

'That's good. Word of warning, though – I'll be announcing new immigration quotas for Hong Kong Chinese tomorrow afternoon. Two hundred thousand this year. The eligibility criteria will be varied: part economic, part cultural, part based on having family in US. But the main new category will be for those who can demonstrate they would be in jeopardy from the Beijing administration. I want to offer a bolt-hole for those in real danger of reprisals when the Chinese army walks in. I know this ought to be done in conjunction with the UN High Commissioner for Refugees, but I've decided to make the announcement tomorrow personally.'

So that was the concession, thought the Consul-General, his face betraying nothing of his thoughts. Fredericks had finally agreed to this mission in return for announcing this new quota and a chance to play saviour to the Hong Kong Chinese. Whether the man was motivated by feelings of humanity or merely a wish for personal popularity was entirely irrelevant. The gesture was everything. And clearly Fredericks had needed to compromise his principles in order to secure it.

Bob Walters opinion of his superior shot up to the ceiling.

In the corner Dan Fluherty roused himself and joined in the conversation.

'I have a statement already prepared for release tomorrow, late afternoon. We can discuss a full press briefing in the morning.'

'Fine by me,' agreed Walters.

'About tomorrow's arrangements, specifically our meeting with the Chinese delegation; just where is this villa? I heard it was way out in the boonies.'

'Not quite – but it is up near the border. The New China News Agency made the arrangements. They own the villa. Should be OK; they always know exactly what they're doing.'

Nodding agreeably, William Fredericks tugged at his belt and crossed back to the easy chair he had occupied previously. At sixty-three his sagging shape made any shirt seem rumpled.

'I hope you arranged an alternative programme for Mrs Fredericks. Not just the usual shopping.'

'Certainly, sir. I believe my wife, Mary, has set up a visit to the Jockey Club's riding-for-the-disabled facility in Pokfulam. That's on the south of the island. They're doing some wonderful things out there.'

Once more Fredericks indicated his approval, nodding his great balding head. He knew how much his wife enjoyed spending time with sick and disabled children. It was not generally known that one of their own grandchildren suffered from cerebral palsy. With an effort he forced his mind back to the other preparations.

'So what do your people say about tomorrow, Bob? Do we anticipate any problems at all?'

The Consul-General – who after much discussion between Cinch and Prioletti had not been informed of the Hong Kong Special Branch's updated threat assessment – smiled confidently.

'Smooth as silk, Mr Secretary. Provided the rain lets up by morning, it should be an excellent day.'

* * *

Ruth Tavistock knew from the fuzziness of the printed page before her eyes that she needed a break. She had read the same paragraph three times in the past five minutes and had still failed to grasp its meaning. There was a faint stabbing pain behind her left eye. Then, as she turned back the page to make one last attempt, the quiet of the room was broken by the urgent ring of the phone on a bureau by the main window.

She answered it cautiously, giving her number but nothing more. That was Special Branch training. After ten seconds of silence during which she thought *Christ, not again!* the line went dead and she lowered the instrument back on to its cradle. Wondering.

Once more the suspicion began to grow. It was the fourth silent call she had received in as many days. Wrong numbers were common enough in Hong Kong's over-wired, over-capacity phone network; usually you would hear a stream of Cantonese followed by a hurried apology before the line went dead. But these calls were somehow different: the definite sense of someone listening in silence at the other end – a malevolent presence waiting in the shadows. It occurred to her to request the technical guys to put a trace on the line, but she rejected the thought of such an invasion of her privacy almost immediately. What would she do if it turned out to be Jack Cinch? How would she explain that to them? She resolved to get a change of number – less fuss all around – and wandered back to the table.

Even as she sat down again, she knew it would be no good now. Her concentration was gone, and the pain behind her eye was spreading to her left temple. Gazing across scattered papers and news magazines strewn across the desk surface, she closed the briefing folder, stretched, and pushed herself up again from the table. She had read as much as she could take for one night.

It was just after midnight when she stepped out through the sliding patio doors on to the balcony of her

Mid-Levels apartment, and looked out across the harbour towards the lights of Kowloon. It was a view she never tired of. The air was cooler now that the rain had come, and the fragrance of dense foliage on the slopes below rose up to bring with it the welcome breath of frangipani.

The stepped layers of roadway spread away beneath her with intermittent dark patches of greenery sprouting on the slopes between levels. Pale concrete lined up in rows to face the harbour, as in some ancient Roman amphitheatre. Down on Kennedy Road an occasional public light bus buzzed back and forth, engine straining, gears grinding, bringing Filipino maids home late from their one night off. Up here in Mid-Levels the coming and going of traffic, and the spill of noise from a late dinner party on the twentieth floor, were the only sounds to be heard, but down on the waterfront the clamour and bustle would continue all night.

She rubbed her eyelids and blinked, the beauty of the scene a balm to her eyes. Beyond the rising slab of the Connaught Building, the blackness of the harbour was lit in places by the intense reds and golds of advertising hoardings over on Kowloon side. A sudden fast-moving light in the distance caught her attention, as an aircraft, probably the last of the evening, charged down the narrow strip of concrete jutting far into the bay and was airborne, turning hard in a wide arc over the island. She wondered how many others were looking down into the harbour at this moment. Would Jack Cinch be on his balcony on Robinson Road, savouring a glass of Jack Daniels and ice before turning in? What did she care anyway, she chided herself. That particular episode was now behind her.

The roar of the aircraft passing directly overhead turned her thoughts to Becker's absence. There were bound to be questions when he returned. Umbrellas would go up. Someone on the fifth floor was bound to ask why he had gone to Japan just two days before the VIP arrived. Then they would need to be shown, or at least be told about, the coded telex received by Special Branch Information Centre. That had originated in the Ginza Headquarters of the National Police Agency and was bounced in via the earth station near Stanley Fort on the south of Hong Kong Island. Recognising immediately its importance, the duty controller had brought it straight to St John-Black's office. In short order, Stephen Lee, Brian Evans and Ruth herself had then been summoned to hear the text.

At that point Stephen Lee had requested and been given permission to involve other support units. It could not wait any longer: he needed now to disseminate information on the threat to the US Secretary of State. This immediately involved the Airport Security Unit, Staff Officer Counter Terrorism, and the Special Duties Unit which was currently under the command of Mel Kale.

Then it had been Ruth's turn. Using what Becker had discovered about the composition of Okamoto's party and their approximate date of arrival, she had set up an immediate check on immigration records of Japanese arrivals. They had concentrated their efforts on arrivals in the last week of August. After this a force of over fifty detectives had been mobilised to follow up generated leads, checking all the addresses given on arrival cards. Now it had to be just a matter of time. Almost certainly Okamoto's team would have given false addresses and would now be lying up in a safe-house provided by the Chiu Chau group who, in Becker's words, had sponsored the visit. Many hundreds of man-hours would now be spent in the search, and the most the authorities could expect from the exercise was the elimination of the innocent and the eventual discovery of the false passport names being used by the suspects. Still, they had to follow procedures – however remote the possibility of success. The problem was that, in that one week alone, over 3700 male Japanese visitors had passed through Kai Tak's arrivals hall and dispersed throughout the city.

Ruth took no part herself in this search operation: it was pure routine. What concerned her now was the Director of Special Branch's final instruction. They had certain details and other vague warnings, but what they still lacked were clues to the motive behind the threatened action. That was where St John-Black had felt Ruth's particular skills might best be employed. Her knowledge of the ideology of the Japan Red Army was as thorough as anyone's in the territory, but even she had to admit she could not connect any of what she knew about the terrorist group with the claims of Chan Ming – or with the facts Becker had recently turned up in Tokyo.

In the late afternoon she had taken a brief walk around the Botanical Gardens, hardly noticing the squeals of Chinese children, not even seeing the monkeys and bears in their cages nestling amongst the richly-flowered rhododendrons. Oblivious to her surroundings Ruth's mind was seething with possibilities, wrestling in particular with the political implications of Fredericks' meeting with the Foreign Minister of the People's Republic.

Returning to her office she had opened up the Special Branch reference section and begun poring over news magazines for clues. She was a great believer in the iceberg theory – that no matter how deeply buried the stratagem might lie, there were always indicators which showed above the surface: the tip of the iceberg. The trick lay in correctly estimating the true extent of the iceberg lying submerged beneath a sea of disinformation and deception. It was this process that the political analyst relished most of all.

She worked feverishly, extracting anything containing coverage of US Foreign Policy in the Far East. When she had finished, the heavy stack of paper fitted awkwardly under one arm. Arriving home, she brewed up a large pot of coffee and set to work.

By midnight she had penned eighteen pages of notes in her bold, distinctive handwriting. The information she had gleaned was drawn mainly from the region's two most influential news publications, *Asiaweek* and the *Far Eastern Economic Review*, with some additional material from a British magazine, *The Economist*. American concern seemed focused on two main issues: import restrictions levied by the Japanese Government which restricted the access of US goods, and the future of the US Seventh Fleet. The first subject seemed to lie outside Hong Kong concern, but the second was of far greater topical interest. There had been much speculation over the future relocation of a small portion of the American military presence to the island of Singapore, where that government was eager to access the vast spending power of the Defense Department. But Singapore alone was far too small to support the size of operation the US had previously enjoyed in Subic Bay. They would need to secure other berthing facilities – and Hong Kong had always provided a friendly welcome for the US Navy.

Ruth knew of the rumours that after 1997 China was to be offered massive payments to allow the development of existing facilities in Hong Kong: at HMS *Tamar*, the Royal Navy base, together with Stonecutter's Island to the west of Kowloon peninsula. And the secret talks scheduled for Tuesday of that week suggested this was now well past the rumour stage. The very fact that their Foreign Minister had agreed to attend at all showed the advanced state of the negotiations.

Ruth had then asked herself an important question: how did all this affect the balance of power in the Pacific?

Thus far, the Soviet Union had lined up with Vietnam to secure for its submarines and warships a legitimate patrol route in the South China Sea and also a sizeable

507

base from which to threaten Japanese oil-supply routes. The US, Japan and an ever more powerful South Korea were the new triad which sought to keep a lid on communist expansion in that theatre. China, as always, went her own way, with a nod towards cooperation with the USA in the field of electronic surveillance of the Soviet mainland.

If Sino-American cooperation in the military sphere were stepped up, she asked herself, how would the Vietnamese react to this new pressure? How far would they go to prevent such an alliance?

These were interesting questions, but where did they get her on the Japan Red Army threat? Not very far, she had to admit.

She knew for a fact that the Vietnamese maintained a very warm relationship with the Marxist-Leninist government of North Korea. And there was ample reason to believe that the Japan Red Army had carried out bombings and assassinations on orders originating inside the Pyongyang government.

That begged the further, more puzzling question: why was a Chiu Chau triad group involved in all this? Could they be forging some sort of alliance? If so, where was the advantage to be gained for their criminal empire? In the past they had always reviled all forms of communism.

She was still debating these questions when there was a ring at the door. When she peered through the fish-eye lens, she could see a man wearing a Hawaiian shirt and blue jeans. It was Jack Cinch.

'It's late, Jack,' she said, after opening the door. 'I was about to go to bed.'

'I know it's late,' he replied, clearly agitated, 'but I must talk to you right now. No funny stuff. Strictly business. Can I come inside?'

Ruth stepped aside to let him in. She closed the door, feeling distinctly uncomfortable about his presence. Involuntarily she folded her arms as she waited for his explanation. Her body language was deafening.

Cinch paced the room for several uncomfortable seconds, working himself up to what he wanted to say.

'It's about the Secretary and this Okamoto thing. There are a few things you ought to know.'

He examined her face for a reaction, but found none. She gazed at him like a parent indulging a child despite obvious irritation at its behaviour.

'Explain.' It was a directive – not a request.

'I couldn't say anything before – hell, I was sworn to secrecy – but you were right when you guessed Reicher wasn't regular State Department. He was in fact a CIA officer, East Asia Division, Operations Directorate. They sent him here thinking he was clean. They claimed he had the specific job of setting up a sting against local passport fraud, but that was just the cover for a much more ambitious intelligence operation.' Cinch broke off his narrative and appealed directly to her. 'Will you not keep looking at me that way?'

'What way is that?'

'Like I shit in your swimming pool or something. Jesus, I'm doing my best to be honest with you.'

'If by that you mean you wish to cooperate with us finally – then proceed. I'm listening.'

As she folded her arms tighter he saw the bitterness that still remained between them. He turned and stepped out on to the balcony and leaned upon the sliding door. Ruth walked after him, following his gaze into the distance. She too decided it was better to look out into the night, at the lights of Kowloon, than at one another. Cinch rubbed his neck awkwardly, collected himself and tried again.

'It was a very sophisticated operation – best I've seen in all my time in the Far East. Right from the start I was told to take on Reicher but let him do his own thing. Even the C-G knew nothing of his real purpose.'

'I'd always thought State Department cover was

taboo. It jeopardises the status of legitimate diplomats.'

'That's right. Fredericks would have broken anyone who even suggested it. CIA get no favours with us. Mutual recriminations run deep, based on the well-known frosty relationship between Bill Fredericks and Phil Kagan. No, this was strictly between Prioletti and myself. It was extremely sensitive, and dangerous for their man Reicher. Prioletti came to me and said they were targeting a local Chinese group which had in the past done work for Vietnamese intelligence.'

Ruth slid past him to lean nonchalantly against the balcony rail. 'What kind of work?'

'You name it. Anything from baby-sitting intelligence officers to forcing their heroin crop through the distribution machine. It's a Chiu Chau connection. Viet intelligence people use heroin to finance expensive operations which can't get government funding. The Chiu Chaus are into that for a big percentage.'

'What kind of operation was Prioletti really running?'

'Disinformation.'

'If the Chiu Chaus were just conduits, then who was the real target?'

'The Vietnamese, of course. The signal Prioletti wanted to send to their politicians was one which would scare their pants off. Enough so they'd put a halt to what the Vietnamese military were up to in the Spratly Islands: attempted resumption of lost territory.'

'The sovereignty dispute ...' said Ruth for her own benefit. She had read about it in passing, had come across it more than once in her recent research that evening. 'China and Vietnam have threatened to go to war over those islands, and the situation becomes increasingly dangerous the closer the Viets come to landing survey crews there. What else do you know?'

'Only what I've just told you. Reicher was friendly with this girl, Ruby Tang – probably his contact. She called him once or twice at the office. Quite a looker by all accounts, and up to her ass in local triads. He played it like an extramarital affair, but there was much more to it than that. When they found him down there in Yaumatei' – Cinch nodded in the direction of Kowloon and grimaced, as if talking of some alien and barbaric world – 'there came an immediate directive from Langley to effect damage limitation.'

'They were worried?'

'Scared to death is how I judged it. I was told to plead ignorance. That wasn't difficult. Truthfully I don't really know that much. I don't have the first idea what Reicher was passing to them, but according to Prioletti it was … provocative.'

Overhead the clouds played hide-and-seek across the moon, and Ruth studied their movements: black silk scarves obscuring a magician's silver ball. Now you see it – now you don't. Prioletti liked to play those games too, she thought. Was Jack Cinch yet another silk scarf, preserving the illusion?

'So why have you come to me now? What am I supposed to do with your confession? If I use it at the office, it's bound to be raised with the Foreign and Commonwealth Office. Trespassing in our back yard. Official complaints. Kiss your career goodbye.'

He thought about that a long time before he answered.

'That doesn't matter now. What Prioletti is doing could jeopardise the safety of the Secretary of State. I believe this Okamoto threat stems from the Vietnamese perception of the old man's purpose in visiting Hong Kong. I think they know about the meeting with the Chinese Foreign Minister. Prioletti is the bastard who's manipulating that perception and he doesn't give a damn about the personal danger to Bill Fredericks. This isn't espionage – this is political in-fighting between Kagan and Kazinski on the one hand, and William Fredericks on the other.'

Suddenly two and two were making more than Ruth thought possible. Suddenly it was not North Korea but Vietnam in the driving seat. But she would need time to check Cinch's claims before laying anything before the DSB. This was political dynamite that could cause a massive rift between the intelligence organisations in the Colony.

'Don't get me wrong, Jack. I've no reason to disbelieve you, but do you have any proof to back up any of these allegations?'

He shook his head, moving back from the shadow of the balcony, and a spill of light from the room splashed over his cheeks.

'You know I don't. Even if I did, I'm not sure I'd supply it. I just wanted to tip your guys a warning. Do what you can to hamstring Prioletti's plan before he gets somebody else killed. That somebody I think may be Bill Fredericks.'

For Ruth the one outstanding question was of a personal dimension. Unable to withhold it any longer, she asked it now.

'So why did you go along with this, Jack? You always said you distrusted the Company. When Reicher was murdered, you could have blown it there and then.'

'Ruth,' Cinch spoke quietly but forcefully, though still unable to look at her directly. 'Prioletti is the worst kind of bastard. He needed a favour badly and he had the leverage to get it.'

'I don't understand. What leverage?'

'Can't you guess?' said Cinch, his face alive with guilt beneath the pale moon. 'He knew about us, for Chrissake! He threatened to use our relationship to get me sent home – maybe even investigated. Do you know what a full CIA investigation of a government officer is like? If he'd really wanted to, he could have easily gotten me two years in a Federal penitentiary for the papers I've passed to you. It's all contrary to good security practice. They would have twisted everything.'

It was all too fast for Ruth to take it in. She needed time to consider things. Was she really the reason he had been forced to go along with Prioletti's operation? Or was that just another clever excuse? God knows, anyone operating in the security field was well versed in half-truths and false legends.

'For God's sake, say something!' urged Cinch, a note of desperation creeping into his voice. 'Don't just stand there staring. Give me something.'

'Like what, for instance?'

'Say you believe me – that would be a start. That now you *understand* the way things were; the way they are. I can't go to my bosses, now that I'm in it with Prioletti up to my neck.'

'I don't know, Jack,' she said coolly. 'I don't know what I believe any more. Not that all that matters anyway. Anything we had going between us is over. What's important now is the safety of your precious Secretary of State.'

Just then the rain falling beyond the balcony ceased abruptly, leaving only the sound of cicadas chirping in the islands of green vegetation below.

'Listen, I just . . .' he started to say.

Suddenly Ruth found his presence a threat. She turned to walk back inside, but as she passed him he caught her elbow and pulled her close, the steely blue eyes imploring. She did not struggle, instead setting her face in a cold, flat stare. In the end he released her arm, and just stood there hugging himself.

'I think it's time you left, don't you?' she said, moving inside, rubbing her arm where his hand had gripped her. 'From now until Fredericks boards that aircraft the days are going to be long and scary. It's late and I suggest you get some sleep now – while you can.'

'What are you going to do – about Prioletti, I mean?'

She had no clear idea yet. Even so she said: 'There'll

be a full Special Branch investigation into the circumstances of the Reicher killing. I don't think the homicide people have made much progress, but that's understandable in view of what you've just told me.' Then she added, quite maliciously, 'Don't worry about your career. I'll see that your name stays out of it. I'll cite another source.'

Cinch's mind was in a whirl, his emotions a pained mixture of hurt and resentment. Anger hovered in there, close to the point where he could no longer trust his tongue. He turned on his heel and strode for the door. In another moment he was gone.

As she heard the click of the door closing, then the sound of the elevator descending, she felt a shiver run through her. That she could have acted so coldly was for her a revelation, and the proof she had needed that she was now free of him. She drew strength from that.

She put on a fresh pot of coffee, and took a pad and pencil from the drawer. Then, while she waited for the coffee to brew, she began to note down everything that Cinch had said.

As Jack Cinch pulled out of St Joan's Court and back on to Macdonell Road, he barely noticed the taxi parked beside the kerb, its roof light gently glowing in the darkness. Or the driver sitting hunched across the steering-wheel, staring blankly up at the lights of Ruth Tavistock's apartment.

Minutes earlier, the same taxi-driver had been gripping the wheel in a state of near frenzy, palms in a cold sweat. But now the rain had ceased and with it 'the voices' that drove him. For tonight at least, he decided, no one need die. In Gwan-Dai's name.

514

BOOK THREE
RED MANSION

NINETEEN

Okamoto's team moved off from the Yaumatei apartment at 05.00 hours in a single white microvan obtained through Red Cudgel's auspices, heading south along Nathan Road, the spinal column of the Kowloon peninsula, and down through the cluttered shop-fronts of Tsim Sha Tsui. In that feeble first light they moved quickly through the near deserted streets, with headlights still burning – though not so quickly as to draw undue attention to themselves. A safe thirty-five miles per hour – that was the briefing. Then one unexpected flash of adrenalin when a police transit roared alongside and passed without interest; it was bringing the first boxes of *dim sum* breakfast back to Tsim Sha Tsui station for the nightshift constables, and to them that was much more interesting.

Where Nathan Road reached the harbour front and Hong Kong Island loomed in the mist beyond, they turned hard left on to Salisbury Road, then threw a sharp U-turn beside the imposing ramped entrance to the Regent Hotel. The Regent's circular driveway was always an impressive sight, more so now in this half-light, with a thousand tiny white lights burning elegantly amongst the bushes. Lines of sportscars and limousines thronged the roadside. To the left, the New World Centre stood in almost total darkness; only a few lights showed where cleaners were busily dusting ivory carvings in opulent showrooms. To the right, the Tsim Sha Tsui harbour front, rendered incongruously modern by the

517

moonscape architecture of the Space Museum and the Hong Kong Cultural Centre, spread out calm, majestic, and utterly deserted.

Turning back upon itself, the microvan moved a few yards along Salisbury Road in the direction of the Star Ferry pier, before cutting into a short access road to the left. Here, between the Regent Hotel and the huge, pale concrete dome of the Planetarium, there loomed another futuristic structure, its twin white barrels rising some sixty feet above the ground. It was a building which generally went unnoticed by tourists – not many Hong Kong residents even knew it was there, and those who did often guessed it to be merely some adjunct to the Space Museum complex. In fact it was the northern ventilator building: one of the structures which kept the many kilometres of tunnels of the MTR underground railway system supplied with fresh air. Specifically, this was one of two ventilation buildings located at either end of the MTR tunnel section where it ran beneath the waters of the harbour.

At the end of the access road the white microvan came to a sudden halt. At once both the front doors sprang open, and abruptly eight men climbed down, slid open the side door, and busied themselves pulling canvas holdalls from the belly of the vehicle. Looking quickly around him, the eighth man wrapped a white dustsheet around the plastic mannequin, and wedged it beneath his arm. All eight were wearing orange overalls and orange helmets stamped with the logo of the Mass Transit Railway Corporation.

Another quick look around him, and Okamoto slid the door closed, banging twice on the side as a signal before the microvan moved off again. Going well, he thought; no one around – just as he had expected. Not even a stroller on the waterfront causeway skirting the New World Centre. Traffic was beginning to move now, but that presented no problem: not now they were safely arrived at the MTR site. Here, only the balconies of the Regent's VIP suites overlooked them, and those appeared deserted for the present. Okamoto gazed up at the tiers of tinted glass and sneered: the rich and famous were obviously still sleeping off their champagne hangovers.

Five steps to the top of the access staircase, and the Japanese could hear the hum of machinery behind the steel door guarding the concrete structure. It was secured by a heavy mortice lock, and would have needed a sledgehammer to open it, maybe even a drill, were it not for their good friend Station-Master Cheung, who so dearly wished to see his little daughter again. Transferring the single leather case containing the sword to his left hand, he extracted the first of the keys from the pocket of his overalls. It fitted snugly into the lock and the door swung open, sweet and clean as sugarcane. Wasting no time he urged them all inside, and eight seconds later the outer door was locked up tight behind them, leaving no outward sign of their presence.

Inside the ventilation tower, Okamoto ran a hand along the rough concrete of the wall until he found a brass light switch and flicked it on. Next he spoke quickly into a small but powerful radio clipped to the breast pocket of his overalls.

'Inside now. Door locked.' He kept it short, speaking in his native Japanese to confound anyone who might be listening on that frequency. He had researched the job thoroughly enough to know that VHF radios were illegal in Hong Kong without a licence issued by the Postmaster General; he also knew that to enforce this law, government communications engineers constantly monitored the frequencies to try and catch illegal transmissions. There was an outside chance that one of them might pick him up, but for the short time needed to communicate with his controller this risk was acceptable.

A disembodied voice spoke back from the handset,

echoing within the chimney of the ventilation building.

'Transmission received. Proceed to the next level.'

The crackling response came back from a tenth-floor suite of the Hyatt Regency Hotel where Rhee, posing as a senior marketing executive with a South Korean firm pushing red ginseng into Hong Kong's lucrative herbal medicine market, had taken a room the previous night. He was standing beside the main window of a suite which looked down into Nathan Road, so the radio reception was near perfect. True, Rhee could not quite see the ventilation building itself, just five hundred metres south of his position, but that did not worry him. Both experience and training had taught him that a good control position was much more important. He had asked for a room that looked down directly into Nathan Road, not because he enjoyed the sight of milling crowds of tourists intent on blowing their life savings, but because he needed sight of the street-level entrances into the MTR system. That was where the action would be later. After the authorities realised what had happened.

With his communications to the San Yee On augmented by his own portable cellular phone and the telex machines available within the hotel, he had all the control he needed to play his part in the coming operation.

Okamoto turned off his radio to conserve battery power, and ordered two of his men to check the upper floors of the ventilation building, where the hoisting gear and the electrical control relays for the air-conditioning plant were situated. Normally the building was not manned unless there was specific work in progress or some fault had been reported, but he knew it wasn't worth taking any chances. The two men came back a few minutes later to confirm what he had expected: no work in progress, apart from themselves, the building was empty.

Okamoto's next move was to locate the staircase

which wound down three flights beneath their feet, terminating in a narrow landing stage. Thus far the diagrams drawn by Station-Master Cheung had proved amazingly accurate. Cheung had not been able to acquire architects' charts from the engineering section in the Kowloon Bay headquarters for fear of detection, but the drawings he had made were more than adequate. His little girl need not now lose any of her tiny fingers.

From those diagrams Okamoto knew that on either side of the landing stage, some twenty-five metres below ground level, there would be a locked steel door. The door he was interested in lay on the right side, and led directly on to the down track: the one heading south towards Hong Kong Island.

'Wait here,' he ordered, and slipped quietly down the staircase. In the dark his fingers scrabbled against damp concrete walls before finding another light switch. This time he slipped the second key into the door, and the lock was easily defeated. The instant it clicked open, he felt a first cold blast surge past the door and whip his face like the breath of a dragon. The Japanese grinned as he realised this was only the piston effect of a train surging through the tunnel, pushing a column of air before it. Then he became aware of distant thunder and a rise of the pressure within his ears. His eyes grew wide with sudden childish excitement.

'The dragon runs,' he whispered aloud, for no one's benefit but his own. 'I must feel the wind as the beast passes by!'

Frantically his fingers scratched at the wall to extinguish the light, then he swung the metal door inward and scrambled out on to the final stairway. The steps leading down to the parapet were in total darkness but he knew he dared not operate the torch hanging at his belt; dared not risk the driver seeing him now and reporting an unauthorised presence. Instead he stayed at the top of the stairs, using the door as a shield against the powerful air current. He was just ten steps away from the parapet below him, and twelve feet above the track.

The dragon's howl rose like the scream of dead spirits in children's games.

He saw the twin spot beams loom ghostly yellow from out of the darkness of the tunnel and heard the whistle of the air blast. The noise of the wheel bogies thundered inside his head. For brief seconds the grey, arched back of the tunnel was lit up with a brilliant light. The beams illuminated the almost biological structure of the tunnel: the overhead strings of power cables, each carrying fifteen hundred volts; the banks of impulse fans; the thick skeins of supply cabling on the far wall. Even with both hands clamped over his ears, balanced on the stairs just twelve feet from the passing train, Okamoto could hear the high roar change pitch as the monster passed. The lights from the coaches strobed wildly across his face and beneath his feet the concrete vibrated in time with the stampeding wheels. Wind buffeted his face, driving him back further against the wall – then sucked him forward again as the train passed on into the depths of the Immersed Tube.

He counted the carriages, knowing there would be eight – there were always eight. Eight coaches, each twenty-two and a half metres in length, making 180 metres in total. The overall stopping distance at this speed, according to Cheung, was approximately sixty to eighty metres, depending upon the driver's reactions. When the last coach had rattled past, and was ticking away into the distance, he had leaned out to watch the red tail-lights recede; realising now why Hong Kong people called these trains 'dragons', for that was indeed what it had resembled: a great metal-jacketed dragon. A long, armoured-steel body snaking its way through the narrow passages. Returning to its lair.

Pulse racing from this first sight of his quarry, Okamoto took a moment to gather his breath, then clicked on the beam of his magnalite torch and began pacing off the stopping distance along the parapet.

William Fredericks, never a fan of the power breakfast, had refused two such invitations that morning. Instead he ate fresh croissants in his room, sitting opposite his wife and poring over the Singapore edition of the *International Herald Tribune*. Later, after showering and dressing, he called Fluherty and told him to inform the Hong Kong people that he was ready to begin the day's programme. At 10 a.m. sharp the special armoured Special Branch vehicle swung into position outside the glass doors of the hotel's main entrance and Fredericks stepped inside. He was attended by Mrs Fredericks and Dan Fluherty, who was already feeding his boss biography notes on Sir Andrew Mackie for their courtesy call at Government House.

Taking the little-used route out through the multi-storey car park behind the Hilton, Stephen Lee directed the motorcade through the restricted access tunnel, to pass under Garden Road into the Murray Road car park and out on to Cotton Tree Drive. It was the shortest and perhaps least expected route for them to take, and only those persons with keys to the two barriers could use it. The alternative was a more circuitous and potentially dangerous manoeuvre right through the logjam of traffic on Queen's Road and Connaught Road, both of which had current works in progress.

The meeting at Government House lasted slightly under ninety minutes, but to Stephen Lee and the Special Branch bodyguards shadowing the VIP's movements it seemed to drag on for several hours. With security men thronging the flowerbeds, the two elderly men rambled through the manicured gardens as if out on a summer stroll together. Totally oblivious to any real or perceived threat, Sir Andrew continued to inspect the azaleas and to appraise the Secretary of State of the

British view – in particular the future projected for Hong Kong as a Special Administrative Region of the People's Republic. As if anyone really cared any more about the British view on that.

The American security party appeared no more at ease with the situation than did Stephen Lee. Keeping close behind the VIP, Lee watched Lassiter and Divine nervously scan the perimeter wall and the dozens of commercial high-rises overlooking the Government mansion.

'Those Jap bastards could be up in any one of those buildings,' murmured John Divine, 'and we'd never even know where the shots came from.'

Tom Lassiter gave him a long hard look of annoyance and turned away.

'Take that one up there,' continued Divine undaunted, indicating the impressive steel and glass wall of the Hong Kong Bank rearing up above the purple rhododendrons. 'I mean, what's to say they aren't up there now?'

For a moment Lassiter seemed to consider this, studying the radical design and solar-efficient construction of the building, which provided a stunning backdrop as well as contrast to the old colonial style of the mansion itself. Then he turned to Divine and, with an intense look of concentration, spoke.

'John, shut the fuck up.'

After the two men had concluded their meanderings through the shrubbery, they went back inside. Fifteen minutes later Fredericks made his farewells on the steps of GH, and heaved his weight back into the long, bullet-proof limousine for the short drive back down Garden Road to the US Consulate-General. With three SB escort vehicles, two motorcycle outriders, and two more cars from SY security, the extended convoy made an interesting sight as it slowed to negotiate the tight turn into the Consulate's covered vehicle compound. Stephen Lee's stomach remained knotted until the motorised gates had closed behind the last car and Fredericks was safe inside the chancery building.

The schedule had Fredericks in conference with the Consul-General and various political counsellors for the next two hours. Lee assumed that he was also being advised by the local CIA station chief on how to approach the negotiations that afternoon. But all Lee really cared about, observing the guarded entrance manned by a marine NCO in full dress uniform, was that here at least the principal was safe. They needed to switch off the metal detectors installed in the main doorway as the Special Branch came through. Pacing their well-practised open V formation, the SB close protection team followed the Secretary of State inside, pausing only a second or so while the marine guard inside an observation booth of bulletproof glass operated remotely the pneumatic lock on the glass inner door leading to the senior admin. grade offices beyond.

Satisfied with arrangements inside the building, Lee then left three men on the corridor outside the meeting-room, and returned to the vehicle compound to position the remainder of his men. Located strategically around the building, the constables swept their arcs of observation with thoroughness and precision, closely monitoring the line of applicants queuing outside the immigration window within the compound, as well as the passers-by on the pavement beyond. Every one of his men was aware of the exact nature of the threat; Lee had spelled it out that morning in no uncertain terms, and he was gratified that he had not so far needed to remind any of them about standards of vigilance. The drivers had already turned their vehicles around for the departure phase, and were now busily checking their radios.

It was here that Jack Cinch put in his first appearance,

approaching Stephen Lee in the compound. He was accompanied by Tom Lassiter.

'So far so good,' he observed, greeting the Special Branch man with outstretched hand.

'So far,' agreed Stephen Lee. 'But not a very auspicious start to the day. One of my guys was hit by a motorcycle on his way into work.'

'Is he OK?'

'Yes, thank God. Just a broken ankle, nothing more. But I had to bring in a reserve to cover for him.'

'So nothing's spoiled then,' observed Cinch. 'Everything still running as smooth as silk?'

Stephen Lee gave a small grimace.

'I'm still not happy with the speed of the motorcade. It's too vulnerable. This time when we move out, I'm going to have it stepped up.'

At this Cinch frowned, stroking his throat speculatively.

'That could pose a problem. We're picking up extra advisers here, and translators too. That means three extra cars in the motorcade. It's hard enough just keeping those five cars together. If you pick it up now, you'll lose them all at the first stop light.'

'I can't help that,' said Lee unswayed. 'Keeping the VIP's limousine sandwiched between my two escort vehicles is all I'm interested in. The rest is just protocol bullshit.'

'That's the way I make it, too,' put in Tom Lassiter, siding with Special Branch on the matter. 'Steve's first priority has to be the old man.'

Though he had said nothing to Cinch as yet, Lassiter still wasn't happy with the other's explanation over the Reicher killing. That dissatisfaction showed itself now in Lassiter's taking every opportunity of disagreeing with Cinch's decisions.

Cinch looked from one man to the other in silent rebuke, sensing the hostility on either side.

'All right, have it your way. I'll pass it on right away.

Suppose I have the remainder of the party leave early, since they're going up by road?'

'That would be better all around,' conceded the Chinese. 'One more thing. When we get to the MTR station in Tsuen Wan, there's quite a distance to walk to the train. That's a danger period. I'll have two concentric layers of armed officers surrounding the man while he's walking, but if you could get the State Department security guys to throw a third ring outside of us, that would help to screen the Secretary from view.'

'You got it,' said Lassiter, grinning.

'You're sure this Okamoto Cell is real?' asked Cinch.

'They're out there all right,' responded Lee. 'Only thing is we've no idea where.'

'Or why they're so interested in William Fredericks,' added Lassiter pointedly. 'Perhaps you have a few ideas on that, Jack?'

'You got me,' shrugged Cinch, wishing a moment later he hadn't said it – seeing Lassiter's satisfaction at that telling little phrase. He studied his watch and turned towards the glass doors leading back inside the chancery. 'Guess I'll go get things moving now. I'm going to ride up to Tsuen Wan with the other group. If I don't see you guys before then, I'll see you on the train.'

Fredericks remained in discussion at the US Consulate-General until breaking for lunch in the basement commissary. Being something of a man of the people, the Secretary of State liked to mingle with his staff and to share at first hand their working conditions. Shortly before lunch concluded, Stephen Lee was approached by Dan Fluherty with a message that Fredericks would depart shortly for the helipad. That was his cue to relay a warning via Special Branch control to the second party, which was waiting at the landing site just outside Tsuen Wan.

The chopper's blades were rotating idly when they

arrived at a private helipad on the waterfront loaned by a pro-US Chinese property tycoon. Owing to restrictions of space, there was room enough for only two bodyguards inside the helicopter, and these seats were taken by Stephen Lee and Tom Lassiter. The other passengers were Fluherty and a few strategy advisers. By the time they arrived in Tsuen Wan there were two mobile escort teams waiting at the landing zone, ready to blaze a trail out to Fung Chik Sin.

All through that drive along the Castle Peak Road, Stephen Lee felt the sweat breaking across his shoulder-blades. The convoy was well armoured and well prepared, but once again it seemed to move far too slowly for his liking. Realising that in this anxious state his perception of time was unreliable, he concentrated instead on the road ahead and the stream of communications coming through his earpiece. As if waiting for the sudden deafening explosion and the madness to begin...

Their time at the villa was like time spent in some dream. It was a run-down Sixties-style villa with a balcony on the main upper floor, overlooking the Castle Peak Road, and servants' quarters on the ground floor. Around the house banana palms and young bamboo grew side-by-side in dense clumps, and from out of this tangle of green came the hum and chirp of many insects. For the security officers each strange sound served only to jangle their strained nerves still further.

After the main party had disappeared inside the house, Lee and his men stood outside in small groups, watching the road, the water to the front and the hillside to the rear. In sharp contrast the Chinese security men from across the border – eight serious-looking young men in utilitarian grey lounge suits – smoked continuously and fixed their gaze upon the men from Special Branch. It seemed as if they at least realised nothing would happen here: that this small piece of Hong Kong was guaranteed safety by the full might of the People's Republic.

And nothing did.

Two hours later Stephen Lee breathed a sigh of relief when signs of movement indicated that the meeting was at an end. He was anxious now to get out of the open: to make the cover of the MTR station as soon as possible.

In central Tsuen Wan local uniformed police had the approach to the underground station well wired. There were steel Mills barriers cordoning off every access point, and Delta Company of PTU were performing crowd control duty in and around the MTR station itself. With green uniforms and top brass everywhere, the atmosphere was charged with a kind of tension not often experienced here in out-of-the-way New Territories.

Then, as the crowds of onlookers already lured by the blue lights and uniforms jostled for sight of the VIP, his slightly overstuffed figure strode away from the stationary motorcade and past the crowd of eager onlookers, then through the great ceramic-tiled concourse and down into the station. All the while Lee's men, immaculately dressed in well-cut lounge suits and understated neckties, maintained the strict geometry of their defensive positions – a two-layer cocoon holding firm against any unauthorised attempt to approach the principal. Eyes shaded by sunglasses against the sun's glare reflecting from concrete structures all around, the Chinese officers watched rooftops and nearby cars, and most of all the hands of people in the crowd.

There were six Special Branch men in suits and four uniform police waiting down on the platform as the procession approached and boarded the train. The whole station had been cleared just prior to the Secretary of State's arrival and there was a senior public relations official and a photographer from the MTR already waiting beside the stationary train to greet Fredericks aboard. In his customary style Fredericks first congratulated the MTR official on the smart appearance of the silver carriages, then his VIP party moved straight into the second car. As the doors closed with a pneumatic hiss, the security men retreated to the third car, enabling Fredericks to speak privately with his aides.

'Like I said before,' murmured Fredericks to Fluherty, 'goddamned waste of time. If I've studied one book on comprehending the Asian mind, I've studied a dozen, and it still doesn't get me any further in understanding these people.'

'Nevertheless, sir,' enthused Fluherty, 'at least we're talking to them. Like it or not you have to maintain a dialogue.'

Fredericks sighed, bored by all the rhetoric, and wishing now merely to return to the security of the hotel and the company of his wife. She was one of the few people he actually trusted to give him an unbiased view of events.

In the driver's cab at the head of the train, operator Suen Sai-kit saw the lights of Tsim Sha Tsui station glowing dimly in the far distance, and he eased back his speed to a comfortable fifty kilometres an hour. Between stations he could easily make eighty, but when approaching stations thirty was the order of the day – if he intended stopping. True, this special non-stopping train had clearance to make top speed back towards Chater station on the Island, but he was taking no chances. He wanted ample time to hit the brakes if the unthinkable happened.

For Suen Sai-kit the unthinkable had nothing much to do with William Fredericks, a man he knew almost nothing about. His caution was entirely personal. In the preceding month there had been two suicides on the City line: both young Chinese women, and both also pregnant. They had hurled themselves from the platform into the path of oncoming trains, deliberately avoiding the suicide pit between the rails, and equally deliberately stretching themselves across them, so their heads and feet had been snapped off like breadsticks. Operator Suen shuddered as he remembered the stories that circulated around the maintenance yards out at Kowloon Bay. The operators involved had been badly shaken: one of them refusing to drive again; the other becoming anxious and withdrawn – seldom speaking to his workmates. Suen had promised himself to keep his speeds down in future. At fifty kilometres he would have some chance to react in time.

The train passed through the momentary glare of Tsim Sha Tsui station, and thundered on into the darkness of its journey under the harbour. Two minutes and forty-five seconds: the longest inter-station stretch on the whole tunnel system. He had barely noticed the dozen or so green police uniforms lining the platform, concentrating hard on the rails. But just as he approached the starting section of the huge Immersed Tube, his subconscious shrieked in horror at the sight before him.

There was a single point of white light in the far distance – where no light ought to be. His first incredulous reaction was that another train must be heading towards him the other way on the down track. But that was impossible! As his fingers faltered on the angled surface of the operator's panel, his eyes could just make out the blurred image of a man in orange overalls – a shape rushing forward to meet him. *Diu lei lo mo*, his brain screamed: Track maintenance!

It all happened too quickly for conscious thought. There were only microseconds available for action. What was left to him was the automatic reaction instilled by successive emergency drills. *Man on the track!* With no time to call out, Suen slammed the heel of his hand hard against the large red button at the centre of his control panel between the speed indicator and the air gauge.

This was the emergency override button which took over from the computer and activated the pneumatic braking system. There was an immediate lurch as the brakes bit; the beast groaned under the strain of its own momentum.

'*Ting ah, ting ah!*' shouted the driver, as the orange shape loomed nearer. 'Lie down, lie down!' he screamed, though knowing the man could not hear him. Let the train pass harmlessly over him!

Still the orange shape did not move; it seemed to approach still faster. When the train struck it, the figure disappeared beneath its wheels and Suen let out an anguished cry. A second later the train stopped dead; this unexpected and violent reaction sending the occupants of the second and third cars slamming into one another; tumbling over and over across the carriage floors.

Immediately Suen grabbed for the PA system microphone.

'Do not be alarmed.' His insides churned with fear for the poor wretch beneath the wheels. Remember procedure, he told himself, fighting to control his actions. First reassure the passengers. 'This is an emergency stop. There is an obstruction on the line.'

'*Mat lan ye?*' demanded Stephen Lee at full volume, as he grabbed a polished upright and hauled himself back to his feet. The carriage seemed full of aides and security men all scrambling about the aisle ahead of him, all shouting and struggling to extricate themselves from the confused heap.

'What the hell's going on?' shouted Jack Cinch, climbing over Lassiter's legs.

'No cause for concern,' bleated the PA. But Stephen Lee was not listening anymore. Something else had caught his attention; his peripheral vision was instantly electrified by the sudden appearance of dark, fast-moving shapes in the tunnel outside the train.

Then he saw feet running along the parapet beside the

window. *In Gwan-Dai's name,* he thought, *this is it! This is really it!*

He slipped back into his native Cantonese for everything that followed, as he called out to his team:

'Men outside the window! Everyone down *now*!'

The Chinese officers hit the floor, drawing their weapons even as they dropped – already looking for available cover. Almost immediately the Americans, too, understood the situation and flattened themselves against the floor. In what now seemed a slow-motion dream, Stephen Lee moved forward towards the second car, where William Fredericks was crouched in the aisle between Fluherty and the officer commanding the SY detail.

Having struggled to reach the VIP through the other bodies, the SB bodyguard got one hand on the man's head and pushed it downwards. Fredericks' head was knocked against the deck, but that could not be helped. Over his shoulder, Lee had barely time to notice his men bring their weapons to bear upon the windows before the first shots came. From outside the car.

The initial volley had a truly terrifying quality: unmistakably machine-gun fire. It flew high over their heads, shattering the reinforced perspex of the windows and doors. In sudden reflex the occupants of the second car ducked still lower to avoid flying splinters. Someone cried out – probably hit by a ricochet. Then came a second volley: this time the deeper, more resonant tone characteristic of high-calibre weapons, followed by a hail of grey, tube-shaped projectiles which cannoned off the far wall before dropping to the floor. Almost on impact, the grey canisters ignited, belching forth clouds of dense grey smoke. Within a matter of seconds it was impossible to see even from one side of the carriage to the other.

'For God's sake cover up,' shouted one of the American team. 'It's gas!'

There was a vain flurry of activity as the fallen men

533

attempted to clamp handkerchiefs, jacket lapels, or anything else which came to hand, over their noses and mouths.

Then, while Stephen Lee manoeuvred himself across the prone figure of William Fredericks, there came a sudden volley of pistol fire; it was his own men attempting to return fire. He realised in desperation that the radio was no good to him down here, underground. He knew also that there was no fallback position into which he could evacuate the VIP. They were totally trapped inside the train while, crouching unseen in the darkness, their attackers had all the strategic advantages. Worst of all, within the brightly-lit carriages the Special Branch men provided easy targets. Blinded by the lights they could see nothing in the darkness beyond the windows but their own startled reflections.

Now, in the pall of choking smoke that erupted into the confined space, Lee knew he had to coordinate a rapid defence in order to repulse this attack. But when the breath he had held so long gave out and he was forced to take another, he realised at once that was the worst thing he could have done. That first new intake of air knocked him sideways, stinging his throat and lungs like ammonia. Then, as the gas particles hit his bloodstream, the powerful agent went to work on his parasympathetic nervous system, provoking the type of intense nausea induced by a full-blooded kick to the groin. His stomach was suddenly gripped by a wave of pain which ran the entire length of his insides, appearing to unite his throat and rectum in one long, burning canal.

Retching uncontrollably, he fell sprawling across his VIP, who lay convulsing before him upon the floor. Consciousness fading, Lee barely perceived the strangled coughs and the violent convulsions of those around him; they were a deadly hallucination now. But long afterwards he would remember the first orange shape kicking its way into the car through a half-shattered window, a black NBC respirator clamped over its face, and the ugly jut of a Viet-style assault rifle clutched in its hand. That was the last thing he saw before the fog took him.

Then there was only blackness.

Just seventeen seconds after the gas was hurled in, Okamoto watched as the security men began to fall like sparrows. It had been a concentrated dose and he knew that the bodyguards would be totally incapacitated for at least fifteen minutes. Perhaps permanently, in some cases, if he did not get aboard quickly and fling wide the doors.

The members of his cell watched their leader intently, finally rewarded by the single hand jerk which ordered their line of orange uniforms aboard. They had been crouching low on the parapet – now they sprang forward, swarming through shattered perspex into the first three of the eight cars. The gas had done its job, there was no further need for caution.

Besides their assault rifles, each man in Okamoto's team was equipped with a protective respirator completely covering his face, and a full set of wrap-around bulletproof body armour which protected the body from neck to groin. On this occasion it was not required: they encountered no resistance whatsoever. Those not already unconscious were so racked with nausea that they could well have wished themselves dead.

One determined figure, the American, Jack Cinch, stumbled briefly through the blinding fog, only to be struck down by a rifle butt. A moment later all was still.

Exiting from the second car, Okamoto ran quickly along the parapet to the front of the train. Reaching the driver's cab, he stopped by its single pneumatically-controlled door and, using the last of the keys provided by Station-Master Cheung, forced it open. The door hissed, then slid neatly aside. Counting breaths to still his heart, Okamoto peered inside and saw immediately how tight the space there really was. The operator lay slumped across the control panel, the public-address-system microphone dangling between the fingers of his left hand. Okamato pushed him away from the seat to get inside, then, stepping over the inert body, he flipped the lock on the connecting door which led back to the first carriage.

Forty-five seconds already gone. They would need to move fast before the MTR control room started asking questions – and sounding alarms.

Kicking aside the door, Okamoto strode back through to the first car and scanned the inert bodies through a caustic, drifting mist. Already his team were at work, four of them stripping weapons from the policemen, prising them from still-gripping fingers, while the two other Japanese stood covering them – legs braced, leaning into their weapons, anticipating the kick that would come if they were forced to unleash a full automatic burst. It took no time at all to locate the bulky frame and thin white hair of the Secretary of State. Pushing aside the unconscious Chinese policeman who lay across him, they hauled William Fredericks clear, and laid him out flat on one of the stainless-steel bench seats to recover.

In spite of all the counting and all the prior meditation, at that moment Okamoto's heart pumped wildly, for this was the most dangerous point of the whole operation: the point at which he had already decided to depart from the agreed schedule.

He gave a nod of recognition at the face jerked upwards towards him between gloved hands.

'That's him.'

The two men supporting Fredericks' body by the armpits hitched up their burden and struggled with their load towards the doors.

'Wait!' Okamoto was trying to make his voice

536

commanding, even inside the full-face respirator.

Instantly all heads turned towards him – quizzical behind the dumbness of their own rubber masks. A thinning mist hung around Okamoto's head.

'Put him back on the seat and check his breathing.'

The two men looked blankly at one another. Finally one of them said: 'But the time. We have no time!'

'Do as I say!' Okamoto took a step forward, pointing an imperious finger towards the seat. The assault rifle hung across his chest; and they could see the long, braided handle of the sword slung high across his back. Okamoto had no need to reach for either in order to reinforce his authority. 'There has been a change of plan. I have decided our aims would be best achieved by remaining here.'

'What about the vans? The boat?'

'Forget them. We are here now. This will be our stronghold.'

The rubber-masked heads stared at each other for a moment, then carried out his order, laying the Secretary of State carefully down on the steel bench, then checking his vital signs. One brushed a smear of vomit from the old man's lip.

As always within their group, it was Okamoto's will which carried the day – even though it had just defined a new and unexpected direction for their operation. His new orders came in a decisive flow of energy.

'Get Miyagi back from the ventilation building. Then two of you secure the rear of the train. The rest of you get those two bags open! They contain everything we'll need to handle the prisoners.'

Okamoto stepped back into the operator's cab at the front of the train. For a moment he looked down at the operating console in confusion. Then, reaching into the breast pocket of his overalls, he pulled out the cab diagram Cheung had drawn for them, and began to match it to the display before him. First he located the radio console's line of coloured keys, immediately to the right of the fault reset button; he pressed the red one marked CONTROL EMERGENCY. The effect of this was to override all current transmissions into the MTR control centre, and to set the train regulator's panel lights flashing like a Christmas tree.

Meanwhile, inside Chater station on Hong Kong Island, six Special Branch officers paced anxiously along the deserted platform, watching the tunnel mouth. At that precise moment Alpha Four, the inspector in charge of the security team covering Chater station, checked his watch – not for the first time that day – and realised there was still a full minute to go before the train should pass through Admiralty station and finally arrive here.

The anxiety he was now feeling had little to do with the train timing. He was too busy worrying about the dangers posed by the huge crowd of people already massing outside the station entrance. If they could clear that one last hurdle, he reassured himself, and get Fredericks safely back inside an armoured limousine, then they were home and dry.

Inside the control room on the first floor of MTR headquarters in Kowloon Bay, the first person to notice the stoppage was the train service regulator for the Tsuen Wan Line. It was something hardly surprising, since it was this uniformed officer's job to monitor that particular line and ensure a smooth flow of service.

Only now the situation presented him with something of a puzzle.

For almost one minute the coloured blips on his diagrammatic board which showed the progress of trains through the system had not moved. As the regulator sipped from a carton of chrysanthemum tea, he frowned at the board and readjusted his glasses. Trains just did not stop inside the 'immersed tube'. Not unless there was some kind of emergency.

His immediate reaction was to call up the train operator on the radio link to ask for an explanation. No answer ... Confused, and worried now, he turned to the console behind him, where the line controller – his immediate supervisor – was calculating loading figures for that day.

'Got a non-mover in the IT.'

'How long's it been stopped?'

'Nearly two minutes now and no response to radio messages. There's another train at Tsim Sha Tsui waiting to follow it through.'

'Warn all affected stations to standby.'

The line controller walked over to the senior regulator's console, read off the train's designator, and picked up the radio handset.

'Train AA06, report your situation, please.' There followed a bleak, worrying silence.

'That's the special train we had instructions on this morning,' offered the senior regulator suspiciously, a note of concern creeping into his voice.

'Train AA06 – this is the line controller speaking,' he tried once more, as if mentioning his rank might produce a quicker response. 'Report your situation!'

A moment later the emergency circuit cut in, and the radio came back in a loud excited babble of English rendered with a staccato oriental inflection.

'Listen to me, line controller, and do not interrupt! I am speaking on behalf of *sekigun* – the Japan Red Army. We have taken control of your train. The American Secretary of State and his party are our prisoners. If any attempt is made to approach the train we will kill every one of them. We have both weapons and explosives, and will use them if forced to do so. You understand?'

Turning around and snapping his fingers loudly to

attract a colleague, the line controller answered carefully – also in English. Immediately his colleague switched on another communications set to monitor the call.

'Yes, I understand. What is it you want?'

'A full list of our demands will be issued shortly. For now it is enough that you make this area safe for us. After that we must speak to an accredited representative of the Hong Kong Government. I will call again in thirty minutes, and then I expect to speak to someone in authority. I remind you now, do not try to approach this train or the prisoners will all die.'

There was an air of numb disbelief at Kowloon Bay headquarters as the first crisis meeting was summoned – just thirty minutes after an urgent call reached the chief controller's desk.

Chief Controller 'Paul Sung had been momentarily stunned. When his mind had assessed the emergency, he immediately ordered the line controller to instigate computer route-switching that would allow the cross-harbour service to continue by using the up-line of the tunnel only. Aware that his hand was shaking, he grabbed the white telephone in the centre of his console and tapped out a number.

'Let me speak with the operations manager.'

'I'm sorry. Mr Cruikshank is in a meeting. Would you like to leave...'

Cruikshank's personal assistant never finished her sentence.

'Then interrupt him now. We have a *tango* emergency.'

Mention of this codeword for a terrorist incident was enough to extract Clive Cruikshank from his meeting with visiting senior executives of the San Francisco Bay Area Rapid Transit. Instantly he had begun a series of hurried phone-calls to the executive members of the MTR board and to the emergency services. Five minutes later the other phone in Cruikshank's office rang and a softly rising Welsh accent said:

'Clive, I hear we have a problem.'

As District Commander of the MTR police district it was Senior Superintendent Taff Owen's job to know about such things the instant they happened. He had picked up news of the crisis from the police control-room adjacent to the MTR's own nerve centre in the Kowloon Bay headquarter building.

'They've taken the special train – the one with the American VIP aboard. God knows how it happened! That's a non-stopping train.'

'Let's think about that later, shall we?' Owen responded calmly. 'We'd better start thinking of the knock-on effects. Start your automated evacuation procedures at Tsim Sha Tsui and Admiralty stations. Get everyone above ground level. Our emergency units are now on their way; they'll cordon both ends of the Immersed Tube.'

'Both stations are already cleared,' said Cruikshank.

'Excellent,' responded the senior police officer.

'We'd better cancel all cross-harbour trains, too, for the time being.'

Cruikshank looked incredulous.

'But I can't do that! The evening rush-hour is just beginning. You know Hong Kong. While that's on, we'll need to keep up a one-direction loading of seventy-five thousand passengers an hour or there'll be a bloody riot. Any greater build-up in the stations would be intolerable – damn dangerous, I should say.'

'I'm going to have to order it, Clive, just until we ascertain the full situation. Divert as much of the traffic as you can through the second crossing-point at Quarry Bay. We can probably allow you to resume again after we've confirmed that the terrorists are contained.' Taff Owen took Cruikshank's silence to mean grudging assent. 'There are a number of things I need to do immediately. So meet me in twenty minutes at the conference room next to the MTR police control room.'

'Do I have any choice?' breathed the operations manager, beckoning to his personal assistant who was waving a second phone in his direction. 'What about the driver we have down there?'

'Just keep cool, and let's move one step at a time. They're in control for the time being but they're not going anywhere. Concentrate on maintaining your service. Tell your people not to approach the train and to make no attempt to contact the terrorists. Put out announcements urging people to find alternative transport. As I said, divert as much as you can of the passenger loading to the Quarry Bay harbour crossing.' Owen's thoughts were now occupied by the threat of rioting as crowds of commuters jammed the other station concourses. In this cloying wet heat, tempers would soon fray. The terrorists had chosen the worst time to strike – but for them, perhaps, the best. 'I'll be back to you as soon as I can.'

In the twenty-minute interval, while the MTR police control room echoed messages in and out of Kowloon Regional Command and Control Centre – RCCC for short – and from there into Headquarters PolMil on the Island, all over Hong Kong radio-pagers began bleeping. Telephone digits were punched in frenzied response as the ripples of official activation flowed outwards from the epicentre in Kowloon Bay.

In a matter of minutes the news was being flashed to the Headquarters PolMil Control Centre – focal point of the force's counter-terrorist response. When the duty controller there called the Commissioner's office on the secure line, James Weldon at once broke off his discussion with Henry St John-Black to take the call.

'They've done what?' he breathed, his great ruddy face horror-struck by the news. Then for the Director of

Special Branch's sake he said softly: 'They've got him. They've got Fredericks.'

St John-Black almost choked. 'Where? How?'

Weldon demanded a summary of the incident so far.

'Who have you informed?' he asked brusquely, stemming an urge to overreact with anger.

'Director of Operations, SO Counter Terrorism, Special Branch Information Centre, and the Director of Criminal Investigation,' came the answer. 'Kowloon RCCC already knows. Foxtrot Company, PTU is currently en route to Tsim Sha Tsui to reinforce Emergency Unit officers in cordoning the station approaches.'

'That'll do for the moment. Who's currently in charge of the incident?'

'District Commander MTR, sir.'

'Fine, I'll be there presently.'

Henry St John-Black continued to listen with rapt attention as Weldon picked up another phone and asked to be connected to Government House. After a few seconds a voice replied: 'Good afternoon, James.' Weldon stiffened as he gave the news to His Excellency the Governor. There was a brief exchange of information, then he put down the phone and in silence began buckling on his Sam Browne belt.

'Good God!' exploded St John-Black finally.

'Yes, Henry, the bastards have actually done it. So much for stepping up security!' Weldon could hardly conceal his bitterness. 'Better get back to your desk and set up the Higher Command Centre for situation intelligence evaluation. Becker was right all along; they're claiming to be the Japan Red Army.'

Entering New May House, Weldon climbed the staircase to the first floor, where the Chief Staff Officer PolMil had opened up the situation room and was waiting to receive him.

'Right then, Bill, let's get on with it. How are they coping over there?'

'Pretty well, sir. The cordon went in two minutes ago. Witnesses at Tsim Sha Tsui station have reported hearing shots fired. There's also a suggestion they used gas of some kind; some people standing near the tunnel end of the concourse collapsed and had to be taken to QE hospital.'

'Anyone in contact with the terrorists?'

'They were speaking to the MTR staff at Kowloon Bay, but that was quite a while ago. One of the emergency unit inspectors at Tsim Sha Tsui station is now attempting to speak to them from the Station-Master's office. He reports talking with an oriental male who claims to be the leader of the group.'

'What language did he use?'

'English.'

'What's the situation about negotiators?' asked Weldon. Like many police forces around the world, the RHKP had spent a lot of time and money on the selection and training of experts to conduct the delicate business of hostage negotiation. Now it was time for them to justify this expense.

'There are two men over at the Kowloon Bay control room, waiting for clearance to begin. They don't have a full team yet, and the incident commander hasn't decided whether to work from the control room or the Station-Master's office down in Tsim Sha Tsui.'

'What's the problem?'

'Well, sir, they have good two-way radio communications with the train at Kowloon Bay but that location is a long way from the incident. The Tsimsy station is bang next to the immersed tube, but they only have a single telephone link, which is controlled from the driver's cab. The negotiators prefer to be close in, just in case they get a chance to go face-to-face with the suspects.'

Weldon knew this 'incident' would be big enough to command international attention, and that within a short space of time the eyes of the world would be focused upon them all. Without pausing, he made a decision, issuing his instructions slowly and carefully.

'Contact Taff Owen now and tell him to get communications moving. We'll play it from *his* end; the MTR control room is the obvious place for our incident centre and support units. We can move forward to Tsim Sha Tsui later if things appear to be going well. Tell him I want to be told the instant these people issue their demands.'

Eighteen metres below ground on the Tsim Sha Tsui waterfront, the passengers of train AA06 began, painfully, to stir. Thick-headed, dazed and disoriented, Stephen Lee came to with that same feeling of nausea he had suffered just before hitting the floor. His mouth was dry and, like his eyes, stung from the gas particles still affecting the mucus membranes. He forced his eyes open with difficulty, at first seeing only a nebulous mass of orange moving around before him. As he rubbed his raw eyelids, he heard someone shout, a grating, guttural sound, and suddenly the orange shapes came sharply into focus; men with sweating faces, respirators pushed up on top of their heads like black helmets. He counted six of them, each man standing braced against the steel uprights, surrounding them on all sides. Then he noticed the assault rifles slung across their bodies, their barrels pointing downwards at the tangled bodies on the floor. There was a shrill recollection of automatic gunfire ringing in his head, but what alarmed Stephen Lee most were the bullet holes in the silvered walls and doors of the carriage. Those bullets had punctured the metal as easily as if it was aluminium foil.

The terrorist's first command was uttered in English. The faces of the hostages turned in response.

'Stay exactly where you are!' The voice seemed to come from the glaring brightness of the overhead lighting, and it paralysed the hostages where they lay. The man who then stepped forward out of the light wore no respirator. Still in shock, Stephen Lee lay perfectly still, but he was checking the slender build and almost girlish face against his recollection of pictures faxed through from NPA headquarters. This was him, all right: Kazuo Okamoto. Slim and goodlooking with intense almond-shaped eyes. There was no resemblance here to the scruffy leftist subversives usually seen in Interpol circulars.

'This train is now under the control of the Okamoto Commando of the Japan Red Army. You are all our prisoners.'

On the other side of the car Jack Cinch uncurled from a foetal position, grimacing as he fingered the swollen cut on the side of his head where the rifle butt had struck.

'We will soon begin negotiations with the authorities,' continued Okamoto. 'In particular, with the United States Government. The exact nature of the concessions we seek do not concern you. But if there is no satisfactory outcome, you will all be killed.'

There was a spontaneous murmur of concern amongst the prisoners, instantly silenced when the barrel of a gun was jabbed in their direction.

'In a moment you will be moved to another part of this train. Anyone who attempts to resist us will be shot.'

Stephen Lee scanned the other members of the security party. Most still lay helplessly entwined upon the floor, not daring to move. With his left elbow he covertly probed the area of his hip, but felt only the emptiness of the plastic belt holster beneath his jacket. The Glock pistols had been removed while they were unconscious. That was good: it made things less complicated. There would be no bloody ridiculous attempts at playing hero. At least for the time being.

'We are now ready to move.'

Unlike many underground railway systems, the cars of the MTR trains were not separated by interconnecting doors, but formed one continuous corridor the full length of the eight cars.

One by one the security men, both Americans and Chinese, were hauled to their feet and pushed back along the connecting aisle to the sixth car. Here they were made to lie face-down on one side of the carriage, while their hands were bound behind their backs with plastic handcuffs. After fifteen minutes there was a single line of hostages stretching from this point forward to the third car. They were laid head to foot to prevent conversation, with a metre of clearance between each hostage.

Finally William Fredericks was made to sit upright in the first car, with Dan Fluherty on one side and the MTR liaison officer and the train's operator on the other. Fredericks watched helplessly as one of the terrorists picked up the leather briefcase containing his confidential briefing notes and handed it to Okamoto.

The Japanese's eyes devoured the pages with interest.

'Mind telling me what this is all about, son?' asked the US Secretary of State, his voice sounding very old.

Okamoto stared back at him for a while, then he finished reading the page he was holding.

'You will know very soon, Mr Secretary,' he said without bothering to look at the elderly politician. 'In the meantime I have an important ultimatum to give your government. Choose one man you can trust to act as messenger.'

After consulting Fluherty, the Secretary of State decided that the best man would be the Consulate's security officer, since he would know what information to give the law enforcement units on the outside. Quickly Cinch was unbound and led forward into the first car. As the big American looked into the cold clear eyes of the Japanese terrorist, his bloodied face clouded with thunder. At once the muzzle of an automatic rifle was pressed against his spine as a reminder of his position.

Okamoto took a written statement from his pocket,

unfolded the paper and began to read from it. Immediately Fredericks' face registered his horrified reaction at the content of the message.

'You can't be serious!'

'But I am, Mr Secretary,' said Okamoto almost smiling. 'It is now 16.22 on Tuesday. If these demands are not met in full by midnight on Wednesday, everyone aboard this train will die – including ourselves if necessary.'

Cinch took the paper held out to him. Suddenly a thought occurred: 'You'll radio ahead?' he asked. 'Warn them that I'm coming out?'

'Of course,' snapped the terrorist, waving him away.

The guard grabbed Cinch's collar ready to propel him back along the aisle, but Okamoto was not finished with him yet.

'Wait! Before you go I have something to show you – so you may tell your friends not to try anything stupid.'

Turning his head, the Japanese spoke rapidly in his native tongue. One terrorist responded with a shouted '*Hai*' and headed into the operator's cab. He returned carrying what resembled a large metal cashbox, which he placed on the seat opposite Fredericks.

First the terrorist removed a waxed paper parcel, unfolded the edges and took out what looked like a coil of ordinary plastic washing-line. Then carefully he located a squat plug of shiny metal with thin red and blue wires protruding from one surface, and placed this gently on the waxed paper. Cinch's eyes widened as the man reached inside his overalls and pulled out a survival knife with a ten-inch blade. His curiosity increased as the man measured out a piece of the white rope as long as his arm, folded it across the blade, and cut it with a single fluid stroke.

'Do you know what this is, Mr Secretary?'

'I do not.'

'Cordtex,' said Okamoto matter-of-factly. 'Also

known as detonating cord or linear cutting charge. High-explosive in a flexible plastic sheath. Quite inert if properly handled, and harmless until electrically initiated.'

All eyes followed the man's movements now as he took out a broad canvas money belt and threaded the cordtex down inside the length of it. His fingers worked nimbly, and in another few seconds he had attached the spike of the metal plug to the end of the white cord, and the protruding wires to a small matt black battery pack which he slid into a pouch beside the belt buckle. When he had finished he took the belt carefully between both hands and turned around.

'Now, Mr Secretary,' said Okamoto, 'please stand up and take off your jacket.'

'What for?'

Okamato's eyes spat fire.

The first swipe caught Fredericks unawares, as the back of Okamoto's small hand lashed at his left cheek. The second and third blows made him cry out.

'Do not question my order. Just do it! Get up now!'

A third terrorist grabbed the Secretary's collar, hauling him up to his feet, then punching the back of his neck. The old man's head jerked like a puppet's as the jacket was stripped roughly from his rounded shoulders. Fredericks said nothing now, allowing the man who had loaded the belt to buckle it around his waist and check the connections. When that was done, he was given back his jacket to put on, then pushed back into his seat.

Fredericks stared down at the broad canvas cummerbund which now encircled his middle. Enjoying the prisoner's discomfort, Okamoto reached out a hand for the slim dark lozenge of the radio-initiator mechanism. There was a single soft click as the unit was powered on, followed by a red flash and a beeping noise to indicate that it was functioning correctly. The sound made Fredericks start.

'Observe, Mr Cinch,' said Okamoto pointing at

549

William Fredericks. 'Your master's body is now wired with explosives. A flick of my finger will cause the cordtex to detonate at one end, with a linear speed of twenty-one thousand feet per second. The effect will be a simultaneous explosion throughout its length, and your Secretary will be cut in half where he sits. Do you understand?'

Fredericks' face went ashen. He looked as if his age had miraculously doubled.

'I understand,' responded Cinch.

'Then go now. Give my message to the chief intelligence officer at the US Consulate. And make sure you tell your friends outside what you have seen here – all about the Secretary's beautiful new belt.'

Without a word Cinch turned and walked back down the aisle, past the line of police and SY men lying trussed upon the floor, and on to the rear of the train. As the door opened and he stepped out on to the parapet, he was already preparing individual descriptions of the terrorists and of the weaponry he had observed. He dropped down into the well of the track and, keeping close to the left-hand rail to avoid touching any live wires in the dark, set out on foot to Tsim Sha Tsui station.

At that precise moment Taff Owen and Clive Cruikshank were together in the conference room adjacent to the police operations centre at Kowloon Bay. The operations manager, now in shirt sleeves, rolled out a diagram of the Tsuen Wan line and began to explain what he had already ascertained from his own staff. This sudden invasion of the control room by the district commander and other senior officers kept everyone on their toes, though most of them were already busy enough answering the urgent shriek of telephones.

Thirty-five minutes later, two more men arrived to join the meeting – one European, the other Chinese. They entered the control-room wearing faded jeans and

T-shirts – a sight never before seen in that room – and each carried a motorcycle crash-helmet and a small rucksack. Apart from their radio-pagers, though these were common enough amongst young men in Hong Kong, it was only the laminated warrant cards clipped to their belts which identified the pair as police officers. The European was broad and well-muscled, and he clutched a leather personal organiser. The Chinese was a wirier individual, with dark skin and bony shoulders: he dangled a packset radio in his right hand.

Taff Owen's thin face registered considerable relief at the appearance of these two fit and tanned figures. Here at last were two men with whom he could now discuss his options – two of the Force's experts. Even before he had introduced them to the MTR people, almost everyone in the room had already guessed that this was the first showing of the heavy mob.

'Clive, let me introduce Mel Kale, acting OC/Special Duties Unit, and Willie Ng, his operations officer. Lads, Clive Cruikshank, Operations Manager, MTR.'

'Clive,' nodded Mel Kale pleasantly. The handshakes were firm and businesslike. 'We made it as fast as we could, Taff,' he continued, consulting the Casio sports timer on his wrist. 'We heard there was a problem down here. Thirty-four minutes from NT depot by motorcycle. Not bad going, seeing traffic's backed up half a mile at the Lion Rock Tunnel. Right, better tell us what you got so far.'

These two men – the advance party of the Special Duties Unit Counter Terrorist intervention force – had left their base in northern New Territories just two minutes after a hurried phone-call from the Staff Officer Counter Terrorism, giving orders that their personal kit and the other team members should meet them at Tsim Sha Tsui MTR station as soon as a helicopter lift could be arranged through the Police/Military Joint Air Tasking Unit.

In theory, before the SDU could be deployed, they needed the authorisation of the Director of Operations, who himself needed to consult the Commissioner. But to Mel Kale this was so much wasted time, and he had not waited for the D.Ops' order. He reasoned that getting into position for advance recce and intelligence-gathering took precedence over any requisite paperwork. He needed to be on the ground sharpish, appraised of the situation, and with a workable immediate action plan in case the terrorists changed their minds and began killing hostages. With this thought in mind, Mel Kale opened his leather personal organiser and prepared to take notes.

'OK, they said we had a train hijack with VIPs aboard, and suspicion of shots fired and gas used. That right?'

'Right. Witnesses on the platform at Tsim Sha Tsui heard what sounded like gunfire. They had to evacuate some of them to hospital after inhaling something emanating from the tunnel. Puking like dogs, they were.'

'Could be CR,' offered Mel Kale. 'An incapacitating agent. If they've got that they obviously know what they're about. Identity of the hostages?'

Taff Owen gave a list of the VIP party and security officers, and watched apprehensive looks pass between the two SDU men.

'Right,' said Kale. 'Better let me have the sequence of events so far.'

Cruikshank used a hard copy from the Chief Controller's console log to explain what had happened, right up to the first radio message from the stricken train – reading verbatim the words of the terrorists' spokesman.

When he had finished, Kale nodded slowly, scribbling everything down, then asked for the exact location and situation of the stronghold. In response he was led out through the police control room and into the MTR control centre beyond. On one long side of the windowless room were three giant console desks with angled displays, one for each of the three railway service lines. An army of blue-uniformed MTR staff hurried between computer screens, their ranks conspicuously displayed in the gold bars on the dark blue epaulettes of their pale shirts.

The four-man conference formed up around the broad panels of the Tsuen Wan line console, on which were arrayed three banks of lights and switches and three recessed telephone handsets. Above the switches a three-section diagrammatic map of the Tsuen Wan line was punctuated by illuminating blips which monitored the progress of trains through the tunnels of the underground system. At strategic points small oblong windows were lit by LED indicators showing the coded identity of the train passing that point.

'Would you mind explaining?' asked Kale, somewhat overwhelmed by the information in this display. Immediately Cruikshank summoned Paul Sung and handed over to him.

'The train system is completely under computer control. The regulation of acceleration, braking and coasting is automatically controlled by our computers. Each section of track has sensors and a microchip memory encoded with safe speeds; the chips are intelligent enough to know the identity of the train passing over them. That information is displayed on this schematic.'

Sung adjusted his gold spectacles and pointed to the angled three-section display.

'On this side we have Tsuen Wan station, where the party boarded and the train service began. On the other end we have Central station, where the train should have terminated. And in between are the many way points for us to track its progress. Here, two stops back from Central, is Tsim Sha Tsui; and the train indicator window here shows the designation of the hijacked train.' The

LEDs showed AA06 in burning red figures next to the down track. 'It's stopped here at track section 08T, the back of the train approximately four hundred metres beyond Tsim Sha Tsui station.'

'Do you mean it's in the tunnel section running beneath the harbour?' asked Willie Ng, pausing at the notes he was scribbling into his own personal organiser – notes which would be important when later briefing his teams in the event of a neutralisation option.

'Not strictly. The train is 180 metres long. Part of it is undoubtedly inside the IT – that's the Immersed Tube under the harbour – but some is still within the bored tube between Tsimsy station and the start of the IT. That means only part of it is actually under the harbour.'

At this point Cruikshank broke in to explain that the Immersed Tube consisted of fourteen prefabricated concrete sections which had been floated out, sunk and then joined together on the sea-floor. The tube, approximately one mile in length, had then been connected to the bored sections on both sides of the harbour, and blown through with compressed air to clear out the water. It had been a remarkable feat of engineering.

'But it's a double tube, right?' asked Kale, his face taut with concentration. 'They were heading for the Island, so it's only the down track that's blocked, isn't it?'

'That's right. This hijacking needn't stop the service; there are cross-overs here and here.' Cruikshank used a ballpoint pen to tap the shiny steel board, indicating a first point between Tsim Sha Tsui and Jordan stations to the north, and a second within the Admiralty complex to the south on Hong Kong Island. 'We could still operate a contra-flow on one side, but we've closed it down on the orders of the District Commander.'

Cruikshank had been half hoping Kale might disagree with this decision, and so allow him to push for continuation of the service. But there was no chance of that – not yet at least.

554

'That's good,' continued Kale. 'So now we have an isolated section of tunnel. The train is stationary for the moment, but is it capable of movement?'

'Not now we've fed new signalling codes into the computers. If the driver attempts to move, there'll be an immediate power cut-out. It's a built-in safety feature.'

'No override possible from inside the train?'

'Well, yes. As a last resort the driver may switch into coded manual mode and proceed at restricted speed, say ten kilometres an hour.'

Kale shot a glance at the District Commander. Something would need to be done to prevent that – and fast. But it was up to Taff Owen, the Incident Commander, to make that decision. When he spoke, the Welsh voice was quietly authoritative.

'Then I suggest, Clive, you bring up a couple of those bloody great yellow maintenance engines of yours and block the tunnel off at Tsim Sha Tsui and at Admiralty. It's bad enough if they start moving around in the IT, but we don't want them wandering around the full system unrestricted.'

The operations manager blinked back his confusion, apologising for not having considered this precaution sooner. Massaging the back of his neck, he instructed Paul Sung to make the necessary arrangements.

'Clive,' said Mel Kale – attempting to reassure the man; he would get more out of him that way – 'try to think of this from the terrorists' point of view. Anticipate their reactions. We want to restrict, isolate, contain, and *then* learn what we can about the inside of the stronghold.'

'Yes, I understand,' he conceded, checking his momentary confusion.

'We need to know exactly what these guys can make that train do before we make any approach. I'd hate to see any of our technical mob run down in the dark.'

The operations manager realised he himself was

construing the problem in terms of normal operations, and that he must shed those blinkers right now.

'Point taken. But it's highly unlikely anyone would be injured in that instance, unless they lay across the track. There's a suicide pit between the rails, and on either side, deep enough for a man to lie down in and avoid injury from a train passing above him.'

'Excellent,' conceded Kale. 'That's the kind of thing we need to know. I'd like you to detail one of your senior operations men to brief Willie on structural, technical and engineering matters. We'll also need access to your workshops, and a train of our own to play with. That OK?'

'I'll set it up right now.' Cruikshank picked up a phone and called Fred Wong, the area manager responsible for the Tsuen Wan line. At the same time the SDU leader stepped aside to speak quietly to Taff Owen.

'Well, looks like you're it, Taff,' he said meaningfully. 'Incident Commander, the man on the spot.'

'Don't think I don't know it. I can feel James Weldon's breath on my neck already. Two years in charge of Airport Division and not even a sniff of a bloody hijack. Six months at MTR, and bingo! Still, we've got the PTU cordon deployed and the negotiators are setting up in a room adjacent to the control room.'

'I presume you'll be controlling from here.'

'That's right. Two radio channels to the driver's cab of the train, and our own patch link to Headquarters PolMil. It's the obvious choice: I can visually scan the concourse and platforms from the master video screens on the regulator's console.'

Kale couldn't restrain a smile.

'Enjoy it while you can.'

'Meaning?'

'That in twenty minutes it'll be out of your hands, mate. As soon as they realise the full political implications of this, PHQ will throw in a Deputy Commissioner as Incident Commander.'

'Suits me bloody fine,' grinned Taff Owen.

Mel Kale shared the humour of the moment, knowing there might be little cause to smile during the hours that followed. From now on it would all be in deadly earnest, with the eyes of the world watching every move they made.

'Right, then, I'd best get along to Tsim Sha Tsui and take a decko. Give us about fifteen minutes. My lads will be choppering in there about half an hour from now. Stay in contact.'

Before moving out, Mel Kale advised Taff Owen, still Incident Commander, that he would stay tuned into channel four of the Kowloon Regional radio network in case of a need for emergency communications. He would re-establish contact by phone the instant he reached the Station-Master's office at Tsim Sha Tsui MTR station.

Taff Owen watched the door swing shut, then just for a moment considered his position. Rearrangements he would need to make: both professional and personal. As a leading member of the Jupiter Players amateur operatic society, he was scheduled to star that evening in the company's production of the musical *South Pacific*. The production was being staged at the Hong Kong Arts Centre, and it was a part he had waited for for a long time: the romantic Frenchman with an interesting past. It was not so far removed from himself, since he had two Eurasian children of his own. Certainly the opening night was already out of the window. Comes with the bloody territory, he told himself, just as the voice of the super-intendent commanding the police control room jerked him back to reality.

'Sir, call for you on the secure line.'
'Who is it now?'
'James Weldon himself, sir.'
'I'm already there.'

* * *

The instant RCCC put the Special Duties Unit on standby, HQ PolMil put through a hurried request to RAF Sek Kong, the military airfield lying midway between the New Territories towns of Yuen Long and Tai Po. Minutes later a pair of Wessex helicopters of No. 28 (Army Co-operation) Squadron rose out of the valley beneath Tai Mo Shan mountain and headed north-east for NT Depot, the run-down collection of Nissen huts and scarred buildings where the unit made its home. As the pilot overflew Sheung Shui police station and circled the trees around the depot, he recognised at once the white expanse of the old parade-ground below him. Then he saw the green camouflage-pattern uniforms of the SDU men and the collection of unmarked transit vans and land cruisers being loaded with kit. When the wheels touched down, the men were already formed up in two sticks on the edge of the square, and the moment the loadmaster gave the thumbs-up they ran out in line, approaching the doors at the four o'clock safety position without needing to be told.

Ordinarily the Wessex could carry up to fourteen men with ease, but since each of the twelve-man team carried an expansive olive-green holdall filled with his personal kit, the load had to be split between two aircraft. The last man aboard each aircraft, the team leader in both cases, gave a thumbs-up to his loadmaster, and immediately the aircraft rose in a flurry of dust and grit. As they swung away, climbing steeply towards the distant silhouette of the Lion Rock, the noise of the engine prevented any detailed conversation. No one spoke anyway, but still a sense of dreadful expectation communicated itself in small looks and glances.

Through the open doorway Inspector Marty Lewis, Bravo team leader, watched a silver line of traffic feed into the Lion Rock tunnel. Then they were over the lush green hump of the Kowloon foothills, and into Kowloon proper. As they overflew Kowloon Tong, the low-rise area of luxury housing directly in the airport glide-path, Kai Tak control halted the jumbo traffic, stacking the planes for an additional five minutes to allow them a clear run towards Tsim Sha Tsui.

Within a matter of minutes Lewis was watching the familiar pattern of intersecting roads sweep by beneath the aircraft wheels: the grimy high-rise blocks crowded with rooftop cocklofts; the grey ribbons of tarmac all but obliterated by steel and rubber. Mile upon mile of grid-locked asphalt.

The aircraft banked sharply, and for a second or two he saw the acres of shipping silhouetted darkly against the silvery waters of the western anchorage. Then the aircraft righted, and Nathan Road swung into place beneath it. From Boundary Street, the northern extreme of old Kowloon, through burgeoning Mongkok, Yaumatei, and even to the very tip of Tsim Sha Tsui, he watched the frantic motion of the rush-hour crowds as if he was observing an entirely separate species. Flying straight down that urban channel reminded Lewis of some half-forgotten space-wars movie.

The approach to Tsim Sha Tsui was like a scene from a 1950s riot. Lured by the sight of police vehicles, their blue beacons flashing, sirens blaring, a crowd of thousands had converged upon the tourist district, choking the wide pavements and spilling on to the roads. Fortunately uniformed branch officers had already cordoned off the six street-level entrances to the underground station with steel Mills barriers, and officers of the Police Tactical Unit had cleared sufficient area to allow emergency vehicles to draw up. District Commander Yaumatei had ordered a stretch of Nathan Road closed between Peking Road and Jordan Road, and police traffic branch was frantically attempting to cope with this problem by diverting the rush-hour traffic out along Kowloon Park Drive.

Jesus Christ, thought Lewis as he surveyed the bedlam; I'm glad I'm not in traffic any more.

He slapped the loadmaster's shoulder and hollered into his ear: 'Take her down, mate.'

The pilots exchanged brief radio communications, circled the great onion-shaped dome of the Kowloon Mosque, and put down on the soccer pitch in Kowloon Park, just west of Nathan Road. Once again PTU had done their job well, securing and clearing the landing site of the vast crowds usually found strolling there. It was about the only location in Tsim Sha Tsui's concrete jungle capable of taking a pair of Wessex helicopters, and luckily it lay within a hundred metres of the MTR. Lewis and his men heaved their gear into a waiting police transit, and were immediately ferried to the main station entrance on Haiphong Road. The transit backed across the wide pavement and right up to the entrance, allowing them to slip discreetly into the underground station out of the prying gaze of the public and the press corps.

Over the past few years the existence of a specialist counter-terrorist unit within the Hong Kong Police had become something of an open secret. Though working and training in absolute secrecy, their infrequent episodes of deployment in siege-busting situations had reaped them a blaze of publicity. Lewis was well aware of the effect their presence would have on the situation if discovered. There would be much excitement amongst the media, accompanied by intense speculation, and there was no way of knowing who might be monitoring such broadcasts. For all these reasons, and to preserve the anonymity of their members, the SDU as always chose to maintain a low profile.

Like most of the rest of the MTR system, Tsim Sha Tsui was a two-floor station built entirely underground by cut-and-cover construction techniques. It consisted of two levels, each 180 metres in length. The upper level formed the commercial area, where ticket machines, automatic turnstiles and a handful of shops were located, as well as a small police report centre. Directly below that, on the lower level, were the blue-tiled platforms where the trains ran through, and where neon-lit advertising hoardings blazed down from the walls above the tracks. Both levels were linked by escalators and tiled stairways, and the whole operation was controlled from the Station-Master's office on the upper level.

When Lewis and his men moved through the outer cordon of PTU guards and passed down on to the upper level, it was rather like landing on the moon. The normally thronged station was now completely evacuated, and the metal roll shutters on the shops were pulled down tight. Outside the Station-Master's office, at the northern extreme of the upper level, four policemen were manning the Forward Control Point: two Chinese constables, a sergeant and a European officer.

When the SDU *foh gei* came through, carrying their heavy kit bags, the European officer looked up immediately from the occurrences book he was inscribing.

'Have to log you and your blokes through, Marty,' said Inspector Donovan, seated behind the desk he had commandeered from the Station-Master.

'What's the situation?'

'Haven't you heard? Some Japs have grabbed the US Secretary of State. They're threatening to blow this whole place to kingdom come. We've secured the station. Nobody here now but police and essential MTR staff manning the control room. Our company commander is in there with the Station-Master, monitoring the radios.'

'What's the latest on the stronghold situation?'

'No movement. They're digging in and waiting for us to get our act together. Come and see.'

Donovan's cleated boots clicked noisily along the tiled floor, the sound emphasised by the echoing emptiness of the place. He led the way down a stationary escalator to platform level. They walked the length of the down-track platform to the farthest point, where the tracks disappeared into the darkness of the tunnel. Here the PTU inspector had deployed the firearms section of his platoon to guard the tunnel mouth: two AR-15 rifles in the hands of sharpshooters, and seven others carrying Remington Wingmaster shotguns. Lewis noted with amusement the section sergeant using a rattan shield to cover himself as he peeked into the tunnel. That served to underline the totally unreal quality of the situation.

'So what's happening in there? Anything?'

'Hard to tell from here. The track dips away as it leaves the station, but you can just make out the tail-lights of the train.'

Lewis leaned out to look into the great circular tube, but the points of red light gave no clue as to distance.

'How far inside?'

'Just a few hundred metres, I heard from upstairs. They're not sure yet, but definitely this side of the harbour.'

'They have it cordoned off on the other side?'

'Yes, Charlie company. Relax. Whoever's inside the train, they're going nowhere for the time being. MTR is bringing in shunting engines to block both ends.'

Marty Lewis continued staring into the forbidding blackness of the tunnel. He had been used to assaulting rooms and buildings, choosing a blind side from which to approach or a weakened partition wall through which to crash, but this was something quite different. The hostages were held inside a solid concrete tube whose thickness was measured in feet, and the only approach was from either end. Obviously the terrorists would have observers positioned in the front and rear cabs, and with the kind of weaponry reported, Lewis did not give much for his own men's chances in rushing the train.

As he made a hurried series of notes in his briefing book, a runner appeared from the upper concourse to inform him that Mel Kale had arrived and wanted to see him in the station control room. Now would begin the planning session that could prove crucial to the safety of the hostages. Between them they had to be ready with a workable 'Immediate Action Plan' within forty-five minutes: one which had a chance of neutralising the stronghold if and when the killing started.

'OK, Ah-Wong,' said Lewis to his team sergeant, a dark-skinned Hakka renowned for his ability to blow the bugle, i.e. drink a litre of San Miguel from the bottle in a single continuous gulp. 'Get the men into black overalls and stand by here. We're going to have the "head shed".'

In the Tsim Sha Tsui control room Mel Kale was on the phone to the Incident Commander at Kowloon Bay. As he had correctly predicted, Taff Owen was no longer in charge there. This operation was serious enough to merit international attention, so was now being handled by the Regional Commander/Kowloon; a senior officer of assistant commissioner rank. As in all terrorist incidents, he had at his disposal an *ad hoc* unit known as the Close Action Group, consisting of officers with all the peculiar specialist skills required for such cases. This unit consisted of the PTU personnel manning the Forward Control Point in the inner cordon, the Police Negotiator Team who would conduct the negotiations with the suspects, a psychiatrist who was a full colonel coopted from the British Military Hospital to advise on the mental and emotional conditions of both the suspects and the hostages, and the Special Duties Unit itself.

When he had finished his call and was fully appraised of the situation at Kowloon Bay, Kale returned to the chart table where Station-Master Cheung had been using engineering drawings to explain the situation in minute detail.

'They must have had first-rate inside knowledge,' said Kale puffing out his cheeks. 'Not many people could have known how to crack the ventilator building.'

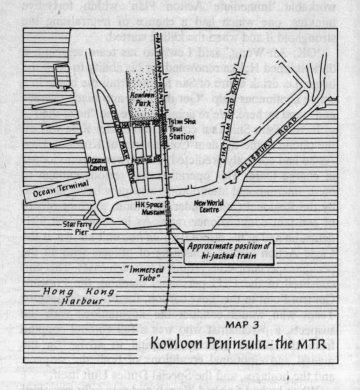

MAP 3
Kowloon Peninsula – the MTR

As Cheung's finger traced the line of the parapet on the drawing, Kale noticed the shaking of his fingers.

'Are you all right, Mr Cheung?'

The man looked nervously at Kale, then down at the table. Suddenly his shoulders collapsed in resignation.

'They have my daughter,' he said quietly.

'Who does?'

'I don't know. I just gave them what they asked for. They said they would cut off her hands and feet if I didn't...'

Quickly Cheung explained how he had been contacted and forced to disclose full details of the MTR's security procedures and tunnel access points. Kale listened carefully resisting the temptation to pass judgement on the man's actions. Now, that was so much water under the bridge.

'Thank you for telling us, Cheung,' he said gently. 'I don't know if we can get your daughter back – we'll just have to wait and see. But what I must know is exactly how much you told them.'

'*Ho, ngoh ji,*' the MTR man nodded, shattered by the result of his betrayal. The shame closed in on him like the walls of the tunnel.

Just then the door opened and the Bravo team leader appeared in the doorway. His raised eyebrows indicated the privacy of the anteroom. Kale took the hint and stepped outside.

'How's it look down there?'

'Not good,' said Lewis, shaking his head. 'Approach routes are bloody limited. The moment we set foot inside that tunnel, they're bound to spray it with automatic fire. If they have explosives, they might also have the rails wired. Even with body armour, my lads would be cut to pieces.' He paused, wet his lips and dropped his voice still further. 'Maybe this is one we ought to walk away from. Tell the government to give these people what they ask for?'

Kale looked down, considering what Lewis was telling him.

'Maybe you're right. I just found out the Station-Master has been supplying them with inside knowledge.'

'Fuck me! Why?'

'Somebody kidnapped his daughter. Threatened to chop her fingers off or something.'

'Bastards.'

'They've done their homework, all right,' sighed Kale, rubbing the back of his neck. Beneath his heavy moustache, the movements of his lips were barely visible. 'That just means we have to do ours twice as well if we want to get our lads out alive.'

'Is Becker in there, Mel?' asked Marty Lewis, concern writ large in his face.

Kale shrugged, indicating his frustration.

'I don't know that yet, mate. Nobody seems to know. Let's get back inside. Best thing we can do now is concentrate on those tunnel diagrams and wait for their ultimatum.'

ome of the many restaurants in Western district. From the
anxious tone of Joe's voice Roman had guessed it was
something important. Joe did not explain further and
Roman did not question him.

Over tea, and afterwards, Joe related what he had
learned from his agents; also his suspected involvement in
the death of the American diplomat.

The girl Kim looking for works at the Basking Peacock
on Kowloon side. She uses the name Ruby Tang,' for

TWENTY

Late that afternoon, about the same time the sound of
Okamoto's voice first broke across the console at
Kowloon Bay, Joe Lai was boarding a jetfoil for the
thirty-mile trip west along the coast of China to the
Portuguese enclave of Macau. Sitting in a window seat
on the starboard side he watched the yellow rock and
lush green cap of Lantau Island slip by, oblivious of the
drama then unfolding beneath Hong Kong harbour.
Even had news appeared on the television screen
mounted above the seats of the passenger cabin, he
might still not have noticed, so wrapped up was he in his
thoughts.

It was a beautifully calm evening, with the setting sun
gilding the surface of the water. As Joe gazed fixedly
through the window, a pair of flying fish leapt from the
water in a series of high slippery arcs before disappearing
again below the surface. An immediate whoop of
pleasure rose from the seats around him. Most of the
people on the jetfoil were going to Macau for one thing
and one thing alone: the gambling. So for them the sight
of the flying fish, bodies burnished gold by the setting
sun, was an unmistakable portent of good fortune.

Even Joe Lai began to wonder if this could be auspicious: perhaps at last his own fortunes were changing.
That day had already proved eventful; with luck the
night would bring still greater revelations.

It had all begun with his call to Roman Fung's office
in Headquarters, when Joe had asked for a meeting in

one of the many restaurants in Western district. From the serious tone of Joe's voice Roman had guessed it was something important. Joe did not explain further, and Roman did not question him.

Over tea and *dim sum* Joe related what he had learned from his agent Philip about triad involvement in the death of the American diplomat.

'The girl I'm looking for works at the Barking Peacock on Kowloon side. She uses the name Ruby Tang.' Joe took out his wallet and showed Fung the picture.

Roman's face registered surprise. 'But that's the same girl *we're* looking for!' He studied the face in the picture to be sure there was no mistake.

'The US Consulate finally came through with a picture from Reicher's apartment. This is the same girl, all right.'

'*Gam ngaam ah!*' said Joe, no less surprised. 'Quite a coincidence.'

Roman nodded slowly, deep in thought.

'I'll give you another coincidence. My team's been ordered to assist investigations into those serial killings of ballroom girls. One of the victims turned out to be a hostess at the Barking Peacock – and according to my woman sergeant, Ruby Tang was the last to see her alive. Apparently the girl became drunk and abusive, so Ruby had to put her in a taxi and send her home. Nobody's seen either of them since.'

Joe refilled both teacups. As he drank he glanced around the restaurant, paying particular attention to the entrance stairway, the memory of Tasker's killing still fresh in his mind. Cautiously his eyes checked each of the young toughs who lounged about reading newspapers or kung-fu comics, for signs of undue interest. Of late he found it hard to relax in these places.

Casually he placed both elbows on the table and clasped his hands before his face to conceal the movements of his lips.

'I had a whisper that Ruby Tang was in serious trouble with the San Yee On.'

'What kind of trouble?' asked Roman with growing interest.

'It seems that when the girl went missing, so did something else of tremendous value. My informant didn't know what, just that the society now wants her dead. They think she's probably hiding out somewhere in Macau.'

Roman's face came alive.

'Macau? I think I can help you there. We discovered Ruby Tang has an elder married sister living there. She runs some kind of cooked food concession at the dog track. Even if Ruby's not at the sister's place, it's a safe bet the sister will know how to contact her.'

A slow smile crept across Joe Lai's face. At last, the light at the end of the tunnel. He clapped a grateful hand on his friend's shoulder.

'*M'goi sai*, Roman. You're better than gold.'

'*M'sai gam gong*,' shrugged the other detective. 'No need to speak so. We're brothers aren't we?'

Roman's cup had hardly been touched; still Joe filled it again to the brim, to demonstrate his appreciation. It was a simple ritual, one of a thousand in everyday life among the Chinese community; but one which gave both men pleasure now: a symbol of the friendship and loyalty that they shared. Brothers in Gwan-Dai.

'What's *your* interest in the girl?' asked Roman, tapping the table top with two fingers. The correct gesture of appreciation for the tea.

'If the San Yee On wants her dead, then she has nothing to lose by helping me nail them.'

For the first time Roman Fung appeared sceptical.

'Do you have clearance from Headquarters to pursue this thing to Macau?'

Joe's eyes were fixed again on the faces moving between tables, his good humour suddenly gone.

569

'I don't have the time for all those memos to Interpol and all the rest of it.'

'What do you mean? Listen, Joe, you'd better...'

'No, *you* listen, *hing dai*! We were given a job to investigate the biggest robbery in Hong Kong history. There haven't been that many things in my life that I could say I was proud of – really proud – but I felt honoured to be entrusted with that responsibility. We worked our arses off, surfaced some pretty good leads; it started to look good. We grew more and more convinced the robbery was the work of the San Yee On. We looked like getting a result. Then one night, as we all sat down to dinner, John Tasker was murdered – *right before our eyes!* The killer was a San Yee On executioner. Ruby Tang is my only chance now. Do you really think I am going to let official channels get in the way of solving this case and finding Tasker's killer?'

At once Roman regretted questioning his decision. He realised the pain Joe still felt.

'You're going to need help, Joe. Who have you got on your side?'

'I have James Weldon's backing.'

'But he can't help you in Macau. You know how it is there. The organisations control everything. You can't even take your detective special with you: if Customs found it, even Weldon couldn't keep you out of jail. You're fast enough with your hands and feet, but what chance do you give yourself if the triads find you first?'

'We'll have to see.'

Exasperated, Roman tossed his chopsticks aside. It seemed Joe Lai was beyond reasoning – obviously determined to get himself killed in his quest for revenge. Both men were embarrassed by the awkward silence that followed. Then, abruptly, Joe took a folded envelope from his pocket and laid it carefully on the table.

'There's one thing I'd like you to do for me. I want you to give this letter to Weldon personally.' Joe's hand closed protectively over the envelope. 'To nobody else. Not to his secretary or Staff Officer – not even to the Deputy Commissioner. Weldon himself. Do you understand?'

'Of course,' muttered Roman irritably, but Joe Lai's request only served to confuse him further. He took the envelope in his hand and tried to look through the paper. 'What's in this that's so important anyway?'

'I'm afraid I can't tell you at this stage. You'll have to trust me. If you have problems getting in to see the Commissioner, tell him you have something from me. That should be enough. I'll be back in a few days. By that time I should have what I need – and you'll have the witness you need for those Gwan-Dai murders.'

'A precious little package, this girl. But don't be so sure she'll give evidence. You know the triad penalty for traitors.'

Joe did indeed. The thirty-six triad oaths were very clear on that score: If I give information to the authorities about my brothers I shall suffer death by five thunderbolts.

It was an ancient punishment. Only nowadays each thunderbolt was delivered by a bullet from a .45 automatic.

After clearing Macau Customs, Joe Lai joined the growing line outside the jetfoil terminal and eventually climbed into the back of a beat-up black and yellow taxi. He was trying hard to put Roman Fung's warnings out of his head.

Of course, Roman had been correct about the detective special. After a brief discussion with the duty officer, Joe had been allowed to store the weapon in the armoury at Waterfront police station, adjacent to the Macau Ferry terminal. Touching the space where the pistol ought to lie, he felt more vulnerable than ever.

'*Gau Cheung, mgoi*,' he told the Chinese driver, as

571

the throaty engine raced away along the sea-front road. Ahead, in the gathering dusk, he could see the garish lights of the Lisboa Casino – a beacon to thousands of excited tourists. The building stood facing the sea, its ornately crowned circular tower of yellow and white stucco rising skyward and resembling the spindle of a giant roulette wheel. Joe loved to gamble as much as the next man, and the sight of this spindle sent a tingle to the tips of his ears. Later, he thought – right now he was heading down-market for the Canidrome, where the dog-racing was held twice-weekly.

The Canidrome lay well away from the main hustle and buzz of Macau nightlife, in an area more appropriate to its seedy status: a run-down stadium lacking the grandeur of the trotting track on nearby Taipa island, and light-years away from the luxury of Hong Kong's race-tracks. Here the presence of loansharks in crocodile-skin shoes and illegal bookmakers operating through handsignals and portable telephones all testified to the presence of organised crime. Joe paid off the taxi, and joined a crowd of Chinese pushing through the turn-stiles. They were shabby men of all ages, who studied form books and folded newspapers in the gloom: all searching for lucky omens as much as any actual evidence of form. Savouring the down-at-heel atmos-phere, Joe marvelled that, despite frequent allegations of fixing and doping, dog-racing could remain as popular as ever with the public. These races were featured on TV back in Hong Kong, and odds were quoted at the Jockey Club's off-course betting centres.

Entering the public enclosure Joe made his way up to the back of the terrace. There he stood and looked around: not at the greyhounds being paraded past the enclosure in their coloured jackets prior to the first race, but instead through the crush of faces and bare brown arms – the excited punters fanning the hot evening air with their race-cards. His eyes picked out several hawkers moving through the crowd, selling everything from ice-cream to dried plums – the delicacies enjoyed by the Chinese at public events. These he discounted: he was looking for a cooked food vendor, and *they* all kept stationary pitches because of the potential danger from the gas burners and boiling fat and water they used.

Then he spotted it: a hawker cart selling *gaai bei* – boiled chicken legs. The cart was crowded close beside the first line of betting windows. Behind it, regularly plucking chicken legs from the steaming tub, stood a Chinese woman: tallish, thirty-ish – and not bad-looking either. A slightly gone-to-seed version of Ruby Tang herself, perhaps.

Joe Lai pressed through the crowd towards the betting windows, aware of a sudden rush of excitement. Behind him an electronic whine sounded through the loud-speakers as the first hare began to run. After it came the baying of dogs, and finally the shotgun twang of the traps springing open.

Above the roars of delight and encouragement the woman continued her vending. '*Gaai bei, gaai bei! Sik gaai bei!*'

Casually Joe stepped up and held out a ten-dollar note. Then, without preface, he said: 'I'm looking for Ruby.'

At once the woman's body stiffened – just for a moment – then she wiped a greasy hand on her overalls and began fishing for change. Joe knew then he had found the sister. Gwan-Dai was indeed smiling.

'You're mistaken, sir. Got no rubies – just got *gaai bei*,' she muttered.

'*Ho ye. Ho sik gong ye.*' Joe congratulated her on her wit. 'I'm talking about your sister Ruby.'

Her eyes stared past him, pretending to follow the race as the dogs streaked round the final bend and passed the cheering enclosure in a series of fluid leg beats.

'Got no sister,' she insisted. 'Only brothers. Two in China mainland, one more in Hong Kong. Now step aside. I've got thirty dollars down, and you're blocking my view.'

As the dogs reached the finishing post she appeared to lose interest in the race. She filled her lungs and continued to call out her wares.

'Listen to me!' insisted Joe, taking her arm firmly. 'There's no point you play-acting. Ruby's in a heap of trouble with the San Yee On. There are people here looking to kill her. You know it – and I know it.'

'And who the hell are you?' she demanded.

'Ruby's only chance.'

The woman looked him full in the face for the first time and asked, 'Hong Kong Police?'

When Joe nodded in confirmation she did not look as surprised as he might have expected.

'You prove that?' she asked.

The woman looked long and hard at his warrant card then back at his face, as if uncertain what she was looking for. She removed the lid of the cooking tub and began to stir the steaming water needlessly with a large steel spatula.

'I don't speak to police.'

Joe Lai had lost count of the number of times he had heard that. It represented the innate mistrust of authority shared by Chinese communities all over the world. *Policemen beat up people and line their own pockets . . .*

'Spare me the lecture,' said Joe impatiently. 'You know what the triads will do if they find Ruby?'

For a long moment her eyes glazed over with uncertainty, then, just as she seemed poised to speak, a rather skinny youth appeared with a handful of coins – only to be shooed away by her.

'*Yau mo gau choh!*' the youth protested sullenly as he turned and stalked off.

The woman dropped her voice to a barely audible

whisper. An unexpected tremor showed itself in her lower lip.

'She said they would come looking for her sooner or later – didn't say anything about police, though. She told me to watch I wasn't followed home. "Watch for strangers," she said, "but who knows what shape they'll come in." After three days I couldn't stand it anymore. She moved out and we agreed to keep in touch by phone. I gave her money and told her to call if she needed anything.'

'Where did she go? Is she still in Macau?'

Ruby's sister sighed deeply, as if a heavy burden had been removed from her shoulders.

'Still here, but I don't know where. Best not to know. Safer that way.'

Joe could see in her face how frayed her nerves had become with worry.

'Would you like to go somewhere and tell me about it? We could meet later if you'd prefer.'

'No!' the woman insisted. 'What I have to tell you can be said here and now. Then you must go at once.'

'If that's the way you'd prefer it, sister.'

'It is,' she said bitterly, 'and if you're not who you say you are, then damn your soul to hell!'

She was a woman who did not waste words. Joe listened to her brief story, aware of the depths of her fear for her own children. He detected a certain resentment of the fact that Ruby had brought them all into close contact with danger and of Ruby's longstanding relationship with the triads who had proved her very undoing.

'You could spend a month searching the brothels and hostels for her, and still not find her,' she said contemptuously. 'But if you truly want to find her before these gangsters, then search the casinos. Ruby never could resist the tables. She'll pawn all her jewellery for them. She gambles practically every night – that's how she keeps her fears at bay for a few hours.'

'There are dozens of casinos,' Joe said, despairing at the enormity of the task before him. 'Could you be more specific?'

She shook her head.

'No. Only to say she stays away from the Lisboa – that would be suicide. I warned her to keep to the smaller places, warned her to stay away in the early evenings. Most of them are open twenty-four hours, anyway. You'll find her at the tables from three in the morning until breakfast time.'

Joe thanked her for her trust in him. He felt he owed her that much reassurance that she had not condemned her own sister to a triad execution.

'Don't worry, I swear by Gwan-Dai I won't rest until she's safe. Believe me, I need her help every bit as much as she needs mine.'

Outside the Canidrome Joe tossed the chicken leg into a litter-bin and caught another taxi back uptown. There were dozens of casinos to check, but he could not begin work until three the next morning. That was good, because right now he needed a decent meal and a rest in preparation for the long night's vigil. After that he knew he could pick up on local gossip by visiting the Hotel Estoril for a relaxing Thai massage. They would know where to find the kind of girl he was looking for.

Back inside the stadium, the dogs were parading for the second race as the skinny Chinese youth who had been shooed away jogged back up the concrete terrace and hovered expectantly beside the four-man knot standing there. The kid was selfconscious beside the older, tougher operators. At length he tugged the sleeve of one of the Chinese – the one wearing gold-framed glasses – and whispered into his ear.

Whatever the grandeur of Government House, the actual

seat of government in Hong Kong is a much less pre-possessing, low-rise granite building located just below the US Consulate-General on Garden Road. Known simply as CGO, the Central Government Offices building houses a miniature parliament chamber wherein the Legislative and Executive Councils meet to advise the Governor in his administration of what has for some time been officially named the 'British dependent territory'. In another part of the same building, however – far removed from the eyes and ears of the media which monitor political proceedings – there is a well-equipped crisis-management facility known as the Civil Coordination Centre, with excellent communications to both police and the military control centres. It was here that Sir Andrew Mackie assembled the team who would assist him in managing this particular crisis.

After James Weldon's first call to Government House, it had needed just thirty-five minutes to locate and bring together the five permanent members of the Governor's Security Committee. In addition to the Police Commissioner himself, these were the Chief Secretary, the Attorney General, the Secretary for Security, and the Political Advisor. Later came the coopted members – those whom the Governor personally invited to sit in and provide the additional specialist information needed for the decision-making process. The US Consul-General was now an obvious choice, together with John Prioletti, the CIA head of station. Then there was Henry St John-Black, Director of Special Branch, and finally the operations director of the Mass Transit Railway.

It was almost 6.00 p.m. before the full session finally got under way.

Sir Andrew Mackie took his seat and called the meeting to order. On the table before him a red-bound folder, bearing a secret classification, lay open at the section headed CRISIS MANAGEMENT, though he knew in that moment that no amount of prior training could have fully prepared him for this. True, he had previously attended courses at a rambling mansion in the Surrey countryside at which senior civil servants were exercised in the management of a wide range of terrorist incidents. But the reality of it was something else.

The other men seated around the table fingered their notes nervously and waited in silence. A slight odour of mildew permeated the air, emanating from the heavy scarlet drapes.

'Gentlemen,' Sir Andrew began, eyeing each one in turn. 'For those of you who may not already know, it seems that an MTR train carrying the American Secretary of State and his entire party has been hijacked by suspected terrorists.'

'Suspected?' John Prioletti muttered with thinly-concealed sarcasm. The Consul-General shot him a reprimanding glance and his eyes dropped to the table, fingers tapping quietly in irritation.

The Governor cleared his throat and continued.

'Before we get down to details I'd like to state our objectives clearly, so we don't waste time on irrelevancies. Jeremy, would you...?'

As Sir Andrew spoke his private secretary took up a felt-tipped marker and inscribed each point on the long, wall-mounted whiteboard to the Governor's right.

'The questions we must answer are these. First: what are the demands of the terrorists and who has the authority to grant them? Second: what is the apparent reason for the incident and how much planning appears to have gone into it? Third: who has executive jurisdiction over the incident? Fourth: how symbolically important are the hostages? Fifth: who are the suspects and how much is known of them? Sixth: what is our policy on handling such incidents, and what is the political cost of the response?'

Having finished reading from his notes, Sir Andrew's gaze now fell upon the Commissioner of Police. 'Could we start with the briefing paper from your people, James?'

Weldon took the papers from the Director of Special Branch and passed them around the table. The delegates read in silence.

SECRET

Special Branch
Royal Hong Kong Police
2nd October, 1993

SPECIAL REPORT TO H.E. THE GOVERNOR'S SECURITY COMMITTEE ON THE HIJACK OF A MASS TRANSIT RAILWAY TRAIN CARRYING A FOREIGN DIGNITARY

1. At 16.07 hours on Tuesday, 1st October 1993, a special train carrying Mr William Fredericks, United States Secretary of State, and a party of advisors and security personnel was hijacked by armed terrorists suspected to belong to the Japan Red Army (JRA).

2. Initial enquiries indicate that the train left Tsuen Wan station at 15.33 hours precisely, carrying only the Secretary's party and one liaison representative from MTR. According to the schedule agreed between SB security and the MTR, the train was to have proceeded without stopping to Chater station on Hong Kong Island where a motorcade was waiting to take the dignitary back to his residence at the Hilton hotel. The journey should have taken approximately twenty minutes. Instead, for reasons as yet unknown, as it approached the cross-harbour section of the system, the train made an emergency stop and was attacked by the terrorists who had gained access on to the track via the northern ventilator building. Indications are that the terrorists used gas, an incapacitating agent, dibenzoxazepine (known by the formula CR), to over-power the security party. This gas is in wide use throughout the world as a riot control agent, and is reckoned to be six times more effective than CS. Aside from the burning effect on mucus membrane surfaces the agent acts upon the sympathetic nervous system, producing effects of choking, extreme nausea, and rendering victims unconscious in somewhat less than one minute.

3. At first MTR control room staff were unable to contact the driver/operator of the train (C/M Suen Sai-kit) but at 16.56 hours radio contact was made with an unknown male who claimed to have hijacked the train on behalf of the JRA. At this time no demands were made other than to speak with the authorities. In accordance with emergency procedure, MTR staff then immediately alerted their own senior staff and informed police (MTR district console). Shortly there-after DC MTR ordered the suspension of train services within the Immersed Tube (IT) and the evacuation of underground stations on either side. Tsim Sha Tsui and Admiralty stations are now under cordon by Foxtrot and Charlie companies, respectively, of Police Tactical Unit (PTU) who are also handling crowd control in the vicinity of station approaches.

4. Staff Officer/Counter Terrorism (SO/CT) was contacted by pager at 17.12 hours, and the Director of Police Operations (D/Ops.) placed the Special Duties Unit (SDU) on immediate standby in case the situation should seriously deteriorate. The officer commanding the Special Duties Unit (OC/SDU) has visited the scene at TST station and is discussing the situation with senior operation staff of MTR at Kowloon Bay headquarters. Police Negotiator Team was activated as were specialist technical support units. All relevant players for full-blown terrorist incident are currently stationed at Kowloon Bay where an Incident Command Centre (ICC) has been set up adjacent to the police control room. In view of the serious nature of the incident the Incident Commander has been designated as the Director of Operations (D/Ops.).

5. First subsequent contact with the suspects was made by DC MTR at 17.21 hours, who was able to ascertain that all persons aboard the train were well and, at present, unharmed. During this communication the terrorists announced themselves as the OKAMOTO CELL of the JRA and dictated a list of demands as follows:

a) A guarantee of a full British or US passport for every Hong Kong citizen wishing to leave the territory before June, 1997.

b) An immediate withdrawal of all US naval units from South-East Asia.

c) A ransom of $20,000,000 (USD) in gold for the release of the Secretary of State.

The suspects set an initial deadline of midnight on Wednesday, 3rd October, by which time they require an agreement in principle to each of the above demands. If an agreement is not forthcoming they threaten to explode charges placed on board the train and within the IT thereby destroying both.

6. At 17.36 the terrorists released one of their hostages, John Cinch, a State Department employee and Regional Security Officer (RSO) at the US Consulate-General. Although claimed as an act of goodwill, actual reasons for his release are unclear at the present moment. However, Cinch was able to give police an extremely detailed account of conditions prevailing on board the train where most of the hostages have been bound and ordered to lie in the aisle. Most alarming of his observations was the claim that the Secretary of State, whilst being otherwise unharmed, has been made to wear an explosive device around his waist which the terrorists claim will be initiated if any attempt is made to storm the train.

7. The train is now located at the northern end of the IT, four hundred metres south of TST station in a position of extremely limited access. In addition, the suspects are believed to have used explosives to booby-trap the front and rear of the train, thus effectively cutting off any possibility of approach or close observation.

ASSESSMENT

8. It has long been recognised by Special Branch that the JRA would like to increase its presence in Hong Kong. Over the past five years they have repeatedly attempted to recruit Chinese students at the Hong Kong University to their cause. One possible motive for this is the infiltration of the student democracy movement with the intention of inciting violence. In a much broader sense, Hong Kong represents one of the most obvious examples of bourgeois capitalism in the Far East and therefore an obvious target for an organisation, like JRA, which still espouses world revolution. As leader of the western capitalist world the United States and members of its government are held to be legitimate targets for terrorist action.

9. Aside from the purely political motive certain facts indicating a connection with organised crime have also come to light. One unconfirmed source has revealed that Okamoto's group came to Hong Kong in early

582

August after first being contacted in Manila by a Chinese businessman. It was the belief of the source that this man represented a group of Hong Kong Chinese with links to local Chiu Chau triad societies. Furthermore, it now seems likely that a portion of the proceeds of the Shatin Jockey Club robbery on Saturday, 15th September was used to purchase weapons and otherwise fund this incident. Taken together these facts suggest a number of possible motives – not least of which is one of simple criminal extortion. Enquiries are continuing with a view to establishing the exact identities of those involved in planning these crimes.

CONCLUSION

10. There is now little doubt but that the suspects are indeed who they claim to be and that they have the weapons and explosives to carry out their threats. Given the excellent tactical choice of location for the hostage-taking, and the degree of planning which must have been involved, we must conclude that we are dealing with a very credible, well organised and highly motivated cell. It must be emphasised that since the Japan Red Army has on numerous occasions demonstrated its commitment to violence there is every reason to believe they would carry through these threats if denied.

R.A. Tavistock
(for Director of Special Branch)

The first person to speak was Bob Walters, the US Consul-General.

'Right off the bat, sir, I have to say I've been in touch with Washington and I'm instructed to offer the services of our Delta Force hostage intervention group. One of their training teams is currently based just outside Seoul. Using their own C-140s, they could be here in just a few hours.'

The Commissioner bridled. The last thing he wanted was another counter-terrorist force running around the place, for he well knew the difficulties and the dangers of crossed lines of command and communication – difficulties which had always hamstrung the US counter-terrorist effort in the past. He looked to the head of the table for a swift response, and was not disappointed.

'Consul-General, I have no objection to your bringing in observers,' said the Governor quite firmly. 'In fact, I would welcome it. Everyone can learn something from these incidents. But there is no question but that the Royal Hong Kong Police will be responsible for the prosecution of this matter. They have their own expertise.'

'I understand your feelings, sir,' countered the American, trying his best to sound reasonable. 'I know you have your own vest-pocket version of a unit. But these terrorists are dug in deep, and we're talking about a senior member of the US cabinet here. I'm afraid, no matter what you say, our President is going to intercede with your Prime Minister.'

Sir Andrew bit back the urge to show his irritation. He was, after all, the representative of Her Majesty's Government, with absolute authority for the day-to-day running of the territory.

'Consul-General, the Prime Minister has already consulted with the officer commanding our own Special Air Service Regiment. He immediately gave his full backing to our people. We anticipate the arrival of an SAS observer team from Brunei by 21.30 this evening. If we do require additional support, it will be to them that we turn. Now, if I've made myself clear, I suggest we devote ourselves to answering the questions on that board.'

There was a blue police transit parked at the junction of Lock Road and Peking Road as Rhee Joon-kil walked out from the Hyatt Regency's main entrance. As he came down the vehicle ramp to street level, he counted eleven green uniforms manning the cordon around the MTR entrance. When he reached the bottom of the vehicle ramp he stood for a moment on the pavement beside the junction, to light a cigarette and take in the scene. Map in one hand, wrist-bag in the other, he gave an excellent impression of just another tourist planning his route.

Affecting also a tourist's ignorance, he pretended not to notice that the metal barriers which cut off access to the MTR also barred the way into Lock Road, and that he was therefore on the wrong side of the cordon. Looking around, he noticed the complete absence of all traffic save for emergency vehicles and huddled knots of onlookers crowding the pavements. On Peking Road the neon hoardings above the bars, jewellers' and electrical goods shops blazed like a forest fire as their proprietors experienced a sudden boost in turnover. Here and there, opportunist hawkers had drawn up their carts to sell stick sugarcane, curried fishballs and other snacks to the ever-growing audience. Outside the open doorways of the shops, spectators gathered to stare intently at the barred frontage of the MTR entrance immediately beside the Hyatt Regency hotel.

After less than a minute a police constable, wearing a blue beret and a red shoulder tab behind his number – to indicate that he spoke English – approached Rhee and asked him to move on. The Korean bowed, apologised profusely in poor English, and set off along Hankow Road towards the Haiphong Road entrance of the MTR. Due to the complete closure of that section of Nathan Road, it took him some little time to survey each entrance on foot. Squeezing through the sweating bodies jamming each street required real effort, and Rhee was reminded of the organised street chaos he had experienced here during Chinese New Year. He crossed Salisbury Road and joined the pedestrians strolling the harbour-front causeway. From there he could observe the police cordon which now surrounded the North Ventilator Building.

At 8 p.m. precisely he found a secluded spot on the causeway and stopped to look out across the harbour, as if savouring the stunning panorama of Hong Kong Island across the water. There was no mist that night; high up in the cleft of Victoria Peak he could see the restaurant lights in the Peak tram terminal burning brightly. Far below, illuminated concrete slabs and walls of light reared out of the darkness, all along the waterfront a jewelled ribbon of hoardings assaulted his senses, advertising names known the world over: American cigarettes, German automobiles, Australian beer, Swiss watches as slim as after-dinner mints, the latest in futuristic audio and visual decks from Japan. To Rhee's left a scattering of pleasure junks and, among them, one police launch rode gently at anchor off Kowloon public pier.

Looking around once again, more cautiously this time, he unzipped the wrist-bag, removed a set of Walkman headphones and placed them over his ears. Bringing the bag close to his face he spoke quickly, in Japanese, to the powerful radio within. He received an acknowledgement in less than ten seconds, and then made his report to the hijackers beneath his feet.

'All exits are well covered, including your original access point. Helicopters were observed landing in Kowloon Park, so presume the hunting dogs are on hand. Remain calm. No mention of our primary demands in news broadcasts, so must conclude the Americans are treating this seriously. Secondary demands well publicised. Already expressions of support on local media. Your position looks strong at this time. Over.'

The response came back distorted by layers of intervening concrete. For a moment a wave of white noise poured from the headphones. Quickly Rhee adjusted the gain of his radio set, and listened.

'... all in good condition and without injury. Have agreed to receive food from the authorities, but have refused to accept a landline at this time due to possibility of it being bugged. No visual contact with security forces as yet. Have heard strange sounds from tunnel walls. Cannot distinguish location of unidentified activity. May have to execute hostage if this reoccurs. No other problems. Out.'

As soon as Becker stepped off the JAL flight at Kai Tak International Airport he knew something was wrong. The airport security police inside the terminal wore bullet-proof vests over their normal blue overalls. The Chinese inspector from Special Branch's airport detachment waiting to meet him at the air-bridge wore a serious expression.

'What's up?' Becker already dreaded the answer. 'Fredericks?'

'Afraid so,' came the quiet, almost inevitable reply.

The Kowloon Bay headquarters of the MTR Corporation is a modern multi-storey office block of orange stone and darkened glass nestling beside one of Kowloon's many chicken-coop flatblock housing estates. As the Special Branch saloon swung through the crowded bus terminus opposite the building's main entrance, Becker saw ranks of reporters and video-camera crews massing outside and asked to be dropped beyond them. He moved quickly down several flights of concrete steps, past another complex which housed the sheds and turntables of the train maintenance yards on one side, and the computerised operations centre on the other. Adjacent to these was the headquarters of the

MTR police district. Becker identified himself to the duty officer at the door and was escorted immediately up to the control centre.

The police response was already well developed. The incident commander, now Ray Doogan, had taken over every available office from which to control the crisis, but the operation was focused around two particular rooms.

In the first room was the police negotiator team: a superintendent and four officers together with the metal cases containing their communications equipment. Doogan had allotted them a separate room to protect them from the noise and bustle going on everywhere else. The second, larger room was occupied by men from the intelligence-gathering units, both operational and technical. Doogan had made this room his own base; he had moved in four portable telephones to augment existing lines of communication with HQ/PolMil, Government House, and other departments supporting the effort.

Doogan himself was barking into one of the phones as Becker arrived. Ever since the incident began, there had been a stream of senior officers turning up at the Forward Control Point on what they called 'reconnaissance trips'. Complaints had filtered back from SDU and other covert units that these sightseers were 'getting in the bloody way!'

'I don't care who they are,' bellowed Doogan. 'Get them all out *now*. No one else to pass through the cordon without my orders. OK!'

His phone hit the cradle with a crash.

Becker smiled to himself. But his eyes devoured the large whiteboard before him. Someone had sketched on it a large-scale tunnel diagram indicating the Immersed Tube, the northern ventilator building and the present position of the hijacked train. Beside that was fixed a paper sheet showing a coloured cutaway diagram of an MTR train, taken from one of the company's publicity brochures. To the right of the board was a set of enlarged black and white photographs of the platform at Tsim Sha Tsui, of the ventilator building, and even some grainy infra-red shots of the rear of the train, which must have been taken from Tsim Sha Tsui station and enlarged many times. Down at the left edge of the board Becker recognised the NPA photographs of Okamoto and his group, enclosed in a thick black border. Photos of the hostages were grouped below these, but bordered in green for psychological differentiation. It was as if the competing teams were playing in some sporting fixture: the senior staff inspector from counter-terrorism had even drawn up a headcount: CROWS 8, DOVES 21. Another board displayed a diary of the incident so far, with exact timings noted and a list of the terrorists' demands and deadlines marked in red.

Across the incident room Doogan noticed Becker's tanned features and tall, wiry frame as he examined the intelligence boards.

'You took your sweet time, didn't you?'

'I got caught up in the biggest blow-job Tokyo has seen in years.'

'Very funny, Becker, but this is serious. We're going to need your help with the names and faces of the hostages. Most of them are your own blokes. You know, you're very lucky that typhoon *did* close the airport, otherwise you could be in there with them now.'

'How is the government treating their demands?' Becker asked.

Doogan squared his shoulders.

'You know the rules. No deals with terrorists of whatever colour.'

'Yes, I know what the politicians say. But the Americans were still prepared to deal arms for hostages with Iran, remember.'

'What are you suggesting, Becker?'

'That it's all bullshit. Governments never know what

they'll concede until it comes down to it. So what have you told the terrorists?'

'We told them their demands have been passed on to Washington, but we're having problems with time differences. That the President needs time to consult his military advisers on any pull-out. And that we need more time to put the whole thing together.'

'Are they accepting that?' asked Becker sceptically.

'Not one word of it.' Doogan shook his head. 'The negotiators say Okamoto hasn't budged an inch. When the psychological flannelling starts, he just restates the deadlines and cuts them off.'

Becker frowned thoughtfully, remembering the words of the *oyabun* of Sakaguchi-gumi.

'You can forget about talking this guy down. He's different.'

'What do you mean "different"? He's a terrorist isn't he?'

'I've just got back from Tokyo,' said Becker staring again at the pictures on the board. 'Okamoto has quite a biography. He's not your average terrorist. He won't wear himself out talking politics, so don't waste your time with the psychiatrist.'

'If you know so much, perhaps you could tell us what drives him?'

'It's difficult for a Westerner to understand. He believes that in some past life he was a samurai. All his life he has been studying the art of the sword. This man is high on Zen. Listen, I've been thinking this through. What he's set up here is a physical *koan*.'

'A what?'

'It's a kind of riddle used to help students of Zen achieve their ultimate enlightenment. Often they're no more than stories which defy comprehension. Sometimes they're questions with no obvious answer. Show me the sound of one hand clapping – that kind of thing. Okamoto has set us a problem which he believes has no answer. He believes his position is unassailable because the moment we try to take him he'll push the button on everything and everyone. He knows we daren't risk that.'

'What if we call his bluff? Surely he doesn't intend to die over this?'

'It's no bluff, Ray. If he fails to secure the concessions he has demanded, I think he will blow the whole lot. Code of honour, loss of face, call it what you like – but I think he'll do it.'

Doogan did not know quite what to make of it all. Such concepts were beyond his experience.

'It's early days yet. We'd expect them to still be pretty resolute after only a few hours. But they'll wear themselves out. I've spoken with Dr Gibson, the psychiatrist, and already he's seen encouraging signs of personality weaknesses. He tells me the people who gravitate towards these underground groups have a strong need to *belong* to something. Basically they're inadequate. He believes that when the strain and tension and the lack of sleep have taken their toll, then we'll hear a different tune.'

To Becker this all sounded very familiar: the usual pre-digested psychological assessment trotted out on such occasions. But in this case it was wrong. Dangerously so. It did not gel with what Becker had himself learned of his adversary. That presumption of inadequacy could be true in most criminal cases of domestic hostage-taking, but urban terrorist leaders were often powerful personalities who inspired their followers to dream with their eyes open. And Okamoto's eyes definitely glowed with some cosmic force.

'I think Gibson's wrong, sir. That mumbojumbo doesn't apply in this case. There's only one way those hostages are coming out – and that's over Okamoto's dead body.'

Suddenly Becker realised he was talking too loud. The room had fallen silent and his was the only voice to be heard. Doogan studied Becker's frowning face, then his eyes strayed momentarily across the drawings on the board. Finally he answered, softly and with a certain amount of dread in his voice.

'You'd better pray it doesn't come to that, son.'

'I stopped praying a long time ago,' said Becker, annoyed by Doogan's seeming refusal to comprehend the situation.

'Hope, then. It's a long sad way down to that train, and with no scrap of cover. Those terrorists have automatic weapons as well as body armour. Mel Kale estimates losses of up to fifty per cent for his own men, and perhaps a hundred per cent of the hostages, if we move to neutralise that stronghold. Make that a hundred per cent casualties, if they blow the charges. And if the immersed tube blows open, we'd have the whole South China Sea in on us. The entire system of tunnels on Kowloon side would be flooded out.'

'Isn't there an emergency floodgate or something to cover that contingency?'

'That's right, there is. Twelve tons of steel. And guess where it happens to be? Right above the stricken train. How many hostages do you think that would crush, if it fell? These bastards planned everything down to the last full stop. Frankly, Mr Becker, I don't see how we could authorise a military option on this one. We're just going to have to wait and see what Washington is prepared to offer.'

Joe Lai had checked into the last available room at the Praia Vista Hotel. He changed clothes and then caught another cab back across Macau to the Estoril Hotel and Sauna, restless with expectation. The Praia Vista was a rambling old place perched high on a hill facing out to sea; its peeling stucco frontage and wooden shuttered windows suggested the *pousadas* of old Portugal. To its rear was an open-air terrace where candles burned in bottles on tables looking down over narrow cobbled streets filled with statues of saints. There were things he loved about Macau that he could not find in Hong Kong: the seafood and the Portuguese wines, and that special Latin change of gear so different from the mad clamour of the streets of Kowloon. Here was a lifestyle far slower than Joe was used to, and that was sometimes just what was needed.

Unless one was looking for action . . .

There was plenty of that too, if you were interested.

Joe realised the coming night could drift into morning before he had finished his work, so he had already decided that a relaxing sauna and massage should unwind him enough to grab a few hours' sleep before getting to work. At the Estoril Sauna the massage girls waited in a room shaped like a goldfish bowl. One wall was a sheet of darkened glass through which male customers viewed the ladies before selecting one to perform the massage. The girl Joe chose from the tiered goldfish bowl was a young Thai with skin the colour of pale caramel and with soft, humorous eyes. She wore a wrap-around skirt of purple silk and a tight bodice of crimson that stopped beneath her arms, leaving her neck and shoulders bare.

She took Joe's hand and led him through a beaded curtain and down a dimly-lit corridor, then into a changing room where Indian carpets covered the floor. Here she helped him undress, smiling pleasantly as she folded his clothes into a locker and handed him a thick monogrammed towel for his waist. Next she secured the locker, placed the key on a leather cord around his neck and led him into a pink-tiled bathroom where she pushed him under a spigot gushing with hot water. As he luxuriated beneath the flow, the girl began to soap his body with an enormous sponge. His pleasure in this was unashamedly childlike, allowing himself to be patted and probed as she layered his reddening skin with creamy soap suds. Then with a grin she slid a soapy hand between his thighs, her touch light as a butterfly. An electric shock of excitement shot through his lower belly as her fingers strayed between his buttocks. Immediately his erection reared out of the foam, and the girl smiled softly.

'Your little brother is awake,' she giggled.

Quickly she sluiced the suds away and fastened the towel back around his waist, then led him to the sauna room.

He opened the door and, when the clouds of pine-scented steam had dissipated, he found himself a place on the second level of wooden benches. There he lay flat out, one hand shading his eyes against the glare of the bare bulbs in the ceiling recess. Two other Chinese were sitting at the far end of the room, relaxing in the heat as they discussed blackjack strategy for their evening's gambling.

After just a few minutes Joe found himself beginning to float; the sense of peaceful equilibrium was returning.

Twenty minutes later the girl's gentle hand on his shoulder woke him from his reverie, and she led him away to a private room fitted with a luxurious bath and a padded table.

She placed a fresh towel upon the table and Joe lay down, his face tucked into the recessed hole that allowed for reading. On the shelf below his eyes someone had left a girly magazine open at the centrefold. He reached down and closed the page over the model's lean, tanned body. A moment later the girl's wise fingers began to probe the muscles of his upper back, seeking out the hidden points of tension as if they were small bones. Joe soon lost track of time as she used all her strength to stretch each muscle and crack each joint in his exhausted body. When finally she urged him to turn over, he heard the faint rustle of silk and saw her skirt slide to the floor. Her legs were long and slim, their golden colour

594

extending into the sparse tangle of black hair below a flat, muscular stomach. Slowly unbuttoning her top, she then poured perfumed oil from a porcelain jar on to both hands and applied it first to her thighs, then to her stomach, and finally to her small dark-nippled breasts.

'You like Thai body massage, yes?'

Rising on one elbow, Joe watched as the girl moved on to the table beside him. She stroked a slippery shoulder against his chest, pressing him flat to the table once more. He closed his eyes in anticipation, and a moment later felt her weight slide on top of him, massaging his whole body with a series of slow grinding movements that began low in her pelvis. He shuddered to her touch, the kiss of her stomach sending ripples through his own.

His body seemed to respond to hers almost at once. She was gentle and comforting, and Joe found her attentions a momentary release from all the pain he had sought to deny within himself.

'I like Thai massage very much,' he told her eventually, trailing one oily finger down the channel of her back and over the curve of her buttocks. 'But I didn't pay for extras.'

The girl smiled at this, running one hand across his smooth, hairless chest.

'What your name?' she asked.

'Joe.'

'You good man, Joe...' She smiled. 'But stupid.' Unexpectedly she moved her face to kiss him lightly on the lips. Before he knew what was happening, she had shifted to straddle his thighs. Her breasts now hung above his face, their dark nipples tight and hard. The next thing Joe felt was the girl's weight sliding down all around him. Automatically he grabbed for her waist and pushed hard into her, matching his thrusts to the rhythmic grind of her behind.

In the urgent animal moments that followed, the girl

said nothing except for the one time she managed to gasp, between breaths:

'Who say anything about paying? Good man go free.'

The Thai girl left Joe asleep and took the room out of service so he would not be disturbed. She came back to wake him just after eleven o'clock, as he had requested, bringing a bowl of soup noodles and a pair of chopsticks.

'Maybe I see you again sometime,' he said, pulling on his jeans. Not looking at her.

'No problem.' She shrugged. 'I know good man not stay with massage girl. Massage girl earn good money but not find good man. Some day I quit, then find good man like you, Joe. One who never know I was massage girl. Then can be happy. Have family.' She seemed to enjoy telling him her plan. 'Tell sons not marry massage girl.'

Joe smiled at that, then fastening on his wristwatch he looked at her.

'Listen, maybe you can help me.'

'If I can. Of course, very happy to help.'

'Do you like to gamble?' asked Joe.

'Every massage girl like to gamble. That's better than sex.'

Once again Joe smiled, this time at the enthusiasm evident in the young girl's face.

'If you wanted to play *dai-siu* early in the morning, where would you go?'

'The Lisboa of course.'

'What if you didn't want to be noticed?'

The girl appeared confused by this.

'What's the point of throwing money across table if nobody notices you do it? That's the fun, isn't it? Big Face!'

He had to agree she had a point.

'I'm looking for somewhere quiet where I won't be recognised. There are people here I'd rather not see.' There was more than a grain of truth in that.

'The Jade Palace small and discreet. Or you try Golden Dragon. That's the one I use if I feel lucky. But after two o'clock it's full of ballroom girls, and you might not get to table.'

Joe tipped the girl a hundred Hong Kong dollars for the information.

When he stepped outside into the tree-lined square, the breeze seemed as warm and damp as the air inside the sauna. From out of the night came the faint ringing of one-armed bandits in a nearby casino. On the street itself the night creatures were into their practised routines of hustling the tourists, soliciting business for the many nightclubs and brothels.

At first Joe Lai hung around the entrance of the Estoril, waiting for a cab or bicycle rickshaw to appear. He had decided to make the Lisboa his next stop. There he would play a few hands of blackjack before beginning his search for Ruby Tang. But, as he stood before the parlour's illuminated sign, the taxi-stand remained empty. He was surprised not to see more people around at this time. A young Chinese with blond flashes in his blow-dried hair lounged in a shop doorway, biting on a stick of sugarcane and spitting the chewed pulp into the gutter.

Deciding he would have to walk, Joe turned away to take a shortcut through one of the many cobbled squares. The man with the sugarcane raised one foot and kicked the door behind him twice. Immediately the door opened, and two more blow-dried heads emerged from the shadows. All three set off quietly across the square, staying close to the walls where the shadows covered their movements.

They followed him along three other streets before they made their move, allowing him to stray deeper and deeper into a warren of dilapidated housing – further away from bright street lighting and police patrols. Joe was making his way across another square, heading for a narrow alley at the far corner, when he saw the same youth from the doorway step out ahead of him. Only this time the stick of sugarcane was a two-foot length of steel pipe.

Joe braced himself, bringing both hands close to his belt.

'*Jo mat ye a?* What's this then?'

The kid stared back at him. He wore a tank top bearing the name of some gymnasium, and his arms showed the massive development of a bodybuilder. He slapped the pipe against the wall beside him; above the hollow ring of steel Joe heard two pairs of feet approach from behind, and he felt the sudden pressure of a steel pipe placed across either shoulder.

'We represent the family of Ruby Tang. Why you looking for her?'

Looking down at the tattooed inner forearms, Joe knew at once there was no point arguing. Where these men were concerned, trying to reason did not enter the equation.

'I came to tell her she won the Mark Six lottery,' he said, trying to gauge the exact positions of the two men behind him.

'Think you're smart, don't you, *jaap chai*?'

The word for detective hit him like a slap in the face.

'Ruby Tang is none of your business, *jaap chai*,' said another voice just behind his right ear. The breath was laden with the odour of chilli sauce and ginger.

'Better go home, *jaap chai*,' lisped the third, a little further off to his left – probably about eight o'clock.

Now he had all three located.

'In that case, I'll be going home first thing tomorrow, sirs,' he offered disarmingly.

The bodybuilder jabbed his metal pipe hard into Joe's chest.

'So you will be, *sai lo*. But before you do, let's see how badly your arse can bleed.'

It was the cue Joe needed.

Slapping the pipe down and away from his chest, he pulled his left knee up into his chest, then shot it backward in one explosive kick. He had expected to catch the man low in the gut, but by pure chance he caught the triad square in the groin and sent him scrunched and choking into the wall. Anticipating him, the man to his right skipped sideways, and Joe's second kick touched only the night air.

No fancy stuff, he warned himself, recalling the advice of his teacher; this isn't the fucking movies. Keep it simple and effective or it won't be the opponent who kills you; you'll kill yourself!

Even as Joe fought to regain his balance, the body-builder in front of him began to react.

'Diu lei lo mo!'

He swung the pipe in a lateral arc, lashing out for the policeman's head. Joe tried not to think what the metal would do to his skull if it connected; he had seen enough postmortems to know how easily bone could shatter. Instead he concentrated upon maintaining his equilibrium; preserving the central line of his defence. Wing Chun masters conceived of the upper body as being divided into two by a centre line running down the breastbone, and then into four by a horizontal line just below the chest. In order to defend these areas, they had devised defensive techniques known as guarding the four gates. Joe knew any attack would have to pass through one of these gates and he adjusted his guard in readiness. The thug's muscular arm curved towards him and instinctively Joe swayed left, diverting the movement and drawing the man's weight past him on his right side. Then, as the attacker's balance faltered, Joe slammed his palm into the man's ribs blasting the air from his lungs and sending him reeling into a low wall bordering a flowerbed.

In that same moment Joe felt the air around his right

ear come alive with sound – and the sickening jolt of metal as it crashed down upon his collarbone. His scream of pain was pure reflex, as was the way he dropped and rolled to cushion the force of the blow. He came upright once more, with no time to assess the damage done to his shoulder before the first assailant was back on his feet.

This time when they moved, their attack was better coordinated. Joe took up a new position, using the wall to protect his injured right side. As the two men circled, feinting and jabbing, looking for an opening, Joe heard the retching of the man he had kicked in the balls; his peripheral vision caught the agonised writhings, and he knew there would be no more fight from that one at least.

Joe realised his chances of survival were improving. The bad guys sensed that too. As if realising they must end it before the cop regained strength and confidence, the bodybuilder muttered a hurried instruction to his partner and relaunched the attack with a nerve-jangling scream.

His fingers twitching from the adrenalin that now flooded his body, Joe Lai turned to meet both his attackers head on. They came in fast with batons swinging, the first triad attempting to grab Joe's collar and then crack open his head. Once again his balance was in error. Joe caught the arm with his own left, and stepped inside, striking the hinge of the man's lower jaw with his elbow. He dodged a second blow from the accomplice's weapon before grabbing the bodybuilder's shoulder and tugging right whilst sweeping the man's legs away to the left. The muscular torso pivoted at the waist, and the man fell heavily on his lower back against the stone cobbles.

As the second triad moved in again, Joe noticed a change in his movements: the educated stance of a kung-fu practitioner. The extravagant open guard might have signified any of the Shaolin styles – Joe could not tell which – but this time, instead of dodging or stepping back, Joe stepped inside, engaging the close combat range in which his beloved art of Wing Chun was without peer. Wing Chun was the art of street fighting, it had been perfected through a thousand street battles in the hell-holes of Kowloon. The punches came direct: cutting, slashing, gouging.

Tuning to the other's movements, Joe accepted the double-arm attack and turned it back at the last moment, trapping both the attacker's arms beneath his own armpits and chopping the attacker's throat with the edge of both hands. Completing the close circular movement, he hooked one arm about the man's neck, cranked his locked elbow high in the air and, as the head began to fall, brought his knee crashing upward to meet it. When Joe released his grip the man fell screaming to the ground. He knew then with absolute certainty that the man's shoulder was dislocated. He had felt the muscle tear and the tell-tale wrenching click transmitted through his grip on the upper arm.

The bodybuilder was on his knees now, struggling to haul himself up off the ground. Joe swept his feet from beneath him and once more the man crashed down hard, screaming in agony a second time.

'All right, little brother, talk to me.'

'Fuck ... your ... arse,' the man gasped.

Joe bent over, grabbing the shoulder straps of the bodybuilder's vest. Then, crossing his hands, he pulled one strap through the other so that both bit into the sides of the neck, closing off the flow of blood to the man's brain just long enough to put a scare into him.

'Tell me what I want to know or I'll choke the fucking life out of you. *Hai bin do nei?*' These words were not normal Cantonese spoken on the street but a recognition phrase used between triads. The question was clear: *Where do you stand?* – meaning, in which society are you enrolled? The man's eyes darted around as fear spread across his face. He was trying to swallow but the pressure on his throat prevented that. Joe released his grip a degree or two, and once more urged him to speak.

'In the second lodge,' the triad gasped with difficulty.

'Say it all,' insisted Joe twisting the straps tighter again. 'All your damn nonsense.'

'Hung Obedience Hall of the Golden Orchid. District of Kwangdung and Kwangsi. The lodge of all Hong Kong triad societies.'

'That's better,' smiled Joe, struggling to control the aggression still boiling within him. 'And the name of your society?'

'The honourable Chiu Chau brotherhood of the San Yee On.'

'*Tat doh?*' demanded Joe. More triad slang: an order to report one's status within the society.

'Four three two official: grass sandal.'

'And the name of your protector?'

The triad writhed in silence.

'Who is your *dai lo*?' demanded Joe again. 'Or do you really want to die out here in the street?'

According to Chinese belief, anyone who died out on the street, away from home and family, became a hungry ghost and must wander the world in misery for ever.

'My protector is Eddy Kwok,' the man whispered with difficulty. 'And when he finds you, he will surely kill you, Lai Hing-keung.'

Recollected images of Buchanan's computer graphics flashed behind Joe's eyelids. Box after box, and the connecting arrows. Eddy Kwok – close associate of Tony Kwan and Johnny Yau.

'Thanks for the warning, little brother. Was it Eddy Kwok who sent you and your brothers to walk me home?'

There was no further resistance to his questions.

'No. It was Macau branch council.'

602

'How did they know I was here?' He realised there was no way the triad implant in PHQ could have warned them. It had to come from somewhere else.

'There was a phone-call to the Double Happiness casino. Someone saw you at the dog track this evening. Someone from outside the society. We were told you were with a Thai chicken in the massage house – nothing more.'

Joe's grip slackened and he stood up. Somewhere in the darkness the two accomplices still lay moaning on the ground.

'Tell Eddy Kwok I can't be scared off that easily. I no longer care what happens to me. I'm here for the girl, and I intend to get her. Tell him to stay out of my way, or else pick a burial plot on the hillside where the *fung shui* is good.'

He kicked at one of the steel pipes as he moved off, sending it ringing across the cobbles. By the time he reached the bright lights of the Avenida do Conselheiro his adrenalin had subsided enough for the stabbing pain in his collarbone to register. He winced as he hauled open a taxi door, thanking Gwan-Dai that his stupid head was still in one piece. For it was stupidity, he realised now, to have been caught out so easily. Next time they cornered him, the men they sent would be better armed.

'Lisboa Casino, *m'goi*,' he told the driver and sank back into the worn leather seat.

At 22.16 hours in the Central Government Offices, Hong Kong Island, the US Consul-General returned to his chair in the Governor's Crisis Committee. He had been absent for a period of one hour and fifteen minutes and now as he resumed his seat he brandished a single typed sheet of instructions received from his own government. It had taken twenty minutes to set up the satellite link necessary for coded communications between Hong Kong and the State Department Building in Washington, which was located out at Foggy Bottom. No one trusted scrambled phone lines any more, and both sides were using computer screen and keyboard to talk. His conversation with Assistant Secretary Richard Nicholson had taken just fifteen minutes, with Nicholson doing most of the talking and the C-G dutifully following the stream of white characters which sprayed across the screen. When it was finished, he pressed a key and took a hard copy.

Now, in the tense atmosphere, Bob Walters addressed Sir Andrew directly.

'Your Excellency, the position is this,' he began gravely. 'In answer to their first demand, our government will undertake to look favourably upon all properly submitted visa applications, and then to raise the matter of Hong Kong refugees at the next meeting of the United Nations General Assembly, which is the proper forum for debates on this question. On the second point, we are reviewing the extent of our naval deployment in the region, with a view to cutting back our forces by thirty per cent over the next five years. However, agreements previously signed with other friendly and allied nations mean that a total pullout at the present time would be completely out of the question. Finally, on the third matter, whilst the policy of our administration is never to submit to blackmail, this Government has reluctantly agreed to pay the ransom of twenty million dollars, to be negotiated in whatever financial instruments are acceptable to the terrorists, provided the Secretary of State and all US citizens held hostage are released unharmed.'

When he had finished speaking, the other members of the committee exchanged meaningful glances. The Commissioner of Police raised one bushy eyebrow in mild surprise. No one had expected anything other than an outright rebuttal of all the demands.

'I see,' said the Governor evenly, masking his own

surprise. 'Pretty much what the FCO said on the immigration business. I'm not at all sure that particular demand isn't just a smoke screen anyway. What do you think, James?'

'I tend to agree, sir. Winning over the local community would be a shrewd move on the terrorists' part. It creates a certain reluctance on the part of government to intervene with force and to be seen as unsympathetic to the future of the local Chinese. So far we've had a few sporadic demonstrations on Nathan Road, just a few marchers with banners; also a few hundred members of the democracy movement meeting in Victoria Park. This meeting passed a resolution of solidarity with the hijackers.'

'That's hardly surprising,' said the Chief Secretary ironically. 'After all, they do have a vested interest.'

James Weldon ignored this remark.

'The point is that, now we have an undercurrent of support building out there on the street, the situation becomes even more dangerous.'

'How so?' asked the Consul-General.

Weldon spread his hands on the table.

'Mr Walters, these are emotional issues. If we go in heavy-handed, it could spark off something very ugly indeed – perhaps uncontrolled rioting on the same scale witnessed here in the 1950s. Let's just consider that for a moment. After the Tiananmen Square massacre a quarter of a million people turned out in Happy Valley to protest. The local population is extremely nervous about what the People's Liberation Army might do here after the 1997 takeover. Many of the poorer families will see these hijack demands as their one chance of escape. We don't want to be seen as frustrating their chances.'

'I trust you've taken precautions on that score, James,' said the Governor cautiously.

'Yes, that's all taken care of, sir.'

In the previous hour all anti-riot police had been

placed on standby, and the fleet of seven Saxon armoured personnel carriers had been deployed to the Regional Headquarter buildings. Companies of Police Tactical Unit not on border patrol, including those still under training, were now on continuous CP's reserve. All leave had been cancelled until further notice, and police formations still performing normal watch and ward duties had been briefed to be ready to go into Internal Security structure and form riot companies at district level at the first announcement of FORMOB II (Force Mobilisation). If that happened, the soft-peaked caps would come off and it would be black riot helmets and gas guns. In spite of these elaborate preparations, it was James Weldon's earnest wish that it would not come to a need for FORMOB II.

'They do seem to have us over a barrel rather,' muttered Sir Andrew Mackie, considering the deepening complexity of the problem. 'Any ideas on how we could buy ourselves room to move, gentlemen?'

Sir Andrew Mackie cast a glance around the table and saw Henry St John-Black casually raise one finger.

'Yes, sir. It would seem we have to somehow discredit the terrorists in the eyes of the public. I rather doubt the Japan Red Army gives a damn about the Hong Kong Chinese, so if we can't discover their true motive for this act, then perhaps we ought to invent one. Then have the Government Information Services feed that to the media.'

The Governor did not like the sound of that one. There were too many likely pitfalls.

'A very shrewd idea, Henry, as one would expect from Special Branch. But I can see all kinds of problems if we start lying to the public. I'd prefer to stick with the truth.' He turned his grey eyes back on to the Commissioner of Police. 'Miss Tavistock's briefing spoke of some kind of conspiracy involving local triads. How are your investigations progressing in that area?'

'Steadily,' said Weldon implying no significant progress. 'I'm afraid it's unlikely to fall into place overnight, sir.'

'And Special Branch?'

St John-Black sighed deeply. Twenty minutes earlier he had received a call from Ruth Tavistock down at Caine House which suggested something potentially explosive was falling into place. For a moment he considered raising the subject of Jack Cinch's release, but then thought better of it. Better to wait until they knew the full extent of what they were dealing with. He sighed once more and shook his head.

'Nothing to add, sir.'

The Governor reviewed the questions on the board: questions he had presented nearly six hours ago. Now, at least, he was clear in his own mind that concessions to the terrorists would be minimal, and that both governments were prepared to face the consequences of that decision. The disappointing fact was that Weldon's counter-terrorist force was giving prohibitive odds on any rescue bid. The three SAS observers now present at the ICC had visited the site of the incident and they supported this assessment. *Only as a last resort* had been their succinct advice.

'So, James, it would seem we're entirely reliant upon the skills of your police negotiators – for the time being, at least.'

One visit to the Forward Control Point at Tsim Sha Tsui, Kowloon, convinced David Becker there was no way he was going back to Hong Kong Island that evening. This was largely a sense of duty towards the men of his unit held hostage inside the stronghold, but that was not the whole of it.

Down in the bright blue-tiled cavern of the lower concourse there was an atmosphere of tension so acute, so darkly terrifying that in spite of all his disciplined training he could hardly bear to leave. He had already spoken at length with Kale about the tactical difficulties inherent in the terrorists' location. In idle moments he had been watching the specialists from technical support branch run out hundreds of metres of cable along the concourse and unpack banks of audio and video surveillance equipment from shiny aluminium chests. Around the fringes of this activity uniformed police stood silent, and aware of their own impotence.

In the silence, they fixedly regarded the dark maw of the tunnel as if a dragon might suddenly come roaring out from it. Above the sound of their own quiet breathing the only noise was the soft clicking of electrical switches. It was like standing beneath a billion kilowatt dam that might burst at any minute.

By the time Becker remembered his promise to meet Ruth Tavistock, it was almost midnight. Walking up the escalator to the first level, he crossed to the police post and used a desk phone to call the SB Information Centre.

'Let's make it somewhere nearby,' he suggested, and from the preoccupation in his voice she did not need to ask why.

'All right then, what about Some Place Else?'

The bar was close enough for him, just across Nathan Road in the lower arcade of the Sheraton Hotel, and immediately outside the cordoned area. But Becker at once rejected this suggestion. It was a favourite watering hole of European police officers, and at a time like this the place would be packed with every off-duty one-pip *bong baan* in the colony.

'Not there, too many other cops. Let's make it the Playboy on Peking Road.'

'Spare my blushes,' said Ruth, deadpan. Topless bars were not exactly her style.

'You've seen worse,' responded Becker. 'Twenty-five minutes, OK?'

'OK. Playboy it is.'

* * *

Ruth Tavistock, accompanied by Cinch, came down the steep, carpeted steps into the twilit bar. Becker waved them over through a red mist born of lasers and cigarette smoke to a wall booth got up to look like a half coconut. He was sitting behind a glass of coke decorated with fruit and ice, toying with the swizzle-stick. As they sat down, Becker glanced about him, into the broad wall mirrors, to enhance his view of the bar. The leather stools lining the illuminated bar front were mostly occupied by Japanese tourists attempting to get drunk as fast as possible while they ogled a half-naked girl vigorously shaking cocktails. The girls here were a cut above usual: failed actresses and models mostly, with figures like prize thoroughbreds and eyes that suggested that everything was negotiable. They wore kitschy little Barbie-doll slippers and lurex cutaway bikini pants that rose in a sharp V-shape across their blade-like hipbones, the spangled costumes framing their flattened stomachs and swooping back over perfect buttocks.

At the far end of the bar one of the girls had noticed Ruth, and now the same soft glow which had turned her breasts a metallic purple painted her sneering lips a lustrous black. Becker knew from old what she was thinking: *What for you bring white girl here – gimme no face?* In some of the wall booths Becker observed tight groups of Chinese men deep in conversation. Elsewhere, in high-backed booths, loners sat curled around squirming hostesses, their fingers dancing in the dark.

As he had hoped, there were no other cops in the place.

'OK, let's hear what's on your mind,' he said to them.

Ruth waited until the waitress had set two beer glasses on the table, made a note on the check, and drifted back to the bar.

'I thought you ought to know,' she began, keeping her

voice soft yet businesslike, 'the situation is now significantly more complicated.'

'How?'

'We now have a second set of demands.'

'What?' Becker's confusion lasted only a moment, then he said quietly: 'Explain.'

Ruth looked across at Jack Cinch and said: 'I think you'd better do this.'

The American leaned in closer, his jaw tightening. In the ultraviolet lighting Becker noticed for the first time his tombstone-like teeth, straight and even: they had probably cost a fortune in orthodontist's bills. Cinch's eyes glinted like Christmas baubles.

'Before he cut me loose, Okamoto handed me a sealed envelope and said to deliver it to the CIA station chief – no one else. As I walked back along the track, I began thinking about what he'd just given me and why I'd been let go. I then assumed that Okamoto didn't want the contents of the envelope broadcast: it was a message for the CIA eyes alone. I wasn't happy about that. Before doing anything with the letter, I knew I had to read it first for myself. When I did read it, I just didn't believe it. That paper was so hot I thought it would incinerate.'

Becker pushed his drink aside.

'So. What did it say?' he asked coolly.

Cinch opened his wallet and took out the folded sheet.

'Here, read it for yourself. I made a photocopy.'

The ultraviolet strip above Becker's head made the paper glow a ghostly white. Impatiently he flattened it on the table and read the typed message.

To the American Government,

It is now known that the imperialist USA has concluded secret agreements with the Philippine Government and with the People's Republic of China. It is further known that these agreements are intended

610

to deny the Vietnamese people their sovereign rights to the Truong Sha island group (known internationally as the Spratly Islands). Although these islands are some 300 nautical miles from the Vietnamese coastline they have, since 1930, been considered an integral part of Vietnamese territory and defended as such against Chinese belligerence. Now the presence of Chinese frigates in the archipelago is joined by a detachment of the American Seventh Fleet bent on constructing bases from which to threaten Vietnam itself.

Such aggressive measures cannot be tolerated by the freedom-loving revolutionary forces around the world.

Accordingly, we the Fighting Okamoto Cells of the United Red Army now present the following ultimatum to the Government of the United States. Unless all aggressive action ceases forthwith and the attached demands are fulfilled before midnight on Wednesday, 3rd October, the Secretary of State for Foreign Relations will be executed by explosion.

Our specific demands are as follows:

a) All US military units and construction crews must immediately evacuate the islands of Itu Abe (10 30′N 114 15′E) and Pagasa (11′N 114 30′E) in the Truong Sha (Spratly) group and withdraw at least 100 nautical miles to allow Vietnamese forces to take full control.

b) In order to dissolve this devilish alliance between the two aggressive powers now drooling over the prize, US naval forces must be seen to launch an attack, sink one of the Chinese boats moored off Itu Abe, and withdraw immediately. No explanation or apology must be given for at least twenty-four hours, or the Secretary of State will die. After the twenty-four hours are up, the USA will claim that the sinking was the result of an accident.

*When both these demands have been fulfilled we will
discuss the method of payment of the $20,000,000
ransom, and the safe return of the Secretary of State and
his staff.*

*We make these demands on behalf of the peace-loving
peoples of the Republic of Vietnam, who are themselves
slow to anger. Be it known, however, that any further
attempt to invade the Truong Sha islands by force will
prove intolerable and will be met with like force.*

*Our friends are monitoring the world media. Do not
attempt to publish this ultimatum, or any portion
thereof, or we shall be compelled to execute the Secretary
of State at once.*

The Fighting Okamoto Cells of the United Red Army

Becker tossed the paper back down on to the table.

'So that's it. Not about Chinese immigration at all.
The real problem is what your navy is doing here in the
South China Sea.'

Cinch responded defensively.

'It's crazy. I'd like to know where he gets such a
ridiculous idea.'

'Then there has been no agreement to grab those
islands?'

'If there has, then the Department of State has no
knowledge of it.' Since the State Department was
supposed to be responsible for all US foreign policy, that
was as good as a denial. 'Believe me, as far as I know, we
have no forces in or near those islands. The dispute has
always lain between Vietnam and China, with the
Philippines and Malaysia just minor players. Now the
Philippines have withdrawn their people altogether.'

'Fredericks has just come from Manila,' said Ruth

significantly. 'Might the Philippines have offered their stake in the Spratlys as a sop to American withdrawal from Subic Bay? After all, a US base halfway between Vietnam and the Philippines coastline would provide an excellent buffer between the two. It could restore confidence all around – and at no personal cost to the Philippines.'

'It's possible,' muttered Cinch uncomfortably, 'but I doubt it. Fredericks would never be a party to anything so ... hawkish.'

'What about this meeting with the Chinese Foreign Minister?' demanded Becker. 'What does that look like if not a conspiracy of hawks?'

Cinch thought about that for a moment.

'From what I heard, Fredericks didn't want that meeting at all. It was the President who suggested it. Or rather Kazinski, the National Security Adviser. Just low-key talks about the future of economic cooperation between our two governments. Arms-length stuff.'

'David's right,' said Ruth. 'Coming at this time, those talks lend credence to Okamoto's claims. It would appear someone wants desperately to stop them taking over those islands. Someone prepared to see the US and China at each other's throats. I shudder to think of the Chinese reaction if the US navy were to sink one of its vessels.'

'They must know we won't do it.' Cinch seemed none too confident in this assertion. 'Our policy says no concessions to terrorists.'

'In public, perhaps,' said Ruth sceptically. 'In private we know things are often very different. The Iran arms deals would have gone through without public knowledge if the Ayatollahs hadn't decided to blow the deal. Maybe that's why these demands weren't announced: to give the US government room to manoeuvre. They could publicly defy the terrorists, secretly pay them a stack of money, and still walk away looking strong on terrorism.

But behind the scenes ships are withdrawn, and a little accident occurs.'

'My God,' whispered Jack Cinch. 'This thing is beginning to sound like one of Phil Kagan's operations gone wrong. I still can't believe I'm hearing this.'

David Becker shook his head, equally incredulous.

'It may sound like a bad joke, but those people actually expect the USA to sink a Chinese ship?'

'What's more, if they don't,' said Ruth softly, 'William Fredericks dies tomorrow at midnight.'

TWENTY-ONE

By 05.15 hours Joe Lai was beginning to despair of his mission. He had spent the whole night looking over his shoulder, checking most of the first and second string gambling establishments with no sign of the elusive Ruby Tang. Along the way he had lost two hundred dollars to the blackjack dealers, drunk four cups of black coffee, and on one occasion felt the icy finger of panic touch the back of his neck. Sitting in at the fan-tan table of one of the harbour-front dives frequented by dock workers, he had felt an insidious pressure around his right lower back and reacted instantly.

'*Jo mat ye?*' the man had asked, terrified by the sudden fingers which stopped just inches from his eyes. 'What's your game?'

'*Mo mat ye, lo yau, gong siu,*' Joe had reassured him, turning his own sudden violent hand movement into a sweeping action which brushed dandruff from the weathered coolie's shoulder. 'Nothing, friend. Just kidding around.'

'*Gong lan siu. M'hai chi sin,*' the man had grumbled, suggesting the wires inside Joe's head must be tangled.

Not Eddy Kwok's boys, after all, thought Joe with relief as he moved on to the next table. Just some middle-aged labourer, nutbrown from years of wharf work, eager to get his twenty bucks down before the buttons were counted. One night of excitement to break the drudgery of workaday life: there were hundreds like him haunting the tables of these smoky glitter palaces, with eyes glinting and ever hopeful.

This coolie would have told his friends at work, over a lunchtime rice box, how this time he must surely break the bank. In the preceding days he would have been watching for lucky omens, and would have been sure not to eat soup (for the word soup is *tong*, which also means to be cut up, and is therefore very bad luck). He would shuck off his greasy work rags and sport a polo-shirt with a fake crocodile on the pocket, and, of course, his lucky jade pendant. Arriving with his friends, he would buy his stack of chips and lose himself amid the brightness and bustle, watching the dice fall until he felt the time was right. He would tour the mirrored pits and select a green baize table on which to do battle. Then he would slip on to a padded chair, light his luxury-length cigarette from a gold lighter, and sit twirling the plastic discs as he concentrated upon the cards. When he won, he would tip the lady croupiers well and play the high-roller. When he lost he would curse all the gods and wonder in vain what he had done or forgotten to do to anger them so. For a while his stack might grow, and with it his face and influence as the herd of other gamblers followed his lead. At times he would claim to discern a pattern in the sequence of reds and blacks on the roulette wheel. And every time the betting board illuminated beneath his stack of chips, his heart would beat like the wings of a bird.

But in the end, as always, he would lose.

Encouraged to bet bigger amounts, he would squander his gains – doubling his bet to recover the loss. Finally, exhausted and greatly relieved, he would leave the table and walk from the casino temporarily the wiser. He would always keep enough money for the cab fare and a box of cakes to take back home for his workmates. On the hydrofoil back to Hong Kong he would tell himself safely that the house always wins; that he was foolish to believe otherwise. But at work, when the cranes and drills stopped for lunch, he would wait for the inevitable questions, and grin like a cat in answer.

'*Dak m'dak a? Yeng m'yeng a?* How'd it go? You win?'

'*Yeng se siu.* Won a little,' he would say. 'Few hundred. Paid for the trip and a little besides. I'm nobody's fool.'

'*Wah! Ho ye lei,*' they would say, congratulating him. For Chinese people love it when one of them beats the bank.

All this Joe Lai knew with certainty because he was Chinese, and because he had done it all himself many times. For Joe life was a kind of casino game: a series of gambles. There were some moments of glory, and sometimes you slunk away from the table flat busted. You played the odds: won a little – lost a little. But there always came a time when you just had to make that one big play – the one the odds don't favour. And you did it because you knew you had to. To prove to yourself you still had the nerve for it. What the hell if you lost the whole stack – for the short time the wheel was spinning and the ball was in motion, all eyes at the table would be upon you. Anybody not prepared to take those chances had no business sitting at the table.

Joe finally found Ruby Tang at the Golden Dragon Casino, one of the places the Thai girl had suggested. She was in the last room on the upper floor, where the ritzier Chinese women played *dai-siu* with hundred-dollar chips. *Dai-siu* was a game anyone could play but, for some reason no one could quite explain, betting on the total outcome of three dice shaken in a cup had always been a favourite with Chinese women.

He recognised her at once from the photograph: a razored, geometric hair design, and just about the most perfect cupid's-bow mouth he had ever seen. The lips were full and sulky, painted first in scarlet and then frosted over with one of those new irridescent coatings that gave her mouth the look of a Ferrari paint job. The black dress with its diamanté lizard brooch was very definitely off the shoulder, and as she sat opposite the pit boss, she occasionally made eyes at him as if that might somehow affect the outcome of the dice.

When the three dice were shaken and uncovered, the rules were always the same – for everyone. If the total number of spots amounted to between four and ten, then the result was *siu* – small; if the total lay between eleven and seventeen the result was *dai* – big. Of course, there were any number of combinations you could bet on, a pair of threes, a total of twelve, at least one five showing, and so on; and the betting table was divided into boxes corresponding to these various combinations. But the majority of the better's money went into two large squares at opposite ends of the board, where the Chinese characters for *dai* and *siu* were inscribed. Cash or chips placed on the winning box drew double the stake in return.

The croupier who operated the automatic dice-shaker stood imperiously between two long betting tables, observing as chips and paper money were laid in small boxes representing each combination. Both tables had opaque glass surfaces beneath which were banks of concealed lights that could be illuminated to indicate the winners. The colours were always bright and exciting – red and gold, yellow and green. The colours of good fortune.

When Joe moved up to the table, he found, as usual, all seats occupied, with a frantic crowd of other gamblers, four deep in places, jostling the players' elbows for a sight of the board. Each time a bell sounded, the winning squares lit up to a din of excited cheers ringing out above grunts of disgust.

This was how the Chinese loved it: frantic, crowded and very, very noisy.

Joe watched Ruby's face grow more excited with each

618

successive bet, but he quickly realised that he was not the only one watching her. In the brief time she had been sitting there the girl had become something of a minor celebrity, and the reason was clear: Ruby Tang had something going – and the crowd at the table was with her.

The chips in front of her were divided into five discrete piles, each double the size of the last: 1, 2, 4, 8 and 16 chips. At once Joe Lai was intrigued, but after only a few minutes of observing how she played he knew exactly what she was doing. She began the sequence by first wagering the single chip on either BIG or SMALL. If she lost she would then wager the second pile of chips, then the next, in ever increasing amounts. Every winning bet brought back all she had previously lost, replenishing her stock of chips; then the sequence would begin anew with the single chip bet. In the casino business they called this 'doubling up' – more correctly, progressive betting.

Joe knew that the system had a certain cock-eyed logic to it, and that the girl could expect modest gains provided she was not unlucky enough to lose five times in succession. Odds against that – at two-to-one for whichever position she backed – ran up to thirty-two to one.

After watching the girl lose four times in succession, then back a winning *dai* on the fifth bet, Joe was surprised to hear an elderly Chinese woman whisper admiringly to her neighbour, 'Such nerves, that's sixteen thousand she just won!' That's when he realised the girl was not playing with hundreds as he had mistakenly assumed. Each of the purple chips represented a thousand dollars.

Impressed with the girl's success, the table was well tuned in, following Ruby's bigger bets hungrily with the queer twisted mislogic that she would always win back what she had already lost. Each time the bet increased, her chances of winning were seen to be greater. Each time the stacks of winnings were arranged and pushed back to her across the glass surface, the whole table responded gleefully.

'That girl really knows how to gamble!'

'She's got the secret, all right.'

'Look she's going for *dai* this time. Quick, get your money down. Follow her.'

Twenty minutes later Ruby had another bad run, and went to the fifth bet once again. Only this time, as she arranged the sixteen thousand dollars into two towers for the last bet, her nerve seemed to falter. This time she was worried. Anxiously she checked the centre of the table where a box of mah-jong tiles was employed to mark the previous sequence of winning bets. A red tile for big; a blue one for small. The last four tiles had been all *dai*, and on each of those occasions she had backed *siu*, losing every time. A nervous hubbub now ran around the table. If she changed her mind now and started betting *dai* and the tide changed to *siu*, she would lose all of her money but, more importantly, she would also lose face. In the end she knew she had to stay with *siu* and trust to the gods to change the sequence for her.

With a show of great bravado she pushed the two stacks of chips into the square marked *siu* and called for another whisky sour.

After a single moment's deliberation the entire table followed her.

Joe watched the *siu* square fill before making his own move. He had been wondering for a while how he could get close to her and had decided he must find some special way of attracting the girl's attention. Now he had sensed that way.

As the table held its breath Joe Lai stepped forward and made a great show of changing five thousand dollars into chips. While he stood gazing up and down the table, he knew every pair of eyes was upon him. Every cent being wagered was now on *siu* so everyone assumed the stranger would follow. Even Ruby Tang, who had not previously noticed the goodlooking Chinese at her table, watched closely his deliberations, confidently expecting him to back her bet. Smiling quietly, Joe nodded an acknowledgement in her direction, then placed the entire five thousand squarely in the window marked *dai.*

There was an immediate collective gasp of astonishment. Faces turned to one another and mouths hissed comments back and forth.

Then the girl croupier was on her feet, slamming her wooden block down hard upon the bell. No more bets! The table waited breathlessly while she adjusted the cuffs of her blouse, prolonging their agony still further. As the lid came off the shaker, heads everywhere craned in from all angles for a sight of the three little devil-faced dice. Elbows jostled in a mad flurry; here and there a desperate cry of encouragement erupted. Lost in the mêlée of bodies, Ruby Tang sat rooted to her chair, eyes concentrating only on the *siu* window, willing it to light up. A silent cry of anguish erupted from her lips.

The lights under the table flickered momentarily before registering the individual numbers. 4, 2 and 6. The result, *dai.*

Sniggering to herself at the crowd's collective sigh of disappointment, the croupier then inserted a fifth red tile into the box and sat down again.

In Ruby Tang's mind there could be no doubt whose fault this had been. She shot a fierce glance in Joe's direction, damning his impudence. Cursing his arrogance. He had obviously diverted the good fortune by betting directly against her.

Striving to maintain his cool, Joe accepted the ten thousand dollars, and asked for a one hundred to be split so he could tip the croupier a fifty. Now that he had Ruby's attention, he elbowed his way around the table until he stood beside her chair.

'You finished yet?' he asked as the noisy conversation resumed.

'Not yet,' she answered. 'I'm here to beat the bank, and if you bet against me again I'll beat you too.'

'*Nei ho dai daam,*' he complimented her. 'You've got a lot of spirit, lady. But if you're to keep playing this system, you're going to need thirty-two thousand dollars. That's a lot of water.'

'That's none of your business,' she spat back, already starting to stack the pile of chips remaining on the table before her. Joe watched her long, perfect neck turn away, and inhaled a rush of expensive perfume as she moved. The sight of her naked shoulders he found faintly arousing; the glow of smooth skin against the black silk of the dress. There was something incredibly suggestive about her simplest movements: the way she rolled her slender bottom upon the chair as she rebuilt each tower of betting chips.

A couple of minutes later she had counted out eighteen thousand Hong Kong dollars into three neat stacks and sat quietly taking stock, occasionally glancing towards her small gold handbag. While the rest of the crowd deliberated over the girl's next move, Joe Lai remained quietly confident. There was no way Ruby could leave the table. Not now he had succeeded so well in getting under her skin.

Aware of the eager eyes all around her, Ruby Tang put out a languid hand to open the handbag, then counted off a sheaf of yellow thousand-dollar notes – until the wager before her amounted to thirty-six thousand dollars. The significance of this auspicious number was not lost on Joe Lai – the number of oaths sworn by triad initiates when entering the lodge. A plea for magical intervention. Without a pause, she ordered the assistant croupier to help her shift the mountain of money on to *siu.*

Continuing her run.

This time nobody moved. Unsure of what to do, the crowd of onlookers stayed out of the game. Their anxiety was palpable: this game was far too charged with lust for revenge.

'Still chasing the same one?' asked Joe. 'Don't you know how to change shoulder when the burden gets heavy?' It was a Chinese expression commonly used to describe the pig-headed as well as the plain stupid.

The faintly-pencilled eyebrows rose quizzically.

'Dare you bet against me once more?'

Joe gazed back steadily, saying nothing, admiring the flames leaping within her brown eyes. She had been Eddy Kwok's girl until Tony Kwan took her to his bed, and he could see now why Red Cudgel had wanted her. Still wanted her. Only now he wanted her corpse.

What a waste that would be! It was time to heal the wounds of battle. This time, as the croupier reached for the bell, Joe leaned across and dumped his accumulated money into the *siu* window.

'I think this time I must follow you.'

'Why so?'

'With such fierce eyes the gods would not dare set the dice against you.'

The ghost of a smile tugged at her full red lips. Then she heard the bell and turned to concentrate fully upon the table. Now it was all or nothing, every cent she had was riding on *siu* and, instead of quietly waiting for the outcome, this time she rose to her feet extending one long red-enamelled talon towards the table.

'*Siu!*' she demanded. '*SIU!*'

Almost immediately a blaze of light appeared in the window beneath her stake money, and above the wild cheers of the crowd Ruby could be heard whooping like a schoolgirl.

Suddenly all that had gone before was forgotten. Suddenly she was Queen of Heaven and Goddess of Mercy all in one. Wildly she cheered as skyscrapers of chips were formed up and pushed towards her across the glass. Borne on the tide of her excitement, she looked left and right for someone she could hug – someone with whom she could share this moment.

Before she realised what she was doing, that someone was Joe Lai.

'*Ho ye! Ho ye!*' she laughed. 'We won! You followed me and we won!'

'That's right,' said Joe, above the din. 'You're a winner now – but only for as long as it will take Red Cudgel to find you.'

The words left her thunderstruck. Her eyes widened with the sudden fear that leapt within her. But she made no attempt to move. There was no longer anywhere to run to.

They had found her!

'Is he ... here?' she managed to stammer.

'Kwan? I don't think so,' said Joe. 'But, then, I wouldn't know. I'm not San Yee On.'

'Not one of them ... Then who?' she asked, reining back her fear. She was intrigued by this man's sudden appearance and she wanted to know more.

'Never mind that. Their soldiers are close and I'm here to help you, so if you want to see another sunrise you'd better come with me now.'

For a long moment she showed no reaction. Ruby Tang just stared into his face, as if mesmerised by uncertainty. Then somewhere inside her the walls came crashing down and she appeared as a child: totally vulnerable. He realised then what the desperate gambling must have meant to her: a temporary relief from her appalling predicament. But Ruby's sense of escape had ended the moment he had walked up and reminded her.

'All right,' she said at last, sensing that this stranger was her only hope. 'I'm in your hands.'

Clearly Ruby had a strong sense of self-preservation. The first thing she did, as the taxi pulled away from the Golden Dragon, was to take Joe Lai's hand and place it firmly between her thighs, staring deep into his eyes.

'What's this?' he asked, caught off balance, though the gesture was not totally unwelcome. 'Some kind of incentive scheme?'

For the first time she smiled. 'Call it something on account. Get me safely away from here and I could really make it worth your while.'

'Don't thank me too soon,' he said coolly. 'I have to get you back into Hong Kong first.'

Before he realised it, her lovely lips were against his – and he was kissing them.

The thinnest sliver of daylight marked the eastern sky as they reached the Praia Vista, but up in Joe's room the bedside lights cast a soft golden glow on the wall. Closing the door he turned her gently towards him and took her face between both hands.

Ruby Tang was no stranger to love, he reflected, her powerful scent now filling his head. All at once his thumbs caught the top of the black cocktail gown and drew it slowly down across her stomach. In the pale light from the lamps her naked breasts shone as lustrously as the silk which recently contained them. Ruby gave a small gasp that was part shock and part anticipation. His mouth bore down upon her, seeking out each breast in turn. She moved her body searchingly against him, pivoting her groin upon his thigh, rehearsing the movements they would soon make. Joe's hand slid down over her lower back to the cleft of her buttocks – then between. His mouth now rose to the warmth of her neck; licking and gently biting. And when he finally arrived at the hot slippery caress of her open mouth, her tongue was waiting to dart into his own.

Without a word he pressed her bottom against the foot of the bed, then slipped off the remaining underclothes leaving only the black dress bunched around her waist. Angling her backwards, upon the cool cotton covers, he took a moment to savour the sight of her naked legs hanging over the edge of the bed, still wearing high black stilettos. Then he buried his head between her thighs. Thrilled by her cries, Joe pressed still harder.

Then came a wilder sense of urgency and he rose and lunged across her body, no longer able to restrain himself. He entered her. Entered her. Entered her. Roughly, and without pausing to remove his own clothes. Urging him onward, her small hand reached down to encircle him, exciting him with the threat of her enamelled fingernails. Then her body began to buck and lurch beneath him. At the end of the tunnel he heard a sudden cry as night exploded into endless white light.

It was 7 a.m. when he woke. He felt her head upon his stomach, her soft hair caressing his thighs and her eager lips teasing his dormant flesh back into a rigid column. He was barely awake as she rose and straddled him, totally naked now, guiding him once again into the centre of her longing – riding him furiously until her cries mingled again and again with his and they both dissolved into a fractured spasm.

TWENTY-TWO

At 8 a.m. on Wednesday morning, when the hospital rush was just beginning, a young Chinese woman walked into the casualty department of the Queen Mary Hospital in Aberdeen with a child strapped on her back and an arm so swollen and discoloured that it made even the casualty nurses wince. From the drab pyjama suit, and the woman's calloused hands and tanned limbs, she was obviously a rural villager well used to a life of hardship.

Sitting her down, the chief nurse removed the foul-smelling bandage from her elbow; it was loaded with a heavy brown sludge of Chinese medicaments. The nurse took one look at the elbow, the purple-green marbling on the bruised flesh, and she called the junior houseman.

Dr Michael Tse listened carefully to the young woman's story as he made his examination. Respectfully, Chan Yim-king explained to him that her family owned some poor agricultural land in a remote area of Lantau Island. Although only a short ferry ride from Hong Kong Island, it was an area with no proper roads, where visitors seldom ventured. Five days ago she had been out in the field lifting vegetables with a small sickle, when she had noticed blood upon her sleeve. From the amount of bleeding she realised that she must have cut herself on the blade, so she sought treatment from a Chinese herbalist in a nearby village. At first the pain had subsided, and all seemed well. But then came the swelling and discoloration, and the pain had returned.

After two days her elbow was almost immobilised. Finally, at her husband's insistence, the young woman had resolved to cross to Hong Kong Island to consult a Western-trained doctor.

Dr Tse examined the cut and found that the scab covering it was well formed, but still soft from the foul-smelling poultice which had covered it. Ignoring the odd shape of the scab – not like a normal blade laceration – he concentrated upon the lack of movement in the arm and decided to send the woman for an X-ray. The swelling could easily be due to torn ligaments, severed tendon or even elbow fracture: he needed to see the X-ray plate before probing further.

When, after twenty-five minutes, the nursing orderly shuffled back along the corridor with the developed sheets, Dr Tse clipped them to the illuminated board for viewing. What he saw made him blink twice and raise his glasses to peer again. Thirty seconds later he called the staff nurse and arranged for the woman to be prepared for minor surgery. The young patient required a great deal of calming, for traditional-minded Chinese find it difficult to submit themselves to such extreme treatment. In the end it was the doctor's mock stern talking-to and the woman's own ingrained respect for authority which overcame her personal fears.

Surgery confirmed what Michael Tse had thought he saw on the X-ray plates. It turned out to be a flattened piece of soft grey metal, about the weight of a two-dollar coin. The metal blob with a fragmented casing of orange metal had lodged between the radius and the ulna, pressing close against the radial nerve. No wonder her arm had been immobilised; the poor woman must have been in absolute agony.

She had not cut herself at all.

She had been shot.

Quickly he closed the wound, placed the metal in a plastic sample dish, and returned to the houseman's station. A moment later he was on the phone, tapping out the number for the report room at Western police station.

In his office at the top of the Au-Yeung Building, Alexander Au-Yeung sat drinking tea and watching a wall-mounted television screen. Beyond the tinted glass of the windows it was a bright clear morning, but as he flicked between the early morning news channels, taking in the hijack summaries offered in a recurring loop of Cantonese and English versions, the tai-pan of Bright Star Holdings quietly seethed.

And with good reason.

At that moment William Fredericks ought to have been safely captive aboard a Chinese tan somewhere off the coast of Macau. Instead he was being held prisoner in a tunnel below Hong Kong harbour, with police standing guard and the whole colony looking on in awe and fascination. He considered the events of the previous evening with equal measures of anger and frustration.

'What the fucking hell is the man playing at?' he had demanded of his younger brother just thirty minutes after the first news bulletin. The reply had brought him little comfort.

'I have no idea. The man is touched with madness!'

'What about Rhee – what does he have to say about this?'

'Only that we must give Okamoto his head.'

'I'll give him his head in a basket!'

'Rhee says our aims can still be achieved. He believes this hijack spectacle and all the media interest will exert still greater pressure upon the authorities.'

'Still achieved! I will kill him for this,' the businessman had thundered impotently, surrounded by a nervous entourage of San Yee On officials. 'He was supposed to be controlling the Japanese. You were meant to control him!'

629

'I have seen enough of this Japanese to know there is no controlling him,' Red Cudgel had answered. 'The damage is already done, so what would you have me do now?'

In the circumstances, Au-Yeung had realised, there was nothing to do now but wait.

Fifteen hours later his mood had not improved significantly but he continued to watch the news reports, wondering what his Vietnamese patrons would make of it all.

He watched closely the night-time shots of Tsim Sha Tsui blaze bright on the screen, the girl reporter pressing her microphone toward some *gwai lo* policeman with a silver band on his cap. The situation was well under control, the policeman assured her, before appealing vainly for people to stand away from the immediate area. The scene then switched to daylight and a snatched interview with the Secretary for Security on the steps of Central Government Office. Amid a surge of eager pressmen the same girl managed to put her question first.

'Mr Deacon, the terrorists have made explicit demands regarding immigration rights for Hong Kong people. This will obviously raise the hopes of those who fear for our future after 1997. Would you care to comment?'

The Secretary for Security did not break stride; he kept moving towards the safety of his limousine, unwilling to be drawn on the subject.

'Government is aware of the feelings of local people, and is currently studying the demands of the hijackers.'

The girl continued, undeterred.

'Mr Deacon, does that mean that the Prime Minister is now prepared to reconsider the British Nationality Bill.'

Turning his back on her, Deacon shouldered his way into the car with a crowd of eager reporters still pressing after him.

'Mr Deacon,' the girl persisted, 'can you confirm

whether there has been any word from the President so far?'

Quickly the burly chauffeur stepped forward to force the door closed as the Secretary for Security threw away his final words.

'No further comment, thank you.'

The government limousine pulled away amid a volley of camera flashes.

Au-Yeung considered her final question himself. Deacon had remained tight-lipped on the subject, but surely the US President was being appraised minute by minute of this situation. He had never been known as a hands-on President, but it was inconceivable that he had not yet been consulted about the behind-the-scenes negotiations.

Okamoto's message would have shaken the smile from the President's face, all right. Now that he thought about it, Au-Yeung, the son of a poor refugee from Swatow, enjoyed the idea of so affecting the most powerful leader in the world.

He snapped off the TV and rotated his chair to face the broad, tinted window and the harbour. Like many Hong Kongers that morning, he was trying to imagine the scene unfolding beneath the calm blue waters below. He recalled his visit to the Mandarin Hotel the previous night.

He had gone with just two of his closest lieutenants, expecting vitriolic condemnation from the Vietnamese intelligence officers with whom he had arranged to dine. To his surprise there had been none. Over a sumptuous dinner at the Man Wah, the Mandarin's exclusive Chinese restaurant, the Vietnamese had expressed their cautious satisfaction with the current state of affairs. That William Fredericks' location was known to the authorities, and that the press were now hyping the situation would only serve to concentrate the US President's mind the more. Okamoto had done well, they said, expressing optimism about the ultimate outcome.

In spite of this there was little doubt in Au-Yeung's own mind that Okamoto had double-crossed them all.

One should never trust to the vanities of a *kai dai*, he mused as he opened a deep drawer beside his knee and spat into the brass pot it contained. Au-Yeung's prejudices were built on old Chinese conservatism, and Okamoto's dubious sexuality had fuelled his misgivings from the very beginning. They are vain and prone to emotion he told himself once again: a most unreliable combination. Perhaps if Chan Ming had shown stomach enough for the job, things would have proceeded more in keeping with his own wishes. *Aiyah!* Instead it seemed that Okamoto had made a deliberate spectacle out of the operation for his own gratification.

What irked Au-Yeung most of all was that he, the tai-pan of Bright Star Holdings and First Route Marshal of the San Yee On, could do nothing now but wait for the outcome. His mood had been tense at the dinner table; the lemon chicken had tasted sour to his tongue.

'Patience,' the Vietnamese intelligence colonel had counselled. 'All is well thus far. So long as our stated aims are achieved, the agreement between us still holds good. Were the true demands delivered to the American Consulate?'

'They were. My younger brother has spoken with Rhee Joon-kil and he received an assurance on this. Okamoto released one of the Americans with a message for the CIA. The man was warned of the need for secrecy.'

'Good. No doubt the lines to Washington will burn white throughout the night.' The Vietnamese had paused there, as if in his mind's eye viewing the ravings of outraged officialdom collected together in the White House situations room. 'Let them wring their hands a while.' He smiled. 'But expect no response from them until tomorrow.'

'Why tomorrow?' Au-Yeung had asked, surprised. 'Wouldn't they want Fredericks back as soon as possible?'

'Of course, but first there will be recriminations. That is the way of governments. And the guilty move slowest of all.'

'Then you are satisfied with the service I have provided?' The Chiu Chau toyed with his brandy, watching the thick golden liquid wash the sides of the glass.

'Indeed satisfied.' The Vietnamese nodded. 'Your speed and flexibility were most gratifying.'

'Then the missing papers are forgotten?' ventured Au-Yeung tentatively.

'Let us say the State Department documents are no longer crucial to our aims. Significant but not crucial. However, that you managed to lose them to a woman was ... most unfortunate.' Submerged within the manicured tones the sarcasm was still apparent. 'The many other items of intelligence provided by Reicher were sufficient for us to reach our decision.'

'Be assured the woman's days are numbered,' said Au-Yeung raising his glass in salute.

Aboard the underground train the hostages had stayed awake into the small hours, alert to each and every sound around them, and nervously monitoring the actions of the Japanese. When any did manage to sleep, it was brief, fitful and ultimately exhausting.

At midnight Okamoto had issued amphetamine sulphate tablets to each of his team, and they remained continuously alert throughout the night. Periodically Okamoto checked the front and rear operators' cabs where he had placed guards to monitor the radio sets. The rest watched over the hostages.

When five o'clock came, Okamoto picked up the soft leather case which carried his sword, and he wandered back to the seventh car to meditate alone. First cleaning the floor with a small towel, he knelt down in the aisle and sat back on his heels in the Japanese fashion, attempting to clear his mind of all useless encumbrance. Now, more than ever, he found this small ritual essential: the attainment of peace in the eye of the storm.

The first part of his ritual was a silent recitation of Buddhist sutras. These were the words of Boddhidharma, the great Zen monk who had first brought the word into China. Then, when his mind was completely at peace, like the mirror surface of a pond upon which no ripple stirs, he drew the katana free of its leather bindings and laid it before him on the floor. As always, he took a brief moment to appreciate the awful, simplistic beauty of the weapon sheathed in its scabbard of lacquered magnolia wood. Then, after bowing before the spirit of the *dojo* with head low and palms flat to the floor, he sat back and grasped the weapon in one hand – symbolically taking possession of the blade. Rising slightly on his left knee he fitted the weapon into the black cloth belt at his waist with an expert flourish.

He paused in this position, exploring his own breathing, aware of his true mastery of posture. His back and neck were straight, his eyes alert and staring directly ahead, as always, in the direction from which any threat would come. Both his slender hands were poised ready: the left encircling the top of the scabbard, thumb and forefinger against the sword guard and ready to ease it free; the right hand resting lightly upon his right thigh, just one hand-span from the katana's braided hilt.

Poised thus between action and inaction, he reflected upon the continuum of energy between both these states. Energy resting, energy moving. Both were aspects of the same ultimate truth. Both of equal importance. Many years of study had brought him to this level of understanding, and taught him to value silence as much as sound. For each defined the other absolutely.

At the centre of his own personal storm, his spirit was now truly at peace.

Then abruptly, in the beat of a dragonfly's wing, he moved for the kill: body rising for a single step, then dropping to add power to the blade stroke. The katana hissed as it left the scabbard, a continuous arc of gleaming steel under the striplights, its razor-edged blade singing a dull note as it parted the foetid air, the curved edge continuing down through an imagined point of contact. Internal energy unleashing itself with Okamoto's sudden cry.

The stroke was everything he knew it would be: swift, balanced, perfect. A cut cleaving the skull and slicing deep into the chest cavity, bringing instant death to his opponent. It seemed a purer form of death than any other he could imagine. A warrior's death.

Okamoto continued his personal devotions in silence. The orange overall was an encumbrance to his leg movements, inhibiting the freedom allowed by the divided skirt he normally wore for this ritual. But his arm movements were bold and assured, like the strokes of a master calligrapher who paints with steel and light. And the picture he painted now was the secret advanced sword *kata* of the Tenshin Shoden Katori Shinto Ryu: the ancient ritual of the School of the True Divine Martial Tradition. It was a tradition which could trace its lineage back into fifteenth-century Japan, and to the founding master Chosai Sensei.

His final movement was a single high flourish with the hilt as he ran the spine of the blade along his left finger, feeding the steel back into the scabbard. Inevitably there was a degree of sadness as he returned the sword to its leather case. A reluctance to let go. For deep inside him something mourned the passing of the old times. That part of him he recognised as the reborn spirit of the samurai Honda Tadakatsu, one of the Shogun Tokugawa's four great generals.

One day, he promised himself, he would relive the man's former glory, die the warrior's death. But until then he would live to inspire terror.

Hunched in the aisle with his back to the bench seat, Stephen Lee watched the Japanese leader stride back towards the front of the train. It had been the man's first shout which had woken him, and thereafter he had watched the swordsman's every stroke with a mixture of horror and morbid fascination. Most of the other hostages were still asleep on the seats, their hands now tied in front to make sleeping possible. They were all exhausted, though in sixteen hours they had hardly moved except to use a latrine bucket provided by the authorities and kept in the last car, which was immediately emptied through the window of the rear operator's cab. By morning the stench had begun to drift back through the tunnel, masked by the smell of chemical decomposants.

Thus far no one had been harmed. The Japanese had imposed a strict discipline, and none of the hostages had been allowed to speak to them, or even to each other. Stephen Lee realised that the only person they were interested in talking to was Fredericks himself, but he had always been too far away to hear what was said.

Lee had heard the demands for Chinese immigration rights, but knew little else of what was going on. To him it made little sense that the Japan Red Army should involve itself in a Hong Kong problem largely ignored by the rest of the world.

As a security officer, Lee concerned himself little with the progress of negotiations. To his mind it was just a matter of time before the talking stopped and the shooting began. Before then he must work out what he could do – if anything – to assist the SDU when they finally appeared. One of the most important things for the technical people was to pinpoint the positions of each of the terrorists, as well as each of the hostages. Obviously the terrorists realised that too, because they had moved the hostages around the train six times already: sometimes in one large group, sometimes in fours and fives, other times singly.

Lee knew that in previous sieges it had been possible to drill through the walls of the stronghold and introduce needle-thin camera lenses with fibre-optic cables to give a clear picture of the situation inside. But, surrounded by a couple of feet of solid concrete on all sides, he knew there was no chance of that now. Their isolation was total. Nor could they be glimpsed by long-range camera, for the same reason. The authorities' only clues would come from sounds picked up by microphones placed at the mouth of the tunnel, and even if the rescuers did make it to the train, they would still be coming in blind. Lee did not give much for their chances of success. Either way, Fredericks would be blown in two long before any rescuer reached him. For all Lee knew, the whole train could have been wired in the same way, primed to blow them all into the world of ghosts.

The terrorists were clearly taking no chances, however, their respirators perched on top of their heads in readiness. Three of the Japanese had exchanged clothes with Lee's men in an obvious attempt to confuse any assault party.

Lee studied the shattered remains of the windows. Outside the train lay darkness and shadow; the cool, pungent air of the tunnel seeped through the broken glass with a hiss. At least the tunnel's ventilation system was holding up.

Inside the belly of the dragon the strip-lights burned continuously. There were nearly thirty people collected in a silence broken only by the occasional sound of footsteps treading the aisle. Stephen Lee turned to examine the faces of his men, some clearly scared, others bolstering morale with whatever aggressive gestures they dared. Each was probably thinking of his family: wives, children, girlfriends.

Then, looking up the train, Stephen Lee succeeded in catching Lassiter's eye. The American was seated on the floor, his legs drawn up and his arms folded across his knees. His head was tilted to one side, resting against a steel upright, eyes coolly following one or other of the terrorists.

When he saw Stephen Lee's thumbs-up, Lassiter forced a grin in response, showing a covertly clenched fist. Making sure the Japanese backs were turned, Stephen Lee raised his eyes inquisitively and cocked his head in Fredericks' direction. Lassiter's reply was a nod which seemed to indicate that Fredericks was still holding up in spite of everything.

Nods and winks, Lee thought, it was all too absurd, and yet it was all they had to sustain each other. To keep hope alive.

At 7.15 the radio in the front operator's cab squawked into life. Okamoto walked through to answer it.

'Mr Okamoto? This is Tom speaking.'

'This is Okamoto – speak.'

Over the radio the negotiator's voice seemed small and distant. An inoffensive kind of a voice.

'I'd like to provide breakfast for everyone aboard the train, if that's all right with you.'

'OK. Send bread and tea, enough for thirty. And hot *dim sum*.'

'I see. Would you like green tea or jasmine tea?'

It was a well-worn ploy of negotiators the world over. Draw the suspects into a protracted dialogue based on making decisions between alternatives. Particularly where food was concerned, if the terrorists could be persuaded to consult their hostages over such decisions, they might come to view their prisoners more as human beings and less as bargaining chips – or victims.

Okamoto smiled to himself before answering.

'Green tea is fine for everyone.'

'And which particular *dim sum* would you all prefer, *ha gau, siu mai, cheung fan*?'

'I leave it to you, Mr Policeman. Fetch the food to within twenty-five metres of the back of the train. Remember, we have strong flashlights and can see you very clearly. Send two persons only, but call me first. If I see anyone approach before we are ready, they will be shot. Is that clear?'

'I understand what you're saying,' said the negotiator, 'but there's no need for that. No one has been hurt so far, and I'd like us to keep it that way. I think you'll agree I've acted in good faith.'

'Then continue to do so if you wish to see your people alive again.' The negotiator's long-winded manner was grating upon him.

'I'll do what you ask, Mr Okamoto. I'm going to arrange the food now, but first I have something to request of you in return. I'd like you to put the Secretary of State on the line so I can speak with him.'

Okamoto's eyes narrowed in suspicion as he pressed the transmit button on the handset.

'For what purpose?' he snapped.

'Before I can win concessions for you, I need to persuade the authorities that Mr Fredericks is still alive and unharmed. If you let me speak to him a moment, it will help us both.'

The Japanese considered this request. There seemed no reason to refuse. Perhaps it would remind those on the outside just whose life they were bargaining for.

'Very well – this once. But do not ask again.'

In the negotiator's room at the ICC three men listened carefully as the spindles of two audio tape-recorders rotated in silence. Throughout the night Ron Sewell, the superintendent in charge of the team of negotiators, had monitored their progress from the Incident

639

Commander's office, conferring closely with Ray Doogan, still the man in overall charge of the incident, on matters of strategy. When morning came it was he who had slipped back into the negotiator's room to suggest that breakfast would be a good time to push for voice contact with Fredericks. After a brief discussion with the strategist, who sat beside the negotiator at all times, assessing the tone of the interactions and suggesting new verbal avenues to explore, the strategy was agreed. If they could not turn this into a two-way thing, then they were wasting their time.

Seated opposite his two subordinates, Ron Sewell glanced across the small table at the strategist hunched over the incident log, and at the negotiator quietly scribbling notes. All three wore light-weight pilot's headsets connected into a common deck which had been jacked into the main MTR city line console. Though their eyes occasionally met, no one actually spoke. They were too busy straining after the slightest click on the line.

Thirty excruciating seconds later a new voice was heard: a voice that suggested education and moneyed New England. One with an accent so polished, the vowels so well enunciated, that it was difficult to tell he was American at all. But there was something else. The negotiators had been trained to detect the high, cracking tone of a man under stress, and they heard it now in the Secretary's voice.

'This is William Fredericks speaking. I've been asked to remind you that you now have less than sixteen hours to comply with the conditions set for my release. After that the train will be destroyed, along with everyone aboard.'

'Mr Fredericks, are you all right?'

'Son, I've been better.' The Secretary's voice relaxed a little. 'I suppose you already know about this explosive belt thing I'm wearing.'

'Yes, sir.'

'Doesn't make much difference. Come midnight Okamoto intends to kill us all anyway. Please tell my wife ...'

Just then the headsets were filled with a sound like a stereo needle skidding across a record, and Fredericks was gone. The strategist sprang forward to check the sockets in the deck. 'Jesus Christ,' he muttered, this gear was always packing up.

'Hello, hello,' called the negotiator, barely able to maintain the quality of calm for which he had been selected. 'Can you hear me there inside the train?'

The silence lasted only a few seconds. When contact was restored it was Okamoto's voice that came back at them.

'You have the reassurance you requested. This foolish old man has not yet been harmed. Tell his wife and his President that will change if we do not soon receive assurances that our demands will be met. Is there any word from Washington?'

'We're doing all we can. I'm sure you're aware there are time differences to contend with ...'

'Do not play games, policeman. I know the time as well as you. In Hong Kong it is 8.14 in the morning. In Washington it is still early evening: 7.14, Eastern Standard Time. The White House has had a whole working day to consider its response. So answer my question!'

The negotiator heard the change of tone, and he sensed the approach of another ultimatum. Lacking the information with which to answer, he looked to the team leader for guidance. Thus far information from the US Consulate had been sketchy, bland, noncommittal. Ron Sewell had been told only that the CIA were coordinating contacts with Washington. If any response had yet come back, it had been strangled at some level higher up the chain. Sewell knew that to feed the terrorists lies now could prove extremely dangerous. Particularly if they had to admit later there had been no genuine contact. At the very least that could risk breaking the tenuous relationship the negotiator had so far established with Okamoto. At worst it could mean the lives of all the hostages.

All this ran through Sewell's mind as he scribbled a hurried message on the negotiator's pad for him to read.

'I'm sorry, I still don't have an answer for you. Obviously the things you have asked for involve communications between governments – not least the Chinese government. Diplomatic channels take time. Inevitably there's a degree of bureaucracy, but we are doing our best. If you'll just give me a little more time ...'

Even as Okamoto cut him off, the negotiator knew he had said too much, had transmitted a subtle air of desperation.

'I shall give you time. Here is your time: four more hours. If I have not heard from the President by twelve noon today, there will be blood. Do you hear me? *Blood!* He must state his readiness to concede on all the points outlined or I will execute one of the hostages and throw his body on to the tracks. They *must* take us seriously!'

Ron Sewell punched one balled fist into his left palm. Damn the bastard!

'I'll convey your message to the authorities, of course, but there's no need for...' The negotiator worked quickly to diffuse the tension, but Okamoto was quick to silence him.

'Enough, policeman. Enough! Now go and attend to breakfast.'

At 8.19, two minutes after Sewell had conveyed the new deadline to the intelligence cell in the Incident Commander's office, Ray Doogan was speaking by secure line to James Weldon in the PolMil control centre at New May House. Weldon had stayed on at CGO until midnight, then called his wife and informed her he would not be home that night. As she had expected, he would remain on hand in case of sudden developments, and for that reason, he would sleep in the officers' accommodation in the PolMil command centre.

'Look, they're not kidding, James,' said Doogan attempting to convey the same urgency Ron Sewell had just conveyed to him. 'If there's no word from the American side soon we could have a disaster on our hands. Surely there's been something?'

Weldon did not disguise his own frustration with the Americans.

'Bugger all of any use. Not since that official handout last night. The Governor is pressing their Consul-General, but I get the feeling their CIA man is the one dictating policy.'

'What's he want to do? We can't just do nothing.'

'I know that, Ray. It's just I'd rather do this with their full backing than have to explain our actions later at an enquiry. Last night Prioletti was talking "wait and see".'

'Very constructive of him,' muttered Doogan sourly. 'But I have to know whether they're going to respond to this latest demand. If not I need to prime the negotiators and prepare to implement the IA plan.' He was trying to imagine the outcome, but the projected casualties Kale had spoken of kept getting in the way.

'Are you ready to mount a military option?' asked the Commissioner hopefully.

Doogan gave a quick snort.

'In a word – no. But we may have to go anyway. If they start killing hostages, what other choice do we have? If it goes that way, it'll be strictly down to percentages. Live bodies out – that's all.'

'That's understood, Ray.'

'Yes, but understand this, from the way they have him

643

wired up you can write off Bill Fredericks at the very first shot.'

The colour drained from James Weldon's face. Those words had a terrifying quality all their own. He took a long breath and held it whilst he pictured the faces of the men aboard the train. The black and white Interpol photographs of the terrorists eased in and out of focus. They existed in another, dreamlike dimension, deep within that black tunnel. How appallingly unreal it all seemed.

'Leave it with me,' said Weldon, his voice suddenly resolute. 'I'm on my way now to CGO to get this thing sorted. In the meantime, if things deteriorate in a hurry, don't hesitate. Do whatever you have to.' He paused just long enough to indicate the gravity of such an authorisation. 'I'm prepared to back your judgement.'

Weldon returned the secure phone handset to its housing and walked back to his desk. Still lost in thought he gathered up the stack of papers lying scattered there and piled them into his briefcase. The morning sitrep from SB was contained in an orange SECRET folder which immediately caught the eye. Inside it were four typed sheets of A4, each page stencilled top and bottom with the red SECRET logo in English and Chinese. He had already browsed through the report. The first section was a rehash of some of the stuff he had seen on the Governor's brief the previous evening. Now there were thumbnail biographies included on each of the terrorists, together with a source report from David Becker giving background on the Okamoto Cell's activities in Metro Manila.

So Becker was back now, thought Weldon, realising he had heard nothing from him in several days. By good fortune he had missed the hijack. Better to have him on the outside where his experience could be used than inside the stronghold where he could not help.

The last page of the sitrep expressed concern over

civil unrest. Crowds had gathered around the cordon on Nathan Road the previous night, and a number of shop windows had been broken by groups of chanting youths. Just before midnight SB had arrested what proved to be triad elements trying to spark off a riot. So far, however, the majority of Hong Kong citizens seemed to be playing it cool. In a colony with a history of street rioting, violence and political unrest, who knew how long that would last.

Weldon had just stood up, intending to leave for CGO, when the PolMil duty officer put through a call from the Director of Special Branch.

'Make it fast, Henry,' snapped the Commissioner. 'I'm on my way out.'

'I don't think I can do that, sir,' said St John-Black in that cool, understated manner for which he was famous. 'Something rather ticklish just came up on the MTR incident. Of critical importance, I'd say. Miss Tavistock is here in my office with a photocopy of what purports to be a second set of demands.'

'A second what?' said Weldon incredulously.

'It was given to her by the released American hostage, Cinch. It raises quite a lot of new questions; suggests our cousins have been less than honest with us. I simply must speak with you immediately.'

'Henry, I've no time for intrigues. A few moments ago Okamoto threatened to execute a hostage if the President doesn't speak to him before midday.'

St John-Black pressed his case with quiet force.

'Sir, I think you'll want to see this letter now. It's addressed to the American intelligence community, and amongst other things it demands the sinking of a Chinese warship.'

'What! But you can't be serious.'

'Indeed I am, sir. What's more, Miss Tavistock has just informed me of the true source of all our troubles.'

'One moment.' His head reeling with impossibilities, Weldon quickly ordered his staff officer, waiting anxiously by the door, to have the driver stand by. CGO would have to wait a few minutes more.

'Stay right where you are, Henry,' he said, returning to the phone. 'I'm coming across.'

At 8.50 he awoke, for the second time, to the sound of voices somewhere in the room, dull and distant. Chinese voices. A single shaft of light breaking through the heavy curtains on to the empty space in the bed where the girl had lain. Joe Lai started awake, eyes scanning the hotel room until he saw her by the foot of the bed, kneeling naked upon the floor watching the television screen. In a movement tinged with dread, the girl brought her hands up to her face.

'What is it?' yawned Joe, sitting up. He looked past her to the screen, massaging the small of his back half-heartedly; it still ached from the hours he had spent at the betting tables the previous night.

'They've done it,' she said softly, her eyes staring ahead, incredulous.

'Done what?' He swung his legs over the side of the bed and walked over to the set, to stand behind her. The TV was tuned to a Hong Kong channel. For the tenth time that morning they were replaying the interview with the Secretary for Security on the steps of CGO. As Joe listened, the phrases fell like cluster bombs in his consciousness. *'Crisis management ... Hostage security ... Japan Red Army.'*

'What the hell's going on?'

The girl turned her head slowly and looked up at him, her eyes brimming with guilty knowledge.

'The San Yee On. They've taken the American alive. What do you think of that, *chai lo*?'

Chai lo she had called him. Cop. Was it so obvious in his manner, he wondered, or was it just that anyone looking for her now simply had to be a cop if they were not a soldier of the San Yee On.

The news highlights gave only a brief report of the incident currently underway on Kowloon side, but the girl's apparent knowledge of it raised more questions than Joe could assess at that moment. Suddenly the significance of Philip's warnings came into focus. A team from Manila with a suitcase full of plastic explosive.

'You knew this would happen, didn't you?' He said it more as a statement of fact than a question.

Ruby Tang shrugged and looked away.

'I knew *something* was happening. There were visitors to entertain at the Barking Peacock. Ah Chan from the mainland.'

'Was that Chan Ming and his gang of *Dai Huen Jai*?'

'Yes. Then there were the Japanese. Chan Ming was engaged to lead the Jockey Club raid, but the Japanese always had another function. I was never given any details about that operation. Safer not to know, *hai m'hai ah*?'

'Is that why Tony Kwan wants you dead?'

The room was already warm from the morning sun, yet she shuddered, her small nipples contracting as if caught in an icy blast. She picked up her clothes and padded into the bathroom, leaving the door open.

'You know who I am, *chai lo*, but I know you, too.' The voice was petulant. Striving to regain face.

'*Hai m' hai ah?*'

'*Hai la!* After the Shatin robbery everyone in Kowloon was talking about the heavy team they put on the case. Jockey Club wanted somebody tough who'd bend the rules and get their money back. They asked for Kuen Wong and got him. Kuen Wong was too clever and too dangerous for his own good. That's why he had to die. The senior Chinese detective on the case was a man no less dangerous. A man very clever and skilled with his hands and feet. A man who had already shot dead three men. That's you, isn't it? You're Lai Hing-keung.'

As he listened to the girl's voice he fished in his jacket

647

on a bedside chair, found a crumpled pack of cigarettes and lit one. He lay back on the bed, one forearm across his head. 'And if I am ... does that make a difference?'

'I don't know,' she said, stepping into the black dress and drawing it up over her smooth hips. 'Maybe I should feel reassured that it's you protecting me, but something tells me you don't have long to live either.'

His fist closed tight on the slim gold lighter.

'Just tell me one thing. Was it Tony Kwan who killed John Tasker?'

'How would I know? I've been here in Macau these past two weeks. Usually he would send one of his *ma jai* to do that sort of job but if he felt it was important enough, if he felt personally threatened, face would require he do the job himself. Did the killer wear a mask?'

A shot of adrenalin hit Joe's bloodstream like pure speed. The blue cigarette smoke drifted across his face.

'*Hai ah!* A Peking opera mask with a black beard.'

For a moment she was silent. Joe repeated the answer. Eventually the girl asked, 'What colour was the mask?'

'The mask? It was red.'

At this Ruby Tang came to the bathroom door, her lips now a lustrous crimson. She looked hard at Joe and held up both hands with the index fingers crossed, forming the Chinese character for the number ten.

'Was there a *sap chi* upon the table?'

'*Hai ah!* Crossed chopsticks in Tasker's place.'

The girl dropped her hands and walked back into the bathroom.

'*Dang a dang.* Wait a minute.'

Joe slid from the bed, and in another second was beside her at the bathroom mirror. She brushed at her hair distractedly, perhaps because she had been reminded of Tony Kwan's potential for violence, but it was impossible to tell.

'I have to know,' said Joe, forcibly turning her around.

'Yes it was him. You already knew that, *chai lo*. The *sap chi* is his signature: a warning to the other societies. The mask is his vanity. In Peking opera the red mask indicates a brave and loyal servant of the emperor. The warning is for you, Joe Lai. Give up, or suffer the same death.'

Joe released her arm and walked back into the bedroom. He dressed quickly, pulling a button from his shirt in his haste, fully aware now of his vulnerability here on foreign ground. When he came to the belt, force of habit made him reach to adjust the position of the leather holster – but of course it was not there. He looked down at his hand, examining its treachery, measuring the small tremors in its outstretched fingers.

'I have to get you back to Hong Kong. That's the only way I can guarantee you protection.'

'Protection for information, is that the deal?'

'We want the names of all conspirators on the Shatin job. I'll get you a good deal from the authorities. Got any relatives overseas? Somewhere to go?'

There was a sigh from behind him and Joe looked round to see Ruby standing at the window looking out, hugging herself.

'Got a father back in Hue and a brother in Da Nang.'

'Vietnam.'

She glanced in his direction then back through the window, to where cargo vessels were wallowing in the muddy waters of the Tai Pa channel.

'Elder sister and me came to Hong Kong with our mother back in '79 aboard the *Huey Fong*. Big ship that one. That was in the days of the open refugee camps. When we landed we were sent to one in Shamshuipo. Ah Ma died there from hepatitis. That would be 1981. I was fourteen. Ah Je was fifteen.'

'That must have been rough,' murmured Joe, knowing that the streets of Kowloon were an unforgiving place if you were poor. Worse without family to protect you. 'How did you survive?'

'We hustled the streets of Mongkok. Slept under the flyover. Picked a few pockets along the way. Slept with anyone who'd feed us both. One night we fell in with a group of boys from the Wo Shing Wo triad group. They were just blue lanterns, not yet properly initiated. Their job was to deliver packets of white powder, and sometimes recruit flesh for their *dai lo*. We got a quick lesson in the need for protection and went to work for Wo Shing Wo as fishball girls.'

Joe found it hard to think of Ruby Tang sitting in the stinking corner of some dreary Chinese ballroom while strangers pressed their sweating hands between her thighs. She seemed too proud for all that. But, then, what did he know of life on the street, or of being alone and hungry?

'How did you come to fall in with the San Yee On?'

'In 1985 they moved into Mongkok in a big way. There were blade wars for a month or two. When it was over the San Yee On took over the Barking Peacock and four other clubs in the same street. Bought them out without a murmur of protest. Two hundred and fifty-two girls came with the furniture. Only one girl tried to leave; she got acid thrown in her face. After that I knew there was only one way out, and that was upward. I made my play for one of the big men; member of the *gung on*. Lucky for me, Eddy Kwok likes small tits. He was running the place himself then. He put me in charge of the other girls at first. Last lunar New Year they made me full hostess captain.'

'And Tony Kwan? When did you first open your *wok* for him?' Joe did not even know why he was trying to hurt her.

Ruby's eyes blazed at him, but he stared back at her without blinking.

'You don't leave a girl anything, do you, *chai lo*?' She

walked past him to the bed. The springs groaned slightly as she sat and lit a cigarette from the pack on the bedside table. The nicotine seemed to bolster her will. 'It's true he shared my bed, for a while. Why should I deny it? You can't imagine the face it brought me. You see, Tony Kwan isn't just anyone. He's Red Cudgel. Do you have any idea what that means? Really means?'

'I think so. It means he's chief enforcer for the San Yee On and a member of the Inner Circle. It means he controls the white powder distribution chains and forces twelve-year-old kids on to the streets. That he screws *bo woo fai* – protection money – from anyone who does business on his turf, even the old ladies with newspaper stands outside his restaurants.'

Ruby Tang sucked nervously on the cigarette, then breathed smoke into the room with each hurried word as she spoke.

'All very well for a policeman to say such things. But Tony Kwan has power of life and death over girls like me. Better to make a friend of him than an enemy. Look at me now.' She held out her hands and studied the slender white fingers, each tipped with burgundy nail enamel. 'Shaking so bad I can hardly hold still. I tell you, *chai lo,* when he decides that's it, then better run as far away as possible. No point in going to the police – he owns them too.'

'That's not true,' said Joe in a defensive reflex.

'*Nei yau mo gau choh?* Are you kidding me? Ask yourself who set up John Tasker for them, if not another policeman. You say you want to protect me, ha! Be sure you can protect yourself first, *chai lo.*'

Suddenly her aggression collapsed. Awkwardly she stubbed out the cigarette and buried her face in her hands, sobbing. As he stood watching, Joe felt the urge to put his arms around her, but something prevented him from doing so. Something inside him still called her Kwan's woman, and although the lovemaking had been

651

very special, in his mind she was still tainted by the association.

After a minute Joe sat down on the edge of the bed to put on his shoes. He returned with difficulty to the necessary questions.

'They say you stole something from the San Yee On, *hai m'hai a?*'

At first she did not answer, just kept staring fixedly at the floor. Finally she forced a laugh tinged with bitterness and raised her head.

'That's the funniest thing of all,' she said, her voice still brittle. 'I don't even have those papers any more. Only no one will believe me.'

'What papers exactly?'

'But, I thought you knew everything, *chai lo.*'

He ignored the taunt and waited for her to finish.

'Kwan had an arrangement with someone at the US Consulate: a man called Reicher. They had me play up to him so I could collect and deliver things on their behalf. Reicher used to sell economic intelligence briefs produced at the Consulate, sometimes political and military secrets too. Anything he could get his hands on.'

'That's a bit out of Kwan's league, isn't it?'

'It wasn't for himself. He does it for big brother Alex Au-Yeung, the First Route Marshal of San Yee On. Part of *his* power derives from a close relationship with the Vietnamese intelligence service. They guarantee his heroin out of the Golden Triangle supply routes as far as the South China Sea, and in return he acts for them in Hong Kong and Macau.'

Joe turned quickly. 'Are you serious?'

With those last few words, the existing pattern of Joe's perceptions had toppled. The simple logic of the triad violence he had witnessed now represented a more sinister association.

'Come on now, Ruby. You don't expect me to believe that? It's not the kind of information you just give away to anyone. How did you come to find out?'

'Pillow talk. Tony Kwan likes to talk.' She said it as if she did not really care what Joe believed. 'He thought it was funny that after fleeing that country I should end up working indirectly for Vietnamese intelligence. I pretended to laugh about it, too. Then he told me the Vietnamese have a long-standing agreement to purchase anything San Yee On can collect. This arrangement protects the Viets themselves from discovery. I believe they call it a masking operation.'

More masks, mused Joe Lai. The symbolism seemed to beset him.

'You were talking about some papers?' he said, steering her swiftly back to his original question.

'They said it was the biggest thing Reicher had ever offered them. He came to the club – I had a room above the club for special guests. I took care of him and he passed me a folder. After he had left, there was some trouble with one of the hostesses. I had to put her in a taxi and send her home. That was when I almost wound up with a knife in my throat. The taxi-driver pulled a blade and tried to drag me inside his cab, but I fought him off and managed to get away. The other girl was already stretched across the back seat. He had the strangest eyes I ever saw. I dropped my bag and those papers inside the taxi as we struggled. I knew Red Cudgel would kill me for losing them; that's why I had to run. I heard later the police found Sor Mooi's body in the Shing Mun reservoir.'

'That's right,' said Joe with a grimace. 'It was cut into five pieces... That means that whoever killed her must still have your folder.'

Ruby's eyes widened.

'Did they ever find the taxi driver?'

Joe shook his head.

'No, and apparently there were no other witnesses. Can *you* remember what he looked like?'

'Let me see. He was pretty weedy – pock-marked face, I think. But there was something really strange about him. It was the festival of Hungry Ghosts and he had a Gwan-Dai mask on the front seat next to him. Not just a miniature – the thing was full-size, like one the kids might wear. I think I can give you the name of the cab company too. It was on the side of the door.'

After a moment's thought Joe Lai picked up the phone to call Hong Kong Island. When he got through to the OSCG *dai fong*, Tiger Cheng was checking witness statements. Cheng listened carefully to his OC's instructions, nodding at each request.

'I'm bringing the witness back on the twelve o'clock jetfoil, and I need backup. They're bound to be watching departure points, so use your warrant card and get on the next boat heading for Macau. Call me at the Praia Vista when you arrive; I'm using my own name. Don't pass this up the chain. Keep it inside OSCG. I want at least twenty armed *foh geis* covering the ferry pier when I arrive in Hong Kong.'

Cheng sensed the urgency.

'Ho, Ah-sir, don't worry. They'll be waiting. Anything else?'

'Yes, I want a safe-house prepared immediately. Don't take any bullshit about paperwork. Shove it down their throats if you have to. After that, warn Roman Fung we're coming in, and tell him we have a lead on his Gwan-Dai killer. That should get him there.'

As he put down the phone Joe Lai felt a surge of aggression – a reaction to the threat he felt closing in from all sides. He knew that, after wrecking their three *fei jai* back there in the darkened square outside the Estoril, the San Yee On would be moving heaven and earth to find him. And after what they had done to Tasker, he did not doubt his own fate if they found him.

'What now?' asked Ruby. Cocking her face toward

654

the sunlight, she looked no more than a little girl. 'You know they'll be looking for us both?'

'I know that,' answered Joe levelly. 'That's why we're going to wait here and talk some more about those documents you lost. After that you're going to tell me everything you know about this hijack.'

In less than two hours Cheng would be there with a handful of the hardest men on the squad. Cheng knew his business, and he would bring only those detectives prepared to rough it with the fighters of the San Yee On.

Ruby Tang looked back towards Joe, studying his eyes and seeking some kind of reassurance there. There was danger ahead of them she knew, and hidden here in the temporary safety of the Praia Vista hotel, she could not help wondering whether this time she had made one gamble too many.

TWENTY-THREE

'I'm sorry, sir, but it's totally out of the question.'

The American Consul-General opened his hands wide in a broad gesture of powerlessness. The room was silent as each of the powerful men at the table listened and waited for the Governor to respond.

'Is it a question of technical difficulties?' asked Sir Andrew Mackie, tapping with a pencil point on the pad before him. As the man in overall command of the situation, everything rested upon his decision.

'Not at all.' Walters fidgeted in his chair. 'I'm sure we could have the necessary secure link set up within the hour. The Secretary of State brought a whole communications team with him, and the aircraft carrier out there in the Lamma Channel has the best satellite communications system in the world.'

'I see. Then it's a policy decision.'

'I'm afraid so. We have a departmental policy document which details the action to be taken in this kind of eventuality. It says negotiations will be conducted locally and top decision-makers must never become involved in the negotiations with the terrorists. In this case I double-checked with Washington. We have a working party set up at the White House, chaired by the National Security Adviser. The feeling there was that it would be inadvisable for the President to speak with the terrorists directly. Such a course would leave us no legitimate reason for stalling. They'd expect immediate decisions every time.'

The Governor's eye rested upon the Commissioner of Police.

'What's your feeling, James?'

'I agree with the logic. The one thing we have to buy is time. Time for the suspects to wear themselves out. Time for them to consider their own fate. There aren't many people actually prepared to die for a cause. Those who are will only do so after they've exhausted all other avenues.'

Sir Andrew nodded in agreement.

'And their threat to execute one of the hostages – do they mean it?'

'Of course they don't mean it!' The voice from the far end of the table was that of the CIA station chief.

'Would you care to explain that, Mr Prioletti,' said Weldon, nettled by the interruption. 'Because I rather think they *do* mean it.'

Prioletti toyed with the heavy graduation ring on his little finger. Ignoring the Commissioner, he addressed his answer directly to the Governor. 'All indications are that these are trained terrorists. Now, these people don't just go into a hijack cold, they undergo extensive training and briefing. Negotiation tactics aren't secret any longer, they've all been well-documented in the academic journals. We must presume these people can read, so they'll already know we'll tie them up in talking to gophers until we're ready to do a deal. Anyone who knows the game wouldn't really expect us to put the President straight on the line. It's just bluff.'

Weldon was staring at the side of the CIA man's face.

'Then why would they make such threats and put their credibility on the line over something they know they won't get? It doesn't make any sense.' He turned his gaze back to the table. 'Your Excellency, I don't think Okamoto is bluffing. I think we're going to lose one.'

'If you're so sure of that, Commissioner,' said Prioletti, at last acknowledging the policeman, 'why don't you order your men in now and finish it?'

'I think you know the reason. As of now the risk to the hostages is far too great for that. Of all the hostage-barricade situations I've studied, I can't think of one that was fraught with so many difficulties. While ever there's a chance of solving this through negotiation, I intend to pursue it.'

'What's left to negotiate? The United States does not make deals with terrorists. How many times do you need to hear that? There's twenty million dollars to play with. The rest is non-negotiable. If your people can't handle it, then step aside. We have a Delta Force team on standby at the Sheraton Hotel. Just say the word and I'll have them go in and clean up this mess.'

'What is it you really want, Prioletti?' snapped Weldon. 'To procure the safety of the hostages, or just to clear up this mess – as you call it – as soon as possible; regardless of the cost?'

The CIA man opened his mouth to speak, but thought better of it. Instead he shook his head, as if in disbelief, and turned away.

At the top of the table Sir Andrew watched Prioletti's eyes flare at the question. He saw him caught flat-footed, just for an instant. But long enough to register guilty knowledge. Enough to lend credence to Weldon's suspicions.

Weldon had met Sir Andrew in an empty office at CGO just prior to the reconvening of the security committee. In accordance with Weldon's wishes Sir Andrew had come alone. The conversation had lasted barely ten minutes. Long enough for Weldon to impart the contents of the second demand note which had been addressed to Prioletti alone.

'The CIA is running a show of its own here behind the scenes,' Weldon had said holding a photocopy of the proof in his hands. 'The Okamoto group wants them to dismantle the operation, and sink a Chinese frigate into the bargain. It seems fairly clear from the wording of the letter that the Vietnamese are behind this hijacking. They seem to think they're the target of some combined Sino-US military operation. This is their way of hitting back.'

'Dear God,' the Governor had said, reading the letter for himself. 'This goes way over my head. It will have to be referred back to Whitehall. Do we have any details of the American covert operation?'

'There's a suggestion of a disinformation campaign. I have Special Branch conferring with the MI6 head of station to try to build up a profile. One thing I can say is that it must be pretty ambitious to provoke this kind of heavyhanded response from Hanoi.'

Now, in the pregnant silence at the table, someone coughed nervously and Sir Andrew's thoughts returned to the room and the current problem.

'I must say, Mr Prioletti, I tend to agree with the Commissioner. Our first concern is for the lives of the hostages, and for this reason alone we must continue to talk. Since there is no possibility of the President of the United States becoming personally involved in the negotiations, then we shall have to improvise. Do I take it that the Consul-General would be willing to act in his stead?'

A look of confusion passed briefly across Walters' face.

'Er ... yes, of course. If they'll speak to me, then I'm happy to do it.'

'Good. Then we offer them the Consul-General instead. Let's hope that is enough.'

In the half-light of the south-bound tunnel just north of Tsim Sha Tsui station, Mel Kale and David Becker listened carefully while the engineer from MTR corporation explained the wiring in the roof and walls of the tunnel. There was not much to tell, he said. There were fifteen hundred volts of direct current in the overhead line, the train's power source, but unless you were earthed it was harmless. The rest was communications and climate control hardware. Their flashlights played around the smooth inner arch of the tunnel, picking out the suspended wires and the metal strips and studs on the side of the wall.

'Funny,' said Kale, checking the track beneath his feet, 'I always thought it would be sort of damp and dusty down here, but it's so clean.'

'That's the piston effect. The trains force a column of air along the tunnels that whooshes out all the dust. Careful where you walk,' warned the engineer. 'If you get your foot stuck in a drainage grating you're liable to break an ankle.'

'That's one for the lads,' said Becker. 'Don't want them going arse over respirator. Come on, let's see how they're doing.'

Ahead of them in the tunnel the yellow headlights of a second train burned through the darkness, the strip neon from the passenger cars spilling out on to the side walls like a bright amber halo. Early that morning Kale had asked for access to the trains in the repair yards at Kowloon Bay, to give his men the chance to familiarise themselves with all the access points and to rehearse their entry tactics. MTR had gone one better. They had shunted in a spare train to within a hundred metres of the Forward Command Post. That gave them an important advantage, because hitherto no one had seemed too sure how much clearance there was between the train itself and the tunnel walls. To the SDU men, for whom speed of movement could mean the difference between success and failure, this point was crucial.

After crawling under, over and around the train, Kale's men now knew at least one very important fact. There was barely enough room to pass along either side of the train when standing fully erect. The problem was that, with each man carrying full kit, a haversack and a sub-machine gun, movement outside the train would be restricted to an awkward shuffle. That would be much too slow – dangerously so. The answer was to keep down low, beneath the level of the train floor and run at a crouch along the broader channel between the wheel bogies and the wall, where there was another foot and a half of clearance.

Passing now along the first car of the practice train, the MTR engineer pointed to a recessed flip lever located beside the second pair of doors.

'This is the door operator I told you about. Throw this, and you bleed the air out of the pneumatic actuator on all five pairs of doors in that car.'

'And then the doors spring open?'

'No. That only breaks the locks. You have to push the doors apart manually, but there's minimal resistance. If you need to open all doors simultaneously, we have a pair of hidden master rescue switches. One of them is here, just outside the operator's cab; the other is in the corresponding position in the rear cab. Here, watch.'

As the engineer operated the flip switch there was a series of loud pneumatic belches along the length of the train, and stale rubber-smelling air filled the tunnel.

Mel Kale slid his fingers between the rubber seals, and the doors slid easily apart.

'OK, that's great. It gives us a good choice of entry points.'

Becker was standing beside the wheel bogies, resting both hands on the glide rail of the door, the floor of the train now level with his chest.

'Fine. But what about this five-foot drop? Our lads will have to give each other a bloody smart leg-up to get inside, won't they? And I can see all kinds of broken legs when they start heaving the hostages out.'

Kale knew the dangers involved in a delayed entry: death to the hostages, a hail of bullets for the rescuers. He looked at his watch and scratched the back of his neck thoughtfully.

'Nobody said it was going to be easy.'

The engineer smiled to himself.

'Wait a minute, gentlemen. There's one other thing you ought to know about accessing this train ...'

Before he could finish his sentence there was a squawk on Kale's radio. A call from the FCP.

At once both policemen felt nervous flutterings in their stomachs, wondering if this was the call they had been dreading. The call to say that the suspects had begun killing hostages.

Kale recognised the voice of Marty Lewis. He spoke back to the radio out of the side of his mouth.

'Go ahead, Bravo Two.'

'Sorry, boss, the technical boys want a word. Good news, they said.'

'Roger, Bravo Two. On our way.'

Dr Lee, the civilian officer who ran Special Projects Section of Technical Support Branch, was waiting on the platform at Tsim Sha Tsui station when Becker and Kale climbed up out of the track well. TSB was the unit which routinely provided technical surveillance aids to specialist units of the police force and to the ICAC, the Independent Commission Against Corruption. Special Projects was where all the mind-blowing stuff was put together and Lee was very definitely the force behind it. A squat Chinese in his middle forties, Dr Lee was well-known for his neat, precise manner, and for the gold penny spectacles which gave him an owl-like appearance. Steeped as he was in a world of micro-circuits and computer load modules, he affected a casual disregard for mere flesh, saving his sweetest words for the computers in his lab.

The two policemen followed Lee to the far end of the platform where the armed tactical unit cordon was still in place, guarding the great arched mouth of the tunnel: two SDU snipers in DPMs standing ready with infra-red scopes. There were electrical cables running the length of the platform, most of them terminating at two trestle tables which had been erected by TSB technicians and which were loaded down with banks of equipment: keyboards, screens, speakers and microphones.

Becker turned to Kale and shook his head.

'Bloody Star Wars or what!'

Dr Lee seemed quietly pleased by the comment. In another moment he tapped one of his technicians on the shoulder, and the junior man moved aside to give him access to one of the master keyboards which controlled all four video graphics screens. There was a brief exchange of Cantonese, too rapid and technical for Becker's ear to catch.

'What do you have, Dr Lee?' he asked, pretending patience. 'Did you manage to photograph the inside of the stronghold?'

'Not quite, but perhaps something just as good. One moment, please.'

Lee's fingers stroked the keys in a fluent sequence and at once the four screens, standing side by side on the trestle tables, simultaneously refreshed their images. Each showed a bright ultramarine background on which was overlaid a series of patches of lighter colours: some moving, others stationary but pulsating. Each of these shapes was composed of a series of coloured layers, like onion skins: large red areas in the middle with darker patches fading to blue around the edges. Towards the centre, blobs of green and yellow appeared and disappeared as the shapes moved around.

For the first few seconds Becker looked on in utter confusion, then abruptly his eyes registered understanding, reflecting the intense colours on the screens.

'Jesus Christ! Are those blobs actually people?'

Dr Lee's attention remained concentrated on the screens as he tapped out a second sequence of keys. A series of menus briefly overlaid one another in one

663

corner of the screen, like playing cards being rapidly dealt one upon the other: too fast for the eye to follow. Along the base of each screen there appeared a numbered scale with a colour-graded diagram beneath. The hues merged like a smeared pallet of watercolours, each one described by a number.

'Infra-red videograms,' said Lee finally. 'These numbers here indicate temperatures. What you are seeing is the temperature signature of each of the bodies aboard the train.'

'Stuff me!' breathed Kale. 'That's bloody brilliant.'

'A refinement of a technique used to locate people buried alive by landslips or collapsed buildings. Not too bad, considering the thickness of the concrete. We placed our sensors at intervals along the parapet in the north-bound tunnel, and aimed them through the adit doors in the central dividing wall. As you can see, the shapes break up a little, but just look at the ones here, and here.' Dr Lee indicated two blobs moving back and forth upon one screen. 'Now let's amplify the image and clean up the signal with this noise attenuator.'

Another stroke of the keyboard and the two blobs filled the screen. This time the central mass was mostly blue and purple, whilst the edges were yellow and white.

'See, the heat signature is different in these two bodies. There's a lower surface temperature at the centre and the extremities of these two subjects are hotter than the ones sitting down.'

'So, what do you think?' asked Kale, sensing now that something of great importance was about to be declared. But what? Dr Lee turned to face the Australian, peering superciliously over the gold spectacles.

'Undoubtedly these subjects are wearing protective clothing. Such materials naturally impede heat loss, and they don't themselves respond to body heat. Hence their lower colour temperature.'

Becker leaned in closer, his expression intense; the

blue light from the screen washing over his face made the chiselled features appear much harsher than before. And more determined.

'It's body armour,' he breathed. 'Got to be. Those blue shapes must actually be Okamoto and his men.'

'So that's the enemy,' said Kale respectfully. 'Looks more like some malignant virus when you see them this way.'

'Isn't that what this is?' asked Becker thoughtfully. 'A viral infection.'

'In that case we must be the bloody cure.' Kale grinned back at him.

'Too right, and it looks like at last we're in business. Now we know precisely where to find each one of them.'

It was the kind of quiet triumph both men were used to: that quite unexpected piece of intelligence which bolsters morale because of the new possibilities it creates.

'That still leaves us with the problem of identifying Fredericks,' said Becker. 'Doc, can this thing give us faces?'

The Chinese turned on him indignantly, whipping off his spectacles.

'Mr Becker, we can do something far better than that. We can set a trace on these heat sources and give you a real-time list of each subject's position and movements. By applying a behaviour analysis to this data we can then identify the leader and the other dominant members of the terrorist group, based on how they act in relation to one another. It's a technique derived from observation of baboons. We can then split the hostages broadly into race on the basis of body mass. And because the Secretary of State is the oldest man aboard, and overweight with it, we can then identify his exact position at any given moment. In short, given a couple more hours we can locate and monitor any of the subjects on that train. By midday I'll be able to tell you everything about them – even when they go to the toilet.'

665

Becker digested the importance of the infra-red videograms, and realised the possibilities were staggering.

'If we match this with the acoustic information coming from the stick microphones aimed at the tunnel mouth, as well as the snatches we're getting on the long-range video camera, we have all the tactical intelligence we need.'

'Agreed,' nodded Kale emphatically, smacking one hand into the other. 'But don't forget, Fredericks is still wearing his little magic belt. Even if we manage to get the others out, the instant the first flash-bang goes in, Fredericks is dead meat.'

'I don't think so.' Becker concentrated his attention on the technical expert, avoiding Kale's sudden look of astonishment. 'Dr Lee, that's a radio detonator he's got in there; what do you reckon it would take to defeat the signal?'

'If you're thinking about *jamming* the signal, you can forget it. Far too risky. Any interference pattern we might generate could just as easily trigger the detonator. As for any physical interference, that depends on the power source. From the description given by the freed American hostage, it sounds quite a small affair. Probably a low-voltage transmitter with the same alkaline battery pack you'd have in your Walkman. If that's the case, the signal might stretch for half a mile in line-of-sight. Any walls or buildings would immediately reduce the signal. Probably a few inches of brick would be sufficient to block it completely.'

'That's what I thought, Doc!' Becker clapped the short Chinese on the shoulder. 'So a foot or so of steel would do it very nicely, thank you.'

Dr Lee slipped his spectacles back on to his nose, his face breaking into a broad smile as understanding dawned.

'Of course. Oh, most certainly. A brilliant idea.'

666

Kale straightened up and folded his arms, watching Becker's glazed expression as the idea appeared to be forming inside his head. As always Becker was infuriatingly guarded when he had something going.

'Mind telling me what's going through that conniving brain of yours, ya pommy bastard?'

Becker turned and looked at him, grinning broadly. Full of mystery.

'A solution to the *koan*, Mel. Something potentially very dangerous for everyone concerned. Come on. You can listen while I explain it to the Incident Commander.'

'When do you expect them to make their move?' asked Tiger Cheng as the jetfoil sped quickly through the choppy waters of the western approach to Hong Kong Island, leaving a broad white wake that was flecked with a scum of discarded plastic bags and soggy cartons.

'Almost at once,' answered Joe confidently. 'Every hour the girl remains alive brings us a step closer to nailing Kwan.'

Ruby Tang gazed ruefully at the closing distance to the Hong Kong waterfront, wondering just what or who would be waiting for her when she stepped ashore.

As the craft neared the Hong Kong-Macau Ferry Terminal complex it veered hard to starboard, cutting the engines and coasting to its berth. Almost before the craft had stopped, two stevedores quickly manoeuvred a narrow gangway into position and a horde of Chinese passengers began shoving eagerly for the exit ramp. Nervously Joe's eyes searched the few staff members lounging at the quayside and again he wondered: when would it come?

Tiger Cheng was the first to disembark, using the combination of his police warrant card and his own impressive build to cut a path to the head of the line of returning passengers. Next came Joe and Ruby, followed by two OSCG men who formed a barrier to Joe's rear,

667

allowing them a head start for the immigration desks. All eyes were alert for any sign of a triad presence as they moved out into the immigration hall. Approaching the desks, Tiger glimpsed an OSCG sergeant in conference with a uniformed inspector of the Immigration Department. The inspector waved the party over, nodding as each man produced a warrant card, and hurrying them through one of the closed desks.

Beyond the gate the twenty men Joe Lai had asked for were posted around the concourse at strategic locations, carefully observing the departing stragglers from the previous arrival: middle-aged Chinese mostly, bearing gifts of cakes and Portuguese wine; the occasional bemused European tourist scanning the boards for exit directions; one or two young toughs in bleached jeans, *fei jai*, strutting through the hall like eager cockerels, joking as they went.

On the bustling pavement outside the terminal Tiger Cheng threw up a hand signal and instantly three OSCG Cortina saloons materialised through a glut of red-and-silver taxis, to pull in close to the kerbside. At once the detectives from the concourse moved in tight around the vehicles, while Joe and Ruby climbed into the back of the first and Cheng eased himself into the front passenger seat. Above the gunning of the engine there came a volley of car doors slamming as the remaining two vehicles filled up, then all three cars pulled out on to the slip-road, weaving expertly between jerking lines of public light buses.

They were well along Connaught Road, the main eastbound arterial route through the business district, before the opposition gave themselves away. Joe's vehicle had just made it through a set of lights on amber when a bright yellow Celica with low-profile tyres darted out from behind a goods truck and sped across on red, narrowly missing a tourist bus turning right into the Star Ferry concourse.

'Showtime!' announced Joe Lai, staring back through the rear window. 'There's the tail. Tell the boys to be ready when they move up.'

As the three-lane tidal flow of traffic weaved its way through the glass towers of Central District, the Celica stood out like a hawk amongst sparrows. It was standing off, three cars back in the outside lane, just matching speed with the first OSCG Cortina. Waiting – not even trying to overtake. Inside the vehicle were four Chinese heavies of a type Joe had seen so often before: mid-twenties, swarthy skin, tank-top vests and blow-dried hair. *Fei jai* – street toughs. Soldiers of the societies. At this distance their tattoos were not visible, their badges of allegiance; but they would be there all right, on arms, chest, back or thigh.

At the approach to the Garden Road flyover the Celica kicked a little and began to move up on the outside. Feeling his pulse quicken, Joe glanced back over his right shoulder to assess the occupant of the front passenger seat as the car drifted into view. The man was darker than the others, with Ray-Ban glasses and the kind of straight clipped moustache the Chinese often associate with gangsters. Joe noticed then that the window was rolled down, but both the man's hands were inside the car, below the level of the window. Out of view. Holding something?

'*Diu lei lo mo!*' cursed Joe. 'That's too close. Get rid of them. Now!'

Cheng grabbed the radio microphone and barked a rapid instruction.

'Ah Fai, lose the tail!'

'Roger.' But at that moment Joe glanced again over his right shoulder into the Celica and saw the man's arms now rise into view clutching something heavy, black and threatening. An automatic weapon. The curve of the magazine triggered images within his memory. For a couple of seconds the triad struggled awkwardly with the

669

long barrel, trying to feed it out through the window.

'That's no tail,' shouted Joe, his voice rising to a near scream. 'They're going to hit us! Everybody down!'

At once, Joe's driver floored the accelerator and the Cortina lurched angrily forward through the traffic, aiming for a gap in the inside lane. It was too late. In that same instant a taxi already in the inside lane moved up, denying them space. The driver swore at the top of his lungs.

When he felt the first smack of a six-round burst stitching the rear wheel arch, Joe was already on the floor with Ruby under him. He knew he had to protect her. She had to give evidence. Then as the Cortina began to weave madly, one stray bullet glanced off the boot smashing the rear windscreen of the offending taxi in the inside lane. Suspecting a collision, the taxi at once screeched to a dead stop to examine the damage, leaving the life-saving gap which Joe's driver needed.

Beneath him, Joe heard Ruby's voice screaming.

'It's me they want! It's me they want!'

'Stay down,' Joe urged her, then he shouted to the driver, 'Get us out of here now or you're back on foot patrol!'

But the driver needed no such inducement to action.

What followed then had the appearance of a well-rehearsed stunt, though there was as much luck involved as skill or judgement. In the same moment Joe's driver found the space to his left and veered into it, the second OSCG vehicle moved up to fill the gap which Joe's vehicle had vacated. Its driver threw the steering-wheel hard to the right, jerked on the handbrake and slewed the vehicle across the carriageway in front of the Celica, blocking it.

The Celica driver was every bit as good as the racing modifications and wide-wall tyres on his car suggested. Seeing he was trapped, he slipped into first gear, pulled hard on the wheel and hit the accelerator with everything. As the tyres protested loudly, the Celica spun expertly around the Cortina and back into the traffic flow.

But in the next moment the triad driver saw the third OSCG Cortina come squealing across from the inside lane to catch the Celica almost broadside, crashing it against the second OSCG vehicle. There was a groan of twisting metal as the Celica's wheels spun hard, its smoking tyres leaving smears of rubber on the road. It was now locked between the two police vehicles which pressed against its doors, sealing them. The Celica was going nowhere. The engine coughed in a cloud of blue smoke, backfired, and then died.

Instantly the Cortina doors were open, and the detectives leapt out on to the road with pistols drawn. Dazed as they were, three of the Celica's occupants still scrambled madly for the windows. Before they were even halfway out, there were half a dozen Smith and Wessons trained at their heads.

'*Mo yuk, chai yan!* Don't move, police!'

The three men froze and raised their hands meekly, without a word.

The fourth man, still trapped in the front passenger seat where the Cortina had struck, looked down at the gash in his arm, and the sixty-degree twist of the bones, and he knew at once the arm was broken. A violent involuntary shaking in his limbs told him that. The assault rifle now lay between his feet, set for auto and splashed with his own blood. Aware of pain in every movement, he left it where it was and hoisted his good right arm through the window.

'*Mo hoi cheung.* Don't shoot,' he managed. '*Tin kei, mo hoi cheung.* For heaven's sake, don't shoot!'

'Throw out the gun!' someone shouted.

'Cannot! My arm is dog meat.'

The detectives moved forward, still aiming their weapons. Behind them civilian drivers were out of their

671

vehicles, trying to make sense of the gridlock which had suddenly choked off Connaught Road. Two detectives were detailed to issue warnings for the public to stay clear, while the three would-be assassins were hoisted against the side of one police Cortina to be searched and then handcuffed.

Sergeant Leung approached the Celica's passenger window carefully from behind, shoving his revolver against the back of the gunman's neck before peering inside the vehicle. What he saw confirmed the would-be assassin's story.

'Under arrest, *si faat gwai*,' growled Leung to the back of the man's head.

'I know my rights, *chai lo*. What are you arresting me for?'

'Illegal tyres, what do you think?'

While police motorcycles were still pouring on to Connaught Road, trying to get the traffic moving again, Joe Lai and Ruby Tang were hurrying on foot through a broad square housing a fruit and vegetable market deep in the midst of Causeway Bay. In front of them Tiger Cheng cut a swathe through the mass of bodies thronging the street, and he led the way to the elevator lobby of a run-down tenement situated between a magazine stand and a shop selling Japanese plastic hobby kits.

The safe-house was a modest apartment on the fourteenth floor, neatly furnished, like most Chinese homes, with that compact modular furniture demanded by lack of floor space. The main window faced one side of the Lee Gardens Hotel, and the rear balcony looked out over the chaos of trucks and litter adjoining the fruit market. It was a place Joe had often used to secrete witnesses, and he knew Ruby would be safe here for the time being, at least. The tenement had been well vetted: most of the block's residents were government servants, and the man who lived in the apartment across the landing was an officer of the Independent Commission Against Corruption, whose people were supposedly beyond reproach. Although Joe had no particular love for the ICAC – like all policeman he resented their power over him – there at least was one less cause for concern.

A babysitting squad of three detectives, two male and one female, was already in residence: people chosen by Cheng himself. As a routine reassurance Joe asked to see the Occurrences Book – the incident log maintained by the squad – and was pleased to see that hourly status reports to the OSCG offices at Police Headquarters were being faithfully recorded. They were not always this sharp; once he had found a babysitting squad so engrossed in endless rounds of mah-jong that the witness had slipped out alone to see a movie. Joe had defaulted all four detectives on the spot.

Tiger Cheng's first action was to call PHQ and discover the result of the stock-car race on Connaught Road. He nodded twice, grunted an acknowledgement, and put down the phone.

'Good news, *dai lo*. Four Chinese males arrested. One with a suspected broken arm. No police injuries.'

'*Ho lan ye!*' said Joe. Fornicating good!

Ruby slumped into a chair, her hands still shaking. Her fear was evident in the foetal posture she adopted: knees pulled up to her chest; arms folded around them as she rocked gently back and forth.

'That was very *ho lan* close,' she said softly.

Joe looked at her, trying not to show how afraid he had been himself.

'They must have been watching the terminal round the clock. Kwan wants you very badly, Ruby. You're one of the only people who can bring him down.'

She stared straight ahead, her face a blank mask.

'I'm afraid, Joe. I'm afraid. He's too strong.'

A detective appeared from the kitchen carrying a tray

loaded with delicate porcelain cups. Ruby turned to watch the man pour tea then offer her one with ritual politeness. She took a sip to calm her nerves.

'The noise of that gun. I can still hear it inside my head.'

'You're safe now.' Joe attempted to reassure her by taking one of her hands between both of his. 'He can't find you here. Only a handful of people know where you are. You'll be safe now, I promise. Look, these men are all armed, and they're going to stay with you here day and night.'

'Won't you be staying here?' She looked suddenly alarmed, fearful he might leave her now.

'I must go to Headquarters. I'll be back later, I promise.'

Ruby fought back her fears, heaving a sigh of resignation. Knowing that she was trapped within the game Joe was playing against the leadership of the San Yee On – and that her life now depended upon his success.

'Very well, Joe Lai,' she nodded. 'Go. You've got me this far. Now I will ask Gwan Yin to protect us both.'

Joe saw the frailty still within the woman's eyes; the child within who feared the dark. So desperate, and so lovely. Her only system was now to wager everything on Joe, and that made him feel good.

He gave her what he hoped was an encouraging smile, then strode to the door.

'Stay with her, Tiger,' he warned the station sergeant, seizing the big man's arm. 'The door stays locked the whole time. Don't open for anyone but me, no matter how senior.'

'*M'sai gong, dai lo.* You don't have to tell me. I've done this kind of thing a hundred times.'

'She's our only real witness against Kwan, and he'll move heaven and earth to get to her now. He'd think nothing of torching this whole building if necessary, and there's no telling which of our own people he has in his pocket – so remember to keep it closed.'

He looked back briefly. Ruby Tang was nursing a teacup and staring with glazed eyes at the television screen.

Joe Lai took the Cortina back to New May House, where he found Roman Fung waiting for him in Sandy Buchanan's office.

'You look good, considering,' said Buchanan. 'I heard about the mess on Connaught Road. Assault rifle? Getting bloody cheeky, aren't they?'

'Not the word I would have used,' shrugged Joe.

'How's the girl?' asked Roman Fung.

'Safe enough for the moment, but with the story she has to tell she's going to need protection for the foreseeable future.'

In the next few minutes Joe detailed the information he had extracted from the key witness. The revelation of San Yee On involvement in the MTR hijack had a predictable effect on his audience.

'Hell's teeth, man!' Buchanan's face registered disbelief. 'I can hardly believe a slug like Tony Kwan cares what happens to his fellow Chinese after 1997.'

'You're not the only one,' said Joe taking a cigarette from his shirt pocket. 'But this is not as clean as it looks. Tony Kwan's been running some kind of intelligence operation for the Vietnamese government; or more correctly his elder brother has.'

'Alex Au-Yeung.' Buchanan's brow furrowed. 'You mean the tai-pan of Bright Star Holdings – the darling of every merchant banker within borrowing distance of Exchange Square?'

'That's right. Do you have shares in Bright Star?' asked Joe.

'Hasn't everybody? The way they've been climbing...'

Joe sucked hard on the cigarette.

'Get rid of them now. What Ruby Tang knows will

take the roof off the Hong Kong stock exchange. We've got Au-Yeung cold. His companies are up to their ears in outstanding loans, with no way of meeting the repayments. As soon as news of his involvement in the Shatin robbery breaks, those shares will begin to plummet. By the time Au-Yeung walks into court you won't be able to give their paper away.'

'What about my dead American?' asked Roman Fung. 'You said you had good information for me.'

Joe proceeded to explain Reicher's involvement with the San Yee On, and how he had met his death at the hands of the same Japanese swordsman now holding the MTR train beneath Hong Kong harbour.

'The same man? You know they're claiming to be the Japan Red Army?'

'I saw the news. Have there been any more developments there?'

'Not much progress regarding the negotiations themselves,' said Buchanan. 'However there was some news this lunchtime. About an hour ago CID raided a wooden hut on Lantau Island and released the MTR man's child who was being held captive.'

'Released who?'

'Oh, you wouldn't have heard. The people behind the hijackers kidnapped the daughter of the Tsim Sha Tsui Station-Master to buy his cooperation.'

'How did our guys find the kid?'

'By sheer bloody good fortune. This morning a woman reported to QM hospital with a bullet wound in her arm which she picked up while out working in the fields. PHQ dispatched detectives to investigate immediately. Luckily she was able to take them to the exact spot where it happened: a rural farming area with only about five dwellings to choose from. They now reckon the triads holding the child must have eased their boredom with a little target practice, and the woman caught a stray bullet. Lucky for us, or we'd still be looking for that kid.'

Our guys surrounded the hut and kicked the door in. Took them completely by surprise. She's probably back home by now.'

Joe shook his head in wonder.

'What's it all about, huh? Can anyone tell me? Why would the San Yee On procure the services of the Japan Red Army to kidnap the Secretary of State? Why would they do that?'

Buchanan gave a snort.

'As police officers, that shouldn't concern us, laddie. Our job is just to prove they did it. Let the courts and the politicians argue about the rest.'

'One thing that still puzzles me,' broke in Roman. 'What was it that Ruby Tang took from the Society that makes them so keen to kill her?'

'United States Government classified information. Ruby Tang was given a highly valuable document by James Reicher on the night he was killed, to pass on to them, and they think she stole it instead. What really happened was that she lost it.'

Roman Fung looked confused. 'So what does this have to do with the Gwan-Dai killer?'

'Do you remember the girl they pulled out of the Shing Mun reservoir?'

'Will I ever forget? She worked at the Barking Peacock, right?'

Joe nodded a confirmation, then proceeded to relate Ruby's version of events the night of her near-fatal brush with the taxi-driver.

'And the document ...?'

'Was left behind as Ruby made her escape. Find your Gwan-Dai killer and chances are we'll get that secret document too.'

Roman Fung gave a shrug.

'Believe me, I don't need any further motivation to look for *that* monster. Six letters I've had from him now, all of them personally addressed. He knows I'm still no

677

closer to finding him, and the smug bastard seems to be enjoying it. Says he's right under my nose but I'm too stupid to notice him – can you believe that?'

'Maybe it's another police officer,' suggested Buchanan. 'That would explain why he appears to know so much about you.'

'A police constable moonlighting as a taxi-driver?' Joe weighed the possibility. 'It wouldn't be the first time. Can you think of anyone who might bear a grudge?'

'Enough to do this?' Roman Fung looked incredulous. 'It's a bit extreme as a means of revenge, don't you think? No this guy, whoever he is, has a more burning reason for doing what he does. The Gwan-Dai tag tells me he thinks he's on some kind of divine mission. Voices inside his head – that kind of kick.'

'So why involve you on a personal level?' snapped Buchanan, to whom none of this insane butchery made any sense at all. 'What's a taxi-driver got to do with you?'

'I don't know...'

And then it struck him. The ghost of a suspicion his conscious mind had been rejecting ever since the first letter had arrived. Too ridiculous, his brain had told him, or was it merely too appalling to consider. A cold shiver ran through him at the very thought of it.

'What is it, Roman?' asked Joe, concerned. He had noticed the look in his eyes.

'Oh, nothing,' lied the murder squad detective. 'Tell me, did your witness get a good look at the taxi-driver?'

'Not bad, she was only an arm's length away. One extra stroke of luck was that she glimpsed the name of the cab company on the side of the door.'

Roman's brain raced and he almost said the name out loud even before Joe could speak – knowing, and at the same time dreading, that he was right. In the end he held his tongue.

'Imperial Chariots of Kowloon,' said Joe Lai.

Roman Fung breathed a sigh of bitter resignation. Then it was true. His own brother. Still he could not bring himself to voice his suspicions before the other policemen present. He sucked air into his lungs to quell the sickness he felt inside.

'All right, Joe, you can leave that with me,' he said bleakly. 'I think I know where to take it from here. You'll get that document as soon as I get my man.'

'Fine by me,' Joe murmured. 'I still have my own pressing business to conclude. Something tells me those papers will give us all the answers we need.'

Roman Fung gave a brief nod of agreement and walked from the room without another word.

'What's wrong with him, I wonder?' quizzed Buchanan.

'He'll be OK,' offered Joe lightly. 'Just overwork.'

'Oh, by the way.' Buchanan snapped his fingers as a new thought struck him. 'A telex came through for you last night. It's here in my tray.'

'Who's it from?'

'Kiwi Rice. In Islamabad of all places. What's he doing out there?'

'God, I almost forgot. He's running a trace on one of the weapons from the Shatin job.'

Joe glanced at the covering memo; it carried a bright red URGENT tag. *Origin: Interpol Section, National Police Headquarters, Islamabad.* He tore open the sealed envelope in a rush of excitement.

Attention LAI Hing-keung SIP/OSCG/HQ-CID/ PHQ

I was right (knew I would be).
Enlisted the help of the ballistics officers here and traced the assault weapon to one of the armaments factories I told you about in North-West Frontier town of Derra. Source of the seized AKM is definitely

679

SUBHANULLAH ARMOURERS, New Aziz Khan Market, Shop No. 9, Derra Bazaar, Kohat Road, Derra Adam Khail.

The proprietor, Haji Rahman Gul (no criminal record), proved difficult. Records of the weapon batch indicate its intended destination was Tanzania. This joker probably does work for the ivory poachers but in this case his paperwork is probably as bent as he is.

Managed to 'acquire' the attached photograph from amongst the old guy's souvenirs. Found it pinned on his wall next to a picture of Arnie Schwarzenegger. The old guy reckoned he'd never done business with Chinese before, but he looks pretty friendly with the two in the picture. Wonder if you know either of them?

Local police very helpful, though not a cold beer in sight. Hope you appreciate this.

Rice

Joe checked the envelope a second time.

'Where's the picture?'

'That must be this one.' Buchanan handed him a second, larger envelope. 'They arrived separately.'

It contained a faxed copy of an enlarged eight-by-ten colour print. From its tones and perspective Joe guessed the original must have been a polaroid snap. In the picture three men stood close together in bright sunshine beside an open shop-front. The old man in the middle wore strange, ragged dress: dark baggy pants and a woollen waistcoat over a white shirt with billowing sleeves which ended at his knees like a skirt; on his head a loose turban sat like a bird's nest. A Pathan probably. Joe had never seen such clothes before, but the two men standing on either side were more familiar. Both were Chinese, each with a Soviet-style assault rifle propped against his hip, posing unashamedly like extras in an old Vietnam movie.

'Look at this, Sandy,' said Joe with a sardonic grin.

Buchanan took one look at the faces. 'Bloody hell, isn't that Eddy Kwok on the left.'

'Yes, and look who's playing Rambo here on the right. It's Tony Kwan.'

They looked at one another for a long moment, incredulous, not speaking. Eventually, it was Buchanan who broke the silence, his great ruddy face splitting into a beaming malicious grin.

'What we have here, my boy, is our first tangible evidence of conspiracy. Oh, the informants have done a grand job but judges always like physical evidence to back up what a witness tells them. This is great!'

Exultant, Joe Lai slid the picture back inside its envelope.

'Together with what Philip and Ruby Tang have to say, this gives me all the *prima facie* evidence I need for an indictment. I mean to have them, Sandy,' he said with sudden vehemence. 'The whole bloody lot of them. Not just for Shatin – but for Tasker, for Ruby, and even for Chan Ming. See if I don't.'

'I believe you, Joe,' said Buchanan picking up the phone, preparing to dial. 'I'd better just give our friends at Immigration a call, and get all our targets placed on the stop-list right away. Can't have them skipping it just when the noose is tightening, can we?'

'No, wait!' Swiftly Joe Lai shot out a hand and cut the connection. 'Not just yet. Too many senior officers see those requests. What's the betting our mysterious High Dragon traitor would leak the news at once, and then Tony Kwan, Eddy Kwok and Johnny Yau would quietly disappear to Taiwan overnight. No, the stop-list is no guarantee of catching them all. We're going to have to bait a hook. But first I'm going to have to take out their spy.'

* * *

In the run-up to the midday siege deadline the mood inside the ICC had turned to one of extreme concern – and with good reason. There had been no reassuring contact with the train in almost three hours, apart from the arranged delivery of breakfast. Two SDU men dressed in catering whites had walked in from the Tsim Sha Tsui end of the tunnel carrying thermos chests with food inside. At a distance of twenty-five metres they were caught in the beam of a powerful flashlight and ordered to set down the chests and walk back out the same way they had come. Since then the terrorists had resolutely refused to answer the negotiator's many attempts at a dialogue.

'It's no good, sir,' Ray Doogan had commented to the Commissioner over the PolMil link. 'It looks as though they intend holding out until the deadline for a straight yes or no.'

It was as Weldon had feared.

'Then they do know their business. They're giving us no way to undermine their resolve.'

The Commissioner thought for a moment.

'How do you rate the chances of an SDU intervention succeeding at this point?'

'That's beginning to shape up,' said Doogan, re-assuringly. 'Becker has an interesting idea. But not without inherent risks.'

'One that will get Fredericks out in one piece?'

'Perhaps. But they say they won't be able to move for at least another two hours.'

'Then until that time, Ray, you'll have to improvise. Get on the line again, try waving the money under their noses – get them thinking about that. Take their minds off this nonsense about direct negotiations with the President. It's a megalomaniac's dream. It isn't going to happen. The Consul-General is prepared to say a few words if necessary, but no other American will speak to them.'

'I understand, sir,' said Doogan wearily and put down the phone.

It was just after 11.30 when Ron Sewell was called into Doogan's office and briefed to buzz the train once more. This time the negotiator was to concentrate on the ransom, telling Okamoto that the twenty million dollars in gold bars would soon be available, and asking how and where it was to be delivered. The negotiator was to tie Okamoto up in a plethora of fine detail, in the hope that the noon deadline might slip by unnoticed. If that failed, he was to plead hard for a postponement.

The negotiator began calling the train at 11.46. There was no reply. He waited exactly one minute, then tried again. And then again after each successive minute. Finally, at twelve o'clock precisely, there was an answer.

'This is Okamoto. What is the decision of the American President?'

The negotiator ignored the question, sticking to the strategy.

'Mr Okamoto, thank you for answering. I have very good news. The gold you asked for has now been collected.' He took a quick breath, attempting to conceal his nerves, and fearful that Okamoto would interrupt before he could finish. 'Obviously that amount of gold will be very bulky. The authorities need to know how you would like it delivered, and where?'

'Mr Policeman, did you hear what I said?'

The negotiator felt his stomach flip. This wasn't working. He was aware of the bitter taste of bile in his throat.

'Of course, Mr Okamoto. I was coming to that, but first . . .'

'Listen!' The Japanese raised his voice only slightly, but it was enough to silence the police negotiator. 'Enough of your clever words. I require answers. Is the US President prepared to negotiate directly with me for the life of his Secretary of State – yes or no?'

683

'No, I'm afraid not. The President has, however, nominated one of his State Department Officers, the US Consul-General in Hong Kong, to speak on his behalf.'

'I see. And in answer to my earlier demands?'

'Discussions are underway. If you could just give a little more time ...?'

'No – no more time. The President must appreciate that we mean what we say. What follows now is the result of his stupidity.'

'Mr Okamoto, wait a moment. The gold ...'

There was only the softest click as the line went dead.

Ron Sewell jumped up from the table.

'Quick, get him back, for God's sake!' Pulling off his headset he ran from the room and out to Doogan's desk in the main Incident Centre.

Doogan was still on the phone to the Forward Command Post at Tsim Sha Tsui station when the shots sounded. The uniformed officers at the mouth of the tunnel started suddenly, clutching at their weapons as two thunderclaps erupted from the mouth of the tunnel. Strange, empty sounds.

It was several seconds before they realised what had actually happened.

When Okamoto eventually returned to answer the radio, he stayed on the line just long enough to say: 'It is done. Now send two men to fetch the body. At once!'

At the Forward Command Post, David Becker and Mel Kale themselves volunteered to carry a stretcher into the tunnel, knowing full well that this would be their only chance of a full recce of the tunnel. Cautiously they picked their way along the track in the meagre glow from the emergency lighting. When they reached the back of the train and saw the dark shape lying crumpled and facedown in the suicide pit, the same numbness they had felt at the first sound of the shots returned. Fumbling in the near darkness they had some difficulty in heaving the big man's body on to the canvas stretcher. There was no sound from the train as they turned to head back. No face was visible in the rear operator's cab, but still Becker felt Okamoto's presence there, silent and watchful – nursing the sword at his side just beyond the grey darkness.

Not until they had re-emerged at Tsim Sha Tsui station, where the light shone full on the corpse's face, did Becker recognise the murdered hostage.

'Oh, God, no,' he murmured, shaken. 'It's Tom Lassiter.'

TWENTY-FOUR

News of the death of Tom Lassiter reached Civil Coordination Centre at 13.17 hours, just ninety seconds after the body was brought out of the tunnel. The Commissioner's staff officer interrupted the Governor's security meeting to inform the Commissioner in hushed tones that Ray Doogan needed to speak with him urgently.

Weldon listened in silence to the full shocking details of the execution. Two bullets through the back of the head. Doogan's voice from the control centre across the harbour seemed very distant, the words somehow unreal – like lines from a film or an anonymous newspaper report.

Weldon chose his own response carefully.

'Very well, Ray, here's what you do. I want a full news blackout on this for the time being. And change the negotiator immediately. Bring the SDU to full state of readiness, and begin preliminary environmental countermeasures. Stand by your phone for further orders.'

No one blamed the negotiator for what had happened, but Weldon knew that such a move was important to compartmentalise the failure.

As Weldon put down the handset he experienced a dreadful sense of release. The situation was no less tense, but at least the waiting was over. He knew now there was only one way it could end.

Back inside the wood-panelled room with the scarlet drapes, Weldon's words brought all other discussion to

686

an abrupt close. He addressed the silver-haired diplomat at the head of the table.

'They have just executed a hostage. An American named Tom Lassiter. One of Fredericks' own security officers.'

In the silence that followed, Walters, the only man present who had actually met Lassiter, bowed his head.

'Dear God in heaven,' he murmured. 'We have to call a halt to this thing.'

One look at the faces around the table told Sir Andrew they were all of the same mind. He knew what he had to do.

Allowing the Chief Secretary to take the chair, the Governor summoned his aide-de-camp and requested an immediate link to the Foreign and Commonwealth Office in London. Priority immediate. Designation FLASH. The call came through within a matter of minutes. After Sir Andrew navigated the nasal whine of the communications officer at the London end, by giving the necessary recognition code, he heard the deep mellifluous voice of the Foreign Secretary himself. In London it was now just 06.30 hrs.

'Good morning, Foreign Secretary. I'm sorry to have to disturb you so early.' There was a slight echo on the line as his words bounced back at him through space. It unnerved him slightly.

'Not at all,' the resonating voice was almost robotic. 'Go ahead. I'm listening.'

The exchange was brief and to the point for, though a life-long diplomat, Sir Andrew was not one to waste words. The Foreign Secretary listened carefully as he concluded his briefing.

'Sir, as Governor of Hong Kong I have responsibility for resolving this mess. However, in view of the political dimensions and the involvement of the US Government I think it only wise and prudent to appraise you of my intended course of action.'

The Foreign Secretary checked his watch.

'Yes, yes, of course. Just leave it with me for now, and stay by the phone. I'll be back to you directly I've spoken with the Prime Minister.'

Immediately the phone was put down, the operator at FCO placed a priority interrupt call to the internal switchboard at 10 Downing Street. Wherever the PM was, he would have to be disturbed. The night-shift operator was still on duty as the call came in; he recognised its priority coding and buzzed it straight through to the private office where the Premier had been hard at work since six o'clock.

The Prime Minister set down his fountain pen to listen to the solemn voice of the Foreign Secretary.

'Our feeling is that the terrorist leader is unstable. Now that he's killed a hostage, further negotiation is not a credible option. They've threatened to blow up the train with all hostages in just over eleven hours. The Hong Kong police are taking this threat very seriously. The Governor intends to order a military option at the earliest opportunity.'

'I see. What chance of success does he give?'

The Foreign Secretary cleared his throat significantly. The PM quickly grasped his meaning. 'Like that, is it?'

'He asked me to stress that it's by no means a foregone conclusion. His men are well trained, but they'll need a large slice of luck, too. He knew you'd wish to forewarn the President.'

The British PM closed his eyes and tried to picture the worst-case outcome. Confined spaces, confusion and madness, and a political fiasco. A flash of anger rose within him and his fist beat upon the desk, shaking the china teacup sitting in its saucer.

'Dammit! If he can't guarantee lives, why is he so eager to abandon negotiations at this early stage?' he demanded fiercely. 'How long have they been down there – even a day?'

'Not quite that long.' The Foreign Secretary wet his

lips. 'Listen, Prime Minister, Sir Andrew is about as cool as they come. He's solid, level-headed, and he knows his ground. I have to say that I entirely concur with his evaluation. Intelligence reports say this Okamoto cell is an extremely violent group. Yes, I know it's been less than a day, and we're used to these things dragging on much longer, but let's not be blinkered in our thinking. Unless we make up our minds to act now, more innocent people may die.'

The Prime Minister tugged his lower lip.

'What's Sir Andrew doing now?' he asked after a lengthy pause.

'He's standing by, waiting to receive your blessing.'

The Premier eased himself from his chair and turned to face the window, nursing the receiver against his shirt. The pale luminescence of the morning sky made sharp silhouettes of the rooftops to the rear of No. 10. How strange, he mused, that the fate of some US citizens and ethnic Chinese held hostage in a place thousands of miles from London should now rest upon his decision. How absurd that this bastion of British colonialism had survived so long.

And that now it was his responsibility.

Steeling himself, he raised the phone to his mouth.

'All right, you can tell him to proceed. But before you do so give me fifteen minutes to speak to the President.'

The lunchtime traffic moved sluggishly through the heart of Wanchai, giving every impression of deliberately frustrating Roman Fung's progress. He was heading home to his family's apartment in a high-rise in Causeway Bay, with Amy Chan seated beside him in the passenger seat, shooting small furtive glances in his direction. As he drove in silence, Amy Chan noticed the way he gripped the steering-wheel too tight, so that the white of his knuckles showed clear through the skin of his slender hands.

Not knowing quite what to say – after the revelation

about Imperial Chariots of Kowloon – wisely she said nothing. She had already seen the suspicion in his face when she insisted on accompanying him.

'Just procedure,' she had assured him. 'You need a witness to cover you. This has to be done by the book!'

The obvious possibilities that Roman Fung might either try to aid his brother's escape, or even throttle the life from his body remained unspoken. Amy was far more concerned with Roman's own emotional state.

When the elevator doors opened on to a narrow landing and he unlocked the door, he could tell at once his mother was not at home. He thanked all the gods for that small blessing. Most likely she was out playing mahjong with neighbours. The apartment was completely empty. Ah Ming's heavy bunch of keys was absent from the hook beside the kitchen god's recess.

The keys with the Gwan-Dai fob!

Amy followed him inside, trying to catch his elbow.

'Roman, remember we don't have a warrant.'

'*Yau mo gau choh.* This is my home. I can do what I like here!'

He made straight for his brother's bedroom and reluctantly Amy followed him. The bed was made up, and magazines and books were arranged on every surface with careful, almost obsessive neatness: all straightly aligned in orderly piles. Music cassettes were scrupulously returned to their cases and neatly stacked along the shelf in rows. In a small drawer beside the single bed Roman found an exercise book containing Chinese poems rendered in exquisitely drawn characters. Some of them appeared to be his brother's own work. Roman threw the book aside, suddenly irritated by such overblown sentiment.

'Joe Lai reckons our taxi-driver may have kept the missing papers which Ruby Tang lost. If they're here, then I'm going to find them – even if I have to rip this room apart.'

Stooping beside the bed, Roman reached beneath it, groping until his fingers brushed the side of the metal chest and dragged at it. They exchanged looks of grim fascination. The fastenings were strong, a padlock securing the hasps on each side.

Roman took a hammer and chisel from the kitchen drawer to break it open. Then, as the lid swung back, he gazed inside at the ordered boxes and packages of his brother's secret world.

A cloyingly sweet smell rose out of the trunk in a foetid blast.

'What in Gwan-Dai's name has he been doing?'

A black zippered case came first to hand, which he passed to Amy before continuing his search. With mounting dread he raised the lid of a cardboard box and peered inside. He saw a collection of about a dozen clear glass jars with screw tops. Each jar seemed to be filled with liquid but before he could examine them further Amy Chan grabbed at his arm.

'Roman, look at this,' she hissed.

She had opened the zipper expecting to find a writing case filled with paper and pens. Instead the plastic loops held a dozen or more wands of finely honed surgical steel. Roman put out his hand and drew one free. The scalpel blade was tipped with a safety cap of near-opaque plastic. He removed the cap and carefully examined the glittering edge. Clean. There was a faint whiff of sterilising alcohol.

'Dissecting kit,' he murmured softly, checking the label on the case: 'YUE WHA China Products'. There was no surprise there: he knew you could get anything in the medical department of China Products store. He slid the scalpel back in its plastic loop, looked meaningfully at Amy, and continued his search.

Inside the trunk was a stack of cuttings from glossy magazines: explicit pictures of European models taken from *Playboy* and *Penthouse*, wall-to-wall flesh. Beneath these he found an album containing photographs of naked girls. Chinese women arranged in poses similar to those found in the magazines. An obvious mimicry – with one notable exception. The girls in the second set of pictures were all quite dead, their corpses positioned like department-store mannequins to ape those of the living models.

Roman Fung's confusion lasted only a second before comprehension dawned across his face and he felt nausea rise up inside him. Pain erupted in his temples. Feverishly he scanned the other items in the morbid collection. Dropping the pictures he removed one of the jars from the box. His hands were sweating as he tried to unscrew the cap. The pain inside his head was now like a knife blade probing at his optic nerve. Unable to release its lid, he held the jar up to the light, his eyes screwing up in horror as he recognised the object bobbing gently from side to side within the clear viscous liquid. The sharp stink of formaldehyde assailed his nostrils.

Amy Chan covered her mouth.

'*Aiyah!* What is it?'

He did not answer, could not answer. An abomination! Silently he continued to watch the fragment preserved within the jar.

'Roman, is it human?' she demanded, her hand still hovering over her mouth.

'Yes, it's human,' he said at last, placing the jar back inside the trunk and moving quickly away from it.

Amy lowered her head, clasping her hands together but otherwise unmoving.

They remained that way for what seemed an agonisingly long time, both of them struck dumb by their gruesome discovery. At long last Amy managed to mumble, almost tearfully:

'*M'ji gong mat.* I don't know what to say.'

He was staring blankly at the wall like the shell-shock victims one finds in military asylums. He shrugged carelessly but there was bitterness in his voice.

692

'*Mo mat ye gong. Hai gam.* Nothing to be said. What's done now is done.'

He threw back his head to release a tortured sigh.

'I'm trying to picture the headlines,' he said. '"Gwan-Dai killer baits brother cop." Has a ring to it, don't you think?'

Amy felt his intense pain. She struggled vainly to find the right words.

'It's not *your* fault, Roman. You can't blame yourself for *this*.'

His reaction was filled with aggression, but it was all turned inward, upon himself.

'He is my family; we share the same blood. Haven't we Chinese always believed in the importance of the family above all things? Isn't *that* our strength? The family protects us, they tell us, and we're all responsible for one another.'

'Yes, but that doesn't mean ...'

'Listen, somewhere out there is a monster with my blood in his veins. Someone who has been terrorising this city, strangling young women with a steel wire and then carving out their sex organs. How can you say I'm not involved – blood carries its responsibilities. I'm responsible for him now. I have to find him.'

When he turned, Amy saw his eyes brim with tears. She placed a hand lightly upon his chest, seeking to calm him. Wanting to relieve his pain.

'*Suen ah!* All right, we can find him together. Let me help you. Where will he be now?'

Roman found it hard to concentrate. His eyes seemed unfocused.

'I don't know. I suppose he'll be starting his shift soon. Maybe he's started it already. He could be anywhere.'

'Then forget him for the moment. He doesn't yet know that we're on to him – he isn't going anywhere. Let's get a grip for one moment. We still haven't found those missing papers.'

'You look,' he told her. 'I've seen too much already.'

Stifling her own fears, Amy began gingerly to empty the metal chest, making a list of its contents in her police notebook. For Roman's sake she would be strong. First she took out the various boxes, envelopes and papers, then placed each of the gruesome jars carefully on the floor beside the bed. What she saw in them was worse than anything she had ever come across in her whole police career. But for Roman's sake she made herself strong enough to do the job – the horror giving way to a feeling of utter sadness.

She found the document she sought at the very bottom of the trunk. It was a slim bound booklet covered by a flimsy orange sheet stamped with the words *Department of State, United States of America*. The spread-eagle crest was unmistakable, and a cutaway window in the cover revealed the official title of the paper: *Draft Agreement between the United States Government and the Government of the Chinese People's Republic on matters of Mutual Security and Economic Cooperation*.

That meant little to her; the English was far too high-blown for her limited command of the language. But when she handed it to Roman, he immediately understood its importance. In spite of the shell-shocked emptiness he felt, still he understood.

'This is what they wanted,' he said.

'What is it, exactly?'

'It's what Reicher handed them just before they killed him. I wonder whether it's actually worth all the lives it has cost.'

As he flicked anxiously through the pages, he heard a startled cry from Amy. Looking around he saw she was holding two more photographs, her hand once again to her mouth.

'What are those?' he asked.

For a moment she seemed to choke upon her words and the colour drained from her face.

'I found these amongst the pictures of all those dead girls,' she stammered. Her frightened eyes watched his face for a reaction.

Roman looked at the two pictures and found a new reason for dismay. He had expected to see more naked death there, but these were different. The first showed a blonde woman, a fully clothed European, striding confidently along the concourse of the Star Ferry Terminal. It was Ruth Tavistock – and it was a shock to know that the killer had begun stalking his colleagues and friends. But the second photograph was an even bigger surprise.

'It's you!' he gasped incredulously. 'Amy, this is you!'

After watching the two Europeans carry away the body of the dead hostage, Okamoto waited ten minutes then reported the execution to his North Korean controller.

'Have they announced it yet in the media?' he asked anxiously.

Pacing his room in the Hyatt Regency, Rhee Joon-kil gripped his radio in consternation at the lack of progress. Okamoto's unilateral decision to remain aboard the train had not come as a total surprise. He knew how the Japanese had always craved recognition for his acts of violence and he realised that the prospect of a worldwide audience had proved too much for him.

But that was Okamoto's own decision. What did he care whether Okamoto lived or died – so long as the operation itself was a success? All battles engender casualties.

'Nothing so far,' Rhee answered into the radio. 'There appears to be a news blackout in operation.'

There was a note of disappointment in Okamoto's reply.

'A strange tactic. Can they actually ignore our victory?'

'Patience. So long as the Americans know about the hostage's death, we are successful. And believe me they

695

do know. The Hong Kong authorities must now fear a bloodbath, but they cannot intervene without the approval of the American government. The White House, however, will fear a scandal: international condemnation if their attempt to take control of the Spratly Islands becomes public knowledge.'

The Japanese realised he was breathing too fast. Stress and fatigue were beginning to take their toll. He tried to relax his shoulder muscles and remain calm. Such lack of control was ... unseemly.

'Is there any news of an American withdrawal from the islands?'

Here at least Rhee had some comfort to offer.

'Their ships have now withdrawn to a distance of one hundred nautical miles. But they are also flying hourly reconnaissance flights over the islands, obviously waiting to see whether Vietnamese forces move in to fill the void.'

'Then we have our first success. We have pushed back the imperialists at least that much. Surely greater things must follow.'

Rhee reacted with caution.

'Small victories can make us careless,' he counselled. 'Now that an American citizen has died, they will feel backed into a corner. So watch the darkness for strange shadows.'

Okamoto smiled grimly at the warning, half hoping they might indeed try to attack the train.

'Relax. We are unassailable. Remember that the switch I hold in my hand could end Fredericks' life in a second. Caution me not – rather tell me how the people on the street judge us?'

'For the moment they are with you. They will follow anyone who promises escape from the butchers of the Chinese People's Army.'

'Excellent. The American government is cornered, and the hands of the Hong Kong authorities are tied.

With popular support on our side they would not dare to fire upon us. It is only a matter of time before the Americans capitulate and sink that frigate.'

In one of the fifth-floor offices of Caine House the direct line rang three times, then ceased abruptly. Thirty seconds later it rang again, and was answered this time at the seventh ring. An emergency communication.

'Yes.'

'It is I,' said the enigmatic voice at the end of the line. 'The family has need of your services.'

At once the policeman who had picked up the receiver reacted in fear.

'You should not have called me here. It's dangerous now.'

'Much more dangerous for you, little brother, if you do not listen carefully to what I say.'

'All right ... I'm listening,' said the police officer, casting about him fearfully, 'but for heaven's sake be brief.'

'Lai Hing-keung has found the girl and brought her back. She is now hidden somewhere on the Island. You must find out where.'

'What then ...?'

'Call me at once. This time there can be no mistakes. She must be washed immediately, and Lai with her, or we are all in the greatest danger.'

'*Fong sam*, Ah Gung, it will be done.'

The instant the line went dead the senior Chinese police officer was back on the phone, calling the Chief Inspector/CID/Admin over in New May House. There was only the briefest delay while the admin clerk summoned her boss and gave him the identity of the caller.

'Good afternoon, sir. Chung speaking,' came the immediate, rather ingratiating reply. 'How can I help?'

'Chung, I'm preparing a report for the CP on budget

overruns. I need a complete breakdown of all the external accommodation we maintain specifically for CID use. I need to check the validity of each case, so I'll expect a detailed breakdown of every safe-house in current use, and a note on the operation it concerns. Is that clear?'

'Yes, sir. It'll be on your desk by four o'clock.'

'Thank you, Chung. I knew I could rely upon you. One more thing, I'd prefer you didn't mention this to anyone in OSCG for the time being. Any suggestion of curtailed budgets tends to cause upset.'

'Of course, sir. You can rely upon my discretion.'

An urgent buzzing on the secure line shattered the tension in the Incident Command Centre. All eyes turned towards Ray Doogan as he grabbed up the phone.

'Yes.' His face was impassive as he listened. 'I see. If that's his decision . . .'

David Becker walked over to Doogan's desk. Kale was already there, watching the Incident Commander expectantly.

'That was Weldon with the Governor's instructions. You're ordered to release the hostages by military intervention at the earliest opportunity. Activate Operation Red Mansion.'

Kale glanced sideways, eyeing Becker keenly. Both men were aware of the gravity of those words.

'Right, it's your operation from this point on,' continued Doogan, deferring to the expertise of the Special Duties Unit. 'How do you want it played?'

Becker went quickly through his requirements, outlining the scenario he envisaged. The Incident Commander listened intently, occasionally nodding approval.

'Can we agree a strategy for the negotiators?' Doogan asked at last.

'Yes. Tell them we're going in, but don't tell them

when. It could be revealed subconsciously to the target in their tone of voice. The suspects will be very sensitive to any changes in attitude by the negotiator. Have the man on the radio promise some concessions – but not complete capitulation – that'd only make them suspicious. Tell Okamoto he can have a live voice link with the Vice-President in say six hours, and make the delay sound plausible. Say the VP has the President's full authority to negotiate on all issues. That'll get Okamoto thinking. But, in return for setting this up, we must first have sight of Fredericks. As a sign of good faith.'

Doogan began filling his pipe, an activity with which to occupy his hands.

'I don't know about that. There was a violent reaction last time we asked for contact with Fredericks. I think he'll refuse.'

'The negotiator must not take no for an answer,' interrupted Mel Kale. 'Sir, the success of Dave's plan depends entirely on us getting Fredericks to the back of the train. Say we're prepared to send forward a negotiator to go face-to-face. Say anything, but get him there.'

Doogan shook his head doubtfully.

'All right,' he said, striking a match and playing it across the bowl of his pipe. 'When do you want to do this?'

Kale glanced at the quartz diver's watch on his wrist.

'We'll need about an hour to get briefed and into position. After that everything depends on how the negotiator sells it. And how Okamoto reacts.'

Fifteen minutes later Becker and Kale were back at Tsim Sha Tsui station, giving the order for kitting up. In the quiet of the upper concourse the two twelve-man teams stripped out of faded jeans and climbed into black flameproof overalls. There was an air of nervous tension which caused some of the men to joke aloud, while others fell silent and locked themselves into the almost devotional ritual of assembling each piece of equipment in turn.

As he pulled on US Army jungle boots, specially blackened to blend with his other kit, Becker was glad to be back with his unit. Buckling on webbing and the low-slung belt-holster reminded him of the years he had spent at NT depot. The hundreds of hours spent pumping neat double-taps into wooden figures inside the killing house – coloured balloons bursting on each eliminated target. He tied the thigh strap and tested the quick-release thumb break on the holster. The Browning HP came away clean, like shaking hands with an old friend. The cool steel of the well-used pistol was welcoming to the touch, and somehow more real than the plastic-framed Glock he now used with the VIP Unit.

He pulled on the balaclava-style flash hood, wearing it pulled back off his head and bunched at the back of his neck. Then came the assault vest. As in a photographer's or a fisherman's utility vest, there were numerous pockets in front; only this one was made from multi-layered ballistic-grade kevlar capable of stopping a .357 round, and the pockets were filled with bulky ceramic plates designed to defeat high-velocity rounds. In place of the standard aviator's leather gloves, Becker used fully-fitted black golf gloves which were thinner and offered greater hand function, with increased sensitivity to trigger pressures.

Lastly, Becker reached into the canvas kitbag, pulled out the Heckler & Koch MP5 carbine and made the safety checks which for years had been his daily routine. His fingers knew the movements and ran through them without conscious interference from his brain. Set the safety-catch to S, release magazine, cock the mechanism, check the breach, release the mechanism, safety-catch to E, ease spring by pulling the trigger, set safety back to S. Satisfied, he released the sliding metal stock, forcing it fully home so that the length of the weapon was reduced to a more manageable twenty inches. Adjusting the buckle position, he brought the webbing sling over his head so it lay over his left shoulder and the weapon sat comfortably level across his stomach, ready to hand.

When all twelve men were kitted up, Becker ordered his team to buddy up and check each other's equipment a second time. The checks were deliberate and thorough, for, after the many years of practice which had led up to this one moment, no one wanted to get it wrong.

It had been decided that, since Kale was the commander of what had been dubbed operation RED MANSION, he would not be numbered amongst the rescue party. Becker, however, who could identify all the police hostages and most of the American hostages too, was the logical choice for assault leader with Alpha team. Marty Lewis would command Bravo team.

'Maybe next time,' commiserated Becker, aware of Kale's personal frustration at not taking part: a soldier's urge for release from operational tension.

Kale responded with characteristic black humour.

'No worries, mate. It's you I feel sorry for. Int cell just warned us they've got a couple of Rottweilers on board. Make sure you banjo those buggers first, eh?'

The final briefing took place in a room behind the Station-Master's office, where a table in the middle was covered by an architect's scale model of the immersed tube and the ventilator building. As both teams spread around the table, Willie Ng, the operations officer, ran through the position and condition of the stronghold, adding as much structural detail as he had been able to glean from the MTR engineers. That done, Mel Kale took the floor, asking Willie to translate his words for the *foh gei*.

'Alpha and Bravo teams listen in!' The group of black-clad figures fell silent, pens poised above leather-bound briefing pads, all eyes concentrating on the big Australian. 'As you all know, we have a stronghold situation aboard an MTR train. Total of eight crows and

701

twenty doves. These numbers have now been absolutely confirmed by technical support division. It's not like the normal building or airplane scenario we usually practice for, nor even one of the shipboard rescues we do, but that shouldn't make any bloody difference. The same basic principles apply: surprise, aggression and speed.

'This operation is codenamed RED MANSION. Its purpose is to neutralise the eight suspects, believed to be members of the terrorist group *sekigun*, also known as the Japan Red Army, and then to release the US Secretary of State and nineteen other hostages. In that order! Do I make myself clear?'

There was enthusiastic assent from the men around the table. Every man there had his share of nerves, but there was no room for doubts now. In such situations no one talked of ifs or buts. They concentrated on success, and on the order in which the objectives would be achieved.

'We've split the stronghold into two areas, with the dividing line here at the door to the ventilator building.' Kale drew the edge of his hand across the roof of the train in a sawing motion to indicate the appropriate position. 'From here on back to the rear operator's cab is Area Two. That's almost six car lengths, or a hundred and thirty-five metres. From here forward is Area One, just two car lengths, but it's in this area that most of the hostages are now located; most of the terrorists too. The assignments are as follows: Bravo team commanded by Inspector Lewis will take Area Two; Alpha team under Chief Inspector Becker will cover Area One.'

Kale heard the muttered comments pass between the men and he moved to silence them quickly.

'This may seem like an unequal division of work to some of you, but the reasoning behind it will become abundantly clear in just a moment. First, let's fill in some more detail, shall we?'

Carefully he lifted the roof off the first two cars of the

702

model train. The interiors were amazingly accurate, with silvered seats and central aisles and doorways all constructed to scale. One by one he named the hostages located in these first two cars, and stuck a gummed circle of green paper in the correct place to represent each. Alpha team men made their own notebook sketches naming the circles one by one as an aid to memory. Kale then continued the exercise, using black circles to indicate the suspects. Instead of names this time they used the numbers which Int Cell had assigned to each suspect.

David Becker watched as the black stickers assumed positional dominance over the green.

'Pre-deployment positions,' continued Kale, 'will be here, on the parapet of the up-track side of the immersed tube – on the opposite site of the dividing wall. That's where the technical boys have their kit at the moment. In this position we're only a few metres away from the train. We have three entry points through the concrete dividing wall into the down-track tunnel, that's here . . .' His finger indicated the door from the lower landing of the ventilator building. 'That's the way the terrorists got in. And also there's the first two adit doors, here and here.'

Only subsequently had Kale and Becker been informed about the adit doors. These were steel communicating doors set into the dividing wall between the two tunnels of the Immersed Tube at intervals of twenty-five metres. They had been incorporated into the design of the IT to facilitate evacuation and rescue into the adjacent tube in the event of a train malfunction or fire, and for this reason they were not fitted with a locking mechanism.

David Becker noted again the positions of these two adit doors he would be working from. The first faced out on to the train's steel sheath at the junction of the first and second cars; the second door was just a few metres beyond the front operator's cab. Once through these doors, it was only a matter of a few steps. He began to feel a little more confident about the promise he had made to Ray Doogan. Provided the diversion worked and Okamoto's device could be defeated, there was every chance of a clean hit.

Kale continued through to the conclusion of his briefing, then he covered the procedure for handling hostages. The men had heard it all a hundred times before, but it still bore repeating.

'The eavesdroppers in the TSD tell us several people have been forced to remove items of clothing. Now this may have been to facilitate searching, we don't know, but bear in mind that some of the terrorists may have switched their clothes with the hostages. Don't just go on those orange jumpsuits. Check faces! Check hands for weapons or grenades. Check the silhouette for trailing wires. Neutralise anyone who appears to be a threat. Treat the hostages as potentially hostile until each one has been restrained and searched by the reception team. We don't expect any of that Stockholm syndrome stuff from cops, but you never can tell.'

Some of the men shifted their feet uneasily. Becker guessed these were the ones, like himself, who knew personally the guys in Special Branch teams held captive on the train.

Before anyone had time to slip into dangerous reverie, Kale offered a final note of caution.

'Remember, gentlemen, you are police officers. These are special circumstances but you remain accountable for your actions. Standard rules of engagement apply regarding use of force and firearms. All officers will submit their personal weapons to force ballistic officers for investigation at the conclusion of the operation. That's all. Stand on your team leader's orders. Good luck.'

The men filed from the room without another word. The only sounds were the heavy thud of rubber-soled boots on the shiny floor and the dull clank of a CS smoke canister hanging from someone's belt as it slapped against a pistol grip.

Becker marshalled his team on the upper concourse, scrutinising all the young Chinese faces for signs of doubt. Fortunately he found none: only the wide eyes and dilated pupils which indicated the nervous energy summoned up by the situation they faced. The senior NCO of Alpha Team, a tall muscular man with the obvious nickname of Rocky, had already issued his own pep talk to his men. Rocky was in excellent spirits, and there was a keen edge to his demeanour which showed itself in a constant clenching and flexing of his gloved hands.

'*Gwok dak dim yeung*, Rocky?' asked Becker. 'What do you reckon?'

'*Mo man tai, dai lo*,' he barked back with boyish enthusiasm. 'No problem, boss. Alpha Team is glad to see you back.'

'Thanks. It's good to be back – I think.' Becker gave enough of a grin to let Rocky know he was kidding.

The NCO responded with cool bravado.

'Ah-sir, *m'sai pa*. No need to worry, boss. Gwan-Dai will be with us.'

Becker smiled as he fitted his radio earpiece and secured it in place with a Band-Aid. A second Band-Aid fixed the wire to the side of his neck, where it fed down across the collar of his black jumpsuit. The transmitter fitted snugly at his throat; a black Velcro strip circling his neck held two plastic discs set either side of his larynx.

Rocky grinned at his team leader, and continued. 'There's a Gwan-Dai in the police report centre. I made sure the boys all placed joss-sticks first.'

Becker took the NBC respirator in his left hand and slapped the sergeant on one shoulder.

'Between you and me, Rocky, so did I.'

'You believe in Gwan-Gung?' asked the sergeant,

surprised that a European should recognise the power of the Chinese pantheon.

'In a situation like this I reckon every little helps.'

When Alpha and Bravo teams were assembled on the lower concourse, Becker and Lewis made another radio check with Kale in the FCC. Communications were still strong and distinct. Kale then warned the Incident Command Centre and requested an update on the condition of the stronghold. By way of answer the Int. Cell reported that their microphones were picking up no sounds outside the train, and only sporadic conversation within. It was a period of low activity probably due to the environmental measures James Weldon had ordered. For the past hour or more they had been forcing extra carbon-dioxide through the tunnel, using the banks of impulse fans in the ceiling. It was not much, nothing you could detect without sensitive equipment: just an extra five per cent. But it was enough to starve out some of the oxygen in the atmosphere, and so reduce the terrorists' activity level along with their awareness. Enough to slow up their reflexes for those crucial milliseconds that could possibly make all the difference.

After a minute's consultation Kale cleared his men through the inner cordon on the lower concourse, and the teams dropped silently into the well of the up-track. Watched by the huddle of PTU constables and TSB civilians, the twenty-four dark figures put on respirators and entered the tunnel mouth. Ahead of them the emergency light glimmered weakly in the tunnel roof, glinting a dull yellow upon the steel rails stretching into the distance: lighting the long walk to the ventilator building.

The path leading straight to Okamoto.

At that same moment in an office on the fifth floor of Caine House, Lee Ming-kwai, the Deputy Director of

Criminal Investigation, sat waiting for a knock on his door.

It was not often he agreed to take direct calls from detective inspectors, much less to see them, but there had been an unmistakable note of urgency about Joe Lai's call and he was well aware of the importance of the case Lai was working on.

'Lee-sir, I need your help,' Lai had gasped down the phone. 'There's not much time. I can't reach the Commissioner. I must speak to somebody of directorate rank at once.'

'Calm yourself, Inspector,' Lee had ordered. 'Now, what are you talking about?'

The inspector had paused to catch breath, but the frustration remained evident in his tone.

'It's a long story, Lee-sir. What's important is I have a witness – a girl who's willing to give evidence against the San Yee On. Only it's not safe now. They've already tried to kill her once today.'

'The San Yee On?'

'*Hai la!* I don't want to say any more. Some of our own people are involved.'

'All right, inspector, you'd better come up.'

His knock sounded loud above the throb of the air-conditioner. Lee squared his shoulders against the back of his leather chair and called out, '*Yap lei ah!*'

Joe Lai entered, looking pale from lack of sleep. His hair was untidy and damp with sweat, and around his eyes the tension had deepened the worry lines into dark crow's feet.

Lee invited him to sit, then, in a gesture of reassurance, he took a pack of Dunhills from his tunic pocket and offered one.

'Inspector, you look like you just crawled over the snake fence up at Lo Wu. Care to tell me what happened?'

Joe cupped his hands around the gold lighter as he

sucked the smoke deep into his lungs.

'This is difficult, but I must tell someone. Since the Tasker homicide I've been working directly to the Commissioner.'

'Yes, I heard about that. Hardly an expression of confidence in the rest of us.'

'No, Lee-sir, but Weldon had to close it down tight because of the fear that the triads had penetrated our directorate. A couple of days ago I got a lead on a girl in Macau who had information about that penetration. Last night I was over there trawling the casinos. Eventually I found her – by good luck more than anything else. I picked her up and brought her back here. Only there was a San Yee On hit team waiting to welcome us at the ferry terminal. Four gunmen in a car.'

Lee Ming-kwai steepled his fingers thoughtfully.

'Yes, I heard about the mess on Connaught Road. All four are now in custody. I doubt they'll give us anything on their bosses. Still, it was good work.'

Abruptly Lee stood and walked around the desk, perching his tall, lean frame on one corner. He looked directly into Joe's face. 'What do you think this witness can give us?'

'The names of everyone behind the Shatin job. Not the trigger men; they were just the little horses. She can tie members of the inner council to the conspiracy – including Tony Kwan and Eddy Kwok. Perhaps the First Route Marshal, too.'

'That would be ... quite remarkable,' said Lee, rising from the edge of the desk. He pulled thoughtfully on his cigarette and wandered behind Joe's chair while his brain assimilated the information. On the wall the framed portraits of Her Majesty the Queen and Princess Alexandra, the Hong Kong police's Commandant General, both hung askew. *Ah Sau*, he thought fondly, remembering that the old woman who dusted his office every morning insisted on superstitiously tilting the upper edges of his pictures so that any devils trying to perch there would slide off. As he straightened the portraits he asked casually, 'And how is the witness after her ordeal?'

'Pretty shaken up,' answered Joe. 'But safe.'

Lee caught the hint of evasion in his words.

'Then thank heaven for that.' Lee stepped back from the wall and continued gazing at the pictures. 'It's obvious you're going to need protection – our best people. That's for yourself and for the witness. I'll set it up right away; perhaps have a word with the D. Ops and get some of the SDU *foh gei* attached.'

'That would be good, sir,' enthused the inspector, sounding somewhat relieved.

'Still, I can't help wondering why you came to me with this.'

Joe Lai turned round in his chair to face his senior officer.

'But I thought I already explained that, Lee-sir. The Commissioner is up to his neck in the terrorist incident. He can't be reached at all.'

'Then why not the Director of Criminal Investigations? Shouldn't he be the first to know?'

Joe cast his eyes downward, the look of pain on his face mirroring a sense of betrayal.

'That's the worst thing. We can't tell the Director any of this. He's the San Yee On's High Dragon.'

Lee Ming-kwai stopped dead and turned.

'*Mei wa?* What was that?'

'It's true. Chan Ham-gar is a senior triad officer.'

Lee stood momentarily stunned.

'I had a sudden feeling you were going to say that, but I don't see how it can be true. Just because the Director is a Chiu Chau. I'm Chiu Chau myself, for heaven's sake.'

'It isn't just that,' interrupted Joe. 'It had to be someone in CID, and someone of directorate rank. The triads have known every move we've made, right from the moment we first opened this case. Two nights ago I pulled in an agent of ours, a police officer who had worked his way into the San Yee On over a period of three years. It was a conversation he overheard between two members of the inner council which gave him the name. He's pretty sure of his facts.'

Lee settled back into the leather chair. His eyes now contained the same faraway look as a chess player planning several moves ahead. For him the pieces had just changed dramatically, and Joe Lai waited to see which way he would move. Joe had always admired the Deputy Director Crime: he was tall and urbane, and looked every inch the classical hero of Chinese literature, the kind of man other men like to follow. But his career had always been overshadowed by that of the Director himself, Chan Ham-gar, a man Joe considered to be nothing more than a self-regarding, self-seeking politician.

Stubbing out his cigarette, Lee rubbed his chin once and folded his arms upon the desk top.

'I don't enjoy going after other police officers. I don't suppose the surgeon particularly enjoys cutting out a cancer, either, but he knows his actions are necessary for the overall health of the patient.'

'Yes, sir.'

'This will be a very delicate operation; it will need to be carefully timed. We don't want to startle the birds from the trees until we're quite ready to move. I will go now myself to CGO and speak with Weldon.' He reached inside a drawer and slid a small notepad across the desk. 'In the meantime you'd better give me the address of your safe-house so I can arrange appropriate cover.'

Joe took out a pen, carefully wrote down an address, and pushed the pad back across the desk.

'Good. I want you to go back and join your witness –

and don't move until you hear from me. There'll be men along within the hour. They'll have signed authorisation from me. Don't speak to anyone else about this for the present. Weldon was right: the fewer people who know the better. I dread to think what would happen to public confidence in the Force if this got out. It could blow us apart. Better go now.'

Joe climbed to his feet and came briefly to attention.

'*M'goi sai*, Lee-sir. Thank you, sir. I feel much better now.'

Lee followed him to the door and shook his hand.

'I want to thank you, Inspector. This force needs more men like you. Men willing to take a few risks in order to get the job done. I'll see to it you are rewarded appropriately.'

Joe shrugged. 'I'm sure you will, sir.'

Lee watched him move along the corridor and out past the security guard on to the main stairway, then he returned to his office and closed the door. The DD Crime stood debating with himself for several seconds before picking up the telephone. The situation was now critical, and there was not much time left in which to act.

'Cheng man, *giu Ah Gung teng din wah*,' he said into the mouthpiece. 'Respectfully ask to speak to Grandfather.'

'*Bin goh giu?*'

'It is the Birdmaster, Grandfather. I must be brief. The girl is being harboured in an apartment in Causeway Bay. Take down this address ...'

Alex Au-Yeung listened to each word, then repeated back the address.

'Lai is very close to us,' continued Lee. 'But for the moment he has confused me with the Director of Criminal Investigation. He believes Chan is our High Dragon.'

'This time we can afford no slip-up,' said Au-Yeung. 'This time Red Cudgel will wash the faces himself, and

711

put an end to this enquiry. Do not worry. You are safe.'

Lee put down the phone having sounded apparently reassured by the Grandfather's intended course of action. In fact this was far from the truth.

His mind was racing with concern for his own safety now as he crossed the room and opened up the large safe which held all his official documents. Below the shelves piled high with the orange folders of secret enquiries was a locked steel drawer. Lee slipped a key from his trouser pocket to open this drawer, and began stuffing wads of documents into his briefcase. It soon held all he would need. There were two passports: one British and one Australian, each with a different name. Then there were the deeds to properties he had accumulated during his police career: the condominium out in Austin, Texas; the five-bedroomed townhouse in Vancouver, Canada; and finally the two adjoining beach houses on the Australian Gold Coast. The bank books were already safely in the hands of his lawyer in Melbourne, a second-level White Paper Fan officer in the Society's Australian wing.

But he had always known he would need liquid assets in the event of a quick escape and, like all Chinese, Lee had placed his trust in the abiding appeal of gold. One by one he removed four heavy plastic tubes from the drawer and placed them inside the briefcase. On a whim he opened up the last tube and smiled appreciatively at the glinting golden image of the South African deer. Each tube had been designed to take a stack of twenty Krug-gerrands: a total of eighty ounces of fine gold. It was enough to buy his way out of any trouble he might encounter at the airports. Last of all he took out his Smith and Wesson detective special, checked the load, and tossed it inside the case.

He was about to snap the locks closed when suddenly he heard an unexpected noise and jerked his head around to see the door communicating with the Director's office swing open.

In a moment of terror Lee Ming-kwai found himself staring at the stony features of the Commissioner of Police himself.

Weldon's face was thunderous – so too was that of Chan Ham-gar, Director of Criminal Investigation, who stood behind him. Lee made a vain attempt at escape, leaping for the door to the corridor. But when he jerked it open he found Joe Lai standing outside, revolver in hand. Lee took one look at the weapon and stepped backwards.

'You seem to have dialled a wrong number, Mr Lee,' said Weldon angrily as he flung the communicating door wide open, allowing Lee to see fully into the neighbouring office, where a technical officer with a headset was seated behind a sound deck. The phone had been monitored and the conversation recorded, along with everything else Lee had said that day. 'All that talk about washing ... Dear me, if that number you dialled doesn't turn out to be a laundry, I'd say you're in a great deal of trouble.'

Weldon relieved him of the briefcase and examined its contents. The gold did not surprise him. It merely served to intensify his anger.

'By God,' he said, shaking with fury. 'This is one cancer I'll enjoy cutting out!'

TWENTY-FIVE

Just before three o'clock, Hong Kong time, Ron Sewell took over in the negotiator's chair and attempted to contact the terrorists' stronghold. More than a little nervous over his first communication with them, he found Okamoto eager to talk.

'This is Ron Sewell speaking,' he began tentatively. 'I have good news. The US Government has indicated its willingness to speak to you directly. However, there are certain conditions attached.'

Okamoto's response was exultant.

'So, you are the new magic talker. What happened to the other man? Did the sound of gunfire scare him off?'

'You mean Tom? He couldn't continue. He felt you no longer trusted him.' It was a standard reply when forced to change negotiator.

Okamoto gave a snort of derision. 'You people mean nothing to me. I hardly think of you at all. If you fail to carry out my instructions, then I must kill hostages. It's that simple. You understand?'

'I understand.'

'Good. Then tell me what the Americans say.'

Carefully, Ron Sewell began to outline the details of the offer, emphasising that the Vice President would speak with the full authority of the President himself. When he came to the condition that William Fredericks be allowed to speak face-to-face with himself from the back of the train, Okamoto reacted with suspicion.

'Why must you see the old man?' he thundered, the

signal breaking up in the negotiator's headset. 'Is this some stupid government trick? Do you think we are children?'

'No trick. Unless I can confirm the Secretary of State is unharmed there will be no contact with the Vice President.'

'In that case I will kill every single hostage.'

Sewell wet his lips nervously, aware of the crucial importance of what he was about to say.

'You could do that, of course, and no one could stop you, but then you wouldn't achieve your goals.' Easy, he cautioned himself, don't rush it! 'You've already shown how tough you can be. How much better now to be magnanimous.'

'Why should I indulge you?'

'Because you understand the political realities at work here. The President is a powerful man. He must maintain the dignity of his position, otherwise he cannot retain the trust of his people. You understand that. He can't just yield without the appearance of having bought something in return. Let them see Fredericks. It cannot hurt. Give the Americans just a little face, then everyone benefits.'

The few seconds it took for Okamoto to make up his mind seemed like an eternity. Ron Sewell sweated every single second, knowing that without this concession the rescue attempt was a non-starter.

'Very well,' agreed Okamoto at last. 'You may come aboard and see him for yourself.'

Sewell felt the sharp sting of stomach acid. His mind grasped for an excuse – any excuse.

'No. I'm sorry, I can't do that.' He tempered the firmness of his tone, hoping to God it would not provoke the Japanese. 'The authorities will not allow me to put myself in danger. Fredericks must come out to me.' Subtly he had slipped in the suggestion that the Secretary of State be allowed off the train.

715

In his headset he heard an explosion as Okamoto laughed out loud.

'You do well to fear us, policeman. Fredericks will not come out, but you may see him in the rear operator's cab. And I will speak to the Vice President not in six hours, but in two.'

Sewell made an attempt at lengthening this deadline, for the sake of appearances, but Okamoto was no longer listening, and in truth the negotiator no longer cared. The line went dead. He pulled off the headset and breathed a sigh of relief.

'OK, it's time,' said Okamoto, aiming his weapon at Fredericks' head. 'Mr Secretary, stand up now, please.'

William Fredericks rose to his feet with difficulty, his gaze fixed on Okamoto. The flesh of his cheeks was blotched and puffy but his eyes remained cool and watchful. As he straightened up, something inside the canvas belt dug into his side uncomfortably, reminding him of the danger of his situation. The cordtex charge around his middle.

'What now, son? Is this where you kill me?' His voice was almost a sigh but there was no hint of anxiety.

Okamoto spoke rapidly in Japanese, and two of the terrorists still in orange overalls moved forward.

'You will go with these men. I have agreed you may speak a few words to the authorities. They are concerned for your health. Do exactly as you are told. If you attempt to run, or if the police try anything, these men will shoot you down at once. Understand?'

Something in Okamoto's tone rekindled the flame of resistance in Fredericks' weary heart, and he knew that if he were to die it was better to go like a lion than a lamb.

'I understand this,' he answered firmly. 'No matter what happens to me, your own lives can be counted in hours. Think about that.'

Okamoto jerked his head once and Fredericks was hustled down the aisle. As the three-man procession made its way back to the last car, it was watched closely by the remaining hostages now sitting up on the bench seats. They had all managed some sleep the previous night, but now, after the murder of Tom Lassiter, they knew a rescue attempt was probably imminent and that they must remain alert and ready to move as and when required.

Stephen Lee remembered his SDU briefing. In the field of VIP protection it was always a possibility that he would find himself taken hostage along with his principal, and so the Unit had been instructed in how to react in such an emergency. Or, in this case, how *not* to. As he glanced down at the orange overall he had been given to wear, the chief caution in his mind was that he must do nothing to intervene once the attack began, or he would surely be cut down in the confusion. He looked up to see the procession reach the far end of the train and disappear into the operator's cab.

At the opposite end, in the front operator's cab, Okamoto got on the radio, still holding the small black radio detonator firmly in his left hand.

'This is Okamoto, you may now send your man forward. I warn you, if there is the slightest threat to us, I'll push this switch and cut him in two. Is that clear?'

'Perfectly,' answered the ICC strategist who was standing in as negotiator. 'He will now begin walking towards you from Tsim Sha Tsui station. He should get there in approximately four minutes.'

At the forward observation point near the mouth of the tunnel Ron Sewell pressed down the Velcro fasteners on his kevlar waistcoat, and pulled over it a high-visibility reflective vest of orange Day-glo with the words POLICE NEGOTIATOR stencilled front and back in both English and Chinese. He was listening carefully to the advice of an SDU inspector on duty there, aware that

717

something drastic was about to happen – and that he would be close enough to catch the fall-out if anything went wrong. From the corner of his eye Sewell could see the OC/SDU calling instructions into a handheld radio: winding up the troops.

'Stay calm,' warned the inspector, 'and walk at a brisk pace. Never run; that's like a red rag to a bull. When you see Fredericks and you're satisfied, press the transmit key on your radio, *once*. If you see Okamoto at any time, press *twice*. Got that?'

Sewell felt for the key. The wire had been fed down along his arm and looped under his watch-band so that the key dangled beside his open palm.

'Got it.'

'When you're done, just turn around and walk away. Whatever happens, don't run. If you hear the sound of gunfire, hit the ground immediately.'

Jesus Christ! Sewell thought. *Why am I doing this?* He peered into the tunnel and thought of all those childish fears once held of things that lurk in the dark. There was a strange hollow feeling in his stomach and he gripped tight the magnalite torch to keep his hands from trembling.

'Take your time. You have four minutes to get there.'

Sewell forced a smile, then flicked on the beam of his torch and climbed down into the well. He began to follow the steel rails leading into the tunnel mouth.

On the parapet beside the ventilation building, David Becker heard Kale's voice in his earpiece: 'Alpha and Bravo standby. You have four minutes to my signal.' Immediately the ache in his calf was forgotten. He glanced over his shoulder at the line of black-masked faces and raised his thumb, waiting as each call-sign from his team confirmed their state of readiness.

'This is Alpha standing by,' he answered.

'Bravo standing by,' responded the disembodied voice

of Marty Lewis, crouching somewhere in the tunnel behind him.

Feeling the sweat prickling like tiny insects, they remained silent and motionless as the muffled sound of voices in the adjacent tunnel filtered through the narrow gaps around the adit doors. Like hungry ghosts they crouched now in the darkness, each man alone with his own private thoughts.

Becker's thoughts comprised a flashing montage of remembered images that merged confusingly into one another in time with the beat of his pulse. Lassiter and Divine happily sounding off in the helicopter on the day they arrived in Hong Kong ... Jason Leung's funeral, with his parents dressed in mourning: white hoods and surcoats tied up with string ... A big moon rising over a rolling green field in mainland China on the night they had grabbed Chan Ming ... But the most affecting image was that conjured up by the old *oyabun* of the Sakaguchi-gumi: the image of a precious stolen sword wielded by a student fencing champion. Inexplicably that now bothered Becker far more than all the guns he might encounter. He forced his mind back to the practice walk-throughs on the dummy train, mentally rehearsing the steps he would take once across the narrow parapet and inside the first car.

Sewell walked the last hundred metres towards the train, feeling his throat begin to tighten and the arched walls close in around him. Above the laboured breathing of the overhead impulse fans he counted the click of his footsteps on the concrete floor, and he let the rising sequence divert his fears. Ahead he could see the lights of the train blazing in the darkness like two giant red eyeballs, and now he understood why the Chinese called it 'The Dragon'.

When he was fifteen feet away from the train, a light flicked on inside the operator's cab, its yellow glare flooding on to the track. Sewell stopped dead, shielding his eyes and waiting for someone to appear.

'Lower your hands.' The oriental voice was harsh. 'Let me see your face.'

Sewell complied, and when his eyes became accustomed to the light he stared up into the window. The man there was no more than a back-lit silhouette. The head pressed close to the glass was deformed by the bulky outline of a respirator.

For a moment Sewell imagined he heard the sea groaning against the outer surface of the immersed tube. Then he heard himself say: 'Where is the Secretary? I must see him and speak to him first.' His voice seemed strange and somehow different – not his own at all.

For several seconds the black shape lingered by the window, then it receded and was replaced by another much heavier figure in a white shirt. Unkempt and scowling, it was quite definitely William Fredericks. The light spilled across the shiny dome of his forehead, highlighting the blunt nose and the baggy cheeks. He looked very, very tired.

'Good afternoon, Mr Fredericks,' Sewell said carefully.

'What's good about it?'

Advised of the contact by a subordinate, Okamoto at once called Kowloon Bay on the front cab radio. He kept one hand folded tight around his AKM assault rifle, so in order to handle the microphone he had to lay down the radio-detonator on the angled surface of the operator's console.

'There, they are talking,' he barked into the handset. 'Now, connect me to the Americans.'

The new negotiator sounded if anything more co-operative than the last. The solicitude added a new edge to Okamoto's mood of irritation.

'Of course. Please stand by. This will take just a moment.'

The seconds passed slowly, with only connecting clicks on the line to suggest that the radio patch was going through. Okamoto tried to imagine the satellite out in space which was waiting to beam his words all the way to Washington; and with each second's delay his patience frayed a little further. He swung around and slouched against the connecting doorway, looking down the aisle of the train. The continuing silence bothered him: a worm of suspicion gnawing deep within him.

'Quickly!' he growled fiercely into the microphone. 'Hurry it up!'

Along the half-lit carriage an untidy litter of hostages stared back at him listlessly. Their accusing faces angered him, and without warning he aimed his weapon and ordered them all to face the floor – then to drop to the floor with their hands behind their heads. While his fingers flexed restlessly against the weapon, his eyes kept up their fierce scrutiny. At the far end of the connecting aisles, through the forest of upright steel tubing, he could now see the open connecting door to the rear cab. He could see a smudge of his own man's orange overall in the doorway, and a speck of white that was Fredericks' elbow.

They looked a very long way off. Then he remembered, from the plans Cheung had given him, that the distance was exactly one hundred and eighty metres.

Suddenly he realised what was bothering him, and was angry that he had not considered it sooner. Too many distractions! The signal from the radio-detonator had only a limited range. If the battery charge had somehow leaked, then it might prove unreliable. Fredericks might even now be out of range. The charge might not fire!

The radio jarred his thoughts. 'Connecting you in five seconds ...'

'No, wait!' he shouted into the handset. 'Not yet!'

Instinctively the hand clutching the microphone groped also for the detonator. His fingers clipped the black lozenge of plastic; it slid down across the console, clattering to the floor before he could catch it. At that point he released the microphone with a gasp, letting the coiled flex swing free and the handset smack against the raised metal footplate. He grabbed for the detonator and came up shouting.

'Bring him back at once. Tell them to bring him back here!'

Inside the first car Miyagi responded immediately. He leapt down from the bench seat where he had been squatting on his haunches, and echoed the instruction with both hands cupped to his mouth. Halfway along the train a third voice took up the cry, until those in the rear cab responded.

Out on the track Sewell heard none of this. He was too busy concentrating on keeping his own voice calm, reining back the tension that would betray his fears. When he saw them cut off the Secretary of State in mid-sentence, he knew at once something was wrong. Fredericks' head jerked suddenly backward, his eyes rolled up, white and scared, and he was gone. This was it, Sewell told himself, his breath quickening. *They're taking him away*, his brain screamed. *Now! I have to move now!*

Without pausing, he turned on his heel and began to move away, his eyes fixed on the circle of light a thousand miles in front of him, which meant safety. Then something brushed his hand and he remembered the transmission key dangling from his wrist. In his haste to depart he had almost forgotten it. His fingers groped awkwardly for the switch, fumbled a moment, then found the reassurance of the button. He pressed it once. Somewhere behind him someone was shouting after him, though in what language he could not be sure. It all seemed like something in a dream. Step after step, he clung to the advice he had been given and kept walking.

Several seconds later there was a bright flash behind

him which illuminated the tunnel, flinging his shadow across the wall in front. A split second behind it came a rocking boom as the percussion wave from the explosion raced after him along the tunnel. Trapped in this confined space, the blast was amplified to a deafening roar and was fired like a bullet along the barrel of the tunnel. The next moment saw the air ripped by automatic gunfire, and in a reflex Sewell dived for the cover of the rails. He scrunched down into the suicide pit and lay there. Dead still.

The instant Sewell had pressed his transmit key, Mel Kale responded to a green light on Dr Lee's portable receiver unit.

'Right, that's it. You're on,' buzzed the signal in Becker's earpiece. The order to move in. '*Red Mansion. Go, go go!*'

Upon the parapet Rocky Hung heard the signal too. Still he waited for a nod from Becker's respirator before grasping the circular handles of the adit door and easing it aside. Taking the same cue, a second team member equipped with a riot gun stepped forward to the doorway and fired off a percussion grenade that rocked the tunnel to its foundations.

It was the same noise which had put the fear of God into Ron Sewell.

Barely a second behind this followed another explosion of a quite different kind, as a shotgun loaded with a rifled tungsten penetrating slug took out the landing door, and Bravo clambered through. They were to be allowed five seconds head-start to get into the bored tunnel before the door came down.

After that Becker's ears were singing, but he knew the noise did not matter any more. He took a quick breath and put his boot to the steel door. It fell inward with a heavy clang, and in the next second he was through the gap with Rocky Hung just behind him. He came up into a crouch, facing into the windows of the second car with his MP5 carbine extended – scanning the silvered wall of the stronghold for the three targets he had been told to expect. Infuriatingly he counted five figures, all now standing and turning his way: some orange, some black. *Too many targets*, he thought. *How many of them are hostages?* Still turning his way.

While the microseconds bled away, Becker scanned the killing arcs. Faces, elbows and shoulders – all of them moving. All the time, black uniforms were pouring through the gap behind him. Then at last he caught sight of a weapon; the angry curve of its magazine. A Japanese, wearing a *hachimaki* bound around his forehead like a kamikaze pilot, was aiming directly towards him.

At this distance Becker did not need to aim his weapon. That process had passed deep into muscle memory years ago. Now it was more like Zen. Awareness was everything.

In a fluid movement he focused awareness upon the white headband of the terrorist, and automatically his body orientation tuned in to that point – the way a radio homes in on a stored frequency. The change lever was set for single shots and he squeezed the trigger twice, bracing the short barrel with the web of his left hand. Then twice more. He did not see the target go down. He did not need to. Though the glass window panel between them had shattered into a flying mosaic of glittering fragments, which obscured his vision, he knew from the solid kick of the weapon and the even tone it produced that the shot had been good.

And by the time the glass had crumbled from the frame it was already too dark to see anything.

Station-Master Cheung listened to the order he had waited for, and obeyed it instantly.

Minutes before the assault went in, he had been briefed by Kale's Operations officer, issued a portable

SDU radio, and positioned at the Tsim Sha Tsui MTR console for a very special purpose: to lower the gigantic sea-door from the roof of the tunnel when the moment came. There was ample time in the station office for him to reflect on his agony when the terrorists had kidnapped his young daughter – and upon the abominable things they had threatened if he did not cooperate. Time also to thank the many gods he had prayed to that now she had been safely returned to him, and that now he had this opportunity to pay them back.

'OK, Cheung,' Kale's metallic-sounding voice ordered. 'Let her go now!'

Throwing the switch proved a very distinct pleasure.

At the junction between the bored tube and the Immersed Tube an electronic circuit sparked in the roof of the tunnel, then a circuit closed, releasing with it the restraints on the north sea-door. Normally the massive twelve-ton steel hatch would have been supported by a hydraulic damping system, and would have taken almost a full minute to close, thereby preventing damage to the ferroconcrete structure of the tunnel itself. Only this time the hydraulics had been overridden so that it fell like a guillotine, severing all the power cables in the tunnel. There was a tumultuous rending and groaning of metal as the twelve tons of steel fell unrestrained, slicing through the Dragon's silver back, dividing the train between the second and third cars. With all power circuits cut, the emergency lighting failed at once and the tunnel was plunged into total darkness.

Okamoto was in the first car when the lights failed. Still suffering the disorienting effects of the percussion grenade, he had stumbled back inside, unsure what was happening. For a moment he believed the charges he had set had accidentally ignited. Not many seconds later he realised how wrong he was, and a fierce cry erupted from his lungs.

'*So be it. Then they shall all die!*'

725

Frantically he squeezed the touch membrane key of the detonator. In the pitch darkness he saw the tiny LED display window flash up a red firing signal. But the cordtex charge around Fredericks' waist did not explode – nor the semtex block attached to the emergency escape door on the rear operator's cab. Both were shielded by the dense metal of the sea-door which now separated them from the first car. Instead the signal woke only the charge on the front escape door. For the briefest instant, while the blast flared just eight feet behind him, Okamoto saw the inside of the train clearly illuminated before him. This was his only glimpse of the attackers now swarming through doors and windows like an infestation of black beetles.

Fortunately for Okamoto, the charge had been placed on the outside of the train, so the blast was absorbed by the operator's cab. Nevertheless it tore open the escape door, which fell forward like the gaping mouth of a fish, flinging Okamoto to the floor.

Just then one of the terrorists thought he heard footsteps on the roof and fired a wild burst of nine-millimetre ammunition into the ceiling.

Becker reached down to snap on the beam of the magnalite torch mounted beneath the barrel of his H & K. He watched it cut an intense, narrow beam through the darkness.

'Condition black; one crow down,' he said to the microphone circling his throat. 'Alpha team going inside.'

Beyond the door in front of him, Becker's torch picked out the face of another orange-clad terrorist now responding to the light source by aiming his rifle. Without pause for deliberation Becker played the torch beam over his target and put a burst of fire through the glass, shattering the man's face. The briefing had said the enemy were all wearing body armour, so he knew it was head shots or nothing.

Inside the car the two other terrorists recoiled defensively, and in those few precious seconds Rocky Hung found the external door switch and released the lock. Lunging forward, he swept the doors apart with one hand and one boot, and the two SDU men launched themselves inside.

It was always going to be a dangerous job: that first entry. It meant they were exposed on both flanks, with wide arcs of fire to cover. Two men simultaneously through the door of a room could share the arcs, the first one taking the majority targets and the second one taking out the rest. But this was different, they would be vulnerable on all sides. They would have to cover one another's back. Rocky drew the short straw finding both remaining terrorists within his arc of fire and under the relentless sweep of his torch beam. There was a sudden flash of uncoordinated fire from one of the crows before Rocky took them both out with consecutive double taps.

Becker put his beam across the inside of the car. Men in business suits lay on the floor, hands over their heads. At the far end he could see shattered wreckage where the sea-door had ripped through the metal tube of the train and crushed it to floor level.

'Nobody move!' he shouted commandingly. 'Everybody stay down!'

But inside the second car no one had any intention of moving as the black shapes poured through the doorway and began checking for further evidence of explosive charges, and frisking those spread across the floor for weapons. There was an odd squelching underfoot, and the sound of spent cartridges skittering across the floor.

'*Dak ge lak!*' called one of the hooded figures. All clear!

Just twenty-two seconds after their activation, Becker clicked on his radio and made his report: 'Alpha leader, car number two cleared and made safe.'

In the succeeding minute a series of similar reports

crackled up the line from the other assault pairs. Kale's terse order instructed the immediate evacuation of surviving hostages. Still working in near darkness with only the light of their torches, a human chain of SDU men began hauling up the hostages and bundling them out on to the parapet, aiming them in the direction of the access stairs leading up into the ventilator building. Four call-signs from Charlie team had moved in there to safeguard the extraction point as soon as the assault had begun, and now they hurried the coughing, choking hostages up into the safety of the ventilator building, where medical teams were waiting to treat them. The remainder of the hostages, those trapped on the other side of the sea-door, would have to be taken out along the tunnel to Tsim Sha Tsui station.

The moment the last hostage was out of the second car, Becker turned aside from the five corpses whose blood now painted the aisle, and hurried out on to the parapet. He was still tense, alert, watchful. What bothered him most now was Okamoto. Becker had heard the terrorist body count rise with each radio report, but as yet there was no mention of their leader. No one had so much as seen Okamoto.

'This is Becker. Did we get Fredericks out yet?'

'Walking him out right now,' came the reply from Kale's radio. 'Shaken but still in one piece.'

'Shit! Thank God!' Becker pinched the microphone to his throat to assist the pickups in carrying his voice. 'How many crows you make that, Mel?'

'Seven reported dead. Did you see Okamoto?'

'Not me. Wait one.'

Quickly Becker checked again with his team. All they had found in the first car was Fredericks' aide, Fluherty, the PR representative from MTR, and the train operator. Then one of the call-signs informed Becker that during the entry there had been an explosion in the operator's cab. The emergency door which constituted the whole nose section of the train had been completely blown off – probably an own goal by Okamoto.

But no corpse to prove it.

Becker slipped cautiously back aboard the first car and played his torch beam over the scene of desolation and the tangle of scorched wiring erupting from the operator's cab. The cab itself was empty, the operator's console wrecked. Then his torch beam pierced the blackness of the gaping hole where the emergency door had once been.

This was the only exit point they had not yet covered.

Before he realised his mistake he had framed himself squarely within the doorway, his flashlight acting as a beacon to whatever lay out there in the dark. There was a small burst of yellow flame in the near distance but Becker never even heard the report. The single rifle shot sped out of the blackness, smacking into his upper chest with sickening sledgehammer force. Catapulted backwards his head struck the dividing wall as he fell, though he felt nothing. He rolled into cover, instinctively groped for the flashlight and snapped it off. He lay there panting in the darkness, feeling his chest beneath the waistcoat for signs of wetness. There was nothing. He felt nothing. Then a rush of joy and triumph when he realised he was still alive. *Thank God for ceramic inserts!*

From the inky blackness of the immersed tube there came the echo of running feet. Not far. Maybe a hundred metres.

Okamoto.

'Alpha leader, come in,' Mel Kale's voice blared within his ear. 'What the hell's going on there?'

'Mel, this is Becker again. It looks like Okamoto's done a runner into the IT.'

'That's bad news. You OK?'

'Yeah, no worries. But I'm going in after him.'

'Absolutely not!' roared Kale. 'Mate, that tunnel's nearly a mile long.'

David Becker did not obey the order. After surviving a high-velocity round to the chest he was in no mood to give up now. After coming so far he knew he must finally confront the beast. Somewhere, out there in the dark, he felt Okamoto breathing. Waiting for him.

'I know that,' he answered levelly. 'I fancy a bit of a walk.'

Behind the mirrored bar of the Barking Peacock night-club, in a storeroom normally filled with furniture, Red Cudgel looked through the haze of yellow incense smoke at fifteen bare-chested triad fighters kneeling before him, and was duly impressed. Beside him stood Eddy Kwok, cold and imperious, wielding the broad flat blade of a silver Chinese sabre.

This was one of those few occasions when the triad officials put on the ceremonial costume of red robes and knotted headbands: for the administration of the blood oath. Eddy Kwok had assumed the mantle and duties of the Vanguard and was now leading the assembled fighters through the twelve verses of a triad poem associated with the rebel organisations of the Manchu dynasty. Beneath the naked red bulb each man looked bronzed and fit, the red cords on their upper arms biting deep into massive biceps, red bandanas of knotted silk tied tight around their foreheads.

Throughout the proceedings Red Cudgel remained seated, observing the ritual – holding court in what triads described as the City of Willow. He watched the sacred bowl pass down the ranks. One by one, the fighters raised it to their lips, using three fingers of each hand, and tasted the blood.

'Bitter or sweet?' demanded the Vanguard of each man in turn. The sword of retribution raised high above his head.

'It is sweet,' each duly answered, and passed the bowl along. As he did so, a heavy drum sounded three times at the back of the room.

Even for a quick-strike hit squad the team had been drawn together with lightning speed. Red Cudgel had received the phone-call in Rhee's room at the Hyatt Regency long before the assault began, and he had made his excuses and taken leave of the North Korean at once. He had already been shamed once that day by the failure of his men to intercept the fugitive Ruby Tang, and he had no intention of failing a second time.

'They are in Causeway Bay and I have the address.'

'You want this done tonight?'

'She can hurt us, *sai lo*,' his elder brother had said. 'Nor will this policeman, Lai Hing-keung, lie down for us.' This time the orders of the First Route Marshal were quite specific. 'No one to be left alive within the safe-house.'

As a first measure Red Cudgel had issued a general recall, and all over Kowloon triad radio pagers had begun screaming.

Kwok had chosen the men personally, selecting only seasoned fighters from the many triad districts. All San Yee On fighters were good with a blade, but this time he wanted only those who could handle firearms well in a confined space. What this job required was discipline – not bravado.

Fifteen men, Red Cudgel had decided; seventeen including himself and Eddy Kwok. Not enough for a blade war but enough to take out a small apartment staffed by detectives armed only with handguns.

When the last of the fighters had drained the bowl, Vanguard took it from his hands, hurled it in the air and smote it with the sabre, smashing it to pieces. The fractured porcelain skittered noisily across the polished wooden floor.

'This is the fate of Ah Chat, who betrayed the monks of Siu Lam,' intoned Eddy Kwok. 'Whose head was broken even as this bowl.'

The next sound heard was the heels of Red Cudgel's

Italian leather shoes clicking across the wooden floor towards the back of the room. Opening a large built-in cabinet, he slid aside the false rear wall and began to dial the combination on a steel door hidden behind. The racks behind it held two dozen brand-new pump-action shotguns.

'It would be better to lose yourself, than lose one of these,' he warned as each fighter came forward to claim a weapon.

Five.... six.... seven.

In the silence now engulfing the train Becker re-adjusted his ballistic waistcoat and continued counting his breaths, as the Master had taught him – refocusing his energy. Then, after several more moments, he slipped through the gaping maw of the operator's cab and dropped noiselessly down on to the track. Crouching low and pressing close to one wall, he waited and listened as the silence pooled around him like thick black oil. He was fortunate to be alive, he knew; the bullet might so easily have veered a few degrees and struck his head, on which there had been no protection. For several seconds, lying on the floor of the train, that single thought had unnerved him, but now, with an effort, he forced his mind back to the Japanese terrorist who waited for him somewhere in the darkness up ahead.

Before moving off he had first fitted a new magazine to the H & K, for he knew there might not come another chance to reload. Then he had rid himself of the leather gloves and the hot rubber stench of the respirator. Both restricted the senses he would need to function in the utter blackness of the tunnel, and he knew that if he were to stay alive now he must tune in quickly to the slightest vibration. From whatever direction. Freed of these encumbrances now he could feel the cool air of the tunnel blow softly against his face, and the rough, porous touch of the concrete wall against his fingertips.

He was hunting in total darkness now, with sound as the only clue to his opponent's position. Ears still straining, he let his mouth drift open to form an air-pocket that would catch and amplify the slightest sound, transmitting the vibration through the bones of his head.

Suddenly a sound in the middle distance impinged on his senses. Ambiguous, indistinct – a suggestion of metal catching on stone. Then silence once more, pooling back around him with only the softness of his own breathing.

Well aware of his enforced blindness, Becker extended his left hand, spreading the fingers like a radar net, attempting to feel his opponent's presence. Not hear but *feel*. Cautiously he began to advance along the outer edge of the rail, two or three steps at a time, pausing regularly to sample the air displacement around him. Instinctively he moved at a half-crouch, transferring the weight between his feet with infinite care. The rubber-soled boots caressed the concrete before each step, testing the ground for grit – anything that might produce a sound and give away his position.

Silently he thanked heaven for the discipline of the *tai-chi* forms he had studied these many years. The near perfect balance they had taught him.

Step after step ... he tried hard not to think of the old Yakuza's words but inevitably he found himself thinking of little else. Okamoto the swordsman: champion student fencer and now brutal assassin and terrorist. A man who could murder in cold blood that which he loved most. A man who could cut off a woman's head, and execute Tom Lassiter without a moment's hesitation. For Becker the search for this man now seemed like a whole life-time's quest crammed into a few brief days of terror. Now here he was, edging his way down this broad stone artery, moving inexorably towards the final confrontation with what had become his own personal nemesis.

Then he heard the noise again, and stopped dead,

dropping down on to his haunches. It was much closer this time. A footfall against a rail, or perhaps a sleeve scraping along a wall, he could not tell for sure. But very close. The dull, muscular thump of his own heartbeat surprised him by its volume. The nerves of the moment were causing his face to itch. Stifling the sudden damnable urge to scratch, he reached down and confirmed the position of the change lever on his machine-pistol. It was set for single shots; which was exactly right, he thought.

If only he stayed alive long enough to use it.

Suddenly his ears caught the dull slurring of the sword leaving its scabbard. A chemical shriek shot through his nervous system. Responding to the sound like an immediate echo, Becker homed in, tracking right with all the speed his muscles could muster. But too slow. Too slow to avoid the powerful smack of the blade as it struck against the barrel of the carbine, jarring it loose from his fingers. In another portion of its steely arc the same swift blow fell just inches wide of Becker's right ear, crashing instead against his shoulder where the ceramic plates parted, and driving the air from his chest.

What followed was like a scene from a nightmare. A reflex finger-jerk brought forth a thunderous burst of fire from the carbine which exploded into the floor. At the instant of the flash which lit the whole tunnel around him, Becker fell sideways under the weight of the sword and caught the terrifying image of the Japanese crouched beside him with the gleaming blade extended in the attitude of a samurai. The young girlish face was twisted into a ghoulish warrior's mask, the steel burning bright in his hand.

As the flash died away, Becker found himself rolling – scrambling desperately to get beyond his enemy's reach. He came back to a crouch, pressed against the parapet on the opposite side of the rails. The sword had cut the carbine from his grasp, and its next blow might come at any second. After the momentary brilliance of the flash, the darkness seemed blacker than before. Only now his vision was haunted by the floating after-image of Okamoto's face.

Stifling a flood of rapid breathing, he listened hard for the next movement, preparing to dive to one side or the other, but no tell-tale sounds were heard. Five seconds dripped noiselessly by. He shifted his weight against the wall, fingers reaching for his leather thigh holster, closing quickly over the butt of his backup weapon: the Browning HP. Instantly a seering pain burned its way down the right side of his body; waves of nausea welled up inside his stomach. The pain seemed to emanate from somewhere beneath his right shoulder. Then he realised the true extent of the damage wrought by Okamoto's powerful sword stroke. Though the razored edge had not cut a single layer of the kevlar, still the force of the blow had been sufficient to smash his collar-bone neatly in two. The pain now became a dense fog inside his head, clouding his perception and dulling his senses.

Somewhere in the darkness around him the terror of his nightmare still hovered. Waiting to kill him.

The choice for Becker was simple: overcome the pain – or die.

Focusing his breathing he tried once more, reaching for the thigh holster in a slow steady movement. Working through the pain an inch at a time. The sound of a single long breath filled his ears. Whether it was Okamoto's or his own he could not quite tell. But at that moment he was sure the Japanese was no more than two sword-lengths away from him.

Listening also.

As his fingers brushed the restraining strap, Becker peeled it back gingerly, wincing at the soft pop of the metal press-stud. Moving quickly away from the sound, he slipped across the track to the safety of the opposite wall. An instant later the sound of rushing air close by exploded into a shower of fiery red sparks at a point on the wall where he had been standing only seconds before – the blade ringing a shrill note upon the parapet edge. *Thank you, O Gwan-Dai!* Becker mouthed silently.

Standing fully upright now, his back to the wall, he slid the Browning from the holster with a great effort and let its weight carry his hand back down to his side. The shattered shoulder screamed back in protest, and the pound or so of blackened steel he had so easily lifted in the past now felt more like an engine block. Raising the weapon to aim it was going to be bloody hell!

After a moment's deliberation he carefully transferred the pistol to his left hand and waited. But the pain of the movement had distracted him, and by the time his brain finally caught up to the sounds nearby he realised the soft rustle of cloth had been the sound of Okamoto moving again.

The Japanese was closing in for the kill; he could feel it – feel the man's deadly aura like infra-red radiation. He was moving in now to finish it all, unafraid of the pistol because in the dark his sword had the advantage. It added a metre or more to Okamoto's reach and the weapon could be wielded in total silence. A handgun, on the other hand, would be wildly inaccurate in darkness, and the noise and flash of a shot immediately gave away the shooter's position.

Now that Becker was armed again he knew he had only one chance to survive and that was to assess the approximate location of his target and empty the whole bloody magazine into it. And if he got it wrong, Okamoto would not miss again. He would close swiftly and slice him up like a watermelon.

Becker had little time to make up his mind. If he waited much longer, Okamoto might even bump into him in the dark, and then anything could happen. Even if he managed to avoid the sword, he knew that his chances in hand-to-hand combat, with a broken collar-bone, were somewhat less than zero.

Think fast, he urged himself, trying to recall every combat technique he had ever learned: the sequences he had drilled in. Drop, roll and fire. Roll in and out of cover. But, without exception, they all demanded the faculty of sight, and so were useless to him now. What he needed was something founded on instinct; something outside the normal combat envelope. In that moment he found his answer. Another school of training. Another kind of awareness. What was it the old man had called it? *The awareness of skins?*

Becker had always been sceptical of the existence of body auras, until his blind old *sifu* had clearly demonstrated the technique. After a lifetime of practice the old man had been able to detect each of the five successive layers of energy which *tai-chi* masters claim surround the body; he had also been able to detect any changes in the quality of that energy. At times he had used this faculty as a means of diagnosing illness in his students. Of the five successive layers Becker had only ever been able to detect the first and second. With eyes closed he had been taught to discern the location of another student from the touch of that second skin, when less than a metre from the man's body. He had never succeeded in locating the third skin, which radiated outwards for a distance of three metres. But that was what he needed to find now. Urgently.

With no time left for deliberation he took the weight of the pistol once more in his right hand. At once the pain filled his eyes with tears. Glad now that he had removed the leather gloves, he sank back on his haunches, allowing his back to drag noisily upon the concrete wall of the tunnel. In the thick blackness that engulfed them he could only imagine the flicker of reaction this sound would produce in his enemy. Okamoto's head would now be scanning in his direction. Stretching out his left arm, Becker spread his fingers again and let his arm pan back and forth, searching the currents of air for something he now only vaguely remembered.

He tried for a reaction a second time, scraping the ground with the muzzle of the Browning. This time he felt something. A ripple of energy, as if a tiny pebble had been dropped into a dark pool. Whatever it was, it was beyond his understanding, and it told him Okamoto was moving his way.

All at once he seemed to awake into a clearer level of perception as he tuned into his opponent's energy. He felt the blade being drawn back – raised up high for the *coup de grâce*. His opponent's advance came in small, careful steps, probing before him for the source of the sound. Becker's yearning fingers resolutely continued to sweep in a slow arc. Searching. Searching. Then he felt it. The merest brush-touch. Like the touch of a soap bubble or the wing of a dragonfly. The arm swung back, playing an arc of fifteen degrees. Fine-tuning. All at once the palm of his hand was warm. Then cold again. Quickly he relocated the source. There it was, the third skin: the energy of life. Breathlessly he pushed forward, feeling the tiny pressure exerted by the infinitesimal surface tension it possessed.

Now he held his breath, dragging his right arm, and the Browning, up to meet the left hand. Tiny beads of sweat prickled his forehead. Suddenly there came an ear-splitting cry as the Japanese made his lunge, but by then Becker was focused and ready. As the skin moved forward, bursting across his palm, Becker's thumb fumbled on the safety, snapped it off, and he fired.

This time, as the flash came, the Japanese reeled away as if dragged backward by the weight of the sword raised high above his head. His face was still twisted in the samurai death shout. Becker's aim followed him down, emptying the thirteen-round magazine in a series of flashes that lit up the tunnel like a stroboscope. The frozen frames describing the warrior's death fall.

When darkness reclaimed the body, Becker dropped

738

the pistol as if his arm was on fire, falling forward on to his knees in a mixture of exhaustion and utter relief. Clutching at the right shoulder with his other arm – struggling to ease the pain. Was it imagination, he wondered, or had he in that final moment, in the final flash, glimpsed something quite unnerving in his enemy's face: contentment, perhaps, to have died in full cry. A warrior's death. Either way, that Okamoto was dead was beyond question.

The sudden cold sensation in Becker's palm told him that much.

TWENTY-SIX

As the elevator doors slid open in the Causeway Bay apartment building, eight triad fighters squeezed out on to the landing. Immediately they took up defensive positions covering the stairwell and both doorways, with shotguns braced against their hips. Leading this attack group, Red Cudgel checked cautiously around him, then padded over to the door where he listened to a stream of muffled voices coming from within. Satisfied there was no mistake, he issued the warning hand-signal to his men and banged on the door with the thick edge of his fist.

'*Hoi moon!* Open up, brothers! We come in Gwan-Dai's name.'

There was no answer. For ten long seconds they waited, shotguns at the ready, while the voices within continued obliviously.

Red Cudgel banged once more, repeating the recognition phrase – louder this time.

'We come in Gwan-Dai's name!'

He waited just ten seconds more before ordering his men to stand clear, then put the shotgun muzzle against the door.

The rending explosion almost blew their eardrums, punching the brass lock clean out and chewing a hole in the wood the size of an apple. Raising one arm against flying debris, Red Cudgel then kicked the door in and drew quickly aside, allowing the first rank of fighters space to let fly an immediate volley into the room. Those first few shots were wild and fast, calculated to stun and remove any immediate resistance to their entry. They rushed inside while the wall opposite the door still erupted in a blizzard of powdered plaster and paint fragments. Shotguns braced, they scanned the room for bodies.

Eddy Kwok was first to fire again. The sound of voices to his left caused him to spin round and put a wild shot into the vacuum tube of a huge Sony television. At once the black box imploded sending a shower of glass in all directions and the voices died with it.

Kwok's face twitched nervously as he scanned the wreckage of the room, realising suddenly that there was nobody there.

'Where are they?' he hissed. 'Where the fuck are they?'

Red Cudgel broke in angrily, the urgency in his voice catapulting the fighters into action.

'Don't just stand there. Check the other rooms! Find Joe Lai!' he ordered.

Red Cudgel himself searched the kitchen while three of his men took the bedrooms. Several seconds later the fighters returned – empty-handed.

'*Mo yan!* Nobody here!'

'*Diu lei lo mo haai!*' cursed Eddy Kwok, stalking across in front of the rattan sofa and kicking out at the tinkling remains of the television set. 'Wrong apartment! Wrong fucking address!'

Red Cudgel swung the shotgun barrel across his shoulder, trying to make sense of what had happened.

'Fool, there's no mistake. It's the right address. I'm sure of it. Our information came from inside Police Headquarters. It was confirmed ...'

Before he could finish his sentence the amplified bellow of a bullhorn came flooding through the open window, rooting them all to the spot. It seemed to emanate from somewhere on the street below.

'You men inside, this is the police. You're

741

surrounded. Put down your weapons and come out.'

Eyes widening, Eddy Kwok looked to Red Cudgel for directions. '*Chai yan!*' he screeched.

In that same instant, while most of the triads still faced the open window, from the open door behind them a voice shouted: '*Chai yan, mo yuk!*'

Red Cudgel and Eddy Kwok turned to see the detectives at the same moment: a knot of Hawaiian shirts under bullet-proof waistcoats. The jaws of the trap that was closing around them. There was a moment of panic as fear ran wild amongst them.

Tiger Cheng would never know just why Eddy Kwok made his move, raising his shotgun barrel in spite of it all. It made no sense – not when the detectives were already crouching, aimed and sighted, in the open doorway. Perhaps it was his last desperate attempt to salvage triad honour. Whatever the reason, the threat left Cheng with no choice: he fired off his revolver without hesitation. There was an awful thud and thwack as bullets struck Kwok's breastbone, shattering his chest. Cheng saw the triad's head snap backwards, the long hair flick across his face as he went down. Then half-a-dozen armed detectives sprang into the room behind him, as Cheng tracked his weapon across the startled faces.

'Nobody move! Drop your weapons!'

For most of the fighters the warning was sufficient. Kwok's twisted and bloody body provided a salutary lesson. But for Red Cudgel it was another story. He had too much to lose if he was taken now.

Cheng's detectives moved forward and with curses began pushing the nearest two triads out on to the landing, stripping the weapons from their grasp. Red Cudgel waited until the first shotgun clattered heavily to the floor, then he made his move. Grabbing the only shirt his hands could reach, he hurled his own man into one of the advancing detectives. The cop's reaction was a defensive reflex: his detective special discharged in a startled burst into the fighter's stomach. The triad made a hollow gurgling sound and fell forward into the detective's arms.

All hell broke loose: shouting and screaming on all sides. Red Cudgel was ready then to take advantage of the confusion. Dropping to his haunches he let fly with his shotgun, aiming for the knees of the detectives. At once two other triads took his lead and discharged their weapons wildly into the mêlée. Ahead of him Red Cudgel saw legs buckle as three men fell screaming to the floor. Whether or not they were policemen he could not tell. But at that point it no longer mattered; he had achieved his objective. Panic. Bodies moving across the field of fire, obstructing the detectives' aim.

Seizing the moment Red Cudgel glanced over his shoulder and measured the distance to the open kitchen door. Less than ten feet. Quickly he cranked off another shotgun round, and before the sound had died away he was already rolling across the bare floor and out through that door. Tiger Cheng waited for a lull, then tore after him, slamming aside two of the triad fighters. When Cheng reached the kitchen door it was closed and Red Cudgel had wedged a chair beneath the handle.

By the time he had smashed his way through, almost ripping the door off its hinges with the ferocity of his kicking, Cheng had lost twenty precious seconds. Looking around he saw the back door leading on to the rear service stairs was wide open.

Running out on to the staircase he peered over the edge. It was then he felt the first bolt of searing pain shoot through his left thigh. There was a bloody rip in his jeans where the shotgun pellets had struck and lodged in his leg. Far below he saw the black shape of Red Cudgel's head spiralling downwards, and could hear the slap of his feet on the stone steps.

'Joe-sir, this is Cheng' – there was no time left for correct radio procedure. 'Kwan is on the service stairs, heading for the back exit leading out into the fruit market!'

Joe Lai was standing by his command vehicle in a side road opposite the target building directing the ambush when his junior investigator passed him the radio. In the back of the white Cortina, Ruby Tang sat nervously, straining to make sense of the transmission.

Joe's greatest concern had been that Red Cudgel might not himself take part in the hit, but remain aloof and observe at a safe distance. They had staked out the building at street level well in advance of the triad team's arrival. They had even deployed a CIB video-camera team in a room in the Lee Gardens Hotel overlooking the target premises. Whatever happened now, it would all be on film for the courts to see.

Tony Kwan's men had pulled up outside the apartment block in four cars and, after posting guards on the getaway vehicles and in the lobby, had moved to the elevators. One of Joe's own men, acting as assistant building superintendent, had observed them entering the elevators, and then passed word back to the command vehicle by concealed radio.

That had been Joe's cue to warn Cheng and his men, already concealed inside the apartment opposite, to stand by to close the trap.

Out on the street the triad lookouts and drivers had been taken in one well-coordinated swoop. When the shooting began, Cheng, peering through the fish-eye in the door opposite, had given the word. Joe had then used the loud hailer to distract the triads long enough for Cheng to make his move across the landing.

Now, amidst the crackle and hiss of the radio, Joe Lai heard the words he dreaded most: Red Cudgel had slipped the net.

Cursing with frustration, Joe tossed the radio back into the vehicle and ordered two detectives to follow him inside the building. Beyond the watchman's cubicle in the ground-floor elevator lobby was a narrow door leading out to the service stairs and the garbage tanks, with an exit door beyond. Checking the load of his personal issue and snapping the cylinder back into position, Joe heard the metallic rattle of the crash bar on the rear exit as it opened.

Red Cudgel.

The door swung wide, crashing against the concrete side of the building. A second later the security alarm began its wail.

Joe pushed past the uniformed watchman and tumbled out through the still swinging door. The yard behind gave directly on to the open street, where the fruit market extended a hundred yards on either side. Heavily-laden wooden stalls and groaning street barrows were set out like a harvest festival. And between these ordered lanes of produce, jamming every inch of space, was the vast eddying current of Chinese shoppers all haggling and jostling for bargains. Joe's head swivelled left and right, frantically searching for the face now so ingrained on his mind. Then a minor eruption in the crowd caught his eye: an old man protesting loudly as the birdcage he carried so proudly was banged from his grasp. Then, in the same direction, a fruit barrow was upended, sending mangoes and melons bowling into the road. A clutch of shoppers was swept aside like corn as the triad fought his way through, threatening anyone in his path.

There came a strangled cry, 'Look out! He's got a gun!' and a shock-wave ran through the crowd.

Joe started forward, weaving in and out of the passing pyjama suits, jinking between hawkers bearing heavy bags on bamboo shoulder-poles. His voice was drowned by the frantic cries of surging men and women.

'This is the police,' he roared. 'Get out of the way!'

Up ahead Joe saw a bottleneck caused by a parked

745

truck blocking off half the street. Red Cudgel was trying to shoulder his way through the gap. A sharp pain clutched at Joe's chest as he realised Kwan was getting away. He followed in frustration, knowing that, in spite of all his hard work and the risks to his men, if the triad made it past the next two streets he would have lost him. Kwan would then disappear like a ghost. There were public light buses and taxis plying on every street corner, ready to stop at a moment's notice. And two blocks away was an MTR station that could take Kwan anywhere in the Territory. Once he was out of sight, San Yee On money and connections could spirit the Red Cudgel safely out of Hong Kong before the night was over.

It seemed like the worst nightmare Joe Lai could imagine.

The other detectives were a long way behind him now, and Joe knew it was up to him alone to prevent Kwan's escape. At that moment his foot trod upon something soft and his weight lurched forward. He slid headlong, like a bowling ball, taking down two young men with him and hitting the hot, sticky concrete with the sickly sweet smell of squashed mango in his nostrils. For a mad moment there were feet all around him, then he kicked and came up once again with fruit pulp smeared on the back of his shirt.

Feeling panic lurch within him, he gazed up ahead, but of Red Cudgel there was no sign.

Coming level with the parked truck, he saw the street was bisected by an alley of run-down shops too narrow for vehicles, and knew that now he would have to make a choice. Seconds were ticking away, even as he stood checking first one direction then the other. 'Which way?' he muttered beneath his breath. '*Which way?*' At the roadside an old man in black pyjamas sat beside a tray of dragon's-beard candy, perching on an upturned bucket. He regarded Joe with mild interest. From the pistol in his hand this was obviously a police officer.

'Which way, *Ah Gung*?' demanded Joe between wheezing breaths. It was at such times that his thirty cigarettes a day showed their effect. 'Man with shotgun ... red shirt ... Which way did he go?'

The old man shook his head, squawking fearfully.

'Not my business! Not my business!'

In a sudden burst of anger Joe grabbed the ancient's jacket, shaking him like a doll.

'Which way? Damn your old face!'

Before the old man could answer, a sharp crack erupted from the alley, followed by a deeper, duller roar as the sound bounced off the walls. Releasing his grip, Joe tore into the alley in time to see a group of young street toughs wheel and scatter for the cover of shop doorways. At once he knew that Kwan had mistaken these for detectives and opened fire. It could only have been a warning shot, for, despite the reek of cordite in the air, no one had been injured. A fat kid wearing twisted spectacles, the first to spot the laminated warrant card on Joe's shirt, rushed towards him waving frantically.

'Ah-sir, *go bin!* Straight ahead. He's heading for the minibus terminus!'

Joe moved off at a lope, following the gentle bend in the alley past a shabby row of Chinese herbalist shops, sensing now that his quarry was very close indeed. Each new face he passed registered the same look of shock which confirmed Red Cudgel had passed that way. The faster he ran, the more the hot, scented air seemed to burn his throat: the cloying medicinal odours of ginger root and Tiger Balm oil filling his head.

Just as his lungs began screaming in protest, the alley straightened out and he spotted the red shirt up ahead. His heart leapt into his mouth. It was Red Cudgel, standing at the far end where the alley merged with a broader street choked with slow-moving minibus traffic. The triad enforcer was catching his breath as his head swivelled left and right, wondering which way to run.

This is it, thought Joe Lai. The confrontation with Tasker's killer he had hoped for – waited for.

The last twenty-five metres of alley between them was empty and beckoning.

Checking his stride to steady his aim, Joe raised the Smith and Wesson in both hands and called out above the din of traffic.

'You and me, Red Cudgel. How about it?'

Suddenly nothing else existed.

At once the triad turned, facing him square on with eyes that blazed like some vicious animal. Joe felt the blood thud-thudding in his ears as his pulse seemed to rise into an extra gear. In that brief snapshot of time the true danger of his situation struck him. Pistol against pump-action shotgun – was he crazy?

Red Cudgel spat on the ground and dropped the barrel of the shotgun into the crook of his left arm, confident of his advantage. He spread his legs to steady himself against the weapon's powerful blast.

'Lai Hing-keung,' he rasped. 'You were a fool not to leave well alone. A fool not to heed our warnings. Now you'll be just like your boss: another hungry ghost!'

At that moment, in the space between them, something moved. An old porter stepping out of an open doorway, pushing a loaded bicycle. Its cross-bar was hung with a pair of heavy cooking gas cylinders.

Joe Lai's eyes widened in horror. His aim was now blocked by the man and his burden.

'Get out of the way,' yelled Joe. 'Run for it. He's got a gun!'

Instead of moving the cyclist peered about him and, seeing Red Cudgel, he froze to the spot.

Laughing softly Red Cudgel lifted the shotgun to his shoulder.

'Go on, Lai. Fire your weapon. Shoot, why don't you?'

Still aiming at the far end of the alley, past the cyclist's shaven head, Joe could see the small black circle of the shotgun muzzle as the triad began to take aim.

'Get out of the way! Out of the way!'

'You can't do it, can you, Lai? Not with this garbage between us. That's the difference between us. I can!'

There was no more time. Joe shouted a last desperate warning and leapt into the open doorway of a Chinese barber's shop. The cyclist turned fearfully, his face twisted in horror, but he reacted far too slowly. At under twenty-five metres there was almost no scatter to the shot, and the full blast struck his neck and left shoulder, spinning him round as he fell. The clang of the cylinders was the only following sound as the bike toppled over and struck the concrete.

Just five metres away, from inside the doorway, Joe Lai watched the cyclist die. His neck half-severed, the victim lay in a gathering pool of his own blood, staring mutely up at the sky with an expression of utter bewilderment.

For Joe the initial nausea quickly gave way to anger.

'Is that what it's all about, Kwan?' he shouted. 'Just kill anyone who gets in your way?'

'*Fai lan si king, chai lo.* Don't waste your spit, policeman. It's over now. Where I'm going, you'll never find me.'

Joe Lai heard Red Cudgel's shoes scuff the concrete as the triad turned, and once again he felt the man slipping away from him. He knew this time he was powerless to prevent it. Desperately he shouted after him.

'You're going nowhere, Kwan. This doesn't end here. Wherever you go, sooner or later I'm going to find you. When I do I'll fuck you up. I'll fuck you up so bad … When word gets around how I ran you out of this territory you'll be finished wherever you go. And the San Yee On with you.'

Red Cudgel stopped dead as Joe Lai's words rattled inside his head. Before him lay the certain freedom of the open street. But behind him was the police officer who had orchestrated his downfall – cornered and helpless. This far he had been lucky, slipping the OSCG ambush back there. If he could just get clear of the police cordon, he could hide out on the Yaumatei waterfront and wait for Elder Brother to arrange a quiet departure for Taiwan. But Joe Lai was one cop he knew he could neither shake nor ignore. The man had too big a personal investment in this case to let go. It might indeed be said later that Lai had singlehandedly run him out of Hong Kong. And Red Cudgel could not afford such a loss of face if he was to maintain his influence when safely in Taiwan. He knew that his only choice was to kill Lai here and now, and make an end of it.

'*Diu lei lo mo chau hai!*' he screeched. 'I'll kill you, Lai Hing-keung!'

Cranking another cartridge into the shotgun chamber, the triad turned and began to advance back along the alley, his Italian leather shoes crunching the grit underfoot. The first vague buzzing of flies was audible as they discovered the open wounds on the porter's shattered body.

Joe heard the footsteps grow louder as his enemy approached. Scrambling towards the wooden uprights in the doorway he tried to peek out into the alley. There was an eruption as the window to his left exploded in fragments of wood and glass.

Cranking yet another cartridge into the breech, the triad began to laugh. 'Dumb fucking cop! That's the way it will always be. Get it through your head, we're too much for you. That's the way it will always be.'

Pressed to the doorway Joe heard the shoes coming closer. All around him, the shop floor was littered with glass fragments and behind him the owner and his half-shaved customer cowered behind an ancient leather barber's chair.

'Old man, is there a back door?' Joe whispered hopefully.

'*Mo!*' quailed the barber, his fearful face as brown and wrinkled as tobacco leaves. 'Ah-sir, we don't want to die. This not our business.'

'*Mo cho!*' hissed Joe irritably, realising now that he was trapped. 'And keep your damn heads down.'

Just then another blast ripped into the doorway, pellets chewing further chunks out of the window casement and showering splinters into his hair. Joe looked down at the snub-nosed detective special in his hand, small and insignificant against the shotgun's power.

'You're all alone, cop,' the triad crowed. 'And I've wasted too much time on you already.'

The footsteps quickened. Ten, maybe fifteen yards away. Joe was cut off and he knew it. That headlong chase through the market had been a mistake. He should have waited for backup! His evaluation reports always said he was too headstrong. But too late to brood on that now.

There was only one chance left – and he took it. Gripping the pistol in both hands he took a long deep breath, silently asking a blessing of the Gwan-Dai, then swung out from the doorway. A little over twelve metres away, his aim passed over the triad's face then dropped towards the ground. Searching. Searching. Red Cudgel caught Joe Lai squarely in his line of sight and lifted the shotgun to his shoulder once again. The taste of blood was thick in his throat – sure now that the policeman was dead.

There was a moment of awful clarity as Joe faced the shotgun and realised he was no longer afraid of death. That he was actually prepared for it.

Focusing his aim on the nearest gas cylinder by his opponent's feet, he steadied himself and, as if in a dream, he carefully squeezed off two shots.

The first shot glanced off the solid metal base, ringing

the cylinder like a bell. But the second went straight to its mark, striking the thinner side wall and exploding the cylinder like a bomb. Its fragments ignited the second cylinder instantly, engulfing the alley in a fireball of burning gas. The shock wave blew in the entire wooden shop front, pitching Joe hard against the barber's chair by the far wall.

In the next second his body dissolved into a hellfire of pain that seemed to centre somewhere between his ears, and unconsciousness took him.

It was some minutes before he recovered consciousness. There were other OSCG detectives now in the alley, and Tiger Cheng stood over him solicitously. A painful ringing continued inside his head, and the voices around him seemed dull and distant.

Beside him the barber and his customer were sitting together on a bench in a state of shock, attended to by uniformed officers. Apart from minor cuts and bruising, both appeared unhurt.

'Kwan?' he managed to ask, already knowing the answer.

Cheng shrugged and shook his head.

'Not much left to tell. Come see for yourself.'

Joe stepped out into the slaughterhouse mess of the alley. Detectives were cordoning off the area with portable stanchions and yellow tape. He had to tread carefully through the gore.

The command vehicle was parked at the end of the alley. When Joe reached it he slumped heavily into the front passenger seat and reached for the portable telephone.

'Get me Weldon,' Joe demanded when the PolMil Duty Officer answered. 'Tell him it's Lai Hing-keung speaking.'

There was a click as the call was parked and rerouted. A few seconds later he heard the familiar Scots burr take over.

'Weldon speaking. Yes, Joe, how did it go?'

Already Joe felt better. Weldon's strength bolstering his own.

'I'd say we broke even. We picked up some of the hardest cases on the Kowloon peninsula, but three of our boys have serious gunshot wounds.'

'I'm sorry to hear that. What about Tony Kwan? Did you make an arrest?'

Joe cleared his throat, remembering that Ruby Tang was sitting immediately behind him.'

'Sir, the principal target is dead.'

'What do you mean, dead?'

Joe caught the surprise in the Commissioner's voice and he couldn't help but interpret it as a rebuke.

'I mean dead, sir,' Joe continued, sensing his own bitterness. 'If it hadn't been him, it would have been me. Right now he's smeared all over an alley in Causeway Bay.'

There was an unexpected change in Weldon's tone.

'All right, laddie, I get the picture. Were there any independent witnesses to this. There'll have to be a full enquiry, and after the Tasker murder we don't want allegations of police revenge killings.'

At first Joe couldn't quite believe his ears. He had a sudden impression of now being on trial for what he had done; as if Weldon was already distancing himself from the operation.

'There were two members of the public there, but I don't know how much they saw.'

'That's good, Joe. Now, how can I help you further?'

Joe thought of all that had happened and how he had placed all his faith in Weldon, and suddenly he felt hollow inside. He had expected Weldon's continued support. This was beginning to sound like a bureaucratic hand-off.

So be it, thought Joe; but he still meant to have his arrest.

'We got Kwan, but he was only the enforcer. I want to pick up the First Route Marshal. I want Alexander Au-Yeung.'

There was an ominous silence on the line.

'I'm sorry, Joe, but for the moment that's not going to be possible. In fact, under the current circumstances it's absolutely out of the question.'

For a second time Joe could not believe his ears. He wondered if the explosion had affected his hearing.

'I don't understand,' he said coldly. 'How is it out of the question? He planned the Jockey Club robbery and this MTR hijack, too. Over half a dozen police officers have died already. We have witnesses, we have evidence – what more do we need?' By the time he finished, he was shouting.

Weldon cut him off there.

'Inspector!' he warned sternly. 'There is far more to this than you could possibly imagine. Now, listen to me. I'm ordering you *not* to go near Au-Yeung for the time being. Do I make myself clear?'

'Yes, sir,' said Joe caustically. '*Ho ching choh!*'

'Good. See me in my office at 8.30 tomorrow morning and we'll discuss the matter further.'

Abruptly the line went dead.

They arrested Roman Fung's brother at the wheel of his taxi in Mid-Levels. The dispatching company had given its full cooperation.

In a routine search of the vehicle they found all the evidence they needed. The glove compartment was stuffed with everything the killer needed to subdue his victims: a hunting knife with a seven-inch blade; a roll of industrial-gauge wire and a set of pliers; one roll of masking tape and a ball of twine. As an added pre-caution, perhaps, there was also a bottle of ether and a pack of surgical pads.

Beneath the front passenger seat they found the Gwan-Dai mask.

Roman Fung himself took no part in these proceedings. True, he had gone along on the operation, intending to confront his brother, but when it came to it he no longer trusted himself to behave as a police officer. The mere fact of his presence there seemed to make the other detectives nervous.

In the OSCG *dai fong* at Police Headquarters he stood aloof, watching them take his brother's fingerprints, rolling each finger-pad across the inked block and then on to the square boxes of the standard fingerprint form. To his surprise the prisoner showed no sign of contrition. He just sat smugly answering the detectives' questions like it was a television interview or something, giving every sign of enjoying this sudden attention.

Distantly Roman heard Amy ask if anyone had thought to call for a psychiatrist. The *foh gei* who answered glanced in Roman's direction, lowering his voice as one does when discussing the sick at their bedside.

Finally Roman could stand it no longer. Approaching the bench where his brother sat, handcuffed to the backrest, he addressed him directly for the first time.

'Just tell me why,' he managed with difficulty. 'For heaven's sake, why?'

Ah Lam turned slowly and regarded him. The previous good humour all turned now into venom.

'You want to know why? Because I'm good at it – that's why!'

Roman felt a hole open up where his heart should have been. Right then he wanted to cry.

'Was it because of me? Of what I am?' he asked. 'I have to know. Was it because I had the police career you wanted? You were jealous. You knew this job was everything to me. You wanted to be caught; that was your way of destroying me. Isn't that true?'

Roman heard hysteria creeping into his voice and for a brief instant the fierce fire in his brother's eyes made him think he had touched a chord. Just as suddenly the fire was gone, and a bitter loathing took its place.

'Whatever I did was because Gwan-Dai commanded me. I heard his voice in the night. It spoke to me in the sound of the rain. That never happened to you. Look at you, Roman Fung the famous detective from the television. The spirits never whispered in your ear, did they? They spoke only to me!'

There was a moment of awkward silence as Roman realised everyone in the room was now staring at the prisoner. In that same moment Amy Chan was beside him. She addressed him formally, aware of all the others in the room.

'Ah-sir, you should go home now. It's just more difficult your being here. You don't want to be around when the psychiatrist arrives.'

'No, you're right,' Roman managed to say, his face a picture of confusion. 'What I need is some air.'

After collecting his jacket she walked him to the lift.

'I could come with you, if you like,' she said as the doors opened and he stepped inside. 'They know what they're doing here.' All that's left now is the psychiatrist report and the teleprinter messages. They can handle that.'

His eyes glazed over as he thought of the teleprinter message which would now need to be circulated to all police formations. In twenty-four hours every officer in the Hong Kong Police Force would know that it was Roman Fung's brother who had committed those horrific murders.

'I'm all right,' he sighed. 'You'd better stay and keep an eye on things. I don't want anyone suggesting we didn't do it right.'

Amy Chan was reassured by this positive note in his voice. She flashed a sudden smile.

'They're bound to say you did everything a good detective should. You closed the case.'

He gave a brief nod.

'You're right. That's what they'll say.'

On a sudden impulse he took Amy's hand and pulled her close, kissing her tenderly.

'What was that for?' she asked, surprised.

'I don't know. For just being here.'

TWENTY-SEVEN

In the Governor's study that evening James Weldon opened his briefcase, glanced quickly across at Sir Andrew Mackie and then laid the slim orange-covered document on the low table in front of the American Secretary of State, who had agreed to this emergency meeting despite his exhaustion.

'Is this it?' asked Fredericks, a trifle incredulously, as he picked it up to read. 'Is *this* the reason for all that I've just been through?'

In the hours since his rescue, Fredericks had first been reunited with his wife, and then he had undergone a thorough medical examination in his hotel room by the Consul-General's personal physician. Apart from moderately high blood pressure, the ordeal he had suffered had apparently left no other ill effects. He had actually thought twice about accepting the Governor's dinner invitation, but when Sir Andrew had indicated the urgency of matters he wished to discuss, Fredericks had finally given way.

There were just the four of them: Sir Andrew Mackie, James Weldon, Fredericks himself, and Walters the Consul-General. A small private dinner followed by brandy and cigars in the Governor's private study. There it had been strictly business. He had listened attentively to Weldon's explanation of events. First the CIA operation which had placed their man James Reicher under cover, and which had resulted in the agent's gruesome murder. Then the link between the San Yee On triad society and Vietnamese intelligence, which had been so cynically manipulated by Reicher's spymasters. And finally the hijack which the Vietnamese hoped would torpedo Sino-US attempts to exploit the Spratly Islands as a key naval facility.

When Fredericks finished reading the draft military and economic agreement which had been so carefully forged by the intelligence department of his own Government, his face was ashen. This had the outrageous signature of one of Kagan's beloved black operations. Only Kagan would have dared.

For a long while he sat silently fuming. He was aware now of his own role as a pawn in Kagan's game. Aware of the true reason the President had asked him to make this Far East trip; the collateral bestowed on Kagan's operation by his meeting with the Chinese Foreign Minister.

With a huge effort at self-control the Secretary of State closed the orange cover and laid the document back on the table.

'May I ask what exactly you intend to do with this information?'

At once Sir Andrew put down his cigar and folded his hands across his stomach, fixing Fredericks with a clear grey-eyed stare.

'That rather depends on you, Mr Secretary,' he began pleasantly. 'Of course, I'm bound to inform the FCO in London, but I hardly think there'll be any kind of action there. After all, we have no wish to harm or embarrass our friends. You have your own statutory bodies for dealing with abuses of power within the intelligence community. I leave it to you to take whatever action you would feel is justified.'

Fredericks could not help thinking there was more to come, and he was not disappointed. Imperceptibly, Sir Andrew's affable manner changed to one of deadly seriousness.

'In your position, I think I'd feel very aggrieved at certain of my colleagues. Their aggressive meddling might easily have drawn the USA into another war here in the Far East. As for yourself, I think you've been quite fortunate in coming through this mess in one piece. Some might think the whole matter should be laid before your House Intelligence Oversight Committee.' Here Sir Andrew spread his hands theatrically. 'But, then again, before calling for a public enquiry one has to consider who is likely to be damaged most by all this. How high did the authorisation for this operation go? That sort of thing.'

'You mean how much did the President know,' said Fredericks bitterly, filling in the blanks.

'Precisely. Those are matters for you to decide, and we would not dream of interfering in any way, unless . . .'

Fredericks breathed a heavy sigh. In his long political experience there was always an 'unless'.

'I'm listening,' said Fredericks sternly. 'What's the condition?'

Here Sir Andrew looked across at the Commissioner of Police, prompting him to continue. Weldon looked first at Walters, who was listening carefully, not daring to say a word, then he returned his gaze to the Secretary of State.

'Prioletti and his senior staff – we want them out of here at once. We can't have them running wild; not in the current political climate. The transition to Beijing rule must be as smooth as possible.'

'That's all?' asked Fredericks suspiciously, knowing that the moment he returned to Washington this simple request could be accomplished with a single phone-call. 'That's the only string?'

'Not quite,' Sir Andrew said softly. 'Clearing out Prioletti and his cowboys is only a part of it. I understand you'll be leaving for home in the morning.'

'That's right, bright and early,' said Fredericks drily. 'I'd love to stay on a few more days, of course, but the trip's been kind of shot to pieces.'

Sir Andrew smiled at this.

'When you do see the President I'd like you to make one further point clear – just so we understand each other. If ever again the CIA tries to run a covert operation here which threatens or endangers our security, we'll have no hesitation in leaking the contents of that document there, and the true circumstances surrounding the MTR hijack.'

Fredericks thought carefully before answering.

'Governor,' he said, his face bland and expressionless, 'are you trying to blackmail the President of the United States.'

Sir Andrew responded, equally deadpan.

'Of course not, Mr Secretary. And are you suggesting that the President had anything to do with this unfortunate business?'

'No, sir. I don't believe anything I've said this evening could be construed in that manner.'

'Good,' said Sir Andrew, relaxing in his chair. 'Then I trust we now understand each other, Mr Secretary?'

'Yes, Sir Andrew,' said William Fredericks at last. 'I think we understand each other perfectly.'

Roman Fung had not slept at all that night. He had stayed up until just before dawn, staring occasionally at an old police graduation picture, assessing his life, looking for some kind of meaning.

He had once read how Buddhist monks sometimes found enlightenment in the contemplation of the simplest of objects: a flower, a grain of sand, even an empty cup. If the truth was to be found in such as these, he pondered, then why not also in a photograph.

When dawn finally came there was still no answer to his question. There seemed no meaning to his life beyond the job he loved so dearly. All his life it had defined him; it was him.

Only now it wasn't.

And neither was he.

That in itself was a kind of answer.

He wrote a short note to his mother, apologising for all the trouble he would cause her. A second one to Amy Chan, too ashamed to say anything other than just goodbye. Then, with tears in his eyes, he put his police revolver into his mouth, squeezed the trigger with both thumbs, and went to join the infinite.

David Becker had arranged to meet Joe Lai that evening in Tsim Sha Tsui. Before then he dropped off the taxi at the Regent Hotel and took an elevator to the tenth floor, where Nishimura was waiting to receive him. Opening the door wide the Japanese police officer – or was it Yakuza? – inclined his head politely, then stood aside to let him in. Becker did not move.

'Thanks but no,' he said. 'There are people waiting for me. I only stopped by to return this.'

Though it was concealed in its leather case there was no mistaking the shape of the Genroku *katana*. Nishimura accepted the sword in both hands, and at once his eyes filled with delight.

'The *katana* of Ikkanshi Tadatsuna! Becker san, you cannot know how much this means to me – or to my *oy-abun*.'

'I think I can guess,' said Becker. 'Strictly speaking, this weapon is still evidence in a murder investigation. Somehow, though, I don't think there'll be a trial now. Tell your *oyabun* I was glad of his help. Now I trust the debt is repaid in full.'

Before the door closed he was already striding back along the corridor towards the elevator.

When Becker reached the waterfront causeway just

762

beside the Regent, he found Joe Lai leaning against the harbour wall, smoking a cigarette and looking out across the water to the lights of the Star Ferry boats hovering in the distance.

'*Ho ma?*' asked Joe, nodding towards the black cotton sling around Becker's neck. 'How's the arm?'

'The arm's fine,' said Becker, carefully easing his back against the wall. 'It's the shoulder that hurts like hell. The doctor says I have to wear these strappings for a full twelve weeks! Can you imagine? Twelve weeks in this heat!'

Joe shrugged his indifference. 'You'll be fine. These things heal quicker than one thinks.'

It was a throwaway remark but Becker knew Joe Lai too well to overlook the second, submerged meaning. The shock of Roman Fung's suicide was still fresh in all their minds. He let a few seconds pass, observing the red aircraft navigation lights winking in the distance, high above Beacon Hill to the north. Then he asked: 'How about yourself? You going to be OK?'

Joe shrugged again and threw his cigarette butt into the water, watching the red arc of its descent.

'We'll have to see about that. Some hurt goes so deep that it never heals.' There was a long moment of silence, then, just as Becker was about to speak again, Joe continued. 'See that tower block across there in Wanchai? That's the Au-Yeung Building. They say it's one of the most prestigious developments in the Territory. What they don't say is that Alex Au-Yeung and his brother stole two hundred and seventy million Hong Kong dollars, and killed ten police officers in the process.'

'Whatever else he did, you can't blame Au-Yeung for Roman's suicide. He was always the most highly strung of us all.'

'Right now I don't know who I blame,' said Joe bitterly. 'All I know is Roman is dead and Au-Yeung's still out walking the streets.'

'Weldon must have his reasons, I guess.'

'Not Weldon,' corrected Joe with an edge to his voice. 'It's the Governor. He's the one with all the reasons. Sir Andrew Mackie believes our economy is in serious trouble at the moment because of this crisis in the property market – poised on a knife-edge. He says the Hang Seng Index is so closely intertwined with Au-Yeung's personal business empire that if he falls it won't hold up. He reckons every single merchant bank in town would lose, one way or another.'

'So they're just going to let him go?'

'Not in so many words,' said Joe, looking sideways at Becker. 'But it amounts to the same. They say he'll be lifted when the time is right – when it's safe to do so. In the meantime he'll be placed on the immigration stop list and kept under close observation. As if he couldn't just hop on one of his yachts and head for Taiwan the minute he chooses.'

Becker knew there was no further point in discussing it. They were both too bound up in all that had gone before. And since when did politicians care what police officers thought anyway?

'So, do you want to get a beer or what?' asked Joe more out of habit than real enthusiasm. Becker side-stepped the invitation as gently as he could.

'Not tonight, Joe. There's something I have to do. Maybe tomorrow night. We'll set up a *bai Gwan-Dai*.'

'Ho! Talking of *bai Gwan-Dai*, we're having a real one up at OSCG the beginning of next week. General invitation. Everyone connected with this operation. Tell Ruth and Kale when you see them.'

'Thanks,' said Becker. 'I will.'

They held their official *bai Gwan-Dai* celebration in the *dai fong* of the Organised and Serious Crimes Group, and this time everyone came – including the Commissioner of Police. That was Weldon's way of bestowing face upon the unit and on everyone connected with the operation. As tradition demanded, it was a rather formal affair, to begin with at least. The ritual rededication was conducted by a Taoist priest dressed in robes of red and gold, who chanted and prayed for what seemed an awfully long time. The ranks of police officers stood respectfully to one side while the baldheaded old monk droned on, filling the room with the incense smoke that poured from a brass pot swinging on the end of a chain.

As a matter of pride, the detectives had spent the whole of the previous afternoon in preparing the room and dressing the altar with fruit and flowers. Tiger Cheng had overseen the proceedings with his customary attention to detail. That morning they had then brought in extra tables, which they arranged at the back of the room and covered with red paper. Then the staff from the rank and file canteen came in to load up the tables with dishes of snacks and traditional roast meats: pork, chicken and duck, their outer skins golden and glazed to perfection.

When at last the priest had finished his devotions, the officers lined up, according to seniority, to pay their respects to the Gwan-Dai. James Weldon was the first to offer up incense sticks, followed by the superintendents, then the inspectors, and finally the rank and file.

As Weldon now approached the main table and picked up the heavy cleaver for the ritual first cut of the roast suckling pig, a single blow which tradition demanded must split the head in two, it occurred to David Becker, standing to one side, that Joe Lai was right about this ceremony. It represented far more than just a good excuse to get blasted in company time, as Mel Kale still described it. Of course, everyone who regularly came to a *bai Gwan-Dai* knew that after the mumbo-jumbo was over the party would continue far into the night, and that they would probably all watch the sun rise from behind the bar at the Double Dragon – and after that off to the Hilton coffee shop for breakfast.

765

But for Becker, and for Joe Lai too, there was more to it than just that. The *bai Gwan-Dai* represented both a confirmation of their shared identity as police officers and a demonstration of each man's position within the extended family of the force. More than just a Chinese pantomime, this simple act of worship was a reaffirmation of their jointly-held beliefs and values – their major underlying belief, despite all bitterness and cynicism, in justice and the rule of law.

And in the spirit of the Gwan-Dai.

NIMROD RISING

Steven Griffiths

It begins when London's season of goodwill is ripped
apart by a bloodthirsty and horrifying outrage. Evidence
of the perpetrators points to a puzzling coalition between
two widely different terrorist groups.

Though hampered by official political constraints, a rogue
power-base within the SIS now decides on eliminating a
major source of global mayhem. To achieve this they
select a very special killer from the shadowy world of
international mercenaries – an ex-marine called Richard
Tyler, codename NIMROD.

There will be one million sterling waiting for Tyler if he
can pull off the most dangerous gamble of his life. For,
surrounded by an army of trained bodyguards, the target
is capable of striking back through his own deadly
network of assassins.

But Nimrod's operation has already been uncovered. And
now the hunter becomes the prey . . .

FUTURA PUBLICATIONS
FICTION
0 7088 4294 1

Futura now offers an exciting range of quality titles by both established and new authors. All of the books in this series are available from:

Futura Books,
Cash Sales Department,
P.O. Box 11,
Falmouth,
Cornwall TR10 9EN.

Alternatively you may fax your order to the above address. Fax No. 0326 376423.

Payments can be made as follows: Cheque, postal order (payable to Macdonald & Co (Publishers) Ltd) or by credit cards, Visa/Access. Do not send cash or currency. UK customers and B.F.P.O.: please send a cheque or postal order (no currency) and allow £1.00 for postage and packing for the first book, plus 50p for the second book, plus 30p for each additional book up to a maximum charge of £3.00 (7 books plus).

Overseas customers including Ireland, please allow £2.00 for postage and packing for the first book, plus £1.00 for the second book, plus 50p for each additional book.

NAME (Block Letters) ....

ADDRESS ....

....

☐ I enclose my remittance for _____

☐ I wish to pay by Access/Visa Card

Number ⬚⬚⬚⬚⬚⬚⬚⬚⬚⬚⬚⬚⬚⬚⬚⬚

Card Expiry Date ⬚⬚⬚⬚